The River of Strange People

JOYCE KERR
FAMILY TREE

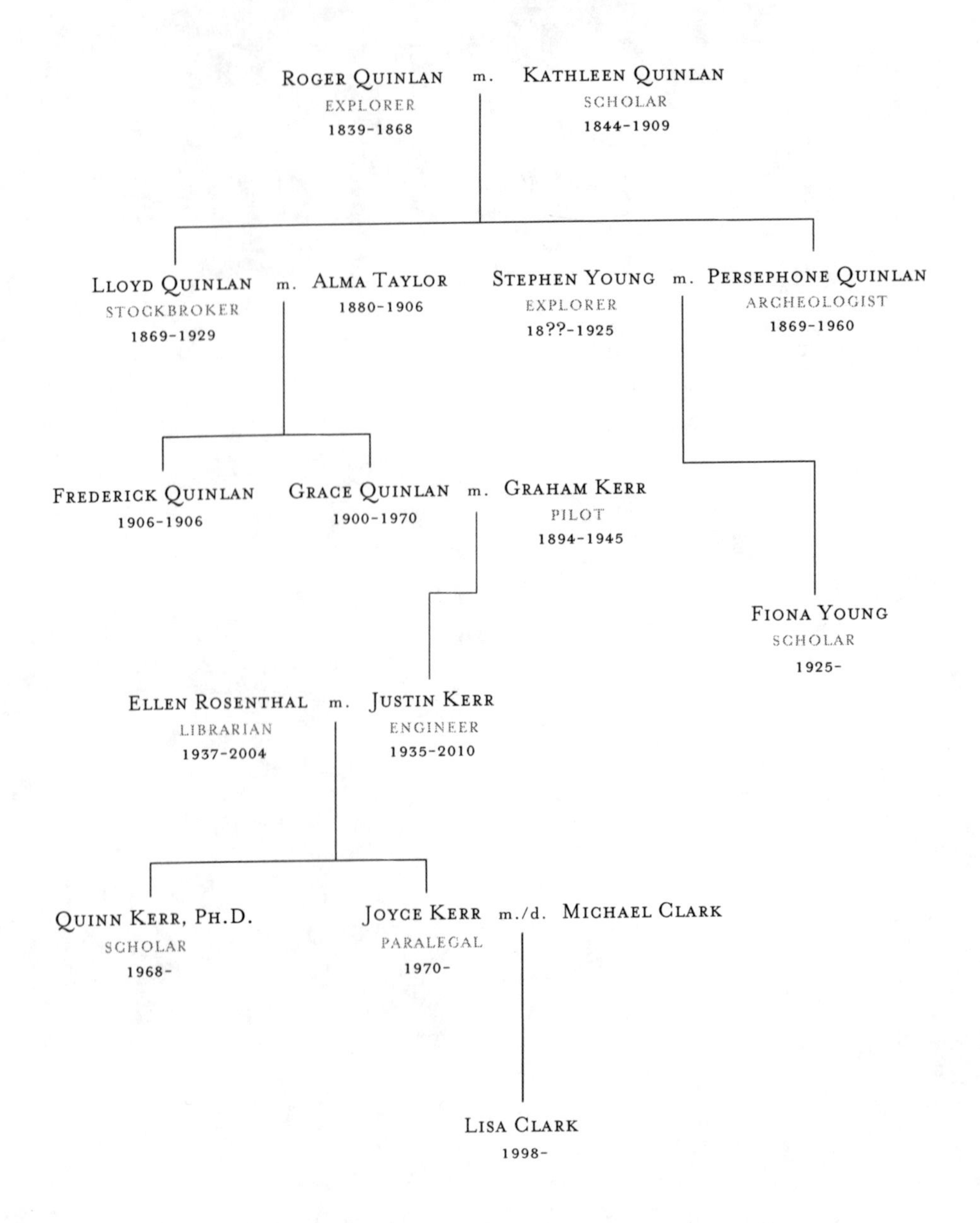

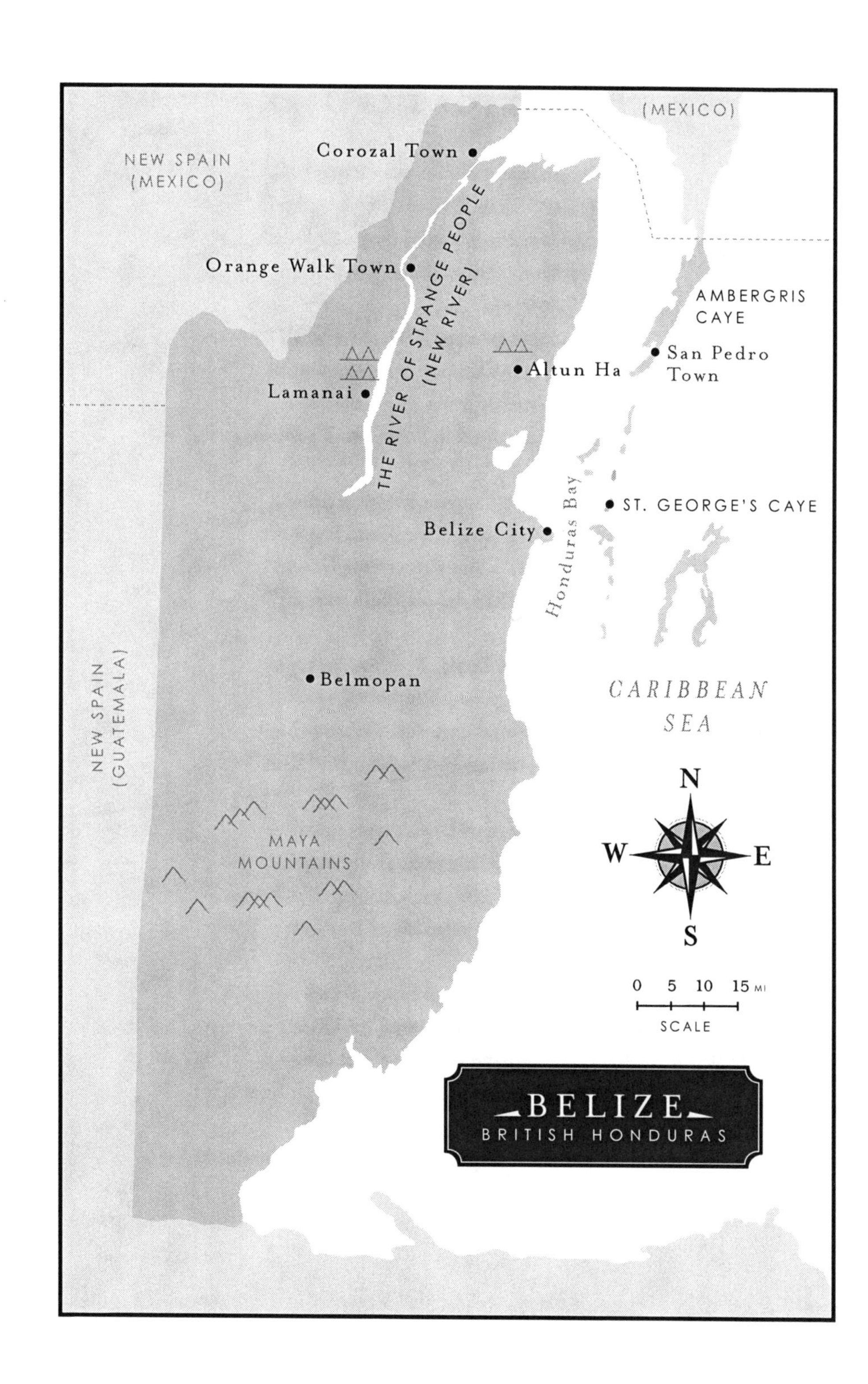

(MEXICO)
NEW SPAIN
(MEXICO)
Corozal Town
Orange Walk Town
THE RIVER OF STRANGE PEOPLE
(NEW RIVER)
AMBERGRIS
CAYE
San Pedro
Town
Altun Ha
Lamanai
Honduras Bay
ST. GEORGE'S CAYE
Belize City
NEW SPAIN
(GUATEMALA)
Belmopan
CARIBBEAN
SEA
N
W
E
S
MAYA
MOUNTAINS
0 5 10 15 MI
SCALE
BELIZE
BRITISH HONDURAS

Sailing for the Dark

Three drunken Fools, out raising hell,
Quit their debauch when they heard tell
That a sneaky thief, whom men call Death,
A drinking mate of theirs just slayeth.

A barman tried to warn the Fools
To keep their distance from the Ghoul
Who's never lost a single battle.
Unfazed, they vowed to hush Death's rattle,

Swearing allegiance, each to th'others,
As if they were true-born blood brothers:
"Tonight we'll slay this traitor Death;
He shall be slain, who all folk slayeth!"

Up leaped the Fools, in drunken rage,
To seek out Death in his village,
Swearing the mad oath that defined them:
"Death shall be dead – *if* we can find him."

Alas, instead of Death, they found
A Chest of Treasure on the ground,
O'er which they fought, each killing th'others –
As if they really were blood brothers.

O'er their fresh-butchered bones Death stepped,
Laughing, as he retrieved his Chest;
And bade us heed the Fools' last breaths:
"Chase your dreams – but don't mess with Death."

– loosely translated from Geoffrey Chaucer's *The Pardoner's Tale*

Note to the Reader

'The River of Strange People' is the Maya name for the river in Belize that whites call the New River. By 'strange people' the Maya meant – and still mean – all the conquistadors, buccaneers, pyrates, explorers and loggers who came up that river over the last 500 years, and forever altered the world the Maya had lived in, undisturbed, for thousands of years before the Conquest.

The Mayan words 'Xibalba' and 'Xhuxh' are pronounced 'She-bal-ba' and 'Shoosh'. (This is because the 16th century Castilian conquerors of the Maya had no letter for the 'sh' sound, so they used 'X' when transliterating Mayan glyphs.)

The historical facts contained in this novel about the ancient and modern Maya, their 16th century Spanish conquerors, the 17th and 18th century buccaneers and pyrates, and the 18th and 19th century British explorers and loggers who colonized Belize, are accurate, except:

- While Lamanai was indeed a great capital city of the ancient Maya, and its Mask Temple is a famous archeological site deep in the Belizean jungle, the cave and the fountain of youth placed at Lamanai in this novel are fictitious.
- While it is true that only four ancient Maya books survived the 1562 Spanish Inquisition, and many Maya shamans were tortured by the infamous *strappado*, the *Lamanai Codex* at the center of this novel is a fictitious book.
- While the buccaneers and pyrates of the 17th and 18th centuries did indeed haunt the islands and coast of modern-day Belize, and behaved in lawless fashion as depicted, the pyrate assaults on Lamanai in this novel are fictitious.
- While 19th century explorers 'discovered' many 'lost' Maya cities in the jungle, Roger and Kathleen Quinlan, like all the characters in this novel, are fictitious.

The wreck of the *General Grant* off the Auckland Islands in 1866 is an actual shipwreck which occurred as narrated, except of course the Quinlans were not really on board.

Finally, the depiction of modern medical efforts to 'conquer death' by activating in our somatic cells the telomerase – the cellular agent which allows cancer cells to live forever – is accurate. Likewise, there truly are renowned scientists who predict that in less than ten years human trials will begin on drugs to make us all immortal ('the cellular fountain of youth'). It remains undetermined whether immortality would really be a good thing.

For Susan Kessler

So many places we haven't seen:
Are you ready to grow young again?

The River of Strange People

Jonathan Rowe

Anchor Brewhouse Books

Anchor Brewhouse Books
47 Anchor Brewhouse
50 Shad Thames
London, United Kingdom SE1 2LY
Phone: 011-44-207-357-6602
jonathanrowe44@btinternet.com

Printed in the United States of America

Rowe, Jonathan, 1954–
Summary: An historical thriller about a modern British biologist seeking to conquer death, who joins forces with an American soldier of fortune, a Belizean archeologist and an American paralegal, to try to retrace the steps of past explorers in their failed quest to discover the location of the fountain of youth, hidden for centuries by the Maya in Belize.

ISBN # 978-0-615-34410-2
I. Rowe, Jonathan II. The River of Strange People
Library of Congress Control Number 2009907279

Cover Design by Savitski Design

The River of Strange People

Death is the price we pay for sex.

–Aristotle

Off old Cape Horn it blows a gale,
I'll be Jonah, you be the whale,
I wanna dive as deep as we can go.

Your ship is sailing for the dark,
Leave your suitcase, take my heart,
Hold me, stow me, love me, very slow.

Why must this hour come to pass?
I look at you and raise my glass.
Our kisses cannot stop the scythe, the hook
– I'll tell it all, in my new book.

– Greg Brown

Prologue
Into the Flames

28 June 1562

Deep in the heart of the Central American rain forest, a huge bonfire burns in the night. Guarding the fire is a circle of Spanish soldiers, their backs to the blaze. The dancing firelight glints in demonic patterns off the soldiers' armor as, visors down, they point their swords out at the dark.

Twenty paces from the tips of their swords, the swath of open ground the soldiers cleared for the fire dissolves into a murky perimeter. To the west looms a huge pagan temple, where the local Maya still practice human sacrifice. To the east lies a vast black lagoon, on whose waters Maya oars make no sound. And in all other directions, shadowy and dense, is the forbidding jungle.

From beyond the dark perimeter come the booming roars of jaguars and monkeys, the crashing of coatis in the thickets, and the piercing cries of oil birds. But these mysterious animal sounds are not what made the Spanish soldiers lower their visors and draw their swords.

What the soldiers fear, they cannot hear, much less see. They fear the eyes in the jungle.

The eyes came to all the other fires this *bandera* has guarded this month, at three other sites along the Yucatan Peninsula. So the soldiers presume the eyes are here tonight at Lamanai, too, just beyond the deep shadows at the jungle's edge, watching this fourth fire of the Holy Inquisition that Friar Diego de Landa unleashed this summer of 1562, to end all pagan idolatry in the Yucatan.

And the soldiers are right.

For interspersed amidst the trees lurk hundreds of hidden Maya warriors, painted for war yet impossible to detect, their angry eyes watching the alien fire, their hearts pulsing with hate. Crouched in the thick foliage, silent and fatal, the painted warriors are interwoven into the very fabric of the rain forest, as seamless and treacherous and violent as the wreath of creeper vines and strangler figs overhead, which are slowly choking to death the trees whose trunks and limbs they've entwined.

In the dark the painted warriors grip sharp obsidian lances and lethal *atlatls*, loaded with wooden spears. From 40 years of defeats, the Maya warriors know their Stone Age weapons can't match furnace-forged Toledo steel. Yet the Maya fear neither Death nor their Spanish oppressors, so the impotence of their ancient weapons never dissuades them from attacking Friar de Landa's fires.

Yet tonight, at Lamanai, the Maya mount no attack. Why, on this one night, at this one place, do the Maya watch from the trees as if paralyzed, while the Friar's fire burns unmolested?

Because human hearts are soft. And because Emilio Alvarez, the Captain of the Spanish *bandera* guarding the Inquisition's blazing *auto-da-fe*, is an expert in the art of torture.

Theoretically, torture is illegal in New Spain, by Crown fiat – although Friar de Landa still authorizes it in extreme cases. But torture, in Captain Alvarez's view, is more than just the blunt infliction of pain on the human body. The artful torturer is also an astute observer of human nature, who locates, with surgical precision, human pressure points, and then administers only the amount of pain necessary to elicit truth and vanquish heresy. In this way, the artful torturer serves God.

At the first two fires in the Friar's Yucatan Inquisition, constant skirmishing kept Captain Alvarez too busy for nuanced observation of the Maya character. But at the third fire, last week in Mani, the fighting was more sporadic, and Alvarez finally got enough time to pinpoint the one soft spot in the fierce Maya heart: the deep reverence with which all Maya idolize their elderly shamans.

So before building tonight's fire at Lamanai, Alvarez first invited all the local shamans to Lamanai – and next, with the Friar's blessing, jailed them all in an old tomb deep inside Lamanai's Mask Temple. Then Alvarez released the oldest shaman, Pel Echem, with a message back to the local warriors: if the Friar's *auto-da-fe* is attacked, all the other shamans will be burnt at the stake.

By this ploy Alvarez created a stalemate. For as much as the Maya hate their Spanish oppressors, they could never bear to see all their honored elders dispatched, before their time, down to the dark caves the Maya believe are the passage to Xibalba, the Maya land of the dead.

So tonight, at Lamanai, the warriors do not attack. Instead, they just glower at the Friar's fire, burning before the temple where their shamans are jailed – a temple their ancestors built two centuries before Jesus was born, and almost two *millenia* before the Spanish came to the Yucatan, with their galleons and guns, and began building fires to try to compel the Maya to worship Him.

Stoking the fire are twelve priests – eight from the Friar's traveling Inquisition, and four conscripted from a local mission. Like ants the black-robed priests work in two passing lines, each priest trudging with an empty gunnysack from the fire, up the steep 200-foot-high steps of the Mask Temple, and vanishing into the inner sanctum at the top; and then, after a few minutes inside, reappearing in the other line, ferrying fuel in his gunnysack back down the steep steps, and out to the fire.

The fuel the priests ferry to the fire in their gunnysacks consists of dozens of small statues of Maya Gods; and thousands of sheets of crumbling fig bark, each folded like an accordion, and bound in animal skin.

Icons. And books – ancient Maya books, called codices.

Thousands of these Maya codices, for Lamanai's Mask Temple holds the world's largest collection of ancient Maya literature. Curious little books, to the Spanish eye – much smaller than European folios, and written in a lost language of mysterious, evil-looking glyphs. But dangerous all the same, for although the Maya shamans claim they can't read the old glyphs, still they chant over the codices during the pagan rites they persist in practicing – replete with orgiastic blood-letting, and human sacrifice – in spite of 40 years' exposure to the civilized teachings of the Christ.

Which is why Friar de Landa ignited this holocaust here in the steaming Yucatan jungle: to purge the Maya forever of their bloody idolatry, through holy fire. To this end, once each priest reaches the *auto-da-fe*, he crosses himself, then casts all the idols and codices from his sack into the flames. With each idol and codex cast upon the fire, skeins of black smoke billow up into the humid night air, swirling in wild chaotic loops, before coalescing into a sooty opaque haze that hovers above the fire – a haze through which the very stars in the night sky can scarce be discerned.

One codex tumbles to the fire's edge, opening to a page with an engraved picture of an ancient Maya shaman. As the heat of the fire curls the codex, the page with the shaman's image writhes in the flames, as if the engraved old shaman himself were being burnt alive on the pyre.

In the hazy firelight, the youngest of the local missionaries conscripted to assist the book burning, Father Antonio Sanchez, stumbles at the base of the Mask Temple, and falls to his knees. Signaling he is unhurt, Sanchez hands the books and icons in his sack to the next priest in line, and motions the other priests to pass. From his knees, Sanchez gazes up at the smoke-obscured stars awhile, then at last stands, and drifts away from the line of priests ferrying books to the fire.

In the darkness no one seems to notice the small lumps under Father Sanchez's cassock, or the way he drifts ever further from the firefly light of the *auto-da-fe*, and ever closer to the dark edge of the jungle. At the far corner of the ancient Maya temple, Sanchez glances back at the priests and soldiers, kneels, and rolls out of sight into a patch of wild herbs growing beside the temple.

On hands and knees Sanchez scrambles the last few yards to the trees at the jungle's edge. There, concealed by the deep shadows, Sanchez stands and raises one hand in silent greeting to an elderly Maya, garbed in a red robe thin as a tomato skin: Pel Echem, the old shaman Captain Alvarez released earlier today – rumored by other Maya tribes to be over 150 years old.

From his cassock Sanchez hands two items to Echem. One is an untitled Maya codex, its cover engraved with a submerged crocodile, which later generations will call the *Lamanai Codex*. The other is a small jade statue of a two-headed Maya God – an indecently priapic Itzamna, the Creator God, joined with the skeletal head of Ah Puch, Lord of Xibalba, the Maya underworld.

An instant later, four pairs of blistered white hands stuff cotton gags into the mouths of Sanchez and Echem, and haul them down to the turf. In the brief scuffle that ensues, Echem drops the *Lamanai Codex*, and the priapic two-headed jade idol, into the brush at the jungle's edge.

The four white slavers tie burlap hoods over their captives' heads, ensnaring them in thick nets of maguey rope, preventing further struggle. Then the four slavers lug their silent faceless bundled captives to the temple, their retreat from the jungle's edge covered by the brandished swords of Captain Alvarez and six soldiers. No Maya warrior challenges the abductions; and none challenges Alvarez, when he retrieves the *Lamanai Codex* and the jade idol from the jungle's edge.

The slavers haul their bundled victims up the temple steps, and stow them in the inner sanctum at the top. For an hour Sanchez and Echem lie there on the floor, while the priests finish destroying the Lamanai library. Then Captain Alvarez releases all the shamans and priests, except Sanchez and Echem; and lets his soldiers relax on the temple steps and watch the fire, still burning strong. Enlisting a Corporal named Ruiz to assist, Alvarez unties Sanchez and Echem, and leads his prisoners down the temple's inner steps, past the ransacked library, to the damp tomb at the base of the temple.

The tomb is twenty paces square, its ceiling twice a man's height. The only exit is the inner steps, where Alvarez posts Ruiz. Four smoking pine torches, mounted on blank plaster walls, cast the only light. The tomb's earthen floor is bare – save for a closed stone sarcophagus in one corner, a tangle of ropes and metal objects by the stairs, and a European chair near one pine torch. On the chair sits Friar Diego de Landa, studying the *Lamanai Codex* and the jade statue.

The Friar doesn't look up when Alvarez escorts his robed prisoners in, binds their hands behind their backs, and bids them stand in silence before His Grace. For several minutes the only sound is the crackling of the *Lamanai Codex*, as the Friar turns its stiff old bark pages.

Aft last the Friar lifts his hawkish face, his hooded ascetic eyes blank as the tomb's walls.

"Father Sanchez, for the love of God, why imperil your immortal soul *for these*" – the Friar waves the statue, and thumps the *Lamanai Codex* – "a lewd idol, and a book in a dead language no one can read anymore?"

Father Sanchez stands mute, staring down at the moccasins on his feet.

The Friar's European chair scrapes earth, as he shifts to inspect his other prisoner.

"And you, Pel Echem, with thousands of Satan's icons and books in your evil lair" – again the Friar waves the statue, and thumps the *Lamanai Codex* – "*what's so special about these two?*"

* * *

An hour later Captain Emilio Alvarez stands atop the closed sarcophagus in the Mask Temple's tomb, hammering a spike into the plaster ceiling, while singing an old troubadour love song:

There is a songbird who nightly moans,
And there is an angel who comes to console;
You are the songbird, my own true love,
And I am the angel, who's come to console.

The ancient plaster falls in chunks from the ceiling, revealing a solid mass of old stone above. But the old stone proves pliable enough for Alvarez to hammer two spikes into it, three paces apart, directly above the ends of the sarcophagus, by the tomb's back wall. Pleased, Alvarez sings on:

There is a lily which time doth consume
And a fountain which keeps us forever young;
You are the lily, come grant me perfume;
And I am the fountain, long may I run.

As he sings, Alvarez screws two butcher's hooks onto the ceiling spikes. Then, gripping one hook, he steps off the sarcophagus and hangs in the air for a ten-count. Satisfied the spikes will hold a man's weight, Alvarez loops a long thick rope through both ceiling hooks, pulling the middle of the rope down to the sarcophagus, so the rope forms an 'M' above the sarcophagus.

Alvarez crosses the tomb to the old Maya, still standing before the Friar's now-empty chair.

"Why do you think the Friar allowed Sanchez to walk out with him into the fresh night air," Alvarez asks the old Maya, "while you're stuck down here in this shit-hole, with Ruiz and me?"

Impassively the old Maya gazes, his face a blank mask, his skin dry as a petrified tree.

"Why do you think, among all the shamans, you were the one I picked to let go this evening?" Alvarez leans in close, crinkling his nose at the fragrant orrisroot the old Maya exudes.

The old Maya, in turn, gags at the reek of Alvarez's sweat-soaked shirt, but stands silent.

"Why do you think four slavers just happened to be waiting at my command in the woods tonight?" Alvarez bares his teeth in a false smile. "Don't you see? *Sanchez betrayed you.*"

At this the old Maya flinches; but then shakes his head emphatically no.

"Oh I know, the missionaries all love you Maya. But human flesh is weak. When I found out Sanchez keeps a Maya bitch" – a flicker in the eyes tells Alvarez the old Maya knows about Sanchez's mistress – "well, then I didn't even need the *strappado* to get the truth from Sanchez."

The Maya darts a quick glance past Alvarez, at the M-shaped rope dangling from the butcher's hooks above the sarcophagus.

"Curious how the *strappado* works? You'll soon find out, old man. Unless you tell me right now, why you asked Sanchez to steal that one statue, and that one book."

Impassively the old Maya gazes at Alvarez, his face again a blank mask.

Summoning Ruiz from the stairs, Alvarado escorts the old Maya to the *strappado.* Ruiz pins the Maya face down on the sarcophagus, while Alvarez binds the Maya's wrists, still tied together behind his back, to the mid-point of the M-shaped rope. Then Ruiz and Alvarado each grip one end of the rope, and simultaneously yank down hard, like sextons tolling a heavy bell.

Their first pull hoists the old Maya's wrists a yard into the air. The Maya's head and feet flop down, his body forming an inverted U; but by standing tip-toed on the sarcophagus, he keeps the weight off his wrists and arms. Methodically Alvarez and Ruiz reach, hand over hand, up the two ends of the taut rope, as high as they can reach; then simultaneously yank down hard again. This second pull hoists the Maya up another yard, lifting his feet off the sarcophagus, his weight now supported only by his bound wrists looped, behind his back, over the middle of the *strappado.*

Two quick pops echo off the walls – the sound of the old Maya's shoulders dislocating from their joints. Next come longer ripping sounds, as the sinews of his shoulders tear away from his bones. Then a brief lull, filled only by the heavy breathing of Alvarez and Ruiz, straining at their taut ropes – before a series of awful shrieks fills the tomb, each fresh scream mixing, in continual cacophony, with the echoes of the Maya's past screams, still bouncing off the plaster walls.

After a ten-count, Alvarez and Ruiz lower the screaming old Maya down, in a controlled fall. But right at the end Ruiz's grip slips, and the Maya drops the last hand's length too fast, hitting the stone sarcophagus face first, cracking his nose. Blood spurts from the Maya's nostrils.

Alvarez waits for the last echoes of the Maya's screams to die off.

Then he murmurs: "Why'd you ask Sanchez to save that one idol? Why that one book?"

The half-broken old Maya spews blood and phlegm, but says nothing.

Without compassion Alvarez wraps a wide cotton bandage round the old Maya's nose, tying it tight behind his head. "Can't let you bleed to death before you confess," Alvarez grunts. "Now tell me: what's so special about that particular statue, and that particular book?"

The old Maya groans, but lies mute.

Alvarez never shouts. "The *strappado* hurts far worse the second time."

Still the old Maya lies mute. So again Alvarez and Ruiz yank down twice on the rope. With the second yank, the Maya's shoulders pop all the way out of their sockets. He screams even louder than before, as the muscles in his back and arms burst, like the ancient bindings of the books outside, cracking in the fire. After another ten-count, the soldiers again lower the Maya onto the sarcophagus. This time he twists his head before Ruiz drops him the last hand's length.

"Why did you come back for that statue," Alvarez presses, "and a book no one can read—"

The broken old Maya gurgles incoherently.

Raising his eyebrows in hope, Alvarez rolls the old Maya on his side.

"I couldn't hear you." Alvarez bends in close. "What's in that little book worth all the—"

The old Maya spits blood onto Alvarez's face.

Alvarez recoils, and glares at the old Maya, murder in his eyes. But the artful torturer never acts in anger. So Alvarez wipes his face on his sleeve, and strolls to the stairs. Without haste he selects two weights from the pile of metal there, and attaches the weights to the Maya's ankles.

"You will be surprised," Alvarado confides, "how much more painful for your shoulders and arms the *strappado* is, with these weights on your ankles."

A third time Alvarez and Ruiz hoist the old Maya twice, raising him again up off his feet, suspending him by his dislocated shoulders for another ten-count. Dark bruises blotch the Maya's arms, as internal blood vessels rupture; and the Maya screams himself hoarse, before the soldiers finally lower him roughly back down onto the top of the stone sarcophagus.

"In the name of the One True God," Alvarez says, "tell me, you faithless heathen: why did you ask Sanchez to steal that statue and that book? Why run such a crazy risk?"

This time the old Maya doesn't even groan. Alvarez pokes the Maya in both eyes, provoking a flinch that reassures Alvarez his victim can still feel pain.

"You are one tough old Indian, Pel Echem. I'll give you that. But in the end you'll confess. Every man does. You cannot escape. You cannot die. That is the genius of the *strappado*. It will never kill you. It will just torment you forever. Till you confess."

The old Maya lies mute. But Alvarez can tell he is listening.

"We'll take a short break now. Give you time to think. But we'll be back, soon. And we'll hoist you all night if we must. We won't stop till you tell us what the Friar wants to know."

The echoes of Alvarez and Ruiz, clomping up the stone stairs, die away.

Lying alone in his ancestors' tomb, his hands bound behind his back, his wrists still tied to the *strappado*, Pel Echem rubs his face against the stone top of the sarcophagus. Searing pain from his broken nose burns through all Pel's nerves. Yet over and over Pel rubs his face against the stone, trying to push the gauze off his nose, hoping to bleed to death, so he can embark for the dark caves of Xibalba, before his torturers return.

But Captain Alvarez tied the bandage too tight.

Giving up on suicide, Pel rolls off the sarcophagus and down onto the earthen floor behind it, pulling the *strappado* rope along with him as he falls. In the dim light from the smoking pine torches, Pel backs up against the far side of the sarcophagus, and gropes the stone carvings there, until his fingers find the *ourobouros*, a depiction of the Maya Creator

God Itzamna as a coiled serpent eating his own tail, symbolizing the circularity of all life and time. Pel sticks his middle finger into the hole at the center of the *ourobouros* carving – but Pel's finger isn't long enough. Into the gloom Pel squints, searching for a long thin stick on the floor. Finding none, he turns and slides backwards, like a crab, until, near the back wall, a small sharp stone jabs his butt.

Tears of pain fill Pel's eyes as he squeezes both hands round the stone, clutching it like death. Rising to his knees, Pel backs his heels up against the wall, and with his bound hands scrapes the sharp stone against the wall, carving onto the old plaster a message he will never see. Under the circumstances all he can manage is one Maya glyph, and a series of lines and dots. When he's done, Pel drops the stone, slides crabwise back to the sarcophagus, and crawls back on top of it, so that when his torturers return, they won't notice the fresh pagan writing on the wall.

* * *

Three hours later, in the dead of night, the *auto-da-fe* still burns, stoked to last till daybreak, as a symbol of the Eternal Light which Friar de Landa's Inquisition is bringing to the poor benighted Maya souls living in the darkness around Lamanai. The dark jungle is quiet now, except for a few oil birds crying in the trees. The jaguars and monkeys and coatis are asleep; the Maya warriors are all abed in their villages; and the Spanish soldiers are dozing on the Mask Temple steps.

Only five men are awake at this ungodly hour. At the outer base of the Mask Temple stand Friar de Landa and Father Sanchez, watching in the flickering firelight as Captain Alvarez and Corporal Ruiz pick their way down the steep temple steps, toting the broken body of Pel Echem. Beneath his thin red robe Pel's knobby, dislocated shoulders sag, like empty husks of maize.

When they reach the ground, the soldiers stand Pel up on his own feet, his hands still tied behind his back. Pel wobbles, but doesn't fall. To prevent escape, the four Spaniards surround Pel.

Friar de Landa shakes the jade idol and the *Lamanai Codex* in Pel's face. "So, you wicked old pagan wizard, the Captain says at last you've consented to answer my questions?"

Peering over his blood-drenched bandage, and shivering with shock and pain, Pel's eyes are frantic, like an infuriated jaguar enmeshed in a hunter's net. But he nods a fierce yes.

"What's so special about these evil curios," the Friar asks, "worth all the pandemonium tonight?"

Pel's vocal chords vibrate. "They're – a key." The rest of his words die in his blood-clogged throat. Pel spits out a mess of blood and saliva, and tries again. "A key," he croaks, "and a map."

"You lie." The Friar waves the *Lamanai Codex*. "There's no map in here. No keys, either."

"The glyphs in the book are the map." Pel spits more blood on the ground. "Instructions."

"You mean, 'directions'?"

Pel looks confused by the Spanish word, but after a racking graveyard cough, nods yes.

"Father Sanchez says you are the only man alive who can still read this book. Is this true?"

Pel darts a quick reproachful glance at Sanchez, but nods yes.

"And this book is a map *to what*?" the Friar asks.

Pel tries to steal another glance at Sanchez, but this time the Friar grabs Pel's jaw and holds it fast. "Don't look to Father Sanchez for the answers! Just speak God's truth, pagan."

Pel twitches with fear. In a voice still wet with blood, he says: "The Lamanai Waters."

The Friar releases Pel's jaw, and jerks his thumb at the dark lagoon beyond the fire. "Who needs a map to find waters at Lamanai?"

"Not the lagoon," Pel says. "Special waters. Waters which slow down Time."

"How can water slow down Time?" the Friar asks.

"The Lamanai Waters strengthen a young man's blood." Pel coughs up more blood. "So he may live four *k'atuns* – generations – before he even begins to grow old."

The Friar's eyes grow cold. "You mean: *the fountain of youth*?"

Pel nods yes. The Friar glares at Pel a long time. But Pel does not flinch.

"Your Grace," Alvarez interjects, "my grandsire reported to General Cortes, that the Maya at Cozumel told him, the fountain of youth was down here, among the Maya at Lamanai."

"And did Cortes, or your grandsire, ever *find* the magic fountain among the Maya here?"

"No," Alvarez concedes.

"Of course not," the Friar says. "In 40 years of searching, no one's ever found the fountain of youth, anywhere in the New World. Don't you see? The fountain of youth is just a fairy tale, like El Dorado, which the Indians use to send us away, always somewhere further down the road."

Alvarez looks down, chastened by the Friar's harsh tone and icy gaze.

"Worse than a fairy tale," the Friar adds, "for the fountain of youth tempts men to dream of living forever in this world, instead of seeking eternal life in the Next World, through faith in Jesus Christ." The Friar shakes the jade idol and the *Lamanai Codex* at Pel. "Your fountain is an evil lie!"

"It is no lie." Pel shrugs. "You asked me what makes these objects special. I told you."

The Friar glares at Pel in angry silence for an entire minute. But then abruptly, the Friar turns to the Spaniards, his eyes feverish and brimming with energy. "Yet does not God often hide His wonders from us? And if there truly is a fountain of youth, here on earth, must it not be His work? And if it truly is here in this jungle, should we not seek it out – to praise it, like all His works?"

All three Spaniards look at their feet, loath to debate the mercurial Friar.

So the Friar debates himself. "A century ago, God granted the Flemish master Van Eyck a vision, which he painted as a triptych for the great cathedral at Ghent. Van Eyck's triptych depicts a band of Christian pilgrims, emerging from a dark forest much like this one" – the Friar gestures at the nearby jungle – "to worship Christ the Lamb. And right beside Him, in van Eyck's vision, was *the fountain of youth.*"

The Friar turns back to Pel, his eyes again cold and severe. "Only one way to learn if you speak the truth, old man. Take us now, to your fountain of youth."

"It's too dark. It's – it's in a cave."

"We'll bring torches."

Pel shakes his head no. "Even with torches, I can't find the passage into the cave at night."

"Then we'll build another big fire right outside the cave. God's light will show you the way."

Pel gets a wily look. "But you preach God's light is brightest at the dawn."

"And so it is. Yet dawn is also when your warriors will return. So we go now." The Friar's tone conveys he will brook no further objections. "Which way, old wizard?"

Pel's eyes search the trees at the edge of the dark jungle.

"It's hopeless – your warriors all went home to bed," the Friar says. "*Which way?*"

Pel sighs. "South," he mutters. "Then west."

"Lead us." The Friar motions for Alvarez and Ruiz to step aside.

Pel takes two lurching steps south, but stumbles, catching himself with his palm on the temple's bottom step, wincing in apparent pain. The soldiers step further back, giving Pel more room. Yet when Pel straightens, he walks much faster than before, with crisp, sure steps. Seeing that Pel is stronger than he first appeared, the Friar turns to Alvarez. "Put him on a leash, Emilio, so he—"

The words die on the Friar's tongue, as Alvarez and Ruiz rush past, chasing Pel, who's now on a dead run – wobbling, like one of Magellan's penguins, because his hands are still tied behind his back, yet nevertheless managing to stay several paces ahead of the soldiers.

Straight at the *auto-da-fe* Pel runs, shrieking: "Only the oil birds will ever see the fountain!"

The next instant Pel Echem plunges head first into the flames.

BOOK ONE:

The Fountain of Youth

Chapter One
Hearts of Darkness

Monday 27 December 2010

Deep in the heart of the Central American rain forest, a small skiff roars up the New River in the dead of night. Squatting in the skiff's prow is an American soldier of fortune, Kip Hunter. On the middle thwarts sit Kip's two young mercenaries, Bruce Tobin and Harry Benz. And back at the stern, manning the rudder, sits their guide, Alfonso something-or-other – a guide Kip already regrets hiring because, even though Al's unlicensed and half-Maya, he just can't shut the fuck up.

A cool breeze sweeps Kip's face as he scans the dense black mangrove along the dark river, searching for any sign of Maya scouts. Even in the bright moonlight, Kip knows he hasn't got a snowball's chance in hell of actually spotting a Maya scout, because Al's cheap little skiff is juddering like it's about to fall apart, blurring Kip's vision; and besides, any Maya scout with half a brain would stand a yard back of the bank, virtually undetectable in the mangrove's deep shadows. At least by Kip, whose 45-year-old eyes see far less than they did in his glory days in the USMC.

But Kip learned, in the Marine Corps, that leadership is often more about appearance than reality. By scanning the riverbank, Kip sets a vigilant example for his two young guns, Bruce and Harry, whose sharp eyes might actually spot something; and even more important, Kip dissuades their chatty guide from asking, again, why in the world Kip wants to visit the Maya ruins at Lamanai in the dead of night, especially since the site's been closed to the public the past two months.

Abruptly the guide's outboard motor coughs and dies, and the skiff lurches to a choppy halt in the middle of the river. Kip whirls to yell at the guide, but in the spooky quiet that suddenly engulfs them, Kip lets the reprimand die in his throat, reluctant to make any unnecessary noise. As the skiff sheers beam-on into its own wake, the guide tilts the motor up and out of the water, leaving the skiff to drift slowly downstream in the sluggish current, away from Lamanai.

"What the hell ya doin', Al?" Kip growls in a low voice.

"You said you want no one at Lamanai to hear us coming," the guide says. "Even though I keep telling you, no one's lived within ten miles of those ruins, since the archeologists packed up and left, ten years ago. But if you want a silent approach, boss, it's time to paddle."

Kip gazes out across the black water at the blank jungle along the New River's banks, utterly bereft of markers or signs to indicate where the hell they are. "You sure we're close?"

"Round the next bend is the New River lagoon," the guide says. "Halfway up the lagoon is Lamanai."

"If you say so." Kip shrugs. "But before we paddle, we gotta put on our war paint."

From his backpack, Kip pulls out three tubes of blackface, and tosses two to Bruce and Harry. The three white men all smear the greasy black gel on their exposed arms, necks and faces; and then pull on black gloves, to match their black clothing and black skull-caps.

Then Kip pitches his tube of blackface back to the guide.

"I don't need this shit." The guide snorts. "My mama says I'm dark enough as it is. She—"

"Not in this bright moon, you ain't. No offense, but you could almost pass for a white man."

Bruce and Harry guffaw. But the guide looks offended.

"Relax, Al." Kip puts on his most conciliatory tone. "All I'm sayin' is, back in the day, a coupla *conquistadores* musta slipped in the back door and spent some quality *siesta* time with a few o' the ladies in your blood line. So now you need blackface to cover up, just like me and the boys."

Bruce and Harry guffaw again. But the guide still looks huffy.

"Ain't no one out on the river in the middle of the night," the guide whines. "Who's gonna see our faces?"

Kip frowns. "We're gonna meet some guys at Lamanai. Can't have 'em see us comin'."

"Helluva place you picked for a meeting," the guide says. "Been closed two months—"

"Cut the chatter, Al, and put on the blackface."

The guide inspects the tube, curling his lip in disgust. "Bugs'll swarm all over this shit."

"Then use bug spray."

"Bug spray don't stop botflies." The guide gets an obstinate look. "I don't get this, boss. If these guys don't know we're coming, what the hell are they doin' out at deserted Maya ruins?"

"You ask too many questions."

"You make me nervous."

"Good. That's the way I like it. Now put on the fuckin' blackface, and let's start paddling."

But Al the half-Maya guide proves just as stubborn as the original pure-bred Maya, who chose death by starvation in caves rather than become Spanish or British slaves.

"This boat's all I have. I have a right to know what kinda trouble I'm paddling my boat into."

Kip glares at the guide, but decides the only way to shut him up is to answer his question.

"The guys we're meeting at Lamanai are there for a religious retreat. Dangerous fanatics. Which is why we need to put on blackface, and paddle real quiet so they don't hear. *Comprende*?"

"They're pure Maya?" the guide asks.

Kip nods yes.

"There's no pure Maya left in this part of Belize."

Kip raises an irritated eyebrow, trying to signal he's fast running out of patience. "These guys are from Guatemala."

"So we're gonna kick 'em outta Lamanai?"

Kip rummages in his backpack. "No. They got permission to use the site. We're just – payin' a visit. Now put on the blackface, before we drift all the way back to Orange Walk."

The guide goes sulky. "I don't want no botflies layin' eggs in the pores o' my face."

Kip jerks his head up from his pack, and gives the guide a long, dead-eyes stare – which always wilted the young Marines under Kip's command in the Gulf. But the guide is made of balkier stuff. Pretending not to notice Kip's stare, the guide picks up a paddle and dips it in the river.

The insolent bastard!

Kip decides he's tolerated enough of this mini-mutiny. From his backpack he pulls out his Smith & Wesson .40 caliber automatic pistol, and points it straight at the guide's heart.

The guide stops paddling, but still doesn't flinch. "You promised me, no guns."

"I lied."

Keeping his pistol aimed at the guide, Kip nods at Bruce and Harry. From a long duffel bag the young mercenaries pull out their AK-47's, snap in the clips, and lay the automatic rifles on the thwarts; and then pull out a dozen grenades, which they stuff in the pockets of their dark green camo jackets.

Kip waves his pistol. "Up to you, Al. Put on the blackface right now, or die in the river."

Still the guide doesn't flinch. "A gunshot'd wake up the Maya you say are out at Lamanai."

"Good point." From his belt Kip unsheaths his long USMC knife, and clambers over the first thwart, eyeing the guide all the way. Bruce and Harry lean out to make room for Kip to pass by.

With a clatter, the guide drops his paddle, and begins slathering on the blackface.

"Good call, Al." Kip re-sheathes his knife, holsters his pistol, and sits on the first thwart, facing backwards to watch the guide. "All our lives'll be on the line this morning, Al. Which means we need *perfect discipline*. Like any military operation. No more dissent. *Comprende*?"

In lieu of a nod, the guide lowers his eyes. Sullenly he finishes applying the blackface, then picks up his paddle, and begins to steer them back on course upriver. The insolent bastard.

Bruce and Harry pull out two more paddles, and begin to pull. But in the dead silence of the pre-dawn jungle, the rustle of water from their strokes sounds like it could be heard for miles.

"Quiet, lads," Kip says. "We got plenty o' time. Quiet is more important than speed."

Bruce and Harry slow their strokes, but still can't avoid making a small lapping noise at the start and end of each pull – the only audible sounds anywhere along the river.

"Maya oars are silent," the guide taunts. "Like mine."

"Shut up, Al," Kip mutters. "They're doin' the best they can."

They all lapse into heavy silence. The New River widens into the lagoon, and they keep paddling south, along the lagoon's western shore. Kip returns to scanning the shore, still thick with mangrove, searching for any sign of Maya scouts. But in the eerie quiet of the dark lagoon, Kip can't help hearing the echo of his own words – spit out during his little showdown back on the river with their dumb-ass guide – about the 'dangerous fanatics' waiting for them at Lamanai.

To soothe his jangled nerves, Kip pictures those fanatical Maya as he hopes to find them: all curled up, and sound asleep. Kip's intel – from his client, Ron Graham – is that there are exactly 17 Maya men out at Lamanai, participating in the religious retreat. No women, no children; just two old shamans, and 15 devout novitiates in their early 20s. Ron says all 17 men sleep together each and every night on pallets in the empty tomb at the base of the Mask Temple. Ron's photos of the tomb showed only two exits: a wood door to the outside, cut by 19th century archeologists; and an inner staircase which leads up from the tomb to the temple's top. So all Kip has to do is simultaneously seize the door and the stairs, and the sleepy Maya should surrender to Kip's superior gun power.

All good, in theory. But even half-asleep, these young novitiates will still be dangerous. They may be pious, but their religion involves lots of blood; and they hail from the most remote, poverty-ridden villages high up in the *Sierra Madre*, where the fiercely separatist Maya raise all their sons hard and mean, always ready to die in the next revolt against the Guatemalan government. These Maya novitiates won't be packing AK-47's, like Bruce and Harry; or even .40 caliber S&W's, like Kip; but they also won't be sleeping far from their obsidian knives, or their *atlatls* – or whatever other Stone Age weapons these violent maniacs wield in their primitive rites.

Kip shudders as he thinks of that blood-thirsty priest in *Indiana Jones*, ripping the heart out of his living victim with his bare hands. Surreptitiously Kip pops six Inderal tablets into his mouth – beta-blockers, to take the edge off the fight-or-flight doubts assailing his aging nerves.

But even beta-blockers can't block the darker doubts creeping into Kip's mind. What if this whole raid is just a set-up? After all, Ron Graham is not Kip's typical outlaw client. Ron's the Director of the Belize Ministry of Archeology, a real mucky-muck – at least as much as any bureaucrat in a shitty little dump like Belize can be called a mucky-muck. But what's worrying Kip is, Ron's also asshole buddies with Kux Ahawis, the radical Maya shaman leading the religious retreat at Lamanai. Ron says he and Kux fell out last month over a two-headed jade icon Kux brought to Lamanai but won't let Ron examine. So Ron hired Kip to steal the icon for him.

But what if Ron's lying?

What if one of Kip's many enemies got Ron to set Kip up for an ambush out at Lamanai?

In the slow-paddling skiff on the moonlit river, Kip conjures Ron Graham's doughy face two weeks ago, when he came to Kip's San Pedro warehouse, lips trembling, and offered Kip $50,000 – American, not Belizean – to mount a river assault on Lamanai, and steal the two-headed jade icon from the Mask Temple, where Ron says Kux Ahawis keeps it under constant guard. Was Kip too quick to say yes? He figured Ron just looked nervous because crime is outside Ron's comfort zone; so once Ron forked over $25K in cash, as a down payment, Kip cast aside all doubts.

But should Kip have asked more questions that day?

Like, for example, where'd the Director of Archeology come up with $25K in cash so fast?

On the other hand, if someone wanted Kip set up, why involve a well-connected politico like Ron Graham? There's so many other, easier ways to take Kip down, if that's your goal in life.

Kip takes a deep breath and tries to relax, hoping the beta blockers'll kick in soon, slowing his heart rate, regulating his breathing, and steadying the mild tremors in his aging hands. Never a good thing, to have shaking hands – especially when you're pulling a gun on 17 religious fanatics trapped in a small tomb of their ancestors. A tomb they believe is the beginning and end of all life, the be-all and end-all, the Alpha and the Omega. Or whatever the hell the Maya believe.

Kip steals a glance at Bruce and Harry. No doubt the young mercs are wrestling right now with their own fight-or-flight instincts. No man's immune from fear. But the young guns probably don't have beta-blockers to pop. And for all their tough talk round the San Pedro bars, the truth is, Bruce and Harry have never seen action anywhere near as hairy as this dirty little war might get.

"Hey, fucker!" Kip hisses over his shoulder at the guide. "You're too close to shore!"

Sullenly the guide points at a narrow beach ahead, with nothing but a short stretch of wet sand, and a splintered wood sign, depicting a submerged crocodile. "That's 'cause we're landing."

Kip peers up the shadowy shoreline, but sees no temples. "Where the hell's Lamanai?"

"Here," the guide says. "That crocodile sign marks the north end of the old settlement."

"Where's the Mask Temple?"

"Two miles to the south. Stay close to the river as you hike, you can't miss it."

"Fuck that!" Kip hisses. "Take us closer to the temple in the goddamn boat!"

"The only other beach is right by the Mask Temple. Your Maya friends'd hear us landing."

Kip looks at the dense mangrove along the shore, everywhere but this beach. The guide's probably not lying. So Kip grabs his submersible diver's backpack, and jumps into the reedy water.

Bruce and Harry follow, AK-47s slung across their shoulders, and pull the skiff's prow onto the beach. The guide stays seated at the skiff's stern.

"Everybody out," Kip orders.

"Our deal was, I stay with my boat."

"Our deal changed. I don't trust you anymore, Al. You're coming with us."

"Whatever you're going to do, I can't help. I've never fired a gun."

"Bullshit. But I'm not givin' you a gun anyway. All you gotta do is walk, and shut up."

After tying the skiff to a huge ceiba tree, the four men set off on a narrow, winding, vine-laden path through the jungle, more or less parallel to the river. The guide leads, with Kip close behind, watching to be sure the guide doesn't try to defect. Bruce and Harry bring up the rear.

The hike is slow and hard, with giant roots tripping them every other step. Kip succumbs to dark thoughts, like why the hell a man of his age and talents can't find something better than jungle work to make a living off of. Maybe it's time to go back to sea diving, like Mel Fisher did when he—

Abruptly the guide stops, grabs a stick, and furiously whacks the brush along the path.

"Hey, you dumb motherfucker!" Kip hisses. "*Quiet* is the goal here."

"*Living* is my goal," the guide retorts. "That snake I just chased off is poisonous."

They resume their march. After half an hour, Kip sees a huge shadowy shape, towering above the jungle canopy inland, to the west. But the guide shakes his head no. Wrong temple.

They march on a few more minutes till Kip sees, with a wild surmise, another huge shadow bulking straight ahead, close by the river. The guide nods yes. Kip signals for the utmost quiet.

Guns drawn, they creep up on the Mask Temple, careful not to step on any branches, and close within twenty yards of the temple, without seeing any sign of a scout. There, in the deep shadows at the edge of the jungle, Kip signals a halt, to review his assault plan, now that he's looking across a swath of open ground at the real temple, instead of just Ron Graham's photos.

The stone steps up the sides of the Mask Temple are steep, but not as bad as some Maya temples Kip's seen. Harry should have no trouble climbing those steps undetected, and then creeping back down close to the tomb via the inner staircase, to block that exit. No problem there.

But the closed wood door on the tomb's east face gives Kip pause. In his backpack, Kip's got four military issue M112 blocks of C-4 plastic explosive, which he plans to use to blow a man-size hole in the door, with the shock and awe of the blast giving Bruce time to fire a few rounds through the hole, before he and Kip crawl in and induce the sleeping Maya to surrender. Unless—

Well, unless lots of things. Like von Clausewitz said, in any military operation, nothing goes according to plan, so you should always plan on having to scrap your plan. Maybe the detonator'll misfire. Maybe the wood door'll withstand the C-4, like Hitler's conference table famously did in 1944. Maybe the hole they'll blow won't be big enough to crawl in through. Or maybe they'll crawl in, only to find the Maya have guns. Or maybe the Maya'll overpower Harry and escape up the inner stairs.

Maybe, Kip thinks, he needs to pop some more Inderal.

Or maybe there's a better way to skin this cat.

Like, how 'bout some hostages? The way Kip did once to seize an ammo dump in the Gulf.

You gotta figure, 17 Maya ain't all peeing and shitting inside that tomb where they're sleeping. They may be re-enacting primitive rites and all, but even cavemen didn't shit where they slept. Come dawn, these fuckers are gonna wander outside, half-asleep, to answer nature's call in the low scrub here outside the Mask Temple. Kip could grab the first one, force the hostage to open the door, and walk in behind him. If anyone inside starts firing, they'll only hit their own guy.

In hushed tones Kip lays out his revised plan. They'll hold off on the C-4 till dawn, while Kip waits to try to grab a hostage. Harry'll wait on the inner stairs, out of sight of the Maya, till he hears Kip enter the tomb. Could be a long wait, since dawn's still an hour off. Bruce'll wait here till Kip grabs the hostage, and then run into the tomb behind Kip. The guide'll sit here with Bruce and shut the fuck up. If he makes any noise or tries to leave, Bruce'll cut his throat, from ear to ear.

The mercs nod assent. The guide shrugs fearful acquiescence.

So Harry climbs the steps and disappears into the temple. Bruce and the guide squat at the edge of the jungle. And Kip, pistol drawn, scrambles across the open ground between them and the Mask Temple, careful not to step on any twigs in the low scrub. At the temple, he sets his backpack down quietly, and stands three feet behind the hinge side of the closed wood door.

And waits, with his pistol drawn.

Which is always the hardest part of any mission.

Kip tries not to let his mind wander. But after awhile he can't help noticing this temple is unlike any he's seen, in his 15 years in Central America. Not as steep as the temples at Tikal, nor as elegant as the temples at Altun Ha; but the Mask Temple's almost as big, and clearly way older.

And it's unnervingly primitive.

Since Kip is at the east wall, he can't see the huge ten-foot angry human face carved into the west face of the temple, which he knows, from Ron Graham's photos, is the reason the building's called the *Mask* Temple. So it can't be the big angry mask unnerving Kip. It's something about the rougher stone of this temple. Or its squatter shape. Or the dark lagoon nearby.

Kip stretches his arms, reminding himself the closed wood door could open at any minute. Better concentrate on the job at hand. Kip visualizes the precise steps he'll need to take, when that door opens. First, three steps round the moving door, and grab the first guy out. Press the pistol to his temple, and hiss a 'shhh' before anyone yells. Then wave everyone who's there back in the doorway, and walk in right behind them. Hopefully with Bruce close on his heels.

Kip takes a deep breath, wondering again if he needs to pop more Inderal.

But he decides against it. Can't risk passing out, when the time for action comes.

Time passes. Slowly.

Noticing an irregularity in the ancient stone he's leaning against, Kip pivots and gazes up the steep face of the temple, and then grins, grimly, as he sees why the stone's different here. Kip's standing at the base of a 200-foot-long stone slide – a slide the shamans no doubt used, back in the bad old days, to dump their victims' butchered corpses, after they'd been sacrificed up top.

All Maya temples have this feature. But this particular stone slide is more overgrown with weeds and moss than any other slide Kip's seen, which is why he failed to notice it earlier. It's so badly overgrown that in most parts the stone and shrubs are indistinguishable, as if the slide itself reverted, some time ago, to a state of nature – the spectacle of all those gruesome deaths, over all those centuries, finally compelling the jungle to reclaim the Mask Temple's slide as one of its own.

The guide said the archeologists left Lamanai what, ten years ago? This looks more like *500*-and-ten years ago. But that's Central America for you. Everything here grows like weeds.

Like the wild herbs poking through the scrub beside the Mask Temple, which Kip kneels to inspect. These herb leaves are bigger than the leaves on any wild herb Kip's ever seen before.

Mindlessly Kip tugs on one of the plants, but it doesn't budge. Kip pulls again, harder, but fails again. Pissed, he sets down his gun, stands upright, bends at the waist, and yanks with all his might on the herb with both hands. At last the roots relent, and the herb emerges from the loamy soil, trailing a massive root system. Holy hell. The damn plant must weigh close to 50 pounds.

Kip drops the herb and shakes his head.

The fuckin' rain forest. Where life runs amok.

Kip retrieves his gun and, for the sake of his aching back, sits on the step beside the stone slide – leaning forward, in case the wood door suddenly opens.

But still the door stays shut, as quiet as the jungle in the night.

In school Kip never gave a damn about history. Yet here, in the near-pitch-dark of the fading moonlight, he can't shake the brooding spirit of the blood-flecked Maya past, all around him.

This place even *smells* like death.

Kip chuckles at his own uncharacteristic skittishness. *Note to Self: next time you go raid an old Maya temple, try to come up with a plan that does not involve standing in the shadow of the spooky old temple for an hour in the dark, right beside the old death slide. Done and done.*

But it can't just be the long bloody history this death slide's seen that's oppressing Kip, because all Maya temples have a death slide. It's something intangible about the Mask Temple, making it feel more primitive than other Maya temples. Like this temple was built by men more violent, and more *fearful*, than the builders of later Maya temples. Not haughty, aristocratic rulers, seeking to cow their vassals into submission by the sheer mass of their arrogant temples; but rather, bare-knuckled rulers, who still understood that they themselves had only recently emerged from the darker chaos of the jungle – and who still understood how thin the line is between man and beast. The builders of the Mask Temple had every reason to be proud of figuring out how to erect such an awesome building, centuries before Europeans built anything like it; yet, to Kip, it feels like they had no illusions that their advanced architectural skills separated them, in any meaningful way, from nature's harsher laws. To the contrary, it's like this huge squat violent and indestructible temple was built, not in defiance of nature, but in submission to its darker force.

A crashing noise nearby startles Kip. Instinctively he drops to one knee and assumes a shooting position, pointing his gun out at the dark jungle. Twenty yards away, Bruce, too, assumes a shooting position, and scans the tree line in all directions through the rifle sight of his AK-47.

But after five anxious minutes, Kip concludes it must've been just coatis, scuffling in the thickets. After waving to Bruce to stand down, Kip turns and takes a leak against the Mask Temple stone, and returns to watching the wooden door next to him.

Time passes. Slowly.

Kip works hard to keep focus. Whenever the beguiling touch of a former lover comes to mind, Kip squashes the image of her fragrant charms at once, by imagining the creak of the wood door beside him opening. Whenever a random family memory comes to mind, like his Marine Corps father scowling the day Kip wrecked his car, or his mother playing Jeopardy at home against the television contestants, or his little sister bawling her head off the day Kip tripped her and she broke all four front teeth, Kip squashes the random memory by reviewing, again, the precise sequence of steps he'll have to follow here, once the wood door opens, which could be this very second. And whenever he finds himself hearing, again, the endless indictments his ex-wife leveled against him, daily, during their short, unhappy marriage, Kip bites his own tongue to stop the noise.

But hardest for Kip to suppress is the fictitious internal dialogue he always carries on with Mel Fisher, the Key West treasure hunter who was Kip's mentor growing up in Florida. Crazy ole Mel, the butt of all jokes, never had two nickels to rub together – till 1985 when, at age 63, Mel found a billion dollar Spanish treasure ship off the Keys. And got the last laugh on everyone.

Mel was a tough old bird, but all those years before he struck gold, even with dozens of creditors circling like buzzards round his door, Mel never broke the law. So in the eternal call-and-shout that plagues Kip's mind, Mel regularly reproaches Kip for resorting to violence.

'*That's piracy, kid,*' Mel says. '*Leave me alone, Mel,*' Kip retorts. '*I'm not lucky like you.*'

At last, to Kip's relief, come the heedless harbingers of the dawn. First the howler monkeys stake out their territory, with huge scratchy roars, like antic children slowly opening un-oiled doors. Next the songbirds chirp, their numbers so immense they soon drown out the monkeys. And last comes another familiar jungle sound, which Kip can't quite place – a rhythmic beating of the leaves, a heavy flapping, like dozens of tents coming loose from their moorings all at once.

Kip puzzles without success for several minutes over that low, throbbing, flapping sound.

Until the first red tinge of dawn shows itself over the tops of the towering trees across the dark lagoon on its eastern shore. Now, in the grubby first light of day, Kip sees the cause of that familiar low, throbbing, flapping sound.

Buzzards.

Dozens of black vultures, swooping in and out of the trees, and circling right above Kip. Spooked, Kip walks a few steps out into the wild herbs, and casts his eye back up at the top of the Mask Temple, where he sees dozens more vultures, perched on the classic Maya roof comb.

What the hell? Kip's not superstitious, but buzzards'd strike anyone as a bad omen.

Kip looks across the scrub at Bruce and the guide. They plainly see the buzzards, too. Kip looks sideway at the wood door, still shut. Something's wrong. He can feel it in his gut.

Something's stirring those buzzards' blood lust. And whatever it is, it can't be good.

* * *

Deep in the throes of the most primordial of human passions, Dr. Clive Phelps remembers what his lover, Gemma Murray, likes best. Slowing the rhythm of his own aggressive thrusting, Clive gently, but persistently, traces small circles round the anterior junction of Gemma's dilated *labia minora*, then steadily shortens the radius of those circles, while accelerating the pace of his circumambient index finger, until the ever-tightening circles reach her smallest, most sensitive, part. As Clive anticipated, the coaxing motion of his circling finger induces Gemma's mouth to form a circle of its own, her swollen lips pursed in an expression of sweet surrender. Closing her pellucid eyes in pure ecstasy, Gemma emits a wild soprano moan, signaling her release.

The sights and sounds of Gemma's pleasure fill Clive with a primitive sense of his own power, causing Clive, in turn, to climax, with a wild rush of blood to his head, followed by a shudder in his loins, as he spills his seed into the dark passageway that leads to Gemma's womb – or, more accurately, medically speaking, the dark passageway that leads to oblivion, because of Gemma's prudent daily use of birth control pills. At the same moment, Clive's arms turn to jelly, and he collapses onto Gemma's supple body, his face parachuting into the pillow beside her head.

Clive knows that the proper etiquette, for lovers canoodling just after dawn in a lush bed in the swanky Jolly Roger resort on Ambergris Caye in Belize, calls for him to raise up on his elbows, gaze wordlessly into Gemma's eyes, and stay with her awhile for an after-glow. 'In the moment', as Gemma likes to say. And honestly, Clive wishes he was the kind of man who could stay 'in the moment.' But almost the instant his sperm departed, Clive felt the bright morning sunlight, flooding through the windows, warming Clive's thighs like a hot reproach. How much time has Clive lost already, dallying in bed? As he rises up on his elbows, Clive sneaks a glance at his travel clock – quickly noting the time, 7:30 a.m. – before gazing into Gemma's eyes, as good manners dictate.

"On the clock again today, are we?" Gemma sighs. "Clive, you really must learn to relax."

"I'm sorry, Gem – it's just, I'm nervous about my telomerase lecture this afternoon."

"Bollocks! You've given that telomerase lecture a dozen times. Everyone loves it. You're a Member of the Royal Society. You've testified before Parliament. Don't expect me to believe a small conference of half-crocked docs on holiday, who only came to Belize to get a sun-burn and probably wouldn't care if you just got up and mooned them all, makes you the least bit nervous."

Wriggling out from under Clive's carcass, Gemma smiles at him, and heads for the loo.

Well, at least Gem's in a jolly mood. A thundering good orgasm tends to do that.

The instant the bathroom door closes, Clive springs out of bed and heads straight for his medical journals, stacked high on the hotel room's desk.

But before he gets to the desk, Clive's attention is diverted by the sight of his entire naked body, captured in the room's full-length mirror. Every day Clive sees his handsome face, in the bathroom mirror; and sometimes even on the telly. But very rarely does Clive see his naked body, even though he's quite fit for a man of 38. And virtually never does Clive see the inspiring sight he now sees: his tumid priapic organ, still swollen from its recent congress with Miss Murray.

Clive cocks his head to contemplate the spectacle of his engorged member, pulsing hard with pure vitality. From a purely clinical point-of-view, the male erection is a tribute to the majesty of the human cell – and to the RNA-encoded telomeres upon which the life of every human cell depends. If only all our telomeres remained healthy and vibrant, we'd live forever; but like Clive's already-flagging erection, telomeres, too, lose steam and become frayed and useless, far too soon.

And then we die.

But is the cure for death, Clive wonders, as simple as the basic rhythms of life, expressed in the act of love in which he was so recently engaged? Perhaps—

Unfortunately, Gemma picks this very moment to pop back out of the bathroom to fetch a hairbrush, and catches Clive in the act of admiring his own life force in the mirror.

"What *is* it about men?" Gemma teases. "You just never get over having a penis, do you?"

Clive grins. "Definitely my favorite organ. I just wish he didn't run out of bullets so fast."

"I'm rather glad 'he' does." Gemma arches an eyebrow. "Or I'd never get a moment's rest."

She laughs and returns to the bathroom, just as Clive's mobile rings.

"Dr. Phelps? It's Robert Margulies at *The New York Times*. You asked me to call early today for our interview, so I hope I'm not too—"

"It's fine. Dawn is the only good time to catch me. Just remind me, your story is about . . . ?"

"Telomerase. Ever since the three Americans won the Nobel Prize last year for discovering telomerase, we've heard a lot about how vaccinating against telomerase may cure cancer. But my editor wants me to do a year-end story about the role of telomerase in aging and death, which we don't hear so much about. I'm told you're the world's leading expert on, well, on death."

"I prefer to say I'm an expert on *mortality*." Clive chuckles. "Sounds better."

"Okay. What's the current focus of your mortality research, Dr. Phelps?"

"Identifying a mechanism to activate telomerase in somatic human cells."

"But isn't everyone else trying to *kill off* telomerase with vaccines, so we don't get cancer?"

"They are," Clive says. "But cancer and immortality are just flip sides of the same coin."

A pause. Presumably the journo is writing down Clive's catchy quote. "In what sense?"

"Cancer cells replicate endlessly," Clive explains, "and are therefore theoretically immortal. Except of course they die when they kill their hosts. So as you correctly noted, the immortality of cancer cells is the problem to which most telomerase research is directed: how to kill cancer cells, before they kill us. But we mustn't forget, cancer cells have mastered the art our somatic cells have not – how to replicate beyond Hayflick's Limit, so they never grow old and die of their own accord."

"What's a 'somatic cell'?" Margulies asks. "And what's 'Hayflick's Limit'?"

Clive suppresses the urge to tell the journo to go look these things up on Wikipedia before wasting Clive's time. But Clive can't do that, because free publicity like this attracts investment money, like bees to honey. Still, realizing this interview'll take longer than he'd hoped, Clive sits down, the steel hotel desk chair cold against his naked bum. "A somatic cell is a non-cancerous cell – a 'good' cell, if you will. Somatic cells are all the cells in your body you want to live forever."

"Got it. I've heard that term before, 'somatic cell' – I just never knew what it meant."

"No problem," Clive says. "Dr. Leonard Hayflick is the scientist who discovered that, during a normal human lifetime, our somatic cells divide about 50 times, which keeps our bodies alive about 75 years, plus or minus – but then our cells hit the limit named for Dr. Hayflick, and stop dividing. Once our cells stop dividing, they grow senescent and die – and we, alas, die with them."

"I thought our skin cells regenerate, like, every day. Or, like, when we get cut, and bleed."

"If you suffer trauma, your skin cells engage in a healing process independent of Hayflick's Limit. And even absent trauma, you may feel you're always getting 'new skin' because, at any moment, about 5% of your skin cells are undergoing their regularly-scheduled recursive divisions. But each skin cell, individually, only divides about 50 times, like most other somatic cells – except those involved in the immune system, which divide more often but still reach a recursive limit."

"So how will you get our somatic cells to replicate beyond Hayflick's Limit?"

"Telomerase," Clive says. "Are you wearing shoes with laces right now?"

"Uh, yeah, I am. Sneakers."

"Splendid. Take one 'sneaker' off, Mr. Margulies, so you can follow with me here. Hold it up, and look closely at the ends of your shoelaces. Are the little plastic bits at the ends still intact?"

"Well, uh, one plastic end is intact, but the other one is really gnarly."

"Brilliant! Your shoelaces will make perfect illustrations of Hayflick's Limit. Let's start with the end where the plastic bit's still intact, shall we? Pull the lace out from the top eyehole in your sneaker there, and pinch the plastic bit between your thumb and forefinger. You with me?"

"Uh, yeah. Got it."

"Good. Now, imagine your shoelace is a cell. Each time the cell divides, the end of the cell gets run through the ringer, just the way the plastic bit at the end of your lace gets jammed in and out of the eyehole, each time you lace up your sneakers. So what happens to the cell is, with each replication, the end of the cell frays, and shortens, just like your shoelace does. Eventually the end of the cell becomes so frayed, it can't go through the ringer anymore, as I gather the other end of your shoelace there no longer can. Can you take hold of that 'gnarly' end a minute now, please?"

"You mean, the end that's already reached Hayflick's Limit?"

"Oh, well done, Robert! Truly, if all my students were so quick, I could spend more time in the laboratory. Yes, take hold of the end that's already reached Hayflick's Limit – the frayed end."

"Got it."

"Remember, the cell is your entire shoelace. So you see, like your shoelace with the frayed end, the cell still has plenty of life left in it, even though the end is frayed. It could keep replicating, unbounded, for many more decades – theoretically, forever – if only we could figure out how to fix the worn-out end of it, so it could keep on going through the eyehole of your sneaker during replication. But you already know how to keep your frayed old shoelace end working, don't you?"

"I spit on it," Margulies says, "and twist the frayed end, and then it goes through."

"Exactly what we all do to repair a frayed shoelace. And the way that cells repair that same problem – the frayed ends of cells, after so many replications – is telomerase."

"So telomerase is like spit?"

"Somewhat," Clive says. "Only telomerase doesn't come from the outside, like our saliva fixing shoelaces does. With cells, the fixer-upper, the telomerase, is already there, inside every cell. You see, in a human cell, the equivalent of the plastic bit at the end of your shoelace is called a telomere, which is what allows the cell to keep replicating. And next to the telomere, in every cell, is the enzyme we call telomerase, designed to repair the telomere, whenever it gets frayed."

"So why doesn't the telomerase fix our cells when our cells grow old?"

"That's the big mystery. Right now in our somatic cells – our 'good' cells – the telomerase just sits there, maddeningly dormant, while the cell grows senescent and dies. That's why we die."

"Then how do you even know telomerase can fix a frayed telomere?"

"Because in *cancer* cells, that's what telomerase does. That's why cancer cells could theoretically live forever. When the telomere at the end of a *cancer* cell starts to fray, the telomerase in a cancer cell leaps into action, repairs the frayed telomere, and the cancer cell keeps on replicating, far beyond Hayflick's Limit – until the cancer finally kills its host."

"So if you can figure out how to activate telomerase in somatic cells—"

"Then you and I can live forever – or at least, until we die from violence."

"In which case," Margulies says, "you'll be the doctor who conquered death."

"Indeed." Clive pauses, to give Margulies time to write down his own catchy words. "Fact is, Robert, death is just a disease, like any other. Waiting for a cure, just like any other disease."

A pause ensues. Clive can almost see the journo's pen, scribbling like mad.

"So, back to my original question, Dr. Phelps: what specific mortality research are you involved in, right now, to activate telomerase in somatic cells?"

"Well, I can't give away state secrets, Robert. We're trying many different compounds and enzymes, to see what's most effective in activating telomerase. But don't worry, we'll find it. As the famous medical saying goes, '*don't think, just try*'. So right now, we're trying lots of different things."

"Are you *close* to conquering death?"

Clive pauses. "The lawyers tell me I have to be very, very careful, answering predictive questions like that. We have investors, you see, and therefore stocks are involved. You have a veritable minefield of securities laws in your country, regarding 'forward-looking statements' and 'safe harbor provisions'. All I'm allowed to say is, we're making very good progress."

"Will there be clinical trials on humans soon?"

"Researchers other than I have already publicly predicted clinical trials of immortality drugs on humans within ten years," Clive says. "I believe it'll be sooner than that."

"Who are these other researchers? I'd like to quote them, if that's okay with you."

Clive hesitates. He hates to give his main rivals free publicity. Better to quote obscure academics. "I'll have my assistant fax you some names before noon. Will that be soon enough?"

"Yes, thank you. How much sooner than ten years d'you think the human trials will be?"

"I wouldn't care to hazard a guess publicly, Mr. Margulies. But I'll be sure to let you know, as far in advance of the clinical trials as the lawyers will allow me to."

"Thank you. By the way, I saw that before you won the Lasker Award and the Gruber Genetics Prize, you also won the Landon Prize back in 2001 – isn't that for cancer research?"

"Yes, it is. I started out doing cancer research, but then got hooked on mortality research."

"What made you switch?"

Clive blinks. An image of his tragic son, Nigel, flashes to mind. "Just a natural progression, I suppose. Like I said before, cancer and immortality are really flip sides of the same coin."

"Okay, thanks. If I find I have more questions later, would it be alright to call you again?"

"Absolutely. If I don't answer, leave me a voice mail, and I'll call back as soon as I'm able."

"Thanks so much, Dr. Phelps. Is there anything else you can tell me that I failed to ask?"

"You were lucky to be born when you were, Robert. I predict you'll never die."

Clive smiles and hangs up the phone. He ends all his interviews and lectures with that line.

Clive turns in his chair, and sees Gemma, showered and standing next to him, dressed in a breath-takingly skimpy sun dress. She's flipping through a tourist brochure.

"Why are you so much sexier *in* your clothes than I am out of mine?" Clive asks.

Gemma inspects Clive's naked body with clinical detachment. "It's a mystery. But what I want to know is, why does Lamanai have to be closed till next week? I really wanted to go there! But there's a day trip we can take to the Maya ruins at Altun Ha. Shall I sign us up for tomorrow?"

Clive looks at the stack of medical journals piled high on the desk.

"I – I need to work, Gem. Why don't you go to Altun Ha without me?"

Gemma puts a hand on one of her lithe hips. "No, love, I'm not going off on a dangerous junket in the primeval jungle without you. Would Wednesday be better for you?"

Clive winces. "Gem, I'm sure you'll be perfectly safe without me. The hotel wouldn't—"

"My safety is not the point. I came down here to spend quality time with you, Clive, away from Oxford and all your work." Ruefully Gemma glances at the stack of journals. "Or so I thought."

"And we've been together every second the past 24 hours," Clive points out.

"Well, if you don't count the three phone calls with your research assistants last night during dinner, and your constant emailing on your Blackberry all through our romantic moonlit beach walk last night, I suppose that would be true. But we're here for a week, Clive, not 24 hours."

"I have a lecture to give this afternoon," Clive pleads.

"Those journals are not for your lecture. They're – actually, I don't know what the hell they're for, or why you felt you had to drag them all the way down here to snarl up our vacation."

"Knowledge moves somewhat faster in medicine, dear, than it does in Maya studies." No sooner are these pompous words out his mouth than Clive regrets them. But it's too late to recant.

"Oh, *believe me*, I know your work is *far* more important than mine." Gemma stretches 'far' out till it's a three-syllable word. "That fact gets drummed into me whenever we're together. And 51 weeks of the year, that's fine with me, Clive. But this one week, while we're down here so close to the land that was once all Maya, couldn't we just *pretend* you think my work is important, too?"

"I *do* think your work is important, Dr. Murray. If you recall, we met because I read your book about Maya medicine – *Rainforest Remedies* – and I rang you to tell you how much I liked it."

"You rang me to quarrel with my thesis that a 'primitive' Maya healer can actually do more good for many human ailments with ancient healing herbs than modern pharmaceuticals do."

"That was just a diversionary tactic, Gem, so I could persuade you to have dinner with me."

"Don't try to charm your way out of this, you smoothie." Gemma sighs. "Clive, I don't want to argue with you. But I also do not wish to spend my holiday watching you read medical journals."

"Precisely why I think you should go to Altun Ha tomorrow without me. Old Maya ruins'll plainly interest you more than me. Meanwhile I'll attend the conference today, and plow through these journals without you tomorrow, and then I'll be more fun later in the week."

"But our holiday'll be half over by the time you come up for air!" Gemma protests. "Clive, I understand you have to attend the conference today. But what's so bloody important about these journals that you've got to read them tomorrow? Why can't they wait till next week?"

Clive looks at the blasted journals, but just can't give them up. "I'm running out of time."

"Why? Who's put a deadline on you? Your investors?"

"My son."

Gemma looks utterly gobsmacked. "Your son? *Nigel*?"

Clive nods. Seeing where this is going, he reaches for his wallet, lying there on the desk.

Gemma peers intently at Clive. "I don't have any idea how Nigel comes into your work. All you've ever told me is, Nigel's very sick, and lives with his mum."

Wordlessly Clive hands Gemma a recent photograph of Nigel Phelps.

Immediately, and involuntarily, Gemma recoils, stifling a gasp at the sight of Nigel's thin white hair, balding at the temples; his withered features; and the deep, wide wrinkles lining his skin.

"This was taken this summer, at Nigel's 9th birthday." Gloomily Clive stares at the photo, though every pixel in the digital image is forever burned into his mental hard drive. "We couldn't have a real party for the little guy, because he has no schoolmates. No friends his age, you see."

"Why – what's—?"

"Nigel has *progeria syndrome*. Accelerated aging. That's why he looks 69, instead of 9. He's got about three years to live. Unless I find a way to turn back the clock for him."

The travel brochure falls from Gemma's hand.

Absently Gemma bends to pick up the brochure. "Why didn't you tell me this before?"

"I don't like to tell people Nigel's the reason I switched from cancer research to mortality research. It sounds – a bit cheesy, I feel. And I don't want to put the poor fellow in the spotlight."

"But I'm not just – 'people'," Gemma protests.

"Precisely why I shared this with you, Gemma. For what it's worth, you're the only person, besides Nigel's mother, who's ever seen this photograph."

Gemma gazes awhile at the photograph of Nigel's preternaturally lined face. Then, with her uncanny knack for locating Clive's weakest point, even when she's not trying to expose him, she asks: "Can activating telomerase in human cells really 'turn back the clock' for Nigel?"

Clive bites his lip. "Probably not." Clive stands, suddenly aware of his foolish nakedness. "But it could stop the sands of time from running out any further on him than they already have."

Gemma raises a dubious eyebrow. "So then, if you were to find the key to activating telomerase, Nigel would stay – like this – forever?"

"Still better than being *dead*, wouldn't you agree?"

Gemma tilts her head, plainly startled by Clive's suddenly sharp tone. "Oh, of course, it's just – I – well, I—" abruptly, Gemma bursts into tears, and buries her head in Clive's shoulder.

Mechanically Clive swings an arm round her back. But the heat and pulse of the woman soon warms him up, and he wraps both arms round her in a true embrace.

"I'm sorry, Clive, I shouldn't have pressed," Gemma sobs.

"It's alright." Clive strokes her hair.

"No, it's not. It was so trusting of you to share all this with me. It helps me understand your obsession with work. But then I had to go and – press ..."

"It's all fine. Really, Gem. I'm glad we got all this out in the open."

Through her tears, Gemma gazes at Clive. "You sure?"

"I'm sure. I want everything out in the open between us. Always."

Gemma wipes her tears away and smiles, playfully giving Clive's naked torso a once-over. "I can see that. But will you be dressing for breakfast, or are you going in the buff?"

"I'll dress. And while I do, why don't you book us two seats to Altun Ha tomorrow?"

"Oh no, Clive, you don't have to—"

"Yes, I do," Clive mutters through clenched teeth. "Like you said, I need to learn to relax."

* * *

At the desk of her father's London hotel room, Joyce Kerr, 40, sits in shock – the condition she's been in, for two hours now – watching the legal representatives of the modern state perform the various morbid functions the law requires, whenever a human death is discovered.

First, there was the brief, horrid examination by the Hilton Hotel's house detective – a retired London cop in an appalling green suit, with an impenetrable Cockney accent, summoned by Joyce only because her 75-year-old father, Justin Kerr, failed to answer Joyce's knocks and calls this morning, even though Justin was so excited last night to get an early start on this, his first full day of vacation in London with his daughter, Joyce. The shock of finding her father dead in his bed had been so brutal, Joyce couldn't recall much from the time she spent with the hotel's green-suited rent-a-cop, except he said 'stand back, Missy, this may be a crime scene' when Joyce got close to the inert cadaver her father had become, to try to glean what happened.

Next came the local Southwark constabulary, who treated Joyce with the officious respect they must, presumably, be trained to give any member of the deceased's family who, so far as they know, is both bereaved and yet, also, a potential suspect in the death – their chilly courtesy prompting Joyce to seek refuge in the desk chair, for the duration of these inescapable formalities.

Last came Scotland Yard, and the London coroner, to investigate the scene, properly. Their arrival turned out to be both good and bad. The good – if anything can be termed 'good' on the day of your father's death – is that Scotland Yard and the coroner soon concluded it was an 'apparent' heart attack, which meant Joyce stopped feeling like the unjustly accused in a Kafka novel. The bad, however, was that 'procedure' requires, evidently, hours of tedious examination to confirm the egregiously obvious fact that Joyce's elderly father died while masturbating.

Because lying on the floor, never expressly acknowledged, yet plainly not unnoticed by any of the various officials passing through the room, is a girlie magazine titled, laconically, 'Gents'.

Oh, this whole ordeal is all too grim, and mortifying, to be actually happening!

And yet it is. As Joyce's 12-year-old daughter, Lisa – currently ensconced, by court order, with Joyce's utterly unreliable ex-husband, Michael – likes to say, 'it is what it is, Mom.'

Yeah, Lisa. It is what is. But what *this* is, if anyone ever makes me spell it out for you, as one day they may, well, it ain't good. Your grandfather – my father, whom I've loved and honored all my 40 years – died jacking off to a bosomy lovely named Tiffany. *If* that really is her name.

So Joyce sits in shock, feeling miserable. Her knuckles ache from drumming them on the desk all afternoon, since this is no-smoking room, and she desperately needs a cigarette. What a bad time she picked to try to quit. Her upper arm itches from the patch, which did not agree with her, and left a rash; and her brain is crying out for the sweet relief a smoke would afford her.

Yet instead of sweet relief, all Joyce has is busty Tiffany, falling out of her preposterously tight top. Thank God Joyce's mother, Ellen, died six years ago, and didn't have to endure this humiliating end to her husband's erratic life. Random words of Justin's assault Joyce's mind: *No matter what you young people think, the need for loving never dies*. OK, Daddy, I believe you. But when you said the 'need for love', did you really mean the need for 'Double-G Tiffany'?

Alone with her own ironic dialogue with her dead father, Joyce chokes back bitter tears.

To Joyce's relief, the lead Scotland Yard detective, Barry Foulds, sits on the bed, ready for a 'convo' with Joyce, as little Lisa would call it. Bad as this convo may be, it can't be any worse than sitting alone with her own dark thoughts about her father's final vulgar moments on earth.

"Do you have any family here in England?" Detective-Inspector Foulds asks.

Joyce shakes her head no – but then remembers her cousin, twice-removed. "Well, I do have one cousin in London, but she's 85 and we're not on speaking terms, and she's been lost in her own little world for 50 years, translating a single ancient Maya codex. So – ah, no, basically."

Foulds gives Joyce a very strange, almost bewildered, look, as he drinks this in.

"Is there a problem?" Joyce asks. "Am I legally required to notify my cousin or something?"

"No." Foulds raises an eyebrow. "Is your cousin, by any chance, named Fiona Young?"

Joyce's eyes open wide. "Yes! How did – how could you possibly know that?"

"I met Dr. Young last year, when she was lying down in front of a digger, protesting the demolition of an unlisted 18th century house in St. Thomas Street."

Joyce gapes. "I – I didn't know Fiona ever left her flat. She's a legendary hermit."

"For this one old house she made an exception. God knows why." Foulds coughs, very dry. "Right. I assume you'll want to take your father's body back to the States for burial?"

Joyce blinks. She hadn't thought this far ahead. "Well, um, Daddy wanted to be cremated."

Foulds brightens. "Ah! That will make things much easier. You're certain?"

Joyce meets the detective's eyes. "Perhaps I'd better call our lawyer, just to be sure."

So Joyce calls her boss, attorney David Burns in Ann Arbor, Michigan, an old family friend of the Kerrs. David is, as always, great in a crisis. After making sure Joyce is okay, David confirms that Justin Kerr's Will specifies cremation and no service. He also tells Joyce he will handle, from Ann Arbor, the arrangements for the London cremation, the death notices, and booking Joyce the earliest flight back home. Half an hour later, David calls back, apprising Joyce he's hired Honor Oak Crematorium in Southwark, apologizing that he couldn't get her on a flight back to Detroit until tomorrow afternoon, and promising to meet her plane. Joyce thanks David warmly, and hangs up.

"All set," Joyce reports to Foulds. "Honour Oak Crematorium will pick up the body. I'll take the ashes home tomorrow afternoon." Joyce blinks away tears. "No muss, no fuss."

"Honour Oak are very reliable." Foulds' eyes size Joyce up a moment. "Will you need any assistance before they get here, Mrs. Kerr? We have someone you can talk to, if you like."

"It's *Miss* Kerr," Joyce whispers. "And no, I'll be alright. Thank you, though."

Foulds nods. His eyes scan the books and papers on Justin Kerr's hotel desk, stopping at a copy Justin made yesterday afternoon, at the British Library, of a 19 July 1868 story in Lloyd's Illustrated Newspaper, about the death of Justin Kerr's great-grandfather, Roger Quinlan:

DEATH OF AN EXPLORER

On Friday 17th July Dr. Lankester held an Inquest in the Grand Hall of the Royal Society for the Improvement of Natural Knowledge, Burlington House, Piccadilly, on the body of Roger Quinlan, aged 29 years. Mr. Quinlan, the only son of the late Chester Quinlan of Mary-le-bone, and formerly a medical student at Christ Church College, Oxford, very recently returned from scientific explorations in the uncharted jungles of Honduras, and was addressing, in excited utterances, a crowd of spectators on the paving stones outside Burlington House, when he suddenly fell down dead.

Two members of the Royal Society, Dr. A.M. Higgins and Dr. J.D. Grove, carried Mr. Quinlan into Burlington House to administer emergency ministrations, which proved ultimately unsuccessful. Thereafter it was determined that the Inquest should be conducted within the Royal Society, even though Mr. Quinlan was not a Member.

Dr. Higgins testified that on Friday morning Mr. Quinlan arrived at Burlington House, and in an animated manner attempted to nominate himself as a new Member of the Royal Society, claiming he'd discovered the lost Mayan city of Lamanai, deep in the wilds of the Honduras jungle; and claiming further, that amidst the ruins there, he had found the fabled Fountain of Youth. When Royal Society functionaries advised Mr. Quinlan that new Members are not permitted to nominate themselves, Mr. Quinlan prevailed upon his wife, Kathleen Quinlan, then in attendance, to nominate him; and when the Society's functionaries further advised that women may not make nominations, Mr. Quinlan created a disturbance, which resulted in Dr. Higgins being summoned to eject Mr. Quinlan from the premises.

Dr. Higgins further testified that, so far as he could determine from brief personal observations, made whilst escorting Mr. Quinlan out of Burlington House, Mr. Quinlan appeared to be, in spite of his manifest excitability, perfectly sober and of sound mind and body; indeed, Mr. Quinlan struck Mr. Higgins as the very picture of robust good health, being unusually tall and impressively strong, quite handsome, and exceedingly fit, although deeply sun-burnt from his recent travels in the tropics.

Dr. Grove testified that, an hour after Mr. Quinlan was ejected from Burlington House, he and Dr. Higgins left Burlington House with the intention of taking their mid-day meal at their club, when they discovered that Mr. Quinlan had, by this time, gathered a crowd of spectators in Piccadilly, just outside Burlington House, and was expatiating upon the topic of his recent explorations in Honduras. Mr. Quinlan produced a beaker of Liquid from the warm south, which he claimed contained waters from the Fountain of Youth; and, with a magician's flair for the dramatic, quaffed the Liquid in a single gulp, before announcing that his Discovery would forever "change the world, for people will now live for many centuries, if not forever."

Then suddenly the beaker slipped from Mr. Quinlan's hand and broke on the paving stones; Mr. Quinlan bent over double at the waist, as if in the grip of a great Ague; his face became extremely florid; and without another word, Mr. Quinlan collapsed upon the paving stones. Dr. Grove examined Mr. Quinlan on the spot, and determined he had succumbed to a raging tropical fever, which had caused his heart to stop beating.

Mr. Quinlan's wife Kathleen, a young woman of remarkable personal attractions, although deeply sun-burnt from accompanying her husband on his travels in the tropics, was barely able to speak, due to her deep distress at witnessing the recent untimely death of her young and vigorous husband. Mrs. Quinlan testified that, for the past two months, her husband had been imbibing small quantities of the waters from the beaker, which he collected during his explorations in the jungle at Lamanai, without any noticeable ill effect upon his health. She testified that she had not drunk the waters from the beaker, but in all other respects, she imbibed the same food and drink as her husband, the past two days. Thereafter Mrs. Quinlan broke down in a paroxysm of sobbing and had to be excused from the proceedings.

The Coroner said that the lamentable case was without a doubt a death resulting from an exotic tropical poison, which originated, apparently, in a previously undiscovered fountain of death, which Mr. Quinlan unfortunately mistook for the fountain of youth.

The jury concurred with the Coroner, returning a verdict "that the deceased explorer expired from the effects of a disease of unknown origin, most likely contracted from imbibing an unknown native poison, acquired during his recent travels in Honduras."

The Coroner thanked the Members of the Royal Society for their humanitarian efforts, and concluded the Inquest by noting that Mrs. Quinlan had donated all the deceased explorer's papers and plaster casts of Indian writing to the British Museum; and assuring the public that all necessary sanitation measures had been taken in Piccadilly, including the covering of the Liquid, accidentally spilled by Mr. Quinlan, with several cubic yards of fresh soil, to ensure that the venomous Poison spilled there would not endanger the public health.

Detective-Inspector Foulds looks up from reading. "Is everyone in your family a Mayan scholar, Miss Kerr?"

"Huh? Oh – no, Daddy's an engineer." Joyce waves an absent hand in the air, as she recognizes, too late, her inadvertent verb tense error. "*Was*, an engineer. And I'm a paralegal."

Idly Foulds paws through the other books and papers Justin left scattered on the desk. "But these all seem to be about the Quinlans, and their search for lost Mayan cities."

As Foulds is talking, Joyce notices that one of the books Foulds just overturned – a handwritten diary by Roger Quinlan's wife, Kathleen Quinlan – now lies open, exposing a stamp inside its cover which was previously not visible: 'Property of the British Library'.

Since the British Library is *not* a lending library, the presence of one of its books here, in the Southwark Hilton Hotel, is irrefutable evidence that Justin must've stolen it yesterday. But – much as the sharp-eyed Foulds chose, presumably from discretion, not to rub Joyce's face in the ample cleavage of buxom Tiffany, lying there on the floor – so, too, sharp-eyed Foulds now appears not to notice the incriminating library stamp, inside the cover of Kathleen Quinlan's diary.

Joyce isn't sure why she feels a need to cover-up her father's latest crime. After all, Justin's stone cold dead. So it's not like anybody's going to charge him, posthumously, with misappropriating an obscure national treasure from the British Library. If Kathleen Quinlan's diary even qualifies as a treasure. Which Joyce sincerely doubts.

But still. It's bad enough the police know all about Justin's fatal obsession with Tiffany. Joyce sees no need to drag her father's name further through the mud, with official recognition that Justin was also, apparently, a book thief. Taking a deep breath, and trying her best to look casual, like an absent-minded grieving daughter, Joyce answers the detective's implicit question, while at the same time closing shut Kathleen Quinlan's diary: "Roger Quinlan was Daddy's great-grandfather. Daddy was hoping we could learn more about Roger on this vacation to London."

Foulds seems to accept this explanation, and prattles on awhile about Fiona Young and Roger Quinlan, and the 'Mayans', as he calls them, though Joyce knows, from her cousin Fiona Young – once a Professor of Central American Studies at the University of Michigan, who helped raise Joyce before she stopped speaking to her – that the original residents of the Yucatan Peninsula and Guatemala are properly known as the 'Maya', not the 'Mayans', and that 'Mayan' is an adjective used only for the language of the Maya. But Joyce listens to

Foulds with only half an ear, because she's trying to reconstruct how and when, exactly, her father filched Kathleen Quinlan's diary from the British Library.

Justin must've swiped it as they were leaving yesterday afternoon, when he made such a fuss about needing to use the toilet. Vaguely Joyce remembers Justin opening his briefcase at the security desk, and then abruptly hurrying off to the restroom, pleading an urgent need, while Joyce alone passed through the security detector, with Justin's briefcase. Then, when Justin came back from the restroom, he must've avoided going through the detector – unbeknownst to Joyce.

Who knew her father was such an adroit and talented thief?

Justin Kerr was a brilliant engineer, and an idealist who used what even he admitted were extreme tactics to try to save the small laser company he co-founded in the 1960s from being sold to a big conglomerate by his greedier partners. Those 'extreme tactics' were later deemed, by prosecutors and juries, to constitute embezzlement. Which Joyce has no doubt is exactly what they were – even though Justin only misappropriated corporate funds to try to weaken the balance sheet and prevent the sale of the company he loved, rather than for personal profit.

Still and all, though, Justin Kerr was no crook. So far as Joyce knows, Justin only broke the law once in his life, and that was part of a complex corporate battle. He was no thief.

Or was he?

Obviously, there were many things Joyce never knew about her father. Ruefully Joyce glances at Tiffany the cover girl, still lying on the floor, directly beneath the man whose dying thoughts were, presumably, all devoted to Tiffany's deep *décolletage*.

"It might be best if you wait downstairs, Miss Kerr, for the Honor Oak men to come." Foulds looks sincerely concerned about Joyce. "Sitting in here alone with the body could be a bit—"

Joyce starts to argue – but then she imagines the sweet relaxation she would feel, deep in her brain, from a cigarette, were she to leave Justin's no-smoking room. There must be someone downstairs she can bum a smoke from.

"Yes, thank you, I will wait downstairs. But would it be okay if first I collect all my father's things? So I don't have to come back in here later?"

Respectfully Foulds nods assent.

Joyce collects everything from the closet and the bathroom – leaving only the empty airplane-size bottles of Scotch, which Justin left littered around the sink – and throws it all into his suitcase. Then she sweeps all the books and papers off the desk into the suitcase, too. She can return the stolen diary to the British Library tomorrow morning, before her afternoon flight.

But seeing the diary causes Joyce to wonder: why in the world did Justin Kerr think Kathleen Quinlan's diary was important enough to risk stealing?

Chapter Two
The Way of All Flesh

Monday 27 December 2010

When the sun rises above the trees along the western shore of the New River Lagoon, Kip Hunter decides he's had enough of the ominous buzzards circling overhead. Time for action.

Pistol drawn, Kip creeps three steps sideways and grabs the handle of the wood door the 19th century archeologists cut into the tomb at the base of the Mask Temple at Lamanai.

What the hell. Time to grip it and rip it. Let the chips fall where they may.

Lightly Kip tugs on the door handle. But it's locked. *Shit!*

Pistol still drawn, Kip scrambles backwards across the open swath of wild herbs between the Mask Temple and the jungle, eyes glued on the door. When he reaches the shadows where Bruce Tobin and the guide stand, Kip says: "New plan. Both of you, come with me. Real quiet."

Back across the open swath of herbs the three men walk, Kip and Bruce with guns drawn.

When they reach the temple, Kip pulls one block of C-4 from his pack, loops it over the door's handle, and lights the detonator. Then he opens his arms, wide as the wings of the circling buzzards, and hurls Bruce and the guide up onto the stone steps of the temple behind the door.

With a deafening blast, the C-4 blows a huge hole in the wood door of the tomb.

Acrid smoke fills the air. At once, a thick cloud of insects emerges from the tomb.

Kip and Bruce leap up from the stone steps, guns drawn. Bruce reaches one arm with his AK-47 through the four-foot hole in the door, and blindly sprays a few rounds into the tomb.

No one returns Bruce's fire.

Kip grabs the guide, and shoves him first through the hole in the door. Still, no one fires.

So Kip pulls a flashlight from his backpack, and follows the guide through the hole in the door, with Bruce right on his heels. As soon as he enters, Kip's nostrils are assaulted by a putrid, sickly stench – not the C-4, but something much nastier, like rancid sweet-and-sour pork.

At first there's no time to wonder what the foul odor is because, from somewhere across the tomb, Kip hears boots tromping. He shines his light towards the footsteps, ready to fire; but just in time he sees it's Harry Benz, AK-47 drawn, emerging through the door from the stairway.

Kip exhales a sigh of relief, but with his next breath, he realizes what's causing the awful stink in the tomb. He smelled it many times in the Gulf. He's smelled it in Belize a few times, too.

It's the fetid smell of death.

In a fast sweep, Kip shines his flashlight around the tomb. Everywhere the air is thick with insects. And strewn across the floor, in a diorama straight out of Dante, are myriad Maya corpses, twisted into the unnatural positions only the dead can assume. Some are prone; some are supine; some are curled in the fetal position. But no one in the tomb is moving, except Kip and his team.

"Mother of God!" The guide makes the sign of the cross. "You bastards killed them all."

In the flickering light of his flashlight, Kip stares in disbelief at the slew of Maya bodies sprawled across the floor. No way one block of C-4 could do this much damage. Did Bruce really squeeze off enough rounds to kill every last one of the Maya, shooting blind through the door?

Impossible. Kip peers into the gloom, wondering if these crafty Maya are playing possum, lying still as death, just waiting till Kip and his mercs put their guns away, before jumping them.

Bruce turns and retches, his vomit splattering onto the face of the nearest Maya, sprawled there on the earthen floor. The Maya doesn't flinch. Doesn't even twitch a single muscle.

A well-trained man can discipline a lot of muscles in his body to stay still, in spite of many provocations. But not the facial muscles – at least not when splattered with human vomit. No way.

These guys aren't playing possum. They're dead as doornails.

A loud thudding noise shakes Kip – which turns out to be Kip's own heart, beating very fast from a sudden surge of adrenaline, overpowering his beta-blockers. Then the light moves very fast across the tomb's floor, straight at Kip, stopping right at his feet – because his wrist has gone limp.

Kip pulls himself together, and sweeps the tomb again with his flashlight. The tomb is empty, except for the dead bodies, and an old stone sarcophagus in one corner. But this time Kip sees, in addition to the insects hovering over the bodies, that the bodies are crawling with maggots.

"We didn't kill these guys." Kip lets his flashlight linger, for the benefit of his young mercs, on the maggots eating one of the corpses. "Maggots hatch fast down here – but not *this* fast."

Having reassured Bruce and Harry they committed no atrocity, Kip sweeps the tomb again with his flashlight, in a slower arc. This time, besides the maggots, he notices, perched atop the closed stone sarcophagus in the corner, a small jade statue. Kip's flashlight projects the statue's silhouette onto the far wall, the projection exaggerating every feature. Most prominent among the silhouetted features are a grotesquely oversized penis, erect and curving upwards like a lethal scimitar, reaching above the statue's shoulders – and the fact that the little statue has *two heads*.

Bingo! Kip strides across the tomb, seizes the two-headed trophy he came for, and stuffs it in his backpack. Mission accomplished.

Hanging from the ceiling above the sarcophagus Kip sees two metal spikes, and scratched on the wall behind the sarcophagus is some Maya graffiti. Briefly he wonders: *Why is the Maya writing so close to the ground? And who put metal spikes in this ancient Maya tomb, since metal was unknown on this continent before the Spanish Conquest? And what were the spikes used for?*

But as fast as these questions enter Kip's mind, he dismisses them as the kind of useless academic questions that geeks like Ron Graham waste their lives trying to answer. With so many dead men lying around, in a room he just broke into, Kip lacks time to ponder old mysteries.

For although Kip's young mercs may be relieved to learn they didn't kill all these guys, still, there's a whole lot of bad shit going down here – shit which will hit the fan next week, at the latest, when Lamanai is opened back up to the public, and these bodies are discovered. Kip's gloved crew won't leave fingerprints; but the crime scene hounds also won't miss the AK-47 bullet holes in the walls, much less the big hole in the door from the C-4. And if the cops somehow find Kip's guide and question him, the guide'll fold faster than a flimsy house of cards.

Kip swings his light away from the sarcophagus, and looks at the trembling guide, standing beside Bruce and Harry in the middle of the tomb. All three of them are staring glassy-eyed at the corpses. Without deciding what to do about the guide, Kip joins them in inspecting the dead.

Kip's eye is drawn first to the two older men, clad in thin red robes, open at the chest. Kux Ahawis, Kip presumes, and the other elder. These two old guys are much more damaged than their young novitiates. In fact, what happened to Kux and his mate is straight out of *Indiana Jones*. Both chests are hollowed out, like dugout canoes, with gaping holes where their hearts should be.

By contrast, as Kip plays his flashlight across the splayed corpses of the young novitiates, he sees no signs of violence, no marks of any kind on their remains, other than the damage from the feasting maggots. Kip's no coroner – and he's sure as hell not going to examine these gruesome corpses up close and personal – but he's seen men dead from bullets, knives, and even strangulation, and he knows these young guys in the Mask Temple died from something else.

"Antil's Curse," the guide intones in a gloomy voice.

Since Kip has no idea what the guide's blubbering about, he ignores him.

Instead, seeing a jade amulet on the neck of the closest corpse, Kip takes a deep breath, swats away the bugs, leans in close, and yanks the guy's amulet free in one swift swipe.

The jade amulet is curved, in the shape of a horn. And it looks like it might be valuable.

Kip drops the amulet into his backpack, and then swings his flashlight across the various corpses again. They all have similar curving jade amulets round their necks.

But before he can order Bruce and Harry to confiscate the other amulets, Kip's gut warns him, something's not right here. What's the body count? Across the corpses Kip swings his light again, this time not lingering on any one corpse, but carefully counting all the dead in the tomb.

Eleven young guys, plus the two elders. Thirteen total. *Shit!*

"Harry!" Kip hisses. "You kill any guys coming in here?"

"No, sir."

"You see anyone on the stairs, dead or alive?"

"No, sir."

"Then there's four young Maya still alive out here somewhere. Time for us to move out."

"Yes, sir." But Harry hesitates. "Sir, with respect, the other four guys probably ran away when their mates died. Or they might be lying dead, in one of the other temples out here."

"Or they might be out hunting, or just sleeping somewhere else, away from all these corpses," Kip retorts. "We have no way of knowing. But what we do know is, we got what we came for. And we just made more noise than a Mexican on the Day of the Dead. So it's time to move out."

The four men climb out the hole Kip blew in the door, and set off on a dead run, two miles through the teeming jungle, clamorous now with morning noise. By the time they reach the guide's skiff, still tied to the ceiba tree, they're all deeply winded.

The whole time, they haven't heard a peep to suggest anyone's tracking them.

But like anyone with any sense in Central America, they fear the reputation of the Maya.

So they just keep moving, fast as they can. They shove the skiff out into the New River Lagoon, and clamber into it. The young mercs paddle furiously, while the guide fires up the motor. Kneeling low in the prow, pistol drawn, Kip scans the silent mangrove along the bank.

The motor kicks in and, swiftly accelerating, the skiff leaps a few lengths out into the river.

Bruce and Harry stow the paddles beneath the thwarts.

And then, without a sound, Bruce and Harry both keel over, sprawling across the thwarts.

At once Kip dives even lower, so his entire body is beneath the top of the skiff's gunwales.

A second later, the guide kills the motor, and also dives below the top of the gunwales.

In the deathly silence of the floating skiff, Kip leans his head back to where Bruce lays, blood spurting from both sides of his throat. Protruding from Bruce's throat are two short sharp wooden spears, still quivering from the force with which they were launched from unseen *atlatls*.

Kip yanks both spears out, but Bruce is dead, for each spear hit a carotid artery, stopping all the blood to Bruce's brain. Keeping below the gunwales, Kip jerks his head across the skiff to Harry, and sees two more spears, in the same two fatal locations, on either side of Harry's throat.

Jesus! These four Maya are as good as any snipers Kip ever saw in the Gulf.

"Antil's Curse," the guide croaks, from his scug at the back of the skiff.

Kip grabs Bruce's AK-47 and, reaching only the rifle and his hands above the top of the port side gunwale, sprays dozens of rounds wildly at the mangrove up and down the western bank of the New River Lagoon. In the air above the skiff Kip sees shards of tree bark spitting up from the hail of bullets. Only after emptying the clip does Kip pull the rifle and his hands back in the boat.

From the mangrove comes no reply.

Kip grabs Harry's AK-47, and rasps at the guide: "This time, when I start firing, reach up and start that motor, and get us the fuck outta here."

"I'll be a sitting duck," the guide says. "I can't start the motor without exposing my head."

Kip points Harry's rifle at the guide. "You're already a sitting duck, Al. If you don't start that fucking motor before I empty this clip, I'll cap you myself with my pistol. *Comprende*?"

Kip glares at the guide a few seconds, to be sure his message got through.

Then he lifts Harry's AK-47 over the portside gunwale, and starts firing.

The guide lifts his head and reaches for the cord on the outboard motor. But before the guide can pull on the cord, four wooden spears appear, silent and quivering, in the guide's throat.

The guide keels over backwards, dead.

Kip's seen enough. Staying below the gunwale, he empties Harry's clip at the trees, tosses his pistol into his seamless submersible waterproof backpack, zips the pack shut, and puts it on his back. Then he takes a deep breath, slips over the starboard gunwale, and plunges into the deep warm water of the New River lagoon.

Kip swims underwater as long as he can, pulling for the east bank. When his need for air grows desperate, he wills himself to stay under longer, by imagining four wooden spears lancing his throat, the instant he pokes his head above water. Finally, with his lungs about to burst, Kip contrives, by rolling his body 180 degrees, to let only his mouth and nose break the calm surface of the lagoon. After gulping fresh moist air into his lungs, he goes back under, and keeps swimming.

When at last he reaches the east bank, Kip grabs hold of the mangrove roots, and hauls himself up from the lagoon into a dense thicket of mangrove. He looks back across the lagoon, half-expecting to see the four Maya using the guide's skiff to cross the water in pursuit of Kip.

But the guide's skiff is still drifting aimlessly along, near the west bank of the lagoon.

Still, Kip knows better than to celebrate. The Maya are legendary trackers.

His only hope is to hike back fast to civilization. And pray they don't hunt him down there.

* * *

As he accepts another glass of champagne, Dr. Clive Phelps gives the comely young Belizean waitress at the cocktail party his most winsome smile. The young lovely returns the smile, her lips as moist and luscious as a newly-replicated cell, laid out in a Petri dish beneath Clive's microscope. As she departs, Clive casts what he believes to be a surreptitious gaze upon her receding form, her shapely backside undulating beguilingly with every joyful step.

Surely, Clive thinks, our Maker – He, She or It – was sending us a very clear message, by designing young women with such enticing forms. If only we could decode that message.

"She's too young for you," Gemma Murray scolds.

"Alas, I fear you're right," Clive admits.

"But not if what you told us this afternoon about telomerase proves true!" exclaims a young man standing nearby, whose name tag proclaims that he is 'Samuel Rivera, Belize Coroner'. "If we all learn to live forever," Rivera continues, "then age won't matter anymore, will it?"

Clive smiles. "Age already seems not to matter to you, Dr. Rivera."

Rivera cocks his head in puzzlement. "I don't know what you mean."

"Well, I hope you don't mind my saying so, but you are very youthful looking, Samuel, for a man who is already Coroner for Belize."

"I'm a rare commodity here in Belize," Rivera says with pride. "A Guy's man."

Gemma raises a perplexed and uneasy eyebrow at this queer remark. But Clive smiles.

"A Guy's man," Clive explains to Gemma, "is a doctor who studied at Thomas Guy's Hospital in London." He turns back to Rivera. "One of the finest hospitals in the world."

Rivera beams. "May I ask: how do the new therapies for aging we read about, like Juvenon and Resveratrol, compare with the telomerase therapy you plan to unveil in the next decade?"

"Like tiny plasters on a war wound." Seeing the pretty young waitress approaching, Clive quaffs down his champagne, and signals for a refill. Truly, she could make any man an alcoholic, for if the only price for perusal of her lovely brown skin and voluptuous form be an empty glass, who wouldn't drain his glass as fast as liquid can pass down the esophageal passageway?

"Tiny plasters on a war wound?" Rivera repeats. "I don't understand."

The lithesome young waitress refills Clive's glass, while Clive indulges a passing fantasy about what it must have been like to live in Belize in the 18th century, as one of the rough-and-ready Englishmen then running the colony, who reputedly took regular advantage of the luscious native girls, whenever they felt the need to release the kind of raw animal desire Clive feels now.

"Juvenon is just a band-aid on the aging problem," Clive says. "All it does is try to slow the decay of mitochondria, the organelles in cells that give us energy. So if you take Juvenon, you may *feel* younger – and my Berkeley colleagues will certainly feel *richer* – but you're still aging at the normal rate. What's the good of that? Resveratrol actually has more potential, but what they're selling now doesn't have much more impact on your longevity than a glass of red wine every day."

"Whereas," Dr. Rivera says, "you hope to stop the aging process dead in its tracks?"

"Exactly." Clive drains his champagne, to be ready in case the very avatar of youth and sexuality passes by again. "With these human hands, I plan to put an end to death by mitosis."

"Sorry," Gemma interjects, "but I don't know what 'mitosis' is."

"Sex," Clive says. "Aristotle was basically right when he said, 'death is the price we pay for sex'. Not in the literal sense medieval Christians believed, where each sex act supposedly shortened your life span by a day. But in the broader sense that all creatures who reproduce by mitosis eventually die. The beasts in the field, the birds in the air, the fish in the sea, and, alas, us – we all die because we reproduce by sex."

"What other way is there to reproduce," Gemma asks, "besides sex?"

"Binary fusion. That's what amoebae and bacteria do. Amoebae and bacteria never die 'naturally', though they can be killed if their food supply is cut off, or if violence destroys them."

"So," Gem teases, "if you find a way round 'death by mitosis', will that be the end of sex?"

"I certainly hope not!" Clive says. "I'm not looking to alter human reproductive mechanisms – I just want to make us immune to organic death. But sex is definitely part of the puzzle, because the human organism is, right now, programmed, from birth, to die. From the moment a girl is born, she carries the next generation in her womb. It's almost as if those unfertilized eggs were pushing her along, towards death's door, before she even gets to wear her first mini-skirt. What I'm seeking is the right combination of enzymes to unbind the telomerase—"

Gemma looks like she's warming up for a frisky retort – but suddenly everyone's attention is diverted by a serious-looking waiter who rushes in, and pulls Rivera off to one side. When Rivera emerges from his private chat with the waiter, he looks very grave – and is focused on Gemma.

"Dr. Murray," Rivera says, "could I have a word with you, and Dr. Phelps, in private?"

Clive exchanges 'why not' glances with Gemma, and they adjourn to a corner with Rivera.

"I need your help," Rivera murmurs to Gemma. "The police have discovered 16 deaths."

"*Sixteen deaths!*" Gemma whispers. "From what?"

"Three were found in a boat, with *atlatl* spears in their throats." Rivera turns to Clive. "*Atlatls* are an ancient Maya weapon. Ten years at this job, I've never seen death by *atlatl* spears."

"And the other thirteen?" Clive asks.

"Worse." Rivera's eyes dart around the room. "I need complete confidentiality here."

"Of course," Clive says. Gemma nods her head in assent also.

"The other thirteen victims were all full Maya. Very rare, these days." Rivera lowers his already soft voice. "Preliminary reports indicate it may have been something, ah, ritualistic."

"You mean," Gemma gasps, "*human sacrifice*?"

"That's what I fear," Rivera says. "And if that happened, in this part of the world, a violent backlash against the Maya is possible. So your absolute discretion is essential to public safety."

"Of course." Gemma says. "But why are you telling us all this?"

"The Belize Police, like my office, have no one who speaks Mayan. You do."

Gemma gapes. "Oh, Dr. Rivera – the Mayan language has over 30 dialects. I know three."

"Well, that's three more than I have now. I need you to come to Lamanai with me tonight, Dr. Murray, and stay two days. Accommodations will be rough. But we'll compensate you for all the inconvenience. Basically, you send us a bill, and it'll be paid, no questions asked."

Gemma turns to Clive, a wild surmise in her eyes.

Clive shrugs acquiescence, already thinking of the journals he'll now get to read in peace.

Gemma turns back to Rivera. "Can Dr. Phelps come, too?"

"We can't pay Dr. Phelps for his time," Rivera says. "But of course we'd be honored to have such a world-famous doctor on site, to observe the autopsies."

Gemma turns to Clive. "Will you come? It'll be far more interesting than Altun Ha."

Inwardly Clive groans. But he can see the writing on the wall. "Why, of course."

* * *

Joyce Kerr opens the mini-bar in her room at the Southwark Hilton. Any other night she'd opt for the cheap wine in the screw-top bottles – the kind of light-bodied wine she drank all through her courtship with Michael, back in the day. But today's been such a long bad day, Joyce finds herself reaching, as her father evidently did last night, for those fiendish little bottles of Scotch.

After emptying two of the little bottles into a plastic cup, and deciding the ice machine is too far down the hall to bother, Joyce toasts herself in the garishly-lit hotel mirror, and bolts down the double Scotch in three gulps. The smoky fumes cause her to choke and cough a bit, but she smiles, thinking how proud her father'd be, that at least she's not smoking her 'cancer sticks'.

And why shouldn't she trade one addiction for another, after a day like this?

Honour Oak Crematorium promised to deliver Joyce her father's ashes, neatly packaged in a mock-Grecian urn she selected, no later than 8 a.m. tomorrow. Delta Airlines agreed not to assess any extra charge when she hauls her father's suitcase back to Detroit tomorrow afternoon. And David Burns drafted a poignant death notice about Justin Kerr for the Michigan newspapers.

Even Double-G Tiffany has, presumably, by this time been retrieved from the floor beneath Justin's death-bed, and appropriately inventoried. By this time, surely, all the reports've been filed, and all the bureaucrats have signed off, on what was, after all, just one more death in the big city.

All the loose ends have been tied up. Except for one.

The diary of Joyce's great-great-grandmother, Kathleen Quinlan.

The little leather-bound diary with its yellowed pages from another time, sitting there across the desk from Joyce – its stamp denoting that it is now, and has been for 142 years, the official property of the British Library. The diary which Joyce's father, barely six hours off the overnight plane from Detroit, and just eight hours before his appointment with Death – assuming the Coroner was accurate in his estimation of the time of Justin's death – went to such great risk to steal, for reasons Justin never bothered to disclose to Joyce, even though he dragged her all the way over to England for his little Christmas holiday investigation into the lives of the Quinlans.

The diary which Joyce really should return to the British Library tomorrow morning.

Joyce cracks open one more little airline bottle of Scotch, quaffs it neat, in a single gulp, and then cracks open the 1868 diary, to find out what the hell is in this little book, worth stealing.

The instant she opens the diary, several pieces of dried leaves, pressed in the book, fall in her lap. As a paralegal trained to preserve evidence, Joyce reflexively scoops the particles into a tissue and puts them in her purse – with no idea why she is saving 142-year-old vegetable detritus.

To Joyce's dismay, the diary is written in tiny spidery handwriting, as old and black and intricately curly-cued as the wrought iron on a fire escape. Yet in spite of the strain on her Scotch-addled eyes, Joyce reads the 23-page diary from beginning to end, escaping into a long lost world.

The Journal Of Mistress Kathleen Allen Quinlan

Tuesday 10 March 1868

Today my life begins anew.

The story I have to tell is a simple one: that of a young girl who yearned with all her heart for nothing more than the freedom to live with the only man she ever loved; who recklessly despoiled her once-spotless Virtue to pursue her passion across sand and sea, to the very ends of the earth; yet about whose ill-starred path Fate hurtled one terrible obstacle after another, along with all the throbbing dilemmas of a restless Age; until at last, after many travails, she came to the New World at the age of twenty-four in the company of the man whom she loves more than life itself, and whom at last she may call 'husband', to start afresh.

But who will read my story, and judge my actions? This haunting question derailed my last attempts at journal-keeping, in London, and again during our New Zealand days; for telling my tale required me then, as I fear it may again, to record certain deeds of mine which, in Mr. Browning's dolorous phrase, were better left undone; and as my imagination conjured my unborn children and their children, reading my journal in some distant, happier time, I could not bear to think of their opprobrium directed at me across the generations; and so I was reduced to staring, hour by hour, day by day, at a blank page blackened with skeins of scored-out words and phrases.

I could have lied. By the simple expedient of altering a few key facts, here and there, and omitting a few unsavory deeds, I could have spared myself all that vexation over my unborn heirs' harsh censure. Yet had I lied to mine own journal, and written a fictional story of my life in London and Australasia, for my future readers, then I feared I might lose all contact with reality, and sink irretrievably into the shadowy world of madness and dreams, from whose seductive bourne few travelers e'er return.

So whenever I caught myself shading the truth, in my London journal or my Australasia journal, I over-scored mine own false words, and compelled myself to write the truth; but then, reading the bald record of mine own dark deeds, I overscored those true words, too, replacing them with new fictions. The result of all my revisions and indecisions was that, after a few days, I abandoned each journal altogether, consigning my London memories, and my Australasia memories, to begin their slow descent into the realm of the forgotten and unrecorded, where I myself shall doubtless one day join them.

But that was another life. Today in the Bay, my life begins anew!

For now I am a completely different person. Gone is the young girl who could not bear to face her former journals; and truly, ever since I paid 'Doctor' Hackett to commit his little murder in his Melbourne surgery, I've had no real cause to fret about the disapproving eyes of my unborn heirs, who might have judged me harshly for my many malfeasances. For 'Doctor' Hackett made it brutally plain that, medically speaking, it is now highly improbable there will be any further issue from my womb; and thus am I, trapped in my barren childlessness, now, in a strange sense, free from all the doubts that previously inhibited me from keeping a journal.

Yet even the loneliest writer, starving in her romantic Chelsea garret, labouring at her art purely for the sake of Truth and Beauty, even she still needs must have some imagined reader, or else why set pen to paper? So how shall I summon now the Will to write, when the only auditor for whom I care was left for dead in that puddle of fluid and blood I discharged onto the grubby floor of Dr. Hackett's sordid back alley surgery?

There can be but one answer to this horrid question: I shall write this journal for the child whose life I wickedly agreed to abort. For of all the crimes and misdemeanors committed in my past life, she is the only one I truly regret. I shall call her Persephone, after the Greek goddess of Spring, because I am myself reborn; and also because, to strike a darker chord, Persephone also means, if I recall my Greek, the murdered one.

So Persephone, my murdered child, may you live again through the words I, your tender murderess, write for you on these pages; and may I always tell you the entire, unadulterated truth; for after all, which of my future sins could possibly shock you, who already know of my cowardly complicity in your murder?

And so, I begin anew:

Dearest Persephone – We came today to the Bay, your father and I, two weary survivors of an awful shipwreck in the Southern Ocean, and an even more desperate eighteen months when we were marooned with thirteen other miserable souls on a barren outcrop of volcanic rock called Auckland Island. Our hardships there were too numerous to record here; and besides, as Mr. Marlowe's famous saying goes, that was another country, and the wench is dead. I mention these past adversities, dear girl, only because they must have colored my eyes as I took in the sights this morning on passing the great guns of Fort George and arriving here at the port of Belize, in this Colony formally named British Honduras, but called by all who dwell here simply: the Bay.

To most visitors I should think the Bay must look a very poor, squalid colonial outpost, with streets of deep wet mud, thick swarms of noxious mosquitoes, and an obscene riot of flimsy wooden shanties, which a strong man could push to the ground with one hand tied behind his back. But to my weary eyes – and R's, too – the tropical ambience of Belize, with its exotic bright flora and soft Caribbean breeze, and its picturesque thatched-roof marketplace perched on the Belize River, teeming with colorfully-clad Indians and half-naked Negroes plying dugout wooden canoes they call dories, seemed as fresh and new to us as Eden must have seemed to the original sinners.

R and I disembarked just as another ship discharged itself of a dozen Americans, refugees from the vanquished Confederacy of the Southern States; and R, who has traveled extensively in the Western Territories of America, engaged these Americans in conversation, with the result that we were directed to a rooming house frequented by Confederate refugees, that of Mistress McDougal. There R and I succeeded, by dint of our well-bred manners and upper-crust accents, in obtaining a room, without revealing the most awful secret one can harbour in a British Colony: i.e., we have no money.

For you see, Persephone, almost all your father's hard-won Australian gold rests on the floor of the Southern Ocean, alongside our ill-fated shipmates and their gold; and the little gold R carried away from the wreck, on his person, was extracted from us by a horrid coachman in New Zealand, as the exorbitant price of effecting our abrupt and clandestine departure from the Bluff, as well as his booking at the very last hour our passage from Wellington to Kingston, and thence to the Bay, before our departure could be discovered. So until R obtains employment here in the Bay, or I muster funds by the more circuitous stratagems I have set in motion, we must live on credit; and therefore didst R stop only long enough here at Mistress McDougal's this afternoon to don a clean shirt and collar, before setting forth urgently to seek a position.

In R's absence, I wickedly enjoyed a long bath, basking in the luxury of having our own private room, instead of being packed in with the poor in steerage, as we were these past three months; and I filled this glorious quiet time by commencing this journal – taking pains to write so small that even with his spectacles R shan't be able to read my words, should he chance upon this journal some time when I am away. But now the time has come when I, too, must summon up my courage and present myself at the local branch of the Bank of England, hoping to acquire money for us, independent of R's exertions, through the stratagem I set in motion behind his back in Wellington, prior to our hasty departure, when I sent a communiqué to London, requesting that a Letter of Credit be sent to me here in the Bay from the Reynolds Foundation.

Faint hope, of course, for it is highly unlikely the Winds of Chance have blown my request home to England and back to the Bay faster than our own ships crossed the same three Seas; yet my errand today is not entirely perfunctory, for I have resolved that whilst I am at the Bank, I shall deposit our last valuable possession into their care.

Adieu for now, Kathleen

12 March 1868

Dearest Persephone –

After two days of worry and unpleasantness, I have finally persuaded the Bank to accept for safe-keeping the wondrous little Codex which Mistress Reynolds entrusted to me in London. Words cannot express my relief!

The delay was occasioned because, unlike our hotelier, the trusting Mistress McDougal, the Bank of England requires genuine coin of the realm, rather than a well-bred woman's elegant manners, before a resident of the Bay may entrust valuables into the Bank's care. So as my wild Irish uncle Padraig used to say, I had to raise a bit o' the ready – and behind R's back, at that. Since opportunities for a woman of Virtue to earn income in the Bay are available only to domestic servants and shop girls, I resorted to taking a pretty keepsake of R's, which I detest as much as the woman whose memory its picture preserves, to the sole pawnshop in Belize City.

Unfortunately, the pawnbroker, Jahlmer Patrous, proved most difficult to run to earth, for he spends his days deep in drink, and engrossed in hazarding his niggling fortune in games of Chance, rather than tending shop; so for two days I tracked vague rumors and faint clews of the gentleman, which took me on a Grand Tour through the Bay's most pernicious taverns and opium emporia, where I gather unescorted ladies normally fear to tread. What an adventure! I could practically hear poor Mum rolling over in her grave in horror at the sights of depravity I glimpsed over the shoulders of the seedy porters guarding the doors of these dens of iniquity. And as for Father – well, had he not already disavowed me, I'm sure he'd have been most pleased to do so again.

But this afternoon I finally located Mr. Patrous, who is a ludicrous roly-poly caricature of a man, straight off the pages of one of Mr. Dickens' novels. Mr. Patrous was stinking drunk, yet still remarkably garrulous; and therefore it was only after protracted and complex negotiation that I succeeded in persuading the inebriated yet loquacious gentleman to return to his shop, whereupon he gave me three crowns for R's detested keepsake. With this, I was able at last to hire the use of a safe deposit box for the Lamanai Codex, thereby granting myself peace of mind.

For four years I've carried that odd little book with me, literally around the Globe, it being the only possession I troubled to save from the shipwreck (which I accomplished by placing it in an oilskin pouch, and then trussing the pouch inside my corset); but here, in the Bay, for the first time in the four years I've possessed the Codex, I suddenly fear that my trunk's lock is no longer security enough for this uncommon treasure. I cannot find any rational basis for my fear, for although thieves and cutthroats certainly abound here in the Bay, yet so too did they abound in steerage aboard both the steamers on which we slept whilst journeying from Wellington to the Bay; and yet somehow now, perhaps because we are so much closer to Lamanai than ever before, I cannot rest for fear of the Codex being stolen by someone who might then beat us to the fountain whose revivifying secrets, according to Mistress Reynolds, the Lamanai Codex unlocks.

But hark! I hear R's heavy footsteps!

Monday 16 March 1868

Dearest Persephone –

Your father and I just had an awful row, precipitated by his discovery that I pawned his detestable keepsake. We made such an awful noise, it is a wonder that Mistress McDougal, who still awaits our first payment, did not come upstairs and evict us at once out onto the muddy streets of Belize, where we should then have had to sleep out of doors with the ruffians at the edge of town, and feel what the wretches feel.

Yet despite all the harsh things R just shouted at me, before slamming the door in my face on his way out, I am ecstatic! The source of my great joy is this: This afternoon, before our row, our 'marriage' was finally consummated!

O it was so sweet and tender, and unexpected. I had just emerged from a bath, wrapped only in a towel, to find R back early from business; and in the looking glass I saw him looking at the graceful line of my long bare neck, which candor compels me to admit is my finest feature, save my dramatic decolletage; and then reflected in the glass I saw that concupiscent gleam in his eye, which I had not seen since before the Wreck. At the same instant Roger caught my eye, and held my gaze, longingly, in the glass. Mindful of how many times these past three years I've been accused of 'pressuring' R by 'leering' at him, I looked down, demurely, though this is not my true Nature, nor is it how I won R's love in Oxford; and yet – it worked! No sooner did I look away than he made three paces cross the room, caught me in his arms, and held me in a tight embrace, whose passion I had not felt since that awful night the General Grant sank.

Modesty prevents me from recording more of the lubricious details, my darling daughter; so let it suffice to say that our commingling was as delicious as the night you were conceived! At last I am free of her spell – the rival whose name I cannot bear to speak, even to you. At last your father is free of her spell, too, and at last he is enough at his ease to love me again as he did in the days before we determined to call ourselves 'husband and wife', when we defied Society's rules with a passion as wild and untamed as that of Heathcliff and Catherine. Except that now, with my rival lying in her watery grave in the Southern Ocean, and with the dark spell that she and her family's money cast over R finally and forever exorcised, R is totally and forever mine!

I should have thrown that locket away months ago, when we were marooned and R first lost his passion for me; only I believed it was to our mutual benefit that he wear it, since everyone always said that she and I were dead ringers. For I shall believe, to my grave, it cannot be mere coincidence that, just four days after I pawned it, the passion pent-up between R and me the past twenty-two months finally burst the dam.

I can write no more; I am delirious with happiness!

18 March 1868 Wednesday

Dear Persephone –

Today I am sorely vexed with R, who has gone away on unnamed business, for seven days. Before leaving, he was very excited, almost raving with excitement, because he has obtained good employment and an advance of income, enabling him both to pay Mistress McDougal, and to open a savings account for us at the Bank of England, so that we might begin to put aside the sterling we shall require to achieve the purpose which brought us here to the Bay: i.e., to mount the long Expedition into the jungle we both yearn to make, to discover if Mistress Reynolds' magical little Codex really does hold, as she promised me, the secret of living a much-extended Life. Yet in spite of my persistent entreaties, R would confide in me neither the name of his employer nor the nature of his position. Instead, he departed in an enormous hurry this morning, kissing me on the forehead as if I were a child, until I insisted on a proper kiss on the mouth; and telling me only that he shall be gone on his employer's business for approximately seven days, and that upon his return we shall be much the richer for his labours.

So here I sit, like a poor little church mouse, with nothing to do but swelter in this beastly heat, and wait. I shall go mad with idleness!

19 March 1868

What joy! Today on the way home from my daily fruitless errand to the Bank, asking for the Letter of Credit which never comes, I discovered a bookseller in Gabourel Lane, just past the Crown Prison; and using a few shillings of the new money R deposited in our account before departing, I purchased two volumes of verse, by Messrs. Arnold and Shelley; along with two of my favorite novels, Ivanhoe and The Count of Monte Cristo.

So now I shall pass this tedious week the way I like best, completely lost in the romance of far-away places and long-ago times, where red-cross knights forever kneel to the ladies in their shields, and bravely joust to win the affection of their beloved damsels; and therefore the secrets which R so discourteously harbours from me shall bother me not one whit!

Saturday 21 March 1868

Without R the days pass slowly. I am nobody's fool (except Fortune's); so I recognize that R's new position, which he refuses to name, is, in all likelihood, illicit. I hope I shan't shock you, Persephone, but to be candid, lawlessness per se does not disturb my conscience, for I long ago ceased to be the good little Angel my mother yearned for me to be; and indeed, I am rather flattered to think R is devoted enough to our cause, and to me, to run certain risks. But I love R so deeply, I cannot help but wonder: how much risk, precisely, is he running? Is he Gaming? Poaching? Smuggling? Pandering? Or something altogether darker? Thieving? Buccaneering? Slaving? Murdering?

To attempt to answer this vexatious question, I walked all round the Port today, calling at the Offices of the Harbour Master, the Post Master, and all the Lumber Companies. At each Office I engaged the clerks in idle chit-chat, before casually inquiring about R and his whereabouts; but in each case, my queries provoked only denials from faces blank as the sea. Worse, I'm sure I saw, twice, lurking behind the bland official denials, a slight twinkling of patronizing pity, as they took me for yet another pathetic woman, abandoned by her beau here in the wilds of the Bay.

For it is common practice here, Persephone, amongst the coarse white men this outpost attracts, to eschew the structured world of domesticity, in favor of the darker freedom of life in the jungle, where, as Mr. Darwin says, the only law is Nature's one immutable law: survival of the fittest. So they come out here, these rowdy refugees from the slums of London and Liverpool and Dublin, and the blighted fields of Ireland, to cut mahogany in the most distant reaches of the rain forest; and they live out in the wild for months, eating and sleeping in uncivilized camps under the stars, hunting wild game and fishing bountiful rivers, and working shoulder to shoulder with boors and brutes like themselves, white men grunting the vilest

English imaginable, and Creole negroes speaking a demotic patois that blends the fractured English they learned as slaves with their own atavistic African tongues; and so, not surprisingly, when these white ruffians return to town, they often feel utterly alienated from the sedate civility their bemused wives have struggled to establish in this profligate place; and one day they just up and desert their wives, choosing to live permanently in the murky shadows at the dark margin of civilization, hunting and fishing for food, and showing up for work in the logging camps only when their money for drink runs dry.

So will R succumb to this same savage seduction? I tell myself I am not at all like those pitiful women, whose drab domestic lives the rude men flee; and that R, still burning with ambition to become the famous discoverer of lost cities in the jungle, is not at all like those barbaric louts who descend into a bestial existence at the outer edges of civilization. But since I am nobody's fool, I also tell myself: the woman in my place is always the last to know.

23 March 1868

Last night I dreamed I was alone in the jungle. Wildly through the vines I hacked my way with a machete, trekking deeper and deeper into the dark, until at last I saw, through the trees, my beloved husband, squatting Indian-style with several men round a campfire in the dark, swigging cane liquor from a gourd they passed, and playing at cards. Since R was winning each hand they played, he had amassed a huge pile of silver; but then one of the men leaped up, calling R a cheat, and challenging him to a duel.

Before my dreaming eyes R and the other man each pulled a vicious hunting knife from his belt, and they wrapped themselves in a single cloak, the way Mistress McDougal told us the Creoles here do; and then they tore at each other, and all I could see was the chaotic pattern of their limbs jousting against each other within the bulging, pulsing cloak, until R finally emerged alone, soaked in blood, but victorious.

I rushed across the ground to throw my arms round him, but R looked at me without recognition; and then there was something worse in his eyes, something closer to hate or even contempt, and then we were no longer in the jungle, instead we were bobbing in the icy waters of the Southern Ocean, the crashing waves trapping us in that awful cave, the screams of the dying echoing off the rocks – and I awoke, drenched in cold sweat, alone in this blank room, my prison in the Bay.

I tried losing myself in the lush cadences of Mr. Arnold's poems awhile, but I am distracted by overwrought fantasies about the black work R must be performing to bring us money. My frenzied imagination envisages R crouching in the dark on a muddy landing by a steaming river in the jungle; then springing, like a jaguar, onto some unsuspecting traveller, and slitting the man's throat with his wicked hunting knife, before casually cutting his victim's money belt away from his waist and disappearing back into the jungle, to await his next victim. O please God may it not be like that!

When R returns I shall make him tell me exactly what labour he is performing that takes him away from me so long.

24 March 1868

Thank God, R has returned, safe and sound! But we've had another awful row.

He's returned with more sterling than any honest man could make in three months, let alone a week. So I demanded to know what dread work he's done, and what dread hands he's joined forces with, to make so much money so fast. Maddeningly, R still refuses to disclose what he's done this past week; but he assures me that, in the eyes of the Bay, his work is entirely lawful. In fact he claims he is working with the Lieutenant Governor himself, on a matter of the utmost secrecy, which he promised to maintain in the strictest confidence. This, R insists, precludes him from confiding the nature of his mission even in me, his faithful 'wife'.

I told him with more venom than I intended that he must think me a perfect little fool, to expect me to swallow such a silly fairy tale. R responded very angrily, calling me an ungrateful woman, who should be praising him for his success rather than pestering him with unfounded accusations; and suggesting that the only reason I am so quick to accuse him of criminal conduct is because of mine own intimate familiarity with lawless behavior. Needless to say, from this point, our discourse descended even deeper into mutual recriminations, which did neither of us any credit.

I am too agitated to write any longer. I gather R intends to rest a few days, and then to go away again, for another seven days of secret work.

Saturday 28 March 1868

I am so ashamed of myself. I am a foolish and untrusting woman, utterly unworthy of Roger Quinlan. When R left before dawn this morning for another week of mysterious labour, I followed him, deceitfully, at a distance, slinking through the sleeping streets of Belize, like Mister Collins' Woman in White.

And where did R go? Straight to the Government House; where the Lieutenant Governor resides! After half an hour there, R went to the docks, boarded an Indian dory with a huge Negro, tall and strong as R, and together they paddled away to the north.

What else can I conclude but that his business must be legitimate after all? Thus have I misjudged and wronged him. Thus was all the turmoil I caused these past four days unwarranted. Thus am I an unworthy 'wife'.

Truly, Persephone, when I stand before the looking glass, I cannot bear to look in the eye the woman reflected there. When blessed with a child, I destroyed you; when blessed with the death of my rival and R's undivided love, I dishonored that love with four days of petulant attacks.

O I deserve to lose the love of this fine man and live out the rest of my days as one of those pathetic women of the Bay, whose husbands have decamped for the woods!

30 March1868

Dearest Persephone:

An embossed invitation has arrived from Mistress Longden, the Lieutenant Governor's wife, inviting us to dine at the Government House with them upon R's return!

Upon reading the gilt-edged card, I fell into a paroxysm of hysterical laughter. Four long years, since the ugly scandal R and I created at Oxford, with our 'shameless love affair', I have assumed that at least I would never again be subjected to the tedium of a high society dinner. Even in Australia, Land of the Convicts, honourable women there shunned me, as a fallen woman; and I assumed social ostracization would be our lot the rest of our lives, no matter where in the Empire R and I chose to go.

But here in the Bay, no one seems to know of our scandalous past; or else what passes for High Society here is still so rough round the edges, it can't afford to shun a useful man like R. But whatever the reason, I must now go buy a suitable gown and hat, along with gloves, shoes and jewellry.

It's been so long since I've been shopping! I confess, my darling, with sinful pleasure my vanity anticipates an afternoon at the mercer's and the milliner's, being fussed over and complimented by envious shop girls, on my pulchritudinous face, and my still fair skin, and my hourglass figure. What a vain and wicked woman I am!

Adieu my lost child, Kathleen

2 April 1868 Thursday

Dearest Persephone –

Time passes slowly here in the Bay. I am restless to the point of distraction.

Shall I tell you why we came here? To find the Fountain of Youth.

Laugh if you like, my darling. I almost laughed, too, when Mistress Reynolds first told me the Fountain of Youth is real; and when she rambled on about how the Indians here in the Bay, the Mayans, were once as mighty on the American continent as the Romans on the European; and how the Mayans mastered many strange arts, including the art of extending human youth far beyond its natural term.

It was July of 1864, and we were sitting in Mistress Reynolds' art studio in Southwark, with its view of London Bridge; and I recall saying, in an effort to keep from laughing in the poor old dear's face, that her reference to 'strange arts' brought to mind Mister Arnold's fine poem, "The Scholar Gipsy", about the Oxford scholar who ran away with a band of gypsies and learned strange arts from them. Since Mistress Reynolds was unfamiliar with Mister Arnold's work, I offered to recite it, for my vanity leaps at any chance to exhibit my recitation talents. She agreed, but after several stanzas seemed to doze off (it being rather a long poem), and so I stopped; but at once she insisted I finish, and at the end she clapped her hands and cried "just so!"

Then she showed me a painting of hers she had never publicly displayed, titled 'The Fountain of Youth'. The painting shows a band of pirates, an Indian priest with a jade amulet round his neck, and a lovely red-tressed young woman in a white gown, all standing in and around a shallow underground river, in a dark cave lit by pine torches. In the near background rough-hewn rock steps lead up and out of sight; and in the distant background, at the top of the steps, a stone door opens up into an empty room with mysterious marks scratched onto the wall. By the river is a small fountain, but it is not the focus of the picture; instead, the Indian priest holds in one hand a bowl full of grey matter, reminiscent of R's anatomy books' depiction of the human brain, and in the other hand, an odd little book, on whose pages the viewer sees mysterious cramped glyphic symbols; whilst the young woman lifts the top of her gown above her thighs and plunges an aboriginal bone needle savagely down towards the region of her own sex.

The painting was macabre, and indecent, but also hypnotically powerful; so I asked Mistress Reynolds why she never displayed it. The old dear cackled and reminded me that, in the world in which we live, she has always had to display even her most demure paintings under a man's name, because patrons and critics are so leery of women painters, and sensual themes; so how could I imagine she could display something as overtly libertine as 'The Fountain of Youth' under any name, male or female?

Then she opened a cupboard and got out an odd little book, bound in jaguar hide, which she called the Lamanai Codex. She said this was the book the Indian priest was holding in her painting, which contains a map to the hidden cave where the Fountain of Youth flows; and if I were to take the Lamanai Codex to the Bay, and ask for an Indian priest near Lamanai named Xhuxh Antil (pronounced 'Shoosh Onteal'), then I would be taken to the temple near the Fountain of Youth and shown what to put in that bone needle so that I could live twice as long as a any other woman.

Burningly it came on me all at once: Mistress Reynolds herself was the red-tressed young woman in the painting! So I asked her, when and where was she born? She replied, in perfect seriousness, that she was born in Port Royal, Jamaica, in 1706.

Well, Persephone, as you can imagine, I judged this whole fantastical tale to be naught but the fond imaginings of an old woman; and this time I could not help laughing aloud. Mistress Reynolds, looking injured by my lack of credence, repaired to the same cupboard; and produced a yellowed parchment entitled 'Record of Live Birth', certified in 1721 by Clement James, a Magistrate of Jamaica, for one India Shaw, born 12 August 1706 in Port Royal. She told me Shaw was her maiden name, before she married Damien Reynolds, her deceased husband; and that she had only obtained the birth record because, back in those days, there was no such thing as a 'passport'; and when her family relocated to the Bay, she needed to prove she was an English subject.

But the document was not what convinced me Mistress Reynolds spoke the truth. It was when she said "now you see, my love, why that poem you recited, by Mister Arnwell" – "Mister Arnold", I corrected her – "yes, dear, you see now why every one of those words rang true for me?" Honestly, Persephone, I did not see, so she recited some of Mister Arnold's words back at me, the lines about how the Scholar Gipsy lived more than two centuries:

> *But thou possessed an immortal lot,*
> *So we imagine thee exempt from age,*
> *And living as thou livest on Glanville's page,*
> *Because thou hadst what we, alas, have not!*

I still failed to understand. "And yet, my dear, in spite of his 'immortal lot', your Scholar Gipsy fled from people, and from life, did he not?" I agreed this was true. "And that is how my life has been, too, dear girl. I thought long youth should be a grand thing. But instead I've lived like those 'shy traffickers, the dark Iberians' in your poem, who can only be happy when they are alone in an inaccessible place, like this studio."

"Why?" I asked her.

"Because for me to stay young so long, many others had to die, before their time; and though they were only vulgar fellows, styling themselves the Brethren of the Coast, the sort of men who live cruel and heedless lives, eagerly seeking their graves before their time, still, there was one amongst them whom I loved and married, until he died young, too; and so all their untimely deaths haunt me, to this very day. In the darkness I see them still, my sad captains, the men who died that I might live so long that I could meet you, dear girl who art so much like me – the living child God never saw fit to grant me. So now I give you this book; but I caution you, Kathleen: be very careful how you use this book, because the Fountain of Youth, paradoxically perhaps,

seems to sow death more often than it extends life; and therefore you must, dear girl, be sure to follow Xhuxh Antil's directions precisely and to the letter."

Then Mistress Reynolds gave me the Lamanai Codex. But she said no more about it; using the remainder of our time that day to brief me for my new position at the Reynolds Foundation, whose important charitable work she was entrusting to me. She originally established the Foundation long ago, to work with Reverend Clarkston and Mr. Wilberforce for the abolition of the Slave Trade; but now I was being asked to redirect the Foundation's efforts towards achieving restitution for the victims of slavery. Mistress Reynolds was exceedingly passionate about the long suffering of the 'Blackies', as she called them; and she moved me to tears with an eyewitness account of an incident in her youth, when she saw an entire galley of African slaves burnt to death after the Belize Wharf caught fire, their awful cries echoing forever in her ears, because their chains prevented them from jumping into the water, as all the free whites did.

Her passion about the suffering of the African slaves distracted me from asking her about her gloomy admonition regarding the need for careful use of the Lamanai Codex; yet had I known, that after that day I should never again see Mistress Reynolds in this World, I should have taken pains to tax her to elaborate further upon that gloomy admonition. But as it was, I was soon bereft; and though I had come to believe her earnest assurance that the Fountain of Youth was real, still I had naught to go upon but an unreadable book, and the name of an Indian priest half a world away.

Wherefore I almost sold the odd little book to the British Museum. But I was passionately in love with Roger Quinlan, who had fled to Australia to avoid the scandal our illicit love had ignited, and seek his fortune in the Victorian goldfields; yet who still burned, I knew, with passion for me, and with ambition to prove himself to the world which had treated him so shabbily; and I felt that Fate had placed this little book in my hands for the specific reason that, as the key to a quest which R could never resist, it would bring us back together. Which indeed it did; for the quest for the elusive Fountain of Youth turned out to be the lure by which I won R back to my love.

5 April 1868

I am miserable and distraught. Our dinner last night with the Longdens was not the tedious high society gathering for which my foolish vanity yearned; it was something far worse. Four other couples were present; all four men were in the same position as R, which is to say, performing labour of an undisclosed and presumably dangerous nature for Lt Gov Longden; but otherwise these four men were as different from R as stone from marble. Everyone sensed immediately that R was the star of the evening; and R of course basked in all the attention, thereby heedlessly exposing us to scrutiny.

One of the lesser lights recalled hearing of R attempting to swim the Channel eight years ago; and this provoked discussion of R's past, and awkward questions about where R and I first met. No one said anything publicly; but when I went out to the privy, I overheard Mistress Baxter and Mistress Clare gossiping furiously in the garden.

"Surely Mistress Longden would never have invited Mister Quinlan to her home, had she known of his past!"

"Expelled from Oxford, my husband said, for robbing graves!"

"Those medical experiments were only the beginning of his infamy!"

"O pray tell, tell!"

"Some years after he was expelled, Mister Quinlan had the bad taste to return from his exile in America and appear, uninvited, at an Oxford garden party, where he seduced two young girls from good families – and then became betrothed to them both!"

"Oh I didn't realize he was the same dark man! As I recall, those two girls were the best of friends, till he drove them apart; and their families were threatening legal action, but – how did it all end?"

"Mister Quinlan eloped to Australia with one; whilst the other fled to London in shame. Propriety forbids me from imagining the life she must lead now: a kept woman on Randolph Street, or, if Fate has been cruel, a madame in a Southwark stew."

"So Mistress Quinlan – she's the one with whom he eloped to Australia?"

"No telling, with a man like that. He might have abandoned the Oxford girl in Australia, and this Mistress Quinlan is a new conquest."

"She does seem somewhat underbred, with that heaving bosom of hers, and those voluptuous eyes, with their heavy lids."

"We must discover more about her background!"

As you can imagine, Persephone, I was in agonies whilst these vicious shrews plotted to dredge up our old troubles; but as I told R later, we have only ourselves to blame for this peril in which we are placed. When we were content to live obscurely at Mistress McDougal's, we were invisible, indistinguishable from all the other human flotsam and jetsam that washes up on the shores of the Bay; but now, because our foolish pride drove us to dine with the Longdens, we shall soon be notorious again.

Never again shall we attend a Society Affair.

Never again shall I let my vanity overwhelm my common sense.

Monday 6 April 1868

Thank the stars, and Roger, that later today we shall quit this miasmic town, built, as everyone in the Bay loves to say, on a tottery foundation of loose coral, stray logwood chips, and discarded rum bottles; to embark on what promises to be a great adventure.

R's next mission for the LG requires him to travel deep into the jungle, up the New River. By happy coincidence, the New River is also where R believes the lost Mayan city of Lamanai was located, so he's decided to make his initial search for Lamanai and its Fountain of Youth now, even though we still lack sufficient funds to mount a full-scale archeological Expedition.

At first R declared, for safety's sake, that I should wait here for his return; but the vehemence of my objections surprised him, and like the good man he is, he agreed to reconsider the matter. How could I be in graver danger at my husband's side, I argued, than left here alone, in this lawless outpost, teeming not only with blackguards and thugs, but worse, with nasty gossips who will soon be circling round me like ravenous predators feasting on a bleeding deer? And how could R think it fair to go looking for the lost city of Lamanai without me, who first procured the Lamanai Codex for him, and then traveled halfway cross the world to persuade him that it is his Destiny to find the fabled Fountain of Youth, whose location the Codex reveals?

The mention of how I chased R to the Victorian goldfields opened old wounds for us both, so we sat a space in silence; but then suddenly he agreed, remarking that it might be prudent for us now to move away from Belize City altogether, and that in the event, traveling with a woman would be 'good cover' for his mission. I was so happy to win R's agreement to take me with him, that it was only much later, in the middle of my restless tossing and turning last night, that I awoke wondering: why should an honest man, engaged in a mission on behalf of the LG of British Honduras, need 'cover', whilst traveling up a river within the borders of the Colony?

Yet should a loyal wife, already humiliated once for her unjust suspicions, even dare to ask such a question of her 'husband'? I think not.

11 April 1868

Dearest Persephone:

We've had so many wild adventures the past five days, I can scarcely record them all. I write now on a rickety wooden table R built under a canvas tarpaulin, as the sun sets over an amazing Mayan temple – yes, we found the lost city of Lamanai!

But as the light is fading fast, I must be brief.

R's mission for the LG turned out to be running guns to rebel Indians!

R presumed I would be frightened away from the trip, once I arrived at the Belize wharf, and saw the long dugout dory loaded with crates marked BSA (which I surmised in a trice stood for 'Birmingham Small Arms', since R was standing there with ammunition belts criss-crossing his shirt); but I decided not to give him the satisfaction. Instead, I walked right up to the dory, and held out my hand to R's Creole guide, Caesar (IF that really is his name, which I doubt), who is the same well-muscled Negro I saw with R two weeks ago. Caesar, naked machete dangling from his waist, helped me find a seat in the middle of the dory, perched on several boxes of BSA guns.

And off we went. Two hard days we navigated the rough seawaters along the coast to Corozal. The first night we slept at an old pirate camp on Ambergris Caye; the second night we slept in the woods outside Corozal. Caesar is an absolute wonder, as strong and indefatigable as R, and he knows the country as well as the Indians. He was born a slave here, in the logging camps; but was freed when he was a teen, by the Emancipation Act. He bears upon his back many wicked scars, and on his arm his former master's brand; but claims to feel no ill-will to whites, an attitude laudably Christian, though not entirely credible, given the black looks he sometimes casts at us.

Somewhere along the coast the Mayan Balche beer loosened R's tongue, and he finally confided in me: we were delivering the BSA guns thirty miles up the New River, near the Mexican border, to a tribe of Indians, the Santa Cruz Mayans, who are at war with Mexico. R also mentioned, off-handedly, that a rival tribe, the Ixaiche Mayans, who are aligned with Mexico, routinely watch the river at Corozal, to try to interdict gun-runners like us. I gathered the Ixaiche murder gun-runners on sight. With spears.

To elude the fatal eyes of the Ixaiche, we rose two hours before dawn the third day, and passed Corozal Town in darkness. Caesar alone rowed, his oars dipping the New River waters as silently as Indians tread the forest paths. The loudest sound we made those two hours was the beating of my heart, Persephone, so wild was my fright.

But I never let the men see my fear!

Once we were several miles past Corozal, we ducked into a small tributary, and tied up at dawn in the shade of a giant ceiba tree. All day we sat there, dozing a little, and talking less; R drinking copious quantities of Balche beer, and smoking a cigar to ward off insects; Caesar drinking from a gourd containing some kind of sweet liquor made from sugar cane, and smoking corn-husk cigarettes; and I, poor I, drinking bad water, smoking nothing, and sweltering like a pretty little pig, in my long calico dress.

When night came, we rowed furthur up the New River, which Caesar says the Mayans call The River of Strange People, after Europeans like us who travel up this river into the deep heart of the jungle. There was no moon, and the clouds dimmed the faint starlight; so most the time I held a pine torch to help Caesar guide us up the river.

It was so exhilarating, Persephone!

The jungle at night is deeper and more mysterious than life itself. It's –
O my light is all gone. I'll resume tomorrow, if I can find the time.

14 April 1868

Dearest Persephone:

For every three days that pass, I find only thirty minutes to write; and so I fear if I don't speed up my tale, I shall fall hopelessly behind in my story.

But I have no complaints. This soul-stirring adventure is precisely the reason I yearned to marry Roger Quinlan the first moment I laid eyes upon him, at the Oxford garden party that provided so much grist for the gossip mill. All my old Oxford friends may look down their noses at me, all they like; but I know that, with R by my side, I am living life to its very top, whilst they are not living at all. They worry about wearing the wrong fashion in the wrong season, or being trapped in a tedious conversation with a person they deem socially inferior; whilst I worry about wearing the wrong sidearm, in case I am trapped in a lonely corner of the jungle by a jaguar!

I wouldn't trade one minute of my life now for their entire miserable existence.

So where was I, in my tale? We made it up The River of Strange People without the Ixaiche detecting us, though much of the time Caesar navigated without the benefit of the pine torch flickering in my tremulous hand, deeming it safer to proceed in just the dim starlight. When we neared the rendezvous point, we searched the jungle for a sign of the Santa Cruz; and as fate would have it, I observed the tell-tale movement of a branch! (Caesar later said I have eyes in the dark like a forest cat.) But how R knew, in the gloaming, with his weak eyes, that the man moving the branch was Santa Cruz, and not Ixaiche, he would not tell. All I know is I nearly fainted when I saw, in the dim starlight, a full-sized red-skinned Indian emerge from behind the branch I'd seen move, his body decorated with ferocious war paint, his eyes brooding and dark as the jungle itself. I was not the only one disquieted by the sight of the fierce red man in full war paint, for in that same instant, Caesar reached for his rifle. But R shook his head no at Caesar, raised his hand in a peaceful salute, and we rowed to shore; and there we unloaded our crates of Birmingham's finest small arms to our Santa Cruz Mayan allies.

Then Caesar guided us much further up the river, deeper into the jungle. On the morning of our fifth day, we came to a very large lagoon. R instructed Caesar to take us slowly along the western shore of the lagoon, because the old Spanish reports, which R found buried deep in the basement in the Government House archives in Belize, indicated that Lamanai was on the western shore of the lagoon.

And then we saw it: an enormous stone temple, covered in moss and foliage, yet still rising out of the jungle, like an antediluvian beast escaping green netting, its distinctive roof comb as unmistakably Mayan as those on the Palenque temples sketched by Catherwood, rising taller even than the tallest trees in the jungle.

Dear girl, I cannot describe the wild emotions I felt seeing that ancient temple, so fabulous and huge and majestic that it defies imagination to think who built it here in this remote jungle – and when! – and yet there it is, an inexorable fact, rising up out of the forest like nothing else on earth, except perhaps the ancient pyramids of Egypt.

We are taught that the New World was peopled only by primitive savages, before we Europeans graced them with our civilization; yet it is plain as the old whip scars on Caesar's back that savages never raised a temple this magnificent, and savages never carved the elaborate drawings that we can see on the ancient stones of this temple, peeking through the centuries of foliage that have failed to obliterate them. Truly, Persephone, our Lamanai temple is worthy of anything that was ever built in Greece or Rome, or London; and more to the point, our temple is as magnificent as any of Catherwood's drawings of the temples he and Stephens discovered at Palenque.

And Roger Quinlan, with a little help from Caesar and me, is the man who has discovered it!

Even Caesar, who seldom shows emotion, was thunderstruck, gaping at the huge temple; and R was more animated and ecstatic than I've ever seen him. For this discovery vindicates all his early Promise, his early brilliance; it is R's revenge against Carver and all the other dons who conspired to expel him from Oxford eight years ago.

But again my light fades, and there is important work to be done.

24 April 1868

Dear Persephone:

We have settled into a hard routine here, R and Caesar and I. We work from dawn to dusk, clearing all the ivy and moss and vines and shrubs that have grown through the centuries into the interstices of the stones of the pyramid we call Ozymandias' Temple. Then we fall into a deep sleep, only to wake at dawn, and work again.

Alas, archeology is not only the exhilarating discovery of lost cities in the jungle; it is mostly painstaking drudgery. Occasionally I feign the exhaustion to which men suppose the weaker sex is prone, and grant myself a brief respite, to collect local flora and herbs, which I press into this journal; but mostly I just work, and work, and work.

We call our principal discovery Ozymandias's Temple because, in the course of cleaning we exposed, on the pyramid's west face, a giant ten-foot mask of a human face, carved into the stone, whose fierce demeanour recalls the 'sneer of cold command' on the 'shattered visage' of Shelley's Ozymandias. The face we uncovered is not handsome, indeed, I find it quite foreboding; but it is a fascinating face for, as Caesar was first to remark, it looks more like the face of an African than an American Indian. R thinks this may be an extremely important find, because it may buttress the argument of certain maverick scholars whom R admires, that the continents of Africa and South America were once conjoined, as one continent; and it may inspire cross-cultural study of aboriginal peoples in Africa and the Americas, to support the compelling hypothesis that perhaps the American Indians are descended from earlier Africans. Or vice-versa.

Yet important though our find may be, archeologically, I confess that the face on Ozymandias's Temple still spooks me. To me, he looks primitive and blood-thirsty. R says I am being foolish, but I will not walk alone by this temple, even in daylight.

R says Ozymandias's Temple must have been built by a very advanced civilization, because of its size and complexity, and the perfect alignment of its stones; and R believes the other large mounds close by must conceal other temples, suggesting Lamanai may once have been the capital of this advanced civilization. I'm sure R is right, because he has already scraped away some of the moss covering another temple, and discovered fascinating, though indecipherable, glyphic inscriptions; yet I still can't shake the feeling that, advanced or not, the people who built Ozymandias's Temple had many inner demons with whom they had failed to come to terms.

In the event, dear girl, you're all caught up now on my adventures – except the one big disappointment, which is that Xhuxh Antil, the Mayan priest whom Mistress Reynolds said could interpret the Lamanai Codex for us, and show us the way to the Fountain of Youth, is dead. We went to the closest Mayan village, Guinea Grass, and asked, in Spanish, for Xhuxh Antil, which inspired great wonderment amongst the Mayan villagers there, who were astounded we knew his name; however, they reported that Xhuxh had gone to Xibalba. When we offered to call upon Xhuxh again, perhaps next week, the villagers explained that Xhuxh would not be returning from his journey, for Xibalba is the Mayan name for the Land of the Dead. Apparently Xhuxh didn't drink deeply enough, from his own fountain, and so he has gone the way of all flesh.

So all we know is, the map to the Fountain of Youth is hidden in the Codex only Xhuxh Antil can read; and the Fountain of Youth itself is in a cave whose hidden entrance only Xhuxh can locate. In short, our only hope of finding the legendary fountain is to conduct a Séance, replete with bi-lingual mystics who speak Spanish and Mayan, and consult with Xhuxh from beyond the grave.

Monday 27 April 1868

R. is elated, for he has discovered a burial chamber deep within Ozymandias's Temple. A stone sarcophagus lies on a slab, decorated with beautiful carvings of serpents, which we take to be Mayan Gods; but, alas, it's empty. Evidently tomb raiders looted it clean, bones and all, preventing us from learning what treasures the ancient Mayans placed in such coffins. Other than the sarcophagus, the tomb is empty, save for strange markings scratched on the back wall, near the floor; and rusted metal spikes, hanging from the ceiling above the sarcophagus. R surmises the spikes were used by the tomb raiders, for it is historical fact the Mayans knew nothing of metal before the Spanish Conquest; and the placement of the spikes suggests they were used to hoist open the sarcophagus.

Yet even with an empty serpent-decorated sarcophagus, and the inscrutable writing on the wall, R is positively giddy with joy, because he says none of the Mayan temples discovered by Del Rio or Stephens has ever contained a tomb. R says this means Lamanai was clearly once a very important place, almost certainly the capital of the Mayans in this region; and if we can only manage to decipher the writing on the wall, we may unlock the key to one of history's greatest lost civilizations.

30 April 1868

We had a disquieting visit today, from an Englishman named Randolph, who says he works at a sugar mill close by. He came to warn us that one of the mill workers was killed last night by a jaguar. The disturbing thing was, we've never seen hide nor hair of the sugar mill workers; and yet they obviously knew we were here, all this time.

3 May 1868

Well, our adventure is coming to an end, because Caesar wants to go home. He says he is no longer a slave; he is a free man, whose services are valued by many, and command a fair price in the Bay. He says he has faithfully discharged both commissions for which he was paid, by LG Longden acting for the BSA, and by Roger (using his BSA advance): he guided us safely to deliver the guns to the Santa Cruz Mayans, and he guided us safely here, to this lost city in the jungle. But now Caesar is tired of working for no pay in the hot sun, clearing foliage all day for weeks on end, on nothing more than R's promise to pay him well when we return to Belize. Who will supply the money, Caesar asks? Who will care so much about an old Indian temple in the jungle, that suddenly sterling crowns will rain down from the heavens on R?

He has a point, our Caesar.

R tried to persuade Caesar that our discovery of Lamanai is the most significant archeological discovery of the century; but with each of R's hyperboles, Caesar's eyes shrank deeper into their sockets, blank and cryptic as the eyes of the scary idol carved on Ozymandias's Temple. Then Caesar interrupted R to say: "In two days time the heavy rains begin. It will be much cooler on the river then. The next morning I will take the dory back to Belize. You and your lady may come with me or not, as you choose. I will leave at daybreak." And with that, Caesar was gone, leaving us alone in the gloaming.

4 May 1868

Dearest Persephone –

Early this morning R took the last of his plaster molds of the inscriptions on the two temples we have cleared. He has taken so many molds, I fear they may sink Caesar's dory; but R says all his plaster casts weigh less than the guns we brought up the river, and they are critical to our enterprise, as they will substantiate his discovery claim.

Then R said we shall use our last two days here to find the Fountain of Youth.

We laughed, of course, as this has been the lone disappointment of our trip: despite what Mistress Reynolds promised, we have been unable to use the Lamanai Codex to locate the fabled fountain.

Still, R is in high spirits, with all the important discoveries he's made here; and this has been a very happy time for us, vindicating my long perseverance in the face of all the slings and arrows of haphazard Fortune (and malicious gossip) which I've endured these past four years, to arrive finally at this happy place.

5 May 1868

The rains have come, exactly when Caesar said they would; and they are truly Biblical in force. So I'm sheltering inside the creepy tomb in Ozymandias's Temple, but now R is at the door which he blasted through the stone wall of the pyramid, for easier ingress to the tomb, and he's beckoning me with a concupiscent gleam in his eye; so that I have no doubt the man intends for us to go make love in the jungle in the torrential rain!

Wednesday 5 May 1868 (later)

As God is my Witness, we found it!

The Fountain of Youth is real; it's here at Lamanai; and we found it!!

R forbids me to record exactly where it is, or what it is, or the embarrassing yet humourous events that led to our discovery of it, or what we did when we found it, in case our writings are lost or stolen. Since R surprised me writing in this journal earlier today, he emphasized that I must not record any details here; and of course I needs must honour my husband's wishes in this crucial matter, as in all others.

So all I can tell you is: we found it!

And now Roger Quinlan – and I, too, I suppose – shall go down in History as the discoverers of the Fountain of Youth!

10 May 1868

Dearest Persephone:

We are back in Belize.

In our absence, the Letter of Credit arrived from England, although there are complications with its precise language, which have prevented me converting it into coin of the Realm. But we used most of our meagre savings to pay Caesar in full for all his time assisting us at Lamanai. Caesar has no idea of our great discovery the last day there; but he is mightily pleased with us, all the same.

We've booked passage to London, where R plans to assemble the leading London newspapers outside the Royal Society in Piccadilly, and there announce that he has discovered the Fountain of Youth. He has a beaker full of the precious liquid, which he carries with him at all times, for display on that momentous day.

R is walking on air, so enthused is he by his incredible and momentous discovery. R talks of being nominated to join the Royal Society, or at least the Archaeological Association; and even of being Knighted. But to my delight, R also talks of our future; and thus he willingly accompanied me yesterday to St. John's Cathedral, where, after a brief ceremony, we completed the paperwork needed for our protection, now that we shall be so much more than ever in the public eye.

Exciting though all these developments be, however, I am distracted by an event that may prove even more miraculous, for me, than finding the Fountain of Youth.

I realized, upon our return, that during our entire five week trip, I never once had to contend with the Woman's Curse. Since I am normally as regular as the Moon, I ruminated about it, until I recalled the last time it came, which was the day I went shopping for the Longdens' dinner party – the 30th of March, according to this journal. So today it has been 41 days – too soon to tell Roger, yet I am beginning to believe that Doctor Hackett erred, when he told me I could never conceive another child.

Or else – dare I say it? – a miracle has occurred within my womb.

15 May 1868

We leave for England this afternoon. I shall pack this journal safely away in my trunk, so that I shall never lose the wonderful memories it records.

Today is the 46th day. I am certain I am with child. O how I pray I am right, and that no complications shall arise from whatever awful injuries 'Doctor' Hackett perpetrated inside me; and that I may deliver into this world a healthy baby!

As soon as we arrive in England, I shall tell Roger, for I know he will insist on placing me in the care of Harley Street's finest physicians.

Yesterday I completed paperwork for the Reynolds Foundation, which I shall post to Mr. Caruthers, the London solicitor to the Foundation, as soon as we reach England. Hopefully the paperwork will resolve the difficulties I have experienced here with the Letter of Credit, because R and I are, again, nearly as poor as church mice.

Yesterday I also tracked down Mister Patrous, and redeemed R's locket which I pawned two months ago. I'm not at all sure why I did that. Guilt, I suppose.

Last night R and I dined with Mister Blake, who plans to buy Ambergris Caye this summer. In spite of our shortage of funds, R entrusted a small sum with Mister Blake, to purchase us a small plot of land on the east shore of the Caye, with a Sea-side prospect. Mister Blake agreed to do so, and to post us the Deed in London once the sale is complete; yet he could not help asking, why in the world should we wish to purchase a small parcel of land, in a Colony where profit can only be made on larger tracts?

To my everlasting delight, R replied that he and I plan to return to Ambergris Caye one day, when we are old and gray, to live in the warm sun in our dotage, and hunt for old pirate treasure, and the odd seashell, along the strand.

* * *

Immediately upon closing Kathleen Quinlan's diary, Joyce Kerr carries the odd little book into her hotel room's tiny bathroom, closes the door, and turns both the shower and sink faucets on full blast, at the hottest settings. After a few minutes, when the air in the bathroom reaches steam bath humidity, Joyce pushes her fingertips against the British Library property sticker on the inside cover of the diary. At once the sticker comes unglued, and she flushes it down the toilet.

Joyce knows she'll never be as adventurous as her great-great-grandmother, who flouted society's rules and laws. But Joyce is pretty sure she has enough pluck to smuggle Kathleen's stolen diary back to the USA tomorrow – without a sticker to attract inquiry from UK or US customs.

Because this book is going to be Exhibit A, when Joyce sues the old bitch, her cousin.

Emerging from the steam bath, Joyce writes out her family tree, as best she knows it, all the way back to the Quinlans, and faxes it to her office in Ann Arbor. Then she calls David Burns.

"I hope I'm not waking you."

"Rust never sleeps," David Burns replies.

"Then how come you sound so groggy?"

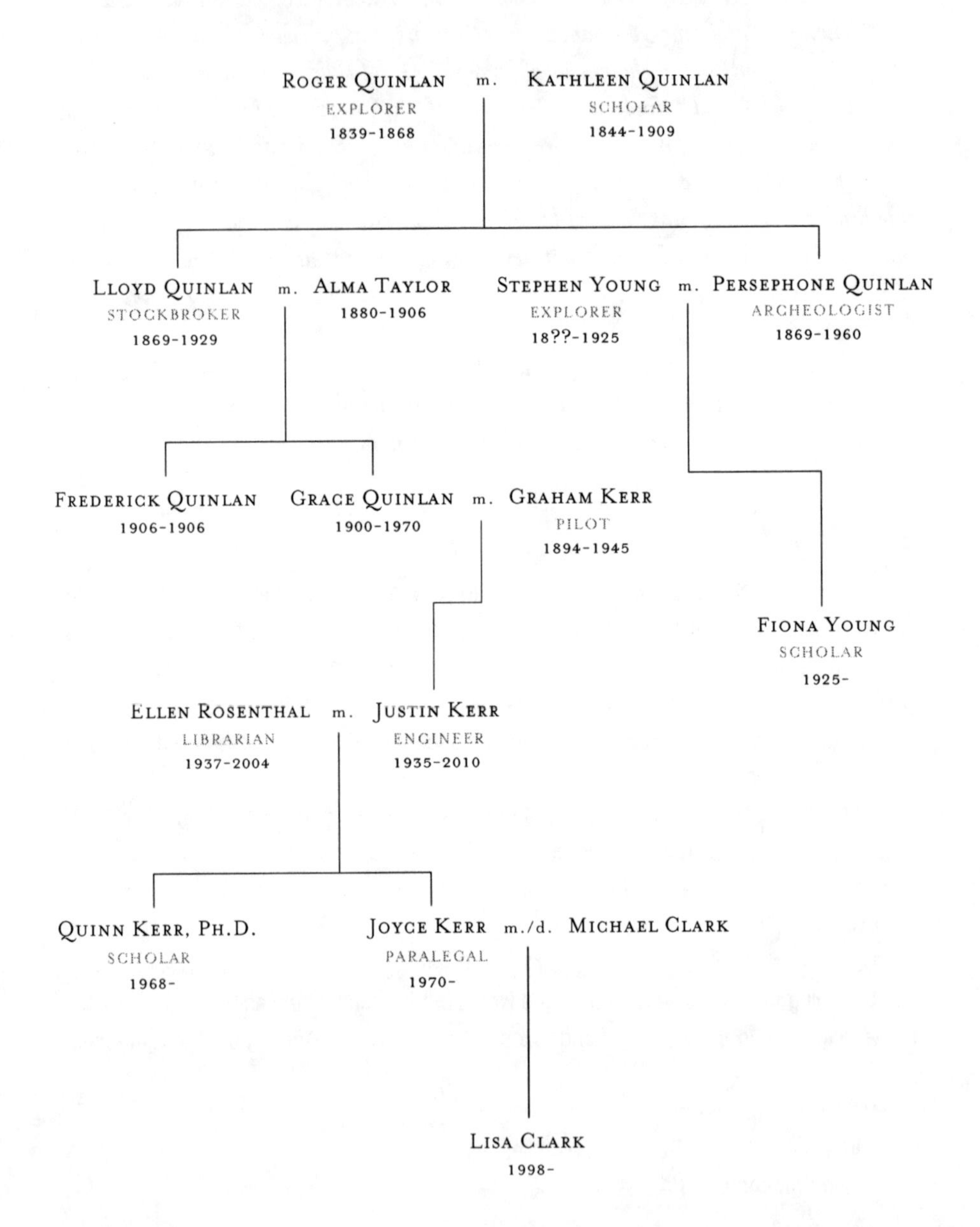
JOYCE KERR
FAMILY TREE
ROGER QUINLAN
EXPLORER
1839-1868
m.
KATHLEEN QUINLAN
SCHOLAR
1844-1909
LLOYD QUINLAN
STOCKBROKER
1869-1929
m.
ALMA TAYLOR
1880-1906
STEPHEN YOUNG
EXPLORER
18??-1925
m.
PERSEPHONE QUINLAN
ARCHEOLOGIST
1869-1960
FREDERICK QUINLAN
1906-1906
GRACE QUINLAN
1900-1970
m.
GRAHAM KERR
PILOT
1894-1945
FIONA YOUNG
SCHOLAR
1925-
ELLEN ROSENTHAL
LIBRARIAN
1937-2004
m.
JUSTIN KERR
ENGINEER
1935-2010
QUINN KERR, PH.D.
SCHOLAR
1968-
JOYCE KERR
PARALEGAL
1970-
m./d.
MICHAEL CLARK
LISA CLARK
1998-

"That's just my vocal chords clearing the whiskey. Once the air reaches my throat, I'll be fine. Hey, I'm sorry I couldn't find you a flight home today, Joyce. Must be awful, alone in a hotel—"

"I'm okay, David. And thank you for all you did today. You're a life saver."

"You're welcome. But I only did it because I'm still hoping, after all these years, to get laid."

Joyce smiles at this old joke. "Good luck, Lancelot. But I'm calling about new business."

"Fabulous! Who's the client?"

"Me," Joyce says.

"No kidding! You're finally going to let me sue that deadbeat ex of yours?"

"No, you silly man. The defendant would be my cousin, Fiona Young."

"The crazy old Maya scholar who tried to get you prosecuted when you were in college, for supposedly trying to steal her precious ancient Maya book – what was it called?"

"The *Lamanai Codex*."

"Right. Well, Joyce, I'm sure you must realize, you can't sue Fiona now for slandering your good name 20 years ago. So what's Fiona done to harm you lately?"

"You get the fax I sent you a few minutes ago?" Joyce asks.

"No, everyone's off today for the holidays. Hang on, I'll go check the fax machine." After a minute Burns returns to the phone. "Got it. Just a one-pager, your family tree?"

"Yes. I thought it'd help, as I explain why I think Quinn and I have a claim against Fiona." Joyce grabs her copy of her family tree. "You see how my family has two branches? One branch ends with Fiona Young. The other branch goes down to Quinn and me."

"Actually, that branch now goes down just to you," Burns says. "Your father was so angry about Quinn running off to India to study with the latest Maharaja, he wrote Quinn out of his Will."

"That's awful!" Joyce says. "Though I suppose Quinn won't care."

"Doesn't matter," Burns says. "There's nothing for you or Quinn to inherit anyway."

"Actually, that might not be true. The Maya codex Fiona accused me of trying to steal back in 1990, well, Fiona told me her mother, Persephone Quinlan, found it while digging up the ancient Maya library at Lamanai in Belize. But that turns out to be a lie."

"How do you know it was a lie?"

"Because I just read the diary of Fiona's *grand*mother, Kathleen Quinlan, which says Kathleen had the *Lamanai Codex* five years before Fiona's mother, Persephone, was even born."

"Slow down a sec." Burns rustles paper. "That side of the family I don't know so well. Okay, Kathleen gave birth to Persephone, who gave birth to Fiona. Got it. But – looking at the family tree, I'm still not seeing why you think the *Lamanai Codex* belongs to you instead of Fiona. So Kathleen had it, she bequeathed it to Persephone, who in turn bequeathed it to Fiona."

"Impossible. The reason Fiona made up the lie about Persephone finding the *Lamanai Codex* while digging at Lamanai is, if it belonged to Kathleen, then it should have passed down *my* side of the family tree, not Fiona's. There was a big lawsuit about this back in 1909, after

Kathleen Quinlan committed suicide. The probate judge in Ann Arbor awarded everything in Kathleen's estate to her son Lloyd, and absolutely nothing to her daughter Persephone."

"How come Persephone got nothing?"

"Beats me, David. I wasn't around in 1909. All I know is, everything Kathleen had was supposed to go to Lloyd – and then Lloyd lost it all when the stock market crashed in 1929. So all of Lloyd's descendants – my grandmother Grace, and my father Justin – never bothered looking into probate matters, because they assumed, like you, there was nothing to inherit. But this diary I just read says there's at least one thing Lloyd never got, which really was his: the *Lamanai Codex*."

A short pause ensues. "So – is the *Lamanai Codex* worth much?"

"Are you kidding, David? Put to one side the old rumor that the codex contains a map to the fountain of youth. Even assuming that's all hooey, it's still one of only five Maya codices in the whole world to survive the Spanish Conquest of Central America. It's gotta be worth a fortune."

"So, if I take this case and win it for you, you'll thank me by retiring on me?"

Joyce smiles, glad she anticipated this objection. "Perish the thought. I might have to go part-time, though, so I have enough time to take the codex and go hunt for the fountain of youth."

"Fair enough – as long as you bring some of the magic water back home for me."

"Beware of what you think you want, David – those magic waters killed Kathleen's husband, Roger Quinlan, back in 1868, at age 29."

"So people actually know where the fountain of youth is supposed to be?"

"No. The Quinlans never said exactly where it was. Not even in Kathleen's diary. And after Roger died so young, no one was much interested in looking for those waters anyway. They figured whatever Roger found was more like a fountain of death than a fountain of youth."

"What about the map in the *Lamanai Codex* – where does the codex say the fountain is?"

"No one knows. Fiona's hoarded that codex for 50 years. Claims she's still translating it."

"But I thought scholars cracked the Mayan code," Burns says, "like 15 years ago, and figured out how to translate all the ancient Maya glyphs."

"They did. And I'm sure they could translate the *Lamanai Codex*, too, if Fiona would ever let them see it. But Fiona refuses all requests to access, or even photocopy, the *Lamanai Codex*."

"Why?"

"Who knows? She's a stubborn old bitch, my cousin. All the other leading Maya scholars are totally pissed at her. Which doesn't bother her one whit, of course."

A pause ensues. "If the codex is so valuable," Burns asks, "why hasn't Fiona sold it?"

It's Joyce's turn to pause. "I'm trying to remember if you ever met Fiona."

"Coupla times, back in the late '80s. She was *very* attractive – I mean, for a lady in her late sixties. Amazing hooded eyes. And smart as hell."

"Right on all counts," Joyce says. "Fiona is also completely obsessed with the Maya, and with the *Lamanai Codex*. Never in a million years would she sell that book. It's her whole life."

"So if we sue her for it, she'll fight us?"

"To the death."

"Don't sugar-coat it, Joyce." Burns chuckles. "Okay, so we've got an 85-year-old lady in London, clinging to a book she loves more than life itself, and you want me to sue her – where, exactly? I'm not licensed to practice in the Old Bailey, or wherever London lawsuits are heard."

"Sue her in Ann Arbor," Joyce says. "Fiona has possession of a book the Ann Arbor probate court said belongs to my side of the family, not Fiona's. The court should enforce its order."

"When did Fiona last set foot in Ann Arbor?"

Joyce pauses to think. "1990. That summer she accused me of trying to steal the codex was her last year teaching at the University of Michigan. Then she retired to London."

"Hmmn," Burns says. "And the order you want enforced, was issued – when? 1909?"

"That's right." Joyce sighs, realizing maybe this lawsuit isn't as simple as she thought.

"You've seen the 1909 order?"

"No," Joyce admits, "it's family legend. But the probate court must have a copy of it, right?"

"Not necessarily. Sometimes old records get lost. But I'll have my paralegal check, when she gets back from London. Listen, Joyce, I'm not trying to give you grief, on the day your father—"

"It's okay, David. I want you to ask hard questions. And don't go easy just 'cause Daddy died this morning. I'm doing this mostly for him. I think this is why he was so bent on coming to London to research family history. But even if I'm wrong about that, I need to know, to-night, if I have a good claim against Fiona. Because tomorrow, before I fly home, I'm gonna go see the old bitch, and demand she give me back the codex. Unless you tell me I'm barking up the wrong tree."

"Alright, I'll be my usual ruthless self, and cross-examine you like any new client. Let's start with the *Lamanai Codex*. How'd Kathleen come to own the codex in the first place?"

"The codex was a gift to Kathleen in 1864, from her painting teacher in London, an old lady named India Reynolds. I have no idea where India Reynolds got the codex."

"Any chance the codex was stolen property?" Burns asks.

"100 percent. I mean, originally it was the Maya's. *Somebody* musta stolen it from them."

"Fair point. Okay. But we don't have a bill of sale, or a gift letter, or anything like that, to prove the codex belonged to Kathleen in 1864?"

"No, but the 1868 diary I'm bringing you says, in 1864, India Reynolds gave it to Kathleen."

"And where'd you get the diary?"

Joyce pauses. "We have attorney-client privilege here, right?"

"Of course."

"Daddy stole it from the British Library yesterday."

A short pause. "Let's say he 'borrowed' it. Sounds better. How long's the library had it?"

"Since 1868. It was in a collection of Roger Quinlan's papers and plaster casts from the Maya ruins at Lamanai, which Kathleen donated to the British Museum right after Roger died."

"Well that's probably good enough to defeat any challenge to its authenticity," Burns says. "Now let's go through your Family Tree, step by step. Is there anyone in the chain, from Kathleen to you, whom Fiona's lawyer might argue was crazy, or acting fraudulently?"

"Are you kidding?" Joyce asks. "Almost all the Quinlans and Kerrs were crazy."

Burns chuckles.

"No, seriously, David. Just go down the family tree. Roger Quinlan thought he found the fountain of youth. Kathleen and Lloyd both committed suicide. Persephone was even nuttier than Fiona – Persephone was still digging in Maya ruins when she was in her 80s. Grandpa Graham came back from World War I with battle trauma, and spent the rest of his days in a VA asylum, till he broke out, stole a plane from Willow Run, and flew east with the intention of ending World War II by killing Hitler – only to crash and die in Lake Erie. Quinn's off chasing the meaning of life in India. Really, Grace and my parents were the only normal ones since before Roger and Kathleen."

"And you, Joyce. You're very stable. Well, at least there's no fraud—" Burns pulls up short.

They both know why Burns stopped. Burns' first client, right out of law school, was Justin Kerr, accused by his business partners of embezzlement – the charges Justin fought for years, in civil and criminal courts of Michigan, ultimately dragging his family into bankruptcy, all in a losing effort, because, at the end of the day, Justin truly did embezzle funds from his partners, although his motive was not self-gain, but rather trying to prevent a buy-out of the company he loved.

"Except for Daddy" – Joyce's voice trembles slightly – "the only other criminal in our family was Roger Quinlan. According to Kathleen's diary, Roger was expelled from Oxford for robbing graves, seduced his wife's best friend before eloping to Australia, left Australia one step ahead of the law for some crime unspecified, went to Honduras and ran guns to Maya rebels in Mexico, and then drank the poisonous water at Lamanai he mistook for the fountain of youth."

"Sounds like a fun guy." Burns laughs. "But since Roger died before Kathleen, he's not in the chain from Kathleen to you. He's irrelevant. Now, Kathleen committed suicide in 1909 – how?"

"Drove off a bridge into a deep river. They never even found her body."

"How'd they know it was suicide, and not an accident?"

"She left a note."

"What was the reason for the suicide?"

"She was caught in a barn on the outskirts of Ann Arbor, with a married professor. *In flagrante delicto*, as they used to say. It was apparently a huge scandal, back in the day."

"Oh, I remember hearing this story from your mother once." Burns rustles paper. "But wait, Kathleen was what, *65 years old* in 1909? Not an age most women have aff—"

"Reportedly Kathleen was even better looking in her sixties than Fiona was at that same age," Joyce says. "All the women in my family age very well – and we're all great-looking."

"No argument from me there." Burns snorts. "What else do you know about Kathleen?"

"Not much. She came to Ann Arbor right after Roger died in London in 1868. She was one of the first women lecturers at the University of Michigan, in the 1870's."

"What subject?" Burns asks.

"Central American studies. The Maya, our family's obsession. Also – I doubt this matters, but to me, it's really strange. Kathleen addressed her 1868 diary to a daughter she says she aborted, around 1865. She calls the aborted daughter 'Persephone'. But then in 1869, when Kathleen gave birth to a live daughter, she gave her live daughter that same name, Persephone."

"That *is* odd," Burns agrees. "But probably doesn't matter. More relevant is what went on in the 1909 court fight between Persephone and Lloyd, after Kathleen killed herself in 1909. Have you ever seen any records at all from that probate case – like the asset inventory?"

"No," Joyce admits.

"Then I'll have my paralegal look for it, in the old court files, once she returns from London. Because Joyce, we really need to know if the codex was listed as an asset of Kathleen's estate."

"Okay. I'll go as soon as the court reopens after the holidays." Joyce frowns. "But – just so I understand, which is better for us: if the codex *is* listed on the asset inventory, or if it's *not* listed?"

A pause ensues. "Well actually, as I think about it, I suppose it doesn't matter much, either way. I mean, if the court order truly says all the assets go to Lloyd, then if the codex *is* listed as an asset, that's one more good thing for us. But if it's *not* listed, we'll just argue that Lloyd – who presumably prepared the asset inventory – never knew the codex existed. So either way, we rely on the court order – and on Kathleen's diary. But tell me about Lloyd. How'd he kill himself?"

"Shot himself in his library," Joyce says, "while reading Conrad."

"*Heart of Darkness*?"

"Is that the one about Central America?"

"No," Burns says, "that's *Nostromo*."

"That's it, *Nostromo*. About a guy who shoots himself on an island off Belize. So the family story is, the stock market had just crashed, the creditors were at Lloyd's door, he was reading *Nostromo*, and he just pulled out his pistol and put an end to it all, *Nostromo*-style."

"Was there probate litigation over Lloyd's estate, too?"

"I don't know," Joyce admits. "Another thing your paralegal will have to investigate."

"Check. But the end result, as far as you know is, Lloyd had nothing left to leave Grace, and Grace had nothing left to leave Justin, and Justin had nothing to leave to you?"

"Correct. So do all the suicides and lunatics in my family somehow defeat my claim?"

"No, although it truly is amazing you turned out as well-balanced as you did, Joyce. Especially with Justin in and out of bankruptcy the whole time you were growing up. But here's the biggest danger I see to your claim: is there any reason to think Justin, or Grace, or Lloyd, knew the other side of your family had the *Lamanai Codex*, and yet *acquiesced* in their having it?"

"Well, I never met Lloyd, or Grace," Joyce says. "But if Daddy'd known, given how desperate he always was for money, I gotta believe he'd've said or done something."

"Fair point. From all my years representing Justin and hardly ever getting paid, I'm sure he never knew he might've had a claim to a valuable Mayan codex. But – just to play devil's advocate here – what if we sue Fiona, and she answers by claiming Grace or Lloyd knew all along that Persephone and Fiona had Lloyd's codex, and it was all okay with Grace or Lloyd?"

"But how could Fiona say that now?" Joyce asks. "She told me Persephone dug the codex up at Lamanai while excavating the famous Maya library there, back in the '20s or '30s."

"Fair point," Burns says. "Okay then, the bottom line is, I think you might really have a good claim to the *Lamanai Codex*, Joyce. Which is why I would rather you *not* go see Fiona tomorrow."

"Why not?"

"Because you're still in shock from your father's death. Not the best time to—"

"I'm going, David. I'm sorry. I get to London about once every ten years, if that; and I haven't seen Fiona in twenty years, since she made such a fuss accusing me of trying to steal a book she must've known full well belonged to me all along. Yet she's also the woman who raised me, as much as my technical mother, who was always too busy for me. So I need to – I need to look Fiona in the eye and tell her I know she done me wrong."

A pause ensues. "Alright. But please be careful when you talk to Fiona. Admit nothing, Joyce, while trying to get her to commit to as many specifics about the codex as you can – where it came from, who knew about it, what they knew and when they knew it, etc. You know the drill."

"I've read a few of your cross-examinations over the years, yes," Joyce says. "But tell me, David, will it be a problem to sue Fiona in Ann Arbor, since she lives in London?"

"A big problem. But we'll find a way across that bridge when we come to it. Please be careful tomorrow, Joyce. In my experience, little old ladies are the most dangerous foes."

Joyce hangs up. She resists her first temptation, to call Lisa. The Judge told Joyce, since she complains about all Michael's encroachments on her time, she better not encroach on his.

But the second temptation she knows she can't resist. So she lights up a cigarette.

Chapter Three
The Brethren of the Coast

Monday 27 December 2010

As dusk settles on the dusty suburbs of Belmopan, Kip Hunter squats near the tree line behind Ron Graham's one-story cottage. In Belize, Ron's shitty little cottage – built of flimsy painted sticks stuck into a concrete slab, smaller than most American mobile homes – is about as upscale as it gets.

Kip's in a foul mood. His feet ache, from double-timing it ten hours through the rain forest. From his armpits he smells the gummy olibanum of the steaming jungle, as if the sap from every vine he passed seeped into his skin. On his gloves is crusted blood, from yanking the Maya spears out of Bruce Tobin's throat; and carved forever on Kip's brain is the memory of Harry Benz's eyes, blank and staring, in the bottom of the guide's skiff, after the Maya spears cut him down, too. Worst of all, Kip still inhales, with every breath, the rancid stench of those 13 dead Maya in the tomb.

Kip has no idea if Ron Graham's married, but he sees no evidence of anyone at home right now, except Ron, fixing dinner in the kitchen. Too bad. Might have been fun to terrorize nerdy Ron with a gun to his wife's head. Because Ron's definitely got a few questions to answer. Now.

Kip makes his move, strong and simple. No gun in sight, just a man with a diver's pack, he walks out of the forest, across Ron's backyard, and opens the back door with one swift karate kick.

Ron Graham whirls, dropping a TV dinner, which splashes onto the formica counter.

"Surprised to see me still alive?" Kip gestures at the kitchen table. "Sit down."

"Why'd you kill Kux?" Ron demands.

"Sit the fuck down."

"I just got a call," Ron persists, "they're all dead. Kux, everyone. You killed them!"

Kip pulls his pistol from its holster. "Sit down, motherfucker. Right. Now."

Ron complies.

Kip sits across the table, his pistol leveled at Ron. "I didn't kill anyone. And they're not *all* dead, either. Four of 'em killed my three men – and I gotta believe those four are still hunting me."

"The call I got was the police," Ron counters. "They said persons unknown attacked the Mask Temple with explosives and guns, and everyone inside is dead. Obviously that was you."

"We blew down the door, and fired a few shots. But the guys inside were already dead, long before we got there." Abruptly Kip stands and glares. "You didn't give the cops my name?"

"Of course not."

"What'd you tell 'em, exactly?"

"Nothing – truly."

Kip studies Ron's face, looking for what poker players call the 'tell' – the signal Ron's lying.

But Ron's face doesn't twitch. "Giving the police your name would be the same as signing my own arrest warrant. Because as soon as they picked you up, you'd just tell 'em I hired you."

"Damn right I would." Kip keeps glaring at Ron.

"But I didn't hire you to *kill* anyone."

"I told you, we did not kill anyone."

"Then who did?"

Kip ignores the question. "How come the cops just happened to call *you*, of all people?"

"I'm Lamanai's site director. The police are coming here in 15 minutes, to pick me up."

"Pick you up!" Kip's heart races. "You mean, as a suspect?"

"No, they just want me out at the site tonight." Ron gestures at a backpack in the front hall. "They're flying me out, to 'assist their investigation'."

Kip takes a deep breath, and sits back down. "Good. Then you can find out where the cops are goin' with this. And I guarantee, you'll see it wasn't my bullets or explosives killed those guys."

"Then what *did* kill 'em?"

"Well, for starters, your pal Kux and the other old guy had their hearts ripped right out of their fuckin' chests."

Ron turns a whiter shade of pale.

"Take a look for yourself tonight. Unless you have a queasy stomach, in which case you might wanna wait for the autopsy. But I'm tellin' you now, they died from human sacrifice."

Ron's shoulders sag, and his eyes go a little glassy.

"You know I'm right, don't you?" Kip presses. "In fact, you're not even surprised by this. You *knew* their rituals might get bloody, so you sent me out there, as what – your stalking horse?"

"No." Ron wipes his hand across his eyes, blinking back what look like real tears. "I had no idea this would happen. Those young men loved Kux, like a father – almost like a God."

"Yeah?" Kip sets his pistol down, but keeps his hand close to it. "Well, they didn't do jack shit for their 'God' Kux after he died. Just left him to rot, like a bad side o' beef at a flea market."

To Kip's surprise, his deliberately harsh words don't get any rise at all out of Ron.

"That's the ancient Maya custom," Ron says. "Instead of burying their worthiest leaders, the ancient Maya offered them as a sacrifice, to the Gods."

"Well, in this case, the Gods weren't quick enough – the maggots and flies got there first."

"To the Maya, the maggots and flies *are* the Gods," Ron replies. "The Maya believe the Gods morph into insects, in order to sustain themselves, and, in so doing, sustain us, too."

"That's some sick shit."

"Not if you take the time to understand it," Ron persists. "Maggots feasting on dead flesh is one of the central natural processes by which all life is renewed, in an endless circle. Time—"

"Spare me the lecture, Ron. I'm really not interested in Maya religion."

"What about the 11 young guys?" Ron asks. "You didn't tell me what *they* died from."

Kip arches an irked eyebrow. "Beats the shit outta me. Those young guys had no wounds I could see – no bruises, no signs of violence, no marks of any kind. Just lotsa maggots."

"Young men don't just drop dead."

"True." Kip glints his eyes at Ron. "Maybe it was *'Antil's Curse'* that got 'em."

Ron's lips tremble, and a flicker of guilty recognition flashes across Ron's eyes, just for an instant. Good. Now Kip knows what Ron's 'tell' looks like. And he also knows that 'Antil's Curse' must be more important than he first thought, when he heard the guide blubbering about it.

Ron grunts, puts on his calm mask again, and asks: "So, d'you get the icon?"

"Don't change the subject, Ron. We're talking about Antil's Curse. And why you gave me bad intel."

"I don't know what you mean."

"You said I'd find all 17 guys sleeping inside that tomb. Instead, four of 'em were off in the jungle, lying in wait with their Stone Age spears. *You set me up, motherfucker!*"

"I did not."

Kip glares at Ron, looking for the 'tell'. But this time no guilt flashes across Ron's eyes.

Instead Ron makes the same point Kip himself made this morning: "If Kux and the rest were infested with maggots, doesn't that explain why the survivors weren't sleeping in the tomb?"

"Maybe. But why didn't you tell me about 'Antil's Curse', before sending me up that river?"

"Antil's Curse isn't important. It's not even real."

"That's not what my guide said. Every time he saw a dead body anywhere this morning, Maya or white, he started burbling about 'Antil's Curse'. What the hell is Antil's Curse?"

"An old pirate spook story." Ron rises. "I've got your money, if you've got the icon."

"Sit down, Ron, and tell me about that old pirate spook story."

"We don't have time. Neither one of us wants the police to find you here with me."

Kip picks up his pistol, and aims it at Ron again. "I like cutting things close. Sit down, motherfucker, and tell me about the pirate's spook story."

Ron sits back down, but over his shoulder he casts a nervous glance out the front window, at the empty street. "In the 17th century a band of pirates supposedly came to Lamanai—"

"What the hell were pirates doing that far inland?" Kip interrupts.

"Fleeing a Spanish warship, the story goes. After a couple of weeks hiding at Lamanai, all but one of the pirates supposedly died of unknown diseases. In the 18th century another band of pirates died, also after visiting Lamanai. After that, the legend spread that the Maya at Lamanai had put a curse on all pirates. But none of this has ever been historically confirmed."

"Who was 'Antil'?"

"The Maya shaman at Lamanai who supposedly cursed the pirates. Xhuxh Antil."

"What reason would Xhuxh Antil have to put a curse on pirates?"

Ron looks out the window. "It's a long story, Kip. We really don't have time—"

Kip slams his fist down hard on the table. "Stop holding out on me, dammit!"

"I'm not holding out on you, Kip."

"You sure as hell are! Why'd my *mestizo* guide look at 13 dead Maya, and the first thing he thinks of is a 400-year-old pirate legend? Why has my guide, who probably can't even fuckin' read, even *heard* of some old pirate legend? And if the Maya curse only went against *pirates*, like you say, why'd my guide think of 'Antil's Curse' when he saw a bunch of dead *Maya*?"

"How can I know what your guide was thinking?" Ron sighs. "But I'll tell you what. I'll give you the only two books that ever mentioned Antil's Curse. Then you can stay here and read 'em, while I go outside and wait in the street for the police. That way you'll have all the information I or anyone else has ever had about Antil's Curse, and you and I don't get seen together. Okay?"

"Where are these books?"

Ron points at a bookcase. "I'll point out the relevant chapters for you to read."

"Alright."

Ron rises. "And while I'm up, I'll get the rest of your cash, too, if you have the icon for me."

Kip smirks. "I'm keeping the icon awhile, till we see how much shit hits the fan over all those dead guys – and till I figure out what's really at stake here, that you're not telling me."

"That's not fair!"

"It wasn't fair to send me up that river without telling me about Antil's Curse, either."

"But I paid you 25,000 dollars to—"

"You didn't pay me anywhere near enough for all the shit you sent me wading into today. So I'm keepin' that little statue as my insurance policy, till I find out how much it's really worth."

"You may not want to do that."

"Are you threatening me?"

"I'm warning you. The legend is, Xhuxh Antil cursed the pirates because they stole that little icon from Antil. So according to the legend, whoever has the icon falls under the curse."

Kip hums a few bars from the theme song of the TV show *Twilight Zone*, whose reruns he grew up on. "Woo—oo! You're really scaring me now, Ron. I might have trouble sleeping tonight."

"Laugh all you like. But you said there were no marks or wounds on the young men out at the Mask Temple, right? And where'd you find the icon? Right there in the tomb with them, I bet."

"Thanks for the warning. But I like living dangerously." Kip grins. "One last thing, though, before you go outside – how'd Kux get the icon, if pirates stole it from Xhuxh Antil centuries ago?"

"The pirates sold it to a collector," Ron says, "whose 20th century descendants donated it to the Belize Museum. This past spring, Kux stole it from the Belize Museum."

"That's a lotta trouble to go to, for one little icon. What makes this icon so special?"

From outside comes the sound of gravel crunching. A Belize Police van pulls up in front.

"My ride." Ron pulls down two small, leather-bound books. "Read these, Kip, and all your questions'll be answered. Chapter 5 in Wyatt; Chapter 3 in Rogers. And don't bother searching my house for the $25,000 – it's in my pack." Scooping up his pack, Ron scoots out the front door.

Kip watches Ron and the cops drive off. Then he hits Ron's fridge for four beers, and eats Ron's TV dinner off the counter, cold, before inspecting the books. Both are cracked and yellowed, and written in old time English. But at least both chapters Ron mentioned are short. Kip checks the publication dates – 1726 for Wyatt, 1752 for Rogers – and decides to read the older one first.

But when he opens Wyatt, five sheets of modern paper fall out, which were folded into the book, right at Chapter 5: a photocopy of a five-page 1724 British Naval memo, replete with Royal insignia. Handwritten across the top of the memo is: "The only historically verifiable facts about Antil's Curse, and India Reynolds (nee Shaw) – including the true ending to Wyatt's tale."

Kip has always preferred to cut to the chase. So on those rare occasions when he reads, he likes to skip straight to the ending. Therefore, it's a no-brainer. Kip reads the Navy memo first.

To: *Hon. Henry Bentinck, Duke of Portland, Royal Governor of Iamaica*
From: *Franklin A. Vaughan, Captain, R.N.*
Date: *6th July of 1724*

With regret I must report that the whole Trade from Great Britain to the Miskito Coast and the Iucatan is presently obstruct'd, and is in grave Danger of being lost entirely to Spain, due to an Accident of serious Consequence that occurr'd last Month at Honduras Bay, resulting in the total Destruction of the Wharf &c. on the Western Shore of the principal Harbour there, at the Mouth of the Belize River.

The White Settlers at Honduras Bay, consisting mainly of unruly Pyrates who claim'd the Benefit of the King's Pardon six Years ago, giving up the pyratical

Life to become rough Logwood Cutters, can not, in all Candour, be rely'd upon to effect Construction of a new Wharf, absent scrupulous Guidance from experienced Engineers, and scores of Leaguers of Rum, to guarantee their Attendance at the Work Site.

The Seamen of his Majesty's Ship Scarborough have erect'd a rudimentary Dock, but we lack Carpenters and Tools sufficient to construct permanent Works, tho' the Need is Urgent; wherefore I beseech Your Excellency to dispatch experienced Engineers from Iamaica with the utmost Expedition, to direct Construction of a new Wharf &c.

It is my Duty to make the Point that, until such Time as a new Wharf &c. is erect'd, the Interests of the Crown in these Parts are in very serious Peril, because the Wharf at the Honduras Bay Harbour is Essential to the effective Deployment of the Royal Navy along the entire Eastern Coast of the Middle Part of America.

The peculiar Circumstances of the Accident at Honduras Bay were as follows:

About two hours before Dawn on 17th June this Year, Edward Jones, a Seaman under my Command, then standing Watch upon the Wharf (the Bay Settlement lacking a proper Water Bailiff), sounded the Alarum, after sighting a solitary Spanish Galleon entering the Eastern Approaches to the Harbour.

Our Ability to respond to the Alarum was regrettably hinder'd, by the Misfortune that the Scarborough was at that Time careen'd along the Strand behind the Wharf, for Cleaning &c., with her starboard Guns pointing directly down into the Sand, and her port-Side Batteries aiming straight up at the Heavens, in no position to menace the Spaniards; wherefore I boarded the only other Vessel in the Harbour equip'd with Cannon, being the Adventure, a slave Galley belonging to the South Sea Company.

By the Time I reach'd the Quarter-Deck of the Adventure, the Spanish Galleon, with the Aid of the Easterly that prevails in these Parts, had clos'd within half Shot. She was sailing Broadside to the Shore, rather than Bow first, which we apprehended as a bellicose Tactic of War; and she had all her Starboard Gun Ports Open, with twenty starboard Cannon aim'd at us, placing in immediate Peril all the Ships lying in the Harbour, including the Adventure, the careen'd Scarborough, as well as the Living Quarters of all the British Settlers in Honduras Bay.

The Danger from the Galleon's Advance being Imminent, I order'd the Gunner to fire at the Galleon; whereupon, in short Order, several Balls found their Marks, and Flames were Visible along the starboard Bow of the Galleon. To our Surprize, however, the Galleon did not return our Fire; but much to our Dismay, neither did she sink, but continued instead to advance upon us, Broadside to the Shore, like an enemy Fire Ship.

In spight of the dark Hour, the Flames on the Galleon's fore-Deck glow'd with Light sufficient for use of a Spy-glass, thro' which I made five Observations, of a most disquieting Nature, viz.: that hanging off the Bolt-sprit End of the Galleon was a humane Skeleton; that the Name of the Galleon had been painted o'er with the words: Batchelour's Dream; that instead of Spain's Colours, she flew the Jolly Rogers Skull and Crossbones; that all fifteen Members of her Crew, visible on the Decks, were cloath'd in the unsavoury Garb of Pyrates; and, most Strange, that all fifteen Pyrates were lying Motionless, sprawl'd across the Decks, as if dead Drunk, or just plain Dead.

The Flames being confin'd to the Bow of the Batchelour's Dream, and thereby producing insufficient Light to penetrate the shroud of Night enveloping her Stern, I could not discern any Steersman at the Helm; nor was I able to discern at such a Distance, any Captain conning her. Indeed, how the burning Galleon was contriving to sail into Port at all was a most perplexing Mystery, for I could see no humane Person on Deck who was upright and engag'd in any sailing Task whatsoe'er.

Apprehending that the Pyrates might be counterfeiting Death, in the Manner of Possums, as a Stratagem to decoy us into letting them sail unmolest'd to our Shore, I order'd all Hands to Arms, and order'd the Gunner to load another Round of Balls; but seeing that the Batchelor's Dream fired no Shot upon us, I delay'd firing upon her again, until we might further plumb her Intentions.

Once the Distance from us to the Batchelor's Dream closed to three Furlongs, Scrutiny thro' the Spyglass reveal'd that here was no Possums' Trick; for all but one of the Pyrates lying on the Decks were Skeletons: their weather'd Cloaths were hanging on Bones utterly bereft of Skin and Flesh, and their Eyes had been pecked clean out of their Skulls. The one Pyrate whose Face retain'd some meager Flesh, was lying on his Back across the Quarter-Deck, in a Captain's Coat; but this pyrate Captain was dead as his Confederates, as evidenc'd by the Fact that he offer'd no Resistance at all to a large Gath'ring of Gulls, who were feasting prodigiously upon his Cheeks and Breast.

At these gristly Sights, a Murmur of Fear arose amongst my Men, and one voic'd what all were thinking, regarding the burning Galleon, viz: that in spight of her Spanish Appearance, and her English Name, she was the ghostly Flying Dutchman, the doom'd Ship of Legend, seeking to Dock at our Port with her Skeleton Crew.

Being a rational Man, I give no Credence to the fantastickal Superstitions of Seamen; yet I do admit, at that dark Hour, by the dim Light of our Lanterns, the Sight of the burning Galleon, with its Skeleton Crew, closing fast upon us without any Sign of humane Navigation, were enough to strike Terror in the stoutest Heart: Wherefore I was unable to quell the wild Talk circulating amongst my Men.

Even my Lieftenants and sub-Lieftenants averr'd, that the approaching Galleon must be of the Devil's Armada, for it is a Fact beyond Dispute in these wild Parts, that only an Indian or a Pyrate can pilot a Vessel unharm'd, in the Pitch of Night, across the Bar and into the Harbour at Honduras Bay, the Entrance being Shoal, the Channels intricate, and the shallow Reefs widely fam'd as the Bone-Yard of many a sunken Ship; and the only Reason Indians and Pyrates can manage such a Feat in the Dark is their light Craft bear no Resemblance to a Galleon in Tonnage or Displacement.

Wherefore, my Third Lieftenant urg'd the firing of further Rounds at the ghostly Galleon, to attempt to blow her to bits, before she ferry'd the Devil to our very Door; in Answer to which my First Lieftenant, who fancies himself a droll Wag, disagreed, saying 'twould be Folly, and a Waste of Cannon-Balls, to fire upon a Ship with Lucifer at the Conn, Fire and Smoak being Lucifer's favour'd Elements.

Brave Jests about Satan sailing the Galleon persist'd amongst my Officers, till she clos'd within two Furlongs, whereupon I espy'd a young Girl on the Quarter-Deck, in a soil'd white wedding Gown, clinging to the Helm: Whereupon I signal'd to her, to turn the Wheel to Leeward, and bring off the Winde, so she might avert a Crash into the Wharf; but I saw no humane Understanding in her wild, distract'd Eyes.

Wherefore I dispatch'd a Pinnace with my six most capable Sea-Men, to attempt to board the Batchelor's Dream and sail her away from the Wharf; but from such a low-lying Craft, boarding the tall Galleon prov'd impossible, without Aid from some Person above, to secure the Ropes: However, the Girl at the Helm, bearing down upon us, with what seem'd malignant Purpose, ignored all Cries from my Men below.

Whereupon I order'd the Pinnace to row clear, and fired repeat'd Volleys at the Batchelour's Dream, in the vain Hope that we might blow her to Bits, before she reach'd the Wharf. Several Balls found their Targets; but none could halt the forward Progress of the Galleon; and all our Gunnery serv'd only to stoke an Encrease in the Fire, which was then raging below the Galleon's Decks.

About an hour before Dawn, the Batchelour's Dream crashed into the Wharf, whereupon the Wharf immediately caught Fire. Two merchant Snows, tied to the Wharf, and loaded with out-bound Logwood, also caught Fire, their Lumber feeding a great Encrease in the Flames, which roar'd all along the Wharf.

Apprehending that the Adventure would shortly be in Flame, I order'd all Hands to jump Ship, onto the burning Wharf, or into the Water, as they judg'd Fittest.

By God's Grace the Winde blew gentle; wherefore my Men, and those of the Adventure, forming a Bucket Brigade with Sea Water, extinguish'd the Fire before it reach'd the Scarborough, or the Living Quarters of the Logwood Cutters.

But the Fire rag'd three Hours after Dawn, before it was finally quell'd, and its Fury destroy'd entirely the Wharf &c., along with both of the merchant Snows, the Adventure, and the Batchelour's Dream. No Lives were lost, save for the Cargo of Negroes aboard the Adventure, who could not be releas'd from their Chains in the Smoaking Hold, before they had all perish'd in the Flames.

The young Girl at the Helm of the Batchelour's Dream surviv'd the Wreck, tho' the Means of her Salvation serv'd only to confirm the superstitious Opinion of the Sea-men, that she was a Witch: For she wander'd off the fiery Galleon, and onto the burning Wharf, in her torn white wedding Gown, oblivious and impervious to the Noise and Smoak of the Wreck; and meander'd safely thro' the Flames, as if she were Proof against Fire, leaping thence onto the Beach, with nary a Burn on her Person.

We arrest'd the Girl, on Suspicion of Pyracy, and Destruction of Property; and interrogated her: Whereupon, when her Name was demanded, the confounded Girl stood Mute; when call'd to account for her reckless Actions in steering a Galleon into the Wharf, she stood Mute; when press'd to explain the Skeleton hanging off the Bolt-sprit of the Galleon which she had been steering with such malignant Purpose, she stood Mute; and finally, when ask'd if she denied being a Pyrate, she stood Mute.

With Naught to be gain'd from interrogating a Mute, I order'd her held in the Brig to await Tryal, assuring her I would see her Hang'd by the Neck before Night-fall.

But a Complication ensued, for it was discover'd, from the Rise in her Belly, that the Girl was Quick with Childe; and more-over, due to the Stress of her fiery Arrival in the Bay, the Girl was in grave Danger of delivering the Childe before its Time. A Surgeon was call'd, and all humane Measures taken; but the result of all the Labour was, the Childe was born Still; and although the Girl barely surviv'd, the Surgeon proclaim'd it a medical Certainty, that she would ne'er again conceive a Childe.

At her Tryal, the unfathomable Girl still refus'd to speak a Word, nor offer'd any Witnesses in her Defence; however, a Logwood-Cutter from the Bay, Geoffrey Howard, came forward and averr'd that the Girl was an Innocent, who should not be hang'd. Howard testify'd the Girl's Name was India Shaw, being the eighteen Year old Daughter of John Shaw, the deceased Owner of a Logwood-Cutting Concern that was, until Shaw's recent Demise, working Land which Shaw claim'd along the Belize River.

Mr. Howard further relat'd that Shaw, along with his Wyfe and Servants, were murder'd here six months ago, by a Band of Pyrates following Damien Reynolds; and that on that same Occasion, Reynolds and his Pyrates – the Brethren of the Coast, as they style themselves – kidnapp'd India Shaw, and forc'd her to board a Galleon they had seiz'd from the Spanish, which was e'en then called the Batchelour's Dream, and taken thence from the Bay to Parts Unknown.

At first I receiv'd the Testimony of Mr. Howard with a sceptical Ear, for he was at a compleat Loss to explain how Miss India Shaw, if that truly was her Name, had been able to sail such a large Galleon, with its substantial Displacement, across the Bar and thro' the shoal Waters and treacherous Keyes that form the Approaches to the Harbour at Honduras Bay, in the Pitch of Night, unless she were also a Pyrate, or, apropos of her most unusual name, an Indian.

However, my Second Lieftenant, deep in the Grip of tender Emotion for the Girl, advanc'd a plausible Theory, viz: seeing that the Pyrate in the Captain's Coat, whom we presumed was Damien Reynolds, appear'd to have died only a short Time before the Wreck, judging by the Zeal with which the Gulls were still feasting upon his Face, e'en as his Galleon menac'd us; mayhap Reynolds had navigat'd the Galleon across the Bar and thro' the intricate Channels, and treacherous Keyes, stationing Miss Shaw at the Helm to steer at his Con; until some Place near the Approach to the Harbour, when Reynolds fell down Dead, from the same Disease which had earlier kill'd his Mates; whereupon Providence, enlisting the Easterly Winde as its Ally, blew the Girl, and the Galleon, safely across the last stretches of shoal Water, and into Port.

Finding this Theory plausible, and relying upon Howard's Testimony that the Girl was Reynolds' Victim, not his Confederate, I dismiss'd all Charges against Miss Shaw; for who knows what Horrors were visit'd upon her Person when she was in the Clutch of the Pyrate, that stole her Capacity for Speech, and left her Quick with Childe?

Once the careening of the Scarborough was Compleat, I transport'd Miss Shaw here, to Spanish Town, where I secured her passage on a British merchant Pink, which sail'd this Morning for London; in which great Capital, I understand, from Mr. Howard, Miss Shaw may have Relatives to care for her. May the Man of Sorrows in His Mercy lend her poor distract'd Soul Grace, for to this Day she still has not utter'd a single Word about her Ordeal. Even more disturbing than her great Silence are the Facts that, in Spight of many kind Offers of Assistance from the gentle Women of the Bay, she insists on wearing only her one soil'd white wedding Gown; and, when signing herself in upon the Pink's Log, she wrote her Name as 'India Reynolds' rather than 'India Shaw.' From these Facts I deduce that, whatever Horrors were visit'd upon her Person whilst she was in the Clutch of the Pyrate, they drove the poor Girl entirely from her Senses.

Tragic though the Circumstances of the Accident were, my Duty compels me to remind Your Excellency, that the present Danger to the Interests of the Crown along the Eastern Coast of the Middle Part of America shall remain most Grave, until the Construction of a new Wharf &c. at Honduras Bay is Compleat.

Kip Hunter folds the naval memo back into the Wyatt book, and finishes off the fourth beer he requisitioned from Ron Graham's refrigerator. Then he rubs his eyes. What a long, bad day.

Maybe he's just too tired to see what's important about this memo. A gripping tale and all – and Kip liked the part where old Captain Vaughan wondered if Reynolds' 'Pyrates' were playing a 'Possum's Trick', just like Kip wondered today if the dead Maya in the tomb were playing possum.

But in the end, this gripping old naval memo strikes Kip as much ado about nothing.

The note on top – Ron's note, Kip presumes – says: "the only historically verifiable facts about Antil's Curse, and India Reynolds (nee Shaw) – including the true ending to Wyatt's tale."

But there wasn't word one in the naval memo about any Maya shaman named Antil. Not one word about a Curse. Not one word about Lamanai or a two-headed Maya idol, either.

India Reynolds (nee Shaw) was there. Whoever the hell she was. But so what?

Basically, all this memo says is, a band of pirates died in 1724, and then sailed like ghosts on the *Batchelour's Dream* into Belize Harbor, spooking the British navy boys and almost burning down the wharf – and killing a ship full of slaves in the process. But it turned out the ghosts weren't really sailing the burning pirate ship, because the pirate Reynolds' woman was still alive, a girl known in the Bay as India Shaw, who later wrote her name as India Reynolds, when she sailed away to London. From her soiled white wedding gown, Kip assumes India Shaw married the pirate Reynolds, sometime after she left the Bay, but before Reynolds died on the *Batchelour's Dream*.

So who cares? And what's the point in all this that Ron Graham thought was so important?

Kip should never have let Ron go. The nerdy geek probably just played Kip for a fool – stalled and distracted him with cheap talk about how these dusty old books would answer all Kip's questions about Antil's Curse, just to buy time so he could run off to Lamanai with the cops.

To pay Ron back for his deceit, Kip turns Ron's house upside down, just in case Ron was lying about the $25,000 he claimed was in his pack. But all Kip finds is ten dollars in Belizean coins. He starts to take the coins, out of spite; but decides the paltry sum is beneath his dignity.

But the dearth of funds in the cheap little dump reminds Kip: where the hell did a nerd like Ron Graham come up with $25,000 cash down to pay Kip in the first place? Has Ron got a secret benefactor backing him? Or is this two-headed idol in Kip's pack worth way more than $50K?

Who knows? All Kip knows is, he's lucky still to be alive, the way Maya *atlatls* were cutting down good soldiers on the New River lagoon this morning. And more than anything, Kip's horny.

All his life, whenever Kip's survived a near-death experience, he's felt a need to affirm life.

Time to go find a good woman. And fuck her brains out.

* * *

For Clive Phelps, the three hours after he whimsically agreed to tag along on Gemma's little adventure with Samuel Rivera are mildly surreal. With Rivera nagging them along, Clive and Gemma bolt down a few hors d'oeuvres, change out of their cocktail clothes and into jungle-ready jeans and chambray shirts, toss a few items into Gem's suitcase, assure the Jolly Roger they'll be back in a few days, and in a matter of minutes are picked up at the hotel dock by a Belize Police speedboat. The boat roars north up the coast to Corozal, around the Bend, and then south up the New River to Lamanai; and with each passing minute, Clive reproaches himself for letting Gemma turn his initial agreement to take one day off to go to Altun Ha into a two-day junket to Lamanai.

Since dark has already fallen, sight-seeing on the three-hour boat ride is impossible; and conversation is also fairly hopeless, because Rivera is on his mobile phone almost every second. First he has a long argument with a Belize Police Captain, Pablo Gonzalez, about whether, after Rivera inspects the dead bodies at Lamanai, they should be transported to the morgue in Belize City. Rivera insists he cannot conduct 16 autopsies out at a remote jungle site, with no electricity for refrigeration, and insufficient indoor space for taking tissue samples, analyzing stomach and bladder contents, and running drug screens. While Clive cannot hear Captain Gonzalez's end of the conversation, he gathers, from Rivera's steady back peddling, that Gonzalez has an answer to every objection. Generators will be brought out; Rivera's assistants can bring out all the necessary refrigeration lockers and examining tables; and Gonzalez will requisition the closed Lamanai museum for Rivera to use as a temporary morgue, with the museum exhibits to be moved out of the way by police constables. The one thing Clive cannot gather, from hearing just Rivera's end of the conversation, is *why* Gonzalez insists the bodies must stay at Lamanai. So when Rivera hangs up, after agreeing to perform 16 autopsies in the jungle, Clive asks why.

"Gonzalez wants everything about this case kept dark," Rivera says, "as long as possible."

"He's afraid of the press?" Clive asks.

"He's afraid of riots. Like I said at the cocktail party, thirteen dead Maya – and three others, dead from Maya *atlatls* – is explosive news in this part of the world. Especially if we don't have a ready explanation for who they were, and what killed them. So until we ID the dead and finish the autopsies, Pablo wants no leaks."

"Is that really possible?"

"Probably not." Rivera shoots a glance at the constable piloting the speedboat. "After all, this is Belize. But at least we have a chance to contain the news, if we do the autopsies on site."

Rivera then proceeds to spend the rest of the trip calling a dozen members of his staff, and alternately cajoling, badgering, begging and ordering them to come join him in 'living rough' out at Lamanai the rest of the week. In most cases the conversation devolves into an argument about whether the particular staffer will be required to give up his or her New Year's Eve.

During these phone calls, it becomes clear that Rivera believes it will take all week to complete the autopsies. Clive begins to see he'll be lucky if his 'two days' at Lamanai doesn't turn into four. With an inward groan, Clive spends the rest of the ride watching the black jungle whiz by, and trying not to think of all the unfinished work he left behind at the hotel.

Most of all, Clive tries not to think of prematurely wizened Nigel, dying by the minute.

When they arrive at Lamanai, Clive sees, tied up at the dock, two other police speedboats, and a small decrepit skiff covered with a big plastic tarp. Also on the dock are two men who introduce themselves as Belize Police Captain Pablo Gonzalez, and Dr. Ronald Graham, the Belize Director of Archeology and Lamanai's site director, who apparently arrived just minutes ago.

Dr. Rivera in turn introduces Dr. Murray and Dr. Phelps, and explains he brought them from the medical conference he was attending, to stay two nights and assist in his examination, because of their 'unique combination of Maya language skills and medical expertise'.

Captain Gonzalez arches a dubious eyebrow, but voices no objection; and orders a constable to take custody of Gemma's suitcase, so they can all get right to work.

The first order of business turns out to be inspecting the decrepit skiff. Pulling a portable floodlight from a duffel bag, Gonzalez switches it on, and pulls the tarp off the skiff, revealing three dead men sprawled across the thwarts. Two have wooden spears stuck in their throats, with crusted blood all round the wounds; the third man also has crusted blood all round open wounds in his throat, with two spears lying beside him on the skiff's decking.

Gemma stifles a gasp, and digs her fingernails hard into Clive's bicep. Clive manages not to gasp, but feels his knees go a little weak. It's been a long time since he's seen human cadavers.

"Coupla Maya fishermen spotted this boat late this afternoon, floating a few miles down river from here," Gonzalez says. "We towed it here, did a quick search, then put the tarp on it."

"Any idea who the dead men are?" Rivera asks.

"The *mestizo* at the stern is Alfonso Canizales," Gonzalez says. "Busted a few times for misdemeanors, but no convictions. It's his boat. He and the boat are both unlicensed."

"And the two white men?" Rivera asks.

"Unlike Canizales, they got no ID," Gonzalez says. "We're running their prints right now."

"Any idea why this unlicensed boat was up here near Lamanai?" Ron Graham interjects.

"Not yet," Gonzalez says.

Rivera slips on rubber gloves and a surgical mask, and bends close to Canizales' throat, examining the wounds made by the four wooden spears impaled there. He pulls one spear out, and studies its bloody end. "This spear went in way too deep to have been thrown, unaided, by a human hand." Rivera turns to Gemma. "What's that ancient Maya weapon that fires spears?"

"An *atlatl*," Gemma says.

"That's it." Rivera turns to Gonzalez. "I can't say for sure, Pablo, until we conduct the autopsies, but I'd guess these spears were fired by *atlatls*, or some modern equivalent."

Gonzalez grunts, and covers the skiff again with the tarp, while Rivera puts the spear he removed into a plastic evidence bag.

Clive smiles, knowing from the cocktail party that Rivera is only pretending not to remember the name of the Maya weapon, to give Gemma a chance to look good and feel useful.

And Rivera's little ploy worked, for Gemma is positively beaming now.

Gonzalez leads the group on a short hike into the jungle.

In the dark Clive doesn't see the Mask Temple until they are within yards of it, when suddenly it rises up out of the jungle, a huge awesome black pyramid of ancient stone blocks.

"Once we saw the three dead guys in the boat," Gonzalez says, "we came up here to ask the Maya, who Dr. Graham gave permission to use this site, if they knew what happened to those three guys. When we got to this temple, we found everyone inside dead."

At the base of the Mask Temple, a uniformed constable stands on guard beside a low doorway cut into the stone. The door itself has a huge irregular hole in its center, and is open wide.

Gonzalez points at the hole in the door. "We found bits of C-4 explosive all around here. The damaged wood is so clean and unweathered, the hole musta been blasted sometime today."

Rivera issues surgical masks to everyone, while Gonzalez explains that, until he can get a generator ferried out to Lamanai, all they've got is four big floodlights he's set up in the tomb – whose batteries won't last long. Then Gonzalez leads them all into the pitch-black tomb, where they huddle just inside the entrance, until Gonzalez switches on the floodlights.

This time Gemma is not alone in expressing shock – Clive, Ron Graham and even Rivera also gasp at the awful sight of 13 human corpses, sprawled across the earthen floor of the tomb.

Rivera goes first to the two elders, whose bodies are by far the most badly damaged.

"Which one is Kux Ahawis?" Rivera asks.

To Clive's surprise, it's Ron Graham, rather than Gonzalez, who identifies Kux. Ron looks deeply distraught. Seeing Clive's curiosity, Ron says: "Kux was a very close friend of mine."

"Dr. Graham's the one who gave these fanatics permission to be here in the first place," Gonzalez says, the studied neutrality in his tone conveying the implicit charge: 'Ron's to blame.'

"As a result," Ron replies, "Dr. Graham's the one whose life is about to turn upside down."

Rivera kneels, and pokes his plastic-gloved hands into Kux's hollowed-out chest.

After a few minutes, Gonzalez asks: "So was it human sacrifice?"

Rivera sighs. "I can't say for certain, Pablo, till we complete the autopsies. But I'm pretty sure man-made tools were used to cut out their hearts. While they were still alive."

"Mother of God!" Gonzalez murmurs.

All six people in the tomb stare at the gaping chests of Kux and the other old Maya.

Clive tries to picture what happened, but his mind blanks at reconstructing the gruesome physiological logistics of human sacrifice – and at the why. *What the hell were these guys up to?*

While Rivera examinines the other eleven bodies, Gonzalez turns to Ron Graham.

"You're sure there were seventeen Maya here in October?"

"Positive. So if your constables find the missing four Maya, we'll know what happened."

"Perhaps," Gonzalez says. "But would that be a good thing?"

Ron twists his neck to stare at Gonzalez. "Wouldn't it?"

"Right now," Gonzalez says, "we've got thirteen Maya victims, three unlicensed victims, and four Maya fugitives. People'll assume either the four Maya fugitives, or the three guys in the boat, murdered the thirteen victims, unless—"

"Unless you find the four Maya fugitives," Ron interrupts, "and they say the deaths resulted from voluntary participation in human sacrifice."

"Precisely. Which story is worse for Belize, Dr. Graham: a mass murder of 13 Maya by four fugitive Maya, or three unlicensed guys, for reasons unknown – or a revival of human sacrifice?"

"Human sacrifice," Ron says, "would trigger a backlash against the Maya."

Gonzalez throws out his hands in a 'just so' gesture. "So if we find the fugitives, fine. But if we don't find them, it may be even better."

Clive suppresses a smile at this wonderful example of positive thinking in a police officer.

"Would it be alright if I go back there?" Gemma asks, pointing behind the sarcophagus.

Ron looks at Gonzalez, who shrugs no objection.

Gemma kneels and inspects the writing on the wall. "Who put this writing here?" she asks.

"No one knows," Ron says. "We ran thermal-oxidation and porosimetry dating tests on the plaster, which showed these marks were scratched here in the 16th or 17th century – the early colonial period, when the Spanish controlled this region. But it's anyone's guess who wrote them."

"The marks at the bottom look like a series of Maya numbers," Gemma says.

"Correct. 666-666-21-4-21-6. We assume it's some kind of coded message. But we've never broken the code."

"And this single glyph above the numbers," Gemma says, "signifies what?"

"We don't know that, either. It's a depiction of a two-headed Maya God. One head is Itzamna, the Maya creator God; and the other is Ah Puch, the Maya God of Death."

"I've never seen a depiction of a Maya God with two heads before," Gemma says.

"It's very rare," Ron agrees. "So we really don't know what that glyph means."

"The, ah, really menacing-looking aroused member of the God in the glyph," Gemma says, "looks almost like the Christian depiction of Death's curved scythe."

Ron cocks his head, and kneels beside Gemma. "You're right. I never thought of that before. But there are many aspects of Maya and Christian theology that have curious overlaps. For example, if you look at the carvings on the sarcophagus" – Ron pauses, while Gemma turns round – "they depict Itzamna again, but this time as a coiled serpent, eating his own tail."

"How does that connect to Christianity?" Gemma asks. "For Christians, serpents are evil; whereas for the Maya serpents are good, because they irrigate the fields where crops grow."

"Yes," Ron says, "but the coiled serpent eating its tail is a symbol almost all religions have, in various forms – it's a symbol of the circularity of all life, and all Time. Here, it denotes the self-sustaining nature of the creator God, Itzamna, who is the Maya equivalent of the Christian God described in Saint John's Revelation – the Alpha and the Omega, the beginning and the end."

Clive tunes out the academic chatter and, girding his stomach, kneels over one of the young corpses – for no particular reason, except he figures he may as well look like he has *some* function here in this tomb of death. Truly, he'd so much rather be back in his lab, studying DNA strips under his microscope, and analyzing the variegated behaviour of cells as they divide, for Nigel's sake. But since he's here, in this murky tomb, Clive studies the jade amulet round the young man's neck. Scanning the tomb, Clive sees similar amulets on almost all the dead. He's about to ask what they are, when he sees Rivera using a Swiss Army knife to cut one of the amulets off the neck of one of the corpses. Gesturing for Gemma to come close, Rivera holds up the amulet and asks if she's ever seen anything like it.

Gemma inspects it a minute, but then shakes her head no.

"All these guys have a similar amulet, except this man." Rivera points to one corpse, without an amulet; and then turns to Ron. "Do you know what these amulets are for, Ron?"

Ron also shakes his head no.

"Our lights are gonna die out soon, Sammy," Gonzalez calls out to Rivera. "So whaddya think? Are you finding signs of trauma on these younger guys I couldn't see?"

"No. We're gonna need to run a lot of tests to figure out what killed eleven young men in one place, with no signs of trauma."

"What are the possibilities?" Gonzalez presses.

Rivera sighs. "Cholera. Poisoned water. Poison gas. But those are all just wild guesses. I'll need tissue biopsies before I'll know anything." He turns to Clive. "But in the meantime, we need to take basic public health measures, don't we?"

Clive figures this is his turn for Rivera to make him look good, so he nods yes.

"Like what?" Gonzalez demands.

"Shutting off the water supply," Clive improvises, "in case it's contaminated."

"Lamanai has no water supply," Ron interjects. "We bring in bottled water."

Clive glances round the tomb. "I don't see any empty water bottles here."

"Kux probably had these guys get their water from the lagoon," Ron concedes. "But the Maya villagers at San Carlos and Indian Church also get their water from that lagoon. And we haven't heard any reports of mass deaths there, have we?"

"We still need to post warning signs around the lagoon in three languages," Rivera says, coming to Clive's aid, "saying 'don't drink the lagoon water, it may be contaminated'."

"Fine," Gonzalez says, "we'll do that. What other public health measures do you want?"

"Quarantine the whole site, obviously," Clive says.

"Already done," Gonzalez says. "What else?"

"Well, we really should make a public announcement about the deaths," Rivera says.

"Why?" Gonzalez demands. "If no one's allowed here except police and coroner personnel, all wearing protective gear, why does the public need to know what happened, before we ID the victims and you finish the autopsies?"

Rivera looks at Clive, questioningly.

Clive decides he doesn't want to annoy either of these guys, so he goes for the diplomatic middle ground. "A public announcement is generally good practice, but if the site is already quarantined, it's not strictly necessary. And since you have good reasons for keeping this quiet … "

Gonzalez nods, evidently pleased that Clive's not making himself too big a pain in the ass.

Rivera also nods acquiescence.

The next moment the first of the lights dies. So they hastily make their way out of the tomb, and head for the old archeologist shacks, where Ron says they'll be 'bedding down' for the night.

* * *

As the first pale gleam of dawn lightens the low gray sky hovering over London's south bank, Joyce Kerr leans against a cold dank stone wall in a narrow passage off Shad Thames, just across from the converted warehouses of Butler's Wharf, where Fiona Young lives. For hundreds of years, Shad Thames was London's roughest slum – the haunt of Dickens' Bill Sykes and the Artful Dodger, as well as many generations of real-life brigands, pirates, thugs and gangsters. But nowadays, with the warehouses all converted to upscale flats, Shad Thames is quite genteel.

Or so Joyce tells herself. In the bleary shadows of early morning, however, the narrow cobbled lane gives her the creeps. The only person visible anywhere along Shad Thames, besides Joyce, is a grouty homeless man with a matted beard, sheltering in a bundle of rags and cardboard in another passage down the lane. The only sounds are the harsh cries of seagulls and sandpipers, coming from the nearby river Thames, echoing in endless cacophony off the cramped warehouse walls. And the only light, besides the pale candescence of the dawn, is the murky glow from the ancient gaslamps affixed to the warehouse walls – twitching flames that dance in jagged patterns off the tangle of irregular metal catwalks three stories above, which connect the riverside warehouses on the north side of the lane with the land-locked warehouses on the south side.

Joyce tucks her chin low into her scarf, to shield her face from the wintry wind blowing down Shad Thames and into the dismal passage where she lurks, and lights a cigarette. She selected this passage because it has two exits, and a clear view of anyone approaching. But it feels so cold and ominous, Joyce is sorely tempted to abandon her post and simply go push the buzzer for Fiona's flat.

Yet she knows that is not a serious option. The last time Joyce buzzed Fiona's flat – on a brief holiday stop in London, thirteen years ago – Fiona coldly told Joyce to go away. And then the squawk box went dead. Before that, the last time Joyce spoke with Fiona was the infamous day in the summer of 1990 when Fiona, then 65 and retiring from teaching at the University of Michigan, falsely accused her cousin Joyce, then 20 and working as Fiona's research assistant, of trying to steal the *Lamanai Codex* from Fiona's roll-top desk in her Burns Park home. After evicting Joyce and filing a complaint with the local police – later dropped by the prosecutor, after David Burns interceded on Joyce's behalf – Fiona made it clear she never wanted to speak to Joyce again.

Hence the need for Joyce to lurk outside Fiona's building, like a thief in the night.

It will take cunning – and a fair bit of luck – to get in to talk to Fiona today.

Right around 7 a.m., to Joyce's relief, a flurry of activity comes to Shad Thames. The porters in the buildings change shifts, the coffee shops open, and commuters begin trudging past Joyce, on their way to Tower Bridge and the City. With so many people now out and about, Joyce shifts her focus from her personal security to reviewing her plan for gaining entry to Butler's Wharf.

Once the hour becomes commercially reasonable, Joyce plans to present herself to the Butler's Wharf porter as a courier from a law firm in the City, with urgent legal documents that must be hand-delivered to Fiona Young in Flat 514. In her hand, Joyce clutches an official-looking envelope, appropriately addressed, though stuffed only with her father's family research papers, so it will be too bulky to fit through a mail slot or the narrow opening of a chained door. Joyce is not quite sure how things will play out with the porter, but she hopes he'll just let her take the lift up to Fiona's floor. From there, Joyce'll pretend to be a courier until Fiona opens her door and takes the chain off, when she'll force her way past the old woman; or, if Fiona won't open the door even to a courier, Joyce'll fall back on her father's death yesterday, to try to shame Fiona into letting her in.

But in the meantime, Joyce huddles in the dismal passage – frigid cold seeping into her feet from the icy flagstones below her flats – smoking, and rehearsing the defiant, self-assured lines she yearns with all her heart to hurl into Fiona's face, if only she can make it into Fiona's flat.

At 7:30, Joyce gets lucky. A delivery truck parks right in front of Butler's Wharf, and begins unloading several bulky couches. To make the movers' job easier, the porter props the building's front door open wide; and then wanders up the street to a small grocery store.

Joyce seizes her chance. Squeezing past the movers with a sweet smile, she scampers into the building, crosses the lobby to the lift, and rides it up to the 5th floor. There she wanders down the corridor until she finds Flat 514, and stands in front of the door, her finger on the buzzer.

An aching fear gnaws at Joyce's gut. She hates confrontations. And Fiona *is* intimidating. But this is one battle Joyce is determined not to shy away from. For twenty years Fiona has treated Joyce like a thief – and all the while, Fiona was the real thief. Shielding her face by holding the bulky envelope with Fiona's name on it up to the spy hole in the door, Joyce pushes the buzzer.

After a long delay, from inside comes the sound of a heavy lock being released.

Then another.

And another.

And finally a fourth lock creaks open.

At last, Fiona opens the door, but only a crack – and she's still got the chain on. Through the narrow opening, she reaches the tips of her gnarled fingers out, as if to take the package.

But as Joyce planned, the envelope, stuffed with Justin Kerr's family research papers – though not with Kathleen Quinlan's diary – is too bulky to fit through the narrow opening.

With an irritated sigh, Fiona closes the door, unfastens the chain, and re-opens the door.

Joyce hands the bulky envelope to Fiona and says: "Daddy died yesterday. These are his family history papers. We can talk about them now or, if you call the porter to throw me out, I'll sue you and we can talk in court. I'd rather not sue you, but if you leave me no choice, I promise I will."

Without waiting for a reply, Joyce pushes past Fiona, through a small foyer, and into a large reception room, which features a postcard-worthy view of Tower Bridge, just two hundred yards away. Rather than sit, Joyce perches on the edge of Fiona's writing table.

Fiona follows Joyce into the reception room, and sets the package on the desk, unopened.

Fiona has aged a great deal in the 20 years since Joyce last saw her. Fiona's skin was always deeply wrinkled, but it's much more saggy and spotted now; and her teeth look like cracked yellow keys on an old piano. She still wears a small metal Maya hoop in her nasal septum, and an antique gold Victorian locket round her neck; and she still walks with the wide-legged gait she learned growing up in the Guatemala mountains – but she uses a cane now, and moves much more slowly. Her eyes are still cloaked with the voluptuous hooded eyelids which are a Quinlan family trait; but beneath those heavy lids, Fiona's once-fiery eyes seem watery and weaker.

"My, my, look what the cat dragged in." Fiona inspects Joyce. "You look well, dear."

Having prepared herself for the possibility that Fiona might start out acting nice, Joyce extracts from her purse a recent photograph of Lisa, giggling on a swing, and hands it to Fiona.

Fiona peers at the photo. "Looks like a very bright girl."

"Smart as a whip. You'd love her, Fiona."

Fiona grunts, and holds the photo back out towards Joyce.

"No, keep it. Please. It's yours."

Fiona shrugs, and sets Lisa's photo down on the desk. Then using her cane as a fulcrum, she pivots and lowers herself slowly into her desk chair, leaning her cane against the desk.

"So where's your Lisa now?"

"With her father. It's his turn to have her for the Christmas holidays. So I came to London to help Daddy with his family research. Only he had a heart attack yesterday. And died."

Joyce chokes back the tears welling up. She is determined not to cry in front of Fiona.

Fiona gazes at Joyce. "I'm sorry, dear. Was Justin – having health problems?"

"No, it was quite unexpected." Joyce feels herself leaning forward, as if her body yearns for a hug from Fiona – the elderly cousin who mostly raised Joyce, all the years her mother and father were busy fighting the endless embezzlement charges and bankruptcies. But there is too much bad blood under the bridge now for any hugs. So Joyce slips off the desk, and turns her back on Fiona, looking out the window. She chooses her next words carefully, not wanting Fiona to know she's seen Kathleen Quinlan's diary – because it's the kind of document Joyce knows might be a great surprise some day in court. "Daddy said he uncovered evidence your mother Persephone didn't really discover the *Lamanai Codex* while digging up the ancient Maya library at Lamanai."

"Of course she didn't," Fiona says. "Persephone got the codex from *her* mother, Kathleen."

Joyce whirls, surprised. "But you told me Persephone dug it up at Lamanai."

"Sounds like a story I might've made up." Fiona shrugs. "What's it matter?"

Joyce starts to argue, but then realizes, if Fiona admits Kathleen once owned the codex, then Joyce has already won the argument. "It matters because everything Kathleen had was supposed to pass to Justin, and now to me. Which means the codex belongs to me, not you."

"Says who?"

"Says the Washtenaw County probate court – when they awarded Kathleen's entire estate to your uncle Lloyd in 1909, and nothing to your mother Persephone."

"Rubbish."

"A court order is not rubbish – it's the law."

"That particular order was rubbish, dear. Kathleen's Will was very clear – she left everything she owned to Persephone, and nothing to Lloyd."

"Then why'd the probate court rule the other way?"

"Because the Judge, Billy Breakey, played poker and went whoring every Thursday night with Lloyd. And he disapproved of Kathleen's affair with a married professor, and he disapproved of an independent woman like Persephone. No court today would uphold Breakey's order, because it was directly contrary to the plain language of Kathleen's Will, which said she wanted Persephone to get everything."

"How do you know all this? You weren't even born in 1909."

"Persephone told me all about it."

Joyce sizes Fiona up. Even at 85, Fiona's still sharp as a tack – and in spite of the watery eyes, there's nothing weak about her mind, or her will. "You'd've made a good lawyer, Fiona. But the problem is, you can't reargue a 101-year-old case. The court ruled; the case is closed. All I have to do is go in and ask the court to enforce its order. And they'll award the codex to me."

"I doubt that, dear. Women have rights these days, which they didn't have in 1909."

"Well, I didn't come here to debate probate law with you – especially since you seem to know so much about it. I came to make you a really fair offer, which you should really say yes to."

"Oh? What offer is that?"

"I know you cherish the *Lamanai Codex*. So even though legally it belongs to me, I'll let you keep the codex until you, ah, pass away – as long as you give me a complete translation now."

"My translation's not finished."

"All right – give me as much as you've got, and a photocopy of the original for any pages you haven't translated yet. And then I'll let you keep the codex the rest of your life."

"That's your idea of a 'fair offer'? I get to keep a book I already have, while I give you a translation you don't have?"

"Twist it any way you like, Fiona – it's still truly generous. You keep an extremely valuable book that rightfully belongs to me, and all you have to do is share your translation – which I promise I won't publish or show to anyone else."

"And if I decline this magnanimous offer of yours?"

"Oh, Fiona, please don't do this! We used to be so close. Please don't make me fight you over this. I miss you so much."

"Really? What do you miss about me?"

"Your way with words, like right now. Your gruff manner. Your salty humor. Most of all, I miss your love – and your wise advice."

"You want my wise advice to you?"

"Always."

"Forget about the fountain of youth."

"Who said anything about the fountain of youth?"

"You did – why else would you still be after the codex?"

"What I'm 'after' is us reaching a settlement, instead of going to court."

"Well, I won't give you my codex, or my translation. And I doubt I have anything else you want, dear."

Joyce puts on a poker face, since she has no idea whether Fiona even has the Ambergris Caye land mentioned at the end of Kathleen Quinlan's diary. "How 'bout the land?"

Fiona gets a cagey look. "What 'land'?"

Joyce feigns anger. "Oh for God's sake, Fiona, don't tell me you stopped paying the taxes on the Ambergris Caye property? Well then I guess you're right, there is no possible settlement."

"No, child, I've paid the taxes on that property, every single year since Persephone died."

"Oh, good," Joyce says – exulting that she bluffed Fiona into admitting she owns the land. "So if you give me the land now, I'll let you keep the codex – but you have to sign an irrevocable document acknowledging I'm the rightful owner of the codex, so it passes to me upon your death."

Fiona stares at Joyce for several seconds, saying nothing, her eyes cloaked in hostility.

Joyce, never a good negotiator, finally breaks the silence, instead of waiting Fiona out. "You're my cousin. You raised me. I don't want to drag you to court. We really should – settle."

In an acid voice, Fiona replies: "That day you tried to steal my translation, little girl, you stole my heart."

"I never tried to steal anything, Fiona! Why won't you believe me?"

"You had my translation in your hand, you little thief!"

"I wasn't stealing it."

"You were stealing my ideas."

"I wasn't stealing! I was trying to learn from you. But since you wouldn't let me see—"

"You were trying to learn what's in the codex – which is the same as stealing the book."

"Your translation isn't the book."

"When a book is written in a dead language," Fiona says, "the translation *is* the book."

Joyce tries to collect her thoughts, but her hands are shaking violently. Worse, Fiona can see Joyce's hands shaking. So Joyce clenches her hands into tight fists, and takes a deep breath.

"I'm sorry, Fiona, but you're wrong. The *Lamanai Codex* is an extremely rare book, probably worth millions of dollars to a collector. Your translation is only worth the publishing royalties for an academic book – a few thousand dollars at most."

Fiona reaches for her cane, her hands trembling, too – though Joyce can't tell if Fiona's hands are trembling with emotion, like Joyce's, or just from old age.

"No, dear, *you're* the one who's wrong – because you measure value only by money. But if you measure value properly, by what a thing can do to help people, then you'll see the original codex is nearly worthless, because almost no one can read it anymore. The translation has all the true value, because the translation is the only way the authors of the codex can be heard again."

Joyce, still struggling to control her shaking hands, stares at Fiona and her crazy nose ring. Arguing with Fiona was always an exasperating exercise that ended with Joyce in tears. "Whatever you say, Fiona. You always have to win the argument. But I'll be the one who wins the lawsuit, unless we make a deal today. Today I'm in a forgiving mood, with

Daddy dying, and all the things I've read about Roger Quinlan. I feel almost – haunted – by Roger Quinlan."

"You have no idea what it means to be haunted by Roger Quinlan," Fiona says flatly.

Joyce shoots Fiona a questioning look, but sees only a blank wall of hostility in Fiona's eyes. "So do you want to make a deal, or not?"

"Not."

"With a lawsuit there'll be news stories, you know," Joyce whispers, playing on Fiona's lifelong aversion to publicity. "All your academic rivals will see the chance to come out of the woodwork and say mean things in the press about you hoarding the *Lamanai Codex* all these years."

Fiona bristles. "I'll not be threatened in my own home."

"I'm not threatening you. I'm trying to help you."

"I don't need your help." Fiona's cane slips out of her hand, and falls to the floor.

Joyce reaches out a hand to pick up the cane – but Fiona bats Joyce's hand away.

Fiona picks up her own cane and points it at the door. "Get out."

Joyce blinks back tears, and picks up the bulky envelope. "I'll be keeping these. For the judge."

"We'll never get to court."

"Why not? Are you ill?"

"Don't get your hopes up. I'm fit as a fiddle." Fiona bares her lips in a snarl, revealing her cracked old yellow piano-key teeth again. "But there won't be anything for your precious judge to decide, dear, if I burn the little book before we get to court."

Chapter Four
Passage to Xibalba

Tuesday 28 December 2010

Kip Hunter is running in the jungle. But no matter how fast he churns his legs, he can't seem to get anywhere, because the thick foliage enmeshes him. Kip flails his arms, casting off the creeper vines and strangler figs; but the sinewy vines swing right back, trying to ensnare him again. Kip thrashes his arms, jerking free of the fatal vines; but now a hail of *atlatl* spears whiz by his head, impaling themselves with repeated heavy thuds on the trunks of nearby trees. Ducking low in the foliage, Kip looks up at the spears, still quivering in the tree trunks – only now the spears are quivering not in tree bark, but in the throat of Kip's old idol, the famous Key West treasure hunter Mel Fisher.

Desperately Kip yanks the quivering spears out of Mel Fisher's throat, and bends close to try to staunch the river of blood flowing out of Mel's carotid arteries; but it's too late, Mel is dead, the maggots are already feasting on him, and round Mel's bleeding neck someone has placed a heavy jade necklace, with a jade amulet hanging from it. Now Kip is holding the amulet, examining it, while Mel's voice is telling Kip to be very careful with the amulet, because it's the key.

The key to what? Kip asks, but Mel has turned his back, and when Kip spins him round, he sees that Mel has two heads – and a gaping hole in his chest, which has been filled with a huge wooden treasure chest, out of which old pirate doubloons and pieces of eight are spilling. Again a hail of *atlatl* spears whiz by, impaling themselves with repeated thuds, this time in the wooden treasure chest where Mel's heart should be. The thuds are getting closer and closer—

With a start, Kip Hunter sits up in bed, wide awake, every muscle in his body tensed.

In the dark he gropes for his backpack, stowed beneath his pillow, and pulls out his pistol.

Were those heavy thuds of *atlatl* spears he heard real – or only a dream?

From above the answer comes: the heavy thud of raindrops, pelting a thin wood roof.

Kip tries to relax, but the room is completely unfamiliar. *Where the hell is he?*

From the other side of the bed he smells jasmine perfume. Oh, right. Desi Something-or-other. The prostitute Kip picked up last night. They're in Desi's San Pedro shack, because Kip decided it wasn't safe to go back to his own place, above his San Pedro warehouse. Since by now the four Maya fanatics have surely traced the guide's boat, and from the guide's friends, they've got Kip's name. Won't be long before they show up at Kip's warehouse. With their *atlatls.*

Kip glances at the bedside clock: 5:30.

Every bone in his body aches from yesterday's ten hour run. Man, does Kip need to hit a big score soon, so he can finish with jungle work. Before jungle work finishes him.

Knowing he'll never get back to sleep, Kip rises and crosses to Desi's back window. Without moving the curtains, Kip kneels and peers out at the darkness, pistol in hand. Desi's shack backs onto the western shore of Ambergris Caye – the undesirable back side of San Pedro, where tourists fear to tread. Instead of a view of the big Caribbean waves and Belize's famous reef, like the snazzy eastside hotels have, Desi's got a glimpse of the dark murky back channel the pirates used to haunt, which separates Ambergris Caye from the mainland.

Right now, all's quiet on the western shore. The water in the dark channel is lapping against the Caye quieter than Bruce Tobin and Harry Benz ever managed to paddle; and the birds and animals in the narrow band of mangrove between Desi's shack and the water are quiet, too.

Kip relaxes, and puts his pistol back in his pack. He gazes at Desi's sleeping brown face, framed by her thick black hair. Recalling how skillful she was in bed last night, Kip's loins stir.

His eyes shift to her kitchen. Desi brewed some Maya root juice for Kip last night – a mixture of herbs she guaranteed would give Kip's flagging libido a 'spark', in spite of his exhaustion from a long day on the lam – and man, was the bitch right! After getting really good wood three times, like he was 18 again, Kip pressed Desi to tell him exactly what was in that shit. Just a few ancient Maya herbs, she told him – coclmeca, gangweo, and a little yohimbe tree bark.

Kip flips on a kitchen light and, finding some root juice left in Desi's sauce pan, quaffs it cold. Then he showers, remembering Desi's limpid eyes, and the beguiling way she has of looking up at a man, while he's doing her, with an expression of rapt amazement, like she's truly awe-struck, and also genuinely curious, like she can't wait to see what's coming next. A fetching expression Desi must use on all her clients, Kip realizes – and probably practices in front of the mirror, in her free time – but which nonetheless had Kip coming buckets last night.

By the time Kip emerges from his shower, the combination of the root juice and the memories of Desi's expressive eyes have Kip feeling, in the pitch dark of the bathroom, like little Kip is standing up as tall and proud as the oversized erection on the two-headed Maya idol in Kip's diver's backpack. Grinning at the idea of himself as a Maya fertility God, Kip swaggers out to the bedroom and, in the dim light from the kitchen, yanks the covers off Desi's warm voluptuous body.

Desi rolls compliantly on her back, while Kip lifts her negligee over her meaty hips and, eschewing foreplay, immediately enters her – marveling at how Desi, even half-asleep, is instantly wet. Without even opening her eyes, Desi's practiced fingers find their way, as if on auto-pilot, down to Kip's groin, and begin fiendishly stroking him, as they did last night while he fucked her.

At first Kip fears he'll come too fast, and miss out on the exquisite build-up she gave him last night, before each release. But then, as the minutes pass, and he keeps humping away, he finds himself distracted by the teary-eyed statue of *Santa Muerte* above Desi's bed – the apocryphal goddess of the dead, who gives the Catholic Church fits, because despite Rome's aggressive campaign to teach that *Santa Muerte* is pagan and Satanic, the poverty-ridden people of Central America just won't stop worshipping her. Kip's confidence begins to wane, as he fears that, though the root juice has him aroused and ready to fire, his aging ammo cartridge may not have had sufficient time to reload, after so much sex so late last night. But just when Kip's doubts are threatening to overpower the root juice driving his pulsing erection, Desi rides to the rescue.

Open flutter those limpid eyes. Oh, Lord. What *is* it about Desi's eyes? Somehow all at the same time they manage to convey total submission, and complete confidence in Kip; and yet also pure delight in being able to participate in his pleasure, and genuine girlish wonder at his manly capacity. Kip feels his heart race, and a wild rush in his head, and then he comes like a fountain.

Man, if there is a God – which Kip sincerely doubts – He is bountiful and good, to let a man as old as Kip still enjoy such raw, unadulterated pleasure of the flesh.

Desi gives Kip a sweet, after-glow kind of smile. "You're sure up early. No pun intended."

Kip chuckles. "A man could fall in love with you, Desi. Real easy."

"Happens all the time. Never lasts past dawn."

"I'm different. And you have the biggest, brownest eyes I've ever seen—"

"I'm sure I do. But even for you, big boy, I don't work for free."

Kip smiles, and reaches for his backpack, tucked under his pillow. But as he pulls out his wallet, in the inattentive rapture of post-coital contentment, Kip carelessly allows the two-headed jade icon to fall partway out onto Desi's bed. Hastily Kip shoves the icon back in the pack.

But those limpid eyes miss nothing.

"You *are* different," Desi says.

"Forget you saw that," Kip growls, as he pays her for the extra roll in the sack.

"You the boss." Desi tucks the bills into her deep cleavage. "But you can't blame a girl for wondering, how's a man who knows nothing of Maya herbs, got a sacred Maya idol in his pack?"

"Desi, I mean it. That Maya idol, which you did *not* see, is big trouble. Forget you saw it."

"Is that why you were up at 5:30, looking out my curtains with a gun in your hand?"

Kip tries to glare at those limpid eyes. But it's no use. Those eyes are just too sweet.

"So who's gonna show up at my door later today, lookin' for you? The law? Or the Maya?"

"The Maya."

"Shit! This is why you didn't want to go back to your place last night?"

Weakly Kip nods again. Desi should be a cop. With those lustrous eyes – even more beautiful, now that she's all riled up – she could get the truth out of any man in a heartbeat.

Desi stomps off to the bathroom, where she showers and dresses.

When she comes out, her tone is all business. "Time for you to leave."

Kip shakes his head. "I like it here. I wanna do you again."

Desi shakes her head no. "I ain't waitin' round to see how your 'big trouble' plays out."

"It's not even dawn," Kip protests. "You can't kick me out in the dark. I love you."

Desi snorts. "You wouldn't know love if it kicked you in the ass."

Kip laughs. "Probably true. But Desi, you're the closest I'll ever come to falling in love."

Desi flips a dismissive hand. "Don't go tender on me. Seriously. I'm outta here, right now."

"Why? It's not like these guys were right on my tail or anything. It'll be hours – maybe days – before they track me here. I haven't even *seen* the fuckers yet."

"You never will. They'll just settle their score with you, and vanish back into the forest." Desi collects her purse. "Look, you eat anything, you leave some coins on the counter."

Desi spins on her heel, and heads for the door. But then she turns back and gazes at Kip, almost fondly. "If they sneak up and catch you by surprise, there's a trap door in the kitchen."

"I saw it last night," Kip says. "Where's it go?"

"Small tunnel, takes you out to the channel."

"No shit! Why'd you put that in here?"

"Wasn't me. This is an old pirate's shack." Desi spins again. Without a wave, she's gone.

So much for the latest love of Kip's life.

Kip peers out the back window curtains again, but all is still quiet on the western shore.

So he flips on the nightstand light, and from his waterproof diver's pack pulls out Ron Graham's old 18th century books. This time he ignores the naval memo, and instead reads Chapter 5 of the Wyatt book, to try to find out what Antil's Curse was, and who India Reynolds was – and most of all, why Ron hired Kip to steal the two-headed icon from Ron's Maya friends.

Chapter V from *A Pyrate's Confession*, by Daniel Wyatt (London, 1726)

In which Fletcher *is elect'd Captain of the* Greyhound, *and new Articles are sign'd; we sail to* Honduras Bay, *and meet crooked* Jack Shaw *at a Slave Auction. Our Reprizals against* Shaw; Shaw's *Daughter bewitches* Reynolds, dividing our Company in Twain. *Cruising with* Fletcher *in the* Caribbee. *The Fate of* Reynolds.

The stiff Resistance put up by the *Dona Esperanza* having cost us five good Rovers, we were in a foul Humour when we considered the Fate of Captain *Gomez*, and his Catholick Crew: Whereupon, the Majority vot'd to cast them all over-Board.

We suffer'd no Qualms of Conscience o'er this black Piece of Work: our only Regret being the Loss of so many able-Bodied Hands, who might have assist'd us in pursuing the Account; but it being a Fact, that the niminy-piminy *Spanish* Nature lacks the enterprizing Spirit requir'd in a good Rover and true, our Regrets o'er not encreasing the Size of our Force pass'd very soon, e'en before we heard the Splash of the last *Spaniard* falling into the *Atlantick Sea*.

The *Dona Esperanza* being such a fine Galleon, and so much larger than the *Greyhound*, Captain *Reynolds* propos'd that we elect a new Captain for our Sloop, whilst he assum'd Captaincy of the Prize, and thereafter that we sail in Consortship. After a Council we agreed, and vot'd *George Fletcher*, a cunning Cut-Throat, new Captain of the *Greyhound*; and drew up new Articles, which I set down here in full Detail, for, as the Reader shall soon see, subsequent Events, to be shewn in their proper Place, placed the Lives of two Members of our Company in Peril, both their Lives hanging in the Balance whilst we, like a Company of weasely sea-Lawyers, reviewed the precise Words writ down in these Articles.

ARTICLES

These are the Rules of the Contract that every Freebooter following Damien Reynolds *and* George Fletcher *must obey, whether cruising at Sea, or marauding on Land, where we recognize no Sovereign or Master; said Lands having been usurp'd from Indians and Negroes; and these Rules shall apply in equal Measure to all, including Captains* Reynolds & Fletcher, *their own Selves:*

I.

The Captain and Quarter-Master each shall receive two Shares of a Prize; the Master, Boatswain, and Gunner, one Share and a half; and other Officers one and a Quarter; all others to receive one Share.

II.

Every Man shall have a Vote in Affairs of Moment, including Election of new Captains, when necessary; and Every Man has equal Title to fresh Provisions, or strong Liquors, at any Time seiz'd, and may use them at Pleasure, unless a Scarcity makes it necessary, for the Good of all, to vote a Retrenchment.

III.

Every Man shall be call'd fairly in Turn, by List, on board of Prizes; but if any Man defrauds the Company to the Value of a Piece of Eight, in Plate, Jewels, or Money, he shall be maroon'd, with one Bottle of Powder, one Bottle of Water, one small Arm and Shot; however, if the Robbery was only betwixt one another, him that was Guilty shall have his Ears and Nose slit, and shall be set on Shoar, not in an uninhabited Place, but somewhere he is sure to encounter Hardships.

IV.

Every Man shall obey civil Command, and if any of us disobeys a Captain, he may punish such a Man according to his Crime, except that a Captain shall desist from doing so, if the Majority of Votes goes against him.

V.

That Man that shall not keep his Piece, Pistol and Cutlash clean, and fit for Engagement, shall be cut off from his Share, and suffer such other Punishment as the Captain and the Company shall think fit.

VI.

He that sees a Sail first, shall have the best Pistol, or Small-Arm, on board her.

VII.

He that shall have the Misfortune to lose a Limb, in Time of Engagement, shall have the Sum of one hundred and fifty Pounds Sterling, or eight hundred Pieces of Eight, and may remain with the Company as long as he shall think fit.

VIII.

No stryking one another on board, but every Man's Quarrels to be ended on Shoar, at Sword and Pistol, thus: the Quarter-Master shall turn the Disputants Back to Back, at so many Paces Distance: At the Word of Command, they turn and fire immediately, if both miss, they come to their Cutlashes, and then he is declared Victor who draws the first Blood.

IX.

Deserting the Ship, or our Quarters in Battle, shall be punished by Death.

IV.

No Person shall Game at Cards or Dice for Money whilst at Sea; and on Shoar, only with Persons not of the Company.

XI.

Talking of Women is strictly forbidden.

XII.

No Boy or Woman shall be allowed amongst the Company. Any Man found carrying any of the latter Sex to Sea, disguised, shall be put to Death.

These fresh Articles being read aloud to the entire Company, we then signify'd our Agreement in the Manner customary to all Brethren of the Coast, *viz:* each Man with his Dagger drew Blood from his fore-Arm, and let it fall freely into a Can of Wine pass'd amongst us by the Quarter-Master; thereafter each Man drank a draught of the Ad-mixture, so that, by the end, we had all drunk each other's Blood, whilst swearing our allegiance to the Company, and Acceptance of the Articles.

Whereupon, Captain *Fletcher* took one Third of the Company with him back on Board the *Greyhound*, whilst the rest of us search'd the *Dona Esperanza* for

Booty and Plunder. We were pleaz'd to discover valuable Provisions, including salted Pork, and many Tierces of Sack and Rum; a large Store of small Arms, with Powder and Shot; and a small chest of Silver and Coin in Captain *Gomez's* Quarters; but of far the greatest Value were the five score and ten Slaves chain'd in the Hold.

To our Surprize and great Delight, these Slaves included many more comely young Females than are usual on Galleys such as the *Dona Esperanza*, wherefore one of our Company, a lusty Cockerel, propos'd that we re-christen her the *Batchelour's Dream*, at which we let off a great Cheer, and thereupon proceeded to live wantonly for three Days, making free with the Negroe Women.

Modesty forbids me to recount the sinful Details of the orgy of Rapine that ensued in the Fo'c'sle those three Days, as we Corsairs used the tender Flesh of the fairest of the Negroe Women to cleanse ourselves of our Seed; other than to confess that I, Daniel Wyatt, as God is my Witness, was a willing and lusty Participant in all the Wickedness that transpir'd there, this being still six Months before I was induc'd to repent my pyratical Crimes, and seek Remission of my Sins from God, through my trew and unfeign'd Faith in Our Saviour Jesus Christ.

The only Man aboard the *Batchelour's Dream* who did not divert himself with the Negroe Women was our Captain, *Reynolds*; wond'ring greatly at his Abstinence, I hail'd him, on the second Day of our Debauching, bidding him join in our Revels. However, *George Mullet*, a case-harden'd Cove, adviz'd me to leave off, least *Reynolds* think I mock'd him, regarding his sad Condition, which *Mullet* said was known to all the Company (save me), *viz*: that in spight of being a strong Man of robust Health, and not yet e'en thirty Years of Age, *Reynolds'* Fundament could not rise, even under Provocation from the most enticing of Strumpets.

I express'd Doubt as to how such a Condition might afflict a Man in the Prime of Life, unless he be a cross-grain'd Snood, who prefers to lie with those of his own Sex; however, *Mullet* swore on his Mother's Grave, that Reynolds was ne'er one to lie unnaturally with Men or Boys, and yet he had seen, with his own Eyes, at a Stew in *Tortuga*, how *Reynolds'* privy Member hung Limp as a Sail on a Ship becalm'd, in spite of the tender Ministrations of two lovesome young Tarts.

Being thus inform'd, I piped down, least I provoke *Reynolds'* Anger, for no Man was more skill'd at Sword-Play, or more Fatal with a Dagger, than he; and I resum'd my Debauches, with nary a Clew that, in but three Days Time, *Reynolds'* sad Affliction would be the Moving Cause of a great Division amongst our Company.

On 12th January of 1724, being the fourth Day after we seiz'd the Spanish slave Galleon, we stopp'd at *Turneffe* Island, for a Council with our brother Adventurers aboard the *Greyhound*. Upon agreeing to sell the Slaves we had seiz'd to the *English* Logwood-Cutters in the *Bay of Honduras*, we sail'd to *St. George's Key*, in the *Bay*, and clear'd a goodly Space on the Shoar, to convene a slave Market there.

The Slaves we had seiz'd being in excellent Condition, &c., compar'd to many I have seen stagger half-dead off of slave Galleys, they might have fetch'd fifty pounds a Head, in *Charles-Town* or *Spanish Town*; but the Logwood-Cutters at *St. George's Key* apprehending that we Gentlemen of Fortune would sell at a large Discount, to be rid of the Burthen, wherefore haggling o'er the Price of ev'ry Slave at Auction ensued, consuming several Hours, during which time our Company made liberal Use of the Tierces of Sack and Rum, seiz'd from the *Spaniards*.

However, early in the Morning of the slave Market, before I was too deep in my Cups, I observ'd a tall Man with a Face hard and flat as an Ax, who, in spight of his gentrify'd Cloaths, I mark'd as a Man who must, in Times pass'd, have gone a-roguing; whereupon my Surmise was soon prov'd Correct, the tall Man making the highest Bid on a young Slave Girl, and coming forward to pay for his new Property, only to stop dead in his Tracks when he saw *Damien Reynolds*, who reach'd immediately for his Sword, with Fire in his Eye.

No Violence ensued at that Time; but the tall Man left Post-Hast, and *Mullet* adviz'd, that in spite of his fine Cloaths, the tall Man was a crooked Rover named *Jack Shaw*, who formerly cruised on the Account with us, as Quarter-Master under *Damien Reynolds*, until those two fell out, in a Quarrel over Spoils.

All totaled, the Logwood-Cutters paid us two thousand six hundred pounds Sterling, for one hundred and ten Slaves, which we divvy'd up amongst the eighty Men then following Captains *Reynolds* and *Fletcher*, according to our new Articles. Well pleaz'd with our handsome Profit in this Venture, we paddle'd our light *Perriaguas* across the Bay, to the Logwood-Cutters' Colony on the *Belize River*.

I presum'd our Purpose in visiting the Bay Colony was to part-take of Rum and Gaming and Whores; however, upon reaching Shoar, I was surpriz'd to find that we were on the Chase, to settle old Scores with crooked *Jack Shaw*. His Pile being the largest in the Colony, it was no hard Work to locate, and surround, the Place, twenty Men on each side; whereupon *Damien Reynolds*, his Sword drawn, kick'd down the Door, and ten of us follow'd our Captain within.

Jack Shaw being away from Home, and his Slaves denying Knowledge of *Shaw's* whereabouts, *Reynolds* inspir'd the Slaves to assist us in our Hunt, by menacing the Throat of one Negroe, with the Point of his Sword; whereupon the Slaves confided that the *Shaws* were most likely hiding in a Cave close by. We search'd Shaw's Lodgings, whilst some of our Company went and dragg'd *Shaw*, along with his comely Wyfe and fair young Daughter, *India Shaw*, out of their Scug.

At the Parlor Door *Jack Shaw* broke free and lung'd at *Reynolds* with a Dagger, but *Reynolds* dodg'd *Shaw's* Thrust, and one of our Company slash'd *Shaw's* Thigh with his Sword, which stopp'd Shaw in his Tracks. Whilst Shaw clutch'd at the Wound that was staining his Breeches red, we reliev'd him of his Dagger, and propp'd him up in a Chair hard by *Reynolds*, for a Parlay concerning Shaw's past Double-Dealing; whilst *Shaw's* Wyfe and Daughter cower'd in a Corner, clutching at each other, like hysterickal Lubbers drowning in a deep, blank Sea.

Reynolds declar'd that *Shaw* was in Breach of his Contract with all us Freebooters serving on Account on the *Greyhound*, for certain precious Jewels which *Shaw* plunder'd in *Porto Bello*, in the middle of April of the Year 1721, from a *Spanish* Admiral's Wyfe, but then fail'd to relinquish, as requir'd by our Articles, for Distribution in equal Shares to all the Fellows of our Company; and that we Brethren of the Coast being honourable Gentlemen, who expect to be treat'd in like Fashion, having for this Reason set Marooning as the contractual Punishment for defrauding the Company, were here to exact the Penalty; however, *Reynolds* express'd grave Doubt whether Marooning be sufficiently harsh Punishment for Skulkery as dastardly as *Shaw's*, seeing as how, at the Time of the Offence, *Shaw* was serving as duly-elect'd Quarter-Master of the *Greyhound*, a position of great Trust, which *Shaw* abus'd with the blackest of Hearts.

Shaw protest'd that he was not Guilty, until our new Quarter-Master, *Hughes*, produc'd a Chest found beneath the Boards in *Shaw's* Bed-Chamber; whereupon, the Lock being broken, and the Jewels inside reveal'd, *Shaw* modify'd his Plea, offering to let us take the Chest and all its Contents, which included ten thousands of Pieces of Eight, in exchange for leaving him, and his Family, in Peace.

To this Plea, *Reynolds* demurr'd, observing that, according to the Terms of our Articles, the pilfer'd Jewels being already the Company's Property, they could not properly be used now by *Shaw* as Barter; and as for the ten thousands of Pieces of Eight, it was *Reynolds'* Opinion that, seeing as how Marooning is the contractual Punishment for cheating Brother Rogues, therefore a Thief in Breach of the Articles needs must give more than mere Money, in Satisfaction of his Crime.

Whereupon several of our Company took Reynolds' Hint, and with the Tips of our Swords, commenc'd lifting the skirts of *Shaw's* Wyfe and Daughter; whilst the squirming Ladies were hard press'd to hold us at Bay, for they were in a Corner, and there were many more Swords thrusting, than they had Hands for their Defence. *Shaw* reaching out to lend Aid to his Women in fending off our Liberties, at once his Hand was lopp'd off with a Stroke of someone's Blade.

Blood gushing from the Stump of *Shaw's* Wrist, he yelp'd in Pain, and soon swoon'd onto the Floor, and within a Minute, fell into a dead Faint; whereupon *Reynolds* remark'd, that since *Shaw* seem'd indispos'd to offer adequate Satisfaction, the two Ladies would have to make up the unpaid Difference.

We pinned the arms of the shrieking Ladies, and began tearing off their Dresses and intimate Garments, whilst unbuttoning our own Horns, in Anticipation of a fornicating Frolick.

However, the Daughter, *India*, scream'd *Wait! I have a Thing which you desire, more than our Virtue*; and *Reynolds* bade us hold off, until he made her Answer, thus: *What could Rogues like us want more, than to see a dainty piece o' fluff like ye, and a lovesome doxy like yer Mum, knock'd off yer pretty pedestals & bugger'd like common Whores?*

A fearsome Speech, well-calculat'd to fright any normal Girl into Silence; however, there was no Quaver in *India Shaw's* Voice, when she reply'd: *Immortality*.

At this *Reynolds* roar'd with harsh Laughter, and mock'd her: *What, be ye a Witch? Or have ye found the Philosopher's Stone, washed up on the shore of Honduras Bay?*

Yet the Girl answer'd in Earnest: *No, I have a Map to the Fountain of Youth.*

In reply *Reynolds* taunt'd the Girl: *Where did ye find yer Map? In a Novel?*

But the Girl reply'd in a resolute Fashion: *My Map's no Fiction. I got it from a Man of Courage, who journey'd deep into the Jungle and discover'd the Fountain of Youth.*

Whereupon *Reynolds* leap'd from his Chair, suddenly flush'd with Anger, and kick'd *Jack Shaw*, lying half-dead on the Floor, full in the Face with his Boot.

So Jack, ye cringin' Sneak, Reynolds cried, *ye kept more than Jewels secret from us then, did ye?*

Jack Shaw groan'd, whilst Blood spurt'd from his Nose, but made no other Answer; whereupon *India Shaw* said, in a calm Manner, with no Hint of Concern for her Father, dying there on the Floor: *'Twasn't my Father gave me the Map.*

Ignoring the Girl, *Reynolds* stepp'd over *Jack Shaw's* limp Body, and reach'd for the Throat of *Shaw's* Wyfe, which he squeez'd hard, whilst demanding of the Fear-struck Woman: *How would your Daughter come by such a rare and valuable Map — unless Jack Shaw stole more than Jewels from us?*

Her Mother quaking in Terror too great to speak, *India Shaw* again answer'd, this Time in Place of her Mother: *An old Pyrate nam'd Jake Palmer gave it me.*

Reynolds releas'd the Wyfe's Throat, but kept his fore-Finger under the Wyfe's Chin, which he tickl'd in a menacing Fashion, whilst still addressing his Words to the Wyfe, and not to the Girl who'd given Answer: *These past six Years, I've met every Rogue in the Caribee; so why is it I never met a Jake Palmer?*

Again *India Shaw* made him Answer, in Place of her Mother: *Because Jake Palmer's rovin' days was done long before any one of us here was born.*

At this *Reynolds* left the Mother, and at last stood Toe to Toe with the Girl, glaring at her with the gut-cutting Eyes that inspir'd us to elect him our Captain; however, *India Shaw* betray'd no Fear, returning his Gaze, an Eye for an Eye.

Whereupon *Reynolds* got a crafty Look, and ask'd her: *If it's Immortality ye be sellin', me Poppet, then why did Jake Palmer's rovin' days ever come to an End?*

India Shaw did not flinch as she hiss'd back at Reynolds: *Because some men tire of rovin' the Seas and want more from Life. But if all you desire is the fleeting Pleasure of the Moment, Pyrate, then rape us and be done with it. Yet if you have the Mettle to chase the greatest Prize of all, you'll forego the Rape, and go with me to seek eternal Youth.*

Reynolds star'd at *India Shaw* a long Time, and verily, I believe in those very Moments, she bewitch'd him. *Let me see the Map*, Reynolds said at last, after which the Girl went to the back of *Jack Shaw's* Dwelling, and return'd with a tiny old Book; however, *Reynolds* flipping through the Pages of the Book, he tossed it on the Table, saying: *There's no Map in here, it's just worthless Indian Scribblings.*

To which the Fear-less Girl made him Answer: *Those Scribblings are the Map, but to interpret them, you must journey far up the New River, to a Place call'd Lemon Eye, and there ask for an Indian holy man, named Shoosh Onteal. Only Shoosh Onteal can read the map; and only he has the key to find, and unlock, the passage to the Fountain of Youth.*

Whereupon, *Reynolds* sneer'd, and reply'd: *Well then, I thank ye, Missy. After me Brothers have their Way with ye and yer Mum, we'll go hunt down yer Shoosh Onteal, and make him take us to the Fountain of Youth.*

At which we rais'd a Cheer, and reach'd again for the Petticoats.

But by now the Girl had cast her Spell on *Damien Reynolds*, and with naught but a Look, she induc'd him to call us off again. *Unless I go with you unharm'd, Pyrate,* India Shaw said, *Shoosh Onteal won't help you, he'll just kill you all.*

At this *Reynolds* snort'd in Derision, and said: *Indian spears are no match for Pyrate muskets.* But *India Shaw* reply'd: *Shoosh Onteal has blunderbusses and muskets, too, which he took from the* Spanish *Army, the last Time they try'd to conquer him, but fail'd.*

Reynolds frown'd, and lock'd Eyes a long Time again with *India Shaw*; but seeing no Way round the Girl, at last he agreed to leave her unharm'd.

My Mum, too, she said, *or I shan't help you gain the trust of Shoosh Onteal.*

To which *Reynolds* agreed, but warn'd her: *If yer Map prove Counterfeit, I promise ye, we'll rut ye like a Pack o' Dogs on a Bitch in Heat; and then we'll bring ye back here, and make ye watch whilst we do yer Mum the same; and by the Time we're finished, ye'll both be so pox-riddl'd and scabrous, ye'll beg us to end yer loathly Lives.*

India Shaw assur'd *Reynolds* her Map was Trew, and it appear'd he believ'd her, e'en tho' 'tis a Fact he must have known, that a Virgin facing a Company of horny Pyrates will tell any Tale, no matter how Fantastick, to escape the Fate she thinks is worse than Death; therefore, I believe she must have cast some Sort of evil Spell, upon our Captain, to render him so Credulous to her Story.

India Shaw went to her Chamber to pack a Trunk, whilst *Reynolds* held a privy Council with our Boatswain, *Hugh Tupman*, a trusty Hell-Hound; thereafter, the Girl returning, she hugg'd her Mother, but ne'er e'en glanc'd at her Father, lying half-Dead in a Heap on the Floor: Whereupon, *Reynolds* escort'd the Girl alone, down to our *Perriaguas*; whilst *Tupman* stay'd behind with us.

When *Tupman* convey'd *Reynolds'* privy Instructions for *Jack Shaw* and his Property, our black Hearts were rais'd, for they shew'd that *Reynolds* was perhaps not under the Girl's Thumb, after all; and I give here a full Account of all that we did, so that it will appear to the Reader, to what a Pitch of Wickedness humane Nature may arrive, if its Passions are not check'd by the Fear of God.

After seizing *Jack Shaw's* Chest, with its Jewels and Pieces of Eight, we separat'd *Shaw* from his Head with an Ax, to make Certain he stay'd Dead; thereafter we each took a fornicating Turn with his Wyfe, as *Tupman* said *Reynolds* desir'd us to do, *Tupman* taking the final Turn, because what rough *Hugh* lik'd best was, to strangle a Woman just as he climax'd his Pleasure, and in this Manner he dispatch'd *Mistress Shaw* to the next World. Whereupon we slay'd all the Slaves, and fired the Dwelling, to leave no Witnesses or Clews to our Crimes there.

However, back at *St. George's Key*, we saw that *Reynolds* was still besott'd by the Story of the *Fountain of Youth*, perhaps due to his sad Affliction, which I suppose would drive any Man to deep Desperation; and therefore, whilst we roast'd Pigs o'er a Fire on the Beach, *Reynolds* announc'd to the Company that we would be setting sail at first Light to the North, and when we reach'd the farthest Pointe of *Ambergris Key*, we would hide the *Batchelour's Dream* and the *Greyhound* in the thick Man-Grove there, and take our *Perriaguas* up the *New River*, to a Place call'd *Lemon Eye*.

One of us ask'd how far up-River *Lemon Eye* was, whereupon, *India Shaw* whisper'd in *Reynolds'* ear, and only then did *Reynolds* reply, 'twas eighty Miles.

I did not like to see a Petticoat playing such a prominent Part in our Council, and neither did many others; whereupon a restless Grumbling could be heard reverberating amongst our Company. One old Fire-eater voicing Objection to making an eighty mile Voyage, in *Perriaguas*, up an unchart'd River, infested with hostile *Indians*, and possibly armed *Spaniards*, too; and another demanding to know what Treasure lay in *Lemon Eye*, that was worth undertaking such a risky Journey; *Reynolds* answer'd that the greatest Treasure in all the World was at *Lemon Eye*: the *Fountain of Youth*; and that once we drank from the Fountain there, we should all remain there-after, Young for Ever-more.

Now the adventuring Gentlemen of our Company being well acquaint'd, from the Monotony of our long Voyages on the blank Seas, with the fanciful Stories seafaring Men share to pass the Time, we had all heard tell of the *Fountain of Youth*; but such Tales we knew bore no more Weight, than Dreams of lush Islands stock'd full with Mer-Maids and Rum; or the vague Promises we oft exchang'd, that one undenominated Date in the misty Future, we would quit our Roving and go a-Shoar, some Place where our Crimes were not Known, and purchase some Settlements with our Booty, to live at our Ease like peaceable Men.

However, 'twas Apparent from *Reynolds'* Voice, that he was not speaking in such a vague and dreamy Manner, of the *Fountain of Youth*; rather, that he regarded the *Fountain of Youth* to be as real as the stones in *London Bridge*, and that his Plan was for us to go there and drink its Waters, without Fear of the mortal Dangers any *English* Man must brave, when traveling in the interior Lands of *New Spain*.

Hugh Tupman ask'd: *Can this* Fountain of Youth *heal a Man who is mortally wounded in Battle*? A Question very much to the Purpose, I thought, for a Rover to ask. To which *Reynolds* said he did not know, except that the magick Waters of the Fountain could work Miracles, and he intended to discover all their Benefits.

Whereupon *Alan Wright* yell'd, across the Fire, what all were thinking: *We know why you're so keen to go there, Damien, so you can sport with your new Bird! But the rest of us don't need magickal Waters just to tame a flutterin' Dove.*

A black Look crossing *Reynolds'* Face, he shout'd several Oaths back across the Fire at *Wright*; but he did not deny the Truth of what *Wright* spake.

Our Quarter-Master, *Hughes*, came to *Reynolds'* defence, accusing *Wright* of violating our Eleventh Article (*Talking of Women Is Strictly Forbidden*), whereupon several Brothers commenc'd Shouting, some taking Sides with *Wright*, saying the Rule against talking of Women could not fairly be applied in a Circumstance such as this, where the Matter at Issue was whether a Woman was exercising undue Influence upon our Captain; but most taking Sides with *Hughes*, who opin'd that a Rule means what a Rule says.

Whereupon *Wright*, the swivel-tongued Whiffler, seeing that the Windes of the Debate were blowing against him, tack'd to the Lee, and lash'd out in a clever Counter-Feint, speaking thus: *was not Captain* Reynolds *his own Self also in violation of the Articles, for bringing a Woman into our Company*?

Reynolds laugh'd, but none other did; and the Silence that followed spake louder than any Words, that the Company believ'd *Wright*, tho' a pewling little Lurcher, was in the Right, in accusing *Reynolds* of being also in Breach of the Articles. But *Damien Reynolds* was a crafty Cove, so he ask'd *George Fletcher* to read the pertinent Article aloud, which *Fletcher* did, thus:

XII. No Boy or Woman shall be allowed amongst the Company. Any Man found carrying any of the latter Sex to Sea, disguised, shall be put to Death.

Whereupon *Reynolds* flung his Palms up at the Heavens, before gesturing at the comely *Miss Shaw*, with her fair Skin and exuberant Breasts, and saying: *Gentlemen, I put it to ye: Is this Female, in any Way, Shape or Form, 'disguised'?*

With one Voice we cheer'd NO!; for *Damien Reynolds* was a fine Captain, and none wish'd to see him put to Death, just for lusting after a pretty little Puss, who might have cast her witching Spell on any of us Corsairs, for in Truth 'twas a hard Thing we ask'd of our Selves, *viz*: To voyage so long upon the Seas, without the Companionship of Women.

Reynolds smil'd, thinking he was Home free; however, one of the trustiest of Hands, old *Will Greer*, called for Quiet; and we grew Silent again, for Greer rarely spake at Council, but when he did, he always made great good Sense.

What *Greer* said was this: *Brothers, debatin' whether* Wright *or* Reynolds *be in Breach is Fools' Work, for no Harm's been done either way that I can see. But Years ago an old Sea Dog warn'd me to stay far away from* Lemon Eye, *because last Century, in buccaneering pyratical Times, a Company followin' Captain* Osborne *got caught in the midst of an* Indian *War with the* Spaniards, *and to save their roguish arses, were compelled to duck up the* New River *which leads to* Lemon Eye. *Whilst they were a-scug in the Woods by* Lemon Eye, Osborne's *bold Adventurers met a treacherous* Spanish *Priest, who seduc'd them with wondrous tales of the magickal Waters at* Lemon Eye, *which he said would keep them, there-after, Young for Ever-more; whereupon* Osborne's *credulous Pyrates drank the Waters which the treacherous* Spanish Priest *gave them, and they all dy'd, to a Man.*

The Hush that follow'd *Greer's* Speech was like the Silence of the Grave.

However, the Girl whisper'd again in *Reynolds'* Ear, whereupon he announc'd that, while *Greer's* old Tale contain'd Elements of Truth, 'twas False in the most important Details. 'Twas Trew, *Reynolds* said, that most of *Osborne's* Company dy'd; but 'twasn't the Lemon Eye Waters that kill'd them, they ran into a *Spanish Bandera* on their way back down the *New River*, and dy'd of Wounds from the fierce Engagement that ensued. However, one Man surviv'd the Fight, and liv'd to tell the Tale; and *Reynolds* said that this Man, *Jake Palmer*, liv'd long past a hundred Years, because he had drunk from the *Fountain of Youth* at *Lemon-Eye*.

We who had been at *Shaw's* Lodgings earlier that same Eve knew, from what *Reynolds* had said there, that he ne'er e'en heard the Name *Jake Palmer*, till *India Shaw* put it in his Head; therefore we object'd to *Reynolds* relying upon the Word of a Girl, especially the Spawn of a thieving Snake such as *Jack Shaw*; however, *Reynolds* answer'd that the Girl's Word was as good as that of any Gentleman of Fortune, for she was vouching for her Story with her Life:

Whereupon *Reynolds* said we were Bound by our blood Oaths to follow him, as our duly-elected Captain.

In the mean Time, *George Fletcher*, having sounded the Inclinations of several Friends, on the Quiet, and finding them oppos'd to joining *Reynolds* on his mad Quest for eternal Youth, saw his own Chance to reach for Power, provided he did it with Cunning, and by Indirection; whereupon *Fletcher*, sounding more like a sea Lawyer than a Mutineer, ask'd if *Reynolds* was not in Breach of a more important Article, being Article III, the same one which *Jack Shaw violat'd*, for not sharing all the Spoils of his Plundering with the Company?

When *Reynolds* demanded to know what Spoils he had not shar'd with us all, *Fletcher* made him bold Answer thus: *The pretty Bird there at your side.*

To which Reynolds reply'd: *But we need her to guide us to the Fountain of Youth.*

However, *Fletcher* would not be rebuff'd so easily, and persist'd in this Manner: *And once we find yer Fountain, Captain, then ye'll share her with the Company?*

No, Reynolds answer'd, *for I plan to marry her.*

Whereupon, *Fletcher* queried: *What should that matter, to a trew Gentleman; did not Teach the Black-beard share his Bride on his Wedding Night, with five of his Company?*

To which *Reynolds* made him Answer thus: *The Tales of Teach are more Legend than Fact, but in any case, I gave her my Word, she would go unharm'd.*

Upon which *Fletcher* seiz'd his Chance, his Voice swelling with Delight at the Sound of his own Oratory, as he declar'd: *If the Time has come, when our Captain's Word to a Woman, is more important to him than his Blood Oath to his Brothers, then I say: the Time has come for us to have a new Captain!*

This cunning Speech fail'd to elicit the big Cheer which *Fletcher* doubtless anticipat'd, but ne'er the less, the Logick of what Fletcher said had Influence over many Hands, and thus it was soon Apparent that we had reach'd an Impasse: The Majority feeling that Reynolds must choose between the Girl and us, but many Others still remaining Loyal to *Reynolds*, these others being perhaps also enchant'd, like *Reynolds*, with the foolish Dream of seeking the *Fountain of Youth*.

Whereupon we agreed, after a Vote, to divide our Selves, for a Time, into two Companies, and to cruise on separate Accounts. Those who wish'd to follow Captain *Reynolds* would sail North on the *Batchelour's Dream*, and thence take the Periaguas South up the *New River*, in pursuit of the *Fountain of Youth*; whilst the Rest would follow Captain *Fletcher* North-East on the *Greyhound*, to cruise for Booty amongst the *Caribbee Islands*. In the end, only eleven Rovers chose to follow *Damien Reynolds* on the *Batchelour's Dream*, to search for the *Fountain of Youth*; whilst sixty-four Rovers followed *George Fletcher* on the *Greyhound*.

For *Daniel Wyatt*, the Choice was hard, because *Reynolds* was, by a very long Stick, the braver, and the smarter, Captain, than *Fletcher*; however, I had no Stomach for the Perils of the Interior of *New Spain*, when the only Reason for going was the fond Hope of restoring Reynolds' wenching Powers, by seeking a Fountain that was likely a Myth, with a Map that was likely a Lie.

Besides, what possible Use could the *Fountain of Youth* be, to a Rogue like me, whose wenching Powers still ran Strong in my Blood; and who assum'd, like all Pyrates, I'd die a violent Death and Soon, long before my Bones grew Old? Even *Reynolds*, bewitch'd as he was by the dainty Fluff, and chasing the foolish Dream of restoring his Prowess, was not so reckless as to claim the magick Waters at *Lemon Eye* could heal a Man who was mortally wounded in Battle; wherefore I chose to follow *Fletcher*, and cruise amongst the *Caribbee Islands*, chasing a fair Chance at a Share of real Plunder, instead of a wild Shot at a vague Promise o' Paradise.

Before parting we agreed to re-unite our two Companies in Consortship again, three Months hence; to which End, we arrang'd to meet, in the Month of April of 1724, in *Charles-Town*, at a little drinking Ordinary we favour'd there.

We on Board the *Greyhound* set Sail for *Porto Rico*, to lie in wait in the Latitude of 18, for the Trade Ships from *Spain*, with their rich Cargoes, and any other Vessels from any other Nations that might pass by. We took two *Spanish* Sloops, and a small Turtler, which we plunder'd, and let go; and further off the Port we fell in with a fine *English* Galley, with twenty Guns, call'd the *Martha*.

Capturing the *Martha* prov'd a Challenge, however, for tho' she were too slow to run from us, yet her Captain, *Wilson*, was a wily Foe, with a Counter-Measure at the ready, for our ev'ry Tack-tick. Whene'er we try'd to come up behind her, *Wilson* manag'd to Tack away, before we could loose a Barrage of Shot to disable her Rudder; and when we dispatch'd our Pinnaces to attack her Rudder from Below, *Wilson* drove us off, by pouring hot Pitch down upon the Hands in our Pinnaces. When we came up Broadside to the *Martha*, with the Design of boarding her with our superior Numbers, *Wilson* repell'd our Attack, by Means of battering Logs his Men affix'd along the Flanks of the Galley, in the Place of the Oars; and when we try'd to use *Wilson's* Logs as Gang-planks, to assist our Boarding, we discover'd his Logs were greas'd, which slow'd our Crossing, leaving us expos'd, like slow swimming Ducks, to the Pistols of the Crew above. All the while, *Wilson's* twenty big Guns were inflicting heavy Casualties amongst us, whilst *Fletcher* was holding back our Fire, hoping to take the Prize Intact.

However, *Fletcher* prov'd a better Captain than I had previously judg'd him, by calling for us to throw onto the Decks of the *Martha*, several new fashion'd Sort of Grenadoes, being Case Bottles fill'd with Powder, and small Shot, Slugs and Pieces of Lead or Iron, with a quick Match in the Mouth of it, which being light'd without Side, presently runs into the Bottle to the Powder, and as it is instantly thrown on board, generally does great Execution, besides putting all the Crew into a Confusion; and under the Smoak of the Bottles, we were able to cross the greas'd Logs, and board the Galley. After a short Fight, *Wilson's* doughty Crew surrender'd, and we were Masters of the *Martha*.

In spight of the heavy Casualties we suffer'd from *Wilson's* stiff Resistance, *Fletcher*, admiring the Pluck and Spirit of *Wilson* and his Crew, invit'd them all to turn Pyrate, and encrease our Company; and to sweeten the Offer, we vot'd to give each Sea-man from the *Martha* who join'd us, a one-Half Share of the Proceeds from the Sale of her Cargo of Logwood and Sugar. By our Generousity, we gain'd eight new Members, who sign'd the Articles, and drank our Blood; whilst *Fletcher* took Pains to ensure that *Wilson* and the Rest of his Crew receiv'd good Treatment, before we put them ashore. Captain *Fletcher* adviz'd *Wilson*, in a gay Humour, to tell his Owners, that their Ship would answer our Purposes exactly, by taking one Deck down; and as for the Cargo, we would take Care to see it carry'd to a good Market.

Having fitt'd up the *Martha*, as *Fletcher* design'd, we re-christened her the *Rose*, and vot'd that rare Fire-eater, *Hugh Tupman*, as her Captain; whereupon we again divided our Company in Twain, and cruis'd in Consortship, taking more Prizes, including a Sloop and a Brigantine. Thereafter we gave Chase to a stout Ship, however, to our Dismay, she out-ran both the *Rose* and the *Greyhound*. This unhappy Event persuaded *Fletcher* that we need'd to lighten our Loads, by selling our Cargo, and thereafter to lye privately for a Time, whilst careening and fitting ourselves for further Mischief; wherefore we sail'd to *Santa Cruz*, a small Island in the Latitude of 18, lying South-East of *Porto Rico*.

After lying privately a few Weeks, we decided to abandon the *Rose*, as being too Slow for the cruising Needs of us Freebooters; therefore we took to the Sea only in the *Greyhound*, confident that we should soon seize a new Ship. But it was a slow Winter for Trade, and we went several Weeks without sighting a Sail, and indeed had almost given up Hope of finding another Prize, when one Evening at Sunset, as I was wond'ring o'er the Fate of *Reynolds* and his mad Quest for the *Fountain of Youth*, I espy'd a Sail at the Edge of the Horizon.

My eyes being weaker than most, ne'er before had I been the First to see a Sail; wherefore I could scarce contain my Excitement, as we clos'd upon our Prey. She was only a small Schooner, and offer'd no Resistance at all, for no sooner had we clapt her on board, and enter'd her, than she immediately struck her Colours and yielded; but ne'er the less, I deluded myself with grand Visions of the fancy Brace of Pistols I should soon claim from her Captain. However, upon boarding her we soon discover'd why she gave us no Fight, for her Cargo consist'd of naught but crate after crate of Calf-skins, and Boot Black, intended for the *Spanish* Army, so they might wrap their Pistols in nice Covers from the Rain, and shine their Boots after walking in the Muck and Mire of *New Spain*; and her Captain was such a miserly Fellow, he carried no small Arms of any Sort.

Since they were *Spaniards*, we consider'd throwing them all o'erboard, in our usual Manner; however, *Fletcher* counsel'd it were not worth the trouble, to have the *Spanish Armada* hunting us, o'er a Cargo of Calf-skins and Boot Black. So we let them sail away in their wretched Schooner, after contenting our Selves with seizing all their Cloathes, which were quite fancy, particularly when compar'd with the Condition of our own, which were extreamly out at the Elbows; and my own Humour improv'd immensely, once I discover'd that the Captain, though miserly with his small Arms, was quite the Dandy in his dress, and the Company insist'd on giving me the Honour of being powder'd, from Head to Toe, with the Contents of the Captain's Powder Bag, so that I could divert the Company with my Impersonation of a mincing *London* Dandy, prancing down the *Pall Mall*.

The Time nearing for re-uniting with *Reynolds*, and those of our Brothers who followed him on the *Batchelour's Dream*, we sail'd to *Charles-Town*, arriving, as agreed, in the middle Part of April, at the Place of Rendez-vous. Two Weeks we wait'd there, diverting our Selves with Drinking and Gaming and Whoring; but none of our Confederates e'er appear'd, nor did we hear at that Time any further Tydings of those who had sail'd with *Damien Reynolds*, to seek the *Fountain of Youth*.

AFTER-NOTE TO THE READER

No doubt, but the Reader will have a Curiousity of knowing what became of *Damien Reynolds* and the rest of our Brothers, and particularly of young Miss *India Shaw*, swept by cruel Fate into the Company of Pyrates, and what were the trew Grounds of the many false Reports that later circulat'd concerning *Reynolds*; therefore, I shall, in as Brief a Manner as I can, give their later History.

In the Month of July, 1725, six months after I renounc'd the pyratical Life, and repent'd my wicked Crimes, thro' my trew and unfeign'd Faith in Our Saviour Jesus Christ, I was sitting in a Tavern in the *Grand Caimanes*, scribbling these Confessions of my passed Sins, when I met a Deserter from his Majesty's Navy, named *Barker*. Sea-man *Barker* report'd that reliable Naval Officers, who arriv'd at the Bay of *Honduras* for careening, only a few Months after we quitted that Place, relat'd that Miss *Shaw*, the Girl who bewitch'd *Damien Reynolds*, and caus'd the Rift in our Company, had thereafter led *Reynolds*, and all the rest of our Company who followed him from *St. George's Key*, into an *Indian* ambuscade at *Lemon Eye*, whereupon they were all slaughter'd, as Revenge for the Murder of her Parents.

Whereupon, according to Sea-man *Barker*, the barbarous *Indians* left the Bodies of *Reynolds* and our other Friends lying in the Jungle, unburied, until all their Flesh was eaten away by Jaguars and Buzzards; and thereafter carry'd the dishonour'd Skeletons, back to the *Batchelour's Dream*, and plac'd them on the Decks, in a skeletal Mockery of a Pyrate Crew. Miss *Shaw* having by this Time lost all her Senses, the *Indians* sail'd the Galleon back to *Honduras Bay*, before leaving her at the Entrance to the Harbour; whereupon, in the Dead of Night, the Girl, mad with Grief and Hatred, sail'd into the Harbour alone, and lit Fire to the Galleon, with the Design of burning down the Colony that had fail'd to come to the Aid or Rescue of her Parents, by ramming her Fire Ship into the Wharf.

Barker report'd that the Royal Navy thwart'd her Plan, by dousing her Fire Ship with Sea-Water, before the Colony burnt; but God, in His infinite Mercy, spared *India Shaw*, who walk'd off the Galleon, and thro' the Flames, unharm'd.

I might not have lent any Credence to *Barker's* Tale of *India Shaw* walking thro' Flames to survive a fiery Shipwreck, but for the Fact that, in the Month of January in this Year of 1726, whilst crossing *London Bridge*, on my Way to the Printer, clutching to my Breast the very Pages of this Narrative, I chanc'd to pass a fair young Woman, of frantick Visage, wearing a tattered white Gown, and battling with the Snow; and I am certain as my Name is *Daniel Wyatt*, that the Young Woman with the frantick Look was none other than *India Shaw*.

I fain would have stopp'd Miss *Shaw*, to obtain more Particulars of her Adventures with *Damien Reynolds*, after our Paths diverg'd at *St. George's Key*; however, I was Certain that, if she remember'd me at all, 'twould not be kindly; and I could not run the Risk of revealing my Presence in *London*, to any other than my Printer, on account of the many Crimes for which I might yet be hang'd.

Wherefore I pass'd by *India Shaw* on *London Bridge*, without addressing her; saying only a short Prayer for her Soul, and a far longer One for my own.

* * *

Kip Hunter closes *A Pyrate's Confession*, but antique phrases keep replaying in his head as, like the *credulous pyrates* themselves, Kip sits *besotted by wondrous tales* from *buccaneering pyratical times* about *the greatest prize of all*: the fountain of youth.

So *that's* what Ron Graham was holding out about. The fountain of youth.

An old legend the whole world gave up on, centuries ago.

And with Damien Reynolds and all his pirates dead, and only India Reynolds (*nee* Shaw) surviving, Kip can't see much reason to get excited about the waters they found out at Lamanai. Probably the same waters that killed the young Maya Kip found yesterday in the Lamanai tomb.

Normally Kip would dismiss the whole thing as crazier than chasing fool's gold.

Except for one thing. Something about this particular fountain of youth legend got an underpaid, but solid citizen like Ron Graham interested enough to offer $50,000 American.

Which has to be just about every last dime Ron has in this world.

Ron – or whoever Ron's acting for – must believe the Lamanai fountain of youth is real.

Kip still didn't see anything in Daniel Wyatt's *Confession* about any Maya shaman named Antil. Not a word about a Curse, or a two-headed Maya idol, either. So there're details still to fill in.

But the big picture is coming clear: the stakes are much higher than just a little jade statue.

Which means Kip's price for delivering the icon just went way up.

Meanwhile, since Wyatt's tale was a hoot to read – all those bad boys running round the Caribbean, doing exactly as they pleased, no rules except the ones they agreed to, no need to be nice to people they didn't like, just fucking any women who crossed their paths, and drinking rum all day long – Kip is more than happy to break open the Rogers book, and read that one, too.

But before diving into another old pirate tale, Kip decides a little recon is in order. So again without moving Desi's curtain, he kneels and peeks out the bottom of her back window.

At first Kip thinks all is fine, as before, along the western shore. But then he spots, at the edge of the narrow band of mangrove between Desi's shack and the water, a single human finger.

The finger is right down at ground level, like it's attached to a man squatting very low in the brush. Kip scans the mangrove more slowly now, and detects the heel of another man, in a moccasin, some distance away from the first guy, and also squatting very low in the brush.

Kip grabs his pistol, and swings his diver's pack across his back. Then he crawls to the front of Desi's shack, kneels and peers out the kitchen window. At once he spots another man –Maya – standing in the shadow of the shack across the muddy road, watching Desi's front door.

But hard as he looks, Kip can't spot the fourth Maya.

Doesn't matter. Any way you count 'em, the Maya have Kip surrounded.

No pointing waiting for the Maya to make their move. Kip opens the trap door in Desi's kitchen, drops down into the old pirate tunnel, and pulls the trap door shut behind him.

The dirt passage is barely four feet high, and it's cold and damp. As Kip crawls along the passage, his flashlight playing off the crumbling old timbers holding it up, it occurs to him that if he encounters any obstruction – say, a cave-in since the last time Desi checked the tunnel, if indeed she's ever checked it at all – Kip's a dead man. Because the Maya'll have him trapped.

But a cave-in is not Kip's biggest worry. It's that fourth Maya he couldn't spot.

What if the guy is waiting for Kip at the end of the tunnel?

Kip tells himself he's just being paranoid. No one would expect a dilapidated old shack like Desi's to have a hidden exit. And without military-grade ground-penetrating radar, which these natives tracking Kip clearly can't afford, you couldn't possibly detect a hidden underground exit.

Even the Maya aren't good enough trackers to spot an old pirate tunnel.

Or are they?

* * *

Shortly before dawn, Clive Phelps wakes, and watches the first light of day seep into the rustic one-room cabin he's sharing with Gemma Murray. Figuring that Samuel Rivera and the police will want to get an early start, Clive reaches for Gemma, hoping for an early-morning shag.

But curse the Gods, Clive's too late, for Rivera is already rapping on the cabin door.

"Hurry! We found one of the survivors. We need Dr. Murray to translate."

In less than five minutes, Clive and Gemma are dressed and riding mules on a winding jungle trail, with Pablo Gonzalez and Ron Graham leading the way, also on mules. Gemma is beaming again, enjoying the adventure of a mule ride at dawn through the rain forest; Clive, on the other hand, is wondering why the hell he's even on this trek, since Rivera got to stay behind.

"We're going to Indian Church Village," Gonzalez calls over his shoulder to Clive and Gemma. "About two miles. As the crow flies."

"How'd your men find this survivor?" Ron asks.

"Apparently he staggered into the healer's hut at Indian Church, very early this morning," Gonzalez says. "When my constable on duty got word from the villagers, he offered to transport the survivor back to Lamanai; but the healer says he can't be moved. On his last legs, she says."

"Who's the survivor?" Ron asks.

"Gave his name as 'Canek'." Gonzalez's tone drips with sarcasm.

"Ah." Ron turns slightly sideways on his mule so he can see Clive and Gemma. "'Canek' is the name all Maya revolutionaries in Guatemala give when captured."

"After the 18th century Maya freedom fighter 'Canek'?" Gemma asks.

"You mean, the 18th century Maya *terrorist* 'Canek'," Gonzalez growls over his shoulder.

Gemma looks deeply offended.

"What was 'Canek' doing at Indian Church?" Clive asks, covering for Gemma's gaffe.

"Damn good question," Gonzalez calls back. "The healer says Canek fell ill walking home to Guatemala. But more likely, the villagers were hiding him. They're all Guatemalan refugees."

"You think the other three survivors are there, too?" Ron asks.

"Probably. But my constables searched the whole village. Couldn't find 'em."

"Did anyone ask 'Canek' where the other three survivors are?" Ron asks.

"He claims not to understand Spanish or English. That's why you and Dr. Murray're here."

"Do we know which Mayan dialect Canek speaks?" Gemma asks.

"No," Gonzalez says. "But the healer speaks Ch'orti Mayan. She couldn't understand him."

"We're hoping it's K'iche' Mayan," Ron interjects, "the dialect Kux Ahawis spoke – which I also speak. Chances are good, Canek comes from the same mountain range as Kux."

"And if not," Gonzalez says to Gemma, "we're hoping he speaks one of the three dialects you speak. Because otherwise we won't be able to find out what the hell happened in that tomb."

They lapse into silence. Clive replays Gonzalez's words in his mind, trying to detect a hint of irony or sarcasm in his tone. But he can't. Obviously Gonzalez is going by the book: he's brought both Mayan speakers. So if Canek dies without being interviewed, Gonzalez cannot be blamed.

The healer's hut in Indian Church Village turns out to be a very small room.

Inside, the young Maya who gave his name as Canek lies on a pallet. He has a classic diamond-shaped Maya face, with dramatic steep-planed cheeks, a broad Polynesian-style nose and full lips. Paintbrush-thick coal-black hair grows low on his forehead. Canek's eyes are closed, his face is drenched in sweat, and his lips are flecked with thick white foam.

And round Canek's throat, Clive sees a small jade amulet.

Beside Canek kneels the healer, an elderly woman with a kind face and deep, furrowed wrinkles all over her face and body, like the skin of an old bulldog. She pours a brown liquid down Canek's throat, causing more white foam to leak from his mouth.

Gonzalez waves his police ID in the healer's face. In Spanish he says: "Wait outside."

The healer is much older and much smaller than Gonzalez. But she stares at him with serene intransigence. In Spanish she replies: "He is dying."

"I know," Gonzalez says. "This won't take long."

"I can't leave him." The healer turns her back on Gonzalez, and gives Canek more water.

In English, Gonzalez says: "You cannot be present for a police interrogation."

In English she replies: "He speaks K'iche' Mayan. I cannot understand him."

"But you'll understand my translator, regardless of whether he speaks Spanish or English."

The healer pulls a blanket up to Canek's chin. "He needs me," she says.

Gonzalez frowns down at the healer. "What's your name?"

"Tumaxh Koreto," the old woman says without fear.

"Well, Tumaxh," Gonzalez sighs, "you can stay – but only if you swear, on all your ancestors' graves, that you will not tell a soul in this world what you hear me or my translator say."

"I swear on all my ancestors' graves," Tumaxh Koreto says, "I will not tell a soul in this world what I hear you or your translator say."

"Good woman." Gonzalez squats beside Tumaxh in the dirt, close to Canek's head, and beckons for Ron to do the same. Gemma and Clive stand behind them.

"Canek, I am Gonzalez of the Belize Police," Gonzalez says, in English.

Ron Graham translates Gonzalez's words, into what Clive presumes is K'iche' Mayan.

Canek stirs.

"I brought a man who speaks your tongue," Gonzalez says. "Can you understand him?"

Ron translates Gonzalez's words, again presumably into the K'iche' Mayan dialect.

Clive sees Gemma nodding, as if she understands K'iche' Mayan better than she thought.

Canek groans. Almost imperceptibly, his head nods yes.

"Good man," Gonzalez says. "Canek, I will not bullshit you. I am no friend of yours. I am just a Belize policeman, doing my job." Gonzalez pauses.

Ron translates into K'iche' Mayan.

"But I am not your enemy, either. Back in Guatemala, you have a mother. Perhaps a wife and children, too, but everyone has a mother." Gonzalez pauses.

Ron translates into K'iche' Mayan.

"You will break your mother's heart, Canek, if you make her spend the rest of her days on this earth wondering what happened to the son she brought into this world."

Ron translates into K'iche' Mayan.

"If you tell me your mother's name, and her village, I will tell her what happened to you. And I promise you, Canek, I will tell no one else in Guatemala."

Ron translates into K'iche' Mayan.

"I have no friends in the Guatemala Police. I have no friends in the Guatemala Army. I am from Belize. I hate the whole Guatemalan government."

Ron translates into K'iche' Mayan.

"What you say will not be told to anyone in Guatemala, except your mother. *Comprende*?"

Ron translates into K'iche' Mayan.

Canek groans. Again Canek nods yes.

"What is your mother's name?" Gonzalez asks.

Ron translates into K'iche' Mayan.

Sounds gurgle in Canek's throat. Tumaxh Koreto rolls Canek onto his side. White foam drains from his mouth. "Xhepel," Canek gasps.

"And what is the name of Xhepel's village?" Gonzalez asks.

Ron translates into K'iche' Mayan.

Canek coughs, scratchy and low, like a child sick with the croup. "San Lorenzo."

Ron mouths silently to Gonzalez: 'That is the village of Kux Ahawis'.

"And the shaman in San Lorenzo is Kux Ahawis?" Gonzalez asks.

Ron translates into K'iche' Mayan.

Canek nods yes.

"And what is your real name, young man?" Gonzalez asks.

Ron translates into K'iche' Mayan.

"Canek."

Gonzalez looks pissed. In English he tells Tumaxh Koreto: "This isn't going to work. We'll have to take this man back to Lamanai now."

"If you try to move him," Tumaxh warns, "he will die. At once."

Gonzalez bites his lip. "How much longer will he live, lying here?"

Tumaxh holds her thumb close to her forefinger, so they almost touch.

Gonzalez turns to Canek. "In a short time, you will make your passage to Xibalba. No one here can hurt you now. So tell me: what is your true name?"

Ron translates into K'iche' Mayan.

Canek utters a few syllables, stops for a racking cough, and then says 'Canek'."

Ron translates into English: "My name, very truly, is Canek."

Gonzalez emits a harsh sound, like a boat motor stalling. "Bah! Have it your way. There are thirteen men dead at Lamanai. And three more dead in a boat. What happened to them?"

Ron translates into K'iche' Mayan.

In a croaking voice, Canek answers.

Ron translates into English: "I love my mother. Tell Xhepel I love her."

"I know you do, young man. So when Xhepel asks me, 'Captain Gonzalez, in the name of God, who killed my son', what am I to say?"

Ron translates into K'iche' Mayan.

Canek answers briefly.

Ron rolls his eyes as he translates Canek's words: "The curse."

"What curse?" Gonzalez asks.

"There's a legend," Ron tells Gonzalez, "that hundreds of years ago, English pirates came to Lamanai and stole a sacred icon and an ancient book. In retaliation, the Maya shaman Xhuxh Antil cursed them, and they all died."

Gonzalez arches an eyebrow at Ron. "That's very interesting, Dr. Graham. Now could you translate my question into Mayan, so I can get Canek's answer?"

"Oh, right." Ron turns to Canek and speaks K'iche' Mayan.

Canek answers briefly.

Ron translates Canek's words: "The curse of Xhuxh Antil."

"If Xhuxh Antil cursed the English pirates," Gonzalez asks, "how did his curse end up killing thirteen Maya, plus this guy?"

"You want me to answer your question," Ron mutters, "or just translate it?"

"Just translate. Please."

Ron translates into K'iche' Mayan.

Canek answers briefly.

Before translating the answer, Ron asks a follow-up question of his own in K'iche' Mayan.

Again Canek answers briefly.

Ron translates Canek's words: "The curse came back on us. We angered the Gods."

Clive arches a questioning eyebrow at Gemma, asking wordlessly if the translation was accurate and complete, because the English version seemed so short. But Gemma nods yes.

"This is horseshit," Gonzalez mutters. Then in a louder voice, dripping with condescension, he says: "Ask him what made the Gods angry at them."

Ron translates into K'iche' Mayan.

Canek answers briefly.

Again Ron asks a follow-up question of his own in K'iche' Mayan.

Canek answers Ron's question at greater length.

Ron translates Canek's words: "We all drank from the fountain, without reading the book. Kux said he didn't need the book, because he knew the formula. But Kux was wrong."

"Is this guy raving?" Gonzalez asks Ron.

Ron nods. "Sounds like it."

"What the hell," Gonzalez says, "ask him if Kux Ahawis killed all the guys in the tomb."

Ron hesitates, but then translates into K'iche' Mayan.

At once Gemma shakes her head violently no at Clive. When Clive shrugs, Gemma whispers very softly in Clive's ear, so only he can hear: "Ron asked him if Kux had the book."

Canek answers at length.

Ron asks a follow-up question of his own in K'iche' Mayan.

Canek answers Ron's question, too.

Ron translates Canek's words: "No, Kux was not to blame. We drank bad water from the fountain."

Gemma shakes her head violently no at Clive, but Clive pushes his hands gently down, like a conductor calming an overwrought violinist. Gemma takes Clive's signal, and says nothing.

At the same time, Tumaxh Koreto shoots Ron a surprised look. To Clive it looks as if Tumaxh, like Gemma, comprehends enough K'iche' Mayan to know Ron is mistranslating.

Gonzalez, sitting closest to Canek, doesn't seem to see Tumaxh's surprised look.

Ron, however, clearly sees it – though he doesn't respond to it.

"Bad water," Gonzalez repeats. "Is Canek saying the guys in the tomb were poisoned?"

Ron translates into K'iche' Mayan.

Gemma nods at Clive, signaling that this time Ron translated accurately.

Canek answers.

Ron translates Canek's words: "Not poison. Kux had the wrong formula."

Gemma nods again, signaling that Ron translated Canek's answer accurately.

Gonzalez looks perplexed. "Wrong formula for what?" he asks.

Ron translates into K'iche' Mayan.

Canek answers.

Ron translates Canek's words: "Because the gunrunner stole the book."

"You sure that's what he said?" Gonzalez asks.

Tumaxh shoots Ron a look that says 'yes, this time you got it right'. Gemma also nods yes.

Ron nods yes to Gonzalez.

Gonzalez turns to Tumaxh and says: "You gave him peyote, didn't you?"

Tumaxh looks down at her hands.

"There will be no legal consequence for you, old woman," Gonzalez says in Spanish. "I just need to know what this man is on."

"Peyote," Tumaxh says in Spanish.

"A heavy dose?"

"He is dying."

Gonzalez rolls his eyes, and says to Ron: "Great. The asshole's not only dying, and lying about his name, he's also so high on mescaline he's raving."

While Gonzalez is complaining to Ron – and indirectly hectoring Tumaxh – Clive notices Canek fumbling with the amulet round his neck. Now he's got it off, and he's holding it in the air.

Ron reaches to take it, but Canek shakes his head no, and mumbles something in K'iche Mayan, before pointing past Ron, to Gemma.

Surprised, Gemma bends down and accepts the amulet.

Canek mumbles a few syllables in K'iche' Mayan.

Ron translates Canek's words for Gemma: "He wants you to have this, because he says yours is the only pure soul here. He wants you to deliver it to his mother, Xhepel."

"Tell him I will." Gemma nods thanks to Canek, and pockets the amulet.

Ron translates Gemma's words to Canek, who nods.

Gonzalez, plainly impatient, says to Ron: "Ask him: where was this 'gunrunner'?"

Ron translates Gonzalez's question.

"Lamanai," Canek says.

Gonzalez throws up his hands. "Canek's gone *loco. Guatemala* is crawling with gunrunners, but Belize hasn't had any gunrunners in over a hundred years."

Canek belches out some more thick white foam, and then utters a few syllables.

Ron translates Canek's words: "Not from Guatemala. *English* gunrunner."

Gonzalez's interest is piqued again, by the apparent return to coherence of Canek's thoughts. "What was the English gunrunner's name? Was he one of the three men in the boat? And who killed those men, with *atlatl* spears?"

Ron translates into K'iche' Mayan.

But a paroxysm of pain racks Canek with convulsions, precluding an answer. Curling into the fetal position, Canek reaches for water, as he gasps for life.

Tumaxh Koreto supplies the water.

While Gonzalez waits for Canek to answer his questions, Ron asks Canek another question of his own in K'iche Mayan.

Gemma's eyes fly open wide, and she looks at Clive in astonishment.

But Canek is past hearing. Probably past comprehension, too.

Clutching at his stomach and his bowels, Canek emits an awful moan.

Tumaxh leans forward, and places her bent, wrinkled hands on Canek's temples. A huge shudder shakes all through Canek's bones; his eyes flicker, like two dying coals; and then his face grows very tense, as his body enters its final death throes.

Together Tumaxh Koreto, Pablo Gonzalez, Ron Graham, Gemma Murray and Clive Phelps watch the young Maya who calls himself Canek twitch alone in the last dark pain of death, before his body stiffens and grows still, and his soul departs on its solitary passage to the dark caves of Xibalba.

* * *

Joyce Kerr checks her watch. Still another hour till she needs to catch a cab for the airport.

But it doesn't matter. She's hit a dead end at the Southwark Borough Archives, trying to prove India Reynolds' claim, recorded in Kathleen Quinlan's diary, that India lived from 1706 to 1864.

After a long search through handwritten death records for St. Thomas Parish (the parish with the best view of London Bridge) in the Borough of Southwark in 1864, Joyce found the death record for India Reynolds, a single laconic row of handwritten data, now stored on blurry microfiche:

NAME	ABODE	WHEN BURIED	AGE
India Reynolds	St. Thomas St.	14 Aug 1864	Unknown

After a quick smoke outside to sharpen her concentration, Joyce scanned the records of marriages and christenings in St. Thomas' parish from 1864 back to 1724. But she found no record of an India Reynolds christening any children, and no record of any child named India christened in the parish during those years. The librarian informed Joyce no birth records were kept before 1837.

The only tax records in the Southwark Borough Archives for the parish of St Thomas were property tax 'Rate Books' for 1791 and 1792. These Rate Books were not indexed, by either street or rate payer's name; and since houses were not numbered in the 1790s, it was hard work to find India Reynolds' house. But after another cigarette, Joyce found the entries for a person named India Reynolds, who paid 10 shillings in taxes on a house in St. Thomas Street, both in 1791 and 1792. The Rate Books for St. Thomas parish for all other years prior to 1864 have not survived.

Finally, Joyce scanned the government Census records for the Borough of Southwark. Since the Census only began in 1831, and was only taken every ten years, there were only four census records for India Reynolds: 1831, 1841, 1851 and 1861. The single row of information recorded by the census-taker for each resident was almost as laconic as the parish death records; and all four census entries for India Reynolds of St. Thomas St. listed her as 'Head' of household, and the only resident of her house; and her 'Condition as to Marriage' was always recorded as 'wid'. But the last four columns of data varied enough from census to census to inspire Joyce to make a small chart summarizing these census entries for India Reynolds:

Census Year	Rank, Profession or Occupation	Age last Birthday	Where Born	If: Deaf-and-dumb, Blind, Imbecile or idiot, Lunatic
1831	Abolitionist	Unknown	Jamaica	
1841	Social Reformer	70+	Jamaica	
1851	Painter	100+	Port Royal	
1861	Painting Teacher	155?	Honduras	Imbecile

Was India Reynolds truly an 'imbecile' in 1861? Kathleen Quinlan certainly didn't think so, in 1864. More likely, Joyce decides, the Census-taker just wrote 'imbecile' because, for the first time, India gave a candid answer about her age – after apparently hiding the truth in the three earlier censuses. The inaccurate entry for India's birthplace in the final census also suggests the census-taker and India were not communicating well that day in 1861 when he visited St. Thomas Street, which could also have inspired the 'imbecile' entry.

But at the end of the day, the census entry of '155?' under 'Age last birthday' doesn't prove that the India Reynolds who died in Southwark in 1864 was born in Jamaica in 1706. The property tax and census records prove that an adult named India Reynolds lived in a house in St. Thomas Street for at least 73 years – a long time, but not fountain-of-youth-long. Yet there's no way to tell if it was the same 'India Reynolds' all those years, or a daughter born-out-of-wedlock and given the same name as her mother. India told Kathleen she had no children; and Joyce knows, from the parish records, that no child was christened 'India' at St Thomas parish during those years. But there were no birth certificates in those days, and there were a lot of places for children to be born and/or christened besides the local parish – especially if a child was conceived in sin.

Since the Southwark Archives can't give Joyce the proof she seeks about India Reynolds' claim to have lived 158 years, Joyce decides to use her last hour in London to go to the National Gallery of Art, and see if they have any information about India Reynolds, the painter.

In the taxi to Trafalgar Square, Joyce tries to focus on the sights, instead of worrying about Lisa, who's no doubt running wild at the mall, while Michael hustles pool in some bar. But now that Joyce's trip to London has been cut short, she has a new worry – how to comply with the Judge's order to have no contact with Lisa this week, so Michael can 'enjoy his vacation visitation rights without Joyce undercutting his parental authority', as he claims Joyce does whenever she talks to Lisa. This trip to London was designed to make mother-daughter phone calls impractical, and sneak visits impossible. Now Joyce will need a new strategy to avoid the very strong temptation she feels to violate the court's order and see Lisa.

What Joyce really needs is a new place to go the rest of the week. But she hates traveling alone. Even at 40, Joyce attracts far too much unwonted attention from wolf-whistling men; and eating alone in a hotel room always makes her feel like a spinster – like her cousin Fiona.

Random snatches of her clash this morning with Fiona replay on the spools of Joyce's memory. *That day you tried to steal my translation, little girl, you stole my heart.* Joyce grinds her teeth at Fiona's unfairness, and reminds herself that Fiona's 'legal' arguments didn't seem to worry David Burns, when Joyce called him just before checking out of her hotel. On the other hand, David was concerned about Fiona's parting shot, the threat to burn the *Lamanai Codex*, even though Joyce told him there's no way Fiona would ever burn the book she loves more than life itself.

The taxi reaches Trafalgar Square. Inside, Joyce scans a catalogue index, listing all the National Gallery holdings, both those on display, and those in storage. Nothing by India Reynolds. But at the end of the index, she finds a pertinent after-note:

SIR BASIL DICKINSON BEQUEST

In his will of October 1909, Sir Basil Dickinson bequeathed 29 pictures to the National Gallery, to 'found a collection of Victorian women painters in London'. Dickinson drowned with the Titanic on 15 April 1912, and after his death an unwitnessed codicil was found in his papers that revoked his first bequest and left his pictures instead to the Belize Museum, in the Crown Colony of Honduras. The 29 pictures thus became the focus of considerable controversy.

In 1924 a Government Committee was established to investigate the matter and confirmed the National Gallery as legal owner. However, in 1959, on the eve of Belize achieving independence, an agreement was reached whereby the pictures were divided into two groups, each of which was rotated for exhibition in Belize and London every five years. This arrangement was reviewed in 1978 after some pictures sustained water damage and for conservation reasons the five-yearly rotation was discontinued. Some 17 pictures were lent to the Belize Museum, with the National Gallery retaining only those works that were most relevant to its collection.

Beneath the catalogue index's after-note is a list of the 17 pictures lent to the Belize Museum, which includes two by India Reynolds: *The Rape of Medusa* and *The Fountain of Youth.*

At the National Gallery information desk, a severe-looking young woman is immersed in studying her computer's monitor. When Joyce asks where she can get information on the Basil Dickinson paintings on loan to the Belize Museum, the ice maiden barely glances at Joyce before telling her, in a clipped tone, that she has no idea where such information might be, but it isn't here.

Joyce stands at the desk a moment, trying to think up a follow-up question, to get the ice maiden to actually look for the answer. But before Joyce can formulate a question, the ice maiden is called away to a back room, and a middle-aged bald man takes her place. The bald man takes one long, lascivious look up and down Joyce, and immediately asks if she needs any assistance.

So Joyce asks him the same question she asked the ice maiden. A few minutes later, the bald man triumphantly produces a loose sheaf of papers on the Basil Dickinson collection, and hands Joyce a copy he says she can keep. She finds these entries on the India Reynolds pictures:

India Reynolds, English (17__? – 1864), *The Rape of Medusa*, 1854.
NG 1168. Oil on canvas, 85 x 62 cm.
Signed 'Damien Reynolds' and dated, bottom right.

Reputedly born on an English plantation in Jamaica before the American Colonial Revolution, India Reynolds was widowed at a young age and moved to Southwark, where she was active in social reform, including the movement to abolish the slave trade. In the 1840s she trained with Dante Gabriel Rossetti, and in the 1850s exhibited a few paintings under the pseudonym 'Damien Reynolds'; but after critics pilloried those paintings, she never again exhibited her work. Before her death in Southwark in 1864, India Reynolds gave art lessons to many young women, including Rebecca Solomon and Anna Eliza Bunden.

The subject derives from the Greek myth regarding the beautiful maiden Medusa who was raped by Poseidon, the God of the Sea, and transformed into the hideous Gorgon. As Medusa sprawls on the floor of Athena's Temple, one side of her face is still young and fair, the other side already ugly and hateful, her red hair turning into writhing serpents, while Poseidon, dressed in the manner of an 18th century pirate, brushes aside Medusa's pleas for help, and departs the Temple with his pirate entourage.

Reynolds Foundation sale, Christies's 12-15 December 1909 (lot 344); bequeathed by Sir Basil Dickinson; on loan to the Belize Museum.

India Reynolds, English (17__? – 1864), *The Fountain of Youth*, 1856.
NG 1169. Oil on canvas, 56 x 74 cm.
Signed 'Damien Reynolds' and dated, lower right.

An allegorical painting in the pre-Raphaelite style, depicting a group of 18th century pirates, an Indian priest, and a young woman with flaming red hair, gathered at an underground river in a cave, with the eponymous fountain and other symbols of eternal youth in the background. The controversial and confusing action of the painting involves a ritual in which the young woman stabs herself near her loins, an act whose recondite meaning is not known.

Reynolds Foundation sale, Christies's 12-15 December 1909 (lot 344); bequeathed by Sir Basil Dickinson; on loan to the Belize Museum

Joyce scans the pages again, noting they have a photo of *The Rape of Medusa*, showing it to be in a style Joyce recognizes as pre-Raphaelite – but no photo of *The Fountain of Youth*.

Joyce smiles at the bald man at the desk, and asks for a photo of *The Fountain of Youth*.

"It's not there?" the bald man scans the sheaf of papers. "How odd. All paintings are photographed – especially those lent to other museums. Let me check."

The bald man disappears into the back so long that Joyce fears she'll have to leave for the airport without an answer. During the long wait, the ice maiden returns to the desk, but doesn't deign to notice Joyce, much less acknowledge that they've previously spoken. At length the bald man returns, looking disconsolate, and says: "I'm very sorry. We don't seem to have any photograph of that particular painting. Perhaps you can ask the Belize Museum for one."

Chapter Five
Telomerase Unbound

Tuesday 28 December 2010

Crawling on all fours, Kip Hunter glimpses sunlight a few yards ahead, seeping into the old pirate tunnel. Quiet as a rat he creeps those last few yards, and sees that the tunnel ends, precipitously, at the bank along the channel. A few yards below he sees the languid waters of the channel; but he can't see anything else, unless he sticks his neck out. Which he's loath to do.

Kip's got two choices. Neither is good. He can crawl out slowly and quietly – and maybe get his head shot off, if the 4th Maya is watching the tunnel exit. Or he can leap out fast, and land with a splash in the channel below – which will surely bring the Maya from Desi's shack in a flash.

Kip decides to avoid making a splash. Slowly and quietly he emerges from the tunnel. Since no one takes his head off, he lowers himself into the channel, and swims underwater with his diver's pack as long as his lungs allow. When at last he surfaces, he looks back at Desi's shack.

No *atlatl* spears whiz through the air. No one is watching.

Kip swims to shore, shakes himself dry, and considers his options. None are good.

He can't go to the cops, because there's no way to explain why the Maya are after him, without confessing to tomb raiding. Worse, the cops could try to pin all the deaths in the tomb on Kip – and if the cops started digging, there's an old American burglary warrant they might find, too.

He can't see shooting it out with the Maya, because Kip's only reliable soldiers were cut down yesterday; and four-against-one are terrible odds.

He could flee the jurisdiction, but travel would be complicated and risky, due to that American warrant – and besides, Kip doesn't want to leave Belize. He wants to stay and get rich from finding the greatest undiscovered treasure of all, the fountain of youth.

He could take the ferry from Ambergris Caye back to mainland Belize, and dodge around some more. But what good would that do? Sooner or later, the Maya would track him down again.

But one thing Kip clearly can *not* do is stand out here in the open, debating his options.

So he decides to head for the Beachcomber – Kip's favorite San Pedro bar and restaurant, located in an edgy neighborhood half a mile from Desi's shack. A *little drinking Ordinary*, as Daniel Wyatt would've called it. At this early hour, the Beachcomber'll be officially closed, but the staff'll let their best customer in to dry off with a few whiskeys. And if the Maya track Kip there, they'll regret it – because the staff at the Beachcomber is always armed and dangerous.

To slow his trackers down, Kip dives back into the back channel, and *swims* to the Beachcomber – watching the shore with every stroke. But instead of danger, what Kip sees lining the shore is the abject poverty of San Pedro. Back here, it's one wretched shack after another, perched on cement blocks, most without glass in the windows – stifling hot little tin cans that breed disease and infant mortality. The grim view gets Kip thinking that he's reached the point where living in his San Pedro warehouse needs to end. Indeed, it's time to quit his adventuring way of life, and *purchase some Settlement with his Booty, to live at his Ease like a peaceable Man.*

Maybe he could follow Mel Fisher's footsteps, and open a pirate museum, here in Belize. Everyone loves pirates these days. He could even shack up permanently with a woman like Desi, in a nice new house on the eastern shore of the Caye, and become a law-abiding citizen.

In the distance Kip sees the Beachcomber, the only two-story building in the area. He tries to see it through the eyes of the Maya, who'll no doubt approach it, soon. Not the easiest building for a three-man team to attack, because Kip won't be sitting out on the 2nd-floor balcony, facing the channel, where they could pick him off with their *atlatls*. The Beachcomber's got three exits: two ground-floor doors, and the fire escape off that 2nd-floor balcony. Which means the Maya'll face a tough choice. If they rush all three exits simultaneously, then each guy'll face a gauntlet of staff, and they risk getting picked off one at a time. But if they stay together and rush one door, Kip'll hear them coming long before they find him inside, and he'll slip away while they battle the staff.

Kip emerges from the channel. He's almost convinced himself the Beachcomber is what Daniel Wyatt would've called *'a safe Scug'*. Almost. But Kip still fears these deadly Maya.

Which, Kip realizes, explains all the cowardly daydreams he was having while swimming in the channel, about shacking up with Desi in a nice house, and becoming a museum curator.

Fear drives a man to flaccid fantasies like those.

Kip arrives at the back door of the Beachcomber soaking wet, which provokes some needling from the kitchen staff. Kip lets them get their yucks at his expense; but when the laughter finally dies down, he warns the staff to watch out for his deadly Maya trackers.

In the upstairs dining room, Kip settles in at a cozy table in a corner, where he can see anyone coming into the room long before they'll see him. He lays his pistol on the bench beside him, and celebrates his latest escape from the Maya by reading Chapter 3 of the Rogers book.

* * *

Chap III from *A Surgeon's Adventures in the Caribbee*, by Bartholomew Rogers (London 1752)

Treating the Rogue Jack Shaw; *a Carriage Accident;* Shaw's *Daughter rescues an Ancient Mariner. The Mariner's Tale of the* Fountain of Youth, *and the curious* Indian *Book with the Map to the Fountain.*

Upon accepting *Shipman's* Invitation to stay for three Months in *Honduras Bay*, I was at once fully employ'd, being the only Surgeon in the Settlement. One of my earliest Patients there was *Black Jack Shaw*. To the greater World, *Shaw* was an infamous Buccaneer, who had sail'd the seven Seas with the vilest of Rogues, and committ'd Felonies as villanous as those of *Black-beard* the Pyrate. But in the peculiar Circumstances of *Honduras Bay* in 1723, *Shaw* was risen to become a Person of Consequence, for this sole Reason: he had sav'd enough Capital from his black Exploits, to enable him to organise, and fund, a logging Enterprize.

The History of *Black Jack Shaw* shews in a bright Light how Narrow is the Line, betwixt the Lawful Privateer, and the Unlawful Pyrate. *Jack* began Life as an honest Waterman upon the *Thames*, until having committed a Murder, he fled to the *West-Indies*. In *Jamaica*, he again found honest Work, as a Fore-Man on a Sugar Plantation, and married a respectable Girl. But he soon fell out with the Owner of the Plantation, and thereafter, having been bred to the Sea, *Jack* sign'd on with an *English* Privateer, rising to become an Officer. Whilst *England* was at War with *Spain*, *Jack Shaw* was a Hero of our Nation, preying upon *Spanish* ships to great Advantage. But the Peace of *Utrecht* left *Jack*, like other Men of Sail, Idle, and lacking any Means to support his Wife and Child. Whereupon, being well train'd by his Majesty's Government, in the Business of living off Plunder at Sea, Jack continued the Way of Life to which he was accustom'd, by turning Pyrate.

Soon he fell in with *Damien Reynolds*, the richest Pyrate besides *Bart Roberts*, and *Jack Shaw* became *Reynolds'* Man Friday. The pyratical Life being good to *Shaw*, he thumb'd his Nose at the King's Proclamation of 1717, declining to turn himself in for the Pardon. But in 1721 he fell out with *Reynolds* in a Quarrel o'er Spoils; whereupon, Shaw desir'd to return to his Wife and Child, to lead a peaceable Life.

The *Duke of Portland*, then Governor of *Jamaica*, refus'd to let *Black Jack Shaw* walk the Streets of *Spanish Town*, or any other Place in *Jamaica*. But the *Duke* was very keen to see the Number of *British* Settlers encrease in *Honduras Bay*, to fortify that tiny Toe-hold of Great-Britain in Middle *America*. Being a practical Man, the *Duke* let it be Known, thro' Intermediaries, that if *Black Jack* were to take up Habitation in *Honduras Bay*, English Law would leave him in Peace. So *Black Jack* went where, as the Saying goes, no Questions would be ask'd. Indeed, in the *Bay*, *Jack* found himself in most familiar Company, for virtually all the Male Settlers residing in the *Bay* in 1723, myself included, had Reason to wish no Light to be shin'd, into the darker Corners of our mutual Past.

Thus it was that *Black Jack Shaw* became a leading Citizen of the *Bay*. Still I trembl'd a bit when the *Shaw* Carriage discharg'd me at the front door of his Manse, for even a reform'd *Jack Shaw* was still a formidable Man. But the big Fellow had been fell'd by a Fever, and lay in a Sweat in his Bed, where he struck no Fear into my Heart. Upon Examination, I discover'd no Buboes or Jaundice, so I commenc'd the standard Treatment, alternating ten Minutes of bleeding from his Fore-Arms, with twenty Minutes Application of cold Towels to his Chest. After two Hours, he shew'd Signs of Improving, so I ceas'd the Bleeding, and instruct'd his Wife to apply the cold Towels for twenty Minutes each Hour thro' the Night.

The Hour was Late when I climb'd into the *Shaw* Carriage, for my return journey to Town, whereupon I was startl'd to discover within the Carriage the *Shaw's* seventeen-year-old Daughter, the uniquely named *India Shaw*. Seeing *India's* Fore-finger fly to her Lips, I did not cry out or betray her Presence. Secretly I was delight'd, to find my Self alone in a Carriage with Miss *Shaw*, for I had reach'd the Time of Life when Thoughts of Marriage come to Mind; and although *India* was not a classic Beauty, for her Years in the Tropicks had redden'd her Skin more than is Ideal, n'er the less, she was the comeliest Lass in the *Bay* Settlement, with a lively Intelligence writ Large in her merry Eyes, and a pleazing intimate Manner with me, that seem'd, to my romantick Imagination, to signal some Interest on her Part.

The *Shaw* Coach-man depart'd at a very fast Clip, with no one apprehending that *Miss Shaw* was within the Carriage. She thank'd me for my Discretion, and apologiz'd for ambushing me in such dramatick Fashion; but she desir'd my Advice on a confidential medical Inquiry, and could think of no other Way to consult with me privily. Miss *Shaw* proceeded to describe her Symptoms, which included Palpitations of the Heart, and Shortness of Breath. But before I could formulate e'en a tentative Diagnosis, our Discourse was interrupt'd by a loud Thud, as our Carriage struck some Thing in our Path, near the edge of Town.

The Coach-man pull'd the Horses to a Halt, and climb'd down to inspect the Damage to the Carriage. I also alight'd, to ascertain what had occur'd. It develop'd that the Thing we had struck was an old blind Beggar, who was lying in a Heap at the side of the Trail. The old Beggar was bleeding copiously from his Fore-head and his left Arm; and was clutching his left Leg round the Ankle, whilst declaiming

Oaths of the most vile and hideous Nature imaginable. One Corner of the Carriage having sustain'd a Dent from the Impact, our Coach-man was matching the Blind Man, oath for oath, cursing him roundly for wand'ring into our Path.

The Coach-man work'd himself into such a Rage o'er the Dent in the Carriage, that he turn'd his Horse-Whip backwards, and struck the old Beggar several Blows to the Head, with the Handle of the Whip. This provok'd *Miss Shaw* to alight from the Carriage, with an indignant Cry, ordering the Coach-man to stay his cruel Hand. Whereupon, the gentle Soul insist'd that the Coach-man and I haul the old Beggar into the Carriage, and take him to my Surgery in Town for Treatment, the Expense of which *Miss Shaw* stipulat'd her Father should bear.

The old Beggar exuded a ripe Stench, redolent of Rum and Sweat and Blood, and of the swampy Ditch wherein he was Struck; but *Miss Shaw* ne'er shew'd any Sign that she notic'd the malodourous Reek. She held the old Beggar's Head in her Lap, pressing her Kerchief to his Fore-head to staunch the flow of blood, as if he were her own Childe. By the time we arriv'd at my Surgery, the old Beggar appear'd much reviv'd, by the tender and charitable Ministrations of Miss *Shaw*.

Miss Shaw bade her Coach-man wait outside, whilst she watched me bind the old Beggar's Wounds. When I asked his Name and Age and Occupation, he reply'd *Jacob Palmer, aged One Hundred and Twenty Two, retired Mariner.* I laugh'd, and told the Ancient Mariner he did not look a Day over Eighty.

Jacob Palmer's only serious Ailment was that his Leg was broken at the Ankle, wherefore I made Preparations for a plaster Cast, in which to set the broken Bone. Thus engag'd, I paid little Heed to the Talk that pass'd between *Palmer* and *Miss Shaw*, until I heard *Palmer* say that the Reason he had liv'd to be so old was, that many Years before, he had drunk from the *Fountain of Youth*.

Working amongst Mariners as long as I had, I was accustom'd to their wild tales, of Sea Monsters and Treasure Islands and Lost Cities in the Jungle, &c.; therefore, hearing a Mention of the *Fountain of Youth*, from an old Sea Dog like *Palmer*, scarce caus'd me to lift an Eye from preparing the plaster Cast.

But old *Palmer* was born a Story-teller. And tho' the Tale he told that Night in my Surgery at the *Bay* had something of the Air of a Novel, such as *Daniel DeFoe* might have penned, ne'er the less, I must confess the Ancient Mariner's Tale enchant'd *Miss Shaw* and, if truth be told, captivat'd me as well.

This is the Story which *Jacob Palmer* told us:

The Fountain of Youth *is not just magick Water; it is a Formula, discover'd by a Tribe of* Indians call'd the Mayans, *in the* Middle Part of America, *many Hundreds of Years ago, at a Place call'd* Lamanai, *deep in the steaming Jungles of the* Yucatan. *The* Indians *at* Lamanai *take the special Waters that flow in a deep Cave there, far beneath the Earth, which are noxious to the Smell, and salty to the Taste; and they mix these Waters with rare Herbs they grow, only at* Lamanai, *and with a thicke silver Pudding they obtain in Trade, from the* Mexica Indians, *and they introduce the combin'd Ad-Mixture into the Body, with the Result that it doubles the Years the Human Body takes to grow Old and Die.*

So I imagine you may be wondering, how did an old blind Beggar such as I, ever find my way to Lamanai? *Well, in my Youth, before I was reduc'd to begging my Bread, I still had my Sight; and believe it or not, in the Year of* 1641, *I was a bold Buccaneer, sailing on the Account under* Stephen Osborne, *near* Campeachy, *with a* Spanish *Man o' War in hot Pursuit. We snuck round the Pointe, and headed South down the* Yucatan Coast, *where we lost our Pursuers in the shoal Waters between* Ambergris Caye *and* Honduras Bay. *In normal Times,* Ambergris Caye *was a safe Snug for us Buccaneers; but in the Spring of* 1641, *we discover'd that the* Cayes *and the* Bay *were crawling with* Spanish *Soldiers, seconded to suppress an* Indian *Revolt in this Region of the* Yucatan.

Which meant we had trapp'd our Selves in the very Jaws of Death, with Spanish *Soldiers in the Front of us, and the* Spanish *Man o' War at our Backs. Our only Chance was to hide our Sloop in the Reeds, and run for our very Lives in our Canoes, up a River into the Interior, where the Man o' War could not follow, tho' we would have to fight our Way thro' any Soldiers patrolling the River.*

The closest River was the one English *Men now call* The New River, *tho' at that Time 'twas known by its* Indian *Name,* The River of Strange People. *A few Hours up that River, we surpriz'd a small* Spanish *Patrol at a Landing, and killed them all, using only our Blades, so when their Bodies were discover'd, 'twould appear they were attack'd by* Indians, *and thus our Presence on the River would not be Detect'd. However, the next Day we encounter'd more Spanish Soldiers, who discover'd our Approach, before we could mount our Assault, and who were Equal in Numbers to our Company. A fierce Battle at close Quarters ensued, with Hand to Hand fighting, in the River and on its Bank. Three Quarters of us Buccaneers died in the Fight, but we kilt twice as many* Spaniards, *with our Pistols and Blades; till at last the* Survivors *fled into the Forest, and we escap'd upriver in our Canoes.*

Whereupon I interrupt'd the Ancient Mariner, for the ostensible Purpose of questioning the Mathematicks of his Tale, tho' for the real Purpose of impressing Miss *Shaw* with my Wit and Waggishness: For if both Sides commenc'd the Fight with Equal Numbers, I said, and thereafter, three Quarters of the Buccaneers died, then the Buccaneers could not possibly have kill'd Twice as many of the *Spaniards,* unless they kill'd Half the *Spaniards* twice.

I was ne'er too Good with Numbers, Guv'nor, old Jake Palmer reply'd, with a Frown, *but I know that only Twelve of my Camaradoes surviv'd that bloody Fray, besides my Self. We that liv'd canoed deeper into the Interior, till about eighty Miles in, we came to a Landing with a Wood Sign, bearing a carv'd Picture of a submerg'd Crocodile, which is the Mark of* Lamanai;

and there we beach'd our Canoes. The Village at Lamanai *was desert'd, however, the* Indian *huts were still strewn with Cloaths and Bedding, by which Clews we knew they had fled in a great Haste. We found two abandon'd* Spanish *churches near* Lamanai, *and in one, we discover'd a wrinkl'd old* Spanish *Priest, hiding in a Confessional.*

Captain Osborne *spoke enough of the* Spanish *tongue to ask this wrinkled old Priest, Father* Sanchez, *where the Indians had fled;* Sanchez *said they were hiding from the* Spanish *Soldiers, deep in the Forest. Osborne decided to kill Father* Sanchez, *to prevent him putting the* Spanish *Soldiers on our Trace; however,* Sanchez *comprehended enough* English *to beg for his Life. Unmov'd,* Osborne *drew his Sword, and advanc'd upon* Sanchez, *shewing no Bent for Mercy, whereupon,* Sanchez *promis'd, if only Osborne would spare his Life, to shew us the* Fountain of Youth.

Osborne *thought* Sanchez *was only feigning Knowledge of the magick Waters, in a desperate Attempt to save his* Catholick *Hide, therefore, when* Sanchez *offer'd to be our Guide, and lead us to the Fountain,* Osborne *suspect'd a Trap, and rais'd his Sword, to kill the Priest. But the Majority of our Company wish'd to see if* Sanchez *could truly take us to the* Fountain of Youth, *wherefore, under our Articles,* Osborne *was requir'd by Rule to desist from killing* Sanchez.

Sanchez *produc'd from a lock'd chest a tiny* Indian *Book, and a small jade Statue of an* Indian *God, with two Heads and an obscene Fundament. Whereupon he guided us deep into the Jungle, and direct'd us to lift a very heavy stone Ring from the Ground, extracting a Gourd full of a Substance none of us Buccaneers had ever seen, like a thicke cold Pudding, coat'd with Silver. Whereafter,* Sanchez *gather'd Herbs from the Forest, and Fish from the River; and took us all to an enormous ruin'd stone Pyramid, where he used the jade Statue to find and open a very heavy stone Door in the Earth, and we all descended down into a deep Cave. Using Torches of pine Knots, we walked a short ways into that Cave, along a secret River that ran under the Ground, until* Sanchez *used the* Indian *Book to find a hidden Fountain in the rock beside the River.* Sanchez *collect'd some Water from the Fountain, which smelt like spoilt Eggs, and using the Book, to get the Portions right, he mix'd the Herbs with a Portion of the Water, and mix'd the silvery Pudding into the Remainder of the Water.*

Osborne *ask'd for Proof that this hidden Fountain, which appear'd quite pewling, was truly the* Fountain of Youth, *however,* Sanchez *reply'd that the only Proof which was Possible, was that from this Day for-wards, we would grow Old only Half so fast as other Men, if only we would drink the herbal Water, and stab our Selves with the silvery pudding.*

To this latter Proposal, Osborne *made violent Objection, asking how we could be sure the Priest would not be giving us Poison; however,* Sanchez *won* Osborne's *Trust, by offering first to follow his own Advise. Whereupon,* Sanchez *drank the Ad-Mixture of Herbs and Water, and upon fashioning a bone Needle from the Spine off one of the Fishes he had collect'd, and burning the end of the Needle in a pine Knot, he filled the Needle with the Ad-Mixture of the silvery Pudding and the Water, and stab'd himself with the Needle.*

With this Assurance of the Safety of the Ad-Mixtures, each of us repeat'd the Process that Sanchez *had used upon him-Self, drinking the odious Water, lac'd with the Herbs, and then stabbing our Selves, by means of the burnt Needles he fashioned off the Bones of the Fish, with the silvery Pudding that* Sanchez *had mix'd with the Water.*

Upon our Return to Lamanai, *we held a Council.* Osborne *said we should now kill* Sanchez, *to ensure our Safety. My Brother* Robin *and I spoke in Protest, that since* Sanchez *had honour'd his Part of the Bargain, we should honour Ours; but* Osborne *counter'd, that* Sanchez *had admit'd, we would have no Way of knowing if the Ad-Mixture was real, or just a Bluff to bilk us, until many Years had pass'd, where-as, the* Spanish *Soldiers might pass this way any Day. Whereupon we vot'd, and* Robin *and I being in the Minority, therefore, our brave Comaradoes slit the Throat of* Sanchez, *who curs'd us all with his dying Breaths.*

We dug our Selves a small Fastness in the Forest, and set up four Batteries of Muskets, in each of the Four Directions of the Compass, to guard us; and we hid there six Weeks, waiting for the Indian *Revolt to die down, and the* Spanish *Soldiers to quit the Region. However, whilst we wait'd, one Buccaneer after another was struck Low, by a terrible Ague, with awful Paroxysms, and alternating Fits of Fever and cold Sweats; and some complain'd of terrible Pains in their Bones, and others in their Bowels; and thereafter some began to cough up Blood, and others to excrete it, and finally, one by one, they began to die.*

And whilst they were dying, some speculat'd that the wrinkl'd old Priest, acting with other-Worldly fore-Sight, that in the End we would kill him any Ways, had inject'd him Self with a slow Poison, in order to win our Trust; and then inject'd us all with the same slow Poison. Others said no, it was God's Curse come upon us, for killing a Catholick *Priest, which had brought Death upon us, one by one. But whatsoe'er the Cause, the Truth was this: one by one my wretched Comaradoes died, till we were only Two, my Brother* Robin, *and me.*

Together we walk'd back to Lamanai, *believing that soon we would our Selves die, in the same miserable Manner as our Comaradoes. The* Indians *had return'd to* Lamanai, *like the Dog to the Vomit, and had burnt the* Spanish *Churches. The* Indians *tied us to a stone Disk, and sharpen'd their Knifes in readiness to cut out our Hearts; but* Robin *spoke* Spanish *badly enough to persuade them we were* English *Buccaneers, not* Spanish *Soldiers.*

There was a young Shaman there, nam'd Xhuxh Antil, X-h-u-x-h A-n-t-i-l, *who said* English *Buccaneers always travel in large Packs, like wild Dogs, and therefore he wonder'd why we were only Two. Wherefore, we told him of our Journey to the* Fountain of Youth *with Father* Sanchez, *and how we drank the odious Water lac'd with Herbs, and stab'd our Selves with the silvery Pudding; and how our fellow Buccaneers had kill'd* Sanchez *after-wards, over our strong Objections; and how they had all died the past six Weeks, leaving us Two the only ones of* Osborne's *Company who were still Alive.*

Xhuxh Antil *was very deeply sadden'd by the News of* Sanchez's *Death, because he said* Sanchez *was a great Friend to the* Indians *at* Lamanai, *tho' he remark'd that* Sanchez *had liv'd a longer Life than any* European *e'er liv'd.* Antil *queried us very close about ev'ry Detail of our Journey to the* Fountain of Youth. *We told him truly of each Event, except we lied about the jade Statue and the tiny Book, which were e'en then in* Robin's *Sack, telling the Shaman that* Sanchez *took the Statue and the Book back to his Church, before our Comaradoes kill'd him there; and by this Deceit, we induc'd* Antil *to believe the Statue and the Book must have gone up in Flames, when the* Indians *set Fire to the Church.*

Xhuxh Antil *seem'd credulous of all that we told him, for he told the other* Indians *to set us Free, after which he ask'd us to shew his Tribe how to use the many small Arms which they had seiz'd from the* Spanish *Soldiers; and therefore we taught them how to fire the various Weapons. However,* Antil *was Evasive when we ask'd him whether* Robin *and I were going to die, in the same miserable Way that our Comaradoes had died; tho' he did say that the* Fountain of Youth *was a Sacred Place for the* Mayan Indians, *and that if a* European *took other* Europeans *there, without any Indian shaman, then the Gods of the Underworld must have curs'd the Intruders, to exact Revenge for this Blasphemy.*

We soon discover'd that Antil's *Tribe had captur'd many* Spaniards. *The* Indians *dragg'd the* Spaniards *up to the top of their Pyramid, where* Xhuxh Antil *ripped the beating Hearts out of the* Spaniards, *who were still Alive, before sliding their Bodies down the Side of the Pyramid. As much as we hat'd the* Spaniards, *seeing them slain in such a barbarous Fashion, made us long for Home; so we ask'd* Antil *for a Canoe, which he generously gave us.*

We paddl'd back down The River of Strange People, *and reach'd the* Caribee Sea, *without further Incident; whereupon we paddl'd along the* Yucatan Coast *to* Ambergris Caye; *however, we could find no Trace of our Sloop which* Osborne *hid there in the Reeds. Whereupon we sat down on* Ambergris Caye, *to wait for a* Buccaneer *Ship to stop for a Careen, and take us a-Board.*

Whilst we wait'd, my Brother Robin *was struck low with the Ague, and soon there were Ghosts in his Eyes, and I watch'd him Die, slowly, and in great Pain, like all our other Comaradoes. After I buried* Robin *in the Sand, I sat down and look'd to the East, waiting for mine own Self to die.*

Many Months pass'd, and I went Blind, from looking into the tropickal Sun; but I did not die, and at last a Buccaneer *Ship, under Captain* Innes, *pick'd me up. Since then I've lived eighty-one more Years, e'en tho' I was already forty-one Years, when I went to* Lamanai. *I do not know why I alone surviv'd, whilst all my Brothers died; but I am certain as my name is* Jacob Palmer, *that I have only liv'd to be so old, because in middle Age, I introduc'd into my Body, the Waters from the* Fountain of Youth.

By the time old *Jake Palmer* finish'd his Story, I had finish'd applying the Cast to his Ankle. I gave him a wooden Crutch for walking, whilst expressing deep Scepticism about the tall Tale with which he'd entertain'd us. When he protest'd mightily the Truth of every Word he had spoken, I challeng'd him to produce the jade Statue with two Heads, which he said his brother stole from Father *Sanchez* and the *Indians*. Old *Palmer* said he long ago sold that Statue to a wealthy slave Trader, who covet'd it for its Jade; but then, to my great Surprize, old *Palmer* produc'd a tiny Book, which he said was the very Book that Father *Sanchez* had used, to create the Ad-Mixtures that gave old *Palmer* his very long Life.

The Book was an Authentick *Indian* book, with a Picture of a Crocodile on its Cover, and folding Pages of antique Bark, full of inscrutable Drawings, of a most obscene and violent Nature. But the Book did not appear to have any connection to the *Fountain of Youth* that I could see. Old *Palmer* said his Time was almost Run, and since he would be dying without Issue, he wanted Miss *Shaw* to have the Book, in Recompense for all her Kindness; and tho' she protest'd that her Actions were naught but what any *Christian* girl would have done in her Place, *Palmer* insist'd that he could not rest in Peace, unless she accept'd his Gift.

Whereupon *India Shaw* agreed, and the Ancient Mariner press'd the Book into her Hands, his aged Eyes burning, as he spoke these last Words to her: If you find a young Swain brave enough to take you to *Lamanai*, *Miss Shaw*, I warrant that *Xhuxh Antil* will still be there; and if you give him this Book, he will shew you the way to the *Fountain of Youth*. You should have no Fear of dying from an Ague, for unlike *Sanchez*, *Antil* is on Excellent Terms with all the *Indian* Gods in the Vicinity of the *Fountain of Youth*; however, you should go as soon as you can, in order that you may stay as Young and Beautiful as you are to-Day, for Twice as many Years as any other Woman may enjoy her Youth.

And with that, old *Palmer* stepp'd out into the dark Night, and was gone.

Once old *Palmer* left my Surgery, I reminded *India Shaw* of her original Purpose, in stowing away in the Carriage. Whereupon I examin'd her, but could discover no Palpitations, nor any Irregularity in her Breathing. So I told her, in a Voice that I hop'd betray'd the warm Affection that I felt for her, that I thought she was the very Picture of good Health. For this she thank'd me, and paid me for my Services; and promis'd again that her Father would pay me for my Treatment of *Jake Palmer*. But at no Point in our Discourse did she give any Hint that she might return my Affection; therefore, in the Exercise of proper Manners, I did not press the Issue. O if only I had found the Courage to speak my Mind that Night!

Since *Miss Shaw* was so Young, and the Book was in an indecipherable Language, I offer'd to keep it for her; however, she declin'd my Offer, and took the Book with her as she return'd to her Father's Home, in her Carriage.

O'er the next three Months, I treat'd many other Residents of the *Bay*, and ev'ry Person I met shar'd the general Opinion, that *Jake Palmer* was a boosy old Rumpot, mightily addict'd to the Punch, whose Tales warrant'd no Credence what so e'er. However, None of these Persons had seen, as I had seen, the *Indian* Book which the Ancient Mariner had given India Shaw; and None of them had heard the deep Conviction in the old Rumpot's Voice, which I heard, when he promis'd *India Shaw* that a Journey to *Lamanai* would bring her protract'd Youth.

During those Months, my Path ne'er again cross'd that of *India Shaw*. However, I often saw old *Palmer*, for he was regularly station'd in the Ditch wherein I first encounter'd him; but I learn'd nothing further of Value from the old Rumpot. Never the less, each Time I saw him, I recall'd his Words that night in my Surgery, until I could recite his entire Tale in my Sleep, as if it were my own Dream.

Three Months after treating *Jake Palmer*, I left the Bay, to make my Home in *Spanish* Town in *Jamaica*. Yet all the Remainder of my Days, my Dreams, both waking and sleeping, have mainly involv'd the *Fountain of Youth*. For many Years I harbour'd vague romantick Phantasies, of riding to *India Shaw's* Door on a fine white Steed, and taking her away with me on a Journey to *Lamanai*, before it grew too late for us to drink at the *Fountain of Youth*, and learn if it be real, or not.

In later Years, as a married Man, and Royal Surgeon to the Governors of *Jamaica*, I abandon'd these vague romantick Phantasies, as being but the Whimsies of Youth. However, in their Place I formulat'd the equally vague Schemes of Middle Age, in which I promis'd my Self that one Day soon, I should mount a serious Scientific Expedition to *Lamanai*, to search for *Xhuxh Antil* and the *Fountain of Youth*, for the Benefit of all Man-kind. Indeed, in my Desk I still harbour a Draft of one such Proposal to the Governor, for just such an Expedition, which I penned one feverish Night some Decades past, well past mid-Night, yet somehow ne'er in day-Time found the Energy to polish and submit for Action.

Now that I am Gray and Bent with Age, the Dream of discovering the *Fountain of Youth* is, of course, far beyond my Reach; yet now more than ever, it is a Dream which haunts me. What if old *Jake Palmer's* Tale were trew? What if there really be a *Fountain of Youth*, just eighty Miles in-Land from *Honduras Bay*? What if I miss'd my Chance, in my Youth, to double my own Life's Span, just as I miss'd my Chance, in my Youth, to love a woman as comely and tender as *India Shaw*, for no Reason other than my own Timidity?

Verily, as some wise Man once said, the Follies we regret the most in old Age, are the Follies we fail'd to pursue in our Youth.

* * *

Kip sets down the Rogers book, and checks out at all the entrances to the Beachcomber. No sign of trouble. Yet. So he pulls out his cell phone, and calls Ron Graham's cell.

"Hey, Ron! Thanks for those old pirate books, dude! Great reads."

"Uh, hi – not the best time for me to talk."

"Make it a good time, Ron. Walk off into the jungle or something."

"Uh, yeah, okay … hang on a sec … uh, okay … so, ah, Kip, what's new?"

Kip laughs heartily. "What's *new*, mofo? Well, let's see. Your Maya friends tried to kill me again this morning, but they missed. Too bad. I'm a tough nut to crack. But that's *old* news, ain't it? I mean, the past 24 hours, that's all they been doin', is tryin' to kill me. For me, it's sure gettin' old."

A pause ensues. Ron fills it, lamely: "The Maya have a relentless quality to them."

Kip laughs again. "No shit? I'm glad you splained that to me, Lucy. That really helps me understand these bad boys. But I tell you what, Ron. I ain't gonna sit around and wait for their next *atlatl* attack. I'm gonna get pro-active. Like your old pirates woulda done."

"Whaddya have in mind?"

Kip chuckles. "Why would I tell you that, Ron? Not since George Washington found himself saddled with Benedict Arnold, has anyone had a more untrustworthy ally than you."

"I'm sorry you feel that way. But I still want to make good on our original deal, for the icon."

"Not till you fill in a few details for me."

"Like what?"

"Well for starters, how come you're so hot to find this fountain the pirates were chasing? If the only ones to survive it were Jake Palmer and India Reynolds, while each time like 12 of their mates bought it, with horrible deaths, what makes finding these waters such a good idea?"

"We archeologists take more risks than you might think."

"Oh, really? Bold adventurers, are ye?"

"I didn't say that."

"No, but as usual, you didn't say anything, Ron. I'm sick of your word games. Right now, I'm three hours from Lamanai. You may think you're safe, with all the cops out there. But you're wrong. The cops can't protect you from me. I'm gonna strangle you with my bare hands, dude."

A long pause ensues. "Kip, I'm really not understanding what you want from me."

"Straight talk. For once. That's all I want, Ron. Straight talk."

Ron sighs. "Okay. Kux Ahawis was rumored by the Maya to be 150 years old. The Maya believe, when Kux was young, he drank from the fountain of youth."

"Which is where, exactly?"

"I don't know. Kux probably knew. I think what he was doing, re-enacting ancient rites out at Lamanai the past two months, was taking his young acolytes to the fountain of youth, to see who the next Kux Ahawis would be. Obviously, things went tragically wrong."

"Where's the two-headed idol with the big cash'n'prizes fit in?"

"You read the pirate tales," Ron says. "What's in those tales is all I know. Rogers says the two-headed idol with the 'obscene Fundament' was the 'key' Sanchez used to 'find and unlock the heavy stone door' to the fountain of youth. Kip, I didn't have to give you those pirate tales. I did it because, like you said, the time for playing games has passed. I'm ready to be a good – ally."

"Don't go tender on me," Kip says, as Desi's words pop into his head. "Seriously."

"Well, what else can I do to keep you from coming out here to kill me?"

"Call the Maya off."

"I didn't sick them on you, Kip. Honestly. They're on their own mission."

"What's their goal?"

"The idol. To them, it's everything."

"What about the codex?"

"The codex is important, too, because it's got a map and the formula. But the amulets the Maya wore on their necks, I think they may be a substitute for the codex."

Kip listens. Then sits in silence. Sometimes the best way to get someone to spill their guts is just to sit quiet, like you're expecting a lot more and you'll be disappointed if you don't hear it.

"The stories about the fountain of youth," Ron continues, "go way back. There were rumors among the other Maya tribes, that the Maya at Lamanai had mastered the art of living long. And there were rumors that the shamans at Lamanai – Kux Ahawis, and before Kux, Xhuxh Antil, and before Xhuxh, Pel Echem, and before Pel, God knows how many others – were living examples of how a man could live to be 150, 175, 200 years old."

Kip continues to sit silent, like he expects more.

"When the Spanish came to Lamanai," Ron continues, "they tortured Pel Echem, the Maya shaman, to find out where the fountain of youth was. But Pel threw himself onto the Spanish *auto-da-fe*, rather than give up the secret. However, the story was, Pel told his one Spanish friend, the Catholic missionary Antonio Sanchez, how to use the idol and the codex. That's the same Father Sanchez, by the way, you read about in the Rogers tale – like 80 years after Pel Echem died."

Kip sits silent. Silence is golden. Why mess with a good thing?

"The curator at the Belize Museum told me," Ron continues, "that last spring Kux Ahawis came and stared for six hours at a painting called *The Fountain of Youth*, by India Reynolds. Six hours! The curator said, before Kux's visit, no one'd asked for that painting in at least ten years."

"What's in that painting?" Kip asks.

"It's got pirates by an underground river, and a Maya shaman, and a codex, and a woman stabbing herself in the groin with a bone needle, like Jake Palmer said he and his mates did. But I don't know what the hell it means, Kip. You can go see it yourself. It's in the basement, but the curator will let you see it, if you make an appointment."

"No, thanks. Whenever I make appointments, cops tend to be waiting when I get there. But if Kux stole the two-headed idol from the museum, why didn't he steal that painting, too?"

"Exactly what I thought. The painting must not have any useful information in it."

"So where's this leave us, Ron?"

"I don't know. But I'm on your side, Kip. Those Maya who are tracking you, called me."

"No kidding."

"What could I do, Kip? They tracked you to my house. I told them I had no idea where you were going. I lied and told them I didn't know why you came to see me, or where you live."

"What else did your Maya buddies tell you?"

"They got your name from the boat you hired to assault Lamanai. Then they figured out you live in San Pedro. I'm sure that's how they hunted you down this morning."

"Evidently."

"But the good news is, the police don't know about you."

"Don't worry, they will. Soon enough."

"I don't think so. They aren't checking with the guide's friends, like the Maya did, because they have no reason to think there might've been a fourth man in the skiff."

"Let's hope my luck holds. For your sake, Ron, as well as mine."

"There's one more thing you need to know. Originally you had four Maya tracking you, but one got very sick. Capt. Gonzalez tracked him down, to Indian Church Village, outside Lamanai. I was there. Before he died he talked about the fountain of youth, but I mistranslated, to protect you."

"And to protect yourself, too, I bet," Kip says.

"That, too," Ron admits. "But there were two women who knew I was mistranslating – the Indian Church healer, and an English scholar Rivera met at a conference and brought along."

"Either of these women narc on you to Gonzalez?"

"No. At least, I haven't been called on the carpet yet."

"Okay, here's the deal, my egghead friend. Even with one Maya down, there're still three fanatics after my ass. Which is three too many. But the one place they will not be looking for me is back at Lamanai. So I'm coming out to see you tonight, Ron. Since my regular troops are all in the morgue, it's time you get your hands a little dirty. I'll be there by sundown."

"Where shall we meet?"

"How 'bout the beach two miles north of the Mask Temple? Cute little crocodile sign—"

"I'll be there at sundown."

"If you bring the cops – or the Maya – I promise you, Ron, I'll hunt you down and kill you."

* * *

"What in blazes was going on with Ron Graham and those translations you kept frowning at?" Clive Phelps asks Gemma, as soon as they're alone, back at their Lamanai cabin.

"Oh my God, Clive," Gemma says. "The last thing Ron asked Canek, just before he died, was: 'do you know where the fountain of youth is'!"

"Was Ron joking?"

"I don't think so."

"And the answer?"

"There was no answer – that's when Canek died. But just before that, remember when Canek gave me this amulet?"

"Because you were the 'only pure soul' in the room."

"Yeah, but what Canek actually said to Ron, who was reaching for the amulet, was 'no, you have an evil aura'."

"An 'evil aura'? Hmmn. I thought Ron seemed a little tense, but 'evil' seems unfair." Clive balances a flashlight so it illuminates a small shard of reflecting glass hanging on the wall, and lathers up for what promises to be a brutal outdoorsy shave. "Why d'you suppose Canek didn't just give the amulet to Tumaxh Koreto? What was 'impure' about *her* soul?"

"She's from a rival tribe."

Clive draws blood with the first stroke. Gotta go easier, shaving in this bad light. "So now what? You aren't really going to San Lorenzo, to deliver the amulet to Canek's mother, are you?"

"No. I'll just post it to 'Xhepel', in San Lorenzo, Guatemala. The villagers there'll make sure the right woman gets it."

Relieved, Clive says: "So take me back to when you first felt Ron was mistranslating."

"The first thing that went wrong was, Gonzalez asked 'did Kux kill everyone?' But instead of translating *that* question, Ron asked Canek 'did Kux have the book?'"

"You're sure Ron was that far off? I thought you didn't know K'iche' Mayan."

"I don't. But the *Popul Vuh* – the Maya Holy Book – is written in Classical K'iche', which helped me recognize some of the modern K'iche' words Canek and Ron were speaking. Also, modern K'iche' turns out to be surprisingly similar to Kaqchikel Mayan, which I do know."

"You're positive Ron mistranslated the question about whether Kux killed them all?"

"You don't have to rely on me – Tumaxh Koreto clearly felt Ron was mistranslating, too."

Clive nods in acquiescence to that point. "So what'd Canek say about 'the book'?"

"That's when things got really weird. Canek said 'no, Kux couldn't get the book from the old woman, so he stole the icon from the museum'."

"An icon? Ron never told Gonzalez anything about an icon – or a book."

"No he did not. Instead, before translating for Gonzalez, Ron asked Canek why Kux stole the icon, and Canek said – I kid you not – 'to unlock the passage to the fountain of youth'."

"And then Ron told Gonzalez something about a fountain—"

"Ron mistranslated both of Canek's answers, and said 'no, Kux didn't kill us, we drank bad water from a fountain'."

"Wow. Were there any other mistranslations?"

"None I could discern. I think Ron knew Tumaxh was on to him. But Clive, don't miss the forest for the trees here. Ron Graham's a well-respected academic, who's published important articles about Maya archeology, which I've cited in my own work. At the other extreme, Canek's a committed revolutionary, from a whole different world. But both these guys were talking like they totally believe the fountain of youth is real, and here at Lamanai. And Ron took a real serious risk, with Tumaxh and me right there, to keep Gonzalez from hearing about the fountain of youth."

"So?"

"So what've you dedicated your whole life to? Finding the cellular fountain of youth, right? For Nigel. For all of us. And these guys, they think the fountain of youth's right here, at Lamanai."

Clive smiles as he rinses his bleeding throat with canteen water. "You're just trying to get me interested in this crazy place, so I don't start getting edgy about all the work I left behind."

"Busted." Gemma slides into Clive's place in front of the makeshift mirror, and brushes her hair. "But I'm also serious, Clive. There've been rumors, all the way back to the days of the conquistadors, that the Maya in the Yucatan were hiding the fountain of youth. Maybe there's something here that could help you in your own work."

"Hmmn. What were the specifics of those rumors?"

Gemma laughs. "Rumors, Clive, don't have 'specifics'. That's what makes them rumors. But generally the story was, the Maya shamans here were living to be 150, 160, 170. Since no one knew how the shamans were living so long, the rumor started: they'd found the fountain of youth."

"Were any of those shaman's ages ever substantiated, medically or historically?"

"Of course not."

"Were there any particular elements or chemicals that were rumored to be in the fountain of youth, which were keeping these shamans alive so long?"

"No, but Ron Graham – of all people – wrote an article a few years ago about two ancient Maya herbs, coclmeca and gangweo, which grow at only at a few ancient Maya sites. And the one and only place he said coclmeca and gangweo are found in huge profusion is here, at Lamanai."

"Are those the two herbs you described in your book as the Maya equivalent of Viagra?"

Deep delight suffuses Gemma's entire face. "You really *did* read my book, didn't you?"

Clive opts against confessing he just skimmed her book, and the Viagra line just happened to stick in his nearly eidetic memory, along with the curious herb names, coclmeca and gangweo.

"You may also recall," Gemma adds, "I wrote that, in addition to treating sexual dysfunction with coclmeca and gangweo, modern Maya healers use coclmeca to relieve arthritis and rheumatism, to build muscle, and" – Gemma's eyes sparkle – "the Maya in Belize brew a mixture of the two herbs they call 'root juice', which an American doctor called the 'herbal fountain of youth'."

"Which American doctor said that?"

"I don't remember. But I can look it up for you when we get back to Oxford."

"Please do. But for now, what say we go find some coclmeca and gangweo samples?"

Gemma breaks into a huge smile. "You mean, I've got you hooked?"

"'Hooked' is a little strong." Clive takes Gemma's hand. "But I'm mildly intrigued. And it's sweet of you to try to make this little junket relevant to my work. Though you don't have to do that."

"I know I don't *have* to. But I really think there's a connection here, Clive. Those rumors about the fountain of youth at Lamanai persisted for centuries. English pirates swore by them."

"Pirates – now *there's* a reliable source."

"You told me the English pirate William Dampier was one of the great early scientists. Quoted by Darwin, friends with Dr. Johnson—"

"Dampier was a special case. Most of the old pirates were just blood-thirsty thugs." Wincing at his own needlessly harsh words, Clive tries to make amends to his lover. "But tell me about the pirates, Gem. What made them think the fountain of youth was here at Lamanai?"

"I don't know. But two separate bands of pirates came here searching for the fountain of youth. After both groups died, nearly to a man, they decided it was a fountain of death, not youth."

"How big were these 'bands' of pirates? And when'd they come to Lamanai?"

"Ten or fifteen pirates each time, I think. One was in the 1600s, and one was in the 1700s. But I'm the wrong person to ask. The real expert on this is – believe it or not—"

"Ron Graham?"

"Spot-on! In that same article I mentioned, Ron had a very lively footnote about the pirate rumors. I remember thinking at the time, the footnote was better than all the rest of his article."

Clive purses his lips. "Gem, I'm a scientist. I can't help it, that's what I am. The fact that a rumor persists, even for centuries, really doesn't prove anything, in and of itself."

"I disagree!" Gemma says. "Ever hear of El Dorado?"

"The mythical City of Gold? Of course."

"You'd say that was just a rumor, persisting for centuries, with no apparent basis in fact?"

"Well no one ever found El Dorado," Clive says, "even the Spanish, who scoured the American jungles fom 1520 till 1850, looking for it. So yes, I'd say El Dorado was just a rumor."

"But they *did* find El Dorado!" Gemma says. "Not the Spanish, but a modern archeologist, who happened to be sitting in just the right place at Tikal about 15 years ago, on May 5th – traditionally the first day of the rainy season here in the Central American jungle – and the sun came pouring through a tiny, perfectly-placed aperture at the top of an ancient Maya temple there, forming a shimmering laser of light, that lit up a half mile path at Tikal in dazzling golden sunlight."

"Oh yes," Clive says, "I've seen photos of that phenomenon – it looked quite remarkable."

"It is. Only happens one day each year, for half an hour. But that path was once the main street of Tikal, which in the 7th and 8th and 9th centuries, was a city of a million people. And on that golden street, I believe, the legend of El Dorado was born. After the Maya abandoned Tikal, in 900, the story of one street of golden light for half an hour one day each year grew, by degrees, into a rumor of a whole city of streets paved with gold all year long. But there was always a seed of truth in the rumor – it's just, in later centuries, we didn't know where to look for that seed of truth."

Clive arches a skeptical eyebrow. "And you think there's a similar explanation for the persistent rumor of the fountain of youth being at Lamanai?"

"I do." Gemma kisses Clive full on the lips. "I just don't know what it is. But I bet *you* could figure it out, my conquistador. The Maya say, once a story is told – like the story of the fountain of youth – then it can't be false, because it could only have come to the storyteller as a lost race memory, left in his blood by his ancestors."

Clive wraps his arms around her, and kisses her back, with passion. "Don't try to distract me from the complete illogic of what you're saying. If I were to believe that Maya 'saying', then if I want the fountain of youth to be real, all I have to do is make up a story about it, and *voila*, it's real!"

"I should've known better than to offer Maya mysticisim to a scientist." Gemma pushes her tongue against Clive's. "But at least you accept my basic point, right? If you're looking for the fountain of youth at Lamanai, it may be something like the golden sunlight at Tikal. Not a literally true fountain, but rather something true in a more poetical sense."

"Well I'm nobody's idea of a poet, my dear." Clive wraps both his hands round Gemma's tight little bum. "But I'd still really like you to show me some coclmeca and gangweo, growing wild in their natural state. The herbal fountain of youth, and all that."

"Great! Only I'm not quite sure where to look – perhaps we should ask Ron, or Rivera."

"Oh, let's *not* do that!" Clive says. "My real purpose here, apart from the pursuit of truth and poetry and the fountain of youth, is just to get you away from Rivera and Gonzalez and Ron, before they dream up another crazy assignment for you. After all, this is supposed to be our holiday."

"Okay." Gemma leers at him. "But in that case, shouldn't we take care of first things first?"

Clive grins, recognizing 'first things first' as their private code for a quick shag. To Clive's great delight, Gemma strips off her jungle gear with reckless abandon, and they make love in their grim little cabin, fast and hard, like two young pagans in the wild.

Afterwards, the lovers dress quickly. But when Gemma reaches for her trousers, whose legs are inside out due to the haste with which they were removed, she forgets she has Canek's amulet in her pocket; and when she snaps the trouser legs back out, an audible crack reverberates in the cabin, as the pocket with the amulet smacks hard against the floor.

"Oh, no!" Gemma cries. When she pulls out the amulet, it's in pieces. Gemma's face falls, and Clive can almost see the tears coming – but abruptly Gemma's crestfallen expression turns to intense curiosity, as she pulls a tiny scroll out of her pocket. "This must've been inside the amulet."

"What's it say?" Clive asks.

"Can't tell. I need better light."

They finish dressing, and walk to a clearing in the forest, where Ron and his archeologists used to eat. At a picnic table Gemma sits down to puzzle over the scroll, which is written in glyphs.

Clive sits beside her, watching Gemma's brow, furrowed in rapt concentration. She does love her work. Which is one of her most attractive features, to Clive – apart from her smashingly fit little body. Things really could work out between them. Of course, Clive thought the same thing when he married Nigel's mother – but Nigel's birth changed everything. Phillipa stopped working, to care for Nigel; and then she grew hostile to Clive, when Clive's response to the tragedy of Nigel's birth was to work harder than ever.

But there will be no Nigel to divide Clive and Gemma.

Unfortunately, there will be no Nigel at all, soon. Unless Clive gets cracking. Soon.

For Nigel is slated to follow Canek down to the dark caves of Xibalba, or the dark abyss of oblivion, or wherever it is we all go, unless Clive – or one of his rivals – finds the formula to unbind telomerase in our somatic cells, and defeat senescence. Clive played it cool with Gemma a few minutes ago, about the idea that the fountain of youth might be here at Lamanai, in some 'poetic' sense, like El Dorado was at Tikal. But in his heart of hearts, Clive is fiercely excited about the idea. Shamans at Lamanai living to be 150, 160, 170. Bands of pirates – young men, presumably, in the prime of life – dying in droves from undiagnosed diseases contracted when they came to Lamanai, seeking the fountain of youth. Not 'evidence', in any scientific sense – but fascinating, all the same. Highly reminiscent of the hypothesis driving all Clive's work, i.e., that immortality and death are much closer cousins than people realize. Flip sides of the same cellular coin.

"It's a list of ingredients," Gemma says. "Part of a formula."

"A formula for what?"

"It doesn't say. But it includes the two herbs you asked me to show you, coclmeca and gangweo. And cinnabar, and salt, and some kind of special water. But the list appears to be a fragment – not the entire recipe. Or formula."

"Does it say where to get the 'special water'?"

"No, but I can show you where they got the herbs, and probably the cinnabar, too."

"Let's go."

The lovers wander off, hand in hand, on Gemma's *ad hoc* tour of Lamanai. After ten minutes of meandering along jungle paths, they come upon the remains of the ceremonial center of Lamanai, including two towering temples, the excavated stone foundations of the Lamanai royal palace, and the weed-riddled ruins of an ancient Maya ball court. They sit for a short rest on the stone bleacher seats lining both sides of the long, narrow ball court.

"What game did the Maya play in a ball court like this?" Clive asks.

"Pok-a-tok," Gemma replies. "The drawings depict it as kind of a cross between modern football and basketball. There was a ring at each end, placed fairly high up, like a basketball hoop, but with the front of the rim pulled down 90 degrees so the hoop was perpendicular to the ground. Then they kicked and bumped and headed a round ball, smaller than a football, up and down the court, without using their hands, trying to put it through the other team's hoop."

"Sounds like fun."

"Not really. The Maya played all their ball games to the death."

"Who died?"

"The losing captain was sacrificed to the Gods. Sometimes, on special holidays, the entire losing team was sacrificed."

"Nice holiday."

"Oh, but it was. Holidays were very important to the Maya, aimed at keeping the Gods happy." Gemma points at a large stone disk in the center of the ball court. "But the reason I brought you here is that disk. No other Maya ball court has one like it. When Ron Graham had it lifted a few years back, he found an ancient Maya clay canister in it, still half full of cinnabar. Since cinnabar was very rare, he assumes they used it in some special ceremony after the ball games."

"What is 'cinnabar'?"

"I don't know. Ron described cinnabar in his article as being a thick, viscuous substance, like cold clammy fresh liver, wrapped in clingfilm. Not liquid, but not entirely solid, either."

"Sounds like mercury, dear."

"Well whatever it is, Ron said there's no cinnabar anywhere near Belize. The closest place the ancient Maya at Lamanai could have gotten this cinnabar was from the Comanche Indians, in Texas. So when the Maya got it, through trade or war, they stored it under that huge disk, which takes, like, five or ten men to lift, and they only used a little of it at a time, on special holidays."

Clive nods, marveling at the huge number of useless pieces of information Gemma has retained in her formidable brain. If Clive were Emperor for a day, he would order all the smart Ph.D.'s in humanities like Gemma retrained and refocused into more useful, scientific pursuits.

Next Gemma leads Clive east, towards the lagoon. This brings them, after a few minutes, to the Mask Temple, with its famous ten-foot human face carved on the west face.

"When was that face carved there?" Clive asks.

"About 2200 years ago," Gemma says.

"Amazing – that guy is the spitting image of our Canek this morning."

"You're right. Shows how isolated the pure Maya are. If you took a Roman sculpture from 200 B.C., you couldn't find an Italian today who resembled the sculpted face, because the

Italians have inter-mingled with other races over the centuries. The same would be true of a Comanche sculpture from 200 B.C.. But not the highland Maya. They are truly a breed apart."

They walk around to the east side of the temple, and are surprised to see no constable standing guard. Poking their heads in the open door of the tomb, they see that the place has been completely emptied – except the sarcophagus – and it now reeks of disinfectant.

"Rivera's wasted no time getting the autopsies started," Clive says.

When they step back out of the tomb, Gemma opens both arms to gesture at the wide swath of wild herbs growing between the Mask Temple and the jungle twenty yards away. Clive kneels and uproots a small plant Gemma identifies as gangweo, depositing it in a plastic bag. But he needs both hands to uproot the coclmeca she shows him, and the 50 pound plant is plainly too big for any plastic bag Clive's got handy. So he settles for some clippings of its leaves and roots.

"Normally we don't allow visitors to dig up the fauna," Ron Graham says.

Clive whirls, and sees Ron standing right behind him.

"But in your case, Dr. Phelps, we'll make an exception," Ron adds, in a bantering tone.

"Thanks." Clive decides to needle Ron back. "Just looking for the, ah, fountain of youth."

Clive rises and looks straight at Ron, Clive's face betraying no irony.

As Clive hoped, Ron's lips tremble, for Ron no doubt realizes Clive's comment conveys the unstated message 'we know you were mistranslating about the fountain of youth this morning'.

"Sorry to intrude like this," Ron says, "but Dr. Rivera asked me to come find you. We've had some, ah, developments."

Clive nods and steps to one side, assuming Ron's focus will be on Gemma.

But Ron's eyes stay locked on Clive.

"Dr. Rivera says the young Maya in the tomb all died of cancer," Ron says. "Canek, too."

"Highly implausible," Clive says. "Cancer is a disease of the elderly."

Ron shrugs. "Not my department. But Dr. Rivera wants to hire *you* now, Dr. Phelps, to review the biopsies. My impression is, he'd like nothing better than for you to prove him wrong."

"Twelve young men, dead of cancer at one time, in one place? That's unprecedented."

"Maybe not." Ron tells Clive the legends of the pirates dying at Lamanai in 1641 and 1724 after seeking the fountain of youth, not realizing Gemma just summarized these incidents for Clive. But Ron's version emphasizes the similarities in the manner of the deaths – the lack of signs of violence on the bodies and the sudden bleeding and 'agues', which Canek also showed, and which Rivera infers the others had, too, from the large amounts of painkillers he's finding in their blood.

"Those 'similarities' are not at all diagnostic," Clive argues. "As Dr. Rivera pointed out last night, cholera, poison water, gas – all are possible explanations for mass deaths of young men which leave no marks and, frankly, are much more plausible than cancer."

Ron arches an eyebrow. "Aren't you the one who says cancer and immortality are 'flip sides of the same coin'? No one knows if the pirates here died of cancer, because cancer wasn't an identified disease in 1641 or 1724. But by the same token, no one can say it *wasn't* cancer, either – and they were definitely seeking the fountain of youth. Now we have 12 young Maya dead of cancer, and we have evidence they were probably seeking the fountain of youth, too. In my field, we seldom achieve 'diagnostic' certainty. But I'm certainly curious to explore the parallels."

"What 'evidence' is there the Maya here died seeking the fountain of youth?" Clive asks.

"Rivera's preliminary toxic screens show the same substances in the blood and stomachs of the Maya that the pirates said they injected and ingested at Lamanai: mercury – what the pirates called a 'silvery pudding' – elevated salt, and sulphur – what the pirates called a 'rotten egg' smell in the water. Why else would the Maya have this same collection of odd substances in their bodies, unless they were following the same formula the pirates followed?"

"What 'formula' is that, precisely?" Clive asks.

"No one knows all the ingredients, or the exact proportions," Ron says, "except one old hermit in London, who's hoarding the ancient Maya codex that reputedly has the formula – and according to the pirates, also has a map to the fountain of youth. But it's got to be a variation on the formula which European alchemists tinkered with all through the Middle Ages."

"Mercury, sulphur, salt," Gemma says. "The three elements of the Philosopher's Stone."

"Precisely," Ron says.

"Sorry," Clive says, "but there's nothing 'precise' about 'mercury, sulphur, salt'. *How much* mercury? *How much* sulphur? *How much* salt? Mercury is highly toxic to humans, and sulphur isn't far behind, so the question of proportions is far from academic. And what're the proportions of the coclmeca and gangweo, and whatever other ingredients they were using?"

Ron stares at Clive with a competitive look. "Who told you the Maya used those herbs?"

"Gemma keeps me apprised," Clive says, meeting Ron's stare, "of all the latest speculations regarding the ancient Maya. But I would say, if there was mercury in the blood or stomachs of the modern Maya who died in the tomb, that's probably what killed them."

"Rivera says not," Ron says. "But you can ask him yourself."

"That I shall," Clive says. "But tell me about the hydrogen sulphide,"

"I don't know what hydrogen sulphide is."

"Sulphur. Does the water at Lamanai smell of rotten eggs, or cause nasty diarrhea?"

"Not when I lived here," Ron says.

Their conversation is interrupted by a rustling in the nearby thickets, followed by Samuel Rivera stepping out to greet them. "Ah, Ron, you found them!"

"Yes, but Dr. Phelps is skeptical about it being cancer," Ron says.

"He should be," Rivera says. "If I release autopsies saying 12 young men died in one place from cancer, my competence as coroner will be questioned. So I desperately need someone with your credentials, Dr. Phelps, to review the autopsies, and the biopsies, in as much detail as you require, and then either point out where I have erred, and correct the autopsies before they are released; or say, I have reviewed Rivera's work, and he is not a lunatic."

"There are forensic oncologists more qualified than I to do this work," Phelps says.

"But none of them is right here, on site, and already privy to a non-public investigation. At this time of year, it'd take me several days to get someone to come here, with qualifications even remotely approaching yours. Which is why we'll pay whatever you think fair to charge us."

"What if there's a leak, while I'm reviewing your work?"

"Then you and I will both have to address the press, and explain that you unselfishly agreed to give up your holiday and help us, because of the extraordinary nature of the situation."

Clive looks at Gemma. But she clearly has no objection to prolonging this little adventure.

"Alright, Sammy, I'll do what I can for you between now and Sunday. But come Sunday, I must go back to Oxford, come hell or high water. Understood?"

"No problem," Rivera says.

"Good. So right now, not counting the two elders, and the three men in the boat, we have twelve young Maya dead, and three unaccounted for, right?"

"Correct."

"And the 12 biopsies all show cancers?" Clive asks.

"Correct. 80% mortality – 12 out of 15 – in 60 days. Has anything like this ever occurred?"

"Not even close," Clive says. "The worst mortality rates ever recorded for cancer were 50%, for Turkish villagers who inhaled erionite mineral fibers – but those deaths occurred over a 24-*year* period. Next worse are American pipefitters working with asbestos in the 1940s – but they had lower mortality rates, and over even longer time periods."

"This is why I need your help," Rivera says. "The world health community will flock around this, like flies to shit. And in this case, I'm the shit."

Clive smiles wanly. "Did anyone observe the health condition of the Maya sixty days ago?"

"I brought them here," Ron Graham interjects. "They looked perfectly healthy to me."

"You have medical training?" Clive asks.

"No. But for two hours, we were squeezed shoulder-to-shoulder, 19 of us, on my friend Manny Santoro's 15-seat launch. If they'd had any obvious signs of sickness, I'd've noticed."

Clive turns back to Rivera. "What type of cancer are your biopsies showing?"

"Extensive cancer in all vital organs. I can't even say which cancer killed any one man."

"And you're finding no trauma on their bodies?"

"Nothing except needle marks around their genitals," Rivera says, "and significant scarring on their penises. The needle marks, I presume, were from injecting mercury. Ron can explain the penis scars better than I."

"Traditionally," Ron says, "the Maya shaman scraped a stingray spine across his penis, and let the blood drip onto burning bark paper so he could read, in the swirling coil of the resulting smoke, augurs and omens of the future. Then he danced before the people, wearing only a paper skirt, to prove by the blood flowing down his legs that he'd truly made the sacred offering."

Rivera hands Clive a thick binder. "Draft autopsy reports for all twelve subjects. Please read them carefully. If you find I am wrong, I shall truly thank you."

Clive skims the draft autopsy for FNU LNU 7 (First Name Unknown, Last Name Unknown). The autopsy begins with the external examination, recording observations about skin condition and the rigor and lividity of the blood; and then moves to the internal examination, describing the incisions made in the skin and bone, the tissue samples obtained, and the removal of the organs. Next it recites the weight of the organs, noting no abnormalities; estimates the age of FNU LNU 7, based on dental measurements and bone length, at between 20 and 30 years old; and summarizes the process for procuring samples for testing tissues, blood, bladder and gastric contents.

The tissue analysis is detailed in a separate attachment, as are the results of the bladder and stomach contents analysis. The autopsy concludes that FNU LNU 7 likely died of adenocarcinoma of the lungs, based on the proliferation of cancer cells in the lung tissues; but the report notes that he might just as well have died from cancer of the pancreas, stomach, colon, testes, liver or brain, because the subject's Stage 4 cancer had not only metastasized to all these organs, but had reached lethal levels in all these organs as well.

Clive looks up from reading. His head is spinning; he struggles to maintain composure. The idea of so many aggressive, accelerated cancers – what could it be, but telomerase unbound?

"You find no error in the procedures with the autopsy?" Rivera asks.

"None," Clive says.

"You find no fault with my conclusions?" Rivera asks.

"With these tissue reports, no other conclusion would be reasonable."

"But you'll examine the bodies, and review the samples, before giving a final opinion?"

"Of course. Though I doubt it's necessary, Sammy, except to show you subjected your findings to review – and to get me up to speed, so we can get to work finding the cause of these cancers." Clive shakes his head, perplexed. "But I have a few general questions about the group."

"Yes, please," Rivera says, "ask away."

"For FNU LNU 7, you estimated his age at 20 to 30, based on bone size and dental observations. Were the others all about the same age?"

"All under age 25," Rivera says. "I used 30 just to be conservative."

"All twelve were ethnically Maya?" Clive asks.

Rivera nods.

"Is there research data I've somehow missed," Clive asks, "showing cancer is a higher risk for young Maya men than for men of other ethnicity?"

"No. Cancer in a young Maya male is as unusual as in any young man."

"Did all 12 victims also have extensive metastatic disease, like the autopsy I just read?"

"Yes," Rivera says. "All twelve had extensive cancer that invaded virtually all their vital organs, with the exception of the heart, of course."

"You gave no opinion as to date of death for FNU LNU 7," Clive says. "Were you able to fix a date of death in any of the other autopsies?"

"No," Rivera says. "With such a long gap between 1 November, when Ron last saw them alive, and 27 December, when the police discovered their bodies, my guesses as to dates of death would lack scientific value."

Clive nods. "Still, I'm interested in your guesses. Off the record."

Rivera frowns. "The man calling himself 'Canek' died today. The 11 in the tomb were dead at least 96 hours before today, based on *rigor mortis*. But the rigor and lividity in those 11 varied widely. I'd guess most had been dead ten days. Some maybe as long as three weeks."

"And the two older men," Clive asks, "whose hearts were cut out?"

"I'd guess they were the first to die," Rivera says. "But I'm only guessing."

Clive glances at Ron. "Ron says you've done some, ah, preliminary toxic screening."

"Yes, we've been finding very high concentrations of peyote – mescaline – in the bodies of all the deceased."

"High enough to be fatal?" Clive asks.

"No, but the peyote was much higher than normal recreational use. These men were using peyote to kill very severe pain. And we've also been finding elevated levels of mercury."

"Mercury is highly toxic," Clive says.

Rivera waggles his hand, like a teeter-totter. "So developed nations tell us. But in places like Belize, mercury is still widely used in traditional medicine – and the jury is still out as to whether mercury is truly as harmful as you all claim."

"Well, it's beyond dispute," Clive says, "that in high enough quantities, mercury is fatal."

"The mercury in these men's blood was nowhere near fatal levels," Rivera says. "And we have not been finding any sign of renal failure or stomach bleeding, which as I'm sure you know, are the signs of acute and chronic mercury poisoning. They just had – elevated mercury levels."

"Excuse me," Gemma says, "but did I hear you say before that the mercury was *injected*?"

"Definitely," Rivera says.

"I've heard of Maya healers using mercury topically, or by inhalation," Gemma says, "but I've never heard of Maya healers *injecting* mercury."

"Neither have I," Rivera agrees. "But we're not finding elevated mercury levels in the stomach tissues, like we are in the blood; and as I mentioned, we've found small perforations in and around the genitals of all the young men, consistent with the use of traditional bone needles."

"How could anyone inject a substance as illiquid as mercury," Clive asks, "without disrupting the osmotic levels of the blood?"

"I assume they diluted it in water, and then injected it into muscles rather than veins."

Clive nods, because Rivera's surely right – Sam's a very capable guy, and besides, the truth is, Clive has no real forensic expertise to bring to bear on this unprecedented calamity anyway. But Clive knows he can't turn down this assignment because, while purportedly 'verifying the accuracy of the biopsies', or whatever Rivera imagines Clive'll be doing, Clive will actually be trying to figure out what these crazy Maya fanatics did to unbind the telomerase in their cells.

Because that *has* to be what happened here. No way 12 young men die of cancer at one time in one place, unless the chemicals they were heedlessly messing with – their crazy ancient Maya formula of herbs and mercury and sulphur and salt, and whatever else they ingested or injected – somehow unleashed the very enzyme Clive's been searching for these past nine years.

And the fact that these were such *young* men who died is compelling. There's a school of thought that says we die because the genes we need in our youth, for sexual reproduction, turn on us in old age, and drag us to our graves – with no Darwinian mechanism to stop those aging genes, because they're so biologically useful in our youth for reproduction, there's no reason for evolution to phase them out. So how fascinating that such young men could activate the telomerase in their cells which, in some cases, turned to cancer and killed them very fast; yet in other cases, evidently bypasses the normal aging process, and lets them live 150, 160, 170 years.

Ron asks: "If a person's on the verge of dying from cancer, are the symptoms obvious?"

"Not always," Clive says. "Some Stage 4 cancer patients suffer weight loss, abnormal sweating and fevers, uncontrolled coughing, bloody stools, and, if they're getting radiation, hair loss. But others carry the cancer inside them, undetected, sometimes right up to the day they die."

"So what if the young men who died here," Ron asks, "were pre-selected to come, precisely because they'd already been diagnosed with Stage 4 cancer?

"An interesting hypothetical," Clive says.

"If they already had Stage 4 cancer when Manny and I brought them here," Ron says, "then maybe it's not so amazing 12 out of 15 died in 60 days."

"Actually," Clive says, "a mortality rate that high would still be unprecedented. Most cancers take much longer than 60 days to kill their hosts. But the idea that the cancers may've developed away from this site is still an intriguing supposition. Although—" Clive turns to Rivera. "Would it be possible to find, in all of Belize and Guatemala, 12 Stage 4 cancer patients who were male, Maya and under age 25?"

"No," Rivera says, "in all of Belize and Guatemala, there aren't 12 Stage 4 cancer patients who are male, Maya and under 25. So it'd be unreasonable to assume the subjects had Stage 4 cancer before they came to Lamanai. This is why I asked to consult with you,

Dr. Phelps. Is my conclusion even possible, that 12 men under age 25 developed cancer in one place and died within 60 days?"

"Anything's possible," Clive says. "And although it's unprecedented, we do know our subjects engaged in unusually risky behavior, injecting mercury and ingesting mescaline. Also, they may have injected or ingested other unknown carcinogenic substances."

"We screened for all standard carcinogens and toxins," Rivera says.

"I saw that," Clive says, "but these men may have used substances that are unidentified cancer-causing agents, outside standard screening procedures."

"Can't you find what they used by testing tissues and blood?" Ron asks.

"Not that simple, I'm afraid," Clive says. "With tissue and blood screens, you have to know what you're looking for, in order to find it. Which is why I'd like to know more about the specific religious rituals these men were participating in."

"I can't help you there," Rivera interjects. "That's Ron's department."

"I'm not aware of any Maya ritual that involves injecting mercury," Ron says, "and I don't know any details of what Kux was doing. Other than what I told you about the pirate tales. Sorry."

"Well, we should do some research," Clive says, "to find out exactly what they were up to."

"Okay," Rivera says. "But that's really up to Dr. Graham, and Dr. Murray."

Everyone nods acquiescence. Then they all stand in awkward silence.

"What about the public health measures we discussed last night?" Clive asks at last.

"The samples from the lagoon all came back negative," Rivera says. "But we've left the warnings up; and we've quarantined the site."

"Any word on the three dead men in the boat?" Clive asks.

"The police've identified the two dead white men in the boat," Rivera says. "They were Americans, ex-Marines. They were in the tomb, because we matched some vomit found on one of the dead Maya to vomit we scraped from one of the dead mercenaries' throats."

"So they're the guys who blasted the tomb door and put bullet holes in the wall," Ron adds.

"But we don't know anything more about who killed them," Rivera says, "except we presume it was the three Maya who are still at large."

"You know," Clive says, "it would really help if the police could locate at least one of the three Maya fugitives, so we could do a comparative physical—"

"Won't happen," Rivera says. "Those three men will never be found."

"You lack confidence in Captain Gonzalez?" Clive asks.

"No," Rivera says. "Pablo's very good at his job. But it's already been 24 hours, and the only one identified is the leader, Kux Ahawis. Ron's friend."

"What about the man, Canek," Clive asks, "who died in the nearby village?"

"That was a false name he gave," Rivera says, "for both himself, and his mother, Xhepel."

"The Guatemala police have gone to Kux Ahawis's village?" Clive asks.

"No," Rivera says, "Gonzalez knew the Maya there would never talk to a Guatemalan policeman, so he sent a Belize constable there, on the quiet. But the villagers still denied knowing of the re-enactment, and denied any of their young men are missing. Same result in all the mountain villages our constable tried."

"A stone wall of silence," Ron adds. "The Maya way."

"What about immigration records?" Gemma asks. "There can't be many groups of 17 Guatemalans who came into Belize around 1 November."

"Only tourists go through immigration here," Ron says. "All Guatemalans and Belizeans cross the border a mile below the official crossing. To avoid fees."

"Don't border patrols stop them?" Gemma asks.

"Few years ago, they tried," Ron says. "But workers in both countries went on strike, till both governments agreed to leave the illegal crossings alone."

"Well, once this story leaks," Clive says, "someone will come forward."

"No," Rivera says, setting his jaw. "Publicity will change nothing. I guarantee you, the families of these men must already know they're missing, yet in 24 hours, no one's come forward."

"Still," Clive says, "someone must be able to trace 17 men missing from work for 60 days."

"Not these men," Ron says. "If they work outside their villages, they give false names."

"Why do they do that?" Clive asks.

Ron looks at Rivera, who shrugs.

So Ron answers: "The Maya leave no tracks."

* * *

The moment Joyce Kerr steps off her plane at Detroit Metropolitan Airport, she sees David Burns, waiting with open arms. The next moment she bursts into tears.

After a long hug from David, Joyce pulls herself together. "Wow, sorry. That was—"

"Delayed reaction," Burns says. "Grief is sneaky that way. You think you got it under control, but the pressure is always building under the surface. And all it takes for the dam to burst is a familiar song, or an old face like mine, or anything else that reminds you of your father."

"Your face isn't that old, David. How old are you now, anyway? Fifty-two?"

"Thirty-nine is the age I give to the women I date."

Joyce laughs. "Maybe you should come with me to Belize."

"When are you going to Belize?"

"First thing tomorrow morning."

"You're kidding! You just got home."

"The whole point of going to London for the week was to be sure I didn't feel tempted to meet Lisa on the sly. The Judge was very clear, because of all the times I've complained about

Michael disregarding the visitation schedule, that he didn't want to hear about me doing it, too. So I realized, if I come back to Ann Arbor now, I'll just be miserable the rest of the week."

"You could always come to the office and get an early start on next year's cases."

Joyce rolls her eyes. "Thanks, David. But as exciting as that sounds, Belize sounds better."

"Can you afford it? I mean, I could lend you some money if you need it."

"No, thank you, I found a really cheap flight, and it's only a four-day trip."

"Okay. But why Belize? We can write to the Land Registry there and get the information on the Ambergris Caye land you think Fiona stole from you."

"I'm not going because of the land. I'm going to find the fountain of youth."

Burns laughs. "Good luck. If you find it, please be sure to save a few long swigs for me."

"Why not come and quaff it down yourself, on the spot? There's still space on the flight."

"Oh, Joyce, I'm too old to do something that impetuous."

"No, you're not. And as much as I hate to say, ever, that I need a man for anything, I must admit the one place a man might come in handy is out in the jungle."

Burns winces. "If only I were the rugged outdoorsy type."

"Who says you're not? You're in great shape. Even for thirty-nine."

"You'd still be better off hiring a guide who really knows the jungle."

"So you're turning me down?"

"'Fraid so. I've just got too many year-end client meetings scheduled this week."

"You're going to regret this, when I call you up to tell you I found the fountain of youth."

"I'll regret it even before you get down there," Burns mutters. "But what's got you so hepped up about chasing after the fountain of youth? It is a myth, you know."

"I wonder," Joyce says. "Fiona certainly believes it's real."

"*There's* a reliable source. Next you'll cite the Quinlans, I suppose."

"No, but I did some research into India Reynolds, the painter who gave Kathleen Quinlan the codex and sent her off to Lamanai to look for the fountain of youth. India Reynolds gave her age to the census taker as 155, and paid taxes on the same house in Southwark for 73 years."

"Did you find a birth certificate for India Reynolds?"

"No, she was born in Jamaica, and before they had birth certificates. But in the Belize Museum, they have her painting of the fountain of youth. So tomorrow I'm gonna go down to Belize, look at the painting, figure out where the fountain is, and then go find it."

"Everyone should have a goal in life." Burns takes Joyce's elbow. "Let's go get your bags."

Later, riding home in Burns's car, Joyce raises a delicate subject that's troubled her all day. "David, I've decided, in all fairness, I can't ask you to represent me against Fiona."

"Why not? I did a little digging around today at the courthouse. I think it's a strong claim."

"Really? What'd you find out? Was Fiona BS-ing me about Kathleen's Will?"

"No, Fiona gave it to you fairly straight. Kathleen's Will did say she wanted her entire estate to go to Persephone."

"Then why'd the court give everything to Lloyd?"

"Persephone was a 'ghost in the nursery'."

"I don't know what a 'ghost in the nursery' is."

"It's probate talk for a secret child no one knew about, who shows up at the probate hearing for the first time."

"But we've always known about Persephone. And she was in Kathleen's Will."

"Maybe *you* knew about Persephone," David says, "but apparently the Will was the first Lloyd, or anyone in Ann Arbor, ever heard that Lloyd had a twin sister. Then, when Persephone produced her birth certificate, Lloyd proved it was a forgery. So – and this is the one place where I don't think Fiona quite came clean with you – the Judge had a little more basis for ruling in Lloyd's favor than just the fact that Lloyd was his poker and whoring buddy, and whatever else Fiona told you about the Judge hating independent women."

"Did you find the asset inventory? Or are you saving that job for your paralegal?"

"No, I found it. The codex was listed as an asset of the estate, which was specifically ordered to pass to Lloyd."

"That's good for my claim, right?"

"Very good. Even better, Persephone probably knew full well she was stealing it, because she lit out for Belize just a few days after the Judge ruled – and just a few days before Lloyd swore out a warrant for Persephone's arrest – *for stealing the Lamanai Codex from him.*"

"How 'bout the Ambergris Caye land? Was that mentioned on the asset inventory?"

"No. So while you're down in Belize, take a few hours and do a full title search on the land. Get the whole history of title and taxpayers, from 1868 forward. And find out what its appraised value is. Then we'll be good to go."

"Okay, but I'm still not comfortable having you represent me, David."

"Why not? I've got an idea how we can get around the problem of Fiona living in London."

"That's not what's troubling me. It's Fiona herself. She's just so damned obstinate. She'll turn this little lawsuit into World War III."

"Waging dirty little wars is what I do for a living," Burns says.

"But not for free. It's one thing for me to impose on you to drag Michael's sorry ass into court, whenever he's misbehaving on custody issues. But Fiona is a whole different kettle of fish."

"Isn't that for me to decide, whether I'm willing to work for you for free?"

"No, it's something we both have to feel comfortable about. And right now, I'm not comfortable with the idea of imposing on you for what could turn out to be hundreds, or even thousands, of hours of legal work I can't pay for."

"You could pay me on a contingent fee basis – pay me a percentage of what we recover."

"I know what a contingent fee is, David. I've also heard you tell many lawyers, 'never, ever take a case on contingency, unless the upside is at least a million bucks'. Because, according to you, by the time you factor in the cases where you uncover bad facts that kill your claim, and the cases where new appellate decisions kill your claim, and the cases where the judge or jury kills your claim, and the cases where you win but the damages turn out to be way less than you hoped, the 'average recovery won't even cover your time and expenses, unless the potential upside in all your contingent fee cases is in seven figures'. Quoth David Burns, nevermore."

"That does sound like me," Burns admits. "But this case might well be a seven-figure case, if the codex turns out to be as valuable as you think it is. How about while you're in Belize, I see if I can get some idea how much the codex is worth?"

Up ahead Joyce sees her house – the only unlit house on the block. "That's fine. David, I've been up almost 24 hours, and I've gotta get up early tomorrow to make my flight to Belize. Let's put off arguing about this till I get back, okay?"

Burns agrees, helps Joyce in with the bags, and offers to hang around while she re-packs for Belize. But she assures him she's fine, alone in her Lisa-less house, and sends him home.

Joyce has one rough moment, when she unpacks her carry-on and finds the urn, with her father's ashes. But she gets through that moment by staying busy. She puts the urn on the fireplace mantel, stows her father's suitcase in the spare bedroom, and dives into re-packing her own suitcase with warm-weather clothes. Then she goes on-line to book a hotel and a guide.

The hotel turns out to be easy – most of the hotels are on Ambergris Caye, where she wants to be – so she chooses one called the Jolly Roger, because they have a few cheap rooms, and a fun-looking pool where you can 'walk the plank' right from the hotel lobby into the pool.

But selecting a guide is harder, because there are dozens of them – and implausibly, they all claim to be 'experts' in Maya history and archeology. Since Joyce needs a true expert in these matters, she digs a little deeper, looking up the many scholars who've published articles slamming Fiona Young for hoarding the *Lamanai Codex*. Among those who've written such articles, there's only one located in Belize: Ronald Graham, Director of Archeology for Belize.

Since Dr. Graham's number is listed on the Belize Government web site, Joyce calls, figuring at this hour, she'll just leave a message. But to her surprise, Ron answers on the first ring.

"Ah, Dr. Graham, hello – my name is Joyce Kerr. I'm Fiona Young's cousin."

"Oh?"

"I read your article criticizing Fiona for not sharing the *Lamanai Codex* with other scholars. I totally agree with you. I'm flying to Belize tomorrow to gather evidence to prove the codex really belongs to me, and not Fiona. But I need a really good guide to take me to Lamanai and show me around – someone truly knowledgeable. Can you recommend a really good guide I can hire?"

A long pause ensues. "For Lamanai, the best guide would be me. I lived there for seven years, back when the site was still being actively excavated."

"Oh, wow! That's so nice of you, but – what do you charge?"

"I don't normally work as a guide. I'll just charge whatever the other guides charge, okay?"

"Sure. This is so nice of you. How will I find you?"

"You'll have to find your own way to Orange Walk dock at dawn on Thursday morning. When you get there, ask for Manuel Santoro. Manny'll bring you by boat to Lamanai, where I'll be waiting for you. You okay with sleeping in a rough shack for a night or two?"

"As long as it's safe."

"I'll personally make sure you're safe, Mrs. Kerr."

Chapter Six
Ourobouros

Wednesday 29 December 2010

An hour before dawn, Kip Hunter enters Ron Graham's cabin at Lamanai. Clapping one hand over Ron's mouth, Kip wakes him up. When he sees recognition in Ron's eyes, Kip pulls his hand away.

"I waited for you last night at the beach," Ron whispers.

"I know," Kip mutters. "I watched you from the trees."

"Then why didn't you show yourself?"

"I don't trust you, Ron. I needed to be sure there was no ambush."

"But I was alone."

"Yeah, I figured that out. But then I went to see Tumaxh Koreto, the Indian Church healer."

"Why?"

"To be sure you told me the truth about the interview with the dying Maya."

"Tumaxh wouldn't've told you anything. She swore on her ancestors' graves."

"She swore not to tell what *Gonzalez or you* said. But she told me what *Canek* said. And she confirmed you translated poorly. Which is why you're still alive."

Ron looks relieved, but then he gets that pissy look Kip saw on him before, at his house. "This is not a safe a place for us to meet. Captain Gonzalez is in the next cabin."

"Gonzo's asleep. I just checked. So fill me in on the investigation."

Ron sits up and dresses while he whispers: "It was cancer. Killed them all."

"Bullshit. I saw the two old guys' chests – their hearts were ripped out."

"But all the rest, including Tumaxh's patient Canek, died of cancer."

"Seemed awful young for cancer."

"Very. Rivera's already got a world expert in cancer here, Dr. Clive Phelps, from Oxford."

"I saw him last night. Kinda short, but looks like a TV star, every hair in place all the time?"

"That's the guy. Phelps says this will be a huge international medical sensation."

"And the lady scholar who knew you were mistranslating – she's Phelps' girlfriend?"

"Yeah. Right away she connected the Maya deaths with the old pirate deaths. She's got Phelps working on what herbs and chemicals the Maya were taking that might've caused cancer."

"What *were* the Maya taking?"

"Same stuff that's in the pirate tales. Mercury – Kux must've found the ancient cache of cinnabar under the Ball Court. And Phelps has Rivera screening for coclmeca and gangweo – those are ancient Maya herbs that—"

"I know all about coclmeca and gangweo. What's the lady's name?"

"Dr. Gemma Murray."

"So, bottom line: are she and Phelps after the fountain of youth?"

"Yes. And those amulets the Maya had on their necks? Dr. Murray broke one open, and found a tiny scroll inside, with ancient Maya glyphs."

"What's the scroll say?"

"Don't know. She claims she's still translating it. But I bet she already knows. She's smart."

"I hate smart women," Kip says. "What about my boys in the boat?"

"The police ID'd 'em, and know they were mercenaries. But they still don't have any idea there was a fourth man in the boat, so you're in the clear."

"Until the Maya catch up with me again."

Ron stands up, fully dressed. "So what're we gonna do?"

"Like I said, we're goin' on offense." Kip dons a wool ski mask, and hands one to Ron. "Put this on. I know it's hot. But we don't want your friends to recognize you."

"They'll recognize my voice."

"Not if you shut up and just do what I tell you."

* * *

Clive Phelps wakes well before dawn. Recalling how his libido was thwarted yesterday morning, by the early trek to Indian Church village, Clive decides today he's not waiting for the first light of day to seep into the rustic one-room cabin he's sharing with Gemma Murray. Like the early bird ready to feast on the worm, Clive reaches for Gemma, primed for an early-morning shag.

But Gemma's already awake and, instead of sex, she's got the Maya on her mind.

"Clive, I know you don't believe in dreams. But I just had this incredible dream, it was so vivid, and it really *makes sense*."

"About what?" Clive reaches for Gemma's breast, not really giving a damn about her dream.

"About the fountain of youth. And the two-headed icon Ron Graham told us the pirates said points the way to the fountain of youth. In my dream, I put the icon up on the sacrificial disk on top of the Mask Temple, and lined it up with the disk at the center of the Ball Court, and at sunrise, on the solstice, like the aperture at Tikal, a stream of golden light shot out, and pointed the way straight to the entrance to the cave that hides the fountain of youth!"

"That's … great, Gem." Clive cuts to the chase, and puts his finger on her sex. "But since today's not the solstice, and since we're here, in this tiny little bed, I figure we may as well …"

Clive rolls on top of Gemma. But curse the Gods, suddenly there are way too many limbs in the bed. It's very confusing. By the time Clive makes any sense out of what's happening, there's a gag in his mouth, his hands are trussed behind his back, and he and Gemma – also bound and gagged – are being marched out of their cabin by two men wearing ski masks.

Clive is completely terrified. Nothing like this has ever happened to him before. As he and Gemma stumble along in the pitch dark of the pre-dawn jungle, Clive tries to get a read on their kidnappers, but all Clive can make out is, they're both taller than Clive, and one's athletic and fit, while the other is a bit on the portly side.

The kidnappers lead Clive and Gemma in the general direction of the lagoon for ten minutes. Then abruptly they're trundled up a path to the Mask Temple, and shoved into the tomb there, which still reeks of ammonia.

Once inside the tomb, the athletic kidnapper bolts the door and switches on a flashlight, which he leaves on the floor, its beam aimed at the middle of the room. He removes Clive's and Gemma's gags, and unties Clive's hands; but leaves Gemma's hands bound behind her back.

Producing paper and pen from his backpack, the athletic kidnapper hands them to Clive.

"Write a short note, Dr. Phelps, apologizing for your hasty departure in the middle of the night, but indicating that urgent matters have called you back to Oxford, with your girlfriend."

"And if I don't write this note?"

"I'll rearrange that pretty face of yours, one tooth at a time, until you do."

Clive's heart skips a beat. The quiet tone of the athletic kidnapper is chilling, and utterly convincing.

"To whom shall I address this note?" Clive asks.

"Who hired you – Rivera, or Gonzalez?"

"Gonzalez," Clive lies.

"Then write it to Gonzalez," the athletic kidnapper says.

At this, the portly kidnapper whispers in the ear of the athletic one. In response, the athletic kidnapper jerks his head as if he'd received unwelcome news, and immediately whips one of his heavy boots around in a vicious kick that lands hard just below the side of Clive's knee.

Excruciating pain racks Clive's peroneal nerve, and he crumples to the ground, clutching at his knee and screaming in pain.

"We're off to a bad start," the athletic kidnapper says in a quiet voice. "Fuck with me again, the consequences will be far worse. Now stop whimpering and address your note to Rivera. Make it nice, and plausible – you're truly sorry to leave him in the lurch, but a confidential emergency arose, so you arranged your own transport, and you're gone."

Clive obeys. Once he hands over the note, the athletic kidnapper – who's armed to the teeth, with a holstered pistol, and a sheath with a huge knife – reties Clive's hands behind his back.

The athletic kidnapper hands Clive's note to the portly one and, after a brief whispered discussion that Clive can't hear, the portly one departs. After he's gone, the athletic kidnapper locks the door again, and positions himself between his captives and the open door to the stairway.

Then to Clive's shock, the kidnapper removes his ski mask, showing himself to be blonde, ruggedly handsome, and in his mid-40's.

"Since you two are so intellectual," the blonde kidnapper says, "we're going to engage in a scholarly exchange. But don't let the highbrow nature of the proceedings mislead you. If you yell or run for one of the doors, I will strike you down, very hard. *Comprende*?"

Wide-eyed, Gemma nods.

Clive, his leg still numb from the sharp kick, nods, too.

"Good." From his backpack, the blonde kidnapper produces a small jade statue, and places it on the ground, within the beam of the single flashlight. It's an odd statue, with two heads, and an enormous erection – a Maya fertility icon, Clive assumes, reminiscent of the two-headed glyph on the wall behind the sarcophagus that Gemma and Ron discussed the first night out here.

At the sight of the two-headed icon, Gemma gasps.

"You recognize this statue, Dr. Murray?" the kidnapper asks.

"No."

"Don't fuck with me, lady. What made you gasp like that?"

"I – I've never seen a two-headed Maya icon before. That's all."

"Oh gimme a break! If you gasp that passionately at the sight of this little guy, what do you do when Clive here pulls out a real Johnson for you to look at?"

At this rude sexual comment, Gemma tenses up, and looks at the ground. This is turning ugly. Clive debates various heroic, though almost certainly futile, options. He could run at the blonde kidnapper and engage him in a struggle, to buy time so Gemma could escape. Or he could kick the flashlight away, so they could both try to escape in the confusion.

But the fact is, Clive loves being alive. He plans to live forever, too. He hates the idea of throwing his life away now, on a risky chance for which he has no training and no experience, without even knowing for sure that the blonde thug is planning to rape Gemma.

"You've seen something like this idol before, haven't you?" the kidnapper presses Gemma.

"No," Gemma lies, without lifting her eyes.

The kidnapper glares at her awhile, then shifts his focus to Clive. "Let's get this scholarly exchange on track, Dr. Phelps. I'm going to ask you several questions. I warn you, I know the answers to most of them. You fuck with me like before, you'll regret it. The purpose of this exercise is to set a good example for Dr. Murray, so she'll get into the spirit of sharing information."

The kidnapper gazes at Clive. In all his life, Clive's never seen eyes so blank and pitiless.

"What did all those young Maya in the temple die of?"

"Cancer, probably. But we don't know for sure, yet."

"Is cancer a common disease among young men?"

"No."

"Have there been any other groups of young men who died at Lamanai in large numbers?"

"Yes. Two bands of pirates died here, in the 17th and 18th centuries. No one diagnosed their deaths as cancerous, but – well, it has crossed our minds there may be a connection."

"Are you aware of any common behaviors among the three groups, other than dying?"

Clive hesitates. By training he hates to give out medical information. But he also hated that kick in the knee. "No one knows for certain what the pirates did. But they may have been injecting mercury, hydrogen sulphide and salt, and ingesting rare Maya herbs, coclmeca and gangweo."

"And you found these chemicals and herbs in the dead men?"

"I didn't. But Rivera found some of them – though he's still checking on the Maya herbs."

"You find jade amulets on the necks of all the dead men?"

"I didn't, but Gonzalez did. Almost all – I think there was one without an amulet."

"What's inside those amulets, Dr. Phelps?"

Clive hesitates again. With no idea what his kidnapper does and doesn't know, Clive decides it's not worth risking a lie over this. "A scroll."

"What's the scroll say?"

"I don't know. It's in glyphs."

The blonde kidnapper turns to Gemma. "What's that scroll say, Dr. Murray?"

"I don't know. I'm working on it."

The kidnapper glares. "You are not so forthcoming as Dr. Phelps."

"I'm sorry. I don't work as quickly as he does."

"I don't think lack of mental agility is the problem. I think you have a bad attitude." The kidnapper clasps Gemma's chin tight between his thumb and forefinger. "Are you familiar with the ingenious device the conquistadors used on reluctant witnesses in the old days, the *strappado*?"

"I know what the *strappado* was, yes."

Clive does not. But he decides not to ask.

"Effective though the *strappado* was, personally I find this modern device much simpler." From his pocket the blonde kidnapper pulls a cigarette lighter and flicks on its flame. "I've never used this on a female. But when held under the male genitals, it never fails to inspire the truth."

* * *

"You're the third person this year to ask to see *The Fountain of Youth*," James Eliot says, leading the way down the stairs to the basement of the Belize Museum. "Before that, in the ten years I've been curator here, no one ever asked about this fascinating painting. Not once."

"Maybe you should put it out on public display," Joyce Kerr says.

"It's a bit too graphic for the general public. As you'll see."

"Who were the others asking about *The Fountain of Youth* this year?"

"A Maya shaman from Guatemala, named Kux Ahawis. And the Belize Minister of Archeology, Ron Graham." Eliot leers at Joyce's chest. "Neither one anywhere as pretty as you."

Even though being leered at by Eliot is disgusting – he looks like Mr. Potato Head in black glasses, with teeth like Roquefort cheese – Joyce flashes Eliot a mildly flirtatious smile. She wants Eliot to be happy, since he's doing her a favor, showing her the painting even though it's in storage and she made no appointment. On the other hand, she doesn't want to encourage him to the point he asks her out, because as bleak as Joyce's love life is these days, it ain't *that* bleak.

But Joyce can do mild flirtation on auto-pilot. What's really on her mind right now is the oddly unsettling fact that her tour guide tomorrow, Ron Graham, was one of two people besides Joyce to come look at this obscure India Reynolds painting. What does Ron Graham care about the fountain of youth? Was that why he was so quick to volunteer to be her guide?

"This building was the old Colonial prison." Eliot gestures down the wide central basement corridor, lined on both sides by small walled cells. The first cell is preserved in its original form, with an old bed and chamberpot; all the others are packed with Maya, Spanish and English artifacts.

Joyce sees pottery, ceramics, marble statuary, huge plaster casts of Maya glyphs and, in the old jail cell Eliot stops at, stacks of framed paintings. Eliot rummages through the stack, pulls out a framed oil painting, and sets it up on an easel in the middle of the cell for Joyce to view.

On the bottom of the frame a plaque says: '*The Fountain of Youth*, by India Reynolds, 17??-1864'. The canvas shows signs of water damage, particularly in the upper left quadrant.

"Regretably this painting was damaged during shipment in the 1970s," Eliot says.

Joyce studies the painting, which matches Kathleen Quinlan's description in her diary: a dark cave, lit by pine torches, with a calm narrow underground river, about four feet deep, judging by several rough-looking pirates standing in it with water up to their chests. Just beyond the river is a rocky plateau where the central characters stand: a young red-haired white woman in a white gown, next to an Indian holy man holding an open book and a bowl full of a silvery pudding, and several more pirates, in tattered 18th century breeches and waistcoats, with scarves holding their long hair out of their sunburnt faces, and assorted swords, daggers, and pistols in their waistbands.

The pirates stand thunder-struck and gaping as the Indian holy man reads from the open book whose pages are covered with Mayan glyphs, while the red-haired woman – India Reynolds, Joyce presumes – lifts her gown far up her thighs, and plunges a primitive bone needle down towards her sex. India does not depict her own pubic region, her forward thigh blocking it from view; nonetheless, as Eliot – and Kathleen Quinlan – said, it *is* graphic. Indeed, this risqué pose would've shocked any Victorians who viewed this painting right out of their gourds.

"It's a trace vulgar," Eliot comments, "but compelling, all the same."

Joyce nods. The fountain itself is in the near background. It's strangely small – more like a gurgle – and none of the people in the painting are paying it any heed. Close by the fountain, scattered around on the rock plateau, are a steaming jug and a large block of salt.

In the distant background, beyond the fountain and the pine torches lining the walls, a winding stone staircase leads up to a heavy stone door in the ceiling of the cave. The heavy door is open, and gives way to a dark space above and beyond the main action of the painting.

"Such a little fountain," Joyce says.

"Strange, isn't it? But that's part of Mrs. Reynolds' artistry. She gives us a tiny spurt, when we might have expected a grand gushing fountain; and she gives us pirates at the tiny spurt she calls the fountain of youth, when we might have expected a conquistador, like Ponce de Leon."

"But Ponce de Leon was supposed to be in Florida, wasn't he?" Joyce asks.

"What makes you think this picture is *not* set in Florida?"

Not wishing to mention Kathleen's stolen diary, Joyce shrugs. "I don't know – maybe because, like you said, there's no Spanish conquistador in the painting."

"Well, you're right. The picture is definitely set in Central America, probably here in Belize."

"How do you know?"

"Mrs. Reynolds left us several subtle clues. Most definitive is the codex the Indian priest holds. Those are genuine Mayan glyphs. Goodness knows where Mrs. Reynolds had come across such glyphs in 1856, but she went to a lot of detail to paint them with precision."

Joyce looks hard at the codex, assuming it's the *Lamanai Codex* – which David Burns told her earlier today by phone has no ascertainable value, because no Maya codex has ever been sold and therefore, with no 'comparable sale', no appraiser will commit to a dollar value. Which led to discord, with Joyce insisting, over David's objections, that she will not allow him to represent her against Fiona on a contingent fee, where the codex's value is unknown and the land is too small to be worth the seven-figure minimum Burns normally uses as his gauge for contingent fee cases.

"Astonishingly meticulous representation, wouldn't you agree?" Eliot asks.

Joyce nods, still arguing with David in her mind. "Does anyone know what the glyphs say?"

"Yes. When I first took this job, I sent a photo of those glyphs to a Maya scholar in California. She told me it's a partial list of ingredients, for some kind of recipe, or a formula."

"What ingredients are listed there?"

"Well, let's see. Salt was one – you see the block of salt in the background – and there were a couple of Maya aphrodisiacal herbs, whose names I don't recall. And – oh yes, cinnabar."

"Why'd you say it's 'probably' in Belize?" Joyce asks.

"Because of the pirates. There was an old legend that, in the 17th and 18th centuries, two bands of pirates traveled to the Maya city of Lamanai, which is in Belize, seeking the fountain of youth. So it seems likely Mrs. Reynolds had that legend in mind when she painted this picture."

"Did the pirates find the fountain of youth?"

"They thought they did, but both times, soon after drinking the waters, the pirates all died. Which gave rise to the legend that an Indian shaman – like this one in the painting – had put a curse on all pirates. The perplexing question is: why Mrs. Reynolds chose that rather obscure legend as the basis for her painting, rather than the far more common legend of Ponce de Leon."

"Wasn't India Reynolds born in the Caribbean?" Joyce asks.

Eliot nods, looking mildly surprised Joyce knows such an arcane fact.

"So maybe," Joyce continues, "India Reynolds heard about the pirates dying at Lamanai, before she moved to London."

"Perhaps. But Mrs. Reynolds was far ahead of her time, because historians have recently concluded that the old story about Ponce de Leon we all learned in school was pure hokum."

"Aren't all stories about the fountain of youth pure hokum?" Joyce asks.

"Well, of course, but historians have discovered de Leon was never even *looking* for the fountain of youth. He went to Florida hunting gold and slaves like all conquistadors; but finding only malarial swamps and invincible Indians, he wrote a long report full of excuses, which the Queen didn't want to read, so she told a minister to summarize it. Sadly for Ponce, the minister she chose was Ponce's arch-enemy, who saw a chance to get Ponce good. He wrote: 'Ponce de Leon, being unable to perform his manly duties, went searching for the fountain of youth to cure his problems." Eliot snickers, and turns unattractively pinkish. "Isn't that delicious – *'unable to perform his manly duties'*? But it was totally false. Like all the conquistadors, Ponce de Leon sired children with every woman who crossed his path, which is the origin of the *mestizos* of Central America today."

Joyce struggles not to show her dislike for this lecherous and possibly racist know-it-all. "If it was totally false, why'd we all learn about Ponce de Leon and the fountain of youth in school?"

"Because early historians were just as lazy as the Queen," Eliot says. "They relied on the rival's summary, and never bothered to read Ponce's actual report. Until very recently."

"But public schools in America are still teaching about Ponce de Leon and the fountain of youth. Just last year my daughter did a big report for 6th grade, reciting the same old story."

"School history books tend to lag about 25 years behind advances in scholarship."

Since the man has an answer for everything, Joyce gives up arguing with him, and studies the painting, looking for clues as to where the fountain of youth is located. But she can't see any. So she asks Mr. Know-It-All where at Lamanai the painting is set.

"Oh, I doubt it's a real place," Eliot chuckles. "I've never heard of any caves with stone stairs shaped like those. In fact, I don't believe there are any caves at Lamanai at all."

"So there's nothing hidden in the painting – like a secret code or something – to tell us where India Reynolds thought the fountain of youth was located?"

"Actually there are many things hidden in the painting," Eliot says. "It's very subtle. When Kux Ahawis had me get it out for him this spring, he stared at it for hours. Since I was stuck down here with him, I stared at it, too – and found several abstruse Christian and Maya symbols, which I had never seen in it before. But nothing about the location of the fountain of youth, I'm afraid."

"Can you point out the symbols you did find?" Joyce gives Eliot another phony smile. "I wouldn't know a religious symbol even if it jumped off the canvas and hit me between the eyes."

Eliot laughs. "Well, the Christian symbols are what we call *vanitas* symbols – they remind the viewer of the transience of earthly life. If you isolate this man's head" – Eliot forms an imaginary frame with his fingers in the air, around a grinning, bald-headed pirate with no teeth – "you'll see—"

"A dead man's skull."

"Very good. Painted in that skull-emphasizing manner, no doubt, to remind the Christian viewer of the inevitability of aging and death. Now isolate the torso of the red-haired woman."

"You mean, India Reynolds?"

"Well, possibly, though we should never assume the painter has put herself in a painting."

"I just have a hunch it's her," Joyce says.

"Alright. You see how India's, ah, luxurious figure is so dramatically corseted beneath her wedding gown that it forms an hourglass shape? Hourglasses are *vanitas* symbols, reminding the Christian viewer how short our time on earth is. The smoke rising from the pine torches, and the bubbles rising from the steaming jug by the fountain, serve the same function. All these *vanitas* symbols were common tropes in Victorian paintings. But what's distinctive here is how Mrs. Reynolds interwove the Christian symbols with two ancient Maya symbols of the *ourobouros*."

"What's the *ourobouros*?" Joyce asks.

"The *ourobouros* is an archetype found in most ancient religions, as well as in alchemy and many mystical philosophies. It represents the cyclical nature of all life, as well as the idea that time has no beginning and no end. For the Maya, the usual expression of the *ourobouros* is a feathered serpent, coiled in a tight circle, and devouring his own tail. The serpent represents the Maya creator God Itzamna; the eating of the tail symbolizes the self-sustaining nature of the creator God; and the coiled circle is a metaphor for the universe having neither beginning nor end."

Joyce peers at the painting. "I don't see any serpents."

"They're not literal serpents; they're very subtle. Step back from the picture a moment, and try to see only the shapes Mrs. Reynolds used. If you look at the composition of people's heads in the painting – India's, and the shaman's, and the pirates surrounding them – you'll see the heads of the entire group form a tight curled circle. And now if you focus only on the pirates' colorful scarves and hats, and India's bright red hair, and the shaman's jade amulet around his neck, those items resemble scores of colored feathers, poking out in all directions from the tight curled circle of heads. And finally, if you look only at the two heads at the very center of the circle – India bowing her small head, as she plunges the bone needle down towards her pelvis, and the much larger pirate with the open jaws facing her – it looks as if the pirate's about to devour her, doesn't it?"

Reluctantly Joyce nods. The guy's a jerk, but he does see things in paintings she would never in a million years see. Benefits of a post-graduate education, she supposes.

"So you see," Eliot continues, "built into the very composition of this pre-Raphaelite painting is the most sacred of Maya symbols, the feathered serpent God, coiled in a circle, eating his own tail. The *ourobouros*. Now when I first saw this, I wondered if I was reading too much into it. After all, why should a Victorian woman like Mrs. Reynolds have been knowledgeable about Maya symbols, which white explorers had only just begun to discover in the 1850s? But then I saw the other serpent depiction she put in the picture. If you look at the pattern of shadow and light thrown onto that winding stone staircase by the pine torches along the cave walls, you'll see—"

"A huge shadowy snake," Joyce says. "I see it. But it's not eating its tail. It's just – it looks like it's just slithering down the stairs, towards the people in the river."

"Quite right. The Maya didn't always depict Itzamna in a coiled circle. Here the Creator God is shown coming down the stairs, as if to tell us that the trip the people in the painting presumably made down those same stairs – after all, the door at the top is flung open, suggesting that's how they entered this cave – is the path to eternal life, symbolized by the Creator God slithering, as you aptly put it, down the steps. But you know what's really enthralling? Only in our time have archeologists discovered that many Maya temples have this same feature: stairs that were constructed with such amazing precision that at certain times of the year – the solstices and equinoxes, or the first day of the rainy season – the light from the sun is funneled through a small aperture in the temple, so that for an hour or so, you see what appears to be a shadowy snake, slithering down the steps. Just like Mrs. Reynolds painted here. Eerie, eh wot?"

"Perhaps India Reynolds was in a real Maya temple," Joyce says, "which inspired her to paint something like this. So is there a winding stone staircase like that – maybe not in a cave, but just anywhere – at Lamanai?"

"Many Maya temples have winding stone staircases inside, including the ones at Lamanai. But there's no pattern of serpents on the stairs of any Lamanai temples. And besides, the first excavations at Lamanai didn't occur until twelve years after Mrs. Reynolds painted this. Indeed, during Mrs. Reynolds' lifetime, the only excavated Maya temples were those

Stephens and Catherwood had discovered at Palenque, in Guatemala. Mrs. Reynolds had probably seen Catherwood's famous drawings of the lost cities in the jungle and so forth. But there's no explaining where she would have seen a pattern of shadows like a serpent going down a flight of stone stairs. That was not discovered, by whites, until after World War II."

Joyce peers closely at the winding staircase, and follows it up to the open stone door, and beyond, to the dark space in the upper corner of the painting. But then she notices for the first time that the dark space is not really part of the painting – it's a six-inch-square swath of black cloth, sewn onto the upper left corner of the canvas.

"What happened there?" Joyce asks.

"That corner of the canvas was damaged so badly in transit in the 1970s it was deemed beyond repair, so someone cut it away and replaced it with the patch you see." Eliot winces. "Not a decision the current curator would've made, I assure you."

"Do you have a photograph of the painting from before it was damaged?"

"Sorry, no."

Joyce gives Eliot her warmest smile. "Oh, surely someone must have photographed this painting before it was damaged. Would you mind looking through your files again for it?"

"There would be no point. I've looked. I regret to say, the Belize Museum has no photograph of this painting from before it sustained water damage."

Figuring Eliot must have more pull with the National Gallery than Joyce did, Joyce pushes her lower lip out in a pout, and asks: "What about the National Gallery in London? Can you contact them, to get a copy of *their* photograph of the painting before it was damaged?"

"The National Gallery doesn't have a photograph of it, either. I'm afraid no one does."

"But didn't galleries *always* photograph paintings, even back in the 1970s?"

"Normally, yes. But all the pre-water-damage photographs of this painting have been lost."

"I hate to be a bother, Dr. Eliot, but it's really important. Would you mind checking again, just to be sure?"

"I already have. Very recently."

"Why—?" Joyce swallows her question, realizing she already knows the answer.

"Because Kux Ahawis and Ron Graham asked me the same questions you're asking."

Chapter Seven
Survival of the Adaptable

Thursday 30 December 2010

An hour before dawn, Kip Hunter wakes his captives in the Mask Temple tomb. After untying them, Kip prods Clive Phelps at gunpoint to walk to the stone sarcophagus and lie face down on top of it, where Kip ties Phelps down, so he can't move.

"You start yelling, I'll hear you first," Kip says, "and I'll come right back and cut your throat."

Phelps nods. He looks like he's got no fight left in him, after 24 hours in this dank tomb.

Kip turns to Gemma Murray. "You start yelling, or try to run away from me outside, I won't bother chasing you. I'll just come right back in here and cut his throat. *Comprende*?"

The lady nods – but still looks defiant.

"Let's go see if you're right about how to use this little toy," Kip mutters.

Gripping the two-headed jade statue in one hand, and his pistol in the other, Kip leads the lady two hundred feet up the winding interior steps of the Mask Temple. Atop the temple she locates the old stone disk, on which untold numbers of ancient Maya were sacrificed over the centuries to the Gods of the Sun and the Rain. Then Kip and the lady sit together on the roof comb beside the sacrificial disk, and wait for sunrise.

For three quarters of an hour they sit in sullen silence, listening to the vibrant sounds of the jungle, waking up – first the booming howls of the monkeys, and then the ear-splitting chatter of the songbirds. Fifteen minutes before sunrise, Kip decides it's time to soften the lady's attitude.

"For what it's worth, Dr. Murray, I'm glad you didn't make me resort to torture yesterday."

The lady stares ahead in stony silence.

"You're pissed at me, aren't you?"

"Yes."

"If I were in your shoes, I'd be pissed, too. But you need to get past this attitude."

"Why should I?" the lady snaps. "You kidnapped us, held us hostage for 24 hours in an old tomb, and threatened to torture us if we didn't tell you what little we know about the fountain of youth. Now you expect me to just forget all that, and act like we're old mates?"

"We don't have to be mates," Kip says. "Just business partners."

"I would never be partners with a man like you."

"Don't be hasty, lady. Think what happens this morning if you're right, and at sunrise this little guy points us the way to the cave where the fountain of youth flows. What happens next?"

"I assume you'll kill Clive and me."

"That's one option, yes. But then what would I do?" Kip pauses, to let the lady think it over. "My expertise is in black ops – kidnapping, assault, torture, assassination, and private military action. But I don't know diddly squat about science or history. Which means I don't have a clue how best to exploit the commercial value of a discovery like the fountain of youth."

For the first time since Kip threatened to light a flame under her pussy yesterday, the lady looks him in the eye. "So you'll hire experts, to tell you how to exploit the discovery."

"But hiring experts ain't like hiring mercs to storm a castle. I got no contacts in science or history, like I do in commando networks. It'd take me months to search out the right guys. Why do all that, when I've got a world-class scientist and his Maya scholar girlfriend, right here with me?"

"You want to *hire us*?" the lady sounds incredulous.

"That would be my preference, yes."

"It'd never work. In case you haven't noticed, there're cops all over this site."

"So? We didn't hear a peep from them all day yesterday."

"But you made Clive write a good-bye note. What happens if they see us back here?"

"Clive tells 'em his emergency got taken care of, so he came back to help again."

"What if someone sees *you*?" the lady asks.

"You introduce me as your colleague, assisting you at no charge to the Belize coroner."

"What makes you think we wouldn't just turn you in to the cops here, first chance we got?"

"I went through your boyfriend's wallet. He's got a son, looks like a tiny old man?"

"That's personal!" the lady objects.

"Very. With a sick kid like that, Phelps can't afford to get on the bad side of a ruthless assassin like me, can he? Kid with a disease like that can't be moved around, so he's an easy target – and I have his address, as well as his pic. So even if I were behind bars, my contacts outside would ensure that Phelps'd pay the maximum penalty, if either of you betrayed me."

"You are an evil man."

"No, just harder-hearted than most people. I don't form emotional attachments. But in my meager defense, I don't enjoy violence, either; and I only resort to it when there's a purpose to be served. Whenever time permits, I try to reason with people first. Like I did yesterday with you, to avoid the need for torturing you. And like I'm doing now, to try to avoid the need to kill you."

The lady blinks. "This is all just too weird. I spent the last 24 hours hatching escape plots, thinking maybe I'd try to sacrifice myself so Clive could escape. And now you're offering to *hire* us."

"Life is full of surprises," Kip says. "Ever read von Clausewitz?"

"The military philosopher? No."

"How 'bout Darwin?"

"Yes."

"Well, Darwin gets misquoted a lot as 'survival of the fittest', but what he really said was, 'survival of the adaptable'. And that's what von Clausewitz preaches, too: 'if you want to survive the battle at hand, stay totally flexible, always prepared to adapt yourself to changing reality'. That's what you and Dr. Phelps need to do: adapt to the changing reality here. Beats the hell out o' dyin'."

The lady stares at Kip like he's a maniac. But he meets her gaze clear-eyed, and after awhile, he senses her attitude may be softening.

"I'll need to discuss your offer with Clive," the lady says at last.

"Of course." Kip stands and stretches. "In the meantime, though, the sun's almost up."

The lady stands up, too. From their two-hundred-foot-high perch atop the Mask Temple, they watch the first shafts of sunlight rise above the tall canopy of the dense rain forest across the New River Lagoon on the eastern shore.

When the light finally comes, Kip hands the lady the two-headed fertility icon, and she sets the icon down in the dead center of the sacrificial disk, with the little guy's aroused pecker aligned with the disk at the center of the Ball Court, visible in the distance to the west. As the lady predicted, the first rays of sunlight from the east glint off the the little guy's pecker, much as the morning sun at Tikal creates the 'El Dorado' effect one day each year. The difference being that the fertility icon doesn't concentrate the sun's rays into an extraordinary golden street of light, like the aperture at Tikal does; rather, when aligned with the Ball Court disk in the distance, the icon serves to reflect the light down towards the rain forest below the Mask Temple.

Kip peers at the ground where the light is pointing – but all he sees is dense foliage. "I can't see anything resembling a cave entrance."

"Remember," the lady says, "the winter solstice was nine days ago. The sunrise then would've been a coupla degrees different from today. So I'm going to wiggle the icon, just a tad, in both directions. You watch to see if it points out anything interesting."

Kip peers again at the ground below, while the beam of light from the icon moves in response to the lady wiggling the icon.

"There!" Kip cries. "That place among the rocks – is it a cave, or winding path?"

"You should go check it out," the lady says.

"We'll both go," Kip counters. "You're not my partner, yet."

"But you'll never find the place unless I stay up here and hold the icon just as it is."

"Don't worry, I've got a bead on it." Kip retrieves the icon, and takes the lady's arm. "We both go. Now."

* * *

Strapped to the sarcophagus in the Mask Temple tomb, Clive Phelps lies alone in the dark, with only his thoughts for company. They're bad company.

In all his life Clive's never been deprived of his freedom. The enforced inactivity is taking a heavy toll. As is the psychological pressure of sitting 24 hours in total darkness, except the brief periods when their kidnapper turned on his flashlight to extract information from them.

Clive counsels himself the depression he's feeling is a normal reaction to such involuntary and prolonged inactivity, for a man accustomed to being constantly busy with work, as Clive is. Many studies have shown the depressive effect of prolonged light deprivation – not to mention the unknown psychotraumatic effect on the brain of breathing ammonia fumes for 24 hours. But no amount of self-therapy can lift Clive's dark mood. Not only is he wasting time, not only is he letting Nigel down, not only is he leaving unattended his quest to conquer death – but worst, it's quite possible he and Gemma will die violently at the hands of their kidnapper. And soon.

Clive recalls the military men he met early in his career, working on government projects. Cold and calculating bureaucrats – bastards, really – but nothing like this nameless blonde American who's holding Clive and Gemma captive. This guy's got ice water in his veins. Clive has no doubt, from the soulless look in his eye, that the guy truly was prepared to hold his lighter under Gemma's vagina, till she told him what he wanted to know. What a nasty piece of work.

The whole thing is beyond crazy. Monday afternoon Clive was living his normal life, giving his well-worn telomerase lecture to physicians, and entertaining lewd thoughts about the lithesome waitress at a cocktail party. By Tuesday morning, for the sake of romance, Clive was riding a donkey through the jungle to watch a Belizean policeman interview a dying Maya separatist, while an otherwise reputable archeologist deliberately mistranslated the interview. Tuesday afternoon Clive got sucked into believing Gemma's patchwork theory of 'evidence' – rife with logical fallacies – that the Maya have been hiding the fountain of youth at Lamanai for 500 years with no one finding them out. Then Wednesday morning, the capper to 36 hours of bizarre events in what used to be the well-ordered life of a rational scientist: Clive was kidnapped at gunpoint, and stuck in a dank dark tomb to watch while his girlfriend was threatened with torture, unless she revealed each and every step in her utterly illogical patchwork theory that the fountain of youth is real.

But if the patchwork theory is so illogical, why's a guy as cold and cruel as their kidnapper running such risks to get all the details of the theory? The kidnapper knows Lamanai's crawling with cops; indeed, he seems to have inside information about their every move. Yet he comes out here anyway, with just one co-conspirator, never seen again, and kidnaps Clive and Gemma, for no purpose other than to force Gemma to tell him what she thinks about the fountain of youth. Then, once she spills her idea about lining up the icon with the solstice sunrise and the disk in the Ball Court, the kidnapper runs another 24 hours of risk that some policeman will wander over to the Mask Temple and find him holding two innocent Oxford scholars hostage – for no reason other than he wants to see if Gemma's right about what happens at sunrise atop the Mask Temple.

Clive shudders to think what'll happen in a few minutes, when sunrise comes, and Gem's dream doesn't pan out. The tomb door'll open, a few rays of sunlight'll filter in, their kidnapper'll chuck Gem's lifeless body into the tomb, and put a bullet in Clive's head. The end.

To distract himself from such dark thoughts, Clive decides to undertake a rigorous scientific review of all the 'evidence' known so far, pro and con, regarding the hypothesis that the fountain of youth is real and hidden in a cave somewhere here at Lamanai:

- Pro: Two groups of pirates, 80 years apart, came to Lamanai, and claimed they went to an underground cave, where a priest showed them the fountain of youth.
- Con: Ron Graham says he and his team scoured every square inch of Lamanai for seven years, with their yard-by-yard grids, and found no caves here.
- Pro: The first group of pirates used a two-headed icon to 'find and unlock' the cave with the fountain of youth – an icon that matches both the two-headed icon the kidnapper has, and the two-headed glyph written on the wall behind Clive.
- Con: The second group of pirates didn't mention any icon, perhaps because the first group of pirates stole the icon from the Maya at Lamanai.
- Pro: The second group of pirates, however, *did* mention an amulet, which they claim their priest used to point the way and open the door to the fountain of youth.
- Con: Regardless of whether one uses an amulet or an icon as the pointer, it's hard to open the door to a cave, in a place where there are no caves.
- Pro: According to the Royal Navy, a woman calling herself India Reynolds – whom the pirates kidnapped – walked off a pirate ship returning from Lamanai in 1724; and a woman named India Reynolds also painted a picture called *The Fountain of Youth* in 1856, depicting pirates visiting a fountain in a cave with a Maya shaman.
- Con: No one has ever substantiated that it was the same India Reynolds who walked off the pirate ship in 1724 and painted the picture in 1856.
- Pro: Fifteen young Maya, led by a shaman reputed to be 150, came to Lamanai last month and injected themselves with mercury and water rich in salt and hydrogen sulphide, and ingested aphrodisiacal herbs and other unknown chemicals, before 12 died of an incredibly fast-developing cancer – cancer being, as Clive always loves to say, the flip side of immortality.
- Con: The local villagers ingest the same aphrodisiacal herbs, and use mercury medicinally, without developing cancer – although something caused the unprecedented cancer outbreak amongst the Maya acolytes at Lamanai.

- Pro: The ancient Maya at Lamanai went to a lot of trouble to hide their cache of mercury under a huge stone disk in their Ball Court, unlike any other Maya.
- Con: Why shouldn't they hide it? Mercury was exceptionally rare in this part of the world.
- Pro: Mercury, sulphur and salt are the three elements medieval alchemists used for the Philosopher's Stone – an early attempt to create a fountain of youth.
- Con: When you start citing medieval alchemists in support of a hypothesis, your hypothesis is in deep trouble.

A flicker of light at the doorway that leads to the interior staircase interrupts Clive's 'review of the evidence'. The light moves towards Clive, erratically, like a torch held in a human hand, bringing with it a scent of smoky pine – and some other musky forest-like fragrances, which Clive can't identify. Into the murky semi-darkness he peers, trying to discern who is approaching.

Then Clive decides his prolonged captivity is making him delusional. Because he could swear that coming towards him, in the dim indistinct light of the flickering torch, are three Maya warriors, in moccasins and loincloths, their bodies glistening with war paint, brandishing hunting knives and ancient sling-shots, loaded with spears.

* * *

Deep in the heart of the Central American rain forest, a 15-seat launch roars up the New River at dawn. The only passenger is Joyce Kerr, sitting cross-legged in the middle of the launch, under its tarpaulin awning. Back at the stern, manning the rudder, sits Manuel Santoro.

Early in the ride, Manny swerves close to the western bank of the river, to show Joyce, from a distance of six feet, a crocodile sleeping in the mud. A little later he cuts the motor to idle, to point out, along the eastern bank, a bat sleeping on the underside of a copan tree, a jabiru stork's nest high in a ramon tree, and a five-foot-tall iguana, so perfectly camouflaged in the mangrove that Joyce can't fathom how Manny spotted it. So she asks how he saw the iguana.

"I pay him to stand in that same place every morning," Manny deadpans.

Joyce smiles. Lisa would've loved to meet this scruffy guide, with his dry sense of humor. Maybe in a couple of years, if Joyce finds a way to pay for a lawsuit against Fiona, and wins, and finds a buyer for the land, or the codex, or both, she'll have enough money to bring Lisa down here for a proper vacation. Lisa would love the Jolly Roger, with its faux pirate decorations, and the lobby with the mock gangplank out to the swimming pool. But by then, Lisa'll be a teenager, who probably won't want to be caught dead hanging out with her mother.

Joyce sighs, hating the precious time she's losing with Lisa, just because Michael – who's doubtless leaving Lisa unsupervised and alone, all vacation, even though it worries

Joyce sick to think of all the trouble a 12-year-old girl can get into – insists on exercising his full rights under the court's orders. Joyce decides to joke back with Manny, and ask him what currency he uses to pay an iguana; but before she can get her question out, Manny speeds away up the river, and the roar and clatter of his rusty outboard motor makes the joke not worth the bother. A cool breeze sweeps Joyce's face as she watches the lush green mangrove along the banks speed by, and soon she drifts into a reverie, imagining her adventurous ancestors, the Quinlans, paddling up this same river back in 1868, running guns to Maya rebels while searching for the lost Maya city of Lamanai.

What a wild pair her great-great-grandparents must have been. Creating a huge scandal in Oxford with their illicit love affair, getting pregnant out of wedlock in the 1860's, running off to Australia to moil for gold and have an abortion, losing most of their gold in a terrible shipwreck – and committing some dark deed that plainly troubled both their consciences – before heading off to Central America, where they ran guns up this river to Maya rebels, discovered Lamanai, and thought they found the fountain of youth. More adventure than their timid and unadventurous heiress, Joyce Kerr, will see in her whole life – and the Quinlans were still in their 20s.

Joyce recalls Kathleen telling her diary she yearned for books to escape into the *'romance of far-away places and long-ago times'* – though Kathleen's own exploits struck Joyce as plenty romantic enough. Yet even Kathleen said, once she came up this river, she found the *'soul-stirring adventure'* she always expected from the moment she met Roger Quinlan. On that journey, Kathleen probably gazed upon these exact same copan and ramon and ceiba trees, towering above the mangrove, that Joyce gazes at now – except unlike her unromantic and unadventurous heiress Joyce Kerr, Kathleen Quinlan saw these trees through the eyes of a daring gun smuggler.

Joyce peers into the deep thickets of mangrove, pretending she's Kathleen Quinlan, riding with Roger and Caesar, as they search for painted Maya warriors lurking in the bush. A branch moves – but it's only a dark green crocodile, sliding into the primeval mud along the river bank. Joyce closes her eyes, re-picturing that crocodile as a painted Maya warrior, waiting along the bank for the Quinlans and their guns. But is this particular painted warrior friend or foe? Is he one of the Santa Cruz Maya, whom Roger has arranged to meet out here along the river? Or is he one of the deadly Ixaiche Maya, toadies of the Mexican government, out patrolling The River of Strange People, to try to stop the flow of guns from British Honduras to the Santa Cruz rebels – by killing the gun runners? With spears.

Eyes tight shut, Joyce re-lives the Quinlans' clandestine voyage up The River of Strange People. Their dugout canoe, gliding silent in the moonlight, sits low in the water, weighted down by rifles. Up at the bow Caesar kneels – naked machete at his waist, cornhusk cigarette on his lips, a gourd of amber-colored cane liquor rolling by his knees – pulling his hardwood paddle through the water with strong silent rhythmic strokes. Back at the stern paddles Roger, somehow contriving to swagger even while squatting in a canoe, his haunches pressed against his heels, his khaki jungle shirt criss-crossed with ammunition belts, drinking his beloved Maya balche beer and smoking a nasty Cuban cigar. And mid-canoe sits Kathleen, perched on the crates of BSA guns in her impractical floor-length calico dress and heavy Victorian petticoats, holding a smoking pine torch in her tremulous hand, and trying not to stare at the angry red welt of his past master's brand burnt into Caesar's arm, and the old scars from his past master's lash, etched like a huge black spider web across the undulating black muscles of Caesar's back.

Then Roger declares, in his calm voice full of a man's loneliness, that it's time to watch the dark forest along the banks for signs of their Maya allies. Now they glide in noiseless tension that spreads through their straining muscles like a creeper vine through which they can almost feel the silent Indians stealing through the forest until Kathleen, with eyes in the dark like a forest cat, sees the fateful branch move – and Roger must decide in a trice whether to grab his own rifle and start firing, or to direct Caesar to paddle to the bank and greet their allies. Yet how can Roger, with his poor eyesight, possibly determine, with only the dim light of the cloud-shrouded moon, and the flickering light of the smoking pine torch – dancing like a firefly in Kathleen's fluttery hand – whether that fateful branch is friend or foe?

Joyce opens her eyes, and smiles at her own foolishness. Along the river banks today, crocodiles still lurk in the reeds, frogs hide in the water lilies, iguana conceal themselves in the mangrove, bats hang beneath the copan branches, and jabiru storks squat in nests high up in the ramon trees – but for better or worse, the days of painted Maya warriors waiting in the bush for English gunrunners are long gone. Today, the only physical dangers Joyce expects to brave are the mosquitoes and botflies patrolling The River of Strange People, enforcing karmic justice by wreaking malarial revenge on yanqui *turistas* like Joyce, for all the multifarious crimes their ancestors committed in the bad old days of the Colony formerly known as British Honduras.

Joyce slathers on more bug repellant, and catches Manny pretending not to notice as she rubs the lotion into the ample expanse of white skin exposed above her tank top. Like her great-great-grandmother, Joyce knows her best feature is what Kathleen called 'the graceful line of my long bare neck – and my dramatic *decolletage*', so Joyce is not offended by Manny sneaking a peek. But Manny isn't the man Joyce had in mind when she put on this slinky tank top this morning.

It's Ron Graham, waiting for Joyce this morning at Lamanai, whom Joyce has in her sights. After arranging for Ron to be her guide, Joyce looked him up on the internet, and found a photo. Not exactly movie-star looks, and a little on the portly side; but Ron has kind eyes, and he's 40, unmarried, and showing signs of settling down, taking an office job as Director of Archeology after living for years in the wild at archeological sites. Plus, as Joyce learned yesterday at the Belize Museum, Ron shares Joyce's interest in India Reynolds and the fountain of youth. So although her picture of Ron still has a lot of blank spots, Joyce has been unable to stop herself from fantasizing like mad the past 24 hours about a love-at-first-sight romance at Lamanai with Ron Graham.

Because unlike Kathleen Quinlan, Joyce badly needs to get her love life into second gear. She's certainly not getting any younger. And maybe there's something in the air at Lamanai. After all, 140 years ago, Joyce's great-great-grandparents paddled up this same river, saw this same rain forest proliferating on the same banks, sweltered in this same moist heat, and ended up making so much love out by the Maya temples in the jungle, they spawned Joyce's ancestors – in spite of Dr. Hackett telling Kathleen, incorrectly, that she was barren from her Australian abortion.

Joyce loses herself a few minutes trying to picture her Victorian ancestors making love in the jungle. Did Roger first remove all those underskirts and corsets Kathleen must've worn? Or did he just throw them all up over her shoulders and thrash about with her in the rain and the mud?

Joyce was never able to picture her own parents having sex – but her great-great-grandparents? Utterly beyond the reach of imagination. Yet one thing she *can* picture is herself having sex with Ron Graham. Joyce is pretty sure she knows what that would be like. In the interest of her own self-respect, she tries not to conjure an image of Ron, red-faced and sweating – he's no youngster, after all – but hopefully gazing rapt into Joyce's eyes, as he moves rhythmically on top of her, holding her without restraining her, one hand on the back of her neck and one hand on her hip, making love with her in the dirt at Lamanai, just as Roger and Kathleen did.

But trying not to think of it is the same as already having thought of it. Still, it probably won't happen. Most things never do. And Joyce only has three more days in this tropical paradise, before she flies home to her routinized life of work for David Burns, shared custody with Michael Clark, and the occasional uninspiring date with divorced Ann Arbor lawyers whose names she forgets before the dates even end. Only three days to see if the febrile waters of this steaming river can heat up Joyce's stagnant love life.

"Hey Manny," Joyce yells, "how come they used to call this The River of Strange People?"

"How'd you know that?" Manny looks impressed. But he's hard to hear.

Joyce moves to the back of the launch, and sits close enough to Manny they don't have to shout over the motor's roar. "My ancestors were the explorers who discovered Lamanai in 1868."

"You mean, *re*-discovered Lamanai," Manny corrects. "The Spanish came to Lamanai in 1562, burned all the Maya books and idols, and built a couple of Catholic churches, to try to convert the Maya. And then in the 1600s and 1700s, pirates came up this river to Lamanai, too."

Joyce frowns. She doesn't like these facts, because they interfere with her romantic conception of the Quinlans as the first whites to discover Lamanai. But as she thinks about it, even though Roger Quinlan was evidently keen on claiming credit for discovering

Lamanai, Kathleen's diary tacitly admits that pirates, and India Reynolds, came to Lamanai before the Quinlans.

"So the Spanish were the 'strange people' the Maya named this river after?"

"The Spanish were the *first* of the strange people," Manny corrects, "to come up this river. For 2000 years, no one bothered the Maya here, till the Spanish came, in metal armor, with horses and cannons and guns. You know what the Maya had for weapons, to fight the Spanish?"

"Bows and arrows?"

"In Michigan, that'd be right." Manny fires up a funky-looking hand-rolled cigarette. "But in the rain forest, trees are too close for bows and arrows. So the Maya used *atlatls*. Ever see one?"

Joyce shakes her head no, while trying not to stare enviously at Manny's cigarette.

"One of the oldest weapons in the world. A small slingshot that shoots a deadly wooden spear with amazing force and accuracy. Maya *atlatls* killed thousands of Spaniards; but their *atlatls* couldn't save them from European germs. In the first 50 years the Spanish were here, three million Maya died from smallpox, measles and flu. That was 90% of all the Maya living at that time."

"How come European germs killed the Maya, but Maya germs didn't kill the Spanish?"

"Because the Europeans had lived for thousands of years in close proximity to farm animals, like horses and cows and pigs, which were unknown in the Americas at that time. So the Europeans had built up immunities the Maya didn't have. Meanwhile, the Maya didn't have any new germs to unleash on the Spanish, because there were hardly any domesticated animals here."

"How many Maya live in Belize nowadays?" Joyce asks.

"There're 30,000 full-blooded Maya in Belize, but six million more in Guatemala and Mexico. And many millions more who are part Maya, like me."

Abruptly Manny cuts the engine, and pokes an inquisitive oar at the bloated belly of a half-submerged crocodile, floating dead down the river. Joyce wonders if he's considering hauling the creature on board, to sell its skin; but abruptly Manny speeds away, leaving the dead beast behind.

"So who were the next strange people up the river?" Joyce asks. "The swashbuckling pirates all women secretly long to meet?"

"Yeah, but you wouldn't have wanted to meet these guys. These weren't pretty Johnny Depp pirates; they were vicious drunks from Europe's darkest alleys, who killed every man, and raped every woman, who crossed their path. Since they almost all died by 35, of scurvy or syphilis or violence, they were even more reckless than the Spaniards. For a long time, when the pirates confined themselves to Ambergris Caye, the Maya just avoided them like the plague; but when the pirates came up this river, the Maya said, The River of Strange People just got stranger."

"And the pirates came up this river looking for the fountain of youth?"

Manny shoots Joyce another impressed look. "If you were on all my tours, I could just let you do the talking, while I sat back and drank beer. Which reminds me. You want a Belikin?"

Joyce can't help looking mildly shocked. "It's not even 8 a.m."

"The River of Strange People is a timeless place." Manny cracks open a can of Belikin, tilts his head back, and pours a deep guzzle of beer down his gullet.

Joyce leans forward. "Do you think there really is a fountain of youth, out near Lamanai?"

"More like a fountain of death. Almost all the pirates who came here died. So they stopped coming, and for awhile things were quiet on The River of Strange People, till the strangest of all strange people came."

"English gunrunners?" Joyce guesses.

"English *loggers*. The gunrunners came later, during the Maya war with Mexico."

"Why were the English loggers the strangest of all strange people?"

"Because to the Maya, money is unimportant. But to the English loggers, money was God."

"But money was important to the Spaniards and pirates, too – they were crazy for gold."

"True, and the Maya thought the Spaniards and the pirates were very strange, chasing a shiny metal that's not at all rare here, and has no value by itself. But the English loggers chased money in a much more diabolical fashion than just digging mines or plundering treasure ships."

"Diabolical? You mean, because the English loggers set up corporations?"

"No, because instead of just chasing gold directly, the English loggers destroyed another natural resource, trees, in enormous numbers, way out of proportion to what the Maya viewed as necessary. To the Maya, trees are a vital part of the sacred life cycle. Trees provide nests for birds and shade for animals and support for vines. They provide gum and resin, and sap, and their bark and leaves are highly prized medicines. Without trees, there would be no rain forest. So the Maya never cut down more trees than they absolutely need, locally, to build boats or houses or bridges, or clear fields for crops to feed themselves. But the English hacked down trees in staggering volumes, for no reason other than to accumulate money. To the Maya, that was very strange."

"Were there specific trees the English loggers cut down?"

"Logwood, for the dyes to put color into clothing, and mahogany, for rich people's furniture. Belize has the world's largest supply of logwood and mahogany. But those trees don't grow in stands, like many trees. Logwood and mahogany are interspersed all through the forest, so you have to seek 'em out, and cut 'em down, one tree at a time; and then drag 'em out, one log at a time. Which led to the other behavior of the English loggers the Maya found very strange."

"The use of organized work crews?" Joyce guesses.

"The use of slaves." Manny gestures at the dense forest along the riverbank. "Imagine the labor required to go in there and cut down the trees, and drag them to the riverbank, through all that dense jungle, and float them 80 miles down the river to the coast, and load them onto ships bound for England and America. If the loggers had paid fair value for all that labor, the price of dining room tables would've risen sky-high in London and New York. But by forcing African slaves to do it for free, they made some serious fortunes."

"Why'd the loggers use African slaves? I saw a movie where there were slave catchers in Central America, hunting Indians with nets."

"*In the beginning* there were slave-catchers in the Yucatan. But they didn't last long, because the Maya were too fierce to be made slaves of."

"But didn't the ancient Maya make slaves of other Maya?"

"Yes, back in the distant past. But by the time the Europeans came, the Maya had stopped slavery, as an inhuman practice. So they were appalled when first the Spanish, and then the British, tried to make slaves of the Maya."

"But if the Maya could make slaves of each other, why couldn't the English make slaves of the Maya, too?"

Manny gazes at Joyce for several seconds, and then smiles. "You're the first person who's ever asked me that. It's a great question. And the truth is, I don't know the answer. Maybe only the Maya can intimidate other Maya enough to make slaves of them. I don't know. All I know is, the Maya had slavery here once; but they simply would not allow the Spanish or the English to make them slaves. Thousands of Maya starved to death in caves, rather than submit to slavery. So finally the British resorted to buying African slaves and shipping them over here. The Africans were fierce, too, but they were so far from their homes, they lost the will to resist which the Maya, so much closer to their homes, never lost. Which is why the majority population in Belize today is black."

"Are you a school teacher, Manny?"

"No. I left school in fourth grade, when I became a boatman."

"How do you know so much history?"

"I just listen to all the tour guides who come out here, spouting their facts."

"But I bet they don't tell it quite like you do."

"I do put a little native spin on it," Manny knocks back more beer. "I hope you don't mind."

"Not at all. If my teachers'd been half as good as you, I might've majored in history."

"What did you major in?"

"Boys." Joyce lights up a cigarette. "And parties. That's where I got this bad habit."

"You're trying to quit?"

Joyce jerks her head up, surprised. "Yeah – how could you tell?"

"The way you tried not to look when I rolled mine."

"I'm glad my boss doesn't notice as much as you." Joyce exhales deeply, enjoying her smoke. "So, I meant to ask: you said the pirates stopped coming up The River of Strange People, because of the curse they thought the Maya shaman put on them. But what happened to them? I mean, where were the pirates when the loggers came to Belize?"

"The pirates *were* the first loggers." Manny knocks back another stiff belt of Belikin. "That's how Belize got started. The Kings of Britain and Spain made a deal to end piracy. Spain gave Britain Belize, with its vast forests of logwood and mahogany, in exchange for Britain agreeing to get serious about stopping piracy. That way, Spainish treasure ships from South America could get through to Spain without being robbed; while Britain got a Central American port, and the logging business. That's how Belize ended up being the only English-speaking country south of Florida."

"But how'd the British stop piracy?"

"The British were much better sailors than the Spanish. Most of the pirates were former British sailors anyway, so the Royal Navy knew all the pirates' tricks. Plus the Royal Navy was smart, and used a carrot-and-stick approach. First, they hunted the pirates hard, to remind them how much better the Royal Navy was than the Spanish Navy at hunting pirates; and then they offered the pirates a full pardon, if they'd come to Belize and work as loggers. Most of the pirates saw the handwriting on the wall, took the pardon and the jobs, and that was the end of piracy."

"But eventually the English loggers replaced the pirates with slaves, because of the cost?"

"The cost, yes, and also the ex-pirates were an unruly lot. They were used to drinking and fighting all day, which is not the most efficient way to extract timber from the forest. Eventually the corporate owners decided using ex-pirates as loggers just wasn't going to work."

"Did the corporate owners ever try to make slaves of the ex-pirates?" Joyce asks.

Manny snorts. "Naw. If you're going to make someone a slave, you don't want him to look too much like you. You might have bad dreams."

Joyce blushes, embarrassed by the naivete of her question, now that she thinks about it. "So where'd the ex-pirates go, after the loggers brought in the African slaves?"

"The ex-pirates found work they were better suited for, on ships or in taverns. Today, their descendants are government bureaucrats. In fact, if you look around Belize today, you'll see how history still rules our lives. The poorest people in Belize are the descendants of the African slaves. In the middle are people like me, part Maya, part Spanish. And at the top of the food chain are the descendants of the Spanish and the English – and the pirates – who still get all the best jobs."

"What about the full-blooded Maya?" Joyce asks.

"They're still here, too, but you have to look very hard to find them. The true Maya want nothing to do with our modern world, because they think the rest of us are so mad with greed for money, and lust for new drugs and toys, we long ago forgot what makes life worth living."

"What would the true Maya say makes life worth living?"

Manny takes his time before answering. "Love, I suppose."

They lapse into easy silence, watching the rain forest whiz by Manny's speeding launch.

Speaking of love, Joyce returns to thinking about Ron Graham. Maybe she'll play a little dumb at first, while getting Ron to tell her what he knows about the *Lamanai Codex*, the pirates, and the fountain of youth rumors. Then she'll hope Ron is the man of her romantic dreams.

Yeah, right. Fat chance of that.

Abruptly Manny cuts the engine to a slow speed, as the New River widens into a lagoon. In the distant reeds along the eastern bank stands a lone fisherman, up to his waist in water, holding a spear high above his head. The fisherman peers into the river, and then hurls his spear down. A moment later he pulls the primitive weapon out of the water, a wriggling fish speared on its tip.

"Maya," Manny says. "From Indian Church Village. Fishing the old way."

With the engine still running slow, Manny veers away from the Maya fisherman, pointing his launch at a dock in front of a small break in the jungle on the western bank. Across the green lagoon they glide, staring at the tops of three ancient Maya temples above the dense rain forest.

"Twelve hundred years ago," Manny says, "instead of all this forest, you'd've seen a huge city there. Back then, 70,000 Maya lived at Lamanai. But one day, around 900 A.D., the Maya just walked away from Lamanai, into the forest. Just like the Maya walked away from all their cities, all across Central America."

"And no one knows why, right?"

"Some people think the Maya population got too big, and they couldn't feed everyone, because of droughts, or because they'd burnt down too much rain forest, making room for their cities and their maize fields. So they reverted to living in small groups and growing only as much food as they needed to eat, putting a natural brake on population growth."

"Do you think that's what happened?" Joyce asks.

"Maybe," Manny says. "That's one theory a lot of archeologists believe."

"What's another theory?"

"The other big theory is, the Maya priests lost their power over the regular people, because the priests tried to end the droughts by killing lots of regular people, and offering their bodies as human sacrifices to the Gods; but then, when the droughts continued, the regular people rebelled against the sacrifices, and started a civil war, and the cities became too dangerous to live in."

"But then why, once the civil war subsided, didn't the Maya just move back to their cities?"

Manny shrugs. "Good question. But if you go with the overpopulation theory, you might as well ask, since the ancient Maya were masters at managing the rain forest, and produced all the food they needed, even during droughts, why'd they suddenly lose the ability to feed their people?"

"So the bottom line is: no one knows why the Maya abandoned their cities?"

"Exactly," Manny says. "All I know is, something awesome must have happened, because their cities were amazing. Look at the Mask Temple there, to the right of the dock. Modern engineers couldn't build anything as symmetrical as that, till laser tools were invented in the 1980s. But the Mask Temple was built before Jesus was born, by people using stone tools. They didn't have the wheel, they didn't have horses, they didn't have metal tools – yet somehow they carried those huge boulders from quarries ten miles away, and carved them into perfect blocks, and aligned them so precisely with the stars that the whole temple worked like a modern observatory. You gotta wonder: *who were those people?*"

Chapter Eight
The Clutch of the Maya

Thursday 30 December 2010

Two hours after dawn, Kip Hunter and Gemma Murray finish a systematic canvassing of the two acres of ground immediately west of the Mask Temple.

"Face it," Kip says, "there're no cave entrances anywhere in this ground."

The lady nods. "Sorry. I really thought the icon would point the way."

"No worries. It was worth a try."

"I guess you can't find the fountain of youth unless you also have the *Lamanai Codex*."

Kip nods. The lady's probably right. He's going to have to go to London and tear the book out of the clutches of the old hermit who's hoarding it.

Kip takes the lady by the elbow and escorts her back to the Mask Temple. To discourage her from trying to run away, he gestures for her to climb first; and in order to prevent her from trying to shove or kick him off the steep temple steps, he stays five big steps behind her all the way up.

But when the lady reaches the roof comb at the top, she turns and looks down at Kip.

Kip doesn't like the purposeful glint in her eye.

"Don't even think about it," Kip says, watching her feet while pulling his Marine Corps knife.

"I'm not just going like a lamb to the slaughter," the lady says.

Kip stops, still three large steps from the top, and looks at her. "How many times I gotta tell you? I don't want to kill you or your boyfriend. I want to hire you."

"You offered to hire us," the lady says, "if we found the fountain. But we didn't find it."

As a gesture of good faith, Kip puts his knife back in its sheath on his hip, and throws his palms open wide. "I still want to hire you. We all need each other to find that damn fountain. Killing you would serve no purpose."

The lady doesn't respond. But she stays put while Kip slides sideway on the giant step. After he slides a safe distance from the lady, he climbs the last three big steps up to the roof comb.

"I still need to talk it over with Clive."

"Be my guest." Kip takes the lady by the elbow, and leads her to the interior steps, where he switches on his flashlight. "Ladies first."

The lady descends the winding two-hundred-foot staircase, with Kip staying close behind her, so his flashlight can light the way for both of them. At the bottom Gemma steps down to the earthen floor of the tomb first, with Kip almost right on her heels.

Kip shines his flashlight across the tomb at the stone sarcophagus.

And gets the shock of his life, when he sees no one lying on top of the sarcophagus.

Dr. Phelps is gone. The ropes Kip used to tie him onto the sarcophagus are gone, too.

Reflexively Kip reaches with his free hand for his pistol.

But he's too late.

A fist of stone – smelling, oddly, just like Desi's jasmine perfume – crashes against Kip's jaw. Blinding stars flash across Kip's vision, his body goes limp, and everything goes black.

* * *

In the faint light from the blonde kidnapper's flashlight, Clive Phelps watches Gemma Murray and the kidnapper step down from the interior staircase onto the tomb floor.

Across Clive's mouth, a short but powerful human hand prevents Clive from shouting any warning to Gemma, the wide squat thumb of the meaty hand digging deep into the masseter muscle above Clive's jawbone, while the last joints of the strong stubby fingers of the meaty hand do the same to the platysma tissues just above the other side of Clive's jaw. At the same time, the other hand of the half-naked Maya warrior standing behind Clive holds a long hunting knife tight against Clive's larynx, dissuading him from trying to slip out of the warrior's grasp. So all Clive can do is inhale the man's strong foresty scent, and watch the action at the doorway unfold.

With no apparent signal, the two Maya warriors crouching in wait at each side of the doorway to the stairs move at precisely the same instant. With astonishing speed and efficiency, one jumps the blonde kidnapper, while the other jumps Gemma.

Clive watches helplessly as the one jumping Gemma puts her in a tight headlock and, at virtually the same instant, kicks her legs out from under her, crashing to the ground on top of her. When Clive glances over to see how the blonde kidnapper is faring, he sees the kidnapper slump backwards against the tomb wall, slide down it, and land in a motionless heap on the floor, his head lolling to one side. So much for the tough-talking soldier of fortune.

Clive's satisfaction at seeing Gemma's would-be torturer knocked out cold is short-lived, however, because now they are all completely at the mercy of three Maya warriors in loin clothes, wielding primitive knives and spears. The warrior holding Clive pushes him forward until he is next to Gemma, and then forces Clive down to the floor beside her.

Since the only light in the tomb comes from the blonde kidnapper's flashlight, now lying on the floor with its beam pointing at the sarcophagus, Clive can't see much. But he can hear the Maya searching the kidnapper's clothing, and rustling in his backpack; and he can hear the metallic clinking of the kidnapper's various weapons being collected.

The warrior holding Clive releases his grip on Clive's jaw and throat, and the warrior holding Gemma releases his headlock on her. Then the three Maya hold a short discussion in Mayan. Clive searches Gemma's eyes for a clue as to what's being said. At first she looks utterly terrified; but then her face relaxes, and she signals to Clive that it will be alright.

One of the Maya drags the still-unconscious blonde kidnapper over and leans his back against the backs of Clive and Gemma. Arranging the three seated whites in a circle on the floor, their backs to each other, their legs splayed out like six spokes of a wheel, the Maya use the ropes, which they removed from Clive a half hour ago, to tie all three whites up, and to each other.

And then, as silent as they came, the Maya are gone.

"What were they saying?" Clive asks Gemma.

"One of them wanted to kill us. But the other two talked him out of it, saying we'd given no offense. The one who wanted to kill us was angry with our kidnapper here, because evidently he stole that two-headed icon from them. But the other two said they've got it back now, and there's no benefit to having the Belize police hunting them for murder."

"Did they say anything else?"

"Along with the icon they found an amulet in his pack, like the one Canek gave me, but unbroken. I got the feeling they were a little more offended by the theft of the amulet than the icon, because evidently our kidnapper yanked it off the throat of one of the dead Maya in this tomb. But in the end, they decided to let him live."

"Well, you promised me an adventure, dear – but next time, let's just go to Altun Ha."

Gemma laughs, but almost at once, her laughter turns to sobbing. "Oh my God, Clive, I was sure we were going to die."

"We're not out of the woods yet. When this bastard wakes up, we'll still have our hands full. Let's yell for help. We're close enough to the staircase, a passerby outside might hear us."

"Might be wise to wait ten minutes, to be sure the Maya are long gone. If they hear us yelling, they might reconsider their decision to let us live."

"Good thought. So – did you find the fountain of youth?"

"No luck. It looked like the sunlight was pointing right at a cave entrance, but when we got down there, we couldn't find any hole in the ground. We scoured the whole area for – well, you know, the whole time after the sun came up. You must have been dying from worry down here."

"I'm alright. Though this ammonia's making me sick. And I'm afraid my body will soon insist on ignoring my social training regarding the elimination of bodily wastes."

"Don't worry," Gem says. "I wet my pants when that warrior jumped me. I'm lucky I didn't have a heart attack – God, he just leaped out of the dark, like a jaguar."

"They were impressive. But how come they all smelled so strongly of – I don't know what it was, exactly – jasmine, or tree bark, or—"

"There were three different scents," Gemma says. "One was jasmine, one was orrisroot, and I couldn't place the third. The original purpose of the scents was so, when hunting in the forest, the Maya's quarry couldn't smell humans approaching, because their body odors were disguised by the various strong natural scents. But long ago the Maya began using these scents in warfare as well as in hunting, with each individual warrior selecting the scent he'll use his entire life, and then putting that scent on before every battle, as ritualistically as he puts on his war paint."

"So that's why the fist that cold-cocked me smelled sweeter than any whore I ever knew?" the blonde kidnapper mumbles, evidently awake now.

Clive grinds his teeth in hatred of this odious bastard.

The kidnapper groans. "Man, that guy's fist was hard as cement. My head's gonna ache for a week."

Clive starts to say 'good', but decides he doesn't want to engage the bastard at all.

The kidnapper scrunches his hips back-and-forth a few times, jostling Clive and Gemma.

"Well, this sure is cozy, ain't it?" the kidnapper says.

Clive cranes his neck as far sideways as he can, in order to catch Gemma's eye and shake his head no, signaling for her not to converse with the bastard.

"Hey, don't be givin' me the silent treatment," the kidnapper says. "I already went through this with your girlfriend outside. I know we got off on the wrong foot, but it's time we join forces."

Clive can't control himself any longer. "Like hell, you bastard. When help comes, we shall ask them to bring a squad of police for you, before they release us."

"A whole squad might be overkill. Since those Maya took my knife and gun, I'm like Samson without his hair. God, I loved that gun – and I've had that knife for 20 years."

"You want me to cry for you – the man who threatened to torture Gemma?"

"Will you two get over that? Please. That was yesterday. Today is a brand new game, with brand new realities, and brand new rules. Like Heraclitus said, 'all things are constantly in flux'."

"Actually," Clive says pedantically, "what Heraclitus said was, 'all things are a-flowing'."

"Same diff, Doc. Look, here's the score, in today's ballgame. The fountain of youth is out here somewhere. And we're awful damn close to finding it. That's why the Maya came back to get the icon, and I assume the amulets, too. They don't want us finding the fountain of youth."

"Why should they care who finds the fountain of youth?" Clive asks.

"Well, I'm not the Maya expert here," the kidnapper says. "What d'you think, Dr. Murray?"

"I think it's impolite for you to talk to us," Gemma says, "without giving us your name."

"Oh, sorry. Excuse my manners. My name's Kip Hunter. Glad to meet you both."

"You'll excuse me if I'm not at all glad to make your acquaintance," Clive says.

"I will forgive you, yes," Kip says. "Because if I were in your shoes, Dr. Phelps, I'd probably feel the same way. But we gotta move forward here. So, Dr. Murray, why d'you think the Maya don't want us finding the fountain of youth?"

"I have no idea," Gemma says.

"Maybe," Kip says, "it's a sacred place to them. Or it's like, the one great treasure the Spanish and the British never managed to take from them. Though I guess the pirates got at it."

"If it's truly in a cave," Gemma says, "then it would make sense that it's a sacred place to the Maya. For they see all caves as passageways to Xibalba."

"Gem, I'd rather we not converse at all with this bastard," Clive says.

"Hey, Dr. Phelps, c'mon now, seriously! You gotta lighten up. We need to join forces."

"Over my dead body."

"Well, that's an ironic way of putting it."

"Not at all," Clive says. "If the Maya hadn't shown up and thwarted your plans, I'm sure you'd be gloating over my dead body right now. And Gem's, too."

"Not so!" Kip says. "If I'd wanted to kill you, I'd've cut your girlfriend's throat outside, and then come down here to finish you off. But I came back down here in peace, to make you an offer."

"Bollocks."

"It's true, Clive," Gemma says. "He did make me an offer. I said I'd have to discuss it with you, of course. But, ah, I really think you should hear him out."

Something urgent in Gemma's voice catches Clive's attention. He can't begin to guess what it is. "Why? He has no leverage over us anymore. Either we'll all starve to death in this tomb or, more likely, we'll be rescued by employees of Captain Gonzalez or Dr. Rivera or Dr. Graham. And once we're rescued, this yob'll spend a good many years behind bars, I'd imagine."

"Even behind bars, I'm dangerous, Clive," Kip says. "You have a son. He has a terrible disease, which I'm truly sorry about, and he has an address, which I know. And just as I'm sure you have colleagues you can count on, when you most need help, I, too, have colleagues I can count on, even when I'm behind my bars. And my colleagues are not so, ah, collegial as yours. So, can we cut the crap here, and get to the chase? I want to make you and Dr. Murray a serious offer."

* * *

"Be careful," Manuel Santoro says, as he ties his launch up at the Lamanai dock.

"Of the jaguars?" Joyce Kerr asks.

"Of the pirates."

Joyce smiles, assuming this is one of Manny's deadpan jokes, and gives him a nice tip. But then she catches the warning in his eyes. "I thought the pirates all turned into bureaucrats."

"The old ones did." Manny guides Joyce onto the Lamanai dock. "It's the *modern* pirates you gotta watch out for." Manny sits back and cracks open a Belikin, while Joyce shakes hands with Ron Graham, waiting for her on the dock. Joyce points quizzically at a brand new sign, in three languages, whose English part says: 'Danger. Lagoon Water Contaminated. Do Not Drink'.

"We're just being careful," Ron says. "We're not sure if the water's bad or not."

For a moment they stand in awkward silence, sizing each other up. Ron's hard to read, but Joyce is pretty sure her tight little tank top is having its intended effect, as Ron gawks at her boobs while she clips on the name badge he says she has to wear, since the site is officially closed. On the other hand, Joyce's first impression of Ron is that he isn't making her heart miss any beats.

"So can we start my tour at the temple with the big scary face on its side?" Joyce asks.

"You mean, the Mask Temple?"

"I'm not sure what its official name is," Joyce says. "It's the temple with a tomb inside, with some strange writing on the wall."

Ron cocks his head at Joyce. "Fiona Young told you about the writing on the wall?"

"No, I read about it."

"The only article ever published about the writing on the wall in the Mask Temple tomb was published ten years ago, in a journal so obscure, even archeologists only read it when they're having trouble sleeping. Since I wrote the article, I'd love to believe a Michigan paralegal read it—"

"Sorry," Joyce smiles, "but I didn't read that article of yours, Ron. My great-great-grandmother Kathleen wrote about the writing on the wall in her diary. Only she called the temple with the tomb 'Ozymandias's Temple', not the 'Mask Temple'."

"When was your great-great-grandmother here?"

"1868," Joyce says. "Kathleen and her husband discovered Lamanai. Or rather, according to Manny, *re*-discovered it, since Manny says the Spanish and the pirates got here first."

"A local chickel-gatherer *re*-discovered Lamanai," Ron says dourly. "In 1854."

Joyce is flummoxed. Bad enough to learn the Quinlans weren't the first whites to discover the lost city in the jungle. But they weren't even the first Victorians? "What's a chickel-gatherer?"

"A guy who traipses through the jungle with a pail, collecting the gum from chickel-trees. You've probably heard of Chiclets gum. It comes from Belize."

"So you're saying the Quinlans did not discover Lamanai?"

"I'm not saying anything, Joyce. *History* says it. The story of the local chickel-gatherer stumbling across Lamanai is on a story-board in our museum."

"But Roger Quinlan's in the British Museum," Joyce counters, "as the discoverer of Lamanai. They've still got plaster casts he made when he and Kathleen discovered Lamanai."

"History is riddled with errors. But I can tell you, by 1858, there was a sugar mill three miles inland from here. The workers all knew about Lamanai a decade before the Quinlans came."

Joyce winces, recalling Kathleen's journal entry about her surprise at meeting 'Randolph' from the sugar mill. Is it true? Were Roger and Kathleen just a couple of posers?

"I'm sorry, Joyce. I can see I've upset you. I didn't mean—"

"No, I prefer to know the truth. It's just unsettling to learn the family legend of the Quinlans discovering a lost city in the jungle, while seeking the fountain of youth, was a load of bull."

"Well, the Quinlans were definitely here. And since they were much better-connected back in London than the chickel-gatherer or the sugar mill workers, they got the credit, for a long time. But you know" – Ron looks down at the ground – "the Quinlans' daughter Persephone, and their grand-daughter Fiona Young, also, uh, stretched the truth from time to time. I'm sorry, but—"

"Don't apologize," Joyce says. "As I told you on the phone, I'm not a big fan of Fiona's. And though I never knew Persephone, I think she stole the *Lamanai Codex* from my great-grandfather."

"And you're going to sue Fiona to try to get it back?"

"I'd like to. A lawyer told me I have a good case. But I can't afford the legal fees."

"Why don't you contact some charitable foundations? I bet they'd be interested in paying the fees for a case like that, aimed at bringing a great treasure of the past to light."

"OK, thanks – I'll try that. But for now, since I'm here, can we go to the Mask Temple first?"

For no apparent reason, Ron's lips start trembling. "Ah, we'll have to make the Mask Temple the last stop, I'm afraid. We've got some, ah, clean-up activities going on there right now."

"Clean-up from what?"

"I'm not allowed to say."

Joyce can scarcely conceal her disappointment. Not only is Ron far more dour and phlegmatic than he was in her fantasies, but he is so distant, he won't even share secrets with her.

So much for the magic power of tight tank tops. Or is Joyce just getting old?

"Well, Ron, what'd I'd like to do today, on our 'tour', is look for the fountain of youth."

"We can do that. Any particular place you want to search?"

"Well, you get the feeling from Kathleen Quinlan's diary that it was somewhere near one of the temples. And it's in a cave."

"There are no caves at Lamanai."

"It's got a hidden entrance," Joyce persists, "with a secret underground river."

Ron rolls his eyes. "Joyce. What we archeologists do for a living is, we map every square foot of a site. In my seven years living at Lamanai, there isn't a single rock in the ten square miles of this site that my team didn't overturn at least twice to see what's under it. We looked specifically for caves, because they're incredibly rich sites for artifacts from all eras. The ancient Maya saw caves as the portals to Xibalba, the underworld, so they performed sacrificial rites in them; and the colonial Maya called caves 'The Grottoes of the Plain', and starved to death in them rather than submit to enslavement. Sadly, there just aren't any caves at Lamanai."

"But India Reynolds—" Joyce stops herself, unsure if she wants to get into this with Ron.

"Yes, India Reynolds painted the fountain of youth in a cave, and both groups of pirates who came here said the fountain was in a cave. That's part of why we looked so hard for caves. There just aren't any caves here, Joyce. I'm sorry."

Recalling the passing reference in Kathleen's diary to a terrible fire India Reynolds said she witnessed in her youth, in which a ship full of slaves perished, Joyce asks Ron if any such fire was ever recorded in the history of Belize.

"That fire did occur, in 1724." Ron arches a suspicious eyebrow. "But since the only document describing that fire is a Royal Naval memo in the Jamaican colonial archives, how do you know about it?"

Joyce gives Ron a warm smile. "I've been looking into India Reynolds' life, trying to figure out if she lived to be 158 years old. I know it sounds crazy, but I really think she did."

"I think she did, too," Ron says.

"You do? Why?"

"Because her name crops up in too many different places, in different centuries, for it to be a coincidence."

"Maybe there was more than one 'India Reynolds' – a daughter or grand-daughter?"

Ron shakes his head no. "A teen miscarriage left India Reynolds barren. And it's too unusual a name for two different women with that name to have so many connections to the fountain of youth. Consider these facts. A 17-year-old India Shaw was abducted by the pirate Damien Reynolds in 1724, to help him hunt for the fountain of youth – with the *Lamanai Codex* as their map. Six months later, India sailed back to Belize alone, in Reynolds' pirate ship; and after seeing the fire you mentioned consume the wharf and the slave ship, India miscarried, was declared barren, and sailed for London, under the name 'India Reynolds', where she was seen on London Bridge in 1726 by one of Reynolds' former pirates."

"How do you know all that?" Joyce asks, arching a suspicious eyebrow of her own.

"I read old pirate stories," Ron says. "Then, 130 years later, a woman in London named 'India Reynolds', using the *nom de paintbrush* Damien Reynolds, paints a picture called *The Fountain of Youth*, depicting pirates and a woman discovering the fountain in an underground river, with a Maya shaman using the *Lamanai Codex* to perform a ritual involving injections of Maya herbs and cinnabar – all as the pirate stories described it. Now that may not be 'proof' that'd stand up in a court of law. But it's enough to persuade me India Reynolds lived to be 158, by drinking from the fountain of youth she discovered with the aid of the codex Fiona Young is hoarding."

"I went to see that painting yesterday," Joyce says. "There's a corner that was destroyed. Have you ever seen a photograph of what was in that part of the painting, before—"

"No. No one has. I looked into that, hard."

"Do you know where that underground river in the painting is?"

"No. No one knows."

"Where could I find those old pirate tales you mentioned?"

From his backpack Ron pulls out a sheaf of loose papers, and hands them to Joyce. "These are copies of the pertinent chapters."

"Thank you." Joyce gives Ron her most inviting smile. "But for now, even though I know you say there are no caves here, could you humor me anyway, and take me on a tour of the temples here, looking for the fountain of youth? I'm sure I'll never get here again – and I'd kick myself if I didn't at least *try* to find Roger and Kathleen's fountain."

Ron agrees. They set off on a brisk hike through the rain forest.

Joyce is immediately cowed by the overwhelming grandeur and wild profusion of the rain forest. Ron points out the enormous magueys and corpulent cedars, mammoth ceibas and giant ramons and huge wild figs; yet there are dozens of other trees he doesn't name, but which still amaze Joyce with their immensity. And beneath all these towering trees are hugely oversized plants which Ron identifies as guayacans and rubber plants, and monsteras and capulins ripe with cherries, with fat bromeliads and termite nests hanging from the trunks, and monkey ladder vines and strangler figs climbing all over everything. Taken altogether, these trees and plants and vines, with their huge leaves, create a heavy veil that screens out most of the sunlight, leaving Joyce feeling smaller and more vulnerable – yet also more alive – than she's ever felt in all her life.

And the noise! Up in the trees Joyce hears kinkajous and macaws and mocking birds – plus dozens of other birds Joyce can't identify – chattering, much louder than she ever heard them at the Detroit Zoo. Rubber-necking through the jungle, trying to see the birds, Joyce keeps stumbling on the gigantic curving tree roots protruding across the rocky trail – till she finally learns the only way to walk in the rain forest without risking a broken ankle is the way Ron Graham walks: head down, eyes fixed always on the path.

But even with her head down on the path, Joyce remains amazed at the fecundity of the rain forest. Snakes and lizards rustle in the dirt; and unseen mammals crash about in the bushes. Into the dense thickets along the trail Joyce peers, trying to discern what animals are crashing within; but then the shadowy thickets themselves distract Joyce with their morbid beauty – live plants growing right out of dead plants, before the dead ones even have time to rot away – and she feels, amid the vegetable excess of the jungle, what a thin line it is that separates the wild splendor of existence from the profound darkness that awaits all living things.

From somewhere above comes a very loud, low-pitched scratching sound, like a child imitating a creaky door opening very s-l-o-w-l-y in a haunted house.

"What's that?" Joyce asks.

"Howler monkey," Ron says.

"No!" Joyce protests. "Monkeys don't sound like that!"

"Howlers do," Ron says. "They're bigger than the monkeys in American zoos."

Joyce considers asking Ron to slow down the pace of the tour, for the sake of her short legs and city feet, but decides the faster they hike, the sooner they'll get to the Mask Temple, which is what she really wants to see.

"This is the Stela Temple," Ron announces. "It's the only excavated temple, besides the Mask Temple, where there's lots of jungle nearby which might conceivably hide a cave. The other two temples are on vast expanses of cleared ground."

The Stela Temple was named for its stone stela, inscribed with 1500-year-old Mayan glyphs, which are in better shape than any 200-year-old tombstone Joyce ever saw in Michigan. The Maya, as Fiona taught Joyce back when they were close, were one of only three civilizations in history to independently invent writing, and they clearly carved their stelae with the intention of keeping their history – the only records of their earthly lives, besides their codices – alive forever.

But Joyce shakes her head at the strange writing itself. Just as she felt that awful day in Ann Arbor in 1990, when she stole a glimpse at Fiona's translation of the *Lamanai Codex*, Joyce finds herself marveling at how scholars like Fiona ever made sense of the cramped Mayan pictograms, with the evil grinning faces and twisted misshapen bodies, all tangled together as chaotically as the forest vines all around Joyce now. More fundamentally, how did scholars like Fiona ever decide this was writing at all? To Joyce, the carvings on the stela look as random as the doodling of a bored high school kid high on pot.

"We're lucky this stone survived," Ron says. "Most stelae were destroyed."

"Who destroyed them?" Joyce asks.

"Rival Maya city-states," Ron says. "The ancient Maya did not fear death, but what they did fear, at least as darkly as we fear death, was being forgotten. So when Maya warriors defeated a bitter enemy, the ultimate act of vengeance was not to drag the vanquished through the dust, like the Romans did; nor even to sacrifice the vanquished to the Gods, like the Aztecs did – and like the Maya did, too. But for the Maya, the real insult was, before the sacrifice, in full view of the vanquished, the victorious Maya would smash to bits any carved stelae like this, which held all the glyphs recording the lives and deeds of the vanquished and their ancestors, so all memory of their lives and deeds would be erased from the earth. For how could later generations honor, worship and feed those whose lives had been erased and forgotten?"

"An insult that makes it hard on archeologists like you?" Joyce asks.

"You're not kidding," Ron says.

They wander around the jungle near the Stela Temple awhile, with Joyce haphazardly poking at the ground, hunting for the fountain of youth. But Joyce finds no hidden cave entrances.

Next Ron takes Joyce to the Jaguar Temple, and the High Temple; but, as he warned, the ground round these temples is so thoroughly cleared, there's no point in searching for caves. Then they go the Ball Court, where Ron describes the pok-a-tok the Maya played to the death, and tells Joyce about the cinnabar Ron found stashed beneath the stone disk in the center of the Ball Court.

In the distance towards the river, Joyce sees one more temple. "Is that the Mask Temple?"

"Yes. But before we go there, Joyce, can I ask you: would you like to go to dinner tonight?"

What the hell. Joyce says yes. They arrange to meet in the Jolly Roger lobby at 7 tonight. Ron isn't the dream man Joyce fantasized about before they met, but he's nice enough for dinner.

Out of nowhere, two uniformed Belize policemen march by. The cops nod at Ron, and then none-too-subtlely check out Joyce's tight tank top. Ron nods back.

"What're the cops here for?" Joyce asks. "Patrolling for pirates?"

Ron's lips start trembling again. "This is highly confidential. For a few more days, anyway. There were 17 deaths here last week."

Ron fills Joyce in on the general facts about the deaths, including the cancer diagnosis, the fact that most of the dead were found in the Mask Temple, and the connection he and 'a few others' are making between this modern mass death scene and the mass pirate deaths centuries ago. Then he leads her to the Mask Temple, where Joyce sees, on the temple's west face, the fearsome 'mask' that spooked Kathleen Quinlan, along with other glyphic writing.

Ron points at a stone engraving of a serpent near the big Mask. "This is the Maya Creator God, Itzamna. Unlike Christianity, the serpent was not an evil symbol for the ancient Maya."

"He's eating his own tail," Joyce says, recalling Eliot's lecture. "The *ourobouros*?"

"Precisely!" Ron looks impressed. "Almost all religions have a version of the *ourobouros*."

"Even Christianity?" Joyce asks, dubiously.

"Sure," Ron says. "Think of the God of Revelation, said to be both the Alpha and the Omega, the beginning and the end. That's the *ourobouros* ideal – a self-sustaining creator like Itzamna, who embodies the circularity of all life and all Time."

Joyce is distracted by a melancholy cry from somewhere above. "Is that an oil bird?"

Ron shrugs. "I'm afraid I don't know my tropical bird calls like I should."

"I'd swear that's an oil bird," Joyce says. "But of course, it can't be."

"Why not?"

"Oil birds are nocturnal. Although" – Joyce gives Ron a lively smile – "oil birds always spend their days *in caves*. You can look it up."

Ron throws his hands up in surrender. "You're too pretty to argue with, Joyce. I give in. There must be a cave somewhere near here, where oil birds nest and the fountain of youth spews like a geyser. I just wish I knew where it was, so I could impress you by finding it for you."

Joyce locks eyes with Ron. He's not great-looking, with his receding hairline and big Dumbo ears. But she's warming up to him. His eyes are even kinder and more intelligent than in his internet photo – and he's got a strong jaw, and no rings on his fingers. And though he doesn't know his bird calls – which Joyce only knows because Fiona taught her – still, Ron's very much in tune with nature. Maybe for once Joyce should go with the plain, good-hearted man, instead of the cocky stud who usually wins her heart – and leaves her feeling as bereft as Michael Clark did.

From close by come more melancholy cries. But these are not the cries of oil birds.

To Joyce's shock, they're human voices, crying for help.

Ron breaks into a run. Joyce follows.

They run around to the east side of the Mask Temple, by the river, where Ron pulls on the handle of a ground-level door – a door Joyce realizes must be the one Roger Quinlan cut in the temple wall. The door is locked, but the sound of Ron pulling on the handle provokes further cries for help, muffled by the thick stones of the Mask Temple, but unmistakeably human.

Ron clambers up the temple's steep stone steps, Joyce following. Up top, as Joyce gasps for air, Ron pulls out a flashlight, and then leads Joyce back down the interior steps to a tomb at the temple's base, where they find two men and a woman tied together, screaming for help.

Ron pulls out a knife, and cuts the ropes, setting all three captives free.

In the dim light of Ron's flashlight, Joyce sees that one man is tall, blonde, 40-something and ruggedly handsome; the other man is short, dark, 30-something and movie-star handsome; and the brunette woman with them is both taller and younger than Joyce.

"Clive! Gemma!" Ron exclaims. "I thought you left Lamanai on an emergency."

"That was a note three Maya warriors forced them to write," the blonde man says, locking eyes with Ron. "Thank God you came along to save us, Ron." He turns to Joyce. "You too, ma'am."

Joyce nods, but her head is spinning. *Maya warriors? In the 21st century?*

"Are you all – alright?" Ron asks.

"We could use a bath," the movie star, whom Joyce infers is 'Clive', answers.

"We're all a little traumatized," the blonde man adds, "from being in the clutch of the Maya. But I'm the only one they hit, and I'm fine. But hey, Ron – you gotta get the cops after these three guys, pronto. They stole the two-headed icon."

Ron locks eyes with the blonde man, and then with the other two. Joyce can't put her finger on it, but there's something *very* strange in the air. The dynamic between these four people is way off. They all seem more nervous than relieved about being rescued, except the blonde man.

"I'll go get Captain Gonzalez," Ron says, looking deferentially at the blonde man. "He'll want statements from all of you, of course ..."

"No problem," the blonde man says, "as long as he sends a posse out after those Maya warriors right away. They've only got about a two-hour headstart. Ron, we need that icon back."

Ron's lips tremble. But he nods acquiescence, and heads for the door. The others follow.

Outside, the three captives squint in the bright sunlight.

"Why don't Gem and I go get Gonzalez?" Clive suggests. "We need to clean up, anyway."

Ron darts a worried look at the blonde man. But the blonde man nods easy approval of the change in plan. So Clive and Gemma run off to fetch Captain Gonzalez.

The blonde man turns his attention to Joyce. "I'm Kip Hunter, assistant to Dr. Murray – the lady scholar you just met. And you are?"

"Oh, sorry," Ron says. "This is Joyce Kerr."

"What brings you out to a closed archeological site?" Kip asks Joyce.

"I invited Joyce to come out here today," Ron answers for Joyce.

"How'd you manage to get yourself *invited* to a closed archeological site?" Kip asks Joyce.

"Her ancestors were among the first explorers to find Lamanai," Ron answers for Joyce.

"No shit." Kip gives Joyce a very cocky grin. "You come from a line of pirates?"

Joyce's heart skips a beat. "You're the one who looks like a pirate." She smiles flirtatiously.

"I'll take that as a compliment," Kip says, smiling back.

"Her cousin is Fiona Young, the scholar who's been hoarding the *Lamanai Codex*," Ron interjects. "Miss Kerr may have a superior legal claim to ownership of the codex."

Kip turns and arches an eyebrow at Ron. "That's very interesting. But I'm trying to strike up a conversation with this pretty lady here, and you are definitely obstructing me. Stand down, man!"

Ron sulks, but complies.

Kip turns back to Joyce. "You got plans for New Year's Eve?"

CHAPTER NINE

The Clutch of the Pyrate

Friday 31 December 2010

Kip Hunter sits at his favorite corner table at the Beachcomber in San Pedro, frowning. "Ron, there are no 'refunds' in the treasure-hunting business."

"Why not? I paid you to get me the icon. You didn't get me the icon."

"Our deal was, you pay me half down, the other half on delivery. You paid half down, and I procured the icon. The only reason I failed to deliver it to you is your maniacal Maya buddies stole it from me before I could deliver it to you. So I'd say we're all square here."

"All square? I'm out $25,000!"

"And I'm out my two best mercs. Plus, I've still got a serious risk of problems down the line with Johnny Law, if they connect me to all these deaths. I'd say 25K barely covers my injuries."

"This isn't a personal injury case. It's a contract. We had a deal."

"I'd like to see the court that would enforce this 'contract' of ours, Ron."

Ron glares across the table at Kip. "I rue the day I met you."

"You been readin' my mail? That's exactly what my ex always used to say."

"You'll get yours one day, Kip Hunter."

"Won't we all? But in the meantime, tell me about the girl. How'd your date go last night?"

"I don't wanna talk about it."

"You fuck her?"

Ron splutters and fumes.

"Bodacious rack like that, and you didn't fuck her? Jesus, Ron, life is too short to let quality pussy like that pass you by."

"I thought the goal here was to use Joyce to get the codex," Ron says, "not just to use her to satisfy the fleeting desire of the moment."

"Oh, *touché*! You got me there. So'd you recruit her to join our ever-growing team?"

"She won't join unless we pay her legal fees to sue her cousin."

"Fine. I assume you told her we'll pay."

"I did not. She says she needs at least $200,000 to cover the legal fees."

"*Two hundred grand?* Who's she hiring to represent her? Johnny fuckin' Cochrane?"

"She says that's the minimum a civil lawsuit costs these days, even in a small town like Ann Arbor. And because Fiona Young lives in London, it could cost more. Since I'm still awaiting repayment of the $25,000 I foolishly fronted you, I did *not* offer to cover Joyce's legal fees."

"Remind me again why we gotta sue this old lady in London. Why can't we just break into her place and steal the damn book?"

"Joyce says the old lady lives in a flat that's more secure than Fort Knox."

"Oh, c'mon. What's Joyce know about home security?"

Ron gets a pissy look. "Joyce says there's a guard at the front door of the building, four police locks on Fiona's only door, and her only windows are up at the 5th story, opening straight onto the River Thames, with a sheer wall of bricks up to them and spotlights from Tower Bridge shining straight at those windows, 24/7. Now I suppose if you're Spider Man, this would be no problem, because you could make yourself invisible, swim down the river, scale the five-story wall with your spider-feet, and break into the flat. But for mere mortals, that place sounds impregnable."

Kip waggles his hand like a teeter-totter. "No place is impregnable. But I agree, that sounds like an unusually challenging target for a break-in. So – let's see. You don't have two hundred large to pay for Joyce's lawsuit. I sure as shit don't have that kind of scratch. What about our English friends – the good doctors. Can they help us here?"

Ron shrugs. "I didn't ask them. You seem to get along with Clive and Gemma better'n I do. Though God only knows how you managed that."

"What can I say?" Kip grins. "Once you get to know me, I'm a charmer."

* * *

At the Jolly Roger, the New Year's Eve mood is building early. The sun hasn't even set, but kids are splashing in the pool with increasing recklessness, and everyone at the bar is already three sheets to the wind. Except Clive Phelps, who's nursing his first and only Vodka tonic of the evening, while glaring at Kip Hunter, seated next to him at the bar.

"Gemma and I held up our end," Clive mutters. "We didn't breathe a word about the kidnapping, the torture threat, or the 24 hours you held us hostage in a dark tomb. Now it's time you held up your end, Mr. Hunter, and leave us the hell alone."

"No can do, comrade," Kip says. "There's still a play we gotta make."

"We're out of time," Clive says. "I have a news conference to attend in an hour. And then Gem and I are on a plane tomorrow morning."

"News conference? Why?"

"We've had a leak about the Lamanai deaths. Dr. Rivera needs me to verify it was cancer."

"You're not gonna tell the press about the fountain of youth and the pirates, though, right?"

Clive casts a highly irritated look at Kip. "We do *function*, Mr. Hunter, even when you're not right on the scene to write all our lines and coach us along, like you did back in the tomb."

"Okay, but I still gotta know, before you go, if you're serious about the fountain of youth."

"Serious? No," Clive lies. "Skeptical, yes. But not serious."

"Are you serious about saving your son?"

"I don't ever want to hear you mention my son again."

"Fine. Are you serious about conquering death?"

"It's my life's work."

Kip opens his hands wide. "Well, then, we're moving in the same direction."

"What do you want from me this time?"

"Two hundred thousand dollars."

"Now you're blackmailing me?"

"It's not for me, Clive."

"Who's it for?"

"Dude named Burns. The Johnny Cochrane of Michigan."

* * *

"Lisa, you shouldn't be calling me," Joyce Kerr says.

"I know."

"How'd you get my number here?"

"Mr. Burns gave it to me."

"I should've guessed." Joyce sighs. "David is such an enabler."

"Huh?"

"Never mind. I love you sweetie, with my whole heart, and I'm very glad to hear your voice. But this call'll show up on your father's phone bill, and then he'll accuse me of instigating it."

"I'll tell them it's not true."

"I know you will. But our judge never seems to listen to you. So what's up?"

"Nothing, Mommy. It's New Year's Eve, and I just wanted you to know I miss you."

"That's so sweet, Lisa. I miss you, too, darling. Are you okay?"

"I'm fine. Have you met a dashing pirate on the beach yet?"

Joyce laughs. "Maybe."

"Really?" Lisa squeals. "What's he like?"

"I have no idea. I just met him."

"Is he handsome and rich?"

"He's easy on the eyes. I haven't checked his bank account. But Lise, there're more important things to look for in a man than good looks and money."

"Like what?"

"Like whether he's strong and independent, and not just looking for a surrogate mother. And whether he appreciates you for your smarts and your passions, and not just your pretty face."

"I think tonight's gonna be the night, Mom! But don't forget to ask the Two Questions."

"Maybe. But I gotta go, sweetie. You do what your father tells you, okay?"

Joyce hangs up, and checks her look in the mirror. The little black dress she's wearing is perfect – at least, it'd be perfect on a woman half Joyce's age. But it doesn't look half bad on Joyce, either. She squints at the mirror, trying to detect any unsightly bulges. But she can't see any. One of the under-appreciated benefits of aging eyesight.

For a few minutes Joyce blow-dries her hair like a maniac, while regretting her penny-pinching decision not to splurge on a hairdresser this afternoon. Why won't the right side fluff up like the left? When she flips off the hairdryer, she hears the phone ringing again. It's David Burns.

"David – not a good move to give Lisa my number here."

"Why not? She seemed like she was really missing you."

"I told you – the Judge is all over me to avoid contact with her this week."

"It's not your fault if Lisa calls you."

"Michael'll claim I instigated it."

"And I'll say he's lying – after all, Lisa had to get your number from me."

Joyce sighs. Arguing with David is as pointless as arguing with Fiona – you can never win. "So what's up, David?"

"What'd you find out at the Belize Land Registry today?"

"The land's worth more than I thought," Joyce says. "About $600,000."

"Great!"

"But still not enough for me to hire you to sue Fiona on a contingent fee." Joyce puts a sharp edge in her tone, to discourage David from re-opening this painful argument. "Still, I found a few odd facts about the land that might interest you. From 1868 to 1909, title to that land was in both the names of Roger and Kathleen Quinlan – even though Roger died in 1868."

"That just means Kathleen didn't bother taking Roger's name off the title."

"For *forty-one years*?" Joyce says. "Okay, maybe. But then in November 1909, Persephone Quinlan claimed title, by filing a quitclaim deed with the Land Registry."

"Who signed the quitclaim?" David asks.

"Kathleen Quinlan – even though, by November 1909, *Kathleen'd been dead for two months*. And I'm no handwriting expert, but Kathleen's signature on that deed sure looked to me an awful lot like Persephone's signature, which was on the same document."

"Was the quitclaim deed back-dated to the summer of 1909?"

"No – that's what's so odd," Joyce says. "It's dated in November 1909. When Kathleen definitely had both feet in her grave."

"Fabulous!" David says. "This is exactly what I was hoping for! Clear evidence of blatant fraud. What happened when Persephone died?"

"That all looked pretty regular to me. Persephone quitclaimed the land to Fiona, before she died. Then Fiona filed the quitclaim deed."

"Which means Persephone learned from her mother's mistake," David says. "Kathleen figured her Will leaving everything to Persephone would be valid, so she didn't bother with a quitclaim deed. But after Persephone lost the Will contest to Lloyd, Persephone had to go down to Belize and file a fraudulent quitclaim deed to transfer the land from her dead mother to herself. So before Persephone died, she did it right, and quitclaimed the land to Fiona, just in case anything went wrong with *her* Will. But all that means is: Fiona's claim to the land is totally bogus."

"Well, I'm glad it's a good claim," Joyce says. "When I find a way to pay you, we'll file it."

"You can't wait that long, Joyce."

"Why not?"

"Because of a legal doctrine called 'waiver'. This is already a 101-year-old claim. The statute of limitations ran out decades ago. You get a short respite, because you just discovered the claim; but the clock is ticking on you, every day."

"How long do I have?"

"Officially, six months. But the reality is, the Judge who gets this case is going to be highly skeptical if we don't file within a few weeks of your discovery of the claim. There's another legal doctrine, called 'laches', and without going into all the gory details, we really need to file this case next week, to be on the safe side. Joyce, let's just file it – we can work out the fees later."

Joyce frowns. "I'm not going to do that, David. I'll find a way to pay you."

"How?"

"Ron Graham thinks a foundation might pay you to bring this case, in the public interest, to get the only unpublished Maya codex out of the hands of the hermit."

"Worth a try, I suppose. But most foundations make decisions with all the speed of a slow-melting glacier."

"We'll just have to try to get them to move faster," Joyce says, in a 'that's that' tone.

A pause ensues. "So how's your search for the fountain of youth going?"

Joyce replays David's words in her head, trying to detect any hint of sarcasm. Finding none, she fills David in on everything she's learned, including not only the Reynolds painting and the pirate stories and the recent cancer deaths and Ron Graham's belief that India Reynolds lived to be 158 and Ron's disappointing conviction that there are no caves at Lamanai, but also the other things Joyce learned yesterday after Kip asked her out for New Year's Eve, including Ron's translation of the writing on the wall behind the Mask Temple sarcophagus, and the disappointing fact that Ron says there is definitely no treasure in or under the sarcophagus, because the sarcophagus is definitely empty and an earth floor like the one in the Mask Temple tomb can't move on big rolling stones like the wood floor in the Maya tomb at Palenque did, when treasure was found in a big room under the floor there in 1948.

David makes one more pitch to file the case against Fiona on a contingent fee, Joyce rebuffs him, and they hang up. Then she walks downstairs. But unlike last night, when Ron Graham was dutifully waiting for her, tonight her date is nowhere in sight. So she sits down at the bar and, with a sigh, orders a Rum Collins. If only men were half as reliable as a Rum Collins.

A cigarette would be nice, too. Unfortunately the pack Joyce bought, in her moment of weakness, is long gone. But she's pretty sure she could bum a smoke from that sallow-faced guy sitting alone across the bar, in the loud Hawaiian shirt. He's a smoker, Joyce can tell. She knows she should have more willpower. But it's New Year's Eve, for Chrissake. If you can't fire up a good smoke on New Year's Eve, when can you? Joyce slips off her bar stool and, drink in hand, strolls over towards the sallow-faced guy.

But before she gets a chance to pop the question, a commotion on the beach distracts her. A huge shout goes up from several people, and there's a horse whinnying, and sand kicking up – and oh, shit. It's Joyce's date.

Kip Hunter dismounts, ties up his horse, and strides into the bar, like a middle-aged version of Kevin Costner in *Silverado*, shit-eating grin and all.

"Sorry I'm late, my lady." Kip bows theatrically. "I'll shoot that horse at dawn, if you like."

Joyce blushes when she sees everyone in the bar staring at them. For they do make quite the couple – the dashing horseman with his wind-blown blonde hair, and the pretty little lady in the hot black dress.

"You look fantastically gorgeous, my lady," Kip says. "Will you forgive me? Or must I shoot myself at dawn, too?"

Joyce laughs and shakes her head no. "Just get me a cigarette, you maniac, and I'll try to forget about all your other faults for a few minutes."

"A cigarette for the pretty lady!" Kip cries. "Surely someone here must—"

The man in the Hawaiian shirt hands a cigarette up to Joyce.

"Thank you sir!" Kip cries. "A gentleman and a scholar! Your generosity has earned you" – Kip pulls a ticket from his pocket – "free admission to the new Belize Pirate Museum, opening in San Pedro sometime this summer, when I get around to opening it. AAARGH there, matey!"

In what seems like a single motion, Kip drops the ticket on the sallow-faced man's table, slaps some money on the bar to pay for Joyce's Rum Collins, and leads Joyce back to his horse.

"What are we doing?" Joyce asks.

"We can't leave my horse here at the hotel," Kip says, all innocence.

"There's no way I'm getting up on that horse in this dress."

Kip gives Joyce a very slow, appreciative once-over, lingering briefly at the plunging neckline of her little black dress, but then cocking his head and intently studying the dress's very short hem. "No one at the bar's gonna complain."

"Not gonna happen."

"A pity." Kip smiles. "But the restaurant's close. We can walk."

Leading the clip-clopping horse, Kip walks with Joyce down the driveway of the Jolly Roger, out onto San Pedro's main drag, and then down a side street. In front of them the darkening sky is streaked red with the last few rays of the dying sunset.

"Do you always ride a horse around San Pedro?" Joyce asks.

"Naw. I was just trying to impress you."

"Well it worked – in all my life I've never had a man pick me up for a date on a horse. If you'd warned me, I'd'a worn jeans and hopped on with you."

"You like horses?" Kip asks.

"Love 'em. I worked on a farm for a year after college."

"No kidding? God – that must've been a blast."

"Not really," Joyce says. "Farmers get up awful damn early. Their chores are tedious. And they get no days off."

Kip smiles. "You're probably right – I just like the idea of working on a farm. But now I understand a little better why you're such a practical lass."

"You got the wrong girl. If I were a practical lass, would I be out on New Year's Eve with a dangerous treasure-hunter I just met – and his horse?"

"Who says I'm a 'treasure-hunter'? I'm Dr. Murray's assistant."

"No, you're not. Ron told me you're after the fountain of youth. Just like all of us."

Kip raises an eyebrow. "Sounds like you got more outta Ron than he got outta you."

"Was he supposed to get something outta me?"

"Everyone wants something outta you, honey."

Well, at least the man's honest. "What do *you* want outta me?"

"All I want from you, Joyce," Kip says, "is to take you horseback riding tomorrow."

"I have a plane to catch tomorrow morning."

Kip groans. "So I've only got this one night to show you the real Belize?"

"'Fraid so."

"Well then, we'd better get started." Kip stops and ties his horse to a fence outside a drab white clapboard house in a very poverty-stricken, ramshackle residential neighborhood.

"We're eating here?" Joyce tries to conceal her dismay.

"The Beachcomber," Kip says. "Best restaurant in Belize."

Inside, to Joyce's surprise, there really is a restaurant – and it's packed. The place has great energy, and Kip knows all the staff, and almost all the customers. After twenty minutes of Kip glad-handing everyone, they finally make it to their table, upstairs in the far corner of a balcony, overlooking a dark lagoon.

"This is quite the place," Joyce says.

"Too bad it's December. Any other time of year, you get great sunsets here. You'd love it."

Joyce stares into his eyes. She's only had one Rum Collins, but this guy's already going to her head. "You're right, I would," she hears herself mumble.

They look at the menus. Joyce orders a salmon steak.

"Would you consider trying their seafood chowder, too?" Kip asks.

"I don't usually eat that much," Joyce says.

"It's New Year's. I really think you'll like it."

Joyce smiles. "Okay."

Kip orders a surf'n'turf, and a bottle of wine.

"So – tell me about your daughter."

Joyce shows Kip a few pictures of Lisa.

"Looks like quite the live wire!" Kip says.

"Lisa's my pride and joy." Joyce smiles. "She tells me to ask all my dates Two Questions, to see if you're the right man for me."

"Shoot."

"If your house was burning down, and you could save only one thing, what would it be?"

"Well, I live above a warehouse, but if my warehouse was burning down, I'd save a jug full of water from the fountain of youth, to keep me young so I could romance you a very long time."

"Do you have a jug full of water from the fountain of youth?"

"Not yet. But I will, soon."

"Okay. Knowing Lisa, I'm pretty sure you'll get an A+ for that corny answer. Second question: if you could have a do-over for any one thing in your life, what would it be?"

"I'd've stayed married a little longer, so I could have a kid as fun as your Lisa."

Joyce laughs. "Were you a shameless brown-noser in school, too?"

"How else d'ya think I got through?"

And so it goes. The chowder comes, and it's delicious. Joyce thoroughly enjoys the conversation, as they kill two bottles of wine with dinner. Kip never ducks questions about himself, but he keeps Joyce talking about Lisa and herself most of the time – which is probably why she's liking the conversation so much. But what the hell, she's having more fun than she's had in years.

"So, Kip," Joyce says at last, "you're very charming. You ride up on a horse – late, but full of extravagant apologies. And you've certainly swept me off my feet here. But why? What do I really know about you?"

"Ah. The moment of truth. It's all downhill for me from here."

"Why? Do you have a criminal record?"

"No, but don't tell anyone, okay? I like having a dangerous rep."

"So why is it all downhill from here?" Joyce asks.

"Because I'm one of those guys who lacks substance."

"What a terrible thing to say about yourself."

"What a terrible thing to have to say about myself."

Joyce laughs. "C'mon. Tell me something. Who are you really, Kip? Where'd you grow up? How long were you married? That kind of stuff."

"Married for two years, before I was 22. Bad idea. No kids, which I used to think was a good thing, till I heard about your Lisa."

"And you're what now – 40?"

"You're too kind. I'm 45."

"Did I hear you say you grew up in Florida?"

"Key West – home of the last real pirates."

"What about the modern-day pirates in Somalia, in the news all the time?"

"Bah, those guys are just sea-bandits. No style, no grace, no sense of the wild freedom that comes from roaming the seven seas. Those guys never go more'n ten miles from Somalia – and all they ever hijack is oil tankers. What would a real pirate want with an oil tanker?"

"So what you like about the old pirates is their freedom?"

"Yeah – and they were much more democratic than everyone else back then. The rest of the world was still on the top-down military model, the captain gives the orders and everyone else obeys or dies; but the pirates, man, they had it all soused out. In the heat of battle, they let their captain run things, because in the heat of battle, you have to, in order to fight efficiently – but all other times the captain had to get the pirates' approval to do anything. I like that."

"But weren't they," Joyce hunts for a word not to offend, "a little violent?"

"Sure," Kip concedes, "but only because grinding poverty and senseless violence was the life that was handed to them, from the cradle to the grave."

"So tell me about the pirate museum you mentioned in the bar."

"Oh, I was just bullshitting that guy."

"But you gave him a ticket."

"That was a movie ticket from last month. Happened to be in my pocket."

"No!"

"'Fraid so. But in my meager defense, the pirate museum's been a dream o' mine for 20 years. Though like a lotta dreams, I doubt I'll ever make it happen."

"Why?"

"Why's it my dream? Or why won't it happen?"

"Both."

"Seems like a pirate museum'd be a real nice way to settle down a bit. You ever been to Mel Fisher's pirate museum in Key West?"

Joyce shakes her head no.

"Pity. Anyway, a friend o' mine runs a jungle lodge here in Belize, inland, and he loves it – but he can never get away. A museum you can close once in awhile, and take a vacation. And I do love the pirates."

"So why won't it happen?"

"Most things never do."

Joyce nods. She still doesn't know anything substantial about this wild character, but honestly, she hasn't met a man this exciting since she met Michael.

On the other hand, look at what a deadbeat Michael turned out to be.

Kip pays the bill. "Could I interest you in a walk on the beach?"

"Can I get another cigarette on the way?" Joyce asks.

"Absolutely, my lady." Kip bums another cigarette, this time from one of the few people in the restaurant he doesn't actually know by name.

"You're very good at spotting the smokers."

"I used to smoke," Kip says. "You can spot 'em a mile away."

"Did you spot me in the Mask Temple?"

"Immediately."

"How?"

"The way you kept fiddling with your hair. And you had a little rash on your arm – looked like maybe the patch didn't agree with you?"

Joyce laughs. "You're scary, Kip. You know stuff you shouldn't know."

"I'm not scary. I'm just plain scared."

"Why?"

"Because a man could fall in love with you, Joyce. Real easy."

"I'll bet you say that to all the girls," Joyce teases.

"I do," Kip smiles. "Only this time, I mean it."

Joyce gazes at him, wanting so much to believe him.

"You have the biggest, brownest eyes I've ever seen," Kip adds.

"Oh, c'mon! You probably say that to all the girls, too."

"I do."

"Only this time you mean it?"

"I do."

"How can I be sure?"

"I can't help you with that one, Joyce. You gotta trust your instincts."

Joyce gazes at him, wondering what it'd be like to kiss him.

"You probably think I asked you out because I knew you'd be going home tomorrow," Kip says. "A safe little vacation fling, with no complications."

"The thought did cross my mind."

"But you're wrong," Kip says. "I've reached the age where I'd like it to be so much more to you than an island fling."

Joyce gazes at him awhile. "I know I should say something – but I don't know what to say."

"Then don't say anything," Kip says. "Silence is golden."

He pays the bill, and they walk outside, away from the horse, down to the dark beach. The waves from the dark back channel lap quietly against the shore. Kip takes Joyce's hand, intertwining his fingers with hers. Then, a quarter mile down the beach, he stops, and folds her into his arms, and they kiss a long, long time.

Kip's a very good kisser. His tongue doesn't probe, like a surgical instrument; and he doesn't suck like a blowfish either. He just takes it easy, and slow, and his lips are very relaxed. He really seems to like kissing Joyce. And she likes kissing him, too. So they kiss a long time, alone on the dark strand.

Their bodies fit well together, too. He's tall, which is nice, and he hugs Joyce with a gentle pressure that makes her feel wanted, but not possessed or owned.

It's not at all bad, to be in the clutch of this latter-day pirate-manque.

Because this guy is good. Very good. But where is this going?

In spite of Lisa's fantasies – and Joyce's fantasies – Joyce is not going the distance with this guy on the first date. It just doesn't feel right. The dramatic entrance with the horse, the smooth manner with all the people in the restaurant, the intense dinner conversation focused all on Joyce, the easy way he got her out alone on the beach making out with him – it's all a little too practiced, a little too effortless. Joyce needs to see a man sweat a little, before she's willing to sleep with him.

"Almost midnight," Kip says. "Where's the mistletoe?"

"I think you already found my mistletoe," Joyce says.

They kiss some more, and head back to the restaurant.

But give this guy credit, he seems to sense it ain't happening tonight.

"So Joyce," Kip says, as fireworks go off all around the island, signaling the midnight hour, "I've had a great time. I'd really like to see you again. A lot."

"Me, too. But I told you, I'm flying home tomorrow."

"You could stay—"

"No, I can't. I've got a job. Lisa's got school."

Kip inhales. "Well, there's another way we could stay in touch."

Joyce cocks her head.

"That lawsuit you're thinking of filing," Kip says, "to get the *Lamanai Codex*. I'd like to go in on that with you."

Joyce blinks. Even through the haze of the Rum Collins and her share of those two bottles of wine, she suddenly senses maybe this was never the romantic date she thought it was. There's a business tone to Kip's voice she hasn't heard in it before.

"I don't know what you mean," Joyce says.

"I've got partners, who'll pay all your legal fees, if you share the prize with us."

"Prize?" Joyce echoes. "You mean the *Lamanai Codex*?"

"Aye, and the bigger prize it'll lead us to – the fountain of youth."

"What If the fountain of youth turns out to be the fountain of death, like it was for the pirates?"

"What better way to die," Kip replies, "than trying to prolong your youth?"

BOOK TWO:

The Witness from Hell

Chapter Ten
The Clutch of the Hermit

Monday 4 April 2011 Morning

The muddy brown waters of the river Thames, swollen from spring rains, are flowing fast and high with the morning tide. From a low gray sky a steady rain falls; and up the river a blustery east wind blows cold North Sea air into London.

Throngs of umbrella-wielding commuters surge both ways along the river's south bank. Those trudging east towards Tower Bridge bow their heads against the wind and rain, tucking their faces into their collars as they advance on the bridge, their umbrellas held out like black shields.

Alongside the eastbound commuters walk David Burns and Joyce Kerr, *en route* to the law offices of Symington & Watt, where Fiona Young's deposition will begin today. Close behind, carting three bankers' boxes of potential exhibits, are the three strays Joyce picked up in Belize: Clive Phelps, Ron Graham, and Kip Hunter.

Trudging beside the Gang of Five are three women in burkas, their faces veiled so only their eyes are visible, like gunners in besieged turrets. Burns also sees many Africans and Asians, and hears many foreign tongues. Plainly ye-olde-steak-and-ale-pie London has undergone a sea change since the days of Sherlock Holmes.

The turbulent wind inhibits all talk, but to Burns's amazement, it doesn't stop Joyce from smoking a cigarette on the way. Somehow, in spite of the furious nor'easter that's bringing tears to Burns's eyes, Joyce – impeccably dressed in an elegant black-and-white striped skirt-and-jacket suit – contrives to shield her cancer stick from the fierce gale and savor her morning nicotine fix.

The Gang of Five crosses under the gray stone anchorage at the south end of Tower Bridge, and enters Butler's Wharf, the old warehouse district of tall brick buildings and narrow streets where Fiona Young lives. Here at last the wind dies down, and they walk in relative tranquillity down Shad Thames, a winding cobble-stoned pedestrians-only lane where Burns sees a tangle of ancient irregular iron-railed catwalks connecting, at crazy angles, the upper floors of the riverside warehouses on the north side of the lane with the landside warehouses on the south side.

"I feel like I just stepped into a Dickens novel," Ron Graham says.

"You did," Clive Phelps says. "This is where the Artful Dodger enticed Oliver Twist into Feagin's gang of child thieves. London's worst slum, for centuries. But it's quite safe now. The docks are closed, the gangsters are gone, and the warehouses are now upscale flats and offices."

They reach the offices of Symington & Watt, on the north side of Shad Thames, where a young woman shelters under the alcove by the front door, her long brown hair wet and curling from the rain. At first Burns assumes she's a homeless beggar – but then he sees her shrewd eyes sizing them all up. The rain-soaked young woman homes in on Clive Phelps. "Dr. Phelps?"

"Yes," Phelps says.

"I'm Sara Hamilton, *London Economic Observer*. I tried to reach you last night for comment on today's story. Would you care to comment now?"

"What story?" Phelps asks.

"About the Fiona Young lawsuit," Sara says, "and the *Lamanai Codex*."

Phelps flashes a smile and starts to speak, but Burns steps between Phelps and Sara.

"We have no comment," Burns says. "We're under a court gag order."

Opening the door, Burns whisks the Three Musketeers into Symington & Watt's lobby. But when Joyce pauses to put out her cigarette on the cobbled stones of Shad Thames, Sara squeezes between Burns and the open doorway.

Instead of entering the lobby, Sara stands in the doorway, facing out, her face inches from Burns's chest. At such close quarters Burns inhales, with each breath, Sara's cheap perfume, and the dank smell of the rain on her hair.

"Are you David Burns, the hardball litigator?" Sara asks.

Joyce snorts and, twisting her slim hips, slips past Sara into the lobby.

Burns tries to follow, but Sara Hamilton slides over, forcing Burns to stop in his tracks, to avoid physical contact with her.

"Can I sit in on today's deposition?" Sara looks up at Burns with young, transparent eyes.

Burns raises an eyebrow. What game is Sara playing? She must know depositions are never open to the press. Is she baiting Burns? If so, for what?

"Did you ask Olivia Watt for permission to attend the depo?" Burns parries.

"Olivia wouldn't take my call," Sara says.

"You wrote a story about our lawsuit without talking to either Olivia or me?"

Sara shrugs. "Olivia refused to talk; and I couldn't track you down."

"So who was your source?"

"You know I can't reveal my sources," Sara says.

"What's your story say?"

Sara hands a rolled-up newspaper to Burns, open to page four. The headline reads: "*Ancient Codex May Explain Belize Cancer Deaths*."

Internally Burns shudders to think what their federal judge in Detroit will do when he finds out this much shit has hit the fan, in spite of his gag order. But Burns keeps a poker face.

"We only made page four?" Burns offers the newspaper back to Sara.

"Keep it, David." Sara winks flirtatiously. "So, can I come in with you?"

Burns stares at her. To his dismay, Sara's perfume, and her flirtatious manner, impact his aging bones more than they should. But then he sees a way to use those allures, jujitsu-style.

Bending forward and down, Burns puckers his lips, as if to kiss Sara. Surprised, Sara shifts sideways to avoid his avaricious mouth – and at that precise moment, Burns slips by her.

"Nice meeting you, Sara." Burns shuts the door in Sara's face.

The lobby of Symington & Watt is a study in understated ostentation: formal marble flooring, rich mahogany paneling, and the obligatory water feature, replete with a gurgling fountain, and shiny golden nymphs chasing shiny golden nymphettes through the spray.

With a jaunty stride Burns approaches the pale stick-thin receptionist, who looks like one of Dracula's victims, after an especially long night of blood-letting.

"Hi!" Burns says.

The pale receptionist gazes at Burns with the same warm look she'd give to something disagreeable she just noticed on the side of her shoe. "Do you have an appointment?"

"Yes!" Burns says.

"With whom?"

"Destiny."

The receptionist gazes at Burns without registering either emotion or response. "Destiny doesn't work here anymore."

"A pity," Burns says. "How 'bout Olivia Watt?"

"I'll ring her."

While he waits, Burns sprawls in one of the luxurious lobby chairs, and unfolds the copy of the *London Economic Observer* Sara Hamilton gave him.

Joyce and the Three Amigos crowd round the back of Burns's chair, to read over his shoulder. So all together they get the bad news.

ANCIENT CODEX MAY EXPLAIN BELIZE CANCER DEATHS

Oxford Doctor Files Secret Affidavit In American Lawsuit

Economic Observer To Ask Court To Unseal Case

By Sara Hamilton, Higher Education Correspondent

Detroit, USA – Oxford cancer doctor Clive Phelps, leader of an international medical team investigating the unexplained cancer deaths of 12 Maya men last year in Belize, has filed a secret affidavit in an American court, attesting that an 1100-year-old Mayan codex may help his team identify the cause of the mysterious cancer deaths.

The ownership rights to the priceless Lamanai Codex are being contested in a sealed lawsuit presently pending in an

American federal court in Detroit. Dr. Phelps' secret affidavit played a key role in persuading the Detroit judge to seal the entire litigation about the rare book, an unusual procedure in American courts, the Economic Observer has learnt.

The lawsuit pits American Joyce Kerr against her London cousin, Fiona Young, known in scholarly circles as the 'Maya code breaker' for her seminal translations of Mayan glyphs. Both cousins claim to be the rightful owner of the Lamanai Codex, one of only five ancient Mayan codices known to survive the Spanish Conquest.

Although Dr. Young has had possession of the codex for 50 years, Dr. Phelps supports Ms. Kerr's ownership claim. According to Dr. Phelps' affidavit, he advised the famously reclusive Dr. Young that the codex could help solve the mystery of the Belize cancer deaths, but she still refused to allow Dr. Phelps' team to access either the book or its translation.

No copy or translation of the codex has ever been published. The only copy of the codex in existence is held by the University of Michigan, under a restrictive contract with the Reynolds Foundation, a charity.

In court pleadings, the University of Michigan and the Reynolds Foundation both deny they have the legal right to release the copy to Dr. Phelps, absent Dr. Young's permission.

Lamanai is an ancient Maya site in Belize (formerly British Honduras), closed to the public since December 2010, when 12 young Maya men were found dead of cancer after attending a closed religious retreat. The only three participants not accounted for are still missing and presumed dead. The cause of the 12 cancer deaths has stymied Dr. Phelps' team of international experts for the past three months.

Citing the "proprietary and privacy rights of the parties", Detroit federal judge Dalton Henderson sealed the lawsuit, gagged all parties, and ordered the London law firm of Symington & Watt to escrow the Lamanai Codex.

The London Economic Observer, which obtained copies of the sealed court pleadings from confidential sources, will ask Judge Henderson today to lift his secrecy order, based on the strong public interest in monitoring public health matters.

"Holy shee-at," Kip Hunter says.

Burns holds his hands up like a traffic cop, suppressing further comment.

Then Burns blusters, nags and whines until the reluctant receptionist escorts the Gang of Five up to the 8th floor conference room without waiting for Olivia Watt to come formally greet them.

The conference room is small but posh. In the room's center is a long rectangular conference table with 12 chairs – five per side, and one on each end. Parallel to the long sides of the table, along the north wall, are floor-to-ceiling windows that look out on a postcard view of Tower Bridge and, across the river, the Tower of London and the financial district – though today the postcard is stained gray by the rainy sky. The windows wrap partway round the east and west sides of the room, giving Burns the feeling they're all standing in a fishbowl.

"Look, gang," Burns says, "first rule of litigation: when you're in the other side's offices, always assume every room is bugged. Even the john. So don't say anything unless you'd be comfortable hearing your exact words played back in a courtroom some day. Anything confidential, save till we go to lunch."

"You really think this room is bugged?" a wide-eyed Ron Graham asks, scanning the ceiling as if he thinks he could spot any listening devices.

"No, but it's not worth risking." Burns waves the newspaper, like a matador taunting a bull. "Judge Henderson will assume this leak came from our side."

"Why should he assume that?" Clive Phelps asks.

"He knows Fiona could've made us sue her in England, since she lives here. But she wanted secrecy so bad, she consented to an American court, just to get our agreement to the secrecy orders. So no way Fiona's the leak."

"What about the University of Michigan?" Phelps asks. "Perhaps they le—"

"The U wants this case buried as bad as Fiona," Burn says.

"Why?" Phelps asks.

"The U's caught between a rock and a hard place," Burns says. "Granting public access to their copy of the codex would breach their contract with their donor, the Reynolds Foundation. But withholding a document that could explain the cancer deaths – and according to you, maybe help conquer death – makes the U look elitist, coddling rich donors at the expense of humanity. Either way, they look bad. So publicity about this case is the last thing Michigan wants."

"Maybe it was someone at the Reynolds Foundation," Phelps persists.

"The Foundation's just a shell," Burns says. "These days Fiona's the Foundation's sole officer, director, trustee and employee – and she doesn't want this lawsuit public, because she looks as bad as the U, for withholding valuable medical information from the world."

"Well," Phelps declares, in the rich baritone TV interviewers love him for, "I still don't believe anyone in this room would violate a judge's order."

"Me neither." Burns scans the ceiling, not because he thinks he can spot an audio bug, but to reinforce that he wants everyone to keep speaking as though they were on tape. "I'm just telling you what Judge Henderson'll think. In the meantime, though, Olivia Watt'll storm in here in a few minutes, mad as hell. You guys are all gonna shut up, and let me handle it. Not a peep. Got it?"

The Three Musketeers all nod yes. Joyce nods yes, too.

The conference room door opens. A Vision of Loveliness sashays in: tall, brown-skinned, slender, shapely – and wearing a skirt shorter and tighter than the most licentious of women wear, even in Burns's most x-rated dreams.

"Olivia?" Burns asks with a wild surmise.

"Nice try," the stunning young woman says. "I'm your court reporter, Ivy Taylor." Ivy hands Burns her card. Flashy opal earrings dangle from Ivy's ears.

"No offense, Ivy, but weren't you, ah, a little cold today?"

Ivy arches a finely-penciled eyebrow. "My office is just round the corner."

"So you get a lot of work from Symington & Watt?"

"Some." Ivy unpacks her steno machine and back-up cassette recorder. "But don't worry. I always stay neutral."

"I don't want you to stay neutral," Burns says. "I want you to root for me."

"Why should I root for you?"

"'Cause I'm suffering from an awful case of jet lag," Burns banters. "My poor body thinks it's four in the morning. That makes me the underdog."

Ivy laughs. "Ms. Watt warned me about you."

"What's Olivia know? She's never even met me."

"Seems like she got her fill o' you over the phone," Ivy says.

"Well, it's hard to make friends on transatlantic calls," Burns says. "Say, am I imagining things, Ivy, or do you have a Jamaican accent?"

"What are you – 'enry 'iggins?" Ivy replies.

Burns laughs. What a great break for a badly jet-lagged man, who's going to be up to his eyeballs in alligators today, to have a smart, saucy, sexy court reporter, with a sense of humor.

Because even before the news story broke, Burns knew he was in for a long, bad week. Olivia Watt will be a complete pain in the ass: testy, humorless, and veddy British. Her client, Fiona Young, will be the witness from hell – imperious, smart and utterly uncontrollable. Because in a deposition, with no judge to enforce rules, old people can get away with murder. Literally.

Worse, the University of Michigan lawyer, Miguel Santos, is a bright young nerd who'll pester Burns to death with technical objections. Since Joyce's claim against the U is weak, Burns will be sparring mostly with Olivia and Fiona – leaving himself open to a Santos sucker-punch.

And worst of all are the three latter-day pyrates on Burns's own team. Since Joyce refused to let Burns do the case on a contingency, she cut a deal with Dr. Phelps, under which Phelps is paying Burns's legal fees, on an hourly basis, in exchange for access to the codex or the copy, and 33% of the profits on any sale. Phelps in turn has some unspecified side deal with his two new Belizean buddies, Hunter and Graham. To Burns's huge irritation, all Three Fools seem to have carnal designs on Joyce; and all three declined to follow Burns's advice to stay away from today's deposition, insisting they must see their 'hardball litigator' Burns break Fiona Young down. So on each break, instead of recharging his batteries, Burns'll have to explain to the Three Blind Mice, defensively, that butts seldom get kicked in real depositions, the way they do in TV trials, and that the only realistic goals are far subtler. This won't sit well with any of them – especially the impatient and demanding Phelps, who's used to getting whatever he wants in life, right now, if not yesterday.

In short, Burns'll be fighting everyone in the room, except Joyce Kerr. So a smart, saucy sexy court reporter is the closest thing to a break Burns is likely to catch all week.

After setting up her machines, Ivy holds the hem of her short tight skirt with both hands, and sits down at the west end of the conference table. Joyce starts unpacking the exhibits the Three Amigos carted in, and squaring them off in stacks along the north side of the table. But Burns slides the stacks across to the south side of the table. Joyce looks up, surprised.

"At home you never face the windows," Joyce says.

"At home we never have this view," Burns counters.

"But if the sun comes out, we'll all be squinting," Joyce says.

"These windows face north," Phelps says, "so the sun'll never be in our eyes."

"Precisely," Burns says. He slides a few more stacks of exhibits across the table, and then takes the first seat on the south side of the table, closest to Ivy.

"Where d'you want the rest of us?" Phelps asks.

"Let's have Joyce next to me," Burns says, "then you, then Ron, then Kip."

They all sit as directed. Conscious that Joyce is right next to him, Burns wills himself not to look at Ivy Taylor's delicious brown thighs, 18 inches away, instead re-reading his depo outline.

The door opens again, and Miguel Santos enters, wheeling a banker's box. Santos, in his late-20s and openly gay, has immaculate black hair, and energetic eyes that miss nothing.

"Darling!" Santos says to Ivy, "I love your earrings!"

Ivy arches that penciled eyebrow again, checking Santos out. "Thanks."

"For the record, Ivy," Burns mutters, "I love your earrings, too."

Ivy looks at Joyce. "It's gonna be a long week, isn't it?"

Joyce snorts. She's not ready, apparently, to be Ivy's pal.

Wistfully Burns wonders if Joyce could be jealous of Ivy. If only.

"Speaking of the long week," Santos smiles, "how long'll this depo last?"

Burns does not smile back. "As long as it takes to get the truth. And the fact that my body's still on Detroit time is not going to slow me down one bit. I told the Hilton we may be here all week."

Ivy looks alarmed. "But you only need me in the mornings, right?"

"Correct," Burns says. "In deference to the witness's age, we agreed to take just three hours of deposition per day. That's why this may take all week."

"Any chance you'll dismiss us from the case?" Santos asks, as he sits in the middle of the five seats on the table's north side, directly across from Phelps.

"Why the hell would I do that?" Burns growls.

"Well, I assume you sued us just to have an American defendant. But now that Fiona's consented to be sued in Detroit, why not let us out?"

"Are you accusing me of improperly suing your client just to create jurisdiction?" Burns puts a hard edge on his voice, just to mess with Santos a bit.

"Oh, no, I—" Santos's voice trails off, and he looks down at his legal pad to collect himself. "I just don't see what you gain by keeping us in the lawsuit."

"I spelled it out for you in the Complaint, Miguel," Burns says. "We want the copy of the *Lamanai Codex* the U forced Fiona to make in 1970 when they hired her."

"But we can't lawfully give you our copy," Santos says, "unless you prove Ms. Kerr owns the original. Yet if you prove that, you won't need our copy."

Burns snorts. "Very tidy. But have you ever heard of settlements?"

"Of course." Santos sounds puzzled. "98% of all cases settle."

"Try this one on for size," Burns says. "Fiona'll never give up the original of the codex – at least, not in her lifetime. Yet we need to see its contents ASAP. So what if Fiona, through the Reynolds Foundation, instructed you to let us copy your copy? Then we could cut a deal with Fiona about the original – maybe she pays us cash for the right to keep the original till she dies, and then it goes to Joyce. A settlement that could only happen if your client is still at the table."

"Have you proposed those settlement terms to Olivia?" Santos asks.

"No. As Ivy was just saying, my phone calls with Olivia weren't all that chummy. But I'm sure once we meet in person, we'll get on like a house on fire."

"You want me to broach this idea to Olivia?" Santos asks.

"Why else," Burns asks, "would I be sharing all these intimate thoughts with you, Miguel?"

The conference room door opens a third time, and Olivia Watt sweeps in. Olivia is 40ish, tall, blonde, fit, and self-assured. She's wearing an expensive-looking red suit that projects power. Her face, which might be attractive in another setting, is pinched into a fierce frown – exactly as Burns pictured her during their tedious trans-Atlantic telephone arguments the past three months.

"Olivia!" Burns rises, and greets his adversary with a formal bow. "Welcome to London!"

Olivia Watt is not amused. "We need to talk."

"On the record?" Burns asks. "Or can we spare Ivy's fingers?"

"Off the record is fine," Olivia says. "My receptionist informs me you've all seen this morning's *London Economic Observer*. So you'll understand why we're canceling the deposition."

Burns feigns shock. "You mean 'temporarily adjourning'?"

"No, I mean 'cancelling'," Olivia says. "Indefinitely."

"I'm sorry to hear that. We'll claim costs, of course." Burns gestures down the table. "I brought my whole team to London. Dr. Phelps is local, but we've still got four transatlantic flights, four London hotel rooms, pre-paid for the week, and four sets of meals." Burns sighs.

"I tried to convince Ms. Kerr we should economize by sharing a room, but she just wouldn't see it my way."

Burns can feel Joyce's eyes burning small holes into his right ear.

"We won't have to pay," Olivia says, "because your side breached Judge Henderson's sealing and gag order, by leaking pleadings to the press—"

"That's not true!" Phelps declares, leaping up.

"Clive!" Burns reaches across Joyce to hold his hand in front of Phelps's face. "We talked about this. Please. Sit."

Phelps sits back down, but his lips still twitch with anger.

Burns fixes Olivia with an earnest gaze. "On behalf of myself, my client and paralegal Ms. Kerr, and my consultants Dr. Phelps, Dr. Graham, and Mr. Hunter, we categorically deny leaking anything to the press. When you depose these good people, you can ask them all about it, just as I may ask Dr. Young about it, in her deposition. But in the meantime, Olivia, if you presume we're at fault and cancel today's deposition on that basis, you err badly – and sanctions will surely ensue."

Olivia puts her hands on her hips, like a human teapot. "Don't try to steamroll me, David. Dr. Young gave up very strong jurisdictional defenses just to get that secrecy order, so you know we didn't leak the story. The University certainly didn't leak it; they want this case swept under the rug. Of course I make no accusations against you or Ms. Kerr. But that leaves only your so-called 'consultants' – and Dr. Phelps is *notorious* for his overly cozy relations with the media."

To Burns's surprise, this time Phelps manages to control himself.

"That may seem logical to you, Olivia," Burns says, "but Judge Henderson will insist on proof, not conjecture or random slanders against Dr. Phelps."

"We're happy to leave this for the Judge to sort out," Olivia says. "But we'll not go forward with this depo until he has a full opportunity to punish the leaker."

"Huge mistake," Burns says. "If you care about your client's best interest, you'll get her in here, sworn and chattering under oath, long before 2 p.m. today."

"What's magic about 2 p.m.?" Olivia squints at her watch. "Oh – that's 9 a.m. in Detroit? But that's my point. We can't proceed till we know the Court's ruling on the newspaper's motion to unseal this case. In fact, I need to start preparing our response to that motion, so if you'll excuse—"

"Olivia, please," Burns opens his palms. "Judging by the size of this place, you must have ten scriveners already drafting your brief. So hear me out. In the States, we have a legal concept called 'justifiable reliance'. It's a winner, every time. Does England have 'justifiable reliance', too?"

"Yes," Olivia says, "but I fail to see how justifiable reliance applies here."

"Right now, it doesn't," Burns says. "That's the problem. But if we could show that someone *justifiably relied* on that secrecy order, it'd give Judge Henderson the good reason I bet he'd love to have, *not* to reverse his own secrecy order just for some foreign newspaper no one in Michigan reads. Yet if you cancel today's deposition, what reliance does anyone here have to show Judge Henderson, when the *Observer* asks him to vacate his secrecy order?"

"We gave up our jurisdictional defenses," Olivia says.

"Judge Henderson could give those defenses back to you," Burns counters. "And then we'd all be back to Square One. Fiona might win her jurisdictional argument, and force Joyce to sue her in London. But then Joyce might just go forward in Detroit against the U and the Reynolds Foundation, without Fiona – in which case, Fiona wouldn't be able to participate in the defense, without creating a jurisdictional basis that would allow us to bring her back into the case. So in other words, we'd all just keep running in a circle, chasing our own collective tails – except the case'd be public then, because none of us could show any real reliance on the secrecy order."

Olivia scowls but says nothing.

"If you include me," Miguel Santos interjects, "five of us traveled an awful long way for this depo. Isn't that reliance?"

"Technically, yes," Burns concedes. "But it won't impress our Judge. So a little money got spent. Big deal. But think how different the hearing on the newspaper's motion'll go, Olivia, if your local counsel – Landau – can say: *Judge, the deposition of Dr. Young has already started, and Dr. Young, justifiably relying on your secrecy order, not only waived all her jurisdictional defenses, but also placed herself in jeopardy, by answering hundreds of plaintiff's questions on the record.*"

Burns pauses to gauge Olivia's reaction. She's frowning hard now. Not knowing Olivia, Burns decides to interpret a hard frown as a good sign.

"*Then* your man Landau could say," Burns continues, "*Judge, it'd be manifestly unfair now to tell Dr. Young, an elderly foreigner who only consented to come before your Court after you assured her, through your rulings, the case would be sealed, 'sorry, dear, but the rules of the game have changed, for the sake of the press, so the secrecy you were promised, and upon which you justifiably relied, is down the drain'*. That's a damn good argument! But Landau can only make that argument, Olivia, if we get this depo rolling before the hearing on the newspaper's motion – which could be right at 9 a.m. in Detroit, because in America, newspapers get to jump the queue."

Olivia squints at Burns. "Mr. Landau warned me what a snake-charmer you can be." She sighs. "Give me a few minutes to speak with my client."

"Sure," Burns says, "but Fiona's going to resist anything she knows is coming from Joyce and her snake-charmer. So you might want to tell Fiona, if she truly thinks we're the leak, and she wants to thwart us by keeping the case sealed, then her best move is to start the depo ASAP."

Olivia looks quite annoyed. "I do not require your assistance in how best to communicate with my client, David." She spins on her heel and exits.

A hush pervades the conference room – the calm after the storm – until Ivy says: "Thanks for not putting all that on the record, Mr. Burns."

"You're welcome. But please call me 'David'. 'Mr. Burns' sounds so old."

Ivy shakes her head, but smiles.

"How old are you anyway, David?" Miguel Santos asks.

"45," Burns says.

Joyce snorts. "David, they can look you up in Martindale."

Burns frowns at Joyce, and then pushes his lower lip out, in a parody of a schoolboy pout. "Okay, technically I'm 52. But I *feel* 45."

"You look damn good for 52," Santos says. "Heck, you look good for 45."

"Easy there, Miguel!" Burns says. "Ivy and I are practically engaged."

"In your dreams," Ivy says, without looking up from inspecting her nails.

"That's where all my engagements are these days." Burns grins. "On the other hand, Ivy, once I win this case and these guys pay me a huge premium for helping them find the fountain of youth, you're gonna regret not snapping me up when you had your chance."

"I never regret nothin'," Ivy says. "You can drive yourself crazy with might-a-beens."

"You got that right," Ron Graham says with surprising intensity.

Burns looks at Graham, on the verge of asking what prompted that random outburst.

But Santos speaks first, looking at Joyce's Three Admirers: "So you guys really think there's a fountain of youth out there somewhere in Belize?"

Burns leans across Joyce again and waves his hand in front of his three consultants. "Whoa! Gentlemen, I know Miguel seems like a nice guy. But he's got a client that wants to take us down. So don't talk to him, ever, except when you're under oath and you've got Ivy's record to protect you." Burns turns to Santos. "And please don't try to get them talking ever again."

Santos blushes. "I – was just – killing time."

"Just kill time with me," Burns growls.

"Okay," Santos says, "do *you* think there's really a fountain of youth?"

"Seems like a fairy tale," Burns says, "but if it's real, I'll be first in line."

"I'll be right behind you," Santos admits. "But does anyone besides Fiona know if the *Lamanai Codex* truly has a map to the fountain of youth?"

"No, but Joyce is entitled to find out if it does," Burns says. "She's entitled to the original of the codex, and your copy – and Fiona's translation, too."

"Well, now," Santos demurs, "*maybe* you'll win on the original, although getting the Judge to reopen a 102-year-old Probate case won't be easy. And we already talked about our copy. But how could you ever get Fiona's translation? That's plainly her work product."

"Not under your contract," Burns says. "The U inked its deal about copying the codex with the Reynolds Foundation, not Fiona. So if the Foundation owns the original, then the Foundation must own the translation, too."

"I don't buy that," Santos says, "but if it's true, isn't that worse for you? The Foundation wasn't a party to the old Probate case. So if you say the Foundation owns both the original and the translation, aren't you left with nothing?"

"That's just a silly shell game," Burns says, though in truth he's more worried about how to finesse the Reynolds Foundation than how to get the Judge to reopen a 102-year-old probate case. "The Foundation and Fiona are one and the same. That's why Olivia represents them both."

"Legally," Santos perseveres, "the Reynolds Foundation's still a separate party from Fiona Young, unless you pierce the corporate veil."

"We'll see about that, young man," Burns says, "once we get all the facts."

To cut off further talk, Burns walks over to the fishbowl window. Santos is a nice kid. But there's nothing to be gained debating the case with him. He's not a decision-maker to be won over. And he doesn't know any secrets worth prying out.

Out the window all kinds of debris are floating up the Thames – chunks of wood, pieces of paper, bottles and cans, even a door – as if a ship recently wrecked down by Greenwich, and the tide is now sweeping the flotsam and jetsam up to London. The floating debris reminds Burns of the penny western history Joyce found for him about Roger Quinlan, which included a brief account of an 1866 shipwreck Quinlan and his wife Kathleen survived in the Southern Ocean – an awful brush with death Quinlan later said was the impetus for his quest for the fountain of youth.

The door opens. Olivia returns, nods at Burns – and leaves open the door.

"We've decided to go forward today," Olivia says. "Although I will need to put a brief statement on the record, David, before we start the deposition."

"Of course."

Olivia steps aside to make room for an elderly woman, pale and gaunt, to follow her in. The old woman, looking like death warmed over, enters slowly, leaning on a cane with one hand, and clutching a tiny book in her other hand.

The old woman's skin is deeply wrinkled, sagging, spotted, and paper-thin. The lines of age run especially deep around her watery old eyes, which are set very deep in their sockets, beneath heavy hooded eyelids. She walks like she's on her last legs.

Burns groans silently. In spite of Joyce warning him Fiona had aged a great deal the past 21 years, Burns was hoping she'd still be a live wire, because you can't intimidate a person near death's door. At least not in a deposition.

Burns rises and sticks out his hand. "Dr. Young, I think we met years ago, in Ann Arbor."

Fiona Young looks up at Burns with piercing brown eyes that seem, in contrast to her tired old body, alert and lively. But Burns finds it hard to maintain eye contact because he'd forgotten about Fiona's nose ring – a native-style metal hoop pierced through the septum of her 86-year-old nose. Around her neck she wears a Victorian photograph locket, closed.

"Am I required to shake your hand, Mr. Burns, even though you've sued me?" Fiona asks, in a surprisingly strong, clear voice, with only a faint trace of a warble.

"Shaking hands is not required, no ma'am." Burns withdraws his hand.

Olivia directs Fiona to the chair nearest Ivy and across from Burns. After easing Fiona into the chair, Olivia sits between Fiona and Santos, and across from Joyce. Fiona shifts her hips 45 degrees, facing Ivy, and away from everyone else – thereby avoiding eye contact with Joyce.

Burns sits and glances at Joyce's hands, fidgeting like mad beneath the table.

"Good morning," Fiona says to Ivy. "Were you born in de Caribbean?"

"Jamaica," Ivy says.

"Paradise on earth," Fiona says, rapturously.

"But so hard to find work dere now," Ivy says.

"Not if you live de old way." Fiona leans forward. "Where can I put my book, *dready dawta*, dat it won't be in your way dis morning?"

Ivy smiles, and points at the corner of the table. "Right dere is fine."

Fiona sets the book down carefully where Ivy points.

"We mustn't let it fall," Fiona says. "Like me, it's very old, and very frail."

Burns gapes, realizing for the first time that the tiny book Fiona carried in must be the *Lamanai Codex*. No wonder rival scholars complain about Fiona. Instead of storing the 1100-year-old book in a climate-controlled museum, and wearing latex gloves to handle it, she schleps it into a deposition like she just picked it up for a pound at the Bermondsey Antiques Market.

Everyone leans forward to gawk, as Fiona sets the tiny book down.

The *Lamanai Codex* looks like an artifact from a lost world. It's smaller than a modern paperback, with jaguar-hide covers as worn and thin as Fiona's skin, on which the only marking is a dark patch on the front cover, in the shape of a crocodile. The codex has no binding; instead, the bare spine shows only a pile of folded page edges. Burns puzzles over what's holding it together, till he figures out the codex is a single long sheet of paper, folded dozens of times and squeezed into a pile, like an accordion – with the covers glued onto the first and last pages. Judging from the rough, lumpy edges of the crumbling pages, the ancient Maya left a lot of wood in their paper.

Burns looks at Olivia. "I think we should put that away, somewhere safe."

Olivia shrugs, and looks at her client.

"It's safest right here with me," Fiona says.

Burns frowns. "Doesn't look at all safe to me. It's falling apart. Each time you touch it, the oils in your hands must be damaging the covers."

"When I got this codex," Fiona says, "the covers were already shot. What's left is a resinous base that hasn't changed in all the years I've handled it."

Burns shakes his head. "Olivia, I've gotta object. The Escrow Order says, if we prevail, you must deliver the book to Joyce in its present condition, without it sustaining any further damage."

"We fully understand our obligations under the Judge's orders." Olivia glares across the table at Phelps. "Unlike some people."

Phelps fumes and splutters, but does not speak.

Fiona points out the window behind her. "To me this book is worth more than all the jewels in the Tower of London. Never would I let harm come to it."

"Then why not store it in a climate-controlled vault?" Burns asks.

"The Judge's Escrow Order does not require that," Olivia interjects.

"The Order requires you to prevent further damage," Burns counters.

"All my life," Fiona says, "I've carried with me this little book, everywhere I've gone. It's like my child. I won't have my child locked up in a vault."

Burns stares at the old woman, with her kinky nose ring, and her watery eyes half hidden beneath the deep hoods of her eyelids. Given her advanced age, she's still astonishingly beautiful.

But is she playing with a full deck?

"Well," Burns sighs, "let's go on the record."

* * *

Transcript of the 4 April 2011 Deposition of Dr. Fiona Young at the offices of Symington & Watt, in the case of *Joyce Kerr* v *Fiona Young et al*, Case No. 11-0098-IP, in the United States District Court for the Eastern District of Michigan. Appearances: David Burns, Esq. for Ms. Kerr; Olivia Watt, Esq. for Dr. Young and the Reynolds Foundation; Miguel Santos, Esq. for the University of Michigan; also present: Joyce Kerr, Dr. Clive Phelps, Dr. Ronald Graham, and Kip Hunter. Reporter: Ivy Taylor, Bridge House, 7 Horselydown Lane, London SE1 2QR.

■ Ms. Taylor: On the record at 9:44. Please state your name and address.

■ Dr. Young: Fiona Young, 50 Shad Thames, Flat 47, London SE1 2LY.

■ Ms. Taylor: (Raises hand) Do you swear or affirm to tell only the truth?

■ Dr. Young: Don't we need a Bible?

■ Ms. Watt: We don't use them anymore, Dr. Young.

■ Mr. Burns: You can swear on the codex, if you like.

■ Ms. Taylor: (Keeps her hand raised) Do you swear or affirm—

■ Dr. Young: (Raises her hand) Yes, I swear to tell only the truth.

■ Ms. Watt: I have a statement for the record. Dr. Young has resided in London since 1990, and has not set foot in Michigan for 21 years. She consented to American jurisdiction for this case only after plaintiff persuaded our Judge to enter an order sealing the entire lawsuit and prohibiting the parties, counsel, and consultants from communicating with anyone outside the case, especially the media. Keeping this lawsuit out of the public eye was essential to Dr. Young, and she would not be here today, were it not for the court's order requiring all of us in this room to keep all pleadings and everything else about the case confidential.

This morning an article appeared in the *London Economic Observer*, reciting confidential information about this case. I have directed our local counsel in Detroit to file a motion, asking our Judge to determine the source of the leak and to sanction the responsible party. In the meantime, we have acceded to Mr. Burns's request to proceed with the deposition, in light of the considerable time and expense incurred by all parties in preparation.

However, the record must be clear that we proceed this morning in continuing reliance upon Judge Henderson's confidentiality order, which includes a provision sealing the transcript of all depositions. If our reliance proves misplaced, and the order is vacated, we reserve the right to move to suppress the transcript of this deposition and to seek dismissal of plaintiff's claims, either for lack of jurisdiction or violation of the confidentiality order.

■ Mr. Burns: Are you finished?

■ Ms. Watt: For now.

■ Mr. Burns: Dr. Young, have you ever had your deposition taken before?

■ Dr. Young: (Long pause) No, I don't believe so.

■ Mr. Burns: Then I'll explain the rules. Ivy here'll take down everything we say, and then type up a transcript, which'll look like the script of a play.

■ Dr. Young: Will this transcript end up in Sara Hamilton's hands, too?

■ Mr. Burns: Let's hope not. As your counsel accurately stated, today's transcript is fully protected by Judge Henderson's sealing order.

■ Dr. Young: So were all the other pleadings. But somehow Sara Hamilton got all of them.

■ Mr. Burns: Evidently. And as your counsel said, sanctions may result. But in the meantime, by agreement, we're going forward now. Okay by you?

■ Dr. Young: (Glares) Uh-huh.

■ Mr. Burns: For Ivy's sake, please say 'yes' or 'no', rather than 'uh-huh' or 'unh-unh'. Okay?

■ Dr. Young: Uh-huh. (Pause.) Okay, yes.

■ Mr. Burns: Also, to help Ivy accurately record what's said, Ivy needs us to speak one at a time. So even though you may often think you know where my question is going, please let me finish before you start your answer, okay?

■ Dr. Young: Uh-huh. Oh, er, yes, okay.

- Mr. Burns: I'll try to do the same for you. But if you pause in the middle of an answer, I may think you're finished, and ask a new question. If that happens, please understand: I'm *never* trying to interrupt you. The whole reason we're here is for you to tell me things. So if I interrupt you, all you have to do is say excuse me, and I'll allow you to finish your answer. Okay?
- Dr. Young: Uh-huh. I mean, yes, okay.
- Mr. Burns: From time to time your counsel may state an objection for the record, which she is required to do briefly and without hinting how she'd like you to answer the pending question. But once your counsel finishes stating her objection, you're required to answer my question, unless your counsel specifically instructs you not to answer on the basis of a privilege.
- Dr. Young: If I must answer anyway, what's the point of the objections?
- Mr. Burns: (Pause) The Court Rules permit me to use this transcript at trial. However, if I want to use an answer where there was an objection, Judge Henderson'll first rule on the objection, and if he decides Ms. Watt was right, then I can't use your answer at trial. But if—
- Dr. Young: If my answers here can be used at a public trial, then what good does it do me to have this deposition sealed? It isn't really secret, is it?
- Mr. Burns: (Long pause) The way this works, Dr. Young, is: I ask the questions, and you answer them. If you have questions of your own, you should direct them to your counsel.
- Ms. Watt: He's right. You and I can talk privately in my office about your question at the break, in about an hour. Let's proceed for now.
- Mr. Burns: Thank you, Olivia. Doctor, when and where were you born?
- Dr. Young: (Long pause) 13th February 1925, in Guatemala.
- Mr. Burns: Did you bring your birth certificate, as I requested?
- Dr. Young: (Nods yes)
- Ms. Watt: (Hands original to Mr. Burns, and copy to Mr. Santos.)
- Mr. Burns: (Reads it) Ivy, let's mark this Young Exhibit 1. My Spanish isn't great. Does this say the village you were born in was San Lorenzo?
- Dr. Young: Yes.
- Mr. Burns: You ever meet a man named Kux Ahawis?
- Dr. Young: Yes, I knew Kux.
- Mr. Burns: When'd you meet Kux?
- Dr. Young: When I was a child. He was San Lorenzo's shaman.
- Mr. Burns: Were you good friends with Kux?
- Dr. Young: Very good friends. (Looks at Dr. Graham) Just like Dr. Graham.
- Mr. Burns: You know Ron, too?

- Dr. Young: Only by reputation. But I know Kux held Ron in the very highest esteem.
- Mr. Burns: Are you aware Kux Ahawis died last year at Lamanai?
- Dr. Young: I saw it in the newspapers.
- Mr. Burns: What was Kux doing at Lamanai before he died?
- Dr. Young: Doesn't Dr. Graham know?
- Mr. Burns: Perhaps. But we're here to find out what you know, Dr. Young.
- Dr. Young: The newspaper said Kux was re-enacting ancient rites.
- Mr. Burns: I know what the newspapers said, too. I want to know what *you* know. Did Kux ever tell you what he was going out to Lamanai to do?
- Dr. Young: (Pause) No.
- Mr. Burns: When'd you last have any contact with Kux Ahawis – phone calls, letters, any type of contact at all?
- Dr. Young: (Long pause) Many years ago.
- Mr. Burns: Ivy, we'll mark as Young Exhibit 2 a letter dated 7 July 2010, addressed to Kux Ahawis, and signed by Fiona Young.
- Ms. Kerr: (Hands original to witness, and copies to all counsel).
- Mr. Burns: You write this letter?
- Dr. Young: (Angry) Where'd you get this?
- Mr. Burns: Is that your signature at the bottom?
- Dr. Young: This was a private letter to Kux Ahawis. How'd you get it?
- Mr. Burns: If you look halfway down the page, you wrote—
- Ms. Watt: Objection. The witness has not testified she wrote it.
- Mr. Burns: What? Someone else signed this letter 'Fiona Young'?
- Dr. Young: I wrote it. But where'd you— (points at Dr. Graham) You! You told the police where to look, and then you stole it for Joyce, didn't you?
- Mr. Burns: Dr. Young, you are not permitted to question Dr. Graham in this deposition. But you are required to answer all my questions. Halfway down the page, you wrote:
- 'Kux, I'm sorry, but I can't let you see the book. I'll burn it before I let you take it. Forget the fountain. Too many have died. You have other work to do, so much more valuable than reviving that old ritual. Your people need you. Stay in San Lorenzo and help them.'
- Dr. Young, the book you referenced there was the *Lamanai Codex*, wasn't it?
- Dr. Young: (Long pause) I don't remember.
- Mr. Burns: You're kidding, right?
- Ms. Watt: Objection! Badgering the witness.
- Mr. Burns: Of course I'm badgering her, Olivia. That answer deserves badgering. Dr. Young, are you seriously asking us to believe just nine months ago, you wrote Kux a letter threatening to burn a book, and now you can't remember what book you were prepared to burn?

- Ms. Watt: Objection! Badgering the witness!
- Mr. Burns: Do you routinely burn so many books you can't remember which ones you were getting ready to burn at any particular time?
- Dr. Young: I do not routinely burn books.
- Mr. Burns: It was the *Lamanai Codex*, wasn't it? The book you told us a few minutes ago you would never harm, because it's like a child to you?
- Ms. Watt: Objection. Compound question.
- Mr. Burns: Dr. Young, why'd Kux ask to see the *Lamanai Codex*?
- Dr. Young: (Long pause) I don't remember Kux asking to see the codex.
- Mr. Burns: Do you remember writing this letter last summer?
- Dr. Young: Yes. I was mistaken earlier, when I said I'd had no contact with Kux recently. I forgot about this letter. I'm very old. Your memory plays tricks on you, when you get old.
- Mr. Burns: What letter or other communication d'you receive from Kux Ahawis, before you wrote Exhibit 2, which prompted you to write to Kux?
- Dr. Young: (Long pause) I don't remember anything from Kux.
- Mr. Burns: Kux told you he was going out to Lamanai, didn't he?
- Dr. Young: I don't remember Kux telling me anything like that.
- Mr. Burns: When you wrote 'forget the fountain', you were referring to the fountain of youth?
- Dr. Young: No. The fountain of youth is just a myth. A terrible myth.
- Mr. Burns: Why is it a 'terrible' myth?
- Dr. Young: Because many people have died chasing that false chimera. Ask Ron. He's written all about the pirates who died looking for it.
- Mr. Burns: If it wasn't the fountain of youth, what other fountain were you referencing in Exhibit 2 when you wrote 'too many have died'?
- Ms. Watt: Objection. There's no evidence that 'too many have died' refers back to the previous sentence about the unidentified fountain.
- Mr. Burns: Olivia, that's an improper way to make an objection. You're obviously supplying an answer to the witness. Please don't do that again.
- Ms. Watt: I was doing no such thing. I resent your implication, and I will continue to state all the many objections your improper questions deserve.
- Mr. Burns: Dr. Young, what fountain were you referencing in Exhibit 2?
- Dr. Young: (Long pause) I don't remember.
- Mr. Burns: You take any medication before you came here today?
- Dr. Young: Only natural remedies. I took sea kelp, wild oats and coleus forskolin for my thyroid, rosehips for my arthritis, calcium for my osteoporosis, and nitroglylcerin for my heart.

■ Mr. Burns: Any of those remedies impair cognitive functioning?
■ Dr. Young: No, but as I told you before, my age impairs my memory.
■ Mr. Burns: You see a physician, from time to time?
■ Dr. Young: Only when I have no other choice.
■ Mr. Burns: But you do have a physician, here in London?
■ Dr. Young: Yes, Dr. Alan Foulds on Mill Street. Very nice young man.
■ Mr. Burns: When'd you last see Dr. Foulds?
■ Dr. Young: Last month. I had a boil on my leg I needed him to lance.
■ Mr. Burns: Has Dr. Foulds prescribed Arisept or any other memory medication for you?
■ Dr. Young: No.
■ Mr. Burns: Has Dr. Foulds, or anyone else, diagnosed you with Alzheimer's, or dementia, or any other cognitive impairment?
■ Dr. Young: Goodness, no. I'm not *that* far over the hill.
■ Mr. Burns: You ever talk to Kux Ahawis about the fountain of youth?
■ Dr. Young: Probably. I've known Kux forever. And it's a famous myth.
■ Mr. Burns: What did Kux and you discuss about the fountain of youth?
■ Dr. Young: I can't recall anything specific.
■ Mr. Burns: You ever talk to Kux about any other fountain?
■ Dr. Young: Probably. I can't recall.
■ Mr. Burns: Is there a fountain in San Lorenzo – in the village square?
■ Dr. Young: There wasn't when I lived there.
■ Mr. Burns: How long d'you live in San Lorenzo?
■ Dr. Young: I'm not sure. We moved around a lot in my childhood.
■ Mr. Burns: Your mother was Persephone Quinlan?
■ Dr. Young: Yes.
■ Mr. Burns: Persephone Quinlan was an archeologist in Guatemala?
■ Dr. Young: Yes.
■ Mr. Burns: Your father was Stephen Young?
■ Dr. Young: Yes.
■ Mr. Burns: And what did Stephen Young do?
■ Dr. Young: (Pause) Stephen was an explorer.
■ Mr. Burns: He died in 1925?
■ Dr. Young: Correct. My father died a few weeks before I was born.
■ Mr. Burns: How'd he die?
■ Dr. Young: Stephen was eaten by a jaguar.
■ Mr. Burns: Whoa! I'm sorry, I didn't know that.
■ Dr. Young: It's okay, I didn't know him. Mum said Stephen took crazy risks.
■ Mr. Burns: So Persephone raised you by herself?

- Dr. Young: My mother did not remarry. But many people raised me. The Maya don't shut their neighbors out, the way Anglos do. So wherever we lived, the whole village helped raise me.
- Mr. Burns: You moved around a lot when you were a child?
- Dr. Young: Yes. For Mum's work.
- Mr. Burns: Were all the villages where you were raised in Guatemala?
- Dr. Young: No. Some were in Honduras. Some in Mexico.
- Mr. Burns: Any in Belize?
- Dr. Young: No, I only lived in Belize a short time as an adult.
- Mr. Burns: What do you mean by a 'short time'?
- Dr. Young: Couple of months. I was in a time of transition then.
- Mr. Burns: Did you go to Honduras and Mexico on a passport?
- Dr. Young: (Shrugs) I was only a child when I lived in Honduras and Mexico. Nowadays we all use passports. But back then, people in Central America crossed the borders without any fuss.
- Mr. Burns: Do you have a Guatemalan passport today?
- Dr. Young: Yes.
- Mr. Burns: Do you have a passport issued by any other country?
- Dr. Young: No.
- Mr. Burns: Have you ever had a passport issued by any other country?
- Dr. Young: No – at least, not that I remember.
- Mr. Burns: Besides Guatemala, Honduras, Mexico, and Belize, what other countries have you lived in the past 86 years – not visited, but lived in?
- Dr. Young: Australia. The United States. And the United Kingdom.
- Mr. Burns: Did you apply to become a naturalized citizen of any of th—?
- Dr. Young: No.
- Mr. Burns: You obtained visas to live in Australia, the US and the UK?
- Dr. Young: I don't – well, here in the UK, I have a visa. But I don't really remember what papers I had in Australia or the USA. It was all so long ago.
- Mr. Burns: Joyce, can you grab the visa app? Thanks. (Hands original to witness, and copies to counsel). Ivy, we'll mark as Young Exhibit 3 a 1970 'Application for United States Work Visa'. Dr. Young, do you recognize this?
- Dr. Young: (Puts on reading glasses, reviews Exhibit 3) Not really, no.
- Mr. Burns: If you look at the last page, is that your signature?
- Dr. Young: (Flips to last page) Oh yes, that's me.
- Mr. Burns: This is a form you filed in 1970, so you could work at the University of Michigan?
- Dr. Young: Yes, I suppose it is. You Americans love long forms like this.

- Mr. Burns: We sure do. Could you read what you wrote on the first page for 'date of birth'?
- Dr. Young: (Long pause, then frowns) I didn't write this.
- Mr. Burns: You didn't fill out the visa application form that you signed?
- Dr. Young: No, that's not my handwriting there.
- Mr. Burns: Whose handwriting is it?
- Dr. Young: (Looks at Mr. Santos, puzzled) Someone at the University.
- Mr. Burns: You did sign the form's last page, indicating 'I attest under penalty of perjury that all the foregoing information is true and accurate', yes?
- Dr. Young: Hmmn.
- Mr. Burns: And what birth date is on the form you attested under penalty of perjury was true?
- Ms. Watt: Objection. Badgering the witness.
- Mr. Burns: What's the birth date written there, Dr. Young?
- Dr. Young: February 13th, 1915.
- Mr. Burns: 1915! So which is right: your birth certificate saying you were born in 1925, or your visa application saying you were born in 1915?
- Ms. Watt: Objection! Your tone is – inappropriate.
- Mr. Burns: (Grins) That's America for you, Olivia. Land of the Free, and Home of the Inappropriate. Dr. Young, what year were you really born?
- Dr. Young: 1925. Obviously 41 years ago someone got one digit wrong for the decade of my birth on the form. I failed to notice, so I signed it.
- Mr. Burns: You still receive a pension from the University?
- Dr. Young: I'm not sure.
- Mr. Santos: Yes, she does.
- Mr. Burns: Miguel, I know you're trying to be helpful. But today I only want to find out what Dr. Young knows, not what you know. So please don't answer any more of my questions, okay?
- Mr. Santos: Can I answer the question you just asked me?
- Mr. Burns: (Rolls his eyes and shakes his head no) Joyce, can you – thanks. (Hands original to witness, and copies to counsel) Ivy, we'll mark as Young Exhibit 4 a 1970 document titled 'University of Michigan Faculty Pension Form 5428'. Dr. Young, you recognize this document?
- Dr. Young: No. (Flips through Young Exhibit 4) But I see it has the same defect. Someone wrote my birth year wrong, and I signed it. (Stares at Ms. Kerr) You've been very thorough, dear, haven't you, digging through my life?
- Mr. Burns: For the record, that is your signature on Young Exhibit 4?
- Dr. Young: (Sighs) Yes.

- Mr. Burns: And you claim the 'February 13th, 1915' birth date on Young Exhibit 4 is not your handwriting, but rather that of a person unknown to you?
- Dr. Young: In the scheme of things, does it matter if I'm 86 or 96?
- Mr. Burns: Does it matter if I'm 45 or 52?
- Ms. Watt: Objection. Irrelevant. Let's move on, shall we?
- Mr. Burns: Dr. Young, where'd you receive your education?
- Dr. Young: In various Maya villages. And from my mother.
- Mr. Burns: Where'd you attend college?
- Dr. Young: I never went to college.
- Mr. Burns: Why are you known as 'Doctor' Young?
- Dr. Young: Harvard conferred an honorary degree on me in 1969. The University of Michigan needed it, to justify hiring me for their faculty. So someone scratched someone else's back. That's how academia works.
- Mr. Burns: Ever been married?
- Dr. Young: (Pause) No. I miss anything?
- Mr. Burns: I'm the wrong guy to ask. Ever have children?
- Dr. Young: No.
- Mr. Burns: Your last employment was with the University of Michigan?
- Dr. Young: Yes.
- Mr. Burns: Any particular reason you retired in 1990?
- Dr. Young: I got old. Happens to us all in the end. No matter how ardently Dr. Phelps wishes it were otherwise.
- Mr. Burns: Why'd you choose London for your retirement?
- Dr. Young: I was too old to go back to living in the rain forest.
- Mr. Burns: Why not just stay in Ann Arbor?
- Dr. Young: It's kind of a one-horse town.
- Mr. Burns: Hey now! It may not be as sophisticated as London, but we're not all country bumpkins there, either.
- Ms. Watt: Is there a question?
- Mr. Burns: Sure. When'd you start work at the University – fall of 1970?
- Dr. Young: August, yes.
- Mr. Burns: What was your exact title there?
- Dr. Young: From 1970 to 1982, I was Professor of History. Then I finally got them to create a separate department for Latin and Central American Studies. The last 8 years, I was Professor of Central American Studies.
- Mr. Burns: Ivy, let's mark this Young Exhibit 5. (Hands original to witness, and copies to counsel) Dr. Young, this is a list Joyce got off the internet of 62 books and articles you published. Is it accurate and complete?

- Dr. Young: (Puts on reading glasses and reviews Young Exhibit 5 at length) Well, I can't see any that are missing. It looks like they're probably all here.
- Mr. Burns: Which ones earned you the moniker 'Maya code-breaker'?
- Dr. Young: Moniker! You use that fancy word with juries, Mr. Burns?
- Mr. Burns: Not if I'm thinking clearly. I'll withdraw the question. Which publications earned you the *nickname* 'the Maya code-breaker'?
- Dr. Young: (Grins) None of 'em, really. They gave me that sobriquet when I translated the glyphs on the temple walls at Palenque in 1966.
- Mr. Burns: (Laughs) Sobriquet, that's a good one. Would you agree you are widely considered the world's leading translator of Classic Maya writing?
- Dr. Young: Once I was. But there are many younger stars now.
- Mr. Burns: Where'd you work before you took the U of M post in 1970?
- Dr. Young: In the field.
- Mr. Burns: Who paid your salary?
- Dr. Young: No one.
- Mr. Burns: How'd you live?
- Dr. Young: Like a Queen. The Maya always took wonderful care of me.
- Mr. Burns: From 1925 to 1970, d'you hold any—
- Dr. Young: No, I never held a salaried position of any kind before 1970.
- Mr. Burns: (Chuckles) You're right, Dr. Young, that is exactly what I was going to ask. But even when your keen intelligence allows you to see where I'm going before I get there, you still have to let me finish my question anyway. For Ivy's sake.
- Dr. Young: For Ivy's sake, I'll try. But can't we cut to the chase here? I'm not getting any younger. Why don't you ask me about the *Lamanai Codex*?
- Mr. Burns: I shall. But first I need to know a little more about your background. Did you reside in Central America continuously from 1925 to 1970?
- Dr. Young: No, I lived in Australia from 1945 to 1960. Otherwise, yes, I lived in Central America all my life till 1970.
- Mr. Burns: What'd you do in Australia?
- Dr. Young: I lived with aboriginal tribes, while studying their culture.
- Mr. Burns: Were you paid anything, by anyone?
- Dr. Young: If you mean money, no. They did not use a cash system. But within the tribal structure, I pulled my weight, so I was fed and clothed.
- Mr. Burns: Why'd you return to Central America in 1960?
- Dr. Young: I got word my mother was dying.
- Mr. Burns: You went home to be with her?
- Dr. Young: Yes, but I was too late. She died before my plane arrived.
- Mr. Burns: I'm sorry. Had you visited her in the years before she died?

- Dr. Young: No. We didn't see each other after 1945.
- Mr. Burns: But then you stayed on in Central America, living in Maya villages, while translating Classic Maya glyphs for the next ten years?
- Dr. Young: Yes. That's when I made my mark as a scholar, in the 1960s.
- Mr. Burns: So just a quick recap: You grew up from 1925 to 1945 in Central America, mostly Guatemala, but some in Honduras and Mexico?
- Dr. Young: Yes.
- Mr. Burns: Then from 1945 to 1960 you lived in the bush in Australia, and from 1960 to 1970 you lived in Central America again?
- Dr. Young: Yes.
- Mr. Burns: Then from 1970 to 1990 you lived in Ann Arbor, teaching at U of M; and finally from 1990 to now, you've been retired, living in London?
- Dr. Young: Correct.
- Mr. Burns: You own your London flat?
- Dr. Young: No, I rent it.
- Mr. Burns: You own any real estate?
- Dr. Young: Just the San Pedro property, out on Ambergris Caye.
- Mr. Burns: You still pay taxes on that San Pedro property?
- Dr. Young: Yes.
- Mr. Burns: Is that book you brought here today the *Lamanai Codex*?
- Dr. Young: Yes.
- Mr. Burns: You understand we contend the rightful owner of the *Lamanai Codex* and the San Pedro property is Joyce Kerr, rather than you?
- Dr. Young: I understand that's Joyce's claim.
- Mr. Burns: You've asserted four Affirmative Defenses to our claim. The First Affirmative Defense says: 'Defendant Young is the rightful owner of the codex and the land, because the 1909 orders of the Washtenaw County Probate Court contravened Michigan law by ignoring the clear intent of defendant Young's grandmother, Kathleen Quinlan, as expressed in her Last Will and Testament, to give her entire Estate to defendant Young's mother, Persephone Quinlan, who in turn left her entire Estate to Defendant Young.' Now I know you're not a lawyer, but I want your lay understanding: what's the gist of your First Affirmative Defense?
- Dr. Young: Your client claims the codex and the land belonged to my grandmother Kathleen, and upon Kathleen's death in 1909, Judge Breakey of the Washtenaw County Probate Court awarded everything to Kathleen's son Lloyd. My First Affirmative Defense is that Breakey's Order should be disregarded because it violated the clear intention of Kathleen's Will, and so her Estate should be deemed to have gone where Kathleen clearly intended it to go: to her daughter Persephone. And then from Persephone to me.

- Mr. Burns: You ever study law or go to law school, Dr. Young?
- Dr. Young: No, but the law is not nearly so complex and mysterious as you lawyers would have us believe.
- Mr. Burns: *Touche*, Doctor. Okay, your Second Affirmative Defense says: 'Defendant Young is the rightful owner of the codex and the land, because Judge Breakey's Orders should be deemed invalid, due to the fraud that was perpetrated upon Judge Breakey by Lloyd Quinlan.' Again, I just want your lay understanding of the gist of that Second Affirmative Defense.
- Dr. Young: My uncle, Lloyd Quinlan, was a nasty little devil, a bald-faced liar and a sniveling cheat. He was also a poker mate of Billy Breakey's, and they went out drinking and whoring every Thursday night on Ann Street in Ann Arbor for twenty years. So it wasn't hard for Lloyd to pull the wool over Breakey's eyes. Which Lloyd did, when he got Breakey to rule against Persephone in the Will contest, by duping Breakey into declaring Kathleen insane when she wrote her Will, when in truth she was right as rain.
- Mr. Burns: What if anything did Lloyd do that you say was 'fraudulent', other than asking Judge Breakey in open court to set aside Kathleen's Will?
- Dr. Young: Lloyd convinced Breakey to rule that Kathleen was insane because she committed suicide. But several of Kathleen's dear friends testified she only committed suicide because of the awful public scandal that erupted after her love affair with a married professor was discovered – a discovery orchestrated by Kathleen's own son, the little devil Lloyd, who hired two teenage boys to walk in on Kathleen and her lover, *in flagrante delicto*, in the horse barn at the county fairgrounds where Kathleen and her lover met to requite their passion. Then Lloyd bribed those boys to lie to Breakey and deny Lloyd hired them to spy on Kathleen. That was a fraud on the court, which means Breakey's order should be thrown out, and the true intent of Kathleen's Will should be followed – awarding all to my mother, Persephone.
- Mr. Burns: Thank you. Now I understand. Your Third Affirmative Defense says: 'Dr. Young is the rightful owner of the codex and the land because Judge Breakey was unlawfully biased against independent women, and therefore his decision should be invalidated and the true intent of Kathleen's Will vindicated, awarding the entire estate to Persephone Quinlan, and thence to Fiona Young'. What's your lay understanding of that defense?
- Dr. Young: Billy Breakey hated all women, especially independent women like Kathleen and Persephone. His decision to ignore Kathleen's Will and award all to Lloyd stemmed from bias against independent women that would not be tolerated today. No modern court should enforce Breakey's biased decision; yet that's what Joyce is asking our Judge Henderson to do.
- Mr. Burns: And your Fourth Affirmative Defense says: 'Partially in the alternative, even if Judge Breakey's Orders are upheld and the entirety of Kathleen Quinlan's Estate is

deemed to have been properly awarded to Lloyd Quinlan, the *Lamanai Codex* was never properly part of Kathleen Quinlan's Estate. Rather, the true owner of the codex, from long before Kathleen Quinlan's birth continuously to the present day, has always been defendant Reynolds Foundation, which was not a party to the 1909 Probate Court proceedings and was therefore unaffected by Judge Breakey's Orders.' What's your lay understanding of that defense?

- Dr. Young: You say the codex and the land were owned by Kathleen, awarded to Lloyd, and should have passed to Joyce. I say no, Kathleen wanted everything to go to Persephone, and then to pass to me. But alternatively, I contend Kathleen never owned the codex at all. It was owned from the 18th century by the Reynolds Foundation, so Billy Breakey's attempt to award it to Lloyd Quinlan was just two wicked boys pissing in the wind. If you'll pardon my French.
- Mr. Burns: No problem, Dr. Young. But I really do think you should consider going to law school. You've got it down.
- Dr. Young: I have more important things to do with the short time that's left me, than to spend my days trying to see how long I can talk about one of two inextricably bound propositions, without talking about the other one.
- Mr. Burns: (Laughs) That's your idea of what we lawyers do?
- Dr. Young: You deny it?
- Mr. Burns: (Shakes his head) No, I suppose not. Dr. Young, when d'you first take possession of the *Lamanai Codex*?
- Dr. Young: 1960.
- Mr. Burns: How'd you get possession of it?
- Dr. Young: I took it out of my mother's trunk.
- Mr. Burns: So when Persephone Quinlan died in 1960, you came back home from Australia, and took possession of her things?
- Dr. Young: That's correct.
- Mr. Burns: What other things d'you get from Persephone?
- Dr. Young: The deed to the land on Ambergris Caye. Some money.
- Mr. Burns: How much money?
- Dr. Young: I don't remember. Not a lot.
- Mr. Burns: Anything else you got from Persephone, after she died?
- Dr. Young: (Pause) Her tools. Her books. Her bed. Her dishes. Some old papers of Roger Quinlan's. And a few other keepsakes.
- Mr. Burns: What specific 'keepsakes' did you get from your mother?
- Dr. Young: (Pause; holds out left hand) This wedding ring, which was Kathleen's originally. This locket, on my neck. Some other jewelry, mostly Maya. An old pocket watch that was Roger Quinlan's. A few gifts Mum'd kept, small items of little value.

- Mr. Burns: The gifts include any Maya artifacts?
- Dr. Young: Yes.
- Mr. Burns: Any of the jewelry or artifacts you got from Persephone Quinlan relate in any way to Lamanai or the codex or the fountain of youth?
- Dr. Young: No.
- Mr. Burns: What'd you do with the Roger Quinlan papers you inherited?
- Dr. Young: Kept them, until recently I donated them to the British Museum.
- Mr. Burns: You also take control of Persephone's personal papers?
- Dr. Young: Yes.
- Mr. Burns: What personal papers did Persephone Quinlan have?
- Dr. Young: Goodness, I don't remember. That was 51 years ago.
- Mr. Burns: What papers do you have today that were Persephone's?
- Dr. Young: (Sighs) I threw most of them out long ago. But whatever I kept, I gave to Mrs. Watt, and she gave them to you, for this lawsuit.
- Mr. Burns: So among the papers you got from Persephone after she died were the Deed and other records about the Ambergris Caye land?
- Dr. Young: Yes.
- Mr. Burns: Also among the papers you got from Persephone were various 1909 probate court documents, relating to the dispute between Persephone and Lloyd over Kathleen's estate?
- Dr. Young: Yes.
- Mr. Burns: Persephone Quinlan leave a written Will?
- Dr. Young: (Pause) I don't think so. I don't remember a formal Will. But perhaps there was one. I can't be sure. It was 51 years ago. And I'm very old.
- Mr. Burns: Persephone have any children besides you?
- Dr. Young: No, I was an only child.
- Mr. Burns: Anyone besides you show up in 1960 and claim any of Persephone's things?
- Dr. Young: No, I was her only heir.
- Mr. Burns: Did Persephone leave any unpaid bills – any creditors?
- Dr. Young: No, Mum paid all her debts.
- Mr. Burns: What about after she died? Who paid for Persephone's funeral, and her gravestone, and her cemetery plot, if you weren't there?
- Dr. Young: (Pause) Persephone was cremated before I got there. But it's possible I used some of her money to reimburse the costs of the cremation.
- Mr. Burns: Who arranged for the cremation?
- Dr. Young: Kux Ahawis.
- Mr. Burns: Do the Maya normally cremate their dead?
- Dr. Young: No, but it was what my mother wanted. So Kux arranged it.

- Mr. Burns: Back to the *Lamanai Codex*. When'd you first see it?
- Dr. Young: In my early childhood.
- Mr. Burns: Your mother had it, even back in the 1920s and 1930s?
- Dr. Young: Yes.
- Mr. Burns: Persephone tell you where she got it?
- Dr. Young: From her mother, Kathleen.
- Mr. Burns: How do you know Kathleen was Persephone's mother?
- Dr. Young: (Long pause) How does anyone know who their grandparents are? Mum told me she was Kathleen Quinlan's daughter.
- Mr. Burns: When and where was Persephone Quinlan born?
- Dr. Young: 19 March 1865. In Castlemaine, Australia.
- Mr. Burns: What documentary evidence do you have, if any, to prove that Persephone's mother was Kathleen Quinlan?
- Ms. Watt: Objection. The witness is not a lawyer, so it is unfair to ask her what documents might or might not constitute proof of a particular fact.
- Mr. Burns: Well, as near as I can tell, the witness is more astute on legal matters than most lawyers. But let's try it this way: how do you know Persephone Quinlan was born in Australia?
- Dr. Young: That's what she told me.
- Mr. Burns: How do you know her birth date was March 19th, 1865?
- Dr. Young: That's what she told me.
- Mr. Burns: You ever see Persephone Quinlan's birth certificate?
- Dr. Young: No. (Looks at Ms. Kerr) Why – does Joyce have a copy of that, too, lurking in those big stacks of paper you've got?
- Mr. Burns: There's no telling what Joyce has in those stacks. (Turns to Ms. Kerr) Joyce, do you have a birth certificate for Persephone Quinlan?
- Ms. Kerr: Yes. (Hands documents to Mr. Burns, who hands copies to witness and counsel).
- Mr. Burns: Let's mark as Young Exhibit 6 a 'Certificate of Live Birth' from Thomas Guy's Hospital, right here in old London town, for Persephone Allen Quinlan. You see the birth date is listed as 10 January 1869?
- Dr. Young: (To Ms. Kerr) Where on earth did you get this?
- Mr. Burns: It was attached to a 'Motion to Intervene' that Persephone Quinlan filed in September, 1909 in the Probate Court in Ann Arbor. Does looking at Exhibit 6 refresh your recollection that your mother was really born in London in 1869, rather than Australia in 1865?
- Ms. Watt: Object to the form of the question. Argumentative.
- Mr. Burns: You can answer, Dr. Young.

■ Dr. Young: My mother Persephone was born in Castlemaine, Australia in 1865. She was the illegitimate child of Roger Quinlan and Kathleen Allen, later Kathleen Quinlan. Shortly after birth, Kathleen abandoned Persephone to foster care in Australia. In 1909 Kathleen wrote to Persephone, begging her forgiveness and inviting her to come to Ann Arbor. But by the time Persephone arrived, some months later, Kathleen had committed suicide. Persephone learned of Kathleen's Will, leaving everything to Persephone, so she went to the Probate Court and intervened in the legal proceedings. But since this was 1909, she feared an illegitimate daughter would have little chance against the legitimate son, Lloyd Quinlan – particularly since Lloyd was thick as thieves with the Judge. So Persephone forged the birth certificate you have there, Exhibit whatever. Six. She lied and told Billy Breakey she was Lloyd Quinlan's twin, born in London the same day as Lloyd, but sent away to Australia when she was just an infant, for reasons unknown. But the truth is, Persephone was born four years before Lloyd.

■ Mr. Burns: How do you know so much detail about all this?

■ Dr. Young: My mother told me the whole story. Many times. We had little dolls of Uncle Lloyd and Judge Breakey, and we stuck pins in them every night before dinner, hoping to cause them to drop dead.

■ Mr. Burns: Did Judge Breakey—

■ Dr. Young: I'm pulling your leg, Mr. Burns. We did not practice voodoo, my mother and I. But my mother was very deeply affected by the travesty of the 1909 court proceedings, which is why I am so familiar with all the details.

■ Mr. Burns: Did Judge Breakey in 1909 believe your mother's tall tale – about being Lloyd's twin sister?

■ Ms. Watt: Objection. How can she know what the Judge believed?

■ Dr. Young: Who knows? As I said, Breakey hated strong-minded independent women. He disapproved of Kathleen's affair with a married professor. He disliked illegitimate children. And he caroused every Thursday night with Lloyd. He was determined to give Kathleen's estate to his whoring mate Lloyd, no matter what Kathleen's Will said. And that's what he did.

■ Mr. Burns: Alright, back to your First Affirmative Defense, that Judge Breakey contravened Michigan law by ignoring the clear intent of Kathleen Quinlan's Will – what are all the specific facts that support that defense?

■ Dr. Young: Facts? Kathleen's Will directed that all her assets should be left to Persephone. Instead of following that clear directive, Breakey gave all her assets to Lloyd. Fact is, that contravenes the law everywhere in the world, even in Michigan. I don't think I *need* any facts besides that.

■ Mr. Burns: But you're aware Judge Breakey found, as a fact, that Kathleen Quinlan was insane when she wrote her Will, as evidenced by the fact that she deliberately drove off a bridge four hours later, leaving a suicide note?

- Dr. Young: Rubbish! You know who witnessed Kathleen's Will?
- Mr. Burns: Is that a rhetorical question?
- Dr. Young: One witness was a physician, and the other was the Dean of the School of Humanities. Both men testified in the Probate Court that Kathleen was perfectly sound and in good spirits when she wrote her Will and asked them to witness it. (To Ms. Kerr) Since you're so good at digging things out, dear, you really should go find their testimony. It was very persuasive.
- Mr. Burns: What specific facts support your Second Affirmative Defense, where you say Lloyd Quinlan perpetrated fraud on Judge Breakey?
- Dr. Young: I have these. (Hands two documents to Mr. Burns).
- Mr. Burns: We'll mark as Young Exhibit 7 the October 11, 1970 Affidavit of Andrew Spink; and as Young Exhibit 8 the October 11, 1970 Affidavit of David Hall. (Looks at Mr. Santos) Sorry, Miguel, no copies for you, I guess. (Looks back at Dr. Young) What are these documents?
- Dr. Young: When I moved to Ann Arbor in 1970, after I settled in at my new job, I sought out those two gentlemen whose peeping, back when they were lads in 1909, provoked my grandmother to drive off that bridge. After much soul-searching, these gentlemen, then old and gray, provided these Affidavits, confessing that in their youth, Lloyd Quinlan directed them to the horse barn at the County fairgrounds on that fateful date in August 1909; that Lloyd paid them to walk in on his mother and her lover; and that Lloyd paid them again, eleven weeks later, to lie to Judge Breakey and deny they'd been working in Lloyd's employ when they made their fateful discovery.
- Mr. Burns: (Reviews Exhibits 7 & 8) You went to all this trouble in 1970, because you anticipated that one day I'd ask you questions about all this?
- Ms. Watt: Objection! It's (pause) – oh, go ahead and answer, Dr. Young. Honestly, though, David, you do take absurd liberties.
- Dr. Young: I obtained these Affidavits in the service of truth, Mr. Burns. History – as your 'consultant', Dr. Graham has written – is a collection of lies and half-truths, perpetrated by the dead upon the living. In this situation, I wanted to be sure, should anyone in the future ask why my grandmother drove off that bridge, that the truth would be available. On the record, as you lawyers say.
- Mr. Burns: (Pause) What specific facts support your Third Affirmative Defense, where you allege Judge Breakey was 'unlawfully biased against independent women', like Kathleen Quinlan and Persephone Quinlan?
- Dr. Young: Do you know where the Bentley Historical Library is in Ann Arbor?
- Mr. Burns: Yes.
- Dr. Young: Go there. Read Billy Breakey's papers, which were donated to the Library when he died. I looked them up, when I moved to Ann Arbor in 1970. But don't send Joyce

to read Breakey's papers for you, Mr. Burns; do it yourself. I promise you'll cringe to think that such a Neanderthal could have served as a judge in the town whose sophistication you were extolling a few minutes ago. If we go to trial one day, you'll need to pick a jury full of men. Because if any woman sees Breakey's papers, she'll vote against your client.

- Mr. Burns: Thanks for the tip. Joyce, can we look at – thank you. (Hands copies to the witness and all counsel) Ivy, let's mark this next one Young Exhibit 9. You ever see Exhibit 9 before, Dr. Young?
- Ms. Watt: This document's in Spanish.
- Mr. Burns: That's the language they speak in Guatemala.
- Ms. Watt: I don't speak Spanish.
- Mr. Burns: Neither do I. But I bet your client does.
- Mr. Santos: I can translate it. (Looks at Mr. Burns) If you want me to.
- Mr. Burns: Thanks, Miguel, but it's not necessary. The words on this form are unimportant. For the record, I believe the title translates to: 'Application for Permission to Excavate Ancient Ruins'. Is that right, Dr. Young?
- Dr. Young: (Looking hard at Ms. Kerr) How'd you *ever* get a hold of this?
- Mr. Burns: Like the Lord, Joyce works in mysterious ways. You ever see this document before, Dr. Young?
- Dr. Young: (Puts on her reading glasses, reviews Exhibit 9) No.
- Mr. Burns: You see that—
- Dr. Young: Mum listed her birth date as 19 March 1875, yes.
- Mr. Burns: You recognize your mother's signature at the bottom?
- Dr. Young: Yes.
- Mr. Burns: And is the birth date also in your mother's handwriting?
- Dr. Young: (Squinting) Yes, I think it is.
- Mr. Burns: Do you know why your mother would lie about her birth date on an Application For Permission To Excavate Ancient Ruins?
- Dr. Young: I can imagine. See the date on this form: 1 April 1955.
- Mr. Burns: (Pause) I'm not following you. Are you saying Persephone was playing an April Fool's Day joke on the Guatemalan government?
- Dr. Young: No, I'm saying that in 1955, Mum was 90 years old. She probably feared a Guatemalan bureaucrat might deny her application to dig out there in the mountains, if he realized how old she was. She probably decided 80 sounded better'n 90.
- Mr. Burns: (Laughs) That's ridiculous. I mean, if 90 is too old to excavate ancient ruins, isn't 80 too old, too?
- Ms. Watt: Objection. Don't belittle my client's answers, David.
- Mr. Burns: It's hard not to, Olivia. In 27 years, I've never had a case where the witness has two birth dates – 1925, and 1915 – and her mother has three: 1865, 1869 and 1875!

- Ms. Watt: Is there a question, or are you just thinking out loud?
- Mr. Burns: Yeah, there's a question. Dr. Young, is your family for real?
- Ms. Watt: Objection. Argumentative and badgering. (To Dr. Young) Don't answer that question, Fiona. I think it's plainly time we all take a break.

Off the record at 10:32 a.m.

* * *

The conference room door closes behind the departing Fiona Young, Olivia Watt and Miguel Santos. Ivy Taylor rises to stretch her lovely long legs. David Burns also stands, to stretch his aging back. And the Brethren of the Coast all rise and pepper Burns with a chorus of questions.

"Why do you let her just blatantly lie?" Clive Phelps demands.

"How come you let her off the hook about the Kux letter?" Ron Graham asks. "It was obviously about the *Lamanai Codex* and the fountain of youth."

"We gettin' anywhere with all this birthday shit?" Kip Hunter asks.

Burns rolls his eyes at Ivy, seeking sympathy. But Ivy misinterprets Burns.

"You want me to step outside?" Ivy asks.

"Oh no, no need for that," Burns says. "But thanks for asking, Ivy."

"Actually, Ivy," Joyce Kerr says, "we could use a few minutes alone."

Ivy meets Joyce's steady gaze, nods curtly, and exits.

"I know you like that short skirt, David," Joyce says, when Ivy's gone, "but Ivy's a little too chummy with Fiona for my taste. All that '*dready dawta*' stuff."

"Also, Ivy's office is just round the corner," Phelps adds. "Like you said, she probably gets a lot of work from Symington & Watt."

"Fair points," Burns says. "Okay, we'll boot Ivy out on all future breaks. Though I will miss those long legs." Burns looks at the Three Blind Mice. "Guys, I warned you: a deposition is like watching paint dry. If you're bored and wanna go sight-seeing, or go visit Clive's lab, feel free."

All Three Fools demur to this offer.

"Okay," Burns says. "Since the walls may have ears, gang, please lean in close while I attempt to answer your questions."

Burns sits on the table with his feet on his chair, facing Joyce, who stays in her chair. Phelps, Graham and Hunter crowd round the back of Joyce's chair, and bend forward, like an American football team huddling before its next play.

"It's good for us," Burns whispers, "when Fiona lies. It opens the door for us later, at trial, to expose the lie. So each time Fiona lies, Clive, try telling yourself 'this is good, I hope she keeps lying, so we'll be able to catch her later'."

"Why not catch her in the lie *right now*?" Phelps asks.

Burns pushes the air in front of him down, like a conductor signaling an orchestra to play *pianissimo*. "Each time we catch Fiona in a lie now," Burns whispers, "we get the joy of rubbing her funky nose ring in it, like when she denied all contact with Kux for years, and then I whipped out her own letter to Kux from last July." Burns nods at Graham. "Great work, Ron, getting that letter."

Graham nods back.

"But what did we actually gain, by catching Fiona in that lie?" Burns murmurs. "*Nada*. All we did was, we gave Fiona the chance, which she jumped all over, to correct her earlier lie; and once she knew we had the letter, she easily sidestepped all the other potholes in that letter, by claiming memory problems."

"Fiona has a very selective memory," Clive grumbles.

"Sure does," Burns whispers. "She can't recall a letter she wrote last year, threatening to burn the codex; yet she recalls 1909 like it was yesterday and she was right there in court with 'Billy' Breakey, even though she only heard those details second-hand, sometime before 1945. But old people get away with that kind of crap in depos."

"So why'd you show her the letter to Kux at all?" Graham asks.

"Cause I wanted to teach Fiona a lesson right outta the gate. Once we produced that letter, you saw her worrying about what else we have in Joyce's stacks of paper. If Fiona's afraid like that, she's more likely to tell the truth. But there's no point in impeaching her every time she lies, cause she'll just correct all her lies, and we'll leave here with nothing. Whereas if we let her lie and she thinks she's gotten away with it, then later we'll have a chance to hang her with it, at trial."

"But won't she play the same game at trial?" Clive asks. "Lie till you catch her, then say 'sorry, my mistake, I'm old' – and just correct her lie at trial, too?"

"Much harder game to play at trial," Burns whispers, "with a jury watching. No jury'll believe she doesn't remember what book she was threatening to burn, or what fountain she was talking about. Which is why I stopped asking about the letter, Ron. We got all we could – and all we need. If you look at the words Fiona used in that letter, they're unfortunately not very precise. There were better ways for her to wriggle out of that letter, rather than pleading memory failure. I was afraid if I kept asking about that letter, she'd think up a better explanation."

"What if she gives a better explanation at trial?" Graham whispers.

"Probably will," Burns murmurs. "But she'll look terrible. No memory at all during the depo, and then at trial suddenly a whole new story about what she was writing to Kux about? The jury'll see through that – and punish her for it."

Burns drops his voice below a whisper. "Kip, I do think we're getting somewhere with all this birthday shit. I'm setting up some very hard questions Joyce and I cooked up for Fiona. But I don't even want to whisper about this right now. If it doesn't work out, I'll explain it at lunch, okay?"

"You got it, bro'." Hunter bumps a fist against Burns's hand, like two MTV rappers.

Burns wonders what sins he committed in a past life to earn him Joyce's Three Admirers as his allies. Oh well, you can't always pick your teammates.

"I got a coupla questions back at you guys," Burns whispers. "Like, how does Fiona afford to live here in Butler's Wharf, and hire a swanky law firm like Symington & Watt? She made no money in Australia, and she says Persephone left her zip – which is plausible, since Persephone was an archeologist who got zip from Kathleen, except the codex and the land she stole, neither of which've ever been sold. But then Fiona spends 10 years in the field with the Maya, and 20 years at U of M, where Latin American studies profs don't exactly rake in big bucks. And I know Fiona's Maya books were never big sellers. Yet when she retires, she moves to this swanky neighborhood? I don't get it."

"She's only renting, David," Joyce says. "Could be a real small flat."

"Some of the smaller flats in Butler's Wharf are still reasonable," Phelps adds. "And even though Symington & Watt is a big firm, Butler's Wharf is not where the really high-priced lawyers in London are found. Olivia's rates may actually be lower than yours."

"Fair points." Burns ducks Phelps' implicit complaint about Burns's bills. "Okay, next: I've heard of women wearing their grandmother's rings. But not on the ring finger of the *left* hand, as if she were married to Roger Quinlan! Did she do that in her Ann Arbor days, too?"

Joyce nods yes. "The past has always been very real for Fiona."

"I guess," Burns says. "Okay, my last question pissed Olivia off at the end. But I'm serious: twenty years it was just Fiona and Persephone, Mom and daughter against the world, but then one day Fiona goes off into the Australian bush, and never sees her Mom again? This – after Kathleen abandons Persephone, and then invites her daughter to a reunion 44 years later, only to commit suicide just before Persephone arrives in Ann Arbor? Is this family *for real*?"

"It was clearly a very dysfunctional family," Phelps says, "where the sins of the mothers kept getting visited upon the daughters."

"Maybe Kathleen got cold feet about a reunion with the child she'd abandoned," Joyce suggests. "In her shoes I'd've been scared to death to face Persephone."

"That might be the real reason," Graham adds, "for Kathleen's suicide."

"Instead of the boys spying in the hayloft?" Burns says. "Makes sense – though I can't do anything about that here. What d'you think about all this, Kip?"

Hunter shakes his head. "I think the old lady's just making it all up as she goes."

Burns chuckles, but then sees Hunter's serious. "You think it's all a lie?"

"The whole kit and caboodle," Hunter says. "I think the old lady's totally schizo."

CHAPTER ELEVEN

Blood in the Water

Monday 4 April 2009 Late Morning

Back on the record at 10:54 a.m. All parties present earlier remain in attendance.

- Mr. Burns: So you were born in 1925, not 1915, correct?
- Dr. Young: Correct.
- Mr. Burns: And Persephone was born in 1865, not 1869 or 1875?
- Dr. Young: Correct.
- Mr. Burns: Which means Persephone was *60 years old* when she gave birth to you?
- Dr. Young: Fifty-nine, actually. Five weeks short of turning sixty.
- Mr. Burns: Did eyebrows go up in San Lorenzo when a sixty-year-old woman got pregnant?
- Dr. Young: I wasn't taking much notice of the outside world back then.
- Mr. Burns: (Laughs) *Touche*, Doctor. How 'bout when you were growing up – were the San Lorenzo villagers amazed at how old your mother was?
- Dr. Young: I don't think they really knew how old she was. (Glances at Ms. Kerr) The women in our family tend to look younger than we are.
- Mr. Burns: I'll stipulate Ms. Kerr is living proof your family has good genes. But it takes more than good genes to give birth at 59. I've heard of women giving birth at 45 or 50, but never 59!
- Ms. Watt: Is there a question?
- Mr. Burns: Sure. Did Persephone Quinlan drink from the fountain of youth, in order to allow her to get pregnant at such an advanced age?
- Ms. Watt: (Exasperated) David!
- Dr. Young: Not so far as I know, Mr. Burns.
- Mr. Burns: Did Persephone Quinlan receive any special medical intervention or treatment to help get pregnant at such an advanced age?
- Dr. Young: I don't know what you mean by 'special medical intervention or treatments'.

- Mr. Burns: Well, I suppose in 1925 there was no such thing as *in vitro* fertilization or advanced hormone therapy, right?
- Ms. Watt: Objection. The witness is not a medical expert.
- Dr. Young: Your question betrays cultural bias. You assume a woman can't get pregnant after 50 without the latest medical wizardry of so-called civilized countries. But in so-called primitive cultures, where people live in much greater harmony with nature than we supposedly civilized folk do, women often give birth in their 50s. The oldest recorded age of a birth mother is 72.
- Mr. Burns: Aw, c'mon, that lady got *in vitro* fertilization, didn't she?
- Dr. Young: (Shrugs) I don't recall. But the Bible says Sarah was 90 when she gave birth to Isaac. And ask Dr. Phelps, there've been women, even in the US and UK, in their late 50s, up to 59, who conceived naturally, without *in vitro* gimmickry, and gave birth to healthy children. Those cases got recorded, because they were unusual in industrial cultures. But in villages in Central America and Australia, no one makes a fuss when a woman in her late 50s gives birth.
- Mr. Burns: Alright, I'll ask Dr. Phelps. (Shaking his head) Did your mother have a nose ring when you were growing up, like you do now?
- Dr. Young: Yes.
- Mr. Burns: Where'd she get hers, and where'd you get yours?
- Dr. Young: (Pause) She got hers in San Lorenzo. I got mine in Australia.
- Mr. Burns: You ever meet your uncle Lloyd, Persephone's brother?
- Dr. Young: (Pause) No. I was four when the little devil died.
- Mr. Burns: If you never met him, why do you call Lloyd 'the little devil'?
- Dr. Young: Because Lloyd felt no remorse about driving his mother to commit suicide after exposing her affair. Only a devil feels no remorse.
- Mr. Burns: How d'you know Lloyd felt no remorse, if you weren't there?
- Dr. Young: My mother said Lloyd shed no tears; he lied to cover his crimes; and after Kathleen died, Lloyd just kept on gambling and whoring. He was a nasty little devil.
- Mr. Burns: You ever meet Lloyd's daughter, Grace Quinlan?
- Dr. Young: No. Grace died shortly before I moved to Ann Arbor in 1970.
- Mr. Burns: You ever speak with Grace Quinlan on the telephone, or exchange letters, or communicate with Grace in any way?
- Dr. Young: No.
- Mr. Burns: To your knowledge, was Grace aware at any time during her life that Persephone, and later you, were paying taxes on the Ambergris Caye real estate that once belonged to Grace's grandmother, Kathleen Quinlan?
- Dr. Young: I have no idea.

- Mr. Burns: To your knowledge, was Grace aware at any time during her life that Persephone, and later you, had possession of the *Lamanai Codex*?
- Dr. Young: I have no idea what Grace knew. I never met her. But her father Lloyd certainly knew Persephone had the codex.
- Mr. Burns: How do you know Lloyd knew Persephone had the codex?
- Dr. Young: Because after Lloyd won the probate case, and discovered the codex was missing, he swore out a warrant against Persephone.
- Mr. Burns: A criminal warrant?
- Dr. Young: I believe so. As you like to say, I wasn't there. But Mum said she came to Central America in the first place to escape Lloyd's warrant.
- Mr. Burns: Your mother said she was fleeing from legal process?
- Ms. Watt: Objection. Calls for a legal conclusion.
- Dr. Young: Mum didn't put it that way. She said her brother swore out a warrant to try to get the codex back, and since he played poker with all the cops and judges, she figured it might be a real good time to move to Central America and take up her interest in Maya archeology.
- Mr. Burns: And once she got down to British Honduras, the first thing she did was start paying taxes on the Ambergris Caye land?
- Dr. Young: Well, I don't know if it was the very first thing she did. But sometime after arriving, she did begin paying taxes on that land, yes.
- Mr. Burns: Let's mark as Young Exhibit 10 a Quitclaim Deed to certain real estate located in the town of San Pedro, on Ambergris Caye in Belize. (Hands copies to witness and all counsel). You ever see this before?
- Dr. Young: (Glances at the document) Perhaps. But I can't be sure. Even though you say I'd be a good lawyer, legal documents bore me.
- Mr. Burns: Me too. But I find this one more interesting than most. If you go to the second page, are those, as far as you know, the signatures of your mother Persephone Quinlan, and grand-mother Kathleen Quinlan?
- Dr. Young: Yes, I believe so.
- Mr. Burns: You see the notarized date of 28 November 1909?
- Dr. Young: Yes.
- Mr. Burns: When did Kathleen Quinlan die?
- Dr. Young: (Long pause, then reads the entire document)
- Mr. Burns: When did Kathleen Quinlan die?
- Dr. Young: 1 September 1909.
- Mr. Burns: You ever happen to meet the person listed as the notary public for this document, Isidro Rios?
- Dr. Young: No.

- Mr. Burns: Do you know whether Isidro Rios made a practice of conducting séances in order to obtain signatures by dead people?
- Ms. Watt: Objection! There's nothing on the face of this document to make us doubt that Kathleen Quinlan signed this while she was alive.
- Mr. Burns: Really? Then how come the small print there, under Isidro Rios's signature, says that old Isidro 'attests that before him on the date stamped came the persons whose signatures appear on this document, and they produced appropriate proof of their identities'?
- Ms. Watt: How do I know the small print really says that? I don't speak Spanish.
- Mr. Burns: It's in English, like all legal documents in Belize.
- Ms. Watt: Oh. (Puts on her reading glasses, and inspects Exhibit 10) I'll withdraw the objection. But your tone is still most inappropriate, Mr. Burns.
- Mr. Burns: A lifelong problem. Ms. Kerr has urged me to seek tonal therapy. Dr. Young, do you know who appeared before Isidro Rios on 28 November 1909, pretending to be your deceased grandmother Kathleen?
- Dr. Young: (Pause) No. I wasn't born until 1925.
- Mr. Burns: But sometimes it almost feels like you were there. (Grins, then looks at Ms. Watt) Is there a question? You bet there is. Before we took our break this morning, Dr. Young, you told me that in 1909 Kathleen Quinlan wrote to Persephone, begging her forgiveness and inviting her to come to Ann Arbor. Do you have the original of that letter?
- Dr. Young: Yes.
- Mr. Burns: May I assume you have it with you now, since your subpoena *duces tecum* for this deposition required you to bring the originals of all correspondence, including envelopes, in your possession involving you, Persephone, and Kathleen?
- Ms. Watt: She has just two letters, David, responsive to your subpoena. (Hands over two original letters, and two envelopes)
- Mr. Burns: Ivy, let's mark as Young Exhibit 11—
- Dr. Young: No, I want to keep those letters. I don't mind you looking at them, but I don't want the originals marked as exhibits. They're too precious.
- Mr. Burns: (Shaking his head no) They're evidence in a lawsuit, ma'am.
- Ms. Watt: David, I've got extra copies of both letters. Why don't we just mark one set of copies, and let Dr. Young retain the originals?
- Mr. Burns: No, the standard American procedure, which we agreed to follow, is for Ivy to take custody of all originals. The *Lamanai Codex*, if I make it an exhibit, will be an exception, because of the Escrow Order. But for all the other exhibits, I want standard procedure followed. I'm sure Ivy'll take good care of all the exhibits, especially these old letters, won't you, Ivy?

- Ms. Taylor: Yes, I will. (Looks at Dr. Young) I keep all de exhibits in de case for my steno machine. Dat way dere's no chance of me losing dem. Den, when de deposition is over, I file dem in a safe in my office until de case is over. Den I give dem back to de lawyers.
- Dr. Young: Dese letters are very precious to me, *dready dawta*.
- Ivy Taylor: I know dat, dear. Dey'll be safe wid me.
- Dr. Young: (Sighs) All right den.
- Mr. Burns: Good. Ivy, I'd like to mark as Young Exhibit 11 a letter dated 8 March 1909, from Kathleen Quinlan to Persephone Quinlan. Young Exhibit 12 will be the accompanying envelope, postmarked from Detroit, Michigan on March 10, 1909. Young Exhibit 13 will be a letter from Persephone Quinlan back to Kathleen Quinlan, dated 1 June 1909. And Young Exhibit 14 will be the accompanying envelope, postmarked from Sydney, Australia on 4 June 1909. Now Dr. Young, can you identify the handwriting on Exhibit 11?
- Dr. Young: Yes, that's my grandmother, Kathleen Quinlan.
- Mr. Burns: You're sure?
- Dr. Young: Positive.
- Mr. Burns: How can you be so sure, if this envelope and the letter inside are the only Kathleen Quinlan documents you've got in your possession?
- Dr. Young: I've seen many other documents Kathleen wrote.
- Mr. Burns: Where?
- Dr. Young: In the Bentley Historical Library, Mr. Burns. Kathleen was one of the first women on the U of M faculty. The Bentley has almost all of Kathleen's papers from her Michigan days, except this letter I have, and the Will and the suicide note, which are still in the Probate Court file. (Looks at Ms. Kerr) I'm surprised Joyce didn't find the Bentley papers for you.
- Ms. Kerr: (Mutters) Joyce only has so many hours in the day.
- Mr. Burns: And Mr. Burns has far too many bright ideas for how Joyce can spend those hours. (Chuckles) So this is Kathleen's writing on the letter. Can you also identify the writing on the envelope that goes with it, Exhibit 12?
- Dr. Young: Yes, that's Kathleen's writing also.
- Mr. Burns: (Shaking his head skeptically) And I suppose you'll tell me you also know for a fact your grandmother licked these stamps on Exhibit 12 in March of 1909, too?
- Dr. Young: As a matter of fact, yes, she did.
- Mr. Burns: (Scoffs) Oh c'mon! How can you possibly know that? Didn't your grandmother have a secretary at the University of Michigan?
- Ms. Watt: Objection. Compound question. Argumentative.
- Dr. Young: Kathleen did have a secretary – but early March, when this envelope was stamped and mailed, was Spring Recess at the University.

- Mr. Burns: But that doesn't prove—
- Dr. Young: Excuse me, I wasn't finished.
- Mr. Burns: Sorry. (Smiles) Go ahead and finish, please.
- Dr. Young: The way I know Kathleen herself put these stamps on the envelope is that I'm a stamp collector. These are Heritage USA stamps, newly issued in 1909, and available that spring only along the eastern seaboard of the United States. When Persephone came to Ann Arbor in September 1909, she found a roll of these stamps in Kathleen's desk. A dear friend of Kathleen's, Professor Raynold Niehoff, told Persephone that Kathleen got them on a trip to New York in February 1909, just before she wrote Persephone. If you look through Kathleen's correspondence at the Bentley, you'll see that all her 1909 envelopes have these stamps.
- Mr. Burns: (Gestures surrender) Alright, can you also identify the handwriting on Exhibit 13?
- Dr. Young: Yes, that's Mum's writing.
- Mr. Burns: And how about Exhibit 14, the envelope containing Persephone's letter to Kathleen? Is there anything about those Australian stamps that allows you to say for sure that Persephone licked those stamps?
- Ms. Watt: Objection. What's the relevance of all these stamps?
- Mr. Burns: Relevance is not the issue, Olivia. American rules only require me to ask questions 'reasonably calculated to lead to the discovery of admissible evidence'. Almost any question meets that standard.
- Ms. Watt: Maybe so. But you're still wasting everyone's time, David.
- Mr. Burns: Humor me, Olivia. Doctor, do you know if Persephone licked these stamps, the way you know Kathleen licked the stamps on Exhibit 12?
- Dr. Young: No, I don't. But that's Mum's handwriting on the envelope.
- Mr. Burns: Do you know if these two letters – Young Exhibits 11 and 13 – were ever submitted to the Washtenaw County Probate Court?
- Dr. Young: Yes, they were.
- Mr. Burns: How do you know that?
- Dr. Young: Mum told me. She submitted the bogus birth certificate we looked at earlier, but Lloyd told Breakey he'd've known if he had a twin sister. Persephone was standing there, the spitting image of Kathleen, but she could see Breakey was leaning Lloyd's way. So she submitted these letters, to prove she was Kathleen Quinlan's daughter. And then even Breakey had to admit, Persephone must be Lloyd's sister. So then Lloyd cooked up the insanity theory, and paid the Spink and Hall boys to lie, in order to deny Persephone her rightful inheritance.
- Mr. Burns: But if Persephone submitted these letters to Judge Breakey, why weren't they retained in the Probate file, like the Will and suicide note?

- Ms. Watt: Objection. How can Dr. Young possibly know what document retention procedures were followed by an American probate court 16 years before she was born? As you well know, David, it's possible Judge Breakey reviewed these letters *in camera*, and then gave them back to Persephone Quinlan once he was satisfied she was Kathleen's daughter.
- Mr. Burns: Ivy, I'd like you to mark this spot in the transcript please, so we can find it later. Olivia, this is the second time this morning you've supplied the witness an answer under the guise of making an objection—
- Ms. Watt: That is most assuredly not what I was doing!
- Mr. Burns: May I finish?
- Ms. Watt: No, you may not. I'm going to finish first. I have a perfect right to state objections for the record, particularly to your outlandish and improper questions, and to state the basis for my objections sufficiently fully so that our Judge back in Detroit, reading this transcript, may know the basis for my objections. That is all I was doing in this case. I was most definitely not 'supplying the witness an answer', and I resent your implication otherwise.
- Mr. Burns: Are you done?
- Ms. Watt: For now.
- Mr. Burns: Olivia, out of deep respect for you, I accept your representation that you did not mean to supply the answer to Dr. Young with your objection. Nevertheless, however good your intentions may have been, it's not proper under American rules to express an objection so fully that you effectively supply the witness an answer she might not have come up with on her own. If this happens again, I'll stop the deposition till we can take this up with Judge Henderson, because I'm entitled to get Dr. Young's testimony, and not yours.
- Ms. Watt: Let's stop right now, call Judge Henderson, and sort this out.
- Mr. Burns: (Shaking his head no) It's only 6:15 a.m. in Detroit. The courthouse phones aren't answered till 8. Besides, Judge Henderson would expect me to warn you twice before taking up his time. So consider yourself warned, for the second time.
- Ms. Watt: For more than the second time, I resent your offensive tone.
- Mr. Burns: I'm getting the feeling I may not make your Christmas card list, Olivia. But I'll soldier on anyway. Dr. Young, since these letters are very important, and since the handwriting is amazingly spidery and small, I'm going to ask you please to read them into the record. Let's start with Exhibit 11, the 8 March 1909 letter Kathleen wrote to Persephone. What's it say?
- Dr. Young: (Puts on reading glasses) Dearest Persephone: I am your mother, who, to her eternal shame, abandoned you in infancy. I write you now to beg your forgiveness; but more importantly, to offer you substantial financial assistance – woefully late though this offer is.

Well can I imagine how you must be tempted to crumple this letter and hurl it against the wall, without reading it. No one could blame you, Persephone, least of all I. But if you're still reading, dearest girl, please understand that unpardonable as my abandonment of you was – and freely I confess, it was an awful deed – still, I've thought of you, Persephone, every hour of every day these 44 years we've been apart. And most earnestly I wish you would come home to me now, and hold my hand in the dark, as I approach the end of my days.

I could offer you excuses. I could point to the heavy social duress under which I laboured when you were born, an unwed mother in a harsh and unforgiving time. But I make no such excuses for myself. The plain and simple truth is, abandoning you to the Melbourne poorhouse was a cowardly, shameful and despicable act. Almost as bad was my failure, all these years, to hire detectives to look for you, another tragic mistake for which I have neither excuse, nor explanation, nor even understanding.

In short, I cannot imagine you would wish to see me now – though I long to see you, dear Persephone, more than you can possibly guess. So I write these few, pathetic lines, in the vain hope that even if you prefer not to see me, you might travel to America anyway, in order to collect an advance portion of the very substantial inheritance I intend to bequeath you. Your father, Roger Quinlan, is long dead, yet he and I accumulated considerable wealth; and although I have a son, your brother, Lloyd Quinlan, he is a pusillanimous little bugger for whom I have no use, who already has too much money of his own, which he squanders on liquor and prostitutes, and therefore needs no further accretion of assets from my estate.

So leave it at this, dear girl: you may contact your mother, if you choose, by writing to Professor Kathleen Quinlan, 217 North Division Street, Ann Arbor, Michigan, United States of America. I should so dearly love to hear from you. But even if I do not, it is my intention to bequeath all my worldly possessions to you, Persephone, and I do hope you shall come to America and claim them in time, before your nasty little brother steals them from you.

With the deepest regret and apologies for all the harm I inflicted on you,

Your Mother, Kathleen Quinlan.

- Mr. Burns: Wow. This letter, Exhibit 11, was among Persephone's personal papers, which you inherited when she died?
- Dr. Young: Yes. But I'd seen it before then. It was part of my childhood, the legacy of the tortured Quinlans.
- Mr. Burns: And after all the lawyer talk, d'you ever get the chance to tell me how Persephone ended up with this original document, instead of the Probate Court keeping it?
- Ms. Watt: Only if you know, Dr. Young.
- Dr. Young: The court clerk gave it back to her. Since no one had formally introduced it as an exhibit, the clerk just gave it back to Persephone.

- Mr. Burns: (Nods) Could you now read Exhibit 13 into the record, which is Persephone's 1 June 1909 response to Kathleen's letter that you just read?
- Dr. Young: Dear Professor Quinlan: You are correct to dread my response. Your words strike me now like rain on crops long dead from drought. All through my childhood, I longed to know: Who were my parents? Why did they desert me? What were their struggles? What kind of people were they? Were they gentle? Were they passionate? Did they suffer? Most of all, why did they abandon me to the orphanage?

  But when I grew up, Professor, I gave up caring about my parents. I'm an orphan. That's all there is to it. My parents are as dead to me now as I've been dead to them all my life. Yet now your letter appears, a bolt out of the blue, like the mirages weary travelers think they see, when they've traveled too long in the Outback. You'd like me to come 'home' and hold your hand, while you prepare to face the dark? Can you possibly imagine how ironic your words sound to me? I faced more darkness in my lonesome childhood than you will ever know in your old age. And I never had a mother to hold my hand.

  But it's plain you're a clever one, Professor, for you dangle before me the enticing prospect of future wealth – while like a magician, you artfully neglect to enumerate the precise sum, instead leading me on to peer behind the curtain, where all is vague and dusky, like you yourself. Still, much as I hate to reward your cleverness, I shall book passage on the first packet to America, and come see you. But not for the reunion. Only for the money.

  Persephone Quinlan
- Mr. Burns: Ouch. Thank you, Dr. Young, for reading these emotionally charged letters into the record. But to return to the mundane world of legal issues where I dwell, I need to ask: these two letters, Exhibits 11 and 13, are the sole basis for your belief your mother was Kathleen Quinlan's daughter?
- Dr. Young: No, that's not true.
- Mr. Burns: What other proof do you have that Persephone was descended from Kathleen?
- Dr. Young: They had the same last name: Quinlan.
- Mr. Burns: Anything else you can point to that you think proves Persephone was actually Kathleen's daughter?
- Dr. Young: Mum was the spitting image of Kathleen.
- Mr. Burns: How do you know that? Do you have photographs?
- Dr. Young: (Pause) Everyone said they looked like sisters.
- Mr. Burns: Who's 'everyone'?
- Dr. Young: Everyone in Ann Arbor, everyone in Guatemala. Everyone.
- Mr. Burns: Anyone who's alive today who could testify to that likeness?
- Dr. Young: (Long pause) No.

- Mr. Burns: Do you have photographs I can look at to compare them?
- Dr. Young: No. There may be one or two photographs of Mum. But Kathleen never sat still for photographs.
- Mr. Burns: Never?
- Dr. Young: Never. She was famous for her aversion to cameras. There are literally no pictures of Kathleen Quinlan. And very few of Persephone.
- Mr. Burns: Is there anything written – a letter, a diary, court testimony, anything at all – where someone wrote down their impression that your mother and grandmother looked like sisters?
- Dr. Young: (Long pause) No.
- Mr. Burns: So besides these letters and envelopes, marked as Exhibits 11 through 14, do you have any other proof that Persephone Quinlan was truly descended from Kathleen Quinlan?
- Dr. Young: Well, there's Kathleen's Will. Why would Kathleen Quinlan name Persephone her sole heir, if Persephone wasn't her daughter?
- Mr. Burns: Anything else? I want to know everything on which you base your claim that your mother was Kathleen Quinlan's daughter.
- Dr. Young: (To Ms. Watt) What happens if I forget something?
- Ms. Watt: Don't worry about that, Dr. Young. It's not a memory test. Just tell Mr. Burns everything that comes to your mind right now.
- Dr. Young: Mum told me she was Kathleen Quinlan's daughter.
- Mr. Burns: Based on what? Persephone never met Kathleen, right? By the time she got to Ann Arbor, Kathleen was dead, right?
- Dr. Young: That's true.
- Mr. Burns: And until Persephone received Exhibit 11 in the mail, she had no idea she was Kathleen Quinlan's daughter, right?
- Dr. Young: That's true.
- Mr. Burns: So the only proof that Persephone was Kathleen's daughter is the two letters, and the last name, and Kathleen's Will – and that's it, right?
- Dr. Young: (Long pause) They looked like sisters.
- Mr. Burns: But there're no photos, no documents recording their physical similarities, and no living witnesses who ever saw them both, right?
- Dr. Young: No.
- Mr. Burns: So in terms of proof you can bring to court, it's the two letters they exchanged, the last name, and the Will – and that's all there is, right?
- Dr. Young: That's all I can remember now.
- Mr. Burns: Now when you were growing up, and you first saw the *Lamanai Codex*, what'd your mother tell you about it?

■ Dr. Young: She said it was a very old book, sacred to the ancient Maya.
■ Mr. Burns: Could Persephone read it?
■ Dr. Young: No.
■ Mr. Burns: Could her friend Kux Ahawis read it?
■ Dr. Young: When I was growing up? No.
■ Mr. Burns: Kux could read it later?
■ Dr. Young: I don't know. Once we started breaking the code, Kux asked to be taught how to read the old glyphs. But whether his studies advanced far enough for him to be able to read the *Lamanai Codex*, I don't know.
■ Mr. Burns: Did you show Kux the *Lamanai Codex* after he began reading the old glyphs?
■ Dr. Young: No.
■ Mr. Burns: Why not? Kux was your pal, right?
■ Ms. Watt: Objection. Compound question. Argumentative.
■ Dr. Young: No particular reason. It never came up.
■ Mr. Burns: Until last year, when Kux asked to see the *Lamanai Codex*?
■ Dr. Young: (Pause) I already told you, I don't remember that happening.
■ Mr. Burns: Can you read the *Lamanai Codex* now?
■ Dr. Young: Not all of it.
■ Mr. Burns: What's the status of your translation today?
■ Dr. Young: I'm still working on it.
■ Mr. Burns: How many pages have you finished translating?
■ Dr. Young: I cannot read a single page of the codex in its entirety.
■ Mr. Burns: Why not? Can't modern scholars translate all the ancient Maya glyphs now?
■ Dr. Young: They can translate all the ones they've seen. But there are glyphs in the *Lamanai Codex* that have never been seen anywhere else.
■ Mr. Burns: What percentage of all the glyphs in the *Lamanai Codex* have you translated?
■ Dr. Young: I don't know.
■ Mr. Burns: Give me an estimate.
■ Dr. Young: It's not possible to estimate.
■ Mr. Burns: Why not?
■ Dr. Young: Translating a Maya codex is a fluid undertaking. Often the translation of a glyph on one page causes me to reconsider tentative translations I had of other glyphs on other pages.
■ Mr. Burns: What percentage of the total glyphs in the *Lamanai Codex*, roughly, do you have either a final or a tentative translation for?
■ Dr. Young: (Pause) Maybe 85%.
■ Mr. Burns: It's true, is it not, that other scholars have repeatedly offered to give you assistance in finishing your translation of the *Lamanai Codex*?

- Dr. Young: Certain opportunists whose real goal is to steal the project have made overtures about working beside me. But I don't consider those to be genuine 'offers of assistance'.
- Mr. Burns: And you've refused all such overtures?
- Dr. Young: Yes.
- Mr. Burns: You've also rejected the suggestion of other distinguished scholars that you should publish a partial translation, right?
- Dr. Young: I'm unwilling to put my name and reputation on an incomplete and possibly inaccurate work. And as I just told you, partial translations of Maya codices are fraught with peril, given the constant revision that goes on as new glyphs are translated.
- Mr. Burns: If you were to pass away before finishing your translation, are there instructions in a Will or elsewhere as to what the Executor of your Estate is to do with your partial translation?
- Dr. Young: I'm not expecting to die anytime soon. (Sneers at Ms. Kerr) Sorry, dear.
- Mr. Burns: I'm not expecting to die soon either, Dr. Young. But Fate cares little for our expectations. Are you saying, if you were run over by a bus on your way home today, you have no arrangements in place, no instructions, for your partial translation of the *Lamanai Codex*?
- Ms. Watt: Are you threatening my client?
- Mr. Burns: Relax, Olivia. I don't own any London busses. And besides, your client lives right here on Shad Thames, a pedestrians-only street. Doctor, I'm just asking – do you have any plans in place for when you pass away? Do you even have a Will?
- Dr. Young: I do have a Will, yes.
- Mr. Burns: Does it address your translation of the *Lamanai Codex*?
- Dr. Young: Yes.
- Mr. Burns: What's your Will say about your translation of the codex?
- Ms. Watt: No, David, we're not going to answer that question.
- Mr. Burns: Why not?
- Ms. Watt: You can't use this intellectual property litigation as a sword to find out the contents of a living person's Will, which is among the most private of all information in our society. No.
- Mr. Burns: I'm not asking for the whole Will. I just want to know what arrangements she's made pertaining to her translation of the codex.
- Ms. Watt: And I'm just saying: No.
- Mr. Burns: I'll bring a motion to compel this information.
- Ms. Watt: You go ahead and do that, David.
- Mr. Burns: Dr. Young, have you ever been to Lamanai?
- Dr. Young: (Pause) Yes.

■ Mr. Burns: How many times did you go to Lamanai?

■ Dr. Young: Four or five times.

■ Mr. Burns: When?

■ Dr. Young: (Sighs) Long time ago. Once in 1945, before I left for Australia. And the rest in the 1960s, when I was back in Central America.

■ Mr. Burns: Why'd you go to Lamanai?

■ Dr. Young: The first time, I was a romantic young girl, like Mr. Tennyson's Lady of Shalot, who'd lived her whole life in the mountains, and had grown 'half sick of shadows', yearning for adventure. Then, as I came of age, I heard a wild tale from my mother, about my grandparents chasing a dream that's haunted Europeans longer than the story of Christ. So I went to Lamanai, like Joyce and all her new boyfriends here, to search for the fountain of youth.

■ Mr. Burns: D'you find it?

■ Dr. Young: No.

■ Mr. Burns: Where at Lamanai, specifically, did you look for the fountain?

■ Dr. Young: All over the site. I was searching for a cave.

■ Mr. Burns: You find any caves at Lamanai?

■ Dr. Young: No.

■ Mr. Burns: What exactly did Persephone tell you about your grandparents' visit to Lamanai?

■ Dr. Young: Mum said Roger and Kathleen came up the New River in 1868, running guns to the Maya, and discovered Lamanai. They stayed a few weeks excavating temples, and in the process found a fountain in a cave, which they mistook for the fountain of youth. Roger bottled up the water and took it to London, but died while announcing his great discovery.

■ Mr. Burns: Who told Persephone all those details?

■ Dr. Young: Kathleen, I presume.

■ Mr. Burns: How would that've been possible? You said Kathleen was already dead when Persephone arrived in Ann Arbor. Exhibits 11 and 13 were the only communication they ever had, right? Yet there's nothing in these two letters about the fountain of youth.

■ Ms. Watt: Objection. Compound, argumentative. And you're asking the witness to speculate about her mother's sources of information.

■ Mr. Burns: Do you know, Dr. Young, who or what were Persephone's sources, for what she told you about Kathleen and Roger Quinlan's discovery of Lamanai and their adventures seeking the fountain of youth?

■ Dr. Young: No, I don't know.

■ Mr. Burns: Do you know if Persephone ever saw a diary of Kathleen's?

- Dr. Young: I don't know.
- Mr. Burns: Have you yourself ever seen a diary of Kathleen Quinlan's?
- Dr. Young: No. (Looks at Ms. Kerr) Do you have her diaries, too?
- Mr. Burns: What made you think the fountain of youth was in a cave?
- Dr. Young: (Pause) Mum told me that.
- Mr. Burns: What made Persephone think it was in a cave? If you know.
- Dr. Young: I don't know. But Ron can tell you, the pirate books say it was in a cave.
- Mr. Burns: Did Persephone read the pirate books?
- Dr. Young: I don't know.
- Mr. Burns: Do you know if Persephone ever talked to Kux Ahawis about the fountain of youth being in a cave at Lamanai?
- Dr. Young: I don't know.
- Mr. Burns: Did you yourself ever talk to Kux Ahawis about the longstanding rumor that the fountain of youth is at Lamanai?
- Dr. Young: (Long pause) When Mum died and I came back to Guatemala in 1960, Kux and I talked about the *Lamanai Codex*. Kux filled me in on the Maya legend that it contained a map to the fountain of youth.
- Mr. Burns: And you began translating the *Lamanai Codex* in the 1960s?
- Dr. Young: Yes.
- Mr. Burns: Does the codex contain a map to the fountain of youth?
- Ms. Watt: Objection. Since that question calls for information that is proprietary and confidential to my client, being her scholarly work product, a translation in progress, I am instructing Dr. Young not to answer the question.
- Mr. Burns: I'm not asking for the translation. I just want to know generally what the *Lamanai Codex* is about. Is it about the fountain of youth?
- Ms. Watt: Same objection. Instruct the witness not to answer.
- Mr. Burns: Olivia, we all signed the confidentiality agreement, which bars us from disclosing any aspect of Dr. Young's testimony. None of us is involved in translating ancient Maya texts. So I think I'm entitled to ask Dr. Young to translate the entire codex on the record, or as much as she can. But I'm not asking that. I just want her to tell us generally what the codex is about.
- Ms. Watt: Signing a confidentiality agreement does not give you the right to access my client's proprietary work product. I stand by the objection.
- Mr. Burns: Then I'll have to file a motion to compel testimony.
- Dr. Young: You go ahead and do that. Do you want to adjourn the deposition until we can obtain Judge Henderson's ruling on this issue?
- Mr. Burns: No, thank you. I'll carry on with other questions, and reserve the right to revisit this topic, along with Dr. Young's Will, after the Judge rules on my motions.

Ivy, let's mark as Young Exhibit 15 the Last Will and Testament of Kathleen A. Quinlan. (Hands copies to witness and all counsel) Is this the document you referenced earlier, Dr. Young, as the clear expression of your grandmother's intent, which Judge Breakey ignored?

- Dr. Young: (Puts on reading glasses, reviews exhibit) Yes.
- Mr. Burns: On page 1 of Young Exhibit 15, your grandmother wrote: 'I hereby leave all my Property, including my Money, my Home and my Personal Possessions, and also including all that I inherited from my deceased husband, Roger Quinlan, including his books and private papers, to our cherished daughter, Persephone Quinlan. I wish to be clear about why I am leaving everything I own to our daughter Persephone, and nothing to our son Lloyd. Although I only learned recently that Persephone is still alive, I have no doubt at all that Persephone is as much a true child of Roger Quinlan and me as her brother, Lloyd. Yet unlike Lloyd, who has had every benefit of his parents' largesse and social standing, Persephone has had to make her own way in this harsh world without any assistance of any kind from her parents. To make amends for this injustice which I caused, I therefore wish to leave everything Roger and I ever had to our daughter Persephone Quinlan, who is the flesh of our flesh and the blood of our blood.' Is that the precise language you feel expresses Kathleen Quinlan's 'clear intent'?
- Dr. Young: Yes. How could Kathleen possibly have been any clearer?
- Mr. Burns: So you claim Kathleen's intent was to leave her entire Estate to her actual daughter – the 'flesh of her flesh and the blood of her blood'?
- Dr. Young: That's precisely what she said.
- Mr. Burns: And she clearly wanted to leave her entire Estate to a 'true child of Roger Quinlan' and herself, right?
- Dr. Young: (Long pause) Well, Lloyd was a 'true child' of theirs, too. But Kathleen was clear she wanted her estate to go to Persephone, not Lloyd.
- Mr. Burns: Gotcha. But the words you rely upon, in claiming you're the rightful owner of the codex and the land, are Kathleen's description of Persephone as 'our cherished daughter' and the 'flesh of our flesh and blood of our blood', and a 'true child of Roger Quinlan and me', right?
- Dr. Young: Yes – the 'cherished daughter' being Persephone, not Lloyd.
- Mr. Burns: But if someone could prove that in reality Persephone Quinlan was *not* a true child of Roger and Kathleen Quinlan, you'd agree that Persephone would not have been entitled, under Kathleen's Will, to inherit the *Lamanai Codex* or the Ambergris Caye land, right?
- Ms. Watt: Objection. (Pause)
- Mr. Burns: What's wrong with that question?
- Ms. Watt: You can't ask a hypothetical question to a lay witness.

- Mr. Burns: It's not hypothetical. Dr. Young says the clear intent of Kathleen's Will was to leave everything to her true flesh-and-blood child; and Judge Breakey should've enforced Kathleen's intent. Fine. I want to know if Dr. Young will admit, if her position is valid, then the converse must also be true: if Persephone was in truth *not* the true flesh-and-blood child of Kathleen and Roger, then Judge Breakey would've been right to give Persephone nothing, as he did.
- Ms. Watt: But then you're asking for a legal conclusion.
- Mr. Burns: (Scoffs) I don't think so. But your objections are on the record. What's your answer, Dr. Young: if in truth Persephone Quinlan was *not* the true flesh and blood child of Roger and Kathleen, would you agree there'd be no clear intent of Kathleen to leave everything to Persephone?
- Dr. Young: Your question is tautological, Mr. Burns. Of course, if Persephone was not the true child that in fact she was, then she would not have been the person Kathleen intended to inherit her Estate. But Persephone was the true child, who was named in the Will, so what's the point in seeing how long you can dance on the head of this pin?
- Mr. Burns: Because there are tests today that did not exist in 1909.
- Ms. Watt: Is there a question?
- Mr. Burns: Yes. Dr. Young, would you be willing to submit a sample of your blood for laboratory testing?
- Ms. Watt: Objection! That's a completely improper request.
- Mr. Burns: With all respect, Olivia, I don't think it's an improper request at all, under the extraordinary facts of this case. Very much to the contrary, I will contend it is both appropriate and incredibly relevant to the dispute.
- Ms. Watt: Poppycock! How could a blood test of my client have any possible bearing on the issues in this case?
- Mr. Burns: (Waves Young Exhibit 12) This envelope has a stamp, Olivia, which Dr. Young testified under oath was definitely licked by Kathleen Quinlan. Modern forensic scientists can extract Kathleen Quinlan's DNA from the back of a stamp – even a 102-year-old stamp. They did it just a few years back, when the novelist Patricia Cornwell got Scotland Yard to reopen the Jack the Ripper investigation. (Turns to Ms. Kerr) Joyce, do you have—
- Ms. Kerr: Yes. (Hands Mr. Burns a stack of yellowed envelopes with stamps)
- Mr. Burns: Thank you, Joyce. (Turns back to Ms. Watt) These are envelopes containing letters written by Roger Quinlan. They also have stamps. A few of the stamps in this stack may have been licked by someone other than Roger, but assuming that modern scientists find exactly the same DNA on all or most of the stamps, I think our Judge will agree that the DNA extracted from the majority of the stamps must be Roger Quinlan's.
- Ms. Watt: (To Ms. Kerr) How in the world did you get those envelopes?

■ Mr. Burns: As I said before, like the Lord, Ms. Kerr works in mysteri—

■ Ms. Watt: No, that's not good enough here, David! As my client testified, she recently donated Roger Quinlan's papers to the British Library, including a huge collection of his letters. If your paralegal has stolen—

■ Mr. Burns: Joyce doesn't steal things and I deeply—

■ Ms. Watt: —or borrowed valuable historical material that is not—

■ Mr. Burns: —resent your accusation!

■ Ms. Watt: —supposed to leave the Library under any circumstances, then we will take all appropriate legal measures!

■ Ivy Taylor: Good people, PLEASE! You need to speak one at a time.

■ Mr. Burns: Sorry, Ivy. Look, Olivia, we didn't touch the papers your client donated to the British Library. What we've got here are letters of Roger that were collected after 1909 by his son Lloyd, along with the envelopes in some cases. This past winter, Ms. Kerr inherited them.

■ Ms. Watt: Why would Lloyd Quinlan have collected Roger's letters?

■ Mr. Burns: Probably the same reason Persephone stole the other ones. Lloyd was Roger's child, too. And like many people who died too young, Roger seems to have inspired morbid fascination in all who followed him.

■ Ms. Watt: (Pause) Alright. I'll accept your representation that Ms. Kerr obtained these envelopes lawfully. But nothing you've said convinces me a blood test on Dr. Young could possibly prove anything of relevance to this case.

■ Mr. Burns: Then you need to re-think it all tonight. Fiona Young's birth certificate proves she is Persephone Quinlan's daughter. So if Persephone was truly the biological daughter of Roger and Kathleen Quinlan, then Persephone must've passed some of the DNA she got from Roger and Kathleen on to Fiona. But if Fiona's DNA doesn't match any characteristics of the DNA we extract from the stamps licked by Roger and Kathleen, then the only explanation is: Persephone wasn't really their daughter. In which case, three of Fiona's Four Affirmative Defenses are out the window. If Persephone wasn't a 'true child of Roger and Kathleen', if she wasn't the 'flesh of their flesh and the blood of their blood', then Judge Breakey's alleged errors and bias, and Lloyd's alleged fraud hiring the boys in the barn, don't matter anymore. No Judge anywhere would've awarded Kathleen's Estate to a person who was *not the daughter she claimed to be*. That's why Fiona's blood test would be very relevant here.

■ Ms. Watt: Well you may think it would be relevant, David, but I don't need to go home and think about it. Dr. Young will not submit to a blood test, and that's that. There's no procedure to require it, and we simply won't do it.

■ Mr. Burns: I agree that Dr. Young is not *required* to submit a blood sample – unless Judge Henderson orders it. That's why I asked if she would provide a blood sample voluntarily. But you should really think more carefully about this, Olivia. Because even if Judge Henderson declines to order Dr. Young to submit to a blood test, your three probate-based defenses are dead in the water, unless Dr. Young agrees to provide the sample.

- Ms. Watt: I don't see it that way. Under the Fifth Amendment to your American Constitution, Dr. Young has a clear right not to incriminate herself.
- Mr. Burns: Yes she does. But I'm not asking Dr. Young to incriminate herself; I'm asking her to incriminate *her mother*. There's no Fifth Amendment right not to incriminate your mother. So if Dr. Young doesn't give us a blood sample now, I'll ask again at trial if she's still unwilling to take a simple blood test to prove *her mother* was related to Roger and Kathleen Quinlan. Judge Henderson will require an answer, in front of the jury. If Dr. Young says no, I'll ask the jury to draw the only reasonable inference: Dr. Young must know or fear she's not really related to Roger and Kathleen Quinlan, because she must know or fear Persephone wasn't truly their daughter. And then your three probate defenses will be worth less than the debris floating out in the Thames. That's why you really should consider my request more carefully.
- Ms. Watt: (Sighs) Alright. But in the meantime, it's almost noon. Dr. Young must be tired. I think we've reached a good time to break for today.
- Mr. Burns: (Shrugs) If Dr. Young is too tired to continue, we'll break. But let's all try to be ready to start at 9:00 sharp tomorrow morning, okay?

  Off the record at 11:42 a.m.

* * *

"You are one fiendish bastard!" Clive Phelps claps David Burns on the back.

"Thanks, I think." Burns glances at the dozens of people lunching at the nearby tables inside the Anchor Tap pub, and then speaks in a much quieter voice than Phelps. "I know I said we could talk freely once we got outside Olivia's offices, but these are closer quarters than I had in mind. Let's keep it down."

"Man, you are paranoid," Kip Hunter says. "You gotta learn to relax."

"We made the news today, oh boy," Burns mutters. "So just because I'm paranoid doesn't mean they're not out to get us."

Hunter laughs, and adds: "Well, I agree with Clive. You kicked some serious butt today, dude." Hunter raises his pint glass. "To our fiendish bastard."

Ron Graham and Joyce Kerr join Hunter and Phelps in toasting Burns.

But Burns refuses to raise his glass. "Gang, it's way too early to celebrate. Litigation's a roller coaster. We drew first blood – but that just means Fiona'll come back strong tomorrow, and kick my butt back, like she did most of today."

"With what?" Hunter asks. "All her probate defenses are gone now."

"Not if she agrees to take a blood test," Burns murmurs.

"No way she'll do that," Phelps says quietly. "She fears that blood test."

"I agree," Hunter says. "You see her face when you asked that question?"

"Not really," Burns admits. "I was too busy arguing with Olivia."

"Pure, unadulterated fear." Hunter looks to the others. "Am I right?"

The others nod yes.

"Fiona might've looked scared," Burns murmurs, "but I still think, once she talks it over with Olivia, she'll agree to a blood test. She's got nothing to lose."

"I agree with David," Ron Graham whispers. "If Fiona doesn't take the test, all her probate defenses are gone. So why not take the test?"

"That makes it two-to-two," Burns mutters. "What d'you think, Joyce? You know Fiona better than any of us."

"She won't take it," Joyce murmurs. "Logically, you and Ron are right. But the longer you went on about the DNA, the more frightened Fiona looked. I've never seen her so afraid."

"But what exactly does she fear?" Burns asks. "Kathleen wouldn't have put Persephone in her Will, and written that letter inviting her to come to Ann Arbor, unless she knew for sure Persephone was her daughter. So does Fiona fear the blood test'll show *Roger* wasn't Persephone's father? Or does Fiona fear it'll show Fiona herself is the problem – that maybe she's not really a Quinlan at all?"

"I bet Fiona fears she's not really a Quinlan at all," Joyce says.

"Agreed," Phelps says. "All that *fol-de-rol* about women in indigenous cultures bearing children after 50? Pure hokum. There's no data to support that."

"I keep tellin' you," Hunter says, "the old lady's just makin' this story up as she goes along."

"What about that stuff Fiona told me to ask you about, Clive?" Burns asks, ignoring Hunter. "The US and UK women getting pregnant in their late 50s?"

"In three highly exceptional cases," Phelps says, "women in their late 50s, in California and England, did naturally conceive and bear a child. And the oldest was 59. But those are the only documented cases of natural conception after 55, *ever*. Three out of billions! Persephone didn't beat those odds."

Burns signals Phelps to keep it down. "But it could have happened?"

"It's so unlikely it's laughable," Phelps says. "Human eggs virtually never last past 50, without laboratory intervention. Far, far more likely that Fiona was a foundling, and Persephone got the villagers to pretend Fiona was her own child."

"But why?" Burns asks. "Why wouldn't Persephone just adopt the kid?"

Phelps shrugs. "Discerning Fiona's motives is hard enough. Discerning the motives of her deceased mother is probably beyond hope."

"I keep tellin' you guys," Hunter says, "the old lady's crazy as a loon."

"I don't think so," Burns says, feelling compelled to answer the man. "I admit Fiona's got a few loose screws. But real nut cases can't give answers as responsive as hers are. She's smart."

"Agreed," Phelps says. "Fiona's ratiocinative processes are really quite formidable, given her advanced age. But you've got her on the ropes now."

"No, I don't," Burns says. "Fiona'll just say she doesn't have to be a blood relative to inherit from Persephone. She'll use the possibility of an unofficial adoption as an excuse to decline the blood test, but keep her probate defenses."

"So maybe we didn't win as much as we thought?" Graham asks.

"You got it," Burns says. "That's litigation for you – a roller-coaster. One minute you think you've won something important, and the next minute it's gone. Also in the cheery news department: Santos told me on the way out that he ran my settlement idea by Olivia and Fiona, but they have zero interest in settling."

The food arrives. Hunter turns up his nose at Phelps's bangars and mash, which leads to some banter about whether English pub food is really any worse than American fast food. Phelps politely participates in the banter, but Burns can see Phelps is stewing inside.

"I can't see," Phelps says, as soon as he finishes eating, "how you'd ever allow Fiona to come back tomorrow and switch her whole story around."

"It's not a question of what I'll allow, Clive," Burns says, "it's what Fiona can get away with. And in a deposition, there aren't many more real, enforceable rules than in a knife fight."

"But she committed herself today," Phelps persists, "to saying Persephone was her natural mother. Doesn't the oath to tell the truth mean anything?"

"An oath only means something," Burns says, "if the witness thinks it means something. And we're a long way from the days when witnesses believed swearing an oath was the same as placing their soul in God's hands."

"Well, I'm going to be very aggravated," Phelps says, "if you let Fiona switch to a new story tomorrow. There's too much at stake here."

"I understand the stakes," Burn murmurs.

"This is already taking far too long," Phelps grumbles. "We know Kux gave his followers cinnabar from the Ball Court, and hydrogen sulphide and salt, and variants of coclmeca and gangweo. But without the proportions, and the other substances Kux fed his followers, my research can't move forward. We desperately need that codex, to give all human beings a new lease on life. This is literally a matter of life and death, David."

Burns puts on a sympathetic face, though he'd like to tell Clive to get a life.

"So I'm expecting you to nail her to the cross tomorrow," Phelps continues.

"I understand your expectations, too," Burns says. "And I'll do my best. But I gotta warn you, Clive, your expectations are unrealistic. Depositions aren't—"

"I know, I know," Phelps says, "we can't win at deposition, we have to wait for trial. I've heard you sing that song. So when's our trial going to take place?"

"We don't have a trial date yet," Burns says.

"You said you were going to get one last week," Phelps says.

"I said I was going to *ask* for one last week," Burns says. "I asked, but we still don't have one. Though it'll almost surely be summer 2012. That's when—"

"2012!" Phelps exclaims. "If medical research moved as slowly as lawsuits, doctors would still be bleeding us when we get sick." Phelps grabs his coat. "Speaking of research, I need to get back to real work. Can you put this on my bill?" Phelps hurries out the door.

"I liked Clive better in Belize," Ron remarks. "He seemed more relaxed."

"That's cause he was gettin' laid regular back then," Kip says. "Now he hardly ever leaves his lab – except to watch this deposition."

"David," Graham says, "in case Fiona does keep her probate defenses, doesn't it seem probable that the real cause of Kathleen's suicide was that harsh letter from Persephone, rather than anything Lloyd or the miscreant boys in the hayloft did?"

Burns nods yes, though he's still brooding over Phelps's abrupt departure.

"Joyce," Graham says, "did people in your family think Fiona looked like Persephone, the way Fiona said Persephone looked like Kathleen?"

"No one on my side of the family ever saw Persephone," Joyce says, "except Lloyd. Persephone only came to Ann Arbor that one time, in 1909."

"But it's still a good question, Ron," Burns says. "Joyce, it's amazing no one in your family ever questioned this whole crazy story. Persephone gives birth at 59, and explains the absence of a father by saying Mr. Young was eaten by a jaguar; yet your family swallowed that story whole?"

Joyce shrugs. "When you say it that way, it does sound like a tall tale. But the Kerrs never talked to the Quinlans, till Fiona moved to Ann Arbor in 1970. Yet by then Fiona was 45, and a famous scholar, doing the same kind of work Persephone did, so it all seemed logical."

"But your parents knew who Persephone was, right?" Burns asks.

Joyce shrugs. "Kind of. Though I remember Mom saying, when Fiona first came to our house in 1970 to introduce herself, Mom had no idea who she was."

"That's the way my family is, too," Hunter interjects. "I've got cousins I've never even met. We all just keep to our own little nuclear units."

Burns nods, pays the bill, and they walk back to the hotel in the rain.

There Hunter and Graham catch a cab for central London, to look through art galleries and antiquarian shops for anything more about India Reynolds and her fountain of youth painting.

"Talk about the odd couple," Burns remarks, watching their cab depart.

"At least those two've stopped hitting on me," Joyce says. "Unlike Clive."

"I thought Clive was in a committed relationship with Gemma Murray."

"When's that ever stopped a man? He told me he's 'thinking of breaking up' with her."

"When did Clive have time to hit on you?"

"Remember outside the pub when I stopped for a cigarette," Joyce says, "while you guys went in and got the table?"

"I thought Clive was just being chivalrous, holding the umbrella for you."

"Chivalry with an agenda. First he scolded me about my 'cancer sticks'. Then he asked me out to dinner tomorrow night."

"You said yes?" Burns says.

"No, I said you and I work every waking minute when we're on the road, except when I call home to talk to Lisa."

"Great answer! Remind me to put you in charge of our firm's client relations."

"It's the truth," Joyce says. "That's what we're doin' this afternoon and tonight, isn't it?"

"'Fraid so."

Inside the hotel, they stop at the business centre, where Joyce faxes a copy of the *Observer* article to Burns's lone associate, Mark Jacobs, back in Ann Arbor, while Burns calls Jacobs at home and tells him to get his sorry ass out of bed and down to Detroit, to defend against the *Observer's* motion, sure to be filed soon. Then they cross the lobby to the lift, as Burns casts a wistful glance at the hotel bar, while several male hotel guests cast wistful glances at Joyce.

Up in Joyce's room, Burns unloads the documents, while Joyce goes in the bathroom to change out of her work suit, and into jeans and a football jersey.

"So whaddo we need to do first?" Joyce asks, as she fires up a smoke.

"You know," Burns says, "if you wanna have dinner with Clive tomorrow—"

"Not unless he brings his girlfriend," Joyce interrupts.

"You're sure it was a romantic pass?"

Joyce rolls her eyes. "You think this girl doesn't know when a man's got love on his mind?"

Burns chuckles. "I suppose you've heard every line in the book."

"It's enough to drive me back to Michael, just to put an end to all the married guys who want to take me out for a test drive."

"Please! If you ever get that desperate, marry me, before going back to Michael." Burns throws up his hands. "I'm not asking you to break our rule against mixing work and romance, I'm just say—"

"So where you wanna start?" Joyce interrupts, in her all-business voice.

"The Reynolds Foundation. Because if I'm wrong and Fiona truly abandons her probate defenses, instead of agreeing to a blood test, then the Reynolds Foundation is the only defense left. But first I have a question. D'you think Roger Quinlan was really Persephone's father?"

Joyce snorts. "Who knows? When Fiona was testifying how she was positive Persephone was born in 1865, I was sure you'd mark Kathleen's diary as an exhibit, and read Fiona the parts about the 1865 abortion. But I was wrong." Joyce cocks her head. "Or – are you afraid to mark the diary, because Olivia might ask where we got it?"

"I'm not afraid to mark it. You got it from Justin. Where Justin got it is not your problem. And I promise, we will get to the diary. But I want Fiona on the record first, on everything under the sun, before she even knows we have that diary."

Joyce nods, drinking this in. "It was interesting today, watching you work."

Burns cocks his head quizzically. "You've worked with me for twelve years."

"But I've never seen you in court or in a deposition. You always send me off to do things behind the scenes. Like Della Street."

Burns laughs. "You aren't old enough to remember Perry Mason."

"But Daddy was. I watched some of the movies they made off the old series with him. It was the only time Daddy ever sat down and watched TV."

"Justin was probably just wishing his own lawyer was as good as Perry Mason," Burns says darkly. "Mason always got his client acquitted. Unlike me."

"Daddy never complained about you, David. He knew he was guilty. He made a bad decision, and took a chance that didn't work out. Not your fault."

"I still think about it, though. It was the kind of close case I could probably win today. But as a famous philosopher said: '*ve get too soon olt, und too late schmart*'."

"Which famous philosopher said that?" Joyce asks. "Yogi Berra?"

"Ponce de Leon. But back to Roger and Persephone. Kathleen said in her diary she aborted a child named Persephone in 1865. Roger's child. But does that mean it's true?"

"Who would lie to her own diary about an abortion?"

"Ah!" Burns says. "How 'bout a woman who knew the true father of her 1865 child was *someone other than Roger Quinlan*, the man she was traveling with when she wrote the diary in 1868? Maybe she was just being careful, in case Roger found her diary and read it."

"But she said she wrote super-small, so Roger couldn't read it."

"Still, she might've worried that Roger could use a magnifying glass," Burns counters. "And remember, their marriage was very troubled in 1868 – they weren't even having sex when they arrived in Belize. So isn't it possible Kathleen invented the abortion, just to cover her tracks?"

"I'm not following you, David."

"If Kathleen truly gave birth to another man's child in 1865, and put that child in foster care while she reconciled with Roger, wouldn't it make sense she might lie about the whole incident, even to her diary, and pretend the child was aborted when in truth the child was put in foster care?"

Joyce waggles her hand. "Maybe."

"So maybe now Fiona fears a blood test'll show she's not related to Roger Quinlan, even if it turns out Fiona really is related to Kathleen and Persephone."

"But why would that matter? Fiona doesn't need to be related to Roger to win this case. She only needs to be related to Kathleen."

"Kathleen's Will says 'a true child of *Roger Quinlan and* me'."

"But would Judge Henderson really care," Joyce asks, "if you proved Fiona was only Kathleen's grand-daughter, and not Roger's?"

Burns mull this over. "Fair point. But there's still a big inconsistency between the 1865 abortion in Kathleen's diary, and Fiona insisting Persephone was born in March 1865."

"Maybe Kathleen got pregnant again, right after delivering Persephone, and then aborted the second child."

"And addressed the whole diary to the aborted child, giving the aborted child the same first name as the earlier child that lived, without ever mentioning the earlier child that lived?" Burns shakes his head. "I can't buy that."

Joyce nods. "You're right, that makes no sense. But if you want something else to keep you awake tonight, think about Fiona's eyes, with those heavy lids. They're just like my eyes, and my brother Quinn's eyes – and the 'voluptuous hooded eyelids' Kathleen seemed to have, judging from the diary. Kind of strange Fiona got the Quinlan family eyes, if she was a foundling who was unofficially adopted by Persephone."

"Maybe not. Kathleen's diary also said her unnamed rival for carnal entanglement with Roger was a 'dead ringer' for Kathleen. So the rival probably had those heavy eyelids, too. Lots of people have those." Burns sighs. "Anyway we're just chasing our own tails on this." He points at the 17 boxes of Reynolds Foundation documents. "We'd better dive into those boxes."

"What are we looking for, exactly?"

"I wanna find whatever document Fiona's gonna rely on tomorrow, to say the codex belongs to the Reynolds Foundation rather than to Fiona personally."

Joyce purses her lips. "I told you before, David, there's no such document. If we find it now, I'm gonna have some serious egg on my face."

"Anyone could miss a single piece of paper in 17 boxes."

Joyce shakes her head no. "I'm telling you, it ain't there. What else you want me to look for as I go through all these old documents again?"

"Anything that sets out the purpose or the bylaws of the Foundation," Burns says, "or the process that's supposed to be followed for appointments and expenditures and so forth. When was the Reynolds Foundation first organized?"

"1788."

"Jesus. Did America even have charities in 1788?"

"The Reynolds Foundation was organized in Great Britain," Joyce says, "where it did business until Fiona moved it to the United States in 1970. Frankly, we're lucky they only have 17 boxes to show for 223 years of operations."

"What were they doing for those 223 years?"

"Working for the abolition of slavery and the slave trade."

Burns starts to read, but then looks up. "Correct me if I'm wrong, but didn't the last and most barbaric country in the world finally abolish slavery in 1863?

"I don't think our country's barbaric. But yes, slavery did end in 1863."

"So what's the Reynolds Foundation been doing the past 148 years?"

"Besides waiting around to provide Fiona a shield to try to hide the *Lamanai Codex* behind? Beats me, David. But here's the box that starts in 1788. Why don't you start there, and I'll start in 2011, and we'll meet in the middle."

"Fair enough." Burns grabs his box.

"But I still don't really get what I'm looking for," Joyce says. "Why do you want the bylaws and official corporate processes for appointments and expenses?"

"Because little charities like this seldom follow the legal formalities all corporations are supposed to follow. So we may be able to beat Fiona's claim that the Foundation owns the codex, by showing that the Foundation never properly authorized Kathleen or Persephone or Fiona to acquire it."

* * *

Joyce Kerr looks up from skimming through her 7th box of the long afternoon. She hasn't met David Burns in the middle yet, but she's getting close. "Hey, how 'bout we eat something besides take-out tonight?" Joyce asks.

Burns winces. "No, I still gotta get my questions ready for tomorrow. But you go ahead. Maybe Kip or Ron'll wanna go with you."

"They're not back from antique hunting."

"How come Kip stopped chasing you anyways?"

"I don't think it was ever me Kip wanted. He's like the pirates in those old books Ron showed us – chasing treasure is all that man lives for."

"Whaddya think are the terms of Kip's side deal with Clive?" Burns asks.

"I have no idea."

"For Kip's sake, I hope he got his deal in writing, like yours. Clive strikes me as a ruthless fucker, who probably eats guys like Kip for breakfast."

"I think Kip can be even more ruthless," Joyce says, "if he needs to be."

"In most cases, I'd agree," Burns says. "But Kip's so starry-eyed about how Clive's gonna kill Death for us all, he might get blind-sided."

"Ron's pretty impressed by Clive, too."

"So am I," Burns says. "Clive's an impressive guy. I just wish he had a little more patience. But hey, you finally ready to try some Indian takeout tonight?"

"I hate Indian food."

"You don't know what you're missing. But I'll tell you what. As a special treat, I'll call for the pizza this time – while you read these four 1860s Reynolds Foundation documents I just found, and tell me what the hell's going on here."

From the ***Reynolds Foundation Correspondence File***

12 June 1864

Nigel M. Caruthers, Esquire
Caruthers & Fotheringill, Solicitors At Law
One Mincing Lane, Tower Hill

My dearest Mr. Caruthers:

I write in the clear apprehension that my days on earth are numbered, and although I devoutly hope I have not been weighed in the balances and found wanting, nevertheless, the writing is on the wall for me: my suzerainty over my little fiefdom, the Reynolds Foundation, must very soon come to an end.

Wherefore I write you, at this critical juncture not only in my life but, more importantly, in the world's affairs, Mr. Caruthers, to request that you execute all legal documentation necessary to effectuate my desire to appoint as my successor as sole trustee, with responsibility for all future affairs of the Reynolds Foundation, a brilliant and passionate young painting student of mine, Kathleen Allen, formerly of Oxford, and presently of London, though I apprehend soon perhaps to be of Australia, if, as I hope, she follows her wild heart there.

I assure you the future of the Reynolds Foundation will be most secure in Miss Allen's capable hands. I am confident she will intelligently assess the final result of the American War – oh pray God, may the Union prevail, and the last of the African slaves at last be set free, in reality as well as in Mr. Lincoln's noble Proclamation – and having assessed that result, Miss Allen will then determine the best future course for the Foundation. For I am certain Miss Allen shares my concern that the miseries of the American blackies will continue beyond the date when the last chain is finally struck from the last neck of the last slave in the New World; and therefore she will determine wisely what actions the Reynolds Foundation might undertake to grant succour and aid to those poor souls whose lives will surely be thrown into complete and utter chaos, once, God willing, they find themselves free men and free women and free children, yet destitute in a harsh and unforgiving land where their family bonds have been shattered and where they shall no longer be welcomed, and where they shall not be able to rely upon the roots that bind most human beings to the land where they live.

To this end, Miss Allen has agreed to present herself at your offices, in the shadow of the Tower of London, in one week's time, on the 19th day of June, at eleven o'clock in the fore-noon, to execute whatever documents you deem necessary to effectuate the transfer of authority to her. I shall endeavor also to attend the ceremony, Mr. Caruthers, as it would give me measureless joy to be present for the passing of the torch; yet I fear my rheumatism, and my gout, may well have darker plans for me on the appointed morning, in which case, I shall wish you to know that I am most deeply sorry not to be in attendance and participating in such a momentous occasion in the history of the Reynolds Foundation.

Let me say in closing, dear Mr. Caruthers, that I am most deeply thankful for all the fine work you have performed for the Reynolds Foundation, and also for the critical role your Grand-father and your Father played in the launch of our charitable work. Your Grand-father was a far-sighted visionary, who understood, far better than I, that in the end Reverend Clarkson and Mr. Wilberforce would win the day, on the question of abolishing the Slave Trade, by appealing to the better Angels of our Nature; for your Grand-father had the confidence that I, as a young woman buffeted by cruel Fate, so sorely lacked, that human beings, in spite of all our failings, do ultimately desire the Good. So know that your Grand-father would be very proud of you and all your fine work, dearest Nigel, as indeed am I.

Faithfully yours,

India Reynolds

* * *

14 December 1867

Nigel M. Caruthers, Esquire
Caruthers & Fotheringill, Solicitors At Law
One Mincing Lane, Tower Hill
London, Great Britain

Dear Mr. Caruthers:

I hope you shall recall our meeting, some years past, at your offices, when I signed the legal documents making me sole Trustee of the Reynolds Foundation.

I regret I have been unable to communicate with you on the regular basis I should have liked. I have been detained by many adventures in Australasia.

However, this fortnight I am embarking for the Crown Colony of Honduras, where I expect to begin at last the important work entrusted to me by Mistress Reynolds three years past. Wherefore, upon arrival in Honduras, I shall be in immediate and urgent need of substantial funds, in order to begin to redress the deplorable injuries perpetrated upon the victims of slavery, in the New World.

Accordingly, I instruct you, by this letter, to post to me, care of the Belize City branch of the Bank of England, a Letter of Credit for the entire balance of funds in the accounts of the Reynolds Foundation, saving only 3000 pounds for payment of incidental future fees and other expenditures in your discretion, as they may arise.

I expect to arrive in Belize City in or around the first week of March 1868. Please do ensure that the funds are present and waiting for me at that time.

Yours most sincerely,

Kathleen Quinlan

Postscript. Oh – I almost forget to inform you of a most critical fact. In the interim, I have been married, so I am no longer 'Kathleen Allen'. Please post the funds to 'Kathleen Quinlan', as that is my legal name now that I am married.

* * *

2 March 1868

Mrs. Kathleen A. Quinlan
Care of the Bank of England
Belize City, The Crown Colony of Honduras

Dear Mrs. Quinlan:

Enclosed per your request please find a Letter of Credit in your favour for 15,438 pounds sterling, being the entire balance of funds in the accounts of the Reynolds Foundation, save the 3000 pounds which you instructed us to withhold for payment of incidental expenditures. This Letter of Credit is fully guaranteed by the London Bridge branch of the Bank of England.

Please accept my congratulations on your recent marriage, Mrs. Quinlan. I should advise you, however, that your request for Foundation funds to be transferred to a woman whose name is not, precisely, the same as the name of the Trustee recorded in our records, was most irregular. However, recognizing that this irregularity arose solely because you are, amongst all our Trustee clients, the only Member of the Fairer Sex, I persuaded our Manager to grant me the latitude to overcome the bureaucratic obstacles inherent in your request. I feel certain that Mrs. Reynolds smiled down upon me from Heaven whilst I did so.

May the Good Lord be with you, Mrs. Quinlan, in your important charitable work.

Sincerely,

Nigel M. Caruthers

Nigel M. Caruthers, Esq.

* * *

11 May 1868

Nigel M. Caruthers, Esquire
Caruthers & Fotheringill, Solicitors At Law
One Mincing Lane, Tower Hill
London, Great Britain

Dear Mr. Caruthers:

We have received, from the London Bridge branch of this Bank, the Letter of Credit you posted 2nd March this Year, on behalf of the Reynolds Foundation, in favour of Mrs. Kathleen Allen Quinlan, in the sum of 15,438 pounds sterling.

We regret to advise you that we have not been able to pay out the monies secured by your Letter of Credit, for the reason that the lady who hath appeared at our offices, claiming the funds, bears identification only in the name of Catherine Larkin Quinlan. In spite of several long and, I regret to say, acrimonious conferences with Mrs. Quinlan, we are not persuaded that she is definitively the person whom you intend the funds to benefit, seeing that you addressed your Letter of Credit to Kathleen Allen Quinlan.

Mrs. Quinlan has advised us, with no little rancour, that she intends to institute legal action against the Bank, to force this Branch to honour the Letter of Credit you posted to us. Please rest assured that our dilatory actions were not taken in any attempt to dishonour the Letter of Credit; rather, we have acted only out of the prudence that all patrons of the Bank of England have every right to expect. If you can provide us assurance us that you intend the monies secured by the Letter of Credit to go to the benefit of Mrs. Catherine Larkin Quinlan, then we shall be only most happy immediately to pay Mrs. Quinlan the sum enumerated supra.

Yours Most Faithfully,

Giles P. Wetherby

Giles Wetherby, Manager

* * *

"No, Lisa, I haven't seen Big Ben yet. We're working very hard here on the lawsuit." Joyce Kerr sits on her hotel bed, holding the phone to her ear with one hand, while stubbing out a cigarette in the ashtray with the other hand. "No, I haven't seen Buckingham Palace, either."

David Burns sits at the small table in Joyce's room, listening to Joyce's end of her phone call with Lisa, while inhaling the delicious warm smell of a freshly-delivered pizza, still in its box, right in front of him.

"Yes, they're all here with us," Joyce says, and then pauses to listen. "No, they're not in the room right now. It's just David and me."

Burns looks at the pizza box with ardent longing. The unusually fast delivery caught Joyce by surprise, thinking she had plenty of time to finish talking with Lisa before the pizza would come. But now, as Burns waits for the phone call to end, the suspense is killing him. This is the third and last pizza delivery place in range of the Hilton. If this pizza is as underwhelming as the other two, then Burns is going to have to give in and take Joyce out to dinner tomorrow night.

"Kip is fine," Joyce says, and then pauses to listen. "No, I haven't made any plans to go out on the town with him. I told you, we're working very hard here." Joyce rolls her eyes at Burns.

Burns looks back at the pizza box. He has high hopes for this one, because at least the makers know how to organize a speedy delivery – no easy feat, apparently, in London. He's really hoping it won't turn out to be like the other two European mutations of pizza, with a thin crust, watery tomato sauce, and an excess of vegetables running loose on top, instead of being melted into a thick wad of cheese and sauce and crust, the way God intended pizza to be made.

"Today was just the first day of the deposition, dear. But it was a very good day. David made a lot of good arguments." Joyce catches Burns's eyes again, and cradles the phone against her shoulder, miming an eating gesture with both hands, and nodding at Burns to go ahead and start eating without her.

Burns doesn't need to be asked twice. He loosens his hands, like a safecracker about to go to work, and then pulls on the sides of the box, opening it. A delicious wave of hot cheesy steam escapes the box and fills his nostrils and lungs. Burns opens his eyes to see what's in the box.

"Don't you have homework, honey?" Joyce asks. "Alright, dear, but don't stay out late on a school night. Just because you're at your father's doesn't mean you need to turn into a zombie."

Burns brings a positive attitude to his inspection of the pizza. But there's nothing good here. Thin burnt crust, runny tomato sauce, and a miserly helping of cheese. Same as the other places. Time to read the writing on the wall. The Brits just don't know pizza.

"Good-night, sweetie. I love you, too." Joyce hops off the bed. "Well?"

Burns shakes his head no, even as he takes a large bite out of his first slice. "Tomorrow you gotta break down and try some Indian food."

"We could take an hour and go out to a restaurant tomorrow," Joyce counters. "Lisa's dying for me to go out on a date."

"Did you tell her you turned Clive down?"

"I didn't wanna get into that with Lisa. But don't change the subject. I want you to take me out to a proper dinner tomorrow. Just one hour off of work, that's all I ask."

"Okay, fine. But while we eat this travesty of a pizza, let's talk about those four Reynolds documents I just gave you. First question: India Reynolds was pals with Reverend Clarkson and William Wilberforce, while they fought to end Britain's involvement in the Slave Trade. That was in the 1780s, right?"

Joyce nods, chewing on her own first slice of pizza.

"Fine," Burns says. "Way to go, India. But then she was still alive *in 1864*? What the hell. She started with young Caruthers's grandfather as her lawyer, and ended with the *grand-kid* as her lawyer? If she was old enough to start a charitable foundation in 1788, how old was she in 1864?"

"I told you before, I went through everything I could find in the Borough of Southwark Archives, and I really think India Reynolds might well have lived to be 158 years old."

Burns snorts. "And Kip calls *Fiona* crazy?"

"He just hasn't gotten to know me yet. But in my defense, there's a passage in Kathleen's Diary – which I haven't shown to any of the Three Musketeers, like you told me – about how passionate India Reynolds got, in 1864, talking about an entire galley of slaves she saw burnt to death when the Belize Wharf caught fire."

"So?"

"So remember that Navy memo Ron showed us?" Joyce asks. "That fire at the Belize Wharf was in 1724."

Burns raises an eyebrow. "That Wharf could've burnt more than once."

"But Ron said, as far as he knows, that 1724 fire was the only one recorded where a galley of slaves was burnt to death."

"Wow. So maybe you're right. But even if 158 is a bit much to swallow, my point for now is India Reynolds must've been at least 100-something when she finally went to see the Big Trustee in the sky." Burns shakes his head. "Okay, next question: If Kathleen Quinlan's maiden name was Kathleen Allen—"

"—and we know it was," Joyce interjects, "from Kathleen's diary."

"—and Kathleen asks Caruthers to send her an LOC for 15,000 quid, and we know from her diary there was a problem with the LOC, and now we see the 'problem' was she couldn't prove she was Kathleen Allen Quinlan, because apparently her ID said Catherine *Larkin* Quinlan, well, what's up with that?"

"Larkin must've been Kathleen Allen's middle name," Joyce says.

"No," Burns says. "There's another document I saw, from 1864, where India Reynolds formally appoints Kathleen Allen as successor trustee; and the lawyer, Caruthers, wrote out Kathleen's full name: Kathleen *Violet* Allen. She signed it that same way."

"Huh. Well, that is a little weird."

"I've been through the Reynolds Foundation documents up to 1886, but I found nothing more on this. Did Kathleen ever get the Foundation money?"

"Yes," Joyce says. "Later in 1868."

"How?"

"By then she was back in London, so she just went to Caruthers & Fotheringill, and they got it for her."

"How'd I miss that?" Burns asks.

"It's not in the correspondence file. There's just a routine ledger entry for it in the summer of 1868."

"What exact name was she using in the summer of 1868?"

Joyce shrugs. "I've never seen anything except 'Kathleen Allen Quinlan'."

"What's the full name on her 1909 Will?"

"Kathleen Allen Quinlan," Joyce says. "Until you showed me that letter about 'Catherine Larkin Quinlan', I'd never seen that name used anywhere."

Burns nods, and eats the rest of his pizza in silence.

"I did find one irregularity in the later boxes, though," Joyce says. "I don't know if this is the kind of minor technical problem you were hoping for. But there is no record of any Foundation funds being spent on the victims of slavery, ever."

"Where'd the money go?"

"No record. There was the one big transfer of £15,000 to Kathleen in 1868, and then everything else went to legal and bank and administrative fees. And Kathleen didn't keep any records of what she did with the £15,000."

Burns shrugs, still thinking about 'Catherine Larkin Quinlan'. "Can't do much with sloppy record-keeping."

"But meanwhile, Kathleen instantly became a woman of means," Joyce says. "When she left Belize City, she and Roger were almost broke. As soon as they got to London, Roger died. Yet right after she got to Ann Arbor, she bought a fancy mansion on Division Street – *the* hoighty-toighty street in Ann Arbor at that time – and soon after she started collecting fine art and all the other loot the creditors took from Lloyd after his suicide. You might wanna ask Fiona if it was Foundation money that paid for Kathleen's lifestyle upgrade."

"Good idea."

"But in the meantime, I'm pretty tired now. Do you mind doing the rest of your reading in your room, so I can pack it in for tonight?"

"Sure, Joyce. I just wish I could get tired, too. But my circadian rhythms are way off. My body thinks it's still afternoon."

"You gonna finish the Reynolds Foundation documents?" Joyce asks.

"No, I'm gonna switch over to those papers you got from New Zealand."

"About the shipwreck? Why?"

"I want to know why Kathleen Allen became Catherine Larkin Quinlan," Burns says, "until the fuss with the Bank in Belize must've caused her to change it back to Kathleen Allen Quinlan."

"People change their names all the time, David."

"Not their *maiden* names. Unless—"

"You think she had another husband in there somewhere?"

"Maybe," Burns says. "But mostly I smell blood in the water here. I just don't know who's bleeding."

Chapter Twelve
Traitor's Gate

Tuesday 5 April 2011 Morning

Still half asleep, David Burns finds Joyce Kerr and her Three Admirers in the Hilton restaurant, finishing breakfast. The mood around the table is tense.

"Any luck in the art galleries?" Burns asks Kip Hunter and Ron Graham.

Hunter and Graham shake their heads no.

"Find any good documents after I left your room?" Burns asks Joyce Kerr.

Joyce shakes her head no. Burns senses she's ticked at the Three Amigos.

"How was your evening, Clive?" Burns asks Phelps.

Unsmiling, Phelps drops a newspaper in front of Burns, open to page two.

Burns narrows his eyes. "Not again?"

"Afraid so," Phelps says. "Worse than yesterday's."

"This is bad, gang." Burns doesn't look at the article. "Yesterday Fiona's attack dog Landau filed a motion asking Judge Henderson to hold us all in contempt of court, for yesterday's leak. Now someone's thrown more gas on the fire."

"What's 'contempt of court' really mean?" Hunter asks. "You hear that phrase, but no one ever says what actually goes down with 'contempt of court'."

"First Judge Henderson'll hold a hearing," Burns says. "Since the motion names the five of us here in London as the likeliest sources of the leak, the Judge'll order all five of us to show up in court in Detroit, to be cross-examined, one at a time, by Mr. Landau, and by the Judge."

"That doesn't sound like fun," Hunter says.

"Won't be," Burns says. "But it could get worse. If Henderson decides the leak came from us, he'll declare one or more of us in contempt. Then, depending on whether he thinks Joyce or I knew about the leak, he can dismiss Joyce's case with prejudice, meaning it can't ever be filed again; or he can fine any of us, or jail any of us for up to 12 months. That's what's 'goin' down'."

"In other words," Joyce says, casting a dirty look at the Three Fools, "when we go to the contempt hearing, be sure to bring your toothbrushes."

OXFORD DON CLAIMS FOUNTAIN OF YOUTH IS REAL

Dr. Clive Phelps claims to have strong evidence: It's real, and it's in Belize

Ancient Mayan codex said to contain map to legendary fountain

By Sara Hamilton, Higher Correspondent

Mortality researcher Clive Phelps, an Oxford don leading an international investigation into 12 unexplained cancer deaths in Belize last year, has attested in an American court he has "persuasive scientific evidence" suggesting the "fountain of youth may well be real."

Dr. Phelps' secret affidavit persuaded a Detroit judge to seal an intellectual property lawsuit, an unusual event in American courts, as reported yesterday by the Economic Observer.

Dr. Phelps attested that an ancient Mayan book, the *Lamanai Codex*, at the center of the lawsuit, might help him solve the Belize cancer deaths. He also attested that the codex "contains a map to the fountain of youth."

Dr. Phelps, whose Oxford colleagues describe him as "absolutely brilliant" but concede "he prides himself on thinking outside the box," also attested he believes the fountain of youth is located near the ancient Maya ruins at Lamanai, in Belize (formerly British Honduras).

Dr. Phelps asked the court to order Fiona Young of London to allow Phelps access to the codex. Dr. Young, a hermit who shuns all visitors, has long been a pariah in academic circles, for hoarding the unpublished codex and refusing access to her translation of it.

Sources close to the case say Dr. Phelps is underwriting the entire cost of the American lawsuit against Dr. Young, to try to obtain the *Lamanai Codex*.

Rival researchers scoffed at Dr. Phelps' unconventional tactics. "Since Phelps preaches to anyone who'll listen that cancer and immortality are flip sides of the same coin, it's no surprise he lusts after the Lamanai Codex," said Dr. Beth Lee of Yale University. "But there are more productive ways to investigate mass cancer deaths than chasing after rare books with secret lawsuits."

Lamanai has been closed to the public since December 2010, when 12 young Maya men were found dead of cancer there. An international team of doctors, under Dr. Phelps' leadership, has been stymied trying to ascertain the cause of the Lamanai cancer outbreak.

American Judge Dalton Henderson will hear arguments today on the Economic Observer's motion to unseal the case in the public interest of monitoring public health matters. The Judge's ruling is expected very soon.

"Believe it or not," Burns says, "I think this one helps us."

"How?" Joyce asks.

"It's so unfair to Clive," Burns says. "A newspaper'll sometimes rough up a secret source a little, to give 'em cover. But a hatchet job like this? Never. If Clive was their source, this piece'd guarantee they'd get nothing more from him, ever."

"You mean this helps Clive in front of Judge Henderson?" Graham asks.

"Helps us all," Burns says. "The *Observer* wouldn't risk pissing off their source by hammering any member of the source's team like this."

"At least, that's what you'll argue to Judge Henderson," Joyce says.

"Absolutely," Burns says, "and I think he'll agree."

"But isn't it a problem," Joyce asks, "that the same article also treats Fiona pretty badly, too? Calling her a 'pariah', and a 'hoarder', or whatever they said."

"So?" Burns asks. "Everyone already knows Fiona's not the leak."

"But *someone's* gotta be the leak," Joyce counters. "Henderson's sure not gonna think it was courthouse personnel."

"No," Burns says. "But how 'bout the University of Michigan?"

"Yesterday you and Olivia Watt both said the U can't be the leak," Graham interjects, "because they look bad no matter what happens – either for violating a donor's wishes, or for withholding a valuable book from the rest of the world."

"Yeah, but look what's happened so far," Burns says. "Two articles in two days, and scarcely a mention of the U. If Sara Hamilton wants to label Fiona an academic 'pariah' for 'hoarding' a rare book, why isn't she also criticizing the U for 'hoarding' their copy of that book?"

"Maybe Sara Hamilton doesn't know about the copy," Graham says.

"She mentioned the copy in passing in yesterday's article," Burns mutters. "I think the U of M's absence from today's article speaks louder than words."

"You think Santos is the leak," Joyce asks, "or someone back home?"

"If Santos did it, he was just following orders. But gang, we gotta keep all this under our hats. If we accuse the U today, then tomorrow's story'll rake the U over the coals, and we'll lose our best defense against the contempt motion." Burns hails a waitress. "Can we pay? We're in a rush."

* * *

"Olivia," David Burns says, "I know you and Dr. Young aren't happy about this new article. We're not happy, either. Dr. Phelps' investigation into those cancer deaths is still pending. It's sensitive stuff. But we're all here. We might as well plow forward today."

"We already created 'justifiable reliance'," Olivia Watt says, "with all the questions Dr. Young answered yesterday. Why should we proceed today?"

"Same reasons as yesterday," Burns says. "We all put a lot of time into getting ready for today. And although Dr. Young answered a lot of questions yesterday, the further we get into this depo, the harder it's gonna be for Judge Henderson to unseal this case. Each aggravating question of mine she answers is one more nail in the coffin of the *Observer's* motion to open this case."

Olivia sighs. "What'd you do before you became a lawyer?"

"Sold snake oil." Burns grins.

Olivia almost laughs. "You are a rare bird, David."

"You spoil me, Olivia. Ready to go on the record?"

Olivia turns to Fiona Young.

"Let's get on with it," Fiona snarls through clenched teeth.

* * *

Transcript of the 5 April 2011 Deposition of Dr. Fiona Young at the offices of Symington & Watt, in the case of *Joyce Kerr* v *Fiona Young et al*, Case No. 11-0098-IP, in the United States District Court for the Eastern District of Michigan. Appearances: David Burns, Esq. for Ms. Kerr; Olivia Watt, Esq. for Dr. Young and the Reynolds Foundation; Miguel Santos, Esq. for the University of Michigan; also present: Joyce Kerr, Dr. Clive Phelps, Dr. Ronald Graham, and Kip Hunter. Reporter: Ivy Taylor, Bridge House, 7 Horselydown Lane, London SE1 2QR.

- Ms. Taylor: On the record at – oh, my watch stopped. What time is it?
- Mr. Burns: According to Bette Midler, no matter what time it is in New York, it's always 1939 in London.
- Mr. Santos: It's 9:02 a.m., Ivy.
- Ivy Taylor: Thank you. Dr. Young, you're still under oath.
- Dr. Young: Yes, dear, I remember.
- Ms. Watt: I have a Statement for the record. Mr. Burns, after consultation with my client yesterday afternoon, we have determined to drop the first three of our Affirmative Defenses, and rely entirely upon our fourth Affirmative Defense. Obviously you and I will need to draft a formal Stipulation to this effect, before completion of this Deposition. But I advise you of this decision now, so you need not waste time asking questions related to the first three Defenses.
- Mr. Burns: (Exchanges glances with his consultants) Dr. Young, Your Fourth Affirmative Defense says in pertinent part: 'The *Lamanai Codex* was never properly part of Kathleen Quinlan's Estate. Rather, the true owner of the codex, from long before Kathleen Quinlan's birth and continuously to the present day, has always been defendant Reynolds Foundation." So are you conceding now that Joyce is the rightful owner of the Ambergris Caye real estate?

- Ms. Watt: Objection. Calls for a legal conclusion. We'll address that, David, when you and I work out the language of our formal Stipulation.
- Mr. Burns: Okay, but I'm just trying to see if I need to ask any more questions about the land. It seems like, if you're relying only on the Fourth Affirmative Defense, that defense doesn't apply to the land. Here, I got a question for Dr. Young. Did the Reynolds Foundation ever own the land on Ambergris Caye that you and your mother paid taxes on the last 101 years?
- Dr. Young: (Long pause) No. Joyce can have that land. (Looks at Ms. Kerr) Think of me, dear, when you sell it for big bucks. That land has always meant a great deal to me.
- Mr. Burns: Why has that land always meant a great deal to you?
- Dr. Young: Besides this ring, it's my only tangible link to Roger Quinlan.
- Mr. Burns: (Long pause)
- Dr. Young: Roger was the one who bought the land, you see.
- Mr. Burns: I guess I see. (Pause) Did the Reynolds Foundation ever buy the *Lamanai Codex*, the way Roger bought the land on Ambergris Caye?
- Dr. Young: (Pause) I don't believe so.
- Mr. Burns: How'd the Foundation acquire the *Lamanai Codex*?
- Dr. Young: India Reynolds donated the codex to the Foundation.
- Mr. Burns: How did India Reynolds acquire the *Lamanai Codex*?
- Dr. Young: I don't know.
- Mr. Burns: How do you know India Reynolds donated the codex to her own Foundation?
- Dr. Young: Mum told me.
- Mr. Burns: Did Persephone tell you her source for this information?
- Dr. Young: Kathleen told Mum that India Reynolds gave the codex to Kathleen in her capacity as the new Trustee of the Reynolds Foundation.
- Mr. Burns: Is there any document that verifies this fact?
- Ms. Watt: Objection, calls for a legal conclusion. You can answer.
- Dr. Young: The only document I know of, which makes it clear the legal owner of the codex has always been the Reynolds Foundation, is the contract I signed with the University of Michigan, pertaining to the copy they made.
- Mr. Burns: That was in 1970?
- Dr. Young: Yes.
- Mr. Burns: How'd that 1970 contract with the University come about?
- Dr. Young: The University – Dr. Winters – had recruited me to teach Central American studies. I was thrilled to be given the opportunity to teach where my grandmother once taught. Then they learned I had no college degree. So we spent a year jumping through hoops to get Harvard to award me the honorary doctorate, which we discussed yesterday, so Dr. Winters could dress me up for the university regents as an appropriate

faculty candidate. Finally it all got done and I arrived on campus in August of 1970, only to discover that the University had a policy mandating that any faculty or staff working on an ancient manuscript were required to make a copy of the manuscript for the University of Michigan libraries. I explained that, although I was working on a translation of the *Lamanai Codex*, I was not the legal owner of the book, so I couldn't agree to let a copy be made, unless the legal owner consented.

- Mr. Burns: And the legal owner of the codex was whom?
- Dr. Young: The Reynolds Foundation.
- Mr. Burns: In August 1970, who were the officers and directors of the Reynolds Foundation?
- Dr. Young: I was the sole officer, director and trustee.
- Mr. Burns: Were there any employees besides you?
- Dr. Young: No.
- Mr. Burns: Well if you were the sole officer, director and trustee of the Reynolds Foundation, then you weren't exactly going to have to sled uphill to get the 'consent' of the Foundation to have a copy made, were you?
- Ms. Watt: Objection. Argumentative and sarcastic.
- Dr. Young: Actually, I took my fiduciary duties very seriously; and for this reason I felt that the University's request to make a copy of the codex, which would have been a hard enough decision for me personally to endorse, was simply not in the Foundation's best interests.
- Mr. Burns: I'm not following this. I would think it would be a no-brainer to make a copy of a rare historical document, just out of general prudence. So let's start with you personally. Why would it have been hard for you personally to allow a copy to be made of the codex?
- Dr. Young: Personally I was concerned that if a copy was made, then rival scholars could access it, and someone might manage to translate the *Lamanai Codex* before me, rendering my ten years of work on the codex worthless. On the other hand, I personally wished ardently to join the U of M faculty, so if it was only a personal decision, I might have let that strong desire conquer my concern about the possible access of rivals to the codex.
- Mr. Burns: Okay, now what extra concerns did the Reynolds Foundation have, in your mind, about a copy being made of the *Lamanai Codex*?
- Dr. Young: In 1970 the codex was, as it is today, the Foundation's only asset. But the value of the codex would be greatly reduced, if a copy became publicly available. As this lawsuit shows, even when a copy is made subject to the strict contractual restrictions we placed on the U of M, the very existence of the copy tempts lawyers like you to think up claims to try to access the copy. So from the Foundation's perspective, it would've been better if no copy had been made.

- Mr. Burns: Any other concerns the Foundation had, in your mind?
- Dr. Young: The other big concern the Foundation had about allowing a copy of the codex to be made related to the specific content of the codex.
- Mr. Burns: What was that concern?
- Dr. Young: (Looks at Ms. Watt) I don't – I'm not comfortable discussing the content of the *Lamanai Codex*.
- Ms. Watt: We object on the basis that the content of the *Lamanai Codex* is confidential and proprietary.
- Mr. Burns: I'm not asking for the content, Olivia. I just want to know the general nature of the concern Dr. Young had that related to the content.
- Ms. Watt: That's an awfully narrow line you want Dr. Young to walk. (Turns to Dr. Young) Can you answer the question without discussing the specific content of the codex?
- Dr. Young: (Sighs) My concern, as trustee of a charitable Foundation dedicated to the improvement of the human condition, was that anything that increases the chances of more people reading the *Lamanai Codex* is not in the best interests of mankind.
- Mr. Burns: Why not? You feared the codex is a dangerous invitation for people to go looking for the fountain of youth?
- Ms. Watt: Objection. Now you're definitely on the other side of that narrow line. I'll instruct you not to answer, Dr. Young, on the basis that the question calls for information that is confidential and proprietary.
- Mr. Burns: Do you feel the codex is dangerous for everyone except you to read, or do you think responsible scientists might be able to objectively assess the risk and benefits of the information contained in the codex?
- Dr. Young: If you mean scientists like Dr. Phelps, who think Death is just another disease to be conquered, then I'd say no, I don't think scientists can be trusted to objectively assess the risks and benefits for mankind of the information contained in the codex.
- Mr. Burns: Are you aware Dr. Phelps won the Lasker Award, the Gruber Genetics Prize, and the Landon Prize for his research which was deemed to have benefitted all mankind?
- Dr. Young: I don't know the names of the various prizes, but I'm aware Dr. Phelps attracts awards the way unwashed children attract lice.
- Mr. Burns: Are you comparing Dr. Phelps's awards to lice in order to imply there is something unsafe or unhealthy about Dr. Phelps?
- Dr. Young: That is precisely what I'm doing. Dr. Phelps and his rivals in the mad race to extend human life remind me of the Chaucer tale about the three fools who went out to kill Death, but got distracted when they found a great treasure chest which Death had placed in their path. Each wanted the treasure for himself so badly, they

ended up all killing each other – thereby ironically 'finding' Death, once they stopped looking for him.

- Mr. Burns: (Long pause) You think you're the only person on the planet who has the objectivity to read the *Lamanai Codex* and not be seduced by its charms, whatever they may be, and end up what – dead?
- Ms. Watt: Object to the form of the question. It's argumentative, and incoherent.
- Dr. Young: I caught the drift of it. No, I don't think I'm the only person on the planet who can safely read the *Lamanai Codex*. But it's a dangerous book to give to mankind generally, Mr. Burns, because most people's objectivity can be compromised by greed; and so, as the Reynolds Foundation's Trustee, I feel a strong duty to protect the codex from publication.
- Mr. Burns: Then why have you spent 51 years working on a translation?
- Dr. Young: When I started the translation, I had no idea how dangerous the codex is.
- Mr. Burns: Do you have any intention of publishing your translation?
- Dr. Young: (Looks at Ms. Watt) Do I have to answer that?
- Ms. Watt: Yes, but your answer is protected by the confidentiality order, so none of these people may disclose your answer to anyone else.
- Dr. Young: That hasn't stopped them so far.
- Ms. Watt: The contempt sanctions will stop them.
- Dr. Young: (Sighs) No, I do not intend to publish my translation.
- Mr. Burns: 51 years of work down the drain?
- Dr. Young: (Shrugs) I don't consider work to be a waste, just because it's not published. Not all of us work just for the sake of winning awards.
- Mr. Burns: But what's the value of work on a translation, if no one else ever reads it?
- Dr. Young: What's the sound of one hand clapping? The Buddhists would say an activity has value if it helps you advance to a higher level of understanding, regardless of its utilitarian value in the marketplace.
- Mr. Burns: (Long pause) So to recap: back in 1970, you were concerned that making a copy of the codex might be dangerous to mankind generally; and that it might jeopardize the market value of the original; and that other scholars might try to steal your thunder and translate it first. Any other concerns you had, back in 1970, for not wanting a copy to be made?
- Dr. Young: None that I remember now, 41 years later.
- Mr. Burns: But the copy did end up being made by U of M, right?
- Dr. Young: Right.
- Mr. Burns: Did you discuss your concerns with the University before the copy was made?
- Mr. Santos: Dr. Young, please don't share any conversations you may have had with counsel for the University of Michigan, because those would be privileged conversations.

- Mr. Burns: Well, the University might feel there's still a privilege, but if their ex-employee wishes to waive the privilege, you have no right to stop her.
- Mr. Santos: (Affronted) Not so! An ex-employee is still obliged to respect the confidential information of their former employer.
- Mr. Burns: People shouldn't walk on the grass, either, but you can't stop 'em when they do. But before we have this argument, let's see if we even have a problem. Dr. Young, without at this point relating the content of your discussions, who'd you talk to at the U about the copy?
- Dr. Young: First I talked to Dr. Winters. Then he brought in a lawyer from the General Counsel's office, who drafted the contract we signed.
- Mr. Burns: Alright. What'd you discuss with Dr. Winters?
- Dr. Young: I voiced the three concerns we just discussed – the risk to the value of the original, the danger of other scholars pirating the work, and the humanitarian issue if the copy were available to people besides me.
- Mr. Burns: What was Dr. Winters's response?
- Dr. Young: He said we could address all my concerns by signing a contract that prohibited anyone from accessing the copy, unless they had the express written permission of the Reynolds Foundation.
- Mr. Burns: And then Dr. Winters got a lawyer to write that up for you?
- Dr. Young: Yes.
- Mr. Burns: Did the lawyer express any concern about the contract being contrary to the strong public interest in wide access to historical documents?
- Mr. Santos: Objection! The question seeks information protected by the attorney-client privilege. Please do not answer, Dr. Young.
- Mr. Burns: You're not her attorney, Miguel.
- Ms. Watt: Dr. Young, I instruct you not to answer on the basis of attorney-client privilege. It's in your best interest to honor the attorney-client privilege with your former employer's counsel, so your former employer remains fully motivated to continue to enforce the terms of the contract they signed, limiting access to the copy.
- Mr. Burns: Back in 1970, before you signed the contract with the U limiting access to the copy, was there any document evidencing your claim that the Reynolds Foundation owned the original of the *Lamanai Codex*?
- Dr. Young: (Shrugs) I don't know.
- Mr. Burns: Your belief, at that time, that the 'legal owner' of the codex was the Reynolds Foundation, was based entirely on what Persephone told you that Kathleen Quinlan supposedly told your mother?
- Dr. Young: I don't know why you say 'supposedly'. Why would either my mother or my grandmother make up a story about someone else besides them owning the *Lamanai*

Codex? Neither they nor I had a crystal ball to foresee that many decades later my ungrateful cousin twice-removed, whom I cared for as if she were my own child, would turn around and reward my love by suing me for the book she knows I care for more than any in the world.

- Mr. Burns: You're surprised to learn Joyce would sue you? The same cousin whom you falsely accused of trying to steal the codex from you when she was only 20 years old? The same cousin you tried to have criminally prosecuted for attempted theft – and now you're surprised to learn she would sue you, even though you've already conceded that the Ambergris Caye land should really have been Joyce's from the beginning?
- Ms. Watt: Objection! Compound and argumentative. You don't have to answer any of those questions, Dr. Young.
- Mr. Burns: No, you don't have to answer my questions on this subject, Dr. Young. But I bet you'll have to answer them in the Next Life. How could you do that to Joyce? Do you know how much pain you caused her when you accused her of trying to steal from you?
- Ms. Watt: Objection! If this continues, we shall end the deposition now.
- Mr. Burns: Your client's the one who insisted on opening old wounds, Olivia, with a gratuitous answer that wasn't even remotely related to the question I asked. (Turns to Ivy Taylor) Please note for the record my motion to strike all of Dr. Young's answer a few questions back, where she carried on about crystal balls and her ungrateful cousin twice-removed.
- Ms. Watt: And I move to strike everything that Mr. Burns said since Dr. Young gave the answer that includes the crystal ball reference.
- Mr. Burns: (To Dr. Young) Let's see if we can stay on track, shall we? My question is simply this: your belief, in the fall of 1970, that the 'legal owner' of the *Lamanai Codex* was the Reynolds Foundation – that belief was based entirely on what Persephone told you, orally, that Persephone said Kathleen told Persephone, right?
- Dr. Young: Yes. Which I considered then, and still consider, an entirely sufficient 'basis', as you call it, for my 'belief' that the legal owner of the codex was the Reynolds Foundation. Why would Kathleen say someone other than herself was the actual, technical owner of the codex, unless it were true?
- Mr. Burns: The way this works, Dr. Young, is I ask the questions, and you answer them. So if you can try to answer my questions with something other than rhetorical questions, we'll move along a lot faster. (Smiles sarcastically) Now, that 1970 contract between the U of M and the Reynolds Foundation, who signed that contract on behalf of the Foundation?
- Dr. Young: I did.
- Mr. Burns: And I think you already said you were, at that time, the sole officer, director and trustee of the Reynolds Foundation?

■ Dr. Young: Yes.
■ Mr. Burns: When were you appointed sole officer, director and trustee of the Reynolds Foundation?
■ Dr. Young: 1960.
■ Mr. Burns: Who appointed you?
■ Dr. Young: The previous trustee, my mother.
■ Mr. Burns: How'd you learn of your appointment?
■ Dr. Young: It was in amongst the papers she left me in her trunk.
■ Mr. Burns: I saw it, too, somewhere in the 17 boxes of Reynolds Foundation files you produced. But before you saw that paper, did you have any glimmer you might end up being appointed as the trustee?
■ Dr. Young: My mother told me years before that she planned to appoint me her successor.
■ Mr. Burns: In your 51 years as the sole trustee of the Reynolds Foundation, what have you done in the way of Foundation business?
■ Dr. Young: I've safeguarded the *Lamanai Codex*.
■ Mr. Burns: Anything else?
■ Dr. Young: I've handled correspondence with accountants and lawyers.
■ Mr. Burns: Anything else?
■ Dr. Young: (Shrugs) No. The Foundation was nearly broke when I was appointed trustee.
■ Mr. Burns: Have you tried to increase the Foundation's endowment?
■ Dr. Young: I'm not a fundraiser.
■ Mr. Burns: What was your understanding of the specific charitable purpose of the Reynolds Foundation?
■ Dr. Young: The Foundation's original purpose was to work towards terminating the Slave Trade, and abolishing the institution of human slavery.
■ Mr. Burns: That purpose was stated in the 1788 incorporation papers?
■ Dr. Young: Correct.
■ Mr. Burns: Have you ever seen any paperwork modifying the original charitable purpose, in light of the end of slavery and the slave trade?
■ Dr. Young: No.
■ Mr. Burns: What's your understanding of the specific charitable purpose of the Reynolds Foundation today?
■ Dr. Young: Safeguarding the *Lamanai Codex* for the benefit of mankind.
■ Mr. Burns: Where'd you get that understanding?
■ Dr. Young: From my mother, who got it from her mother.
■ Mr. Burns: Are you aware of any specific actions Kathleen Quinlan took to benefit the African-American victims of slavery?
■ Dr. Young: No.

- Mr. Burns: Is there any specific action your mother Persephone or you took to benefit the African-American victims of slavery?
- Dr. Young: Without funds, there hasn't been much we could do.
- Mr. Burns: Where'd the money go?
- Ms. Watt: Objection. Vague and ambiguous. What money?
- Mr. Burns: There's a ledger entry for the Foundation, from the summer of 1868, showing a payment from the Foundation to your grandmother Kathleen of £15,000. Do you know what that money was used for?
- Dr. Young: No.
- Mr. Burns: That payment to Kathleen left the Foundation with only minimal funds, a condition that has persisted right down to the present day. Do you not consider it part of your duties, as the Foundation's sole officer, director and trustee, to investigate whether the money withdrawn by Kathleen in 1868 was used for an appropriate charitable purpose?
- Dr. Young: This is the first time I've ever heard anyone suggest the money was not used for an appropriate purpose.
- Mr. Burns: How could the purpose possibly have been appropriate, when the the Foundation's only official purposes – terminating the Slave Trade, and abolishing slavery – became moot five years before 1868?
- Ms. Watt: Objection. Argumentative.
- Mr. Burns: Did Kathleen spend £15,000 in 1868 on abolishing slavery and the slave trade?
- Dr. Young: I doubt it. As you said, slavery was abolished before then.
- Mr. Burns: Did Kathleen spend £15,000 – which was a boatload of money, in 1868 – on security measures for the Lamanai Codex?
- Dr. Young: I already said, I don't know what she spent the money on.
- Mr. Burns: Don't you think it's your duty to find out?
- Dr. Young: Now? That money was taken out 57 years before I was born.
- Mr. Burns: But it's the reason the Foundation doesn't have any money today. Don't you feel you have a duty to find out whether the Foundation might have a claim against Kathleen's Estate to get the money back?
- Dr. Young: No. I think making claims based on what happened a hundred or a hundred-and-fifty years ago is patently ridiculous.
- Mr. Burns: (Chuckles) Well if you're not going to try to get the money back, and you're not fundraising, why not just close down the Foundation?
- Dr. Young: I assume that's what'll happen when I pass away.
- Mr. Burns: And then what'll happen to the *Lamanai Codex*?
- Dr. Young: I plan to leave it in the care of someone who will safeguard its secrets.

- Mr. Burns: Who specifically are you planning to leave it with?
- Dr. Young: I haven't decided.
- Mr. Burns: Really? I know your counsel doesn't like it when I ask about busses, but I have the same question about the original that I asked yesterday about the translation: suppose you walk out of this deposition and get hit by a bus. What would happen to the *Lamanai Codex*?
- Ms. Watt: Objection. You are trying, just like yesterday, to use the back door to find out the contents of my client's Will.
- Mr. Burns: No, I'm not. Your client's Will can't possibly apply to the *original* of the codex, because your client now claims the original isn't owned by her personally, but rather is owned by the Reynolds Foundation. (To Dr. Young) Does the Reynolds Foundation have a plan or procedure that kicks into effect regarding the disposition of the *Lamanai Codex*, when you die?
- Dr. Young: No. Well – hold on a minute. When I moved the Foundation from the UK to the US in the 70s, the American lawyer did explain what happens under Michigan law if I die without naming a successor trustee. I don't really remember – something about the bank taking over control. But whatever it is that happens by law, I guess that's a plan or procedure.
- Mr. Burns: So the bottom line is, you don't know what would happen to the *Lamanai Codex*, if you didn't wake up tomorrow morning?
- Dr. Young: That's right. But as I said yesterday, I'm not planning to die anytime soon.
- Mr. Burns: You said Persephone appointed you trustee in 1960. Who appointed Persephone?
- Dr. Young: Her mother, Kathleen Quinlan.
- Mr. Burns: When?
- Dr. Young: 1909.
- Mr. Burns: (Bares his teeth in a sarcastic smile) Before or after Kathleen committed suicide on September 1st, 1909?
- Ms. Watt: Object to the sarcasm. That's beneath you, David.
- Mr. Burns: You overrate me, Olivia. Look, Dr. Young, we've already established that the Deed for the Ambergris Caye land got signed over to Persephone a coupla months *after* Kathleen drove off that bridge. Did the same thing happen with the Reynolds Foundation appointment – or did Persephone get appointed before Kathleen kicked it?
- Dr. Young: (Impassively) You have copies of all the Foundation records. I don't remember the exact date of the appointment.
- Mr. Burns: Me neither. (After a whispered conference with Ms. Kerr, hands a document and copies to the witness and all counsel) Let's mark as Young Exhibit 16 an August 30, 1909 document titled 'Appointment of Successor Trustee', signed by Kathleen Quinlan.

- Dr. Young: Looks like Kathleen was still alive when this got signed.
- Ms. Watt: Wait for a question, Dr. Young.
- Mr. Burns: Yes, this was signed the day before Kathleen's suicide. As if she were putting her affairs in order, before taking her final leave.
- Ms.Watt: Is there a question?
- Mr. Burns: Sure. Before Kathleen appointed Persephone trustee, who appointed Kathleen trustee of the Reynolds Foundation?
- Dr. Young: India Reynolds, the founder.
- Mr. Burns: When did India Reynolds appoint Kathleen?
- Dr. Young: 1864. You must have the document about that.
- Mr. Burns: So far as you know, was anyone else ever a trustee of the Reynolds Foundation, besides India Reynolds, Kathleen Quinlan, Persephone Quinlan and you?
- Dr. Young: No.
- Mr. Burns: What was Kathleen Quinlan's maiden name?
- Dr. Young: (Pause) Allen.
- Mr. Burns: What was Kathleen's middle name before she got married?
- Dr. Young: (Long pause) I don't know.
- Mr. Burns: You don't know your grandmother's middle name?
- Dr. Young: No. Sorry. She died 16 years before I was born.
- Mr. Burns: Mark as Young Exhibit 17 a document dated 17 June 1864, titled 'Appointment of Successor Trustee'. (Hands copies to witness and all counsel) Ever see this before?
- Dr. Young: I don't think so.
- Mr. Burns: You see the signatures of 'India Marie Reynolds' and 'Kathleen Violet Allen', at the bottom of the document where Mrs. Reynolds appoints Kathleen Violet Allen successor trustee of the Reynolds Foundation?
- Dr. Young: (Pause) Yes.
- Mr. Burns: Do you recognize your grandmother's signature there?
- Dr. Young: Yes, that's Kathleen's signature.
- Mr. Burns: So the 'Kathleen Violet Allen' appointed sole trustee of the Reynolds Foundation on 17 June 1864, that was your grandmother, later known as Kathleen Quinlan, yes?
- Dr. Young: That was my grandmother.
- Mr. Burns: So your grandmother's middle name was Violet?
- Dr. Young: Yes, I guess so. I always heard of her as Kathleen Allen Quinlan, the way it's written on her Will.
- Mr. Burns: Ivy, mark as Young Exhibit 18 a letter dated 14 December 1867, from Kathleen Quinlan to Nigel Caruthers, counsel for the Reynolds Foundation. (Hands copies to witness and all counsel) Ever see this before?

- Dr. Young: (Puts on reading glasses, reviews letter) No.
- Mr. Burns: You recognize your grandmother's signature there?
- Dr. Young: (Pause) Yes, that's Kathleen's writing.
- Mr. Burns: You see at the end, where she explains that, in the four years since she was appointed Trustee of the Foundation, she's had a name change, and she's no longer Kathleen Allen, but now Kathleen Quinlan?
- Dr. Young: Yes.
- Mr. Burns: Ivy, mark as Exhibit 19 an 11 May 1868 letter from Giles Wetherby, Manager of the Belize City Branch of the Bank of England, to Nigel Carruthers, solicitor for the Reynolds Foundation. Ever see this one before?
- Dr. Young: No.
- Mr. Burns: You don't want to look at it, just to be sure? It comes right out of your Reynolds Foundation records.
- Dr. Young: (Sighs, puts on reading glasses, reads it) I don't remember seeing this letter before. Like you said, there are 17 boxes of old records.
- Mr. Burns: Have you ever heard your grandmother referred to as 'Catherine Larkin Quinlan', or even 'Kathleen Larkin Quinlan'?
- Dr. Young: I don't know. I told you, I never knew her middle name.
- Mr. Burns: Hmmn. When did Kathleen Allen marry Roger Quinlan?
- Dr. Young: I don't know.
- Mr. Burns: Sometime after 1865?
- Ms. Watt: Objection. If she doesn't know, she doesn't know.
- Mr. Burns: Well yesterday the witness testified that Persephone was born in 1865, and that Persephone was the illegitimate child of Kathleen and Roger. So the witness must have some inkling when Roger and Kathleen were married. What do you know on this subject, Dr. Young?
- Dr. Young: You're right, they were married sometime after 1865.
- Mr. Burns: How do you know that?
- Dr. Young: From just what you said. My Mum said she was illegitimate. The 1909 letter from Kathleen said she and Roger were Persephone's parents. So Roger and Kathleen must have gotten married sometime after 1865, and before 1868, when Roger died.
- Ms. Watt: David, we waived our probate defenses. What possible relevance does Kathleen's wedding date, or her middle name, have to our sole remaining defense, the Reynolds Foundation's ownership of the codex?
- Mr. Burns: As I explained before, Olivia, relevance is not the test for questions in an American deposition. All I have to do is show that a question is 'reasonably calculated to lead to the discovery of admissible evidence'. Normally that loose standard allows me to ask questions without being required to give you a road map of where I'm going. But

if you want a road map, here it is. We've got an 1868 letter from the Bank of England, questioning whether Kathleen Quinlan was really the same Kathleen Allen who was originally appointed trustee of the Reynolds Foundation in 1864. But if Kathleen Quinlan was not the proper trustee, then her appointment of Persephone, and Persephone's appointment of Dr. Young, were all invalid appointments. In which case, the contract between the Reynolds Foundation and U of M is invalid, because it wasn't signed by a legally authorized trustee of the Reynolds Foundation. (Hands a document to witness.) We'll mark as Young Exhibit 20 the 1868 'Journal of Mistress Kathleen Allen Quinlan'.

- Mr. Santos: Is there a copy for me?
- Mr. Burns: Sorry, Miguel, it's so long we just made the one copy. Do you mind following along over Olivia's shoulder on this one?
- Mr. Santos: (Grumbles) Okay.
- Mr. Burns: Dr. Young, is that your grandmother's handwriting?
- Dr. Young: (Flips through a few pages of the copy of the journal, then looks at Ms. Kerr in utter disbelief) Where on earth did you find this?
- Mr. Burns: Ms. Kerr inherited Exhibit 20 from her father, Justin Kerr, who passed away in December. Do you recognize the handwriting as that of your grandmother?
- Dr. Young: (Nods yes)
- Mr. Burns: If you'll look at the first entry there—
- Dr. Young: I'd like to read this.
- Mr. Burns: You can take your copy home this afternoon, if you like.
- Dr. Young: No, I'd like to read it now.
- Mr. Burns: No, I need you to answer a few questions, first, Dr. Young, so the record is clear as to what you yourself know, without the benefit of what you learn from reading the whole diary. So if you'll look at the first entry, please, for Tuesday 10 March 1868, right under the words 'The Journal of Mistress Kathleen Allen Quinlan', you see the second paragraph, where she writes: (Puts on reading glasses, and squints to read his copy) '*This haunting question derailed my last attempts at journal-keeping, in London, and again during our New Zealand days*'. Dr. Young, have you ever seen any other journals your grandmother kept, besides this one you're holding now?
- Dr. Young: (Long pause) No.
- Mr. Burns: If you keep reading, she writes: '*for telling my tale required me then, as I fear it may again, to record certain deeds of mine which, in Mr. Browning's dolorous phrase, were better left undone; and as my imagination conjured my unborn children and their children, reading my journal in some distant, happier time, I could not bear to think of their opprobrium directed at me across the generations.*' Dr. Young, do you know what deeds your grandmother is referencing here?
- Dr. Young: No.

- Mr. Burns: Have you, as one of the 'unborn children' she was imagining here, ever directed 'opprobrium' at Kathleen Quinlan across the generations?
- Dr. Young: No.
- Mr. Burns: Was Kathleen Quinlan ever convicted of any crime?
- Dr. Young: Not that I know of.
- Mr. Burns: Skip ahead to the entry for 24 March 1868, where Kathleen writes: '*R responded very angrily, calling me an ungrateful wife, who should be praising him for his success rather than pestering him with unfounded accusations; and suggesting that the only reason I am so quick to accuse him of criminal conduct is because of mine own intimate familiarity with lawless behavior. Needless to say, from this point, our discourse descended into mutual recriminations which did neither of us any credit.*' Dr. Young, do you know what 'lawless behavior' your grandmother was 'intimately familiar' with?
- Dr. Young: Why are you tormenting me with this? I already told you, I am unaware of Kathleen committing any crimes or misdemeanors.
- Mr. Burns: What about Roger? Do you know any crimes or misdemeanors he committed, that might lead to 'mutual recriminations'?
- Dr. Young: (Pause) Roger was expelled from Oxford, after he was accused of robbing graves for bodies to further his medical studies. Whether those accusations were true, and whether back then those actions would have constituted a crime or a misdemeanor or what, I do not know.
- Mr. Burns: If you'd flip back to the entry for 10 March that we were looking at earlier, there's a sentence that reads: '*For you see, Persephone, all your father's hard-won Australian gold rests on the floor of the Southern Ocean, alongside most of our ill-fated ship mates and their gold*'. Do you know what events that sentence references?
- Dr. Young: Kathleen and Roger survived a tragic shipwreck in the Southern Ocean in 1866.
- Mr. Burns: The ship that wrecked was the General Grant?
- Dr. Young: Yes.
- Mr. Burns: What do you know about that shipwreck?
- Dr. Young: The General Grant left from Melbourne in May 1866, which is late autumn down under, eastbound for London. A few days out of port the ship got lost in a deep fog, and wrecked against the rocks of Auckland Island, south of New Zealand. Most of the passengers and crew drowned. A small band of survivors, including Roger and Kathleen, were marooned on an uninhabited island for 18 months, until a whaling ship rescued them.
- Mr. Burns: You know this from your mother?
- Dr. Young: Yes – and I've read about it, too. It's a famous shipwreck, because many passengers were carrying the gold they'd found in Victoria.

- Mr. Burns: Salvagers are still searching for the wreck?
- Dr. Young: Not anymore. Too many salvagers died over the years trying to find it. New Zealand finally made it illegal to search for the General Grant.
- Mr. Burns: Does that really keep treasure-hunters away?
- Dr. Young: Probably not.
- Mr. Burns: But no one's ever found the gold from the General Grant?
- Dr. Young: No – at least, no one's admitted finding it. And most of it had Bank imprints, so even if you find it, you couldn't cash it today without someone recognizing it.
- Mr. Burns: How did Roger and Kathleen survive the shipwreck?
- Dr. Young: Roger Quinlan was a champion swimmer at Oxford. He swam out of the water where the ship wrecked, carrying Kathleen on his back to safety.
- Mr. Burns: Wow. If you turn to the next entry in the diary, for 12 March 1868, in the second paragraph Kathleen wrote: "*I resorted to taking a pretty keepsake of R's, which I hate as much as the woman whose memory its picture preserves, to the sole pawnshop in Belize City.*' Who is the other woman referenced there?
- Dr. Young: I don't know.
- Mr. Burns: Flip to the next entry, 16 March, where near the end of that entry she writes: '*At last I am free of her spell – the rival whose name I cannot bear to speak, even to you. At last your father is free of her spell, too, and at last he is enough at his ease to love me again as he did in the days before we determined to call ourselves 'husband and wife', when we defied Society's rules with a passion as wild and untamed as that of Heathcliff and Catherine. Except that now, with my rival lying in her watery grave in the Southern Ocean, and with the dark spell that she and her family's money cast over R finally and forever exorcised, R is totally and forever mine! I should have thrown that locket away months ago, when we were marooned and R first lost his passion for me, only I believed that it was to our mutual benefit that he wear it, since everyone always said she and I were dead ringers.*' Dr. Young, does reading that passage refresh your recollection as to who the rival was, who ended up dead on the floor of the Southern Ocean?
- Dr. Young: No.
- Mr. Burns: Flip ahead to the entry for 5 April 1868, where Kathleen writes: '*One of the lesser lights remembered hearing of R attempting to swim the English Channel eight years ago; and this provoked discussion of R's past, and awkward questions about where R and I first met.*' Dr. Young, do you know where Roger and Kathleen first met, or why questions about it would be awkward?
- Dr. Young: No. (Cracks one of her knuckles very loudly)
- Mr. Burns: (Pause) Dr. Young, are you alright?
- Dr. Young: (Inspects her hand, and then nods) Don't worry, Mr. Burns. I can still feel pain.

- Mr. Burns: A short ways down the same page, Kathleen recounts two women gossiping about Roger: '*Some years after he was expelled, Mr. Quinlan had the bad taste to return from his self-imposed exile in America and appear, uninvited, at an Oxford garden party, where he proceeded to seduce two young girls from good families – and then became betrothed to them both! Oh I didn't realize he was the same dark man! As I recall, those two girls were the best of friends, till he drove them apart; and their families were threatening legal action, but – how did it all end? Mr. Quinlan eloped to Australia with one; whilst the other fled to London in shame.*' Dr. Young, who was Kathleen's best friend in her Oxford days?
- Dr. Young: I don't know.
- Mr. Burns: Was Kathleen the one Roger eloped to Australia with – or was Kathleen the one who fled to London?
- Dr. Young: I don't know.
- Ms. Watt: Mr. Burns, I'm trying to give you the wide latitude you say American deposition rules permit. But is it not abundantly clear that Dr. Young doesn't know the answers to your questions about the details of her grandmother's life sixty years before Dr. Young was born?
- Mr. Burns: It's clear Dr. Young says she doesn't know many details, yes. But I've only got a few more questions on this exhibit. Dr. Young, if you look again at the end of that long first entry in the diary, Kathleen writes of Roger: '*and the little gold he carried away from the wreck, on his person, was extracted from us by a horrid coachman in New Zealand, as the exorbitant price of his efforts in effecting our abrupt and clandestine departure from the Bluff, as well as his booking at the last hour our immediate passage from Wellington to Kingston, and thence to the Bay, before our departure could be discovered*'. Do you know why Roger and Kathleen needed to depart New Zealand in an abrupt and clandestine fashion?
- Dr. Young: No.
- Mr. Burns: If you look at the next entry, for 6 April 1868, Kathleen writes: '*And how could R think it fair to go looking for Lamanai without me, who first procured the Lamanai Codex for him, and then traveled halfway across the world to persuade him that it is his Destiny to find the fabled Fountain of Youth, whose location the codex contains. The mention of how I chased R to the Victorian goldfields opened old wounds for us both.*' Dr. Young, does that paragraph refresh your recollection that it was not Kathleen who eloped to Australia with Roger, but rather she was the one who chased him there afterwards?
- Dr. Young: I see those words here, but I don't have any recollection of ever hearing anything about that, no.
- Mr. Burns: Was Roger Quinlan married more than once?

- Dr. Young: I don't know. (To Ms. Watt) I'm very tired, dear. Can we stop this torture now?
- Ms. Watt: Certainly. Let's take a break, David.
- Mr. Burns: But can we make it a short break? We've still got a lot of ground to cover. Off the record at 9: 55 a.m.

* * *

David Burns stands by the conference room window, looking out at the drab gray day. Along Tower Bridge, the cars and trucks are all at a standstill, belching exhaust, because the motorized drawbridge in the middle of Tower Bridge is up, to let a mock pirate sloop, loaded with tourists, pass through. In the distance, beyond the Bridge, Burns sees the rough waves of the river slapping against the algae-covered rocks by Traitor's Gate, where the warders used to ferry their prisoners by boat into the Tower of London, for torturous depositions.

An image of the old dungeons inside the Tower flashes into Burns's mind: the dark dank stones, the heavy rusting iron chains, and the grim tools used to aid the interrogations back in the day – metal tongs, braziers with hot pokers, and the infamous rack, used to stretch the deponent literally to the breaking point.

Is Fiona near her breaking point today? Are the modern torture tools of depositions – the tidy squared-off stacks of exhibits – racking Fiona towards capitulation? Sure feels like it. But Burns worries he may be fooling himself, under-rating Fiona's determination to resist, in order to justify to himself why he is showing Fiona so much of his hand at such an early stage of the litigation.

Behind Burns, the Brethren of the Coast are huddled conspiratorially round the table, whispering, in compliance with Burns's instructions. Joyce is out in the street, cadging a quick smoke; Ivy is also gone, wherever she goes on the breaks; and Fiona, Olivia and Miguel are off in Olivia's private office.

Clive Phelps joins Burns at the window, and whispers: "This Reynolds Foundation thing is a big problem for us, isn't it?"

"Yes, it is," Burns mutters.

"Isn't there a rule that contracts have to be in writing?" Phelps asks.

"No," Burns says. "Which oral contract is bothering you?"

"The one where India Reynolds supposedly gives the codex to Kathleen Quinlan in her role as trustee, rather than as a private individual," Phelps mutters. "It's a ridiculous story, but how are we supposed to disprove it?"

"I'm not sure we can," Burns says. "With all the witnesses dead, there's not much we can do to disprove Fiona's story about that."

"So you're giving up?" Phelps asks.

"Not at all," Burns says. "I think we're making excellent progress."

"How? Where're you going with all these questions about the shipwreck?"

"I'm probing," Burns says, "for some other ways to attack the Reynolds Foundation defense, that don't require bringing back witnesses from the dead."

"In other words, we're getting nowhere slow?" Phelps asks.

"Depositions are slow going," Burns says, trying not to show his irritation.

"Well it's fairly nerve-wracking to be paying you by the hour," Phelps says, "when I can't see any rhyme or reason to your questions."

"Look, Clive," Burns mutters, "at some point you just gotta have a little faith in me."

The conference room door opens and Olivia Watt walks in. Burns cocks his head quizzically. It's too early for Fiona to be coming back already.

"Dr. Young's gone home," Olivia announces. "She's not feeling well."

"Is she coming back later?" Burns asks.

"Tomorrow," Olivia says. "We'll start again at 9:00."

"What'd we get today, 53 minutes?" Burns grouses.

"I wasn't keeping track of the time," Olivia says.

"Not much to keep track of," Burns says. "At this rate, this deposition's gonna last till May."

"I doubt that," Olivia says, "But given her age, I'm unwilling to push her."

Burns stares at Olivia, trying to discern if she's worried about the way her client bolted. But Olivia's a good poker player. Her face shows nothing.

"So we'll see you all tomorrow at 9:00," Olivia says. She exits.

Burns debates a radical impulse. What the hell.

"Excuse me a second, Clive," Burns says. "I've got an idea that might speed things up."

"I'm all for that," Phelps says sarcastically.

Burns picks up two copies of the next two exhibits in his stack – two accounts of the shipwreck he read last night – and walks out into the hall.

"Olivia!" Burns catches up to her, and hands her both sets of the exhibits. "I think it'd be good if you and Fiona read these next exhibits before tomorrow."

"Alright," Olivia accepts the exhibits with a look of mild surprise.

"And then, if it's agreeable to you," Burns says, "tomorrow, before we dive into the acrimony of the deposition, maybe we could have a short meeting with only our clients, to talk about what these exhibits mean, for this lawsuit."

"You mean a settlement discussion?" Olivia asks.

"Kind of. Our meeting should certainly be protected by the usual rules about settlement discussions – like nothing that gets said can be used against anyone, it's all confidential, etc."

"A settlement discussion in the middle of a deposition," Olivia says, "is unorthodox."

"I know," Burns says. "But I really don't think it'll take all that long. And I think it'll be helpful for everyone. After that, we can get right back into the depo."

The lift opens, and Ivy, Joyce and Santos all walk out. Burns waves, but then turns his back on them, to signal he'd prefer not to be interrupted.

Ivy, Joyce and Santos all go back in the conference room.

"Do you want Miguel to be present for the discussion?" Olivia asks.

"I think not," Burns says. "Let's limit it to you and me, and Fiona and Joyce. I want Fiona to feel as little pressure as possible."

"I'm all for that," Olivia says. "Shall we meet in my office, then, at 8:45?"

"Great," Burns says. "Please be sure Fiona gets a chance to read her copies of these exhibits beforehand."

Olivia nods, and walks off down the hall to her office.

Back in the conference room, Burns fills everyone in on Fiona's early adjournment, and the plan to meet at 8:45 tomorrow with just clients and lawyers, excluding Santos. Burns also asks Ivy to come at 8:45, in case Fiona changes her mind about the meeting and decides she wants to go ahead with the depo.

Everyone starts packing up their boxes and briefcases. Santos is the fastest, so he wishes everyone a good day, and leaves.

Once Santos is gone, Phelps asks: "Is it a settlement meeting tomorrow?"

"Not really," Burns says. Just the first step in a slow dance towards a settlement."

"Well, I'd like to attend the meeting also," Phelps says.

"Olivia wants clients only. To keep Fiona from feeling pressured. But you should be here, so I can consult with you if we start making any real progress."

"Oh, I'll definitely be here," Phelps grumbles.

Suddenly Ivy yelps, and points at the edge of the table, where the *Lamanai Codex* is sitting. "I picked up the exhibits you marked," Ivy says, "and it was under them. I didn't touch it."

"Wow," Joyce says, "I guess Fiona really was feeling sick. To forget this."

"What're we gonna do with it?" Hunter asks, with a big grin.

"Not whatever you're thinking, Kip," Burns chuckles. "Ivy, you wanna keep the codex with the other exhibits till tomorrow?"

"No-o-o-o thank you," Ivy says. "My insurance is nowhere near high enough to cover that thing, if it gets lost or stolen on my watch."

There's a knock at the door. Miguel Santos returns, apologizing for leaving his watch on the table.

"Miguel!" Burns says. "Guess what? The case is over."

Santos looks shocked. "Why?"

"Fiona left this behind." Burns points at the *Lamanai Codex*. "Evidently she's decided to abandon all her defenses and give us the codex. So we're off to Detroit this afternoon. You may still be able to book a seat on the flight."

Santos gapes at the codex, and then looks dismayed. "Does Olivia know?"

"No." Burns smiles. "You don't think I'm misinterpreting Fiona's intentions here, do you?"

Santos finally sees that Burns is joking. "I'll get Olivia."

While Santos is gone, the rest stand in dead silence, staring at the faded engraving of the submerged crocodile on the front cover of the codex.

Olivia returns with Santos. "Thank you all, very much, for your honesty."

Burns laughs. "Honesty, schmonesty. We were just being practical, Olivia. It's so hard to find a buyer these days for a 9th century Maya codex."

"Oh, I think I could find a purchaser for that piece," Hunter says.

Olivia reaches for the codex, but hesitates, and then looks at Ron Graham. "Is there a special way I should handle this?"

"You should wear latex gloves," Graham says, "and slide a piece of wax paper under the codex before you pick it up, so you don't damage the covers."

"This is a law firm," Olivia says, "not a sandwich shop. We don't carry wax paper and latex gloves. Any tips that are, ah, more practical?"

"Sure," Ron says. "Slide the codex carefully along the table onto your palm, and then hold it flat on your palm, so you don't squeeze it."

Olivia does as instructed. "I'm taking this straight to the firm's safe."

Chapter Thirteen

Dead Reckoning

Tuesday 5 April 2011 Evening

"That was a really nice dinner." Joyce Kerr unlocks the door to her hotel room. "Thanks for taking time to do that."

"My pleasure." David Burns lingers in the hall.

"You gonna guard my door tonight?" Joyce teases. "Or you coming in?"

"I'm coming in," Burns says, "but then we're getting right back to work."

"I figured." Joyce sighs, and sits down on the bed. "Except I'm goin' on strike, unless you massage my aching feet for two minutes."

"Alright." Burns sits beside her on the bed. "Two minutes."

"Really?" Joyce slips off her shoes, and swings her legs up onto Burns's lap. "Never again will I wear high heels in London. Those cobblestones – aargh!"

Burns takes one of Joyce's stockinged feet in his hands, and begins rubbing it. Although Burns normally finds the female foot completely unarousing, the feel of Joyce's hot nylons sliding through his fingers is exquisitely erotic.

"You have nice feet," Burns mutters.

"You have nice hands," Joyce counters.

He switches to the other foot. Then he notices the two *General Grant* exhibits, lying beside Joyce's pillow. "So what'd you think of those bad boys?"

"I haven't read them yet."

"Joyce! I really think those two documents are the keys to this whole case."

"If you remember, Mr. Fun, you gave me 38 other things to do this afternoon."

"Okay, sorry." Burns finishes the foot massage in silence, and then points at the Reynolds Foundation boxes. "I'll finish reading this crap, while you read those two exhibits, okay?"

"Okay." Without taking time to change her clothes, Joyce curls her legs underneath her, like a cat, and reads both *General Grant* documents.

Chapter Six From *New Zealand Voices: Narratives of Shipwreck Survivors* (Dunegin & Sons, 1898)
Narrative of Joseph Jewell, Survivor of "General Grant" Wreck

The *General Grant*, an American clipper, 1095 tons, Captain William Loughlin, sailed from Hobson's Bay, Melbourne on the 4th of May, 1866, with 83 souls on board (crew and passengers), and a full cargo of wool, hides and gold for London. She was insured for £165,000, based on the gold in her safe; but rumors circulated that the passengers, who included many successful miners, carried twice as much swag in their trunks and on their persons, in amounts unreported and uninsured. She sank in twenty fathoms of water on the uninhabited west coast of Auckland Island on 14th of May 1866, with 68 lives lost, 15 making it to shore. During a very weary sojourn of 18 months on the Auckland Island, 5 more lives were lost. On 21 November 1867, a Norwegian whaling ship from the Bluff, New Zealand chanced upon the 10 surviving castaways and rescued them.

It is now 22 years since those awful events. Yet the particulars of the wreck are as fresh to my mind today as when the ship sank. I was 30 years old, newly married, and I had signed on as a seaman aboard the *General Grant*. My new bride, Mary Ann Jewell, then 24, was sailing with me. The first day out at sea, Captain Loughlin signed Mary Ann on as the ship's stewardess, due to the unusually large number of women passengers. For both of us it was our first, and last, sea-voyage as members of the crew. Everything about the work of a ship's crew was new to us.

Captain Loughlin set our course out of Melbourne southeast across the Southern Ocean, along the Great Circle Route. This route was used by all the clipper ships in those days, to take full advantage of the strong winds that blow from west to east below the 45th parallel.

Nothing noticeable occurred until the dawn of 11th May, when a dense gray fog descended upon us, so thick we could not see the bowsprit from the port bow. This same dense fog enveloped us constantly for the next 64 hours.

Captain Loughlin assured the panicky passengers that we were in little danger, because we were sailing in open waters that would take us well south of New Zealand, and yet well north of the volcanic islands at the edge of the Antarctic Circle. But the Captain doubled the watch, for fear of running into a rogue iceberg, or an uncharted island.

Unable to shoot the sun or stars, the Captain assured the passengers he would navigate our ship the way the pirates sailed in olden times, by dead reckoning. We members of the crew were advised not to inform the passengers that, in truth, dead reckoning is little better than a stab in the dark.

On the night of Friday 11th May the wind died away to nothing, as it does many nights in winter in the Southern Ocean, leaving us unable to steer the ship. All night we floated blind, adrift in the deep fog. I did not sleep a wink, every slap of the waves against the ship causing me to fear we had struck an iceberg.

Saturday morning 12th May when the wind rose, the Captain tacked hard to port for several hours. From this the passengers and crew concluded that the Captain must have believed we had floated too far south in the night.

The same sequence transpired Saturday night and Sunday morning. All the wind died around 22:00, we floated blind in the fog all night, and at dawn, when the wind rose, the Captain sailed us hard to port, through the fog, indicating he believed again that we had drifted too far south in the night.

On Sunday night 13th May the wind died again around 22:00, and as always, the rudder lost all grip. That night we were at the mercy of a nasty short sea. At the same time, the fog began to lift, for the first time in 64 hours. At once came the cry of "land ho!" from both watchmen above. A mile off the port bow we saw, by the moon and stars, a small rocky island.

Captain Loughlin consulted his charts, and concluded it must be one of the Auckland Islands, meaning that we were about two hundred miles off course. The hope was expressed that the island we'd glimpsed off the port bow was the southern tip of the main Auckland Island, and that we'd soon be clear of all land.

However, at 23:00, the watchmen's cries came again. This time the land they'd sighted was dead ahead. Soon, by the dim light of the moon and stars, we saw every mariner's worst nightmare. Dead ahead, two miles away, and rising 400 feet high, straight out of the dark and frothing sea, loomed the dark cliffs of a large deserted island. Our sails hung limp and silent in the windless night, as the ocean swells pushed the *General Grant* inexorably towards the dark island's rocky cliffs.

The Captain ordered the sea plumbed. But we could find no bottom in that deep water. This meant that we could not steer clear of the dark island by "club hauling", which is dragging the anchors along the sea bottom.

The Captain consulted his charts again, and determined that the first island sighted must have been Disappointment Island. This portended that we were now drifting straight at Auckland Island. The chart showed Auckland Island running 27 miles, north to south, and that our path a mile south of Disappointment Island was taking us towards the dead center. This portended that, unless Providence sent us a breeze, we would wreck on the rocks of Auckland Island in about an hour's time.

The Captain ordered us to square the yards, in the hope that we might pick up even the ghost of a wind, by which he might sail us clear of the danger. But even with the yards squared, there was no luff at all in the sails.

The decision was made to leave the 21 children asleep below decks. But all the adult passengers came up top, even Mrs. Quinlan who had been sick in her cabin all week. All the crew came up top as well, as there was no work to be done anywhere on a helpless ship floating on the tide.

The *General Grant* was drifting beam-on to the urging rollers, her bow facing parallel to the dark island. So we 62 adults stood along the port side rail, watching the black cliffs grow larger as we approached the island. Nary a word was spoken. The only sounds were the creaking of the ship's timbers, the slatting of the empty sails, and the slapping of the waves against the ship. For an hour we huddled along the rail in our oilskins and blankets, each of us alone with his thoughts.

Who knows what the others were thinking at that dark hour? Pathetically some of the first class passengers had trundled out their trunks and suitcases, as if they expected the steward and Mary Ann would soon be loading them onto a private gondola, instead of an overcrowded lifeboat. All the miners featured bulges in their clothing, from gold they'd packed on their persons. Many of the miners also carried more of their swag, tied in blankets. But all the insured gold was still in the ship's safe, where it no doubt rests to this very day.

The more practical souls on board twisted their necks backwards and up, to count the seats on the three lifeboats that hung from ropes above the quarter deck. The longboat had 22 seats; the pinnace and gig, 7 each; 36 seats, for 83 people.

One of the sailors, Corn Drew, caught me counting seats, and pulled Mary Ann and me aside. In a whisper Corn explained that the longboat could actually hold 30, and the pinnace and gig 12 each. He said the usual procedure was for 14 sailors to man the three boats, first rowing the women and children to land, and then coming back to pick up the men.

I felt somewhat reassured by this information. But Mary Ann pointed out that on this ship, we had 21 children, and 25 women, so some of the women would have to stay behind with the men. In response to that, Corn laughed the driest laugh I ever heard. He said he was never much good at arithmetic in school, but out here in the Southern Ocean, 'numbers don't mean nothing'.

When we pressed him further, Corn confided it was no point counting seats on the lifeboats, on account of it would be nigh on impossible to launch the boats at night, in such a rough short sea. Besides, Corn said, lifeboats would be of little use to anyone out here at the ends of the earth, for where would you land? In the

Southern Ocean the islands are few and far between, and they're all made of volcanic rock, with no beach or anchorage for landing.

I asked Corn what would happen to us. He said only, in his laconic sailor's way, that he reckoned we'd 'all be gettin' mightily wet afore dawn'.

We fell back into silence. I held Mary Ann's hand, and put on my bravest face, but fear gnawed at my guts. Instead of staring ahead at the black cliffs of Auckland Island, I began staring down at the dark waves of the Southern Ocean, wondering how long a human being can live, after being plunged into those icy waters. I was pretty sure the time would be measured in minutes, not hours.

The newspaper headline, *Lost at Sea*, came to mind. Soon I was swept away by random images from the old pirate tales I'd read as a boy. In my mind I conjured grim pictures of overcrowded lifeboats, bobbing like tiny corks out on the big swells of the vast ocean, packed with thirst-crazed survivors, dying by degrees. I looked at the men and women beside me along the rail, and tried to picture us as ragged castaways, dying of thirst on the lifeboats, drinking the blood and sucking the marrow from the bones of the dead, before pitching them overboard and drawing straws to decide who we'd kill and eat next.

To escape such black thoughts, I squeezed Mary Ann's hand, and willed myself to remember our sweet courtship. I thought of the small church at the edge of Melbourne where we were married, and our brief honeymoon, riding horses in the brisk autumn air, along the trails outside of town, which the miners use when they ride to Victoria to hunt for gold.

But these recollections brought to mind a silly quarrel we had during our honeymoon – over what, I could not even then recall – and how stubbornly I had dug in my heels, insisting that Mary Ann must be the first to apologize and seek reconciliation. Looking down at the dark icy waters, I vowed to myself, and to our Maker, that, if Mary Ann and I were lucky enough to escape this great peril in which we had been placed, I would never again allow my foolish pride to waste another precious moment of the short time which God grants us here on earth, in silly quarrels or petty occupations of any kind.

A discussion nearby caught my ear. The Chief Officer, Bart Brown, was trying to quell talk of a curse, which was supposedly connected to a consignment of wool and hides originally intended for another ship, the *Bristol*. The *Bristol* had sunk, just outside Melbourne harbour; so with a return voyage impossible, the owner had arranged with Captain Loughlin to send his wool and hides to London on the *General Grant*, instead of the *Bristol*. But the rumor was that, when the dockers were loading the wool and hides originally intended for the *Bristol*, all the rats jumped off the *General Grant*, signifying that we, too, were cursed.

But then some of the men from steerage said it wasn't the wool and hides that cursed us. It was all the gold we had on board that gave God ample reason to forsake us. If we wanted to have any chance of survival, these men said, we should dump all the gold overboard at once.

This radical idea provoked the gold miner James Teer to intervene in the discussion. Teer was by far the biggest and strongest man on board, with only Roger Quinlan, another miner, coming close. Teer was a natural born leader of men. Without raising his hand, or his voice, without violence or even the threat of violence, Teer spoke a few quiet words to the men from steerage, and then there was no more wild talk of curses, and no more talk of dumping gold overboard. I remember thinking then, if any of us survived the wreck, it would be Teer who would be the leader, or possibly Quinlan.

Soon we were close enough to the island to see, near the base of the massive gray cliffs, rhythmic flashes of moonlight, as the ocean's waves broke on the fatal rocks at the base of the cliffs. Then just beyond the flashes of moonlight we observed, at the water line, a few smudges of pitch black along the dark line of cliffs. After some discussion and pondering, we agreed that the dark smudges must be water-filled caves at the base of the gray cliffs.

By this time the waves had pushed us so close we could hear the mammoth boom and roar of the breakers crashing against the rocks, and we could see that up close, the gray cliffs were even larger and more jagged than they'd appeared from a distance. Our ship began to sway violently, pitching and rolling with the waves. The noise increased in volume as we approached the outer edge of the breakers.

With a shiver we struck the rocks. The impact snapped off the bowsprit and jib-boom, and slammed us all hard against the rail. A few people fell, but no one went overboard. Women screamed, but their human cries were scarcely audible amid the deafening boom and roar of the sea hurtling against the huge cliffs.

The ship sheered off to stern, with a sharp twist that unbalanced us all again. Still none fell overboard, but we were close to panic, and braced ourselves for the next impact. Then gradually we realized that the collision had driven the ship back outside the breakers, where a rip tide was dragging us south. The bow was pointing straight at the cliffs, which were still close, and the general swell of the sea was still pushing east, towards the cliffs; but we were outside the fatal breakers, and the southbound rip tide we were riding was stronger than the general swell of the sea.

Gradually hope mounted. It seemed too much to believe, that we could ride a rip tide for twelve or thirteen miles, and then sometime near dawn round the southern tip of the island, without ever again crashing into the breakers, whose huge noise reminded us constantly how close the fatal rocks were. But since hope was all we had, we soon succumbed to its seductive siren call.

For thirty minutes we rode the rip tide, as Reverend Sarda led many of us in fervent prayers, beseeching the Almighty that our good fortune might hold.

But sometimes even fervent prayers go unanswered.

About a mile south of the first impact, the rip tide petered out; and at once the waves pushed the *General Grant* into the breakers again. There, beneath cloudy cliffs, and sheets of foam, our ship again struck the submerged rocks.

This time the first impact was on the port bow, and snapped the spanker boom. The keel squealed and crunched on the rocks, and the ship lurched hard to starboard. At once we struck more submerged rocks, this time on the starboard bow, breaking the rudder and knocking the seaman at the wheel hard against the wheel-house wall. Blood gushed from his forehead, as another sailor ran to his aid.

This time the big ship did not bounce back outside the breakers. Instead, the surging waves pushed us between the two sets of rocks we'd just struck, and pointed our prow straight at the cliffs. Our screams were lost again, in the mighty roar of the waves, and the ripping of the ship's wood against the rocks.

Then someone yelled "the cliffs are opening!" In the moonlight I saw a huge black smudge, straight ahead, darker than the cliffs. Before anyone grasped the peril, we felt ourselves being sucked into the mouth of a huge cavern at the base of the cliffs, hewn out of the rock by centuries of sea and wind pounding the cliffs at the water line.

Of course, natural science instructs us that no known earthly force could have sucked us into the cavern. So I suppose what happened was, the waves pushed us in there. But so fast did it happen, and so abruptly did we exchange the open, moonlit, night sky for the pitch-black, rocky ceiling of that cavern, that afterwards all the survivors swore we had felt as though we were in the grip of some unnatural and unworldly Force, sucking us into that cave.

Both sides of the ship scraped against the cave's rocky walls. I saw, in the last vestiges of the moonlight from outside, that from the mouth of the cavern inwards to a distance of about 50 yards, the walls were sheer, with no ledge or outcropping or handhold big enough even for a bird to rest. Beyond 50 yards, the cavern was too black for anyone to know what was there. We could not see how deep the cavern was, or what its walls looked like back in its black interior. Indeed, as we drifted in deeper, it got so black that even with the ship's lanterns, I could barely see my shipmates beside me, and I could see absolutely nothing beyond the ship's rails.

We huddled on the poop deck, terrified, waiting to hear the prow crash. But instead the scraping on the walls subsided, as the cavern opened wider. Salt spray lashed the deck, and the air around us dropped by several degrees in an instant, with the air temperature falling to a level much colder than even the frigid night air that prevails at the 51st parallel of the Southern Ocean in May.

For several awful minutes, with no sound but the slapping of the waves, our ship drifted deeper and deeper into the unseen dark. I was not the only one aboard who thought that this dark cave at the very end of the earth which was swallowing us whole must be the mouth of Hell.

Bart Brown, a practical man, ordered soundings. They showed the water was 20 fathoms deep, roughly five times the height of the ship. When we'd drifted into the cavern about two lengths of the ship, perhaps 120 yards, the main mast crashed into the cavern's roof. Large shards of timber and huge chunks of rock fell onto the bow. Women shrieked, and I remember an Irish woman's lovely soprano voice calling out to the Virgin Mary to protect us in our hour of need.

Noise was everywhere, as the mainmast and the foremast both ground against the ceiling, each rocking wave bringing more snapping timber and rocks crashing down on the bow. Whether this was Hell or not remained to be determined. But it was clear the *General Grant* had reached its last port of call.

Captain Loughlin consulted with his officers, and also with Roger Quinlan and James Teer. They all agreed that trying to launch the lifeboats in the inky dark of that cavern would be suicide. So the Captain declared we would try to hold out till dawn on the poop deck, and hope that enough daylight would creep into the cavern then to allow the launching of the lifeboats off the stern.

The mothers went below and roused the children, and brought them up to the poop deck. For four hours we stood there in the dark, man, woman and child, huddled in blankets, jostled by the falling tide, with rocks pelting the bow and the abandoned quarterdeck, amid the constant din of the ship's timbers grinding ceaselessly against the rocks, and the sea crashing incessantly in the echoing sound shell of that cavern. They were the loneliest four hours of my life.

Around 5:30 that awful morning, without warning, a huge shudder shook our feet, and a moment later, in a jumble of spars, rigging and rocks, the mainmast crashed through the middle of the quarterdeck, leaving an enormous gaping hole in the ship's center. At once greedy fathoms of water filled the hole, and the ship tilted, angling perilously down towards the prow.

Screams echoed off the rocky walls, as waves swept the quarterdeck. The ship lunged a few yards deeper into the cavern, but then stabilized, at about a 15 degree angle, when the foremast jammed against the cavern roof. People cried for lifeboats. But after talking with Quinlan and Teer, the Captain again declared that in such inky darkness, we couldn't get a boom safely over the stern with the tackle needed to launch the boats. So still we waited for the dawn, listening to the ship's seams opening below the waterline, and feeling the hold filling with water.

At last we heard the raucous cries of seabirds. A few minutes after, the grubby dawn began creeping into the cavern. In the first light we saw the ship's front half was utterly destroyed. Then, as more light oozed in, we saw that the cavern closed at the back, with no outlet, and that all its walls were sheer, with no ledges, no outcroppings, no handholds of any kind. About this same time the morning wind rose – the wind that could have saved us, had it come six hours earlier. But now the wind was our enemy, for it roiled the sea water inside the cave into a foaming whirlpool, which buffeted and pounded our dying ship.

For reasons unknown, Captain Loughlin went up to the wheelhouse, leaving Bart Brown, Roger Quinlan and James Teer to supervise the launching of the lifeboats. A boom was got over the stern, with the necessary tackle; and the pinnace was launched, with four sailors aboard (Aaron Hayman, Peter McNevin, Andrew Morrison, and David McLelland).

But the tide was rising now, so before taking anyone else on board, the sailors decided to test the waters. They had to row like demons to move the small boat at all through the surging water, to get clear of the *General Grant's* stern. Then crossing the rising tide in the cave proved even more arduous, and harder still was crossing the awesome breakers outside. Ten hard minutes those four men pulled, climbing the crest of each wave, then disappearing down into the trough, only to reappear on the crest of another wave. But finally we could see them bobbing out on the far side of the breakers, all alone in the blankness of the Southern Ocean.

Our spirits buoyed by their success, we loaded the gig with salt pork, fresh water and tins of bouilli. Bart Brown, leaving his wife on deck, boarded the gig, with James Teer, Corn Drew and another sailor, David Ashworth. With the extra weight of the provisions, it took five minutes hard slog just to drop the gig into the water, clear of the *General Grant's* stern. But at last we got her down safely in the water.

"Women first!" the Captain shouted from the wheelhouse, gesticulating downwards, to indicate he expected some of the women to jump into the swirling water, and then be picked up by the gig. "No more'n five!" the Captain cried.

But there was no mad stampede of volunteers. It was a long jump down into the rough waves, and we couldn't see an inch below the dark surface of the choppy water. Though we knew the depth of the water, back where the soundings were taken, was twenty fathoms, we had no way to gauge the irregularities along the cavern's floor, so the possibility of jumping onto hidden rocks loomed in our minds. Also, the water itself was swirling and treacherous. For these reasons, the women all wished to wait, hoping they'd be put in the longboat, which was already down on the deck, ready to be launched.

Roger Quinlan began organizing the loading of the longboat, while the Captain kept shouting for women to jump, and the women kept shrinking farther from the rail. As the longboat filled, first with eight sailors to row, and then with the 21 children, it became clear the longboat lacked room for any of the women, except those carrying infants. Then the Second Officer, Jones, declared that the longboat would not be launched, until the gig was filled. At this point my wife, Mary Ann Jewell, reluctantly volunteered to jump down to the gig.

I tied a rope round Mary Ann's waist, and helped her to a foothold on the splintered rudder. From there, brave Mary Ann, who could barely swim, leaped. Her skirts billowed out like a giant kite, till she hit the water with a splash, and plunged deep into the frothing waters. Everyone gasped, and for the longest time she was gone. But the rope I had secured up top pulled her back up, like a cork, and she began thrashing in the water. When I saw that Mary Ann was not strong enough to swim 30 yards through those rough waves to reach the gig, I jumped in after her.

My heart clenched when I hit the water, for it was even colder than I'd feared. But all my thoughts were to save Mary Ann, so I fought my way up through the dark foaming waves of that awful cavern, and swam to her. I put Mary Ann on my back and carried her the 30 yards to the gig, where James Teer hauled us both aboard. It was by far the bravest thing I ever did in my whole life.

No other woman was willing to follow Mary Ann's example, so Teer invited a mining friend of his, Patrick Caughey, to jump. Caughey jumped, and in the wink of an eye, another passenger, Nick Ellis, jumped. Caughey and Ellis swam to the gig, where Teer hauled them in. Since Ellis was married, with three children, there was some shouting back and forth, urging Mrs. Ellis to jump. But Mrs. Ellis declined, choosing instead to board the longboat with her youngest child. So then a sailor, Billy Scott, jumped, and swam to the gig, where Teer hauled him in.

There was still space for three more, but the tide was rising, so we set off. Fifteen hard minutes Teer and the dry sailors rowed against the rough waves, while those of us who'd been swimming huddled in blankets, our teeth chattering like skeletons in the wind on Guy Fawkes Night. The mighty rollers tossed and pitched us, and when we got to the breakers, our little gig bounced wildly off the submerged rocks. But somehow Teer and the sailors got us across those breakers, and out into the open sea.

The pinnace was waiting for us, but at a much safer distance from the breakers than we had reached. Before rowing out to join her in the search for dry land, our rowers took a short rest, and we all looked back into the cave.

What we witnessed, when we looked back, was a sight so awful, the memory of it still haunts my dreams. In my waking hours it troubles me even worse.

For just then, the crumbling foremast of the *General Grant* succumbed, at last, to the hours of steady pressure exerted upon it by the cavern roof, and broke off. When the foremast broke off, the ship rolled forward about ten yards, and at the same time pitched downwards another five yards.

There was a mad dash of men and women leaping into the longboat, which was already overcrowded with sailors and children. The next instant the icy sea engulfed the poop deck, sweeping the longboat, along with all the people in the longboat, as well as all the people still standing on the poop deck, overboard.

The longboat hit the waves with a heavy crash, and was immediately swamped with water. People were piled in there two-deep, while others, who'd fallen off the deck and into the water near the longboat, grabbed onto its sides. In less than a minute, the longboat sank like a stone, spilling everyone in it back out into the general maelstrom of the frothing waters and the screaming people.

At the same time the *General Grant* was also sinking, very fast, creating a huge suction that pulled anyone too close to the big ship down under the waves, never to come up again.

Only two men had managed to stay aboard the *General Grant*. One was Captain Loughlin, whom we saw frantically scrabbling up the mizzen mast's rigging, racing the water nipping at his ankles. The other was a crazed goldminer, whose name I never knew, clinging like death to the mizzen mast itself. The last I saw of these two, Captain Loughlin had stopped climbing, and turned to wave a white handkerchief; while the crazed miner was laughing and waving a blanket full of gold. To whom they were waving, I could not discern. The next instant they were both gone, and with them, the last of the *General Grant* sank beneath the waves.

Away from the huge suction of the *General Grant*, the water in the cave was thick with struggling bodies, desperately clutching and grabbing at each other. Since those bodies that were still alive may have included Bart Brown's wife, and Nick Ellis's wife and three children, Mr. Brown and Mr. Ellis insisted we had to go back into the cavern and attempt a rescue. Teer was strongly opposed, saying that what had just happened to the longboat would surely happen to us, too, if we went back in, meaning we'd be swamped and we'd all drown without saving a soul.

It was a very brief disagreement. What ended the dispute was the realization that the screams in the cavern were already subsiding. It became plain to all that going back in to try to rescue the three souls for whom we had space would be pointless. We knew it would take us fifteen minutes to row the gig back across the fearsome breakers and into that cavern. By that time we could all see there would be no one left alive, for there was nothing afloat in that cavern for anyone to grab onto. In the deep whirling vortex of that awful cavern, both the ship and the long-boat had sunk without a trace, leaving nary a stick of wood behind. Even Bart Brown and Nick Ellis agreed to abandon the idea of attempting a rescue.

So we sat and watched, helpless, as the bodies of their families, and our ship-mates, disappeared from view, one by one, till the cavern was silent as the grave.

But then out of the darkness we saw a man, coming towards us, swimming an awkward one-armed sidestroke. He was using only his right arm to pull himself through the heavy waves, because two women were clinging to his left arm behind him, as he swam with his right, dragging them through the water. Teer was the first to realize it must be Roger Quinlan, whom the Captain had said was once a champion swimmer at Oxford. Yet even though Quinlan was still a young man, what he was attempting struck me as impossible. I myself was a young man, and although never a champion, I was a strong swimmer; yet I had barely made it thirty yards in those heavy waves, with only Mary Ann on my back. Quinlan was attempting to swim 300 yards, all the way through the waves and across the fearsome breakers and out to us, with two women in tow.

But for awhile it seemed he might make it. Then, near the mouth of the cavern, something happened, and Quinlan's left arm fell abruptly down into the water, causing both women to lose their grips on his arm. There followed a frantic and confused thrashing of many limbs in the water. Then one of the women suddenly shot up out of the water, as if she'd launched herself off something under the waves, and latched onto Quinlan's neck with a death grip. Quinlan nearly went under from the impact of the woman landing on his neck, and from her weight pressing down on his shoulders. But somehow he managed to stay afloat, and then he turned and yelled at the woman, persuading her to loosen her death grip on his neck, and to hold on instead to his left arm, as before.

In the time this took to accomplish, the other woman never came up for air. There was no chance for Quinlan to attempt to rescue her, with the first woman hanging onto his arm. Quinlan's strength seemed nearly spent, so we called out to him, to see if he wanted to try treading water inside the cave till we could reach him. But he did not hear us, and launched himself into the breakers.

With rescue impossible on the submerged rocks of the breakers, there was naught for us to do but watch and pray for him and the lady. Incredibly, Quinlan made it across the breakers. We hauled both him, and the woman, who turned out to be his wife Catherine, on board.

With 11 in the gig, plus the provisions, we were badly overloaded. So the pinnace rowed to us, and we evened up the loads. Both boats then lay-to for some time, just outside the breakers, in case the other woman, Kathleen Allen, who had been a close friend of the Quinlans, or any of the other passengers or crew, appeared. But except for the sound of the crashing breakers, all was silent inside the cavern that had become the watery tomb of the 68 souls who perished that awful morning before our very eyes.

At last we set out to look for land. We rowed all day to Disappointment Island, but finding no place to land, we tied up for the night on some rocks at sea. The next day we rowed round the north cape of Auckland Island, to Sarah's Bosom, which is the sailors' name for the anchorage officially known as Port Ross. At Sarah's Bosom, we effected a landing, and immediately gathered timber for a fire, because we were all suffering greatly from cold and wet.

Finding that we had but one lucifer match in our possession, we carefully selected a well-sheltered spot among the rocks to build our fire. We huddled round the fire to warm ourselves and dry our clothes as best we could. We all assumed that Mrs. Quinlan, who had been ill on the *General Grant*, and perhaps others among us, would soon succumb from the terrible shock of our ordeal, and from being drenched and cold for more than 24 hours. But to everyone's surprise, Mrs. Quinlan recovered very quickly, and insisted on doing her full share of the work, as we set about making a survival camp.

Since we had no other matches, we did not allow our fire to die out at any time for the next 18 months, which required constant vigilance on all our parts. Our provisions being in very short supply, we also built a rock cistern to trap fresh rain water, and then we went to look for food.

We searched for several days for the provisions reportedly laid away a few years back by H.M.C. steamer Victoria, and also by the Southland steamer, for castaways. But we found nothing. We eventually found Captain Musgrave's hut at the far southern end of the island, but there were no provisions there, either. We did, however, leave a note, carved in wood, describing our position and begging for rescue. (I understand our note was found many months later, and a rescue operation was about to be launched, when we were rescued by chance.) We also found some pigs and goats nearby, and their flesh proved luxurious.

The rest of the time, however, we subsisted on a relentless diet of seals and mussels. As a result, our party suffered mightily from dysentery.

James Teer naturally took charge of our party, and for many months, no one objected to his leadership. Teer was a very capable and judicious leader, who always took the hardest and least pleasant tasks for himself, so others would have no cause to complain. He also insisted, very wisely, that we all needed to keep constantly busy, so as to avoid falling into the deep malaise that often afflicts castaways. To that end, Teer kept us constantly occupied.

We regularly gathered piles of wood, and burned them as signal fires. We rotated lookout duty, to be sure we would not miss any passing ship. We sent out hunting parties nearly every day, weather permitting. We built rough shelters, and from seal skins we fashioned all manner of clothing and bedding, including caps, coats, trousers, shoes, moccasins, and even dresses for the two women in our party. We even fashioned ourselves new underclothing from seal skins, for both the men and the women. When spring came, we found a garden left behind by Captain Musgrave, salvaged some seeds, and planted a few potatoes and collards. We also built a small sail boat, decked over with seal's skin.

But in spite of our constant signal fires, day after day after dreary day, there was no sign of succour. Every day the horizon out at sea was naught but a blank gray slate. Almost every day it rained, unless it snowed. We'd landed at the onset of the long southern winter, when the days in June and July are as dark as December and January are in London. Yet we had known from the moment we arrived that the winter would be harsh, so we girded ourselves for it, and together we survived it.

But as the weather warmed, in the late months of 1866, and the days lengthened into what passes for summer in the forbidding clime of Auckland Island, the monotony of our isolated island existence began to get the better of some of us. Petty quarrels broke out amongst the men. At first I dismissed these petty quarrels, as merely the unsurprising consequence of our long ordeal, and our enforced close quarters. And of course, true to my vow to our Maker, shortly before the wreck of the *General Grant*, I avoided all the petty quarrels myself. But in the early months of 1867, as the days began to shorten and the southern summer drew towards its close, the quarrels grew more contentious, and more personal.

The main subject of dispute, at least in terms of time spent quarreling over it, was whether we should continue to eke out our meager existence on the island, even through another harsh winter out there on the very edge of the Antarctic Ocean; or whether we should build a bigger sailboat than the one we'd already built, and try to sail across the Southern Ocean to New Zealand, some 350 miles to the north. Bart Brown was adamant that we should build a bigger boat and take our chances on the open sea, before winter struck us low again. James Teer took the more conservative position, that we had survived one winter, and we could survive another the same way, and therefore we should await rescue, however long that wait might prove to be.

But this dispute over the boat was not the only bone of contention, for Teer, who was always in favour of any kind of work to keep us busy, never opposed the building of a bigger boat, even though he opposed sailing it. The bigger issue smoldering under the surface involved some of the men chafing under James Teer's strict leadership, and favouring Bart Brown, who was perceived to have a lighter hand on the tiller. And beneath the leadership issue there were still other issues, less often discussed, but involving deeper emotions.

One of the men had discovered that Roger Quinlan not only saved himself and his wife by swimming out of that awful cavern, but he'd also managed to save a few ounces of gold, which he'd strapped to his body before the wreck. The value of the gold Quinlan saved was far from a fortune. But its discovery brought back harsh memories of the wreck that had cost so many lives, including the lives of Bart Brown's wife, and Nick Ellis's whole family. From the time the gold was discovered, Quinlan and his wife were ostracized to a degree, and there was much grumbling behind their backs. Some began claiming to remember seeing Roger Quinlan spending much more time in the company of Miss Allen than in the company of his wife, who was ill in their cabin. Some even insinuated that Mrs. Quinlan had deliberately shoved her friend, Kathleen Allen, to her death, when it was clear that Roger Quinlan could have saved them both.

The focus on the conduct of Mrs. Quinlan back in the cavern soon brought out even uglier feelings among some of the men. Unchivalrous comments were made that revealed a deep-seated jealousy of the two men in our party, Roger Quinlan and I, who had the comfort of our wives to give us feminine solace, in that bleak place, which the others lacked.

With rancour running high in our ranks, we suffered a great setback near the end of summer, in February 1867. The oldest member of our party, David McLelland, fell violently ill. In spite of the tender ministrations of the ladies, and the best efforts of all of us to grant David the sustenance to survive his illness, David developed a very high fever. The closest thing we had to a physician was Roger Quinlan, who'd studied medicine briefly at Oxford, before leaving under what I later learned were highly dubious circumstances. Quinlan did his best for David, but without any medicines, could not save him.

On the 18th of February, 1867, David McLelland, aged 62, departed this life.

We buried David upon the sand hill on Enderby Island. Prior to his death, David had stated that he was born in Ayr, Scotland, and had, for some years, been employed by the firm of Messrs. Todd and McGregor, in Glasgow. Upon our return to Great Britain, Mary Ann and I visited David's wife, who still resides in Partick, Glasgow.

David's sudden death struck us all very low. The previous winter we'd all witnessed 68 of our fellow passengers and crew perish in a single stroke of Fate, including Bart Brown's wife and Nick Ellis's whole family. Yet I think most of us, excepting perhaps Bart and Nick, whose private thoughts I cannot guess, had all tried very hard to stow that tragedy away, doing our best never to think about what happened back in that dark cave, for fear that dwelling on the lives lost would only bring us all to the same dark end. But David's death let the demons loose. From that day forward I was never again able to quell the memories of what I witnessed in that cave, and I believe the others suffered from the same problem. A general despair gripped our camp, and then serious trouble ensued.

After David's death, the men chafing under James Teer's strict leadership began, for the first time, blatantly disregarding his orders. One man even threatened violence to Teer's face. Since Teer was so much larger than all of us, except Roger Quinlan, who was loyal to Teer from beginning to end, I assumed the threat was meaningless. But I was wrong.

For beneath the incessant quarrels, and the mounting resistance of some to Teer's orders, lay the deeper malady. Jealousy, the green-eyed monster that lurks in the hearts of all men, I suppose. The resentment of Roger Quinlan and me, or I should say of our wives, boiled over, and violence erupted.

So many years have passed, and those involved are long dead, so there is no purpose to be served in naming names. But one evening in late February an incident did occur, in which two men initiated an assault with unmistakeable sexual overtones against Mrs. Quinlan; and although mercifully James Teer and Roger Quinlan beat it back, and Mrs. Quinlan was not harmed, nevertheless, our party was hopelessly divided in the aftermath, as to what the consequences should be.

The upshot was, that very night four men lit out to form their own, separate settlement. They were Bart Brown, Andrew Morrison, Peter McNevin, and Billy Scott. Two had been involved in the attempted assault of Mrs. Quinlan; the other two were merely friends of the wrongdoers who'd tired of what they termed 'Teer's tyranny'. Let God be their only Judge; I shall not name the two wrongdoers.

In spite of what had happened, we wished these four men no harm. We took considerable pains to be sure that they, in their new settlement, had fire, derived from ours. We also gave them the small sailboat which we'd all laboured to build, for it was plain that they were the party that favoured the use of a boat.

Almost at once they decided to sail for New Zealand. They packed about 30 gallons of water in seal gullets, and some seal's meat, and the flesh of three goats, and about twenty dozen of eggs – all cooked. They also carried a very small stove which Billy Scott had constructed, and some charcoal to burn in it.

But they had no charts. They had no compass. They had no nautical instrument of any type, nothing with which to shoot the sun or the stars. They did not know the course, believing erroneously, as we all did at that time, that New Zealand was east north-east, when in truth, as the rest of us only later learned, but did not then know, New Zealand is due north, or perhaps a degree or two west of north, from the Auckland Islands.

Their boat left on the morning of the 22nd of February, 1867. The wind was from the southwest, but it shifted that first night to come out of the northwest, with rain. The wind blew very hard that first night, causing us all to think back to that awful night of May 13th and 14th of 1866, when even the slightest of breezes would have saved 68 souls. But on this night in February 1867, we feared there was too much wind, for the fierce storm blowing all through that night imperiled the lives of our compatriots, out on the open sea in their tiny boat.

Still, we felt that if they survived that first night, they had an excellent chance of finding New Zealand, for the next seven days and nights featured fine weather, seldom seen in those parts. Those seven days gave them ample time to reach New Zealand; or, if the first night's storm had dissuaded them from trying for New Zealand, we guessed they might have changed course and headed east, for the Campbell Islands, which they knew, as we did, lay only 100 miles due east – an easier navigation feat, lying on the same latitude, and a shorter haul.

Later, of course, after we were rescued, we learned that those four men never reached New Zealand, or the Campbell Islands; and that no sign of any of those men, or their boat, was ever seen again.

We who stayed settled back into our weary existence on Auckland Island. Perhaps inspired by the example of our adventuresome compatriots, we hit upon the idea of building a small model ship, and carving onto its deck a plea for help. We launched our ship a few weeks after the others had sailed away, without much hope that it would get anywhere. As it turned out, some months later it drifted ashore on Stewart Island; but by that time we had already been rescued.

In the meantime, we harvested our collards and potatoes, and stored as much goat and pig meat as we could; and then we hunkered down in readiness for the long winter of 1867. As James Teer had predicted, we again survived, by the same means we survived the first winter – by staying together, huddled in our rough huts, keeping as busy as we could, and eating mussels and seals until the dysentery got so bad we just ate the collards and potatoes.

On 19 October 1867, after seventeen months of keeping fruitless watch, we sighted a sail. In a state of euphoric excitement, we lit huge bonfires on the highest visible points, but to our despair, the ship passed us by. In the aftermath of this crushing disappointment, we built another boat, just to be ready. Then on 19 November 1867, to our amazement, we sighted another sail. This time we not only lit the bonfires, but we launched our boat, and attempted to reach the passing ship. Yet again, all our efforts went for naught. For the next two days, our party was at its lowest pitch. But on 21 November 1867, our prayers were finally answered. The whaling brig *Amherst*, sailing from the Bluff, headed straight for the island, saw our fires, and rescued us, after 18 months as castaways.

Aboard the *Amherst* we were treated like kings. We reached the Bluff safe and sound, where the good people there opened their homes, and their hearts, to us. Due to their many great kindnesses, our return to civilization was relatively painless, save for some dissension that arose from discrepancies in people's testimony at the Court of Inquiry, where the insurers were bent on assigning blame for the wreck to Captain Loughlin, and where there was some unpleasantness regarding the Quinlans and the ambiguous circumstances surrounding the incident where their friend drowned while Roger was trying to rescue her. But once these matters were laid to rest, we all enjoyed a pleasant convalescence in the Bluff, save for the Quinlans, who ignored the physicians' advice and left the Bluff abruptly, for parts unknown, immediately after the Court of Inquiry concluded, perhaps to put an end to any further discussion of their friend's death.

It might be thought that my account of the disaster should end with our rescue and convalescence. But the lure of the gold in the hold of the *General Grant* proved too strong. In 1868 searchers landed on Auckland Island, and tried to find the cavern by thorough searching of the coast from the high bluffs along the western edge of the island. However, no trace of any cave was discovered by this method, and it was concluded that the cavern could only be located from the sea. Enlisting the aid of James Teer, the tug Southland from the Bluff next attempted to locate the deadly cavern in 1869, with the hope of raising the wreck and salvaging the gold. The enterprise failed when Teer could not locate the cavern, and the terrible weather along the west coast of Auckland Island finally drove the Southland back home. In 1870, the 48 ton schooner Daphne sailed from the Bluff, with David Ashworth from our party as its guide. This expedition ended even more disastrously than the Southland's, as six men were drowned when their small search boat was swamped while attempting to reach a cavern that David had tentatively identified as being possibly the tomb of the *General Grant*. Sadly, but perhaps also instructively, David Ashworth, who survived 18 months with us on Auckland Island, was among the six who died in the failed salvage attempt.

Will the *General Grant's* gold ever be recovered?

Is any treasure hoard worth all the loss of human life which this one seems to cause?

I won't attempt to answer these questions. But I also won't be sailing on any future salvage ships that seek the *General Grant* and her vault of gold. I'm too busy making good on my vow, never again to waste my time on earth in petty occupations.

* * *

VERDICT OF THE COURT OF INQUIRY FOR THE COMMONWEALTH OF NEW ZEALAND CONCERNING THE WRECK OF THE GENERAL GRANT

THE BLUFF
FRIDAY, 13 DECEMBER 1867
MR. IAN PRESCOTT, MAGISTRATE

The Verdict of this Court of Inquiry is as follows:

FACTS

On 4 December 1867, eight men and two women, the survivors of the crew and passengers of the American ship *General Grant*, were landed at Bluff Harbour, by the whaling brig *Amherst*. They were rescued from the Auckland Islands on the 21st of November 1867, 18 months after the *General Grant* was wrecked on the 14th of May 1866.

General Grant, belonging to Messrs. Boyes, Richardson & Co. of Boston, United States, left Melbourne 4th May 1866, bound to London with a cargo of wool, hides, splenter and 2576 ounces (73 kg) of gold, insured by Spence Brothers for £165,000. *General Grant* sighted the Auckland Islands on 13th May and, with the weather being thick, the ship got too near the land. There being no wind, a strong current carried her the following day on to the rocks on a bold shore where she got jammed in a cavern, and broke up. In attempting to land 68 lives were lost by the swamping of the boats.

There were 15 survivors and after remaining on the island till the 22nd February 1867, the chief officer and three of the crew left in a boat with the intention of endeavouring to make the coast of New Zealand. Their present whereabouts are not known as they have not been seen again. One other survivor of the wreck died on the island.

The names of the ten survivors brought off the *Amherst* were:

Crew	Passengers
Mary Ann Jewell, Manchester	Patrick Coughey, Ulster
Joseph Edwin Jewell, Devonshire	Nicholas Evans Ellis, Boston
David J. Ashworth, Newcastle	Catherine Larkin Quinlan, Oxford
Cornelius Drew, Dublin	Roger Martin Quinlan, London
Aaron Nathan Hayman, London	James Teer, Ulster

The names of the four survivors of the wreck who are still missing are:

Bartholomew N. Brown, New Jersey
Peter A. McNevin, Inverness
Andrew Morrison, Edinburgh
William N. Scott, South Shields

The crew lost, so far as they are known, are:

William H. Loughlin, Capt, New York
B.F. Jones, 2nd officer, Massachusetts
Magnus Anderson, carpenter, Sweden
Henry Charles Keding, steward, Illinois
Unidentified Purser
Unidentified Assistant Cook
Beatrice Alice Brown, New Jersey
Wm. K. Ferguson, Sydney
Wm. F. Sanguilly, Paris
David McLelland, Glasgow
Unidentified Cook
5 Unidentified Seamen

The passengers lost, so far as they are known:

Rev. Father Anthony Sarda, Trieste
Abigail Ellis and three children, Boston
Elizabeth Ott and five children, Hartford
Franklin Jenkins Oldfield, London
Edward Aloysius Ray, Wellington
Leonard Jenkins Edels, Sussex
Harrison F. Dean, Liverpool
Kathleen V. Allen, Oxford
Emma Oldfield and two children
Elizabeth Simmons Ray

Lost Passengers, cont'd

August Leonard Samson, Bristol	Mrs. Samson and three children
George Samson, Bristol	George H. Mitchell, Melbourne
Deborah Ames Ellis and three children	Paul Johnson, Pennsylvania
John J. Fitzgerald and 1 child, Belfast	Andrew Alan Laing, Melbourne
Jedediah Quincy Woodrow, Virginia	Henry Wainsford Tibbits, London
Elizabeth Roberts and three children	Polly Molloy, Melbourne

13 unidentified passengers in third class cabins and steerage

ISSUES

The questions raised at the Inquiry pertained primarily to the question of the Captain's competence. Three particular issues were advanced:

(1) Should the Captain be held accountable for the wreck due to his navigational errors, which contributed to the *General Grant* being hundreds of miles off course on the day of the wreck?

(2) Should the Captain be held accountable for the wreck due to any tactical errors that contributed to the *General Grant* becoming inextricably wedged in the perilous cavern where it foundered?

(3) Should the Captain, or anyone else, be held accountable for the decision to delay the launch of the lifeboats, which is said to have contributed to the loss of 68 lives?

Finally, two questions were raised regarding the conduct of the survivors:

(4) Do the particular circumstances of the death by drowning of 68 persons in the cavern where the ship foundered warrant the filing of any criminal charges, for homicide or criminal neglect, against the crew and passengers who rowed the pinnace and the gig away from the cavern?

(5) Do the particular circumstances of the drowning death of Miss Kathleen V. Allen, of Oxford, England, warrant the filing of criminal charges against any of those involved in her attempted rescue?

FINDINGS

Captain William O. Laughlin of New York was an experienced sea captain who sailed clipper ships for over twenty years with no record of fault.

For sound commercial reasons related to the very substantial amount of gold on board, the owners of the *General Grant* instructed Captain Laughlin to make the speediest possible journey to London, by means of the Great Circle Route. As this route has only been used with frequency the past few years, due to the new commercial demands for speed in ocean travel arising from the Australian goldfields, Captain Loughlin had never before sailed the Great Circle Route.

However, the Great Circle Route has many virtues. It avoids the need for sailing straight into the teeth of the westerly Trade Winds that hinder the progress of all ships sailing west from Australia to Europe. It also avoids the notorious hazards of rounding Cape Horn, experienced by ships sailing east from Australia to Europe with the Trade Winds at their backs. Instead, the Great Circle Route takes maximum advantage of the curvature of the Earth, as well as the very strong westerlies that prevail in the sub-antarctic regions of the Southern Ocean, and results in a much shorter journey than any other route from Australia to Europe.

On the other hand, the Great Circle Route requires sailing through the most desolate and uninhabited region of the world, where temperatures routinely fall below zero degrees, and conditions are always forbidding and stark. It has been pointed out that Captain Loughlin was provided with the very latest of charts for the entire Great Circle Route. However, the Court finds that, due to the infrequency with which the route was used until relatively recent times, even the latest charts are not entirely reliable, as they still contain significant defects.

By way of highly pertinent example, testimony was given that, after rescuing the survivors of this wreck, the brig *Amherst* took time to leave, at prominent places on Auckland Island, two depots of dry clothing, blankets, matches, tools, compasses &c., for the use of future castaways (each depot carrying the customary warning that "the curse of the widow and the fatherless shall light upon the man who opens this box with a ship at his back"). As part of defining the positions of the depots distinctly, the latitude and longitude were taken at both points, and it was found that the Aucklands are placed on the Chart 35 miles to the south of their actual location. This glaring error is sufficient to account for the fact that the *General Grant* is the third ship to wreck on Auckland Island in the last four years.

On the first issue, it has been argued that, had Captain Loughlin adhered to the course indicated on his charts, the *General Grant* would have missed the

Auckland Islands by over two hundred miles, and this wreck would not have occurred. However, no man can be expected to navigate without some degree of error during 64 hours of continuous thick fog, whilst traveling in open waters, particularly when the ship was becalmed for over 20 of those hours. The Court notes that Captain Loughlin took several prudent measures, including the doubling of the watch and the use of dead reckoning to navigate. Moreover, while the Captain's dead reckoning obviously missed by quite a bit more than a mile, the fact that the Chart erred in its placement of Auckland Island by 35 miles is, by itself, sufficient reason to find Captain Loughlin blameless on this issue.

On the second issue, it was argued that the Captain should be held accountable for allowing his ship to become wedged in the tight cavern where it foundered. The Court acknowledges that the particular predicament of a ship becoming lodged in a cave appears to be unprecedented in recorded maritime history. However, that fact does not, by itself, imply fault on the part of the Captain. The Captain raised the sails and attempted to catch any breeze he could, but there was simply no wind at all that night. The plumb line showed the sea was far too deep for club-hauling. No other means exists to steer a drifting ship away from danger. Once the ship hit the breakers, it was at the mercy of the rocks, which the survivors all say guided the ship into the cavern with astonishing speed. Therefore the Court can find no tactical error committed by Captain Loughlin

On the third issue, James Teer and Roger Quinlan persuasively testified that in the rough short sea of the night of the 13th and early morning of the 14th, the lifeboats could not have been safely launched in the dark, either outside or inside the cavern. However, it was also argued that the lifeboats could have been launched more expeditiously once the morning light rose, had the Captain personally supervised their launch, rather than going up to the wheelhouse.

The Court agrees that the Captain's absence at this critical time is troubling. What possible good could the Captain do in the wheelhouse of what was, by then, a doomed ship? On the other hand, the Captain did not completely abandon the task of loading and launching the lifeboats; rather, he delegated it to three very capable men.

It would be all too easy for this Court, sitting high and dry on our bench in the Bluff, with full benefit of hindsight, to say that it might have been better if the boats had been launched faster once the morning light came. But no one present in that cave had any way of knowing that the big ship, which had held together in the cave for over six hours, would suddenly break apart, making every minute lost in the loading process look, with benefit of hindsight, critical.

Moreover, as Mr. Teer and Mr. Quinlan persuasively testified, the task of loading 83 panic-stricken people onto lifeboats with seats for only 36, and space for perhaps 18 more, was never going to be an easy task, no matter who attempted it. Further, the harsh conditions of the Aucklands cast very serious doubt as to whether any of the children and nursing mothers, who were the only passengers who might have escaped the cavern had the longboat been safely launched, would have been likely to survive the severe hardships endured over two long sub-antarctic winters by the hardy survivors who testified before this Court.

Therefore the Court finds no fault on the part of Captain Loughlin or anyone else in the timing of the launching of the lifeboats.

As to the fourth issue, which was only raised incidentally in the course of Mr. Ellis's testimony, the Court finds no cause to warrant the filing of criminal charges against any of the survivors who were manning the pinnace and the gig at the time the 68 lives were lost in the cavern. It was argued that there was space for nine more people in those boats when the drowning deaths occurred; and that neither boat attempted to row back into the cavern and effect a rescue. However, the Court finds that the boats left the cavern in the good faith belief that they would be able to return and ferry those left behind to safety; and the Court further finds that, once the *General Grant* sank so rapidly, spilling 68 people into the cavern waters, the pinnace and the gig could not safely have re-entered the cavern. Even if they could have reached the victims in time, which is highly doubtful, rescue would have been impossible because the pinnace and the gig would surely have been immediately capsized in the same manner as the longboat was. Therefore the Court finds no cause for criminal charges to be filed against anyone on this issue.

As to the fifth issue, which was also only raised incidentally, in the course of Mr. Ellis's testimony, the Court has very strong misgivings. Nick Ellis testified that, as Roger Quinlan was in the process of rescuing both his wife, Catherine Quinlan, and their friend Kathleen Allen, Mr. Ellis saw Catherine Quinlan deliberately pull Roger Quinlan's arm down so that she could shove Kathleen Allen away from him, leading to the drowning of Kathleen Allen. The Court was initially inclined to discount Mr. Ellis's testimony, because it is plain Mr. Ellis's conscience is sorely vexed by the fact that he jumped to safety while leaving his wife and three children behind on the *General Grant*, to die shortly thereafter in the cavern. The Court also finds credible the testimony of Roger Quinlan, corroborated by other survivors, that Mr. Ellis carries an irrational grudge against both Mr. and Mrs. Quinlan, based on Mr. Ellis's claim that his own family members would still be alive, but for the failure to get the longboat launched before the *General Grant* broke apart, a failure which Mr. Ellis, alone among the witnesses, attributes to Mr. Quinlan.

However, Mr. Ellis's testimony regarding what he saw Catherine Quinlan do was corroborated by Mary Ann Jewell, a person who appears to bear no grudge against either of the Quinlans, and who worked side by side with Mrs. Quinlan for 18 months on many tasks, without rancour or disagreement. Yet after hearing Mr. Ellis's testimony, Mrs. Jewell came forward and added her voice to his, and even expanded on one point, testifying that she believes she saw Catherine Quinlan force Kathleen Allen down under the water, and then propel herself up 'like a cannonball' by pushing her feet down on Kathleen Allen's drowning body.

On the other hand, there were seven other people in the gig, including Mrs. Jewell's husband and three other experienced seamen, all watching intently the same dramatic rescue attempt by Roger Quinlan which occupied the attention of Mr. Ellis and Mrs. Jewell. None of these seven witnesses directly contradicted the testimony of Mr. Ellis or Mrs. Jewell; but all seven clearly felt they could not corroborate the testimony, either. Rather, these seven witnesses made three points that impressed the Court about the difficulties in determining what, exactly, was happening out in the water:

First, the gig was almost a hundred yards away from the spot where Kathleen Allen drowned, and it was bouncing up and down in a very rough sea;

Second, the witnesses in the gig were all peering from a day-lit location into a dark cavern; and

Third, there was a great amount of thrashing about in the water by all three people involved in the rescue attempt, which made it difficult for anyone to be sure what exactly was happening at any particular point in time.

Indeed, on this last point, it was evidently so difficult to tell who was who out in the water that even Mrs. Jewell conceded, since Catherine Quinlan and Kathleen Allen were so similar in age, size and appearance, she did not know which had been rescued and which had drowned, until they were hauled aboard the gig; and even then, Mrs. Jewell said she was not really certain which lady it was who had survived until the evening of the next day, after they reached dry land, and Mrs. Quinlan set about to share rough sleeping accommodations with Mr. Quinlan.

Furthermore, Roger Quinlan, who was closest to the incident, not only denied any criminal act by his wife (as Catherine herself did also), but Mr. Quinlan made one other important point. In the 18 months that the survivors lived together in close proximity, not once did Mr. Ellis or Mrs. Jewell, or anyone else, openly level the accusation against Mrs. Quinlan that, so far as Mr. Quinlan was aware, was publicly stated against his wife for the first time in this Court of Inquiry.

On balance, then, this Court does not feel competent to decide the issue of whether criminal charges are warranted against Catherine Quinlan in connection with the death by drowning of Kathleen Allen on 14th May 1866. However, this Court has already contacted the Office of the Prosecuting Attorney for the Bluff, to arrange for a Warrant to detain Mrs. Quinlan here in the Bluff, as a Material Witness to a possible homicide, until the proper authorities can conduct a more detailed investigation. Messrs. Teer, Caughey, Ashworth, Drew, Hayman, Jewell and Quinlan, as well as Mrs. Jewell and Mr. Ellis, are also requested to remain in the Bluff for the next several weeks, until the Crown's investigation is completed.

* * *

"Well, that was certainly intense," Joyce Kerr says.

"What do you think those two documents mean?" David Burns asks.

"I don't know. But I'm pretty sure you'll have some hard questions about all this for poor old Fiona tomorrow."

"Since when is she 'poor old' Fiona? She's the enemy!"

"I suppose." Joyce leans forward on the bed and hugs her knees. "But I still love her. And I'd feel bad for anyone who had to answer all your questions."

"Why?" Burns wills himself not to look at Joyce's slender thighs, taut and tensed on the bed, where she still sits like a cat. "Clive says there's no rhyme or reason to my questions."

"He's right." Mischief dances in Joyce's eyes. "You're like a wild ride at an amusement park, always changing speeds, always throwing Fiona off balance."

"Clive feels the wild ride is taking us nowhere, slow."

"He might be right about that, too. But it's still fun to watch."

"I'm glad you're enjoying the show," Burns mutters.

"I am, because I can never figure out where you're going. Like at the end this morning. I was sure you were going after Kathleen's different names to set up an argument that all of her actions as trustee were invalid, and so Fiona lacked authority to sign the contract with the U about the copy. But then all of sudden you were using Kathleen's different names to go after the idea of maybe Roger had two wives. And now that I've read these shipwreck documents, I get the feeling you're really going after something else. Though I'm not sure what."

"I'm not sure what I'm after either," Burns confesses. "And meanwhile the guy paying the bills is getting very restless. So I'd like to figure out if there's a way to use these New Zealand documents to force an early settlement."

"Fiona will never settle. She's way too stubborn."

"But Fiona couldn't get out of there fast enough today," Burns counters. "I touched a raw nerve with the diary, asking about Kathleen and her rival."

"Yes you did," Joyce concedes. She stands up beside the bed, lifting her arms and arching her back in a long languorous stretch, which shows off her ample chest to great advantage. This time Burns's willpower is inadequate. To avoid ogling Joyce, Burns resorts to closing his eyes, as if concentrating deeply.

"I just wish I knew," Burns continues, eyes closed, "which nerve exactly I struck. Something's clearly out of whack, when the Court of Inquiry lists 'Kathleen Allen' as the one who died in the wreck. Because we know that the Mrs. Quinlan who survived called herself 'Kathleen Allen' in 1864, when she was appointed Reynolds Foundation trustee; and also called herself 'Kathleen Allen Quinlan' most of the time after the wreck, except that weird little interlude with the Belize City branch of the Bank of England, where she was 'Catherine Larkin Quinlan'."

"The Court of Inquiry must've mixed up the names," Joyce says. "Some poor clerk got told to write up lists of the survivors and the dead. But with the ship records gone, and only ten survivors to question, errors got made."

"Maybe. But I feel there's more to this than a clerk's error, because Roger and his lady, whichever one she was, lit out of New Zealand just one step ahead of a warrant. And for some reason, in her diary she was Kathleen Allen Quinlan; but her ID in Belize City five months later said 'Catherine Larkin Quinlan'."

"You think she switched names to dodge the warrant?"

"Maybe." Burns opens his eyes and sees Joyce sitting on the bed again, but this time with her feet on the floor, in a much less provocative pose. "But then I can't explain why she switched names back again in Belize City."

"What'd they use for ID in those days? Did they have passports?"

"I don't know. I think maybe just birth certificates. But whatever they used for ID, I'm sure it all ended up at the bottom of the Southern Ocean."

"Maybe not," Joyce says. "Kathleen said in her diary she saved the *Lamanai Codex* in a waterproof pouch. Maybe her ID was in the pouch, too."

"*If* you believe the diary." Burns says. "We always assume Kathleen wouldn't lie to her diary, but the diary is what's out of whack with everything else."

Burns falls silent, trying to reconstruct what he knows of Kathleen's life. He can almost draw a straight line from 1844 to 1909 – except for the inconsistencies between the diary and the shipwreck documents.

"What kind of settlement do you think you could get Fiona to agree to?" Joyce asks, interrupting Burns's thoughts about Kathleen Quinlan.

"I don't know." Burns shrugs. "That was just wishful thinking, really."

"You're not having fun representing me anymore?" Joyce teases.

"You're fine. But hanging out with Clive is getting old fast."

"Clive is certainly easier to take in small doses," Joyce concedes.

"Still, I can't try to rush a settlement just 'cause Clive's in a hurry to battle Death. Because it's going to take a lot more pounding before Fiona gives up the codex."

"I don't really care about the codex."

Burns gapes. "You don't?"

"Not really," Joyce says. "That's Clive's big deal."

"But don't we all care about finding the fountain of youth?"

"Not me."

"Oh c'mon! You want me to believe if Clive manages to make the fountain of youth safe, or uses it to work out a new rejuvenation drug, you wouldn't try it?"

Joyce laughs. "You're right. I'd try it – but only if I knew it was safe. And I'm not convinced Clive can really make it safe."

"I wouldn't bet against him," Burns says. "Clive's been pretty successful in everything else he's tackled in life."

"Yeah, but now he's messing with stuff people were never meant to mess with." Joyce runs her fingers through her hair. "Anyway, Clive can chase the big prize. I just wanna try to enjoy the actual life I've got, right now, before it's gone."

"So the codex truly isn't all that important to you?"

"No, David, it's really not."

"Well, you're my client, not Clive. You want me to give up on trying to get the codex?"

"Oh no. You should still try to get it, for Clive's sake. I'm just saying I'm happy now, no matter what happens."

"You mean, because we've got the land?"

Joyce nods, and then breaks into a huge smile. "I'm gonna try Lisa again."

While Joyce dials Michael's number, Burns tries to formulate some questions for Fiona. *Was your grandmother Kathleen a ghost? Or was your grandmother really named Catherine Larkin, only after she drowned her best friend Kathleen from Oxford, she decided to call herself Kathleen Allen after that, in honor of the woman she murdered?*

With half an ear Burns hears Joyce sparring with Michael to get Lisa on the line. The problem with formulating sarcastic questions to ask Fiona is, they won't produce anything useful. Burns winces, recalling Clive's 'no rhyme or reason' comment. Burns doesn't like to admit it, even to himself – and certainly not to Joyce – but Clive struck a raw nerve there himself. Most cross-examiners know where they're heading before they even start, and the result looks smooth and polished. Burns, by contrast, learns by going where he has to go; and the result often looks chaotic. 'A wild amusement park ride' is putting it kindly.

Burns looks at Joyce, and his heart aches. She's so gorgeous, with her out-of-date bangs and her out-of-fashion heavy eyebrows, and her always-in-style wicked little body. She's so fun, too, with her light, teasing manner, her wide heart-breaking smile, and her rare wit. For years Burns has carried a torch for Joyce. And yet – she's so utterly unattainable.

Joyce has Lisa on the line now, and her entire body is suffused with the joy of explaining that 'David won a big part of the case today', and 'yes, it means we might get some money', but 'no I don't know how much and it won't be for a long time'. Burns wonders if it's wise to give so much information to a 12-year-old. But that's Joyce. What you see is what you get.

Joyce hangs up, beaming. "Lisa's very excited about the land."

"So are you."

"Yes I am. If we can sell it, the money'll help me so much. To buy things for Lisa I could never afford, and to – change the way I live." Joyce reaches for a cigarette. "Though Lisa thinks instead of selling it, we should just go live on it." She lights the cigarette. "Can you imagine? She has no idea how fast she'd get sick of San Pedro. And how she'd miss all her American comforts."

"I'm going to lose you, aren't I?"

"Weren't you listening? I said *Lisa* wants to live in Belize. Not me. No thanks. "

"No, I mean, you're going to quit working for me, aren't you?"

Joyce takes a long drag on her cigarette, and then meets Burns's eyes square on. "Yes."

Burns nods, acknowledging her honesty, and struggles to control his emotions. It's bad enough having Joyce decline all his romantic overtures. But at least he gets to see her, almost every day. Now – Burns can't bear to think of it.

Joyce cocks her head sympathetically. "I'm sorry, David. I know you'd rather have me stay. But I don't want to work full time all my life if I don't have to."

"You should do what you want to do, Joyce. Though where I'll find another paralegal like you, I can't imagine. How'd you ever get those New Zealand documents?"

"I saw a mention of them on the internet." Joyce pops a breath mint in her mouth. "So I ordered them through an inter-library loan service. Only it turns out you can't get inter-library loans from New Zealand. So then I called the library in New Zealand and asked them to copy the documents for us. Turns out they have a policy that won't allow them to copy more than 30 pages from any single book. So I got someone to read me parts of the books, until I could figure out which pages would be best for us. Then I got her to copy them for us. They only got to Ann Arbor the day before we flew here."

Burns looks at Joyce, trying not to get misty-eyed about the idea of her leaving him. But vaguely he realizes that was an uncharacteristically long answer Joyce just gave. Short, straightforward answers are much more her style. Could it be that she's rattling on so long about inter-library loan services because she, too, feels bad about the idea of leaving Burns?

"Are you sure you can really retire on $600,000?" Burns puts his toe in the water, just to see if there's any chance of finding a way to get Joyce not to quit.

"I won't retire. I'll just find something fun to do part time." Joyce gets up and walks over to Burns. "But thank you, David, for talking me into suing Fiona – and thank you so much for winning on the land."

Joyce bends a little at the waist, and kisses Burns softly on the lips. Softly – but all too briefly, to Burns's way of thinking.

"Since the condemned man doesn't smoke, he gets a farewell kiss instead?"

"Who says it's farewell?" Joyce teases.

Then to Burns's utter amazement, Joyce sits down on his lap, perching herself on Burns's right thigh, and throwing a very friendly left arm around his neck and shoulders. Their eyes lock. His are questioning; hers are frank and fun. Then she looks down at his chest, and her right hand starts messing with the buttons on his shirt. The faint pressure from Joyce's fingertips on his chest provokes a huge adrenaline surge all through Burns's body, and deep in his aging loins, he can feel an erection stirring.

"Now that I've decided to stop working for you," Joyce says, "my rule against mixing work and romance no longer applies."

Joyce kisses Burns full on the lips again, this time a little longer, and with a little more pressure. After the kiss is over, Joyce pulls her head away to a normal distance, and searches Burns's eyes. He meets her gaze awhile, wordless for once in his life.

But then he decides there are better forms of non-verbal communication than gazing at Joyce's eyes. So he reaches for the base of Joyce's head, to bring her lips back close, and encounters no resistance. They plunge into an all-out passionate kiss, which lasts until Burns feels his lungs running short of oxygen.

"Upon further reflection," Burns says, when he comes up for air, "I've decided maybe it is a good idea if you retire, Joyce. Effective immediately."

Chapter Fourteen
The Ends of the Earth

Wednesday 6 April 2011 Morning

The Australian cab driver stops at the bollards blocking Shad Thames. "Can't tike you any fudduh, mite," the cabbie says. "Ye'll have to hoof it from heah."

The Gang of Five alights on Horselydown Lane, and all look up in amazement at the clear, sunny skies. Clive Phelps pays the cabbie, while Joyce Kerr lights a cigarette, and then they all start walking towards Shad Thames.

But when David Burns, bringing up the rear on the narrow sidewalk, stops to poke his head in Ivy Taylor's office, the other four don't notice and keep walking. "Hey, Ivy," Burns says, "can I trouble you for the original of that diary I was using yesterday?"

"No problem, mon." Ivy opens her steno case and pulls out Kathleen Quinlan's journal, which Burns puts in his briefcase.

"You know, there's a chance we may not go on the record at all today."

"I know." Ivy closes up her steno case and heads for the door. "Mrs. Watt called me this morning to let me know that might happen."

Burns tries to act unsurprised. But what does Olivia's call mean? Is she anticipating a settlement this morning? Or just that Fiona'll go home early again?

"But don't worry." Burns holds the door as Ivy walks outside, enjoying a good long look at those great long legs, as always on full and joyous display. "I'll be sure you get paid the same as if you were cranking out transcript pages."

"That's very nice of you, Mr. Bur – er, David." Ivy locks the door and, wheeling her steno cart, walks besides Burns towards Shad Thames.

"You're welcome," Burns says. "But I need a favor, Ivy. When you set up in the conference room, can you flip your back-up cassette on as soon as you sit down, and just leave it running all morning, even before we go on the record?"

"OK." Ivy shoots Burns a sidelong glance as they walk side-by-side down Horselydown Lane. "You don't trust Mr. Santos to leave your consultants alone?"

"It's not aimed at anyone in particular." Burns lies, since Ivy's guess is dead right. "I just might need to know what gets said in there all morning."

"You prefer that no one but me knows the tape's on?" Ivy asks.

"That would be my preference, yes," Burns says. "If it's okay with you."

"No problem, mon. I'll turn it on before I sit down. Dat way no one will see."

"Thanks, Ivy. I owe you one."

Up ahead Burns sees Joyce stop at the corner of Shad Thames, waving the Three Amigos on ahead to Symington & Watt, while she waits. Joyce looks up and down Shad Thames, but never at Burns and Ivy, as if to convey that Ivy's latest heart-stopping miniskirt is beneath her notice.

Burns braces himself for a tart exchange. But Joyce greets Ivy cordially, with no sarcasm.

"Looks like we've got a little problem, David." Joyce points down Shad Thames to the front door of Symington & Watt, where a uniformed constable with a black-and-white pith hat is preventing the Three Musketeers from entering.

"What's up?" Burns asks the constable when he, Joyce and Ivy reach the door.

At high speed the constable utters a series of clipped syllables, probably in English, but his Cockney accent is so thick Burns has no idea what was said.

"Burglary here last night," Phelps translates for Burns. "We can't go in until Olivia comes down and personally verifies our identities."

"Anything taken?" Burns asks.

The constable emits another torrent of sounds, also presumably English, but again Burns has no idea what was said. Again he looks to Phelps.

"Nothing seems to be missing," Phelps says, "except the petty cash till was emptied out. But they're still checking."

Burns glances at the undamaged front door, and then up the brick walls, where all the street-side windows seem intact, too. "How'd the burglars get in?"

"Roof," the constable says.

"No one was hurt, I hope?" Burns asks.

The constable shakes his head no.

Olivia arrives, verifies their identities, and they all enter, except the constable, who stays by the door. Olivia escorts them all up the lift to their usual 8th floor conference room. Straightaway Ivy sits down, opens her steno machine, and begins to set up. The others, except Olivia, plop their briefcases and boxes down on the table, and then stand awkwardly, looking at Olivia.

"So a bit of excitement here last night?" Burns asks.

Olivia purses her lips. "'Excitement' is not the word I'd choose."

"But the constable said they didn't get much, right?" Burns asks.

"No, but they destroyed our big skylight down the hall," Olivia says.

"Why break into a law firm?" Burn asks. "Not a big cash business."

Olivia darts her eyes at Phelps. "They were after the codex."

"Oh my God!" Burns says. "I forgot you kept it in your – did they get it?"

"No," Olivia says.

"Phew," Burns says. "So ... how d'you know they were after the codex?"

Olivia looks at Burns like he's joking. "We have been hogging the headlines the past two days, David. The proverbial cat's out of the bag."

Burns scoffs. "A little publicity is no reason to leap to the concl—"

"I agree with Ms. Watt," Phelps interjects.

Burns shoots Phelps an irritated look, but Phelps ignores it.

"The cell research community," Phelps continues, "is all in a dither over those articles reporting my connection to this case. One of my rivals must've tried to beat me to the codex."

"Cell researchers don't know how to commit burglaries," Burns argues.

"But they can hire someone who does," Olivia counters.

"Were these guys professional thieves?" Kip Hunter asks.

"The police think so," Olivia says. "They certainly dodged our security cameras skillfully."

"Meaning someone paid a lot of money," Phelps says, "to get the James Bond type guys. Only something like the codex would be worth that."

"Oh, c'mon," Burns says. "You don't need James Bond to break a skylight and dodge a few cameras."

"But only the best guys can come in off the river," Phelps argues. "That takes special equipment and training."

"They came off the river?" Graham asks.

Hunter shoots Phelps a sideways glance, whose import Burns cannot decipher.

"That's correct," Olivia says. "A boat with a crane."

"Wow," Graham says. "That *is* a lot of effort, just to break into a law firm."

"Why not just come across from an adjacent building?" Burns asks.

Olivia shrugs. "The police say they definitely used a boat with a crane."

"How come the Tower Bridge watchmen didn't see it?" Graham asks, pointing out the window at the watchtowers on Tower Bridge.

"You'll have to ask the police that," Olivia says. "Maybe they were asleep."

"More likely the guys on the boat called ahead," Hunter says, "and told the watchmen they were coming. Routine night maintenance. That's what I'd do."

Olivia arches a very disapproving eyebrow at this comment. Burns rushes to cover up for Hunter exposing his rougher edges. "Okay," Burns says, "even if it was James Bond, how would some lab guy know where to go hire James Bond?"

"Are you kidding?" Phelps asks. "Ever hear of industrial espionage?"

"You make cell research sound like a rough racket," Burns says.

"It is," Phelps says. "I guarantee you: a competitor of mine organized this."

"If these guys were so professional," Burns asks Olivia, "how come they couldn't get into your safe?"

"They did," Olivia says. "Drilled through the steel, and opened it right up."

"Then why don't they have the codex?" Burns asks.

"I couldn't open the safe yesterday. The lock's very finicky. I didn't have time to fool with it, so I simply took the codex down the street to our safe deposit box at NatWest."

"Why didn't you just give it back to Dr. Young?" Phelps asks.

"She was asleep," Olivia says. "Mr. Burns wore her out yesterday."

"Well, I'm glad no one got hurt," Burns says, "and I'm glad you didn't put the codex in the safe, Olivia. Shall Joyce and I come down to your office now?"

"At this point, I don't think that would be a good idea," Olivia says.

"Why not?" Burns asks. "Yesterday you were all for it."

Olivia fixes Burns with her severest frown. "'All for it' seems a bit of an exaggeration. But in the event, things have changed since yesterday."

"How? If they didn't get the codex, the break-in hasn't changed anything."

"But yesterday's hearing in Detroit has," Olivia says.

"Why?" Phelps interjects. "Did the Judge rule on the *Observer's* motion?"

"No," Burns says. "He's holding off on a decision till next week, so Olivia and I can be there to argue the motion ourselves."

"But," Olivia adds, "Mr. Landau said it was clear to everyone the Judge is leaning very strongly in favor of granting the *Observer's* motion."

"My associate gave me the same report last night," Burns admits. "But I still think it could be productive for Joyce and me to meet with you and Fiona now, at least for a few minutes."

Olivia shakes her head no. "Fiona's very tired."

"But she's here, right?" Burns says. "You didn't call us to cancel today."

"She's in my office," Olivia says. "But she's not in a good frame of mind for a friendly chat."

"Why don't we just talk a little, and see how it goes?" Burns says. "If things get testy, we can always come back down here and carry on with the depo."

Olivia ponders this idea, and then makes a gesture with her shoulders that seems to indicate acquiescence in the meeting. "Just don't say I didn't warn you."

While the Three Blind Mice wait in the conference room with Ivy, Olivia escorts Joyce and Burns down the hall towards her office.

"I'm still not buying this idea of cell researchers hiring James Bond to break into a law firm to steal the codex," Burns mutters. "It's too far-fetched."

Olivia motions Burns and Joyce into an unoccupied office. "I didn't want to say this in front of the others. But the burglars didn't stop after breaking in here. They broke into Fiona's flat, too."

"Oh, shit," Burns says. "Then I guess it really was about the codex."

"Did they harm Fiona?" Joyce asks.

"No," Olivia says, "but they frightened her half to death. She woke up and saw two masked men in her bedroom – but she hit an alarm before they could stop her. Then they picked her up, like they were going to kidnap her; but the clanging of the alarm must've changed their minds, as they dropped her back on the bed and ran out the front door."

"My God," Joyce says. "How'd they get in her flat? Her door's got all those police locks."

"They came in via her river side balcony. It was quite a feat to get onto that balcony. That's why Scotland Yard says these were indeed professional thieves of the highest caliber."

"And that's why you want me to go easy this morning," Burns says.

"You simply must," Olivia says. "Fiona's very badly shaken by the whole ordeal. They turned her reception room upside down, before they went after her in the bedroom."

"I will behave myself," Burns says. "For a change."

"I'll believe it when I see it," Olivia says.

On that upbeat note, Olivia ushers them further down the hall, into her corner office, which is smaller than Burns expected, but richly furnished in traditional blues and reds – and with windows on both the north and east, affording a great view of the river, especially downstream.

Fiona Young is sitting in a chair beside Olivia's elegant rosewood desk, her cane propped against the wall, her purse and the *Lamanai Codex* on the desk. Fiona does not rise or offer any greeting. Olivia sits at her desk, while Joyce and Burns sit in two chairs facing Fiona and Olivia.

"Would it be okay," Burns says, "if we use first names, just for this little meeting?"

Everyone looks at Fiona. She hesitates, but then nods yes.

"Good," Burns says. "Fiona, Joyce and I are truly sorry to hear about your ordeal this morning. We can imagine what an awful shock that must have been."

Fiona sets her jaw very tight.

"We realize that break-in would never have happened to you," Burns says, "or to this law firm, if someone hadn't leaked our lawsuit to the press. We also realize you think someone on our side was the leak, and we respect your right to think that. For what it's worth, if I had any information that someone on my team was the leak, I'd turn 'em into the Judge myself. But I honestly don't think it was anyone on our side of the table. I'm not saying that to start an argument; I'm just saying it so you don't think I'm sitting in here condoning the leaks. Far from it."

"Who do you think was the leak then?" Fiona demands.

"The University," Burns says.

"That's ludicrous, David," Olivia interjects. "The University is the last party that wants publicity about this case."

"And so far the only party that's achieved that goal," Burns counters. "Clive got mocked big time. Fiona was called a pariah. But there was no mention of the U 'hoarding' their copy." Burns throws up his hands. "But I promised not to argue this morning, Olivia, so forget I even said that."

He turns back to Fiona. "I don't know who the leak is, Fiona. But I'm as concerned about it as you are. Which is part of why I wanted to sit down this morning, just the four of us."

"They stole my locket," Fiona says. "And slashed open the spine of every book I own."

Joyce gasps. "My God, Fiona. You have thousands of books. That's—" Joyce's eyes open wide. "They must've been in your flat for hours."

"Hours," Fiona repeats, tersely.

"What were they looking for inside your books?" Burns asks, while noting that Fiona's neck is indeed missing the gold locket she usually wears. "The codex is small, but it's not *that* small."

"My translation, I assume," Fiona says.

"Did they get your translation?"

Fiona shakes her head no.

"How'd they miss it?"

"It wasn't in my flat last night," Fiona says.

"How come?" Burns asks.

Fiona looks at Olivia. "I'd rather not answer that question," Fiona says.

Burns throws up his hands in a surrender gesture. "That's fine. It's not important. I'm just glad the translation wasn't there, so they couldn't get it. And I'm sorry about your books."

"Me, too, Fiona," Joyce says, with feeling. "I know how much those books mean to you."

Fiona gazes at Joyce, but Fiona's face remains a blank mask.

"So," Olivia says, "before we start today, I want to confirm this is a settlement meeting, so everything that's said in here is confidential and can't be used in the litigation or anywhere else."

"That's our understanding also," Burns says.

"Good," Olivia says. "What's on your mind this morning?"

"I need to explore some uncomfortable subjects," Burns says, "and since everything we do in this case seems to end up in the papers, I thought it'd be better to discuss these subjects privately first." He turns to Fiona. "But I promised Olivia I'd go easy this morning, and I will. I'm not here to cross-examine you, or to start an argument. On the contrary, I'm here to throw all my cards on the table, so you can see them. Normally I would never do this. It's bad strategy, bad tactics. But this lawsuit is as painful for Joyce as I think maybe it is for you. And this is the only way I can think of to 'cut to the chase', like you asked me to do that first morning of the depo."

"That'd be nice," Fiona says. "I'm not getting any younger."

"You and me both." Burns says. "Did you get a chance to read those New Zealand documents I gave Olivia yesterday?"

Almost imperceptibly Fiona nods.

"Good," Burns says. "I found aspects of those documents puzzling, when I looked at them in light of the diary I was asking you about yesterday. So I have a theory I want to run by you. And let me admit, right up front, this theory can't be proved – unless someone orders a blood test."

"Which Judge Henderson will never do," Olivia says, "especially now that we've given up our probate defenses."

"Agreed," Burns says. "So this is just a theory. A long time ago in Oxford there were two young women, best friends named Kathleen Allen and Catherine Larkin, who were 'dead ringers' for each other, probably right down to their heavy hooded eyelids. One day a dashing fellow named Roger Quinlan crashed a garden party, and swept both Kathleen and Catherine off their feet."

"We read the diary last night too," Olivia says, "after you introduced it."

"So then you already know Roger seduced them both." Burns pauses, hoping to get a rise out of Fiona; but she doesn't bite. "And even though Kathleen Allen stirred his heart more, Catherine Larkin had more of the family money Roger lusted after, to pay for the extravagant archeological expeditions he hoped to launch, to vindicate himself in the eyes of the Oxford dons who'd booted him out of university. So when Roger was forced to choose, he ditched Kathleen Allen and married Catherine Larkin; and when Miss Allen's family kicked up a fuss about Roger having seduced their daughter, he eloped to Australia with Catherine, who became Mrs. Quinlan, to dig for gold in Victoria." Burns waggles one hand. "Frankly, I don't quite get why Roger was out digging for gold, which is awful hard work, if Catherine had family money."

"Sometimes family money can be hard to access," Fiona says, "especially if you've just caused a big scandal and eloped with the father's favorite child."

"There you go!" Burns says. "That musta been it. So old Roger digs for gold in Victoria for a coupla years, and hits a nice strike. But then things get murky. Because Kathleen Allen is also in Australia by 1865, and her diary says she aborts Roger's child there, whom she calls Persephone in her diary. And then Roger decides to go home to England. So like a lot of British gold miners in the spring of 1866, Roger books passage to London on the *General Grant*. Also on board, according to the Court of Inquiry, were a 'Catherine Larkin Quinlan', and a 'Miss Kathleen Allen'."

"You are coming to the point sometime soon?" Olivia asks.

"You sound like Dr. Phelps," Burns says, hoping to back her off a little.

"Perish the thought," Fiona says.

"During the nine days the *General Grant* was at sea," Burns says, "before wrecking against Auckland Island, the stewardess, a Mary Ann Jewell, noticed two key facts, which you saw in the documents you read last night. First, Mrs. Quinlan spent most of those nine days sick in her cabin. Second, Mr. Quinlan spent most of his time in the company of the Quinlans' 'close friend', Kathleen Allen. And since Catherine and Kathleen looked so much alike, when the *General Grant* wrecked, and Roger and Catherine and Kathleen were all thrown in the water, and Roger was only able to save one of the two women, the other survivors, watching from the lifeboats, couldn't tell for sure whether Roger was saving Kathleen or Catherine. In fact, even after Roger and the woman he saved were hauled into the gig, Mary Ann Jewell still wasn't sure which one had been saved. But 36 hours later, when the lady who'd been saved made arrangements to bed down with Roger, then everyone assumed the lady must be Mrs. Quinlan."

Outside Olivia's window, with its panoramic view of the Thames, Burns sees a small tug boat pulling two flat barges, loaded with rusty iron containers, up the river.

"Now since you want me to speed along," Burns says, "let's cut right to the December 1867 Court of Inquiry. The Magistrate heard testimony from the survivors about how Roger Quinlan saved his wife from drowning, but was unable to save their friend, Miss Kathleen V. Allen. So Mr. Prescott, or perhaps his clerk, listed 'Miss Kathleen V. Allen' among the passengers lost at sea. But then, as you know from reading the diary, just 3 months later, in March of 1868, Mr. Quinlan was married to a woman who styled herself, at least in her own diary, 'Mistress Kathleen Allen Quinlan'."

"So there must've been some confusion," Olivia says. "What's the point of all this, David? You've been obsessing about historical errors the past three days. Birth dates that get written down wrong on forms, and names that get jumbled up on documents. People make small mistakes, and if documents last long enough, later generations find those mistakes confusing. Who cares?"

"I don't think this was a small mistake, Olivia. The lady who went to Lamanai with Roger Quinlan in 1868 was the same lady who acquired the *Lamanai Codex* from India Reynolds in 1864. And in between, she saved the codex from the 1866 shipwreck by carrying it in a waterproof pouch beneath her corset. Almost as if the codex were her child. And that lady definitely didn't die in that dark cave, or the *Lamanai Codex* would've gone down with her, and we wouldn't all be sitting here now. But that lady, whom both our clients refer to as their ancestor, called herself 'Kathleen Allen Quinlan' when she wrote privately to her diary – yet when she went to the Bank in Belize in May 1868, she couldn't produce ID in that name, because her ID was in the name 'Catherine Larkin Quinlan'. Now I suppose people could get confused between Kathleen and Catherine, especially if they spelt Catherine with a k. But it's a lot harder to mix up Allen and Larkin. And the lady who survived the shipwreck couldn't prove the 'Allen' part, which is what the Bank was looking for, even though she called herself Kathleen Allen Quinlan to her diary. Why would that be?"

"I can't imagine," Olivia says. "Why?"

"Because Kathleen Allen switched places with Roger Quinlan's real wife," Burns says, "and started calling herself Mrs. Quinlan, right after Kathleen drowned the real Mrs. Quinlan, Catherine, out there in that cave."

"The Court of Inquiry didn't find the murder allegation conclusive enough to issue more than a material witness warrant," Olivia points out. "Why do you think you know more now, at all this distance, than the people who were so much closer to the events 144 years ago?"

"Because I've got one thing the Magistrate didn't have: Kathleen's 1868 diary. But you asked me not to argue. As I said, this is only a theory, which I thought best to air privately, here in your office, for the purpose of exploring whether a settlement might be possible to our lawsuit."

"Does your theory," Olivia asks, "include a motive for the alleged murder?"

"Love," Burns says. "Kathleen drowned her rival because she saw her chance to make the choice Roger wasn't able to make – or at least, wasn't getting around to very fast. He'd already knocked Kathleen up and run out on her, yet they still had enough of a bond for her to chase him all the way to Australia and entice him with the *Lamanai Codex*, and by that 'ploy', as she put it, she won back his love. Yet there they all were, on the ship for London, and he's still married to Catherine, and Kathleen has to settle for stolen love back in her cabin, or out on deck in the thick fog, or wherever they went. So when they were all three out swimming in that cavern, with everyone else dying all around them, and there was only one man strong enough to swim his way out of there, and he tried to save both women, Kathleen seized her chance and drowned her rival."

"But there were nine witnesses watching everything that happened," Fiona says, "and only two of them said they thought a murder occurred."

"Another reason why this is just a theory," Burns says. "But the interesting part to me is, the witnesses got it backwards. They accused Catherine of drowning Kathleen, because the witnesses didn't realize that Kathleen and Roger pulled their little switcheroo after Catherine drowned. Although the witnesses were all surprised that 'Catherine', who'd been so sick on the ship, and then spent over 24 hours soaking wet in freezing temperatures, not only didn't perish, she was suddenly hale and hearty and pulling her weight on all the chores, just like the men. But we who've seen the diary know that miraculous recovery occurred because it was Kathleen, not Catherine, who survived the shipwreck."

"Why would Kathleen would run the risk of switching identities?" Olivia asks.

"Because Roger and Kathleen knew they were either going to die out there in the wastes of the Southern Ocean, or, at best, they were going to be marooned with thirteen other people for a very long time," Burns says. "In the world they lived in, Roger couldn't just start sleeping with a new woman, without getting married first. But the only man of the cloth on the *General Grant* was Reverend Sarda, and he went down with all the others in the cave."

"You think they switched names just so they could have sex?" Olivia asks.

"I wouldn't say 'just'," Burns says. "Speaking unfortunately from personal experience, I can tell you 18 months is an awfully long time for a 52-year-old man to go without a woman's love – and Roger was, what, 27? And you can see from Kathleen's diary she was a passionate gal. So I can't imagine either one of them would have fancied 18 months of what the Victorians used to call 'self-abuse' – especially with their lover right there in the next hut."

"But the diary you had us read," Olivia counters, "says they didn't have relations for many months after the Wreck."

"An ironic result of what happened in the cave," Burns concedes, "but when Roger and Kathleen were first marooned, they couldn't have known Roger was going to lose his spark. People in their 20s never assume there's going to be any problem with sexual function. Besides, I'm really not saying it was 'just' for love they made the switch. They were in an utterly unique situation, Olivia, out there literally at the ends of the earth, with 13 other people they barely knew – and nobody there was checking IDs, that's for sure, because everything those people had was at the bottom of the ocean, except the codex and a few ounces of Roger's gold. So Roger and Kathleen made a fresh start. Got 'married' in an instant, just by telling the others that Kathleen was Mrs. Quinlan. Which might explain why Kathleen used quotation marks all through her diary, whenever she referred to Roger and herself as 'husband and wife'."

"But if this switch had really happened," Olivia says, "why wouldn't she just carry on calling herself Catherine Larkin Quinlan the rest of her life?"

"She tried to," Burns says. "When they got to the Bluff, she got new ID in the name of Catherine Larkin Quinlan – probably her only safe option, because the folks at the Bluff seemed to know the names of the first class passengers with great specificity. So she probably feared being exposed, if she tried to get new ID issued in the name of Kathleen Allen Quinlan, because some of the other survivors might've known that wasn't Mrs. Quinlan's true name. I don't know. But she clearly tried to be 'Catherine Larkin Quinlan', to the outer world, for at least the next six months."

"But why not for the rest of her life?" Olivia asks again.

"Because after Roger died, she needed to access the £15,000 pounds that was just sitting in the Reynolds Foundation," Burns says. "She'd already told Caruthers to send the LOC to Kathleen Quinlan, but he made it out to 'Kathleen Allen Quinlan'. And then the nit-picking sticklers at the Bank of England in Belize City declined to give the money to Catherine Larkin Quinlan. So to get the money she had to change her name back to Kathleen Allen Quinlan."

"How'd she do that?" Olivia demands.

"I don't know," Burns concedes. "Near the end of her diary she mentions a 'ceremony' in Belize City that Roger agreed to participate in with her, anticipating that his discovery of the fountain of youth would put them 'more in the public eye'. Maybe she and Roger pulled off a quiet little marriage in Belize City, and then used the new marriage certificate to get Kathleen new ID. I haven't had time to ask Joyce to research how ID worked back then, so I don't really know. But I know she switched back to Kathleen Allen Quinlan before her arrival in Ann Arbor in 1870."

"How would a blood test help prove this theory of yours?" Olivia asks. "Are you asking us to agree to an exhumation of Kathleen Quinlan's body? Can they get blood from the bone marrow of hundred-year-old corpses now, too?"

"Probably," Burns says. "But there's no corpse of Kathleen Quinlan to exhume. When she drove off that bridge, her body was never found."

"I didn't know that," Olivia says. "So then, whose blood do you want?"

"Fiona's."

"We've been over this, David!" Olivia exclaims. "What part of N-O don't you understand? Fiona is not giving any blood samples, and that's final."

"Fiona might not have a choice," Burns says. "See, under American rules, if a lawyer uncovers evidence of a crime committed by someone other than his own client – that is, someone with whom he has no attorney-client relationship – then he may have an ethical duty to report the information to the authorities. Notice I said 'may', not 'must'. It's a fairly tricky ethical rule. The lawyer has to make his own judgment call as to how strong the evidence really is. But in some cases, if he decides to keep the evidence under his hat, and the authorities later decide the evidence was strong enough the lawyer should have reported it, the lawyer who sat on what he discovered can be sanctioned for hiding the information, or even prosecuted. So in most cases an American lawyer will cover his butt and report any evidence of crimes he uncovers during a deposition – because it's just so much safer to report it than to risk being second-guessed later."

"Is an American lawyer ethically required," Olivia asks, "to report crimes he thinks were committed 145 years ago, even if the perpetrator is dead?"

"Probably not," Burns says.

"Then why are we even talking about this? Whatever happened back in 1866 is ancient history, and whether your theory is right or wrong, whether there was or wasn't a murder, whether it was Kathleen or Catherine, who cares? The perpetrator's long dead, so what is there to report?"

"I think the perpetrator's still alive," Burns says.

Olivia looks at Burns like he's a complete lunatic.

"There may even be a warrant still pending for her in New Zealand," Burns continues, "although like you said, it was only a material witness warrant back in 1867, because the Magistrate wasn't sure the evidence was strong enough to charge her on the spot. But that's what's so great for us, because the ambiguity in the strength of the evidence gives me the *right*, but not the *obligation*, to report what I've learned. So we all have some room to maneuver here."

"No one lives to be 167 years old," Olivia says.

"Unless they drink from the fountain of youth," Burns says.

"Oh good grief," Olivia says.

"So what's your theory?" Fiona asks.

"You are Kathleen Quinlan," Burns says. "The fountain of youth killed Roger, but it worked for you. You gave birth to Roger's son, Lloyd, and moved to Ann Arbor. When you got to the point that you looked just too ridiculously young to be a 65-year-old woman, you faked your death, by driving off a bridge, and leaving a suicide note; and then came back a few weeks later as your own daughter, Persephone, a totally fictitious person. You tried to Will all your belongings to yourself, but Judge Breakey and your son screwed you, so you swiped the codex and the land and went back to Central America as Persephone; and to raise some cash to live on, you sold the two India Reynolds paintings to Basil Dickinson. Then when Persephone started looking too young for a 90-year-old woman, or whatever age she was supposed to be, you got Kux Ahawis to help you die again, and you came back as Fiona – the girl no one outside Guatemala had ever seen, because she'd supposedly been away in the bush in Australia her entire early adult life. Was Kux the one who showed you and Roger where to find the fountain, and what to do when you got there?"

"I think you've lost your mind, David," Olivia says. "Seriously."

"Well, my circadian rhythms are certainly way off," Burns concedes. "But why do you think your client has such amazing recall of events that occurred before 1925? Why do you think she gave up three defenses, rather than agree to take a simple blood test? She's not afraid the test will show she's unrelated to Roger or Kathleen; she's afraid the test will show she's *too* related to the woman who licked the stamps on both the Kathleen Quinlan letter, and the Persephone Quinlan letter, too. An exact DNA match among all three. That's why she gave up those defenses so fast – to get me to stop barking up that tree."

Burns pauses to gauge the impact he's having. Olivia's still looking at him like he's raving mad. Joyce is looking at him like he's nuts, too. Fiona looks indignant – but watchful, too.

"The thing is, Olivia, I wouldn't have to convince the authorities I'm right," Burns says. "I'd only have to report all these facts, and let them serve Fiona with a simple subpoena compelling her to give a blood sample, which courts routinely enforce in criminal investigations. And if for some reason they decided not to serve a subpoena, well, if the press got hold of this story, you know a hue and cry would ensue until someone ordered the subpoena, just to shut the press up."

"But you couldn't lawfully go to the press," Olivia says, "because you're bound by Judge Henderson's confidentiality order."

"Actually, in America the duty to report crimes trumps confidentiality orders entered in civil cases," Burns says. "For obvious reasons, the authorities don't want lawyers who may know about crime to be gagged by anything. But I wouldn't have to go to the press, Olivia, because as you pointed out, Judge Henderson's likely going to vacate that confidentiality order next week anyway. And then the press'll get the transcript of this fascinating two days we've spent together, and they'll come to me. And I'd be free to show them these New Zealand documents, helpfully underlined, and I'm pretty sure they'd be able to connect the dots."

"So after all this pretense of a friendly meeting," Fiona says, "you're threatening me?"

"I am not threatening you, Fiona," Burns says. "Threatening you to induce you to settle a civil case would be extortion. I am not extorting you. You are free to do whatever you want to do. All I've done is tell you what I know about something that happened 145 years ago which might not even have been a crime, and how I have a theory about how the possible perpetrator of this possible crime might possibly still be alive, if someone wanted to bother to run some DNA tests on some old stamps, and on your blood. That kind of ambiguous stuff is nowhere near extortion, which is why your counsel hasn't stopped me from laying out this whole theory to you. And there's another reason I'm not threatening you."

Fiona glares at Burns. "What's that?"

"Joyce specifically instructed me not to threaten you," Burns avoids Joyce's eyes, and keeps talking fast, to be sure Joyce doesn't contradict him, "even though I advised her, as my client, that we could put you in a very tough spot, if I went to the authorities with all this. Joyce doesn't want that, Fiona. She still loves you. And frankly, I don't want it either. I only laid out my whole theory for you so you'd be motivated to think hard with Joyce and me about how we can settle this whole case, right now, and make everyone happy, even you."

"It's true, Fiona," Joyce says, picking up the ball and, to Burns's delight, running with it. "In spite of everything, I still love you, and I really don't want you to get hurt."

"Then why'd you sue me?" Fiona asks with a hard edge.

Burns almost answers, but decides he should let Joyce speak for herself.

Joyce takes a deep breath. "You have things that belong to me. The money from that land will make a huge difference in Lisa's life. And mine, too."

"What about the money from the codex?" Fiona asks.

Joyce hesitates. "I'll let David talk about that." Joyce takes a deep breath.

"That's— " Burns says.

"Sorry, David, I wasn't finished." Joyce takes another deep breath, and then words come tumbling out. "I just want you to know, Fiona, I was not the person who leaked all this to the press. I hate it that we promised you confidentiality, and then the rug got pulled out from under you. I know you think of me as a little sneak thief. But you're wrong, Fiona. I wasn't trying to steal the codex all those years ago. And I didn't leak this case to the press either. I'm not like that." Joyce turns to Burns. "That's all I wanted to say."

Burns smiles. "Anytime you wanna talk, Joyce, go right ahead. I think these ladies are sick of listening to me. And frankly, who can blame 'em?"

"No, David, they need to hear what you have to say," Joyce says. "Because I know it'll be fair. Just like I 'instructed' you." She shoots Burns a very fast sly smile, and then her face relaxes into an interested listener's expression.

Burns turns to Fiona and Olivia. "Well now you see what I'm up against. I want to be the 'hardball litigator' that Sara Hamilton and Clive think I am; but my client, who's the only one who matters, wants me to be fair. So I have no choice. Here's what I was thinking. And as you know, Olivia, most of the time when lawyers make offers, they start by asking for the moon, so they can seem reasonable when they gradually come down to what they really wanted all along. But unfortunately I can't do that here, because Joyce doesn't want me posturing like that. So this is the real offer. If Fiona doesn't like it, I truly have nowhere else to go."

"Enough with the preamble," Olivia says. "What's the bottom line?"

"Fiona quitclaims the land to Joyce," Burns says. "That's easy; we already won that. Joyce lets Fiona keep the codex. That's hard, because I really think I could win that one for Joyce. But settlements are supposed to be hard on everybody, so that's what Joyce gives up. Also, Joyce agrees that the entire settlement'll be confidential, and we'll make the new confidentiality agreement a binding part of the settlement, so even Henderson will never want to undo this one."

"And it'll apply to everyone – even your consultants?" Olivia asks.

"Especially our consultants," Burns says. "Even though, as I said before, I truly believe U of M leaked this story, in exchange for the kid-glove treatment they've received from the Observer."

"Well you've given us something to think about on that," Olivia concedes. "But normally I'd expect the *Observer* to be a little more subtle about it."

"Sara Hamilton strikes me as very green," Burns points out.

"She's brand new," Olivia confirms. "But the Observer has editors with plenty of experience dealing with confidential sources."

"Also, Sara's the 'Higher Education Correspondent'," Burns continues, "so it makes sense she might've found out about this case from the U."

"But Clive Phelps is also in higher education," Olivia counters, "and he's notorious for trampling patient confidentiality to curry favor with the press. This leak fits Clive's M.O. to the T."

"Maybe so," Burns says, "but that second article ridiculed Clive, and quoted no one in his defense. No newspaper does that to its own source."

"Maybe even the press is finally sick of Clive," Olivia says. "Look, all I know is, someone leaked those pleadings – and it sure wasn't Fiona."

"I agree, no one in this room leaked anything. But back to our offer. In exchange for Joyce letting Fiona keep the codex, and for a new bullet-proof confidentiality agreement, Fiona gives Joyce three things. First, Fiona signs an irrevocable document giving Joyce the codex when Fiona dies. I'm not sure exactly what that document will be, since Wills are always revocable; but I'm sure you and I can figure that out, Olivia. Second, Fiona, as Reynolds Foundation trustee, authorizes Joyce to make a copy of the U of M copy, ASAP. And third, Fiona agrees to tell Joyce and me now, off the record, where the fountain of youth is, how it works, and the gist of what's in the codex."

Burns puts on his best poker face, even though he assumes the third condition will get shot down, possibly on the spot. But to his surprise Fiona just sits there, looking at the *Lamanai Codex*, sitting on the edge of the desk.

"Will you give us a few minutes, David?" Olivia asks.

"Of course," Burns says. "But if you don't mind, I'd rather not go back and hang out with the Three Blind Mice just yet. Is there somewhere else Joyce and I can wait?"

"You may use the office we stopped in this morning," Olivia say, "if I may rely upon you and Ms. Kerr not to look at any of the papers on the desk in there?"

"Absolutely!" Burns says. "We'll just look out the windows and try to work out where exactly Clive's burglars came in off the river, James Bond style."

Burns and Joyce exit, and walk in silence to the other office, which allows Burns's words to rattle in his head longer than usual. Which lets his own Freudian slip hit him: 'Clive's burglars'.

"I'll bet they really were *Clive's burglars!*" Burns says, as soon as they close the door behind them in the unoccupied office.

"Now you have lost your mind." Joyce laughs. "But all that other stuff about Fiona being Kathleen, and she drank from the fountain of youth and it worked – you really think that's true?"

"Fiona sure seemed to be taking it seriously."

"When'd you figure all this out?"

"Last night after you went to bed. The hidden benefit of jet lag is, I have lots of time to spin crazy theories in the middle of the night. But stay with me about Clive a sec. This could be critical. You remember when we came here this morning, none of us knew about the burglary, right?"

Joyce nods.

"If anybody'd known, they'd've mentioned it in the cab," Burns says.

"No one knew till the constable at the door told us," Joyce says.

"Right. But that constable didn't say anything about *the river* – he just said the break-in came through the roof."

"No, but Olivia said the river," Joyce said.

"Yeah, but only *after Clive said it*. I'm positive Clive was the first one to say anything about the river, because I remember Ron was surprised, and said 'they came off the river?' – and *then* Olivia confirmed that the burglars used the river."

"You're right. I remember Ron saying that, too, and I remember Kip looked at Clive kind of funny. So okay, Clive was the first one to say it was the river. But what's that really prove?"

"How'd Clive know that? We were with him the whole time, from when we first heard about the burglary till he said 'river'; so who put that idea in his head?"

Joyce mulls this over a few seconds. "You're wrong."

"I am? Well, good, I suppose. I really don't like thinking of Clive as a bad guy. Even though he gets on my nerves. He's wound so tight."

"Look who's talking." Joyce gives Burns a nice kiss on the lips.

Burns folds his arms around her, but keep his hands from wandering. They are, after all, in a law office. "So why I am wrong about Clive and the river?"

"Because you stopped to flirt with Ivy," Joyce says. "And I stopped to – to keep an eye on your flirting, if you want the truth. But that meant the Three Blind Mice talked to the constable for a few seconds before we got there. That must be when Clive found out about the river."

"Hmmn," Burns frowns.

"You don't like it when I'm right and you're wrong, do you?" Joyce teases.

Burns kisses her on the mouth, long and slow. But to his eternal shame, instead of focusing on the softness of her lips, the sweetness of her breath, or other Shakespearean conceits, Burns is still thinking about Clive and the river.

"Actually, for the record, I love it when you're right and I'm wrong. And I admit I'm wrong plenty, Joyce. Which is one of many reasons I don't want to lose you as my paralegal."

"BUT—," Joyce says.

"How did you know there was a 'but' coming?"

"I could hear it coming as soon as you admitted you're wrong plenty. No way you'd say that, unless there was a really big 'BUT' coming."

"Well, you're right about that 'but', Ms. Know-It-All. But – BUT – you're wrong about Clive and the river."

"Why?"

"Because Ron was standing with Clive when they spoke to the constable outside our presence. Yet Ron was still surprised when Clive mentioned the river upstairs. If the constable told Clive about the river, it could only have happened when Ron was standing right there with Clive; but then Ron wouldn't have been surprised to hear about the river, just a minute later, up in the conference room."

Joyce leans back, not breaking their embrace, but far enough to get a better look at Burns's eyes. "You thought that up while you were kissing me?"

"Guilty as charged."

Joyce pretends to get indignant. "And here I thought I had your whole, undivided atten—"

Burns kisses her on the lips again, and this time lingers even longer.

"There," he says, gasping exaggeratedly, "I didn't think of anything but you that time."

"And as a result, it was better, wasn't it?"

Burns grins. "Much better."

"You need to learn to leave work behind sometimes."

"Fair point. But right now you need me to keep thinking. As your lawyer. Because we gotta figure out what to do about Clive."

"You mean, besides cut the little pretty boy's balls off?"

"Yes, besides that. And in a minute we're going to get their counter—"

A knock on the door interrupts Joyce. Olivia looks in. "We're ready."

Once Burns and Joyce settle back in their chairs in Olivia's office, Olivia says: "We have three very serious concerns you didn't cover in your offer."

"Only three?" Burns jokes. "I must be losing my edge."

Olivia does not smile. "Any one of these kills the deal, if you can't solve them for us. First is the transcript of this deposition you talked us into going ahead with. What good does it do Fiona to settle? Once the transcript becomes public, which it clearly will – Henderson'll rule against us, the press already knows about this depo, so they'll ask for the transcript – then all those things you threatened may happen anyway, even without your assistance. The press may connect the dots, the authorities may cave in to pressure, and Fiona may get a subpoena for a blood test."

"I did not threaten anything," Burns clarifies. "But I hear your concern. And I agree, it's a very serious concern. Here's the thing, though. In America, there's no press right of access to deposition transcripts, unless and until they're filed with the court. But if we settle, we're not gonna need to file anything, except a one-liner saying we settled confidentially."

Fiona frowns, and shakes her head no. "Sara Hamilton wasn't supposed to get the pleadings either. Yet she got those; so she'll get the transcript, too."

"And not just Sara Hamilton," Olivia adds. "The American press is on this story now, too. Copycat stories appeared yesterday in several American newspapers. We can't settle with you because the transcript of this deposition will take away the confidentiality we need in any settlement."

Burns nods. "Okay, but the transcript can only become public—" Burns hesitates, thinking it through, and then snaps his fingers "—if there's a transcript. So how 'bout we agree *not to order it*. I'm sure you can get Miguel to agree to that – if he won't agree, he might as well just write the Judge a letter that says 'I am the leaker'. But if no one orders the transcript, Ivy won't type it up, and there won't be anything for the press to get their hands on."

"Ivy'll still have it in her machine," Olivia says. "And on her backup tapes."

"We'll buy those from her." Burns turns to Fiona. "You trust Ivy, right?"

Fiona nods yes. "Ivy would never burn me."

Burns opens his palms. "Problem solved. There won't be any transcript to be leaked."

Olivia frowns awhile, but finally nods yes. "Okay, I agree. But this discussion leads right into our second concern. Even if there's no transcript, there were a lot of witnesses to this deposition. We need to plug the leak to the press. So we need to be able to go forward with our sanctions motion."

"That's fine with us," Burns says. "Joyce and I have nothing to hide. We can settle with you today, but hold off filing our notice of settlement with the court, until after the Judge holds a contempt hearing on your sanctions motion. That way you get your hearing, and I guarantee Judge Henderson will be relentless in trying to find out who the leak is."

Olivia looks at Fiona. Fiona looks at Joyce.

"Who do you think is the leak, Joyce?" Fiona asks.

"Not Clive," Joyce says. "He's a phony, like Olivia said. He bowls you over at first, with his great looks and fancy manners. Yet I can see he's not a good person. I wish I had never made any deal with him. But if you'd seen Clive's face when he first saw that Tuesday story, you'd know he wasn't the leak."

"What about the other two?" Fiona asks. "Dr. Graham and Mr. Hunter?"

"I'd be shocked if either one is the leak," Joyce says. "Ron seems like an honorable person – and by the way, Fiona, a huge fan of yours. Ron thinks you're the only Maya scholar who really understands the Maya, and makes sense."

"Is Mr. Hunter also an honorable person?" Fiona asks.

"No," Joyce concedes. "Kip is most definitely not an honorable person. But I know him a little better than the other two, and – well, if Kip was the leak, I'd know it. I'd *feel* it." Joyce shrugs. "I know that probably sounds a little lame, but I really don't think it's Kip."

"But if either Kip or Ron is the leak," Burns says, "or Clive, it's fine with us if they pay whatever price the Judge orders. So if we hold off formally entering the settlement until your motion is heard, does that address your concern?"

Fiona looks at Olivia, who nods yes.

"Our last concern may be the hardest of all for you," Olivia says. "But it's also a deal-breaker for us, if you can't give us what we need."

"Can I speak to this one, dear?" Fiona asks.

"Of course," Olivia says.

Fiona looks at Joyce. "You said I have things that belong to you. But if you believe Mr. Bur—er, David, who says I'm 167 years old, then you'll see why I feel those things are really still mine." Fiona smiles. "But I don't mind giving you the land now, and the codex when I pass. Not at all. I'm proud to see what a fine young woman you've become, dear. I see now I was terribly wrong to judge you so harshly when you were young. I truly apologize for that. And I want you to have my things, all of them."

Fiona reaches and picks up the *Lamanai Codex*, and cradles it in her lap.

"But this little book," Fiona continues, "is very seductive, and very dangerous. As much as I love it, I should've destroyed it, years ago, before I took the University job. But back then, as I'm sure you recall, translating the book was my only real joy in life, besides watching you grow up. And once I let the University make their copy, well, after that destroying the original would've served no purpose." Fiona looks up from the book, straight at Joyce. "The reason I contested your lawsuit was, I didn't want you to have a book that could do so much harm. Yet I see now that you will make good decisions about the codex, Joyce. I trust you. But I do not trust Dr. Phelps."

Joyce nods. "Me neither."

"If he gets his hands on the copy," Fiona says, "he'll get it translated by some smart young graduate student, and then he'll go find the fountain of youth, and bottle it and sell it, and many, many people will die. Because Dr. Phelps just doesn't understand that we're not supposed to play God like that."

Fiona and Joyce gaze at each other for awhile, evenly, with no words. Burns tries his best to stay quiet, but sometimes he just can't keep his trap shut.

"Clive says he can test the various components first," Burns says, "and assess the risks and tinker with—"

"Hogwash," Fiona says.

"So the bottom line is," Olivia interjects, "we'll agree to your entire offer, as long as you agree not to let Clive or your other consultants access the copy of the codex, and not to tell them any of what Fiona says to you in here, off the record. What Fiona tells you in here is for you two only; and the copy is for Joyce only. Otherwise there's no deal."

"When you say the copy is for Joyce only," Burns says, "you mean, for Joyce or people she deems trustworthy?"

Olivia frowns. But Fiona nods yes.

"But Joyce has already admitted she thinks Clive's a phony," Olivia clarifies. "So Dr. Phelps cannot be one whom Joyce allows to access the copy."

Burns looks at Joyce, and coughs. "That's a hard one for us."

"Because Clive agreed to pay your fees?" Olivia asks.

"No," Burns says, "because Joyce signed an agreement with Clive, promising him access to the codex or the copy, if she obtained either one."

"But what consideration did Clive give for Joyce's promise?" Olivia asks. "Clive's promise to pay your fees, right?"

"It's arguably a privileged agreement," Burns says. "So the specific ter—"

"I don't need to know the details," Olivia says. "My point is, if you waive your fees, that gets Joyce out of her obligation to Clive, for failure of consideration." In a slightly snide tone, Olivia adds: "*If* you'll waive your fees."

Burns snorts. "You may think I'm too greedy to waive my fees. But believe it or not, I offered to do this case for free, and Joyce wouldn't let me." He wags his finger at Joyce. "And now that's coming back to bite us in the butt."

"Why?" Olivia says. "If you waive your fees, Clive can't complain."

"I don't think it's that simple. Even if I waive my fees, and refund everything Clive's paid so far, Clive can still say he kept his end of the deal. He promised to pay any fees that were assessed; and he kept his promise. So he'll tell the court '*if Burns wants to waive his fees, that's his business; but in the meantime I'm entitled to what Joyce promised me: access to the copy*'."

"Then we can't have a settlement," Fiona says. "I'm sorry, Joyce. But I couldn't live with myself if I unleashed all kinds of misery on the world, without at least trying to stop it. I trust you, dear. But I don't trust Dr. Phelps at all."

Joyce nods. "I understand, Fiona. It's my fault. I should never have signed that deal with Clive. But I didn't want to take advantage of David. And I couldn't afford the fees any other way."

Olivia stands. "Well, thank you for your time, both of you. I admit this was more productive than I thought it'd be. And I'm sorry we can't find a way out of—"

"Wait." Burns holds up his hand. "Before we all give up, I might have a way out of this. It's tricky, and I can't promise anything till I go talk to Clive."

"He's still down the hall, isn't he?" Olivia asks.

"Unless he got impatient and left," Burns says, "which I seriously doubt. But the idea I've got will require me to stick my own neck out way further than I like. I really don't mind waiving my fees. But I do care about my freedom."

Burns looks out the window, where a lone seagull is guarding a nest on a derelict pier. He looks back at Fiona.

"Here's the deal, Fiona. It's illegal for anyone, even a lawyer, to threaten someone with criminal exposure just to get them to settle a civil lawsuit. That's called extortion. If I did that, I could go to prison."

"Well, you threatened me a few minutes ago," Fiona says. "I know you denied it was a threat, but that's what it was."

Burns smiles. "I understand it felt that way to you, Fiona. But legally I didn't threaten you. All I did was show you some highly ambiguous evidence I've collected about a crime that was maybe committed 145 years ago, by someone who might turn out to have the same DNA as you, if anyone were motivated enough to bother testing the DNA from you and some very old stamps. If I'd been anywhere near the extortion line, I'm sure Olivia would have put a stop to it right away. But with Clive, the leverage I have on him is about something far more recent, and the evidence I have may be a lot less ambiguous."

"So Clive *was* the leak!" Fiona cries.

"No, it's not about the leak. But it's better for all of us if I don't say what it is. All I want you to know is, I want this settlement to happen badly enough, for your sake and for Joyce's, that I'm willing to stick my neck out. But Clive's a very bright boy, and he can afford to go hire a real smart lawyer, so when I try to talk him into giving up his claims against Joyce, if I get too close to the extortion line, he'll crucify me. So if I'm going to run this very serious personal risk for you, Fiona, to clear this last problem, then I gotta know for sure we've got a deal, and you won't backtrack on me, or come up with any new conditions, or new problems, right?"

"You want to draft our settlement now, and everyone sign it?" Olivia asks.

"I don't need that now," Burns says. "You can write it up, when I go talk to Clive. What I need now is for Fiona to shake hands on our tentative deal with Joyce. Fiona's word is good enough for me."

Immediately Burns can see he pushed the right button. For the first time ever, Fiona smiles at Burns without sarcastic intent.

Joyce walks over to Fiona, and they shake hands.

"Give me a hug too, dear," Fiona says.

So Joyce bends, just as she did last night in her hotel room to kiss Burns, and hugs Fiona in her chair. Fiona and Joyce come out of the hug a little moist in the eyes. But only a little, because they're both cut from the same tough Quinlan cloth.

"The other thing I need, Fiona, is for you to trust me," Burns says. "I want you to tell me everything, off the record, just between the four of us, before I go in there to meet with Clive. I promise I'll never share any of it with Clive. But I need to know why I'm sticking my neck out like this. You understand?"

"You want me to tell you all about the fountain, where it is and how it works, and why the book's so dangerous," Fiona says, "*before* you talk to Clive?"

"That's right," Burns says. "And then I still might fail with Clive. But if I know why you think the fountain and the codex are so dangerous to mankind, I'll be fully motivated to do everything possible to get rid of Clive, including running risks I wouldn't normally run. And if I fail, you won't be bound by the tentative deal you and Joyce just shook hands on, because we can't deliver your third condition; and I still won't be able to use anything you tell me now against you."

Fiona looks at Olivia.

"You want Fiona to perform part of her obligations under our deal," Olivia says, "before we know for certain we have a deal?"

"That's right." Burns rises. "You should discuss this privately, while I go make sure Clive stays put. I'll tell him I'm not allowed to disclose any details of our discussion with you, but we need him to stay, in case we go on the record later. Then I'll just wait with Joyce in the other office, till you're ready."

"This is a very unorthodox request, David," Olivia says.

"I know. But what I have in mind for Clive is worse than unorthodox."

Chapter Fifteen
Execution Dock

Wednesday 6 April 2011 Late Morning

On his way to the conference room, David Burns catches a small break. Ivy Taylor's outside the conference room, on her way to the loo.

"Ivy!" Burns catches her arm. "I saw your cassette running when I left the conference room with Olivia. Thank you. But how soon did you turn it on?"

"Before I sat down," Ivy says. "Just like we talked about."

"Fabulous! We're probably gonna need that tape, to help Fiona as well as Joyce. So when I come back a little later this morning, and ask you to step outside, can you take the tape player with you and rewind the tape? So it'll be ready if needed."

"Is someone gonna complain about being taped?" Ivy asks.

"Maybe," Burns admits. "But if they do, I'll back 'em right off, and tell 'em it's standard practice. You won't need to say anything. Just look innocent."

Ivy strikes a provocative pose, worthy of a runway model. "Do I look innocent to you?"

Burns covers his eyes. "I plead the Fifth on that one. But if anyone makes trouble, Olivia and I'll both make sure nothing comes down on you. Okay?"

"Ja mon."

After asking Clive and the others, including Santos, to stay patient, Burns heads back for the unoccupied office. But Olivia Watt and Joyce intercept him.

"Well?" Burns asks.

"Fiona trusts you," Olivia says. "Is Clive still here?"

"Standing by," Burns says. "As long as we need him."

Olivia leads the way back to her office.

Fiona's standing by the east window, staring across the river.

"You have a great view, Olivia," Burns says. "What are we looking at?"

"Wapping," Olivia says.

"Where they used to hang the pirates?" Burns asks.

"I wouldn't know," Olivia says. "History's not my thing."

"That's right," Fiona says. "Execution Dock was at Wapping Old Stairs."

"The Dock's not there anymore?" Olivia asks.

"Rotted away," Fiona says, "before even I was born."

Burns moves right beside Fiona. "Where is Wapping Old Stairs?"

"There." Fiona points a gnarled and sun-spotted finger out at a bend in the river. "Right beside that old pub Dickens wrote about, the Town of something."

"The Town of Ramsgate," Olivia says. "I've been there. It's lovely."

"In the old days the Town of Ramsgate had a lovely view of the hangings," Fiona says. "And then for months after, they got to look at the corpses rotting in the tide."

"Ugh," Olivia says.

Out by the Town of Ramsgate pub, a battered old trawler chugs past an old pitch-covered piling, sticking out of the river. Burns points at the old piling.

"Is that a remnant of Execution Dock there?"

"Not likely," Fiona says. "But that's about where it was. Do you know why they built Execution Dock so far out in the river?"

"So all the sailors on the river could see the hangings?" Burns guesses.

Fiona shakes her head no. "Because Admiralty lacked jurisdiction on land. By law, they could only hang pirates at sea."

"The Thames counted as 'the sea'?"

"It's a tidal river. Mark my words, one day the Thames will overflow its banks, and wash this cruel city away." Fiona grabs her cane and walks back to her chair beside Olivia's desk.

They all sit down again.

Fiona looks at Burns. "You want to ask me more questions?"

"Why don't you just tell us what you think we need to know," Burns says.

Fiona nods. "Alright. But where should I begin?"

"Where's the fountain of youth?"

"You really don't know?" Fiona asks. "It's in my diary."

"No, it's not," Burns says. "Roger wouldn't let you write any details."

"But earlier, when I described India's painting, I wrote about the stairs in the cave with the fountain, that led up to a room '*with mysterious marks scratched onto the wall*'. I didn't realize it then, because I hadn't been to Lamanai – and by the time I did go there, I'd forgotton about that entry in the diary, or I'd've torn it out – but there's only one place at Lamanai with writing on the wall."

"The burial chamber in the Mask Temple," Joyce says.

"Yes," Fiona says. "The ancient Maya built the Mask Temple directly over the cave, to hide the entrance."

"That's why I heard oil birds there," Joyce murmurs.

Fiona nods; but suddenly looks concerned. "Has Clive seen the diary?"

"No," Burns says. "Only Joyce and I have seen it."

"But it's in the conference room right now?" Fiona asks.

"No, I've got the original," Burns says. "I borrowed it from Ivy this morning. And you've got the only copy."

"Thank God," Fiona says. "We wouldn't want Clive – or even Ron or Kip – to know where to look for that cave."

"Have I read about caves beneath Maya temples before?" Burns asks.

"Yes," Fiona says. "Three years ago an enterprising young archeologist took infrared photos of several Maya sites from a military plane. He found a few unknown caves, hidden right beneath old temples. Luckily Lamanai's a minor site, and relatively isolated, so they probably won't fly over it for quite awhile. Then again, they might fly over it tomorrow, for all I know."

"But Ron Graham must know about those flyovers," Burns says, "and the caves they found hidden under temples at other sites."

"Ron's a bright man," Fiona concedes. "He may already suspect there's a cave under the Mask Temple at Lamanai. But the entrance is very hard to find."

"Where is it?" Joyce asks.

"The sarcophagus is on a slab that rolls away. It's not as elaborate as the hidden door the Maya built into the floor of the Temple of Inscriptions at Palenque, because the Mask Temple at Lamanai is much older. But it's the same basic idea. If you push on the center of the *ourobouros* carved onto the side of the sarcophagus, the whole slab swings back on stone rollers."

"But tourists and archeologists stand in there all the time," Burns says. "How come no one's ever noticed the rollers?"

Fiona shrugs. "They're well hidden. Alberto Ruz worked inside the burial chamber at Palenque every day for four years, with no idea there was a hidden room below. One day in 1948 Alberto poked a stick in the right hole, tripped the lever, and almost killed his whole team when the entire floor rolled out from under them. The Mask Temple isn't quite so treacherous as that, but if you ever decide to go see the fountain, don't stand behind the sarcophagus when you push on the *ourobouros* – the slab rolls back much faster than you'd expect."

"Kip showed me an old pirate tale about a two-headed fertility icon that supposedly opens the door to the fountain of youth," Burns says. "Was that all malarkey?"

"No, it's true," Fiona says. "In the carving on the side of the Mask Temple sarcophagus, the center of the *ourobouros* is very deeply recessed, to avoid anyone accidentally tripping the lever. The oversized phallus on that two-headed fertility icon was perfectly fitted to enter the recessed hole in the *ourobouros*, and trip the lever. Other objects could probably trip the lever, too, but they'd have to be just the right circumference and length to fit in the hole."

"Do I detect pagan symbolism here?" Burns chuckles. "The fertility god makes love to the self-sustaining serpent carved on the coffin of the long-dead-but-still-venerated leader of Lamanai, which opens the door down to Xibalba, the land of the dead, where the fountain of youth flows?"

"You may find it humorous," Fiona scolds, "but it was serious business to the ancient Maya. And the fountain down there is still seriously lethal."

"Sorry." Burns tries to look contrite. Though contrition is not his strong suit.

"How'd you find that hidden door back in 1868?" Joyce asks.

"Your diary said it was funny circumstances," Burns adds.

"More embarrassing than funny." Briefly Fiona hides her face in her hands. "Oh, dear. Our last full day at Lamanai, it was raining cats and dogs. Roger wanted to make love, but the only dry place was the burial chamber in the Mask Temple. A young Maya shaman walked in on us *in flagrante delicto*. We assumed he'd be very angry with us for defiling the temple. But he viewed making love as the perfect form of worship in that place. When we told him we had the *Lamanai Codex*, and we'd come to find the fountain of youth, he did exactly what India Reynolds said he'd do: he took us to the fountain, and showed us what to do."

"But your diary said Xhuxh Antil was dead," Burns says.

"It was Xhuxh's successor who walked in on us," Fiona says. "Kux Ahawis. After Kux showed us what to inject, and what to drink, he expected us to give him the codex. But Roger refused. Roger felt he needed something tangible, besides the phial of fountain water he'd taken, and the samples of the herbs I'd saved, to validate his discovery claim. So we parted on very bad terms with Kux. In fact, we were fortunate our guide, Caesar, was in a rush to leave at the crack of dawn the next day. Because decades later, after Kux and I became friends, Kux told me he came back that next day with a band of warriors, to take the codex away from us by force. But we'd already headed down the river with Caesar."

"Where'd you save the samples of the herbs?" Joyce asks. "In your diary?"

Fiona looks horrified. "Don't tell me they're still in there?"

"No, there's nothing inside the diary now," Burns says.

"They fell out when I first opened it," Joyce says. "But I saved them."

"Oh, do take pains to ensure Dr. Phelps never gets those!" Fiona says. "Those are the missing pieces of the puzzle Clive's seeking, the ingredients he can't identify for the formula he's trying to reconstruct from the autopsies."

"Clive thinks the herbs were derived from coclmeca and gangweo," Joyce says, "because he found something close in all the cancer victims' stomachs."

"He's close," Fiona says, "but those are special variants of coclmeca and gangweo, which the Lamanai shamans grew only for use in the fountain ritual."

"Did Kux know how to grow the variants of those herbs?" Burns asks.

"Yes," Fiona says "although Kux wanted to look at the codex last summer, now that we know how to read it, to be sure he had the variants right."

"But you wouldn't let Kux see the codex last summer," Burns says, "and no one could read it back in 1868. So how'd Kux know what to do when he took you and Roger there – and how'd he know what to do there this past fall?"

"For centuries," Fiona says, "a small group of Maya shamans have passed the knowledge of how to grow the variants down the generations. Xhuxh told Kux, and I'm sure Kux told the young men who went to Lamanai with him last autumn. And the amulets Kux and his followers wore contain a scroll with most of the formula."

"What exactly did you and Roger drink and inject?" Burns asks.

"Kux mixed the herb variants of coclmeca and gangweo into the fountain water," Fiona says, "which is rich in sulphur and salt, and we drank it. Then Kux burnt the end of a bone needle, to sterilize it – something the Maya figured out, centuries before Europeans did – and we injected the muscles nearest our private parts with cinnabar diluted in fountain water. So the 'formula' is what Clive has deduced – except he doesn't know the proportions, or the precise herb variants."

"How do you know what Clive has deduced?" Burns asks.

Fiona covers her mouth. "Oh dear, I shouldn't have said that."

"Well then, Mr. Burns will drop it," Olivia interjects. "Won't you, David?"

"Yeah, that's fine," Burns mutters, though he's dying to know the answer. Does Fiona have a spy in Clive's lab? How else could she know his deductions and thoughts? But why would she feel guilty telling Burns – unless the spy's Kip or Ron?

"Did you have any physical reaction from those substances?" Olivia asks, filling in the awkward silence resulting from Burns's last question.

"The water smelt dreadful," Fiona says, "but Kux told us to be sure not to vomit, or we'd lose the benefit of the herbs. I was also very tender from the injection, and Roger and I both had unspeakable diarrhea for several days after. It made the journey back down The River of Strange People most disagreeable."

"If Kux knew the formula, why'd he want the codex so bad?" Burns asks.

"It's a sacred book which pirates stole from the Maya," Fiona says, "or rather, pirates stole from Father Sanchez, who was keeping it safe for the Maya. Kux felt it was high time for the book to be returned to the Maya. Also, he felt Roger and I owed him the book, for taking us through the ritual at the fountain of youth."

"Did Kux warn you the fountain of youth might kill you?" Burns asks.

"Yes, he warned us," Fiona says. "Though Kux didn't understand the full extent of the danger, which is set forth in the *Lamanai Codex*, because that knowledge was lost over the centuries. But he warned us it was a risky proposition."

"Why'd Kux take you to a fountain normally used only by Maya shamans?"

"Because we had the book," Fiona says, "and because Kux held Roger in very high esteem, for running so many guns to the Maya rebels in Mexico."

"The English gunrunner who stole the book," Burns murmurs.

"What?" Fiona asks.

"Nothing – just thinking out loud," Burns says.

"You have to speak up for me," Fiona says. "My hearing is starting to go."

"How'd you later become friends with Kux, after parting on such bad terms in 1868?"

"In 1909, when I fled from my own son's warrant, I sought Kux out. By that time he'd moved up to the mountains, and become a great leader of the Maya in Guatemala. That's when I got my nose ring, to blend in better with the San Lorenzo villagers, in case Lloyd's detectives came looking for me. Kux and I made peace then, and I promised Kux I'd return the codex one day, but I wanted to keep it till I figured out how to translate it. But then when I finished my translation, I decided I had to break that promise to Kux, because the contents are just too dangerous."

"So your translation is complete?" Burns asks.

Fiona hesitates. "You can't use this against me, right?"

"I'm not planning to use anything against you anymore, Fiona."

"I finished years ago. But my translation's even more dangerous than the codex, because it's written in a living language. I should probably destroy it – but I can't bear to, because it was my life's work. Yet I also can't bear to look at it. So I put my translation away in a safe deposit box at the Bank years ago. That's why the thieves last night couldn't find it in my flat."

"Maybe you should keep the codex at the Bank, too," Burns suggests.

"I have four police locks on the door to my flat, and an alarm by my bed. You'd think that'd suffice." Fiona sighs. "I need the codex by me. It's my last link to Roger. And to the past."

Fiona stares out the window at a Thames Water Police boat, racing by.

Burns leaves her alone a few moments, but then to get her talking again, he asks: "How does the Reynolds Foundation fit in with the codex?"

"It doesn't. As you said, I spent the Foundation money on myself. I'm not proud of that. But it wasn't as bad as you made it sound. When Roger died, I was distraught – and terrified I'd soon be dead, too. That's how I forgot my journal was in amongst Roger's papers, when I donated them to the British Museum. But when I saw I was going to live, I was flat broke with a new baby. Lloyd." Fiona rolls her eyes. "Slavery was finished, India was dead, and I was so very tired of being poor. The Foundation money gave me the security Roger's death had taken from me."

"I'm not judging you, Fiona," Burns says. "I'm just wondering how the 1970 U of M contract about the copy got written with the Foundation as a party."

"That was for you." Fiona smiles. "Even though you were only a lad in 1970, I was always worried this day might come. After all, I'd stolen the codex from Lloyd, in violation of Breakey's order. For decades no one cared about the codex, but in the 1960s, when we started cracking the Mayan code and translating the glyphs, other scholars started pressuring me to share the codex. I was worried someone might investigate the codex's provenance, and challenge my legal right to it. Then I remembered the Reynolds Foundation. I'd never shut the Foundation down, because I felt so guilty about taking almost all the money. I saw I could use the Foundation, as a shield."

"So you weren't thinking of me personally," Burns says, "just some lawyer, somewhere, coming after you, on some unknown day?"

"Yes – as of 1970. But when you began helping Justin Kerr in the 1980s with his legal problems, I began to expect it'd be you personally, David, who'd come after me." Fiona turns to Joyce. "And that's why I flew off the handle at you that summer day in 1990, dear. By then I'd translated enough of the codex to know how dangerous it is, and I'd become so worried about Justin discovering his legal right to it and selling it to pay his legal fees, that I decided to retire and move to London. When I caught you holding the codex, I was sure all the chickens had come home to roost. So I lashed out at you. I'm sorry I hurt you so much, dear."

Joyce looks down at the carpet, but nods acceptance of the apology.

Fiona looks at Burns. "I tried to make karmic amends to the Foundation, when I laid down in front of a digger last year to try to stop demolition of India Reynolds' old art studio in St. Thomas Street. But in the end my bad deed of taking the Foundation money and the paintings caught up with me, when you found that old Bank letter. If I'd known that letter was in those old files, I'd've thrown it out, though Olivia told me that's not allowed. But I never knew it was written, and I'm too old to read 17 boxes of records – and I didn't expect your questions to go so far back in time."

"Well I'm almost out of questions now," Burns says. "But I'm curious – does the *Lamanai Codex* say why the ancient Maya abandoned their cities?"

"No, although it was written in the last quarter of the 9th century, just before the Collapse, which places it much closer to the mystery than the four other codices extant. But the *Lamanai Codex* only tells about Lamanai, which was always fairly isolated from most of Maya civilization.

"But what the *Lamanai Codex* does tell us, which is a vital lesson, is that the Lamanai people walked out on their leaders because of the fountain of youth. Over the centuries the shamans there had stumbled, through trial and error, on the formula of mixing the cinnabar and herbs with the sulphur water, and drinking part of the mixture while injecting the other part. And they had learnt, from bitter experience, that although the fountain of youth doubled the life span of a few lucky ones whose constitutions were strong enough to withstand the assault of those substances on the human body, they could not predict who exactly would be so lucky. They knew that each person who went through the ritual had a 13 in 14 chance of dying within a few months."

"Even Clive would have to admit," Burns says, "those are some seriously bad odds."

Fiona nods, very serious. "In the beginning, only the shamans and rulers went through the ritual, and those who died from the fountain of youth regarded it as a great honor to serve their Gods and their people in this way. They'd bring a group of young men from the upper class to the fountain, knowing only about 1 in 14 would survive; but the ones who survived would become the religious and political leaders of Lamanai. Like all the Maya, the people at Lamanai venerated the wisdom of their elders – but at Lamanai, the elders lived to be far older than anywhere else.

"But problems arose when the shamans began injecting commoners, hoping to discover, through trial and error, whether some types of people were more likely to survive the fountain. Basically, the shamans were doing what Clive would call gene research – looking for people like me, who happen to have the right genetic make-up to survive the chemical onslaught without developing massive cancer. People who can be tinkered with – and maybe bred – to live far longer than God intended. But the Maya at Lamanai learned what Clive'll also learn, if he ever works out the formula and starts fooling around like that: people won't stand for someone playing God.

"At Lamanai, the people revolted. There was a very bloody civil war, the leaders were killed, many thousands died, and the city was forever abandoned. Which is what would happen in our time, too, if some doctor, or drug company, or western nation, ever developed the capability to double the lives of a few people, while the rest either die in the experiment, or live normal length lives. People wouldn't stand for that. And you can bet your life, there'd be blood in the streets."

"But even without the *Lamanai Codex*," Burns says, "Clive might develop the precise formula anyway. Like you said, he already knows the ingredients, from testing the tissues of Kux's followers for every substance under the sun. All he has to do is find the variants of the herbs, and get the proportions right."

"Right now Clive thinks there's still another element he hasn't identified," Fiona says. "Ron says that's why Clive's obsessed with finding the fountain – he thinks he can't find the missing element, without testing the actual waters."

At the sound of Ron's name, Burns raises an eyebrow, and catches Olivia's eye. Fiona picks up on Olivia looking extremely uncomfortable.

"Oh dear, I didn't mean to say that," Fiona says. "Ron didn't tell me your strategy or anything like that. He just keeps an eye on Clive. For safety's sake."

"It's alright," Burns says. "I'll forget I even heard his name in here."

"You're obliged to," Olivia admonishes, "as part of our agreement that what Fiona says in here doesn't go beyond us four. But rest assured, this firm would never have permitted Fiona to obtain from that source any of your confidential information or internal litigation strategies or such. We were assured that the information the source provided was strictly limited to medical matters that have never been at issue in this litigation."

Burns stifles a very strong desire to tell Olivia to get off her friggin' high horse and eat a little humble pie, now that she's been caught with her hand in the cookie jar. But that would serve no good purpose. So Burns puts on a genial smile instead. "It's okay, really. No harm, no foul."

"Based on what Ron says," Fiona says, "I'm hoping Clive remains obsessed with identifying the missing element for some time. It took the ancient Maya centuries to find the formula. Right now, Clive's only got another 50 years or so."

"But one day some scientist will find the formula," Burns says. "If not Clive, then one of his colleagues. Or students. Or rivals. Sooner or later, it'll be found."

"Which is another reason I've never destroyed the *Lamanai Codex.*" Fiona turns to Joyce. "Because the day may come, dear, when you may have to publish it – along with my translation – as a warning to the world."

Joyce nods, looking very serious. Burns gazes at Joyce a moment, trying to guess what she's thinking. But as usual, Joyce looks like a modern version of the Sphinx: utterly inscrutable – though a little more wry than the original Sphinx.

Fiona evidently misinterprets Burns's silence as an expectation that she'll keep talking, even though Burns feels Fiona's covered all the essential points.

"So I guess that just leaves the question of whether I'm a murderess." Fiona looks out at the river, avoiding eye contact with everyone, even her lawyer.

"Fiona," Olivia says, "you don't have to—"

"I don't suppose you'll believe me," Fiona says to the river, not acknowledging Olivia, maybe not even hearing her, "but I honestly don't know. I admit, in my heart I wanted my old girlfriend dead. And I admit, at that moment, with Roger dragging us out of that dark cavern, and scores of people drowning all around us, I distinctly remember thinking no one would ever know, if I gave Catherine a little shove. The way everyone else was dropping like stones and vanishing beneath the waves, I knew if I gave her just the slightest push, sick as she was, in that icy water she'd fall 20 fathoms down to the ocean floor, and never be seen again. But God's truth is, I honestly don't know what happened, in the final thrashing about.

"The witnesses at the Inquiry were right to be confused. It was sheer pandemonium in that water. The water was so icy cold, it numbed our minds, as well as our limbs. And long before we got swept into that icy water, we were already thoroughly exhausted, all of us, not just from being awake all night, but more from the strain of knowing, each instant of that long night, that we were probably going to die. You can't imagine the stress of those eight long hours, waiting to die. I still see those huge ugly cliffs, looming like a monster in the dark. I still feel us getting sucked into that cavern, like a giant octopus had grabbed the whole ship. I still feel the rocks pounding the ship, every few seconds, all night long; and the ship slowly breaking apart, and the timber falling all around us, and we're huddled back there, praying for light, but assuming the ship'll break apart at any moment and we'll all be thrown into the deep, freezing sea.

"And there were so many false hopes. Just like always in life. When first we bounced outside the breakers, we thought perhaps the rip tide would save us – even though we knew the odds were very long against us. Then when we were wedged in the cavern, but the ship didn't sink, we thought we could hang on till dawn – even though we could hear the falling rocks blasting the front and middle of the ship to smithereens. And then, when the light came, we thought we could get away in the lifeboats – another false hope. And when Roger saved me, I thought we'd be ferried to safety, and picked up in a few weeks – not 18 months.

"And the falsest of all the false hopes was my belief, when we first landed at Sarah's Bosom, and I told the others I was Mrs. Quinlan, that at last I was free of Catherine, free of Oxford, free of the past. But as Mr. Joyce so wisely wrote decades later, 'we walk through ourselves'. And these past 145 years, I've never escaped my memories of that awful night in the cavern.

"And neither did Roger. He truly believed he murdered Catherine. I don't say this to lay blame off on Roger; I say it only to show how murky the incident was. Roger said after he dumped most of his gold, and found Catherine and me in the water, and was pulling us free of the others, he caught a glimpse of Captain Loughlin up on the rigging, ghosts in his eyes, waving his white handkerchief as the big ship went under. Roger thought then the Captain's face was the face of death. But afterwards he said the face of death turned out to be, for Roger, the face he saw every night when he closed his eyes, the rest of his earthly life: the face of the wife he chose not to save.

"Because that's what Roger thought happened. That's why he carried Catherine's picture with him, in a small locket, till I finally pawned it in Belize City, to try to free Roger from her haunting. I used to tell Roger, *no one thinks you killed Catherine. Mr. Ellis and Mrs. Jewell say I killed her, though they never accused me once the entire 18 months we were cast away on Auckland Island. But no one thinks you killed her, Roger.* To free him from his guilt, I even tried telling Roger that I definitely did it, that I pulled his arm down just like Mr. Ellis said, and pushed Catherine down, and propelled myself off her plummeting body to save myself, just like Mrs. Jewell said. But Roger didn't believe me.

"And I didn't believe me either. Oh, I wanted Catherine dead. And somewhere deep down in his heart, so did Roger. Which means we were guilty of wishing we could do what only God should do: determine how long a person's span of days shall be. And for our sins God punished Roger and me by letting us find the fountain of youth at Lamanai – another place where people have been guilty of trying to usurp God's prerogative to determine how long a person's span of days shall be. And then He showed us how arbitrary and cruel life can be, when people try to meddle in His business. God granted me the long life I thought I wanted – but only after taking Roger away forever. Then he left me here on earth, alone and loveless, with my long memory.

"In my youth I assumed God did not exist, because he never spoke to me. I thought of God as a fiction invented to try to keep wild hearts like mine from living and loving as freely and naturally as people like the Maya do. Later, after what happened in that awful cave, I assumed that even if there is a God, He'd surely turned his back on me. So I stole the Foundation money and the paintings, without remorse, and I stole love from other women's husbands without remorse, too. I even considered suicide, though I soon discovered I lacked the courage for that dark deed. A deed much easier said than done, it turns out. But I thought of God in those days as the harsh God of Matthew Arnold, condemning each of us to live alone, like so many separate islands – the God 'who bade betwixt our shores to be/The unplumb'd, salt, estranging sea'.

"But after I faked my suicide and fled from Ann Arbor, to live among the Maya, Kux Ahawis taught me to think differently about God. He persuaded me that God takes many forms, and speaks many languages, on many different frequencies. He may speak Spanish to Catholics, or K'iche' Mayan to Kux, or He may, with people like me, speak in no language at all, but instead just let the events of my own life be His message to me. And so it was, after many years with the Maya, that I came to feel the *Lamanai Codex* was given to me as both a gift and a burden, and that the only way to redeem my many sins was to guard the dangerous knowledge I gained from my visit to the fountain of youth.

"Yet for all my efforts to redeem myself, I still do not know if I am a murderess. All I know is, Roger's arm went down. Maybe I pulled it; maybe Roger lowered it on purpose; or maybe his arm just got tired and dropped. Then we all thrashed about a few seconds, and Catherine went under. Maybe I pushed her; maybe Roger pushed her; or maybe she just dropped like a stone. She was by far the weakest of the three of us, and she'd been quite ill. But I'll never know.

"All I really know is, I redeemed the locket I pawned in Belize – Roger's wedding locket, stolen from me last night – so that, along with wearing on my finger the ring Roger gave me in Belize, I should also have to wear round my neck, all my life, Catherine's wedding photograph. Partly as penance, partly as remembrance – but mostly as simple self-punishment."

Fiona stops speaking. A long silence ensues, in which the only sound is the distant slapping of the tide, eight stories below, against the building.

Fiona stares out at the river. Burns looks out there, too, watching the random traffic on the Thames – a sleek glass tourist boat, a couple of tiny kayaks, and an empty barge, leaving a huge V-shaped current in its wake.

Burns wishes he could think of the right thing to say; but he can't.

At last Joyce walks over to Fiona and gives her cousin a squeeze on the shoulders. Fiona nods, but still won't look at Joyce, or anyone.

Burns stands, and signals to Joyce and Olivia he's going down the hall to talk to Clive. He closes the door; but almost at once the door opens again, and Joyce steps out into the hall.

"Please be careful," Joyce says.

"With Clive?" Burns asks. "Or when I go drink at the fountain of youth?"

Joyce's eyes open wide. "No! She said it's 13 to 1 you die there. Don't you believe her?"

"Sure I do. But I gotta do something to close the 12-year gap between you and me."

"The gap's already closing," Joyce says, "because I feel so awful I put you in this position. If you don't get back here real quick, my worry lines are gonna be dug in so deep, your new girlfriend's gonna look like a wrinkled prune."

* * *

"Miguel, Ivy, can you give us a few minutes alone?" David Burns asks.

"Sure," Miguel Santos says.

"No problem." Ivy Taylor rises, and picks up her cassette player.

"You can leave your steno machine here for now," Burns says.

Ivy looks up, a little surprised; but then she gets it, and waives the cassette player. "I just need to rewind my backup tape."

Nice touch. Like it's her regular routine. Burns smiles at Ivy, and nods.

Ivy leaves, cassette player in hand. Santos follows her out.

The Brethren of the Coast are standing by the window, their backs to the river. Burns joins them in a circle, with Kip to his left, Ron to his right, and Clive opposite. Burns holds up one hand to shield his eyes from the glare of sunshine reflecting off the glassy high-rise across the river.

"Looks like we should claim the north side of the table today," Graham says.

"Probably won't be a depo today," Burns says, shifting to stand closer to Graham, so he's not looking straight into the sun's harsh reflection.

"Does that mean we have a settlement?" Hunter asks.

"Almost," Burns says.

"Fantastic!" Hunter says.

"What're the terms?" Phelps asks.

"I'm not allowed to say," Burns says.

"Under my contract with Joyce, you're required to tell me the terms of any settlement," Phelps says. "You need these gentlemen to leave us alone?"

"No, I'd like them to stay," Burns says. "And actually, it's *Joyce* who's required by that contract to tell you the terms of any settlement, not me."

"Well, then, where's Joyce?" Phelps demands impatiently.

"She's catching up with her cousin. But even Joyce can't tell you the *proposed* settlement terms, till we clear the last two hurdles and it's fully agreed."

"Are we allowed to know what the last two hurdles are?" Phelps asks.

"Yes," Burns says. "One is, Fiona remains very angry about the leaks."

"So am I," Phelps says. "Yesterday's article will put a serious dent in my grant-raising."

"I told them you're as unhappy as they are about the leak. Though I had to concede you're far more adept at working the press than Fiona is. But in the end, I think we'll get by that issue. I've offered to let them go forward with their sanctions motion, and have a full-blown contempt hearing with Judge Henderson, before we enter the settlement. Anyone got a problem with that?"

Burns searches the faces of the Three Fools, but no one objects.

"Olivia's mulling that idea over right now," Burns says.

"What's the other hurdle to the settlement?" Phelps asks.

"Olivia wants to know how you knew the burglars came in off the river."

Phelps blinks, then opens his palms, all innocence. "Someone mentioned it this morning."

"Who?" Burns asks.

"Not sure, really," Phelps says. "Why is this important?"

"Because Olivia's obsessing about it," Burns lies. "It is her law firm that just got broke into, after all. Can you remember where you heard that the burglars came off the river?"

Phelps knits his handsome face into a look of intelligent concentration. "From Olivia, wasn't it? When she ushered us all up here."

"No," Burns says, "you were the first one in this room to mention the river."

"No, actually I was not." Phelps's rich baritone voice is firm and filled with confidence, though still quite pleasant. "I'm absolutely certain it was Olivia."

"How many times this week," Burns counters, "did you hear me ask Ivy to read back one of Fiona's answers so I could get the exact words?"

"I don't know," Phelps says.

"Never," Hunter interjects. "Do you have an eidetic memory?"

"No," Burns says, "just a damn good memory for what gets said."

"It's quite a useful gift," Hunter says.

"Yes and no," Burns says. "My social life suffers from it. But my point is, Clive, unlike you, Olivia and I have both been trained, by years of depositions, to listen to who says what, and to be able to spit it back verbatim, much later. And I can tell you, Olivia's right: you were the first person in this room to say 'river'."

"He's right, Clive," Graham adds. "I remember I was surpris—"

"Well then," Clive interrupts, "I must have heard it from someone else."

"Who?" Burns asks. "Who'd you talk to about the burglary, Clive, before we came up here to the conference room?"

Phelps hesitates, but then brightens. "The constable downstairs!" Phelps says triumphantly. "He must've told me they came in off the river."

"Ron," Burns says, "when we first came up to this room, you were quite surprised to hear about the burglars coming off the river, weren't you?"

"Floored." Graham turns to Clive. "Don't you remember me saying 'wow', or something?"

"No, I don't remember that," Phelps says.

"I do," Burns says. "What Ron actually said was 'they came off the river?' in response to you saying 'only the best guys can come in off the river', because it 'takes special equipment and training'. Then, after Olivia confirmed that you were right about the burglars coming off the river, and added the fact that they used a boat with a crane, *that's* when Ron said 'wow, that is a lot of effort to break into a law firm'."

"Alright," Phelps says. "So that just shows I must've heard it from the constable downstairs. Like I just said. What's all the fuss about here?"

"You couldn't have heard it from the constable downstairs," Burns says, "because Ron was right next to you the whole time you were talking to the constable, and Ron didn't hear anything about the burglars coming off the river."

Even as he's uttering what he thought was a can't-lose line, Burns sees a way out for Clive: the constable's Cockney accent. If Phelps is fast, he'll say Graham must not've understood the constable any better than Burns, who couldn't follow a word the constable said. So Burns moves fast to distract Phelps from thinking about that Cockney constable, with a new false hope.

"So is there anyone else, Clive, whom I can tell Olivia you talked to, where you must've heard about the river entrance?" Burns gives Phelps a sympathetic look. "I know this is annoying as hell, but we're so close to a settlement, which we all want; yet Olivia's on the warpath about this break-in – as you or I would be, if our offices were burgled – so I gotta clear this up for her."

Phelps nods, and knits that handsome brow again in concentration. After a solid minute, he shrugs. "Sorry, I can't think of anyone else. And I'm sorry to have to challenge the memory you plainly pride yourself on, David, but my colleagues – who are, after all, the world's top scientists – always defer to my memory, in any context, because my memory is widely regarded as infallible. And I am absolutely certain: Olivia was the first to say the burglars came in off the river."

"But Olivia's absolutely certain," Burns says, "you were the first one to say 'river'. If I go back and just say you deny it, that won't get us over the hurdle."

Burns notes that Phelps isn't asking Hunter what he remembers. Since it's already three against one, it seems like Phelps has little to lose by asking. On the other hand, Phelps probably doesn't want to ask because the question itself would implicitly concede that the memories of others matter. Or maybe he's worried Hunter'll jump on the chance to stab Phelps in the back.

"Well then, why not tell Olivia I must've *assumed* it?" Phelps turns and gestures at the river behind him, framed by the window. "Not an unreasonable assumption, for an office building that is, after all, located right on the Thames."

"Actually, it'd be a ridiculous assumption, Clive," Burns says. "This is an eight-story building with a sheer face of floor-to-ceiling windows on the river side that even Batman couldn't climb with his Bat-feet. So to come off the river, you'd have to use a boat with a crane. But no one would assume the burglars catapulted acrobatically off a boat with a crane to get on the roof, when there are two adjacent apartment buildings, with roofs the same height, which any burglar with half a brain could enter. So everyone would assume, if they heard of a skylight break-in, that the burglars simply walked over from one of the two easily-accessed adjacent roofs, rather than catapulting off a crane from a boat out in the river."

"If a river entrance is such a ridiculous assumption," Phelps counters, smiling, "and it's so much simpler to enter this building off the roof of an adjacent building, then why did the real burglars, in point of actual fact, choose to enter via the river?" Phelps's face tightens around his smile, his eyes glinting with confidence that Burns cannot refute this argument.

"Because these particular burglars had been instructed to be prepared to make a second stop," Burns says, "in case the codex wasn't here at Symington & Watt. And when the codex turned out not to be here, then, in point of actual fact, old chap, they moved a short ways down Shad Thames to Fiona's flat – a flat that can only be entered by very acrobatic burglars catapulting themselves onto Fiona's balcony off a crane on a boat in the river, because Fiona is a legendary hermit who never opens her door to anyone, and breaking down Fiona's door, with its four police locks, would take so long and make so much noise that the police would arrive long before the burglars got inside to search for the codex."

Burns flashes Phelps a mirror-image of Phelps's own tight-faced smile, now fading fast. Phelps's jaws twitch with anger, and he almost glares, but then his face relaxes back into his usual arrogant, yet confidently genial, countenance.

"Well, David," Phelps says, "you asked me to help you find another argument for Olivia. Yet each time I do, you shoot it down. Hence I can only conclude you don't truly desire my help on this. But at the end of the day, the simple truth is: Olivia was the first, in this room, to say 'river' – and she can't prove otherwise."

"Unfortunately, she can." Burns looks at Phelps with dead eyes, and lets the silence grow thick. "There's a tape recording," he finally adds.

"What?" Phelps hisses. "Someone's been secretly taping us?"

"Not secretly," Burns says. "Whenever a court reporter sets up for a deposition, the first thing she always does is turn on her backup tape. It runs all the time, except when she's out of the room, like now. I know for a fact Ivy's tape was on this morning, 'cause I noticed it running."

"Have you listened to this tape?" Phelps asks.

"No," Burns admits. "So if you're feeling lucky, we can bring Ivy back in, and listen to that tape right now. And if I'm wrong, I'll owe you a major league apology, Clive. But if I'm right – and I guarantee you I am – then we'll all have a problem. Because once we listen to that tape, then it's evidence of a crime, and I'll be ethically obliged to turn it over to Scotland Yard. Right now, like you said, it's just my memory – well, and Olivia's and Ron's memories, too – that you were the first to say 'river'. But like you said, memories are fallible, so we really don't have any 'evidence' to turn over to Scotland Yard at this point. I could be wrong. Olivia and Ron could be wrong. But tape recordings are like fingerprints. They aren't fallible."

"What do you want, Burns?" Phelps asks, his voice now hard and cold.

"I want you to hire a solicitor," Burns says, "and—"

"You're my solicitor," Phelps says.

"No, I'm not," Burns corrects. "I'm Joyce Kerr's attorney."

"I pay your bills," Phelps says. "You're my solicitor – attorney. Whatever."

"No, I'm not your attorney, Clive," Burns repeats, "and I'm not your solicitor either. My professional duty is to Joyce, and only to Joyce."

"Then Joyce has a duty to me," Phelps says, "through our contract."

"Joyce's contractual obligations to you," Burns says, "are entirely different from the professional duty a lawyer owes a client."

"Don't split hairs with me," Phelps says.

"I'm not splitting hairs at all," Burns says. "A lawyer's professional duty to his client is vastly different from a mere contractual obligation."

"You have a professional duty to protect me, since I'm paying Joyce's legal bills. If you don't protect me, I'll see to it you go up on serious charges."

"There are no claims or 'charges' you can bring against me, Clive," Burns says, "because I owe you no duty. You're not my client. The fact that you agreed to pay Joyce's legal bills creates no duty between me and you."

"Well then I'm going to retain my own solicitor for this," Phelps says.

"Exactly what I just asked you to do," Burns says. "And then I want you to run by your solicitor an idea I have, which is the best way out of this mess for everyone, including you."

"I'm all ears," Phelps says.

"First understand," Burns says, "it would be illegal for me to propose that you release Joyce from your contract with her, in exchange for my promise not to report you to the authorities. You know why it would be illegal for me to do that?"

"That's extortion," Phelps says.

"Precisely," Burns says. "So be sure to tell your solicitor, Burns is well aware of the laws against extortion, and he's not proposing anything like that."

"Then what are you proposing?" Phelps demands, impatiently.

"As part of the settlement Fiona and Joyce have almost reached, I'm gonna buy from Ivy all the steno sheets, and all the backup tapes, from these past three days. There won't be any other record of what happened here this week, including what happened in our little meeting first thing this morning. Then I'm gonna put everything I buy away in a bank deposit box, without ever listening to the tape from this morning. That way I won't have any obligation to report you, because like you said, human memories are fallible. And that safe deposit box won't ever be opened, unless someone gives me a reason to consider opening it. Think of it as Pandora's Box. A box that's better for everyone if it just stays shut."

"What would be a reason for you to open the box?" Phelps asks.

"You mean a reason for me to *consider* opening the box? Well, if someone tried again to steal the codex or the copy, that'd be a reason I'd consider opening the box. If some violence were done to Joyce or Fiona or me, that'd certainly be a reason I, or my executor if I were to end up dead, would consider opening the box. A story in the press about the details of Fiona's deposition would make me consider opening the box. Or if you were to try to enforce your contract rights against Joyce, that'd be a reason I'd consider opening the box."

"This is extortion," Phelps says.

"No, it's not," Burns says. "Ask your solicitor. All I'm saying is, I plan to do nothing with the tape that'll be resting safe inside Pandora's Box. Meanwhile you're entirely free to choose whether you pursue your contract rights against Joyce to try to access either the codex or the copy. And if you do, I'll be free to open Pandora's Box, or not, as I choose. And you wanna know the best part?"

Phelps stares at Burns, but doesn't bite.

"You have six years to make up your mind," Burns says. "That's how long the statute of limitations is on any contract claims you might want to bring against Joyce. So you have six years to sit back and be sure that I'm really not going to open that box, before you have to decide finally what you're going to do."

"How long is the statute of limitations on whatever you think I might be charged with?" Clive asks.

"I have no idea," Burns says. "I'm not an English lawyer, and I couldn't ask Olivia, 'cause I didn't want her to know I had any inkling about who might have been behind the burglary of her offices and Fiona's flat. As you can imagine, if Olivia knew you were involved, she'd insist on full prosecution. So you'll have to ask your own solicitor how long the statute of limitations is in England for two counts of conspiracy to commit burglary, or whatever they call it here when you hire some very bad boys to climb up on a crane on a boat and break into an office building and then a private residence. 'Cause it really doesn't matter to me how long the statute of limitations is on your crimes."

"It should matter to you," Phelps says. "Because one of us might lose his leverage before the other one does."

"I have no idea what you mean by 'leverage'," Burns says. "I know I haven't mentioned anything about having 'leverage' over you. I'll be buying a collection of materials from Ivy, including her customary back-up tapes, and I'll be storing them in a safe place, as I do whenever a case is settled. As I mentioned, I have no plans to open those materials I get from Ivy. There are a few events that might cause me to *consider* opening those materials, and, in the spirit of good communication, I shared those events with you. But I don't consider that to be 'leverage', and I'm sure your solicitor will feel the same way."

"Your semantics games don't interest me, Burns," Phelps says. "Let's get straight to the heart of the matter. What happens if my six years to bring an action against Joyce comes and goes, and yet the statute of limitations has not yet expired on any crimes that might have been committed in connection with last night's failed burglaries? How do I know you won't just wait those six years, and then open Pandora's Box?"

"What could I possibly gain by doing that?" Burns asks. "You ever hear of a prosecutor or a cop jumping for joy when some lame-ass shows up, six years late, claiming to have evidence about a completely cold case? And think what the evidence would be. Not an eyewitness or even a nice piece of physical evidence. Just an old tape whose meaning would take at least an hour to explain, and which would be useless unless the authorities went out and found all the several witnesses who'd be needed to corroborate my complex explanation about why you saying 'river' first on the tape was supposed to be significant. Chances are, if I waited that long, instead of coming after you, they'd ask me why I suddenly opened the box after waiting six years. Why would I want to bring that kind of grief down on myself? I don't have a grudge or a vendetta against you, Clive. If six years pass quietly, this is one sleeping dog who will just keep on dozing."

"You really think you've got it all figured out, don't you?" Phelps asks.

"No, I do not," Burns says. "Because I truly don't know you, Clive. And the little I do I know is pretty scary. I know you're impatient enough, and reckless enough, and obsessed enough with finding the fountain of youth and saving your son, to hire burglars to try to steal the codex, when I was on the verge of winning a great settlement."

"You said no one ever wins in deposition, and trial was in 2012 at the earliest."

"So I was wrong," Burns admits. "But those aren't reasons for you to start consorting with world-class felons. You surprised me yesterday, or whenever you hired those guys, by letting your obsession drive you to do something very dumb. And that means you may surprise me again, by letting your obsession drive you to do something very dumb tomorrow, too. Or next week. Or next month. Or next year.

"For example, I can easily imagine you waiting a year, to let the interest in the burglaries die down, and to let the witnesses's memories fade, and *then* suing Joyce to try to get information about the fountain. That would be really dumb and a terrible thing for all of us, but there's absolutely nothing I can do to stop you, if your obsession compels you to be dumb again.

"So don't tell me I've got it all figured out. All I know is, right now I'm not planning to open Pandora's Box, because opening it will bring serious problems, and a storm of terrible and unrelenting publicity, down on all of us. But whether you'll be dumb enough to do something in the future to make me reconsider whether I have to open that box, I can't even begin to predict. And I'm certainly not smart enough to guess what you'll do in five or six or seven years, or whenever you decide you might have more 'leverage' on me than you think I have on you. Which is why I won't even be looking up the statute of limitations."

"What about Ron and Kip?" Phelps points to the two men from Belize, who've been standing like two petrified trees in the rain forest. "They have a right to a percentage of any profits from the sale of the codex or from the discovery of the fountain of youth."

"There's no fountain of youth out there, Clive," Burns lies, "no matter how much you all wish it were otherwise. And the codex'll never be sold. So there ain't gonna be any spoils for you to quarrel over."

"Joyce agreed to just sit on the codex and the copy?" Phelps asks.

"I told you before," Burns says, "I can't disclose the settlement terms."

"This is a dark piece of work, Burns, and you know it. How can my solicitor reach you?"

"I'll be back in my Ann Arbor office on Monday." Burns shakes his head. "But I guarantee your solicitor is not gonna call me. He's gonna tell you to count your blessings, Clive. You think yesterday's article might hurt your grant-raising? Whaddya think a felony prosecution would do for your reputation?"

"Sounds like you're threatening me again," Clive says.

"Now you're grasping at straws," Burns says. "I kept Ron and Kip in here to protect myself. Maybe you think you can buy Kip, because Kip likes to play the pirate; but I really don't believe Kip's integrity is for sale, at any price. And I doubt Ron's integrity is for sale, either. So you're not gonna get anywhere trying to make up threats these guys know didn't occur in here."

Everyone stares at each other in silence for several moments.

Outside the river water is completely still, as the tides are turning.

"You gonna refund the payments I made to you already?" Clive asks.

"Why would I do that?" Burns asks. "Someone might misconstrue that as an attempt to pay you not to enforce your contract with Joyce. But like I've told you at least three times, you're free to do whatever you want with your contract rights against Joyce. Just as I'm free to do whatever I want with Pandora's Box."

"Surely you don't expect me to pay your future bills on this case?"

"I'll be sending the last bill to you," Burns says, "just like always. But if you don't pay, I won't be shocked. And since the case is over, Joyce and I'll check out of the Hilton this afternoon. Ron and Kip, you should do the same, so there won't be any more expenses on Clive's tab."

"Very white of you." Phelps walks to the conference table, shoots his cuffs, and picks up his briefcase. Then he walks back to the window and offers his right hand to Graham. But Graham folds his hands, and looks away. To Burns's delight, Hunter also looks away, so Phelps doesn't bother offering Hunter a hand.

Phelps walks past Ivy's steno machine, but stops at the door.

"How can you fellows just walk away from the *fountain of youth*?" Phelps asks all three of them. "The greatest undiscovered treasure in all the world. The greatest gift anyone could hope to give mankind: a whole new lease on life. *Decades* more of life! Don't you have any imagination? Don't you have any heart?"

All three stand silent.

"Petty little fools," Phelps mutters as he exits.

Burns follows Phelps out of the room, to be sure he doesn't hassle Ivy – or try to steal her cassette player. Once Phelps is on the lift, Burns rounds up Ivy and Santos, and Joyce and Fiona and Olivia, and herds them all into the conference room with Hunter and Graham.

"Joyce and Fiona have reached a settlement," Burns announces. "The terms are confidential. But the University can join in, if it wants."

"What do you want from us?" Santos asks.

"The University agrees to follow any written instructions you receive from Fiona regarding the copy," Burns says.

"We've always done that," Santos says. "The only instruction we could not follow would be a request to destroy the copy."

"You agree not to order a transcript of Fiona's deposition," Burns says.

"That's fine."

"You agree that Fiona can go forward with her sanctions motion," Burns says, "so we can find out who leaked those stories to the Observer."

"That's fine with us," Santos says, poker-faced.

"Actually," Olivia says, "Fiona and I have decided it's better to drop the motion now. One less thing for the press to write a story about."

"That's smart," Burns says. He turns back to Santos. "And you sign a final settlement agreement with the strongest possible confidentiality provision."

"That's fine with us," Santos says.

"I hope so," Burns says. "Some of us couldn't help noticing the second *Observer* article didn't mention the University."

"Why should they mention us?" Santos asks. "We're just bystanders who got dragged into other people's fight."

"Bystanders hoarding supposedly valuable medical information," Burns says, "just to uphold an unusually restrictive donor contract. Normally you'd expect the press to trash a public university acting in such an elitist fashion."

"I'm sure we'll get our turn to be scorched a little," Santos says.

"Not now," Burns says. "Unless whoever's leaking this keeps leaking it."

"Are you threatening me?" Santos asks.

"Why does everyone thinking I'm threatening them today?" Burns retorts. "All I'm doing is making predictions about the future."

"Perhaps it's the edge to your voice," Santos says, "and the way you were staring so hard at me when you said someone might get scorched if the leaks don't stop, like you thought the University might be the leak."

"Perish the thought," Burns says. "Anyway, I'm glad we were able to settle, so everyone can get on with their lives. It was nice meeting you, Olivia. Can you send me a draft of the formal settlement papers by Monday?"

Olivia nods. "Nice meeting you, too, David. Spending three days with you has been like spending three weeks with any other lawyer."

"I'll take that as a compliment." Burns turns to Fiona. "It was also really great getting to know you a little, Fiona. I learned a lot listening to you today."

Fiona offers her gnarled hand, and they shake. Fiona gives Joyce a hug, and they wish each other well and promise to stay in touch.

Then Fiona wags a crooked forefinger at Hunter and Graham. "You two," Fiona scolds, "need to stop chasing the fountain of youth."

Hunter folds his arms across his chest and glowers at her.

Graham says: "Phelps will never abandon his quest, you know."

"It will destroy him," Fiona predicts. "Don't let it destroy you too, Ron."

"Someone needs to keep an eye on Phelps," Graham counters.

"No, they don't," Fiona says. "Clive'll keep the whole world posted on every brilliant step he takes to try to extend life. You have better things to do with your time, Ron."

"Like what?" Ron asks. "What can an archeologist do, that could possibly match the exhilaration of searching for the fountain of youth?"

"Why don't you put together an exhibit about Kux Ahawis?" Fiona says. "So people remember Kux for his wisdom, and for the fine work he did on behalf of the world's poorest people, instead of just for last year's tragedy."

"That's a good idea," Graham concedes. "I'll do that."

"And what about you, Mr. Hunter?" Fiona asks. "You're almost as mad for the fountain of youth as Dr. Phelps. How can we keep you out of trouble?"

"Can't be done," Hunter says. "I live for trouble. But don't bother worrying about me this summer. I'll be busy trying to launch a new pirate museum on Ambergris Caye."

"A museum? That's not enough to keep a romantic like you out of trouble," Fiona says. "You need a new dream, to replace the fountain of youth."

"You gave me one," Hunter says. "A new lease on life."

"I did? That's wonderful." Fiona trills her 'r'. "What is it?"

"The easiest dive I ever heard of," Hunter says. "Since everyone knows that wreck's right up against the island coast, and there's only 27 miles of coast to search, finding the *General Grant's* gold's gotta be easier than stealing candy from a baby."

EPILOGUE
The Writing on the Wall

Friday 8 April 2011

The air inside the ancient tomb at the base of the Mask Temple is oppressive.

"Jesus, it's hotter'n'hell in here," Kip Hunter complains, taking a long deep swig of water from his canteen.

"Careful how much you drink," Ron Graham admonishes. "This could take awhile."

"It's alright," Clive Phelps says, gesturing at the two extra canteens slung across his chest, along with the three empty 20-litre jugs he's carrying. "I brought extra drinking water, just in case."

"Well in that case ..." Ron quaffs a deep draught from his own canteen.

Ron notices Clive doesn't drink from his canteens. But he doesn't think anything of it.

After herding Kip and Clive a safe distance back from the sarcophagus in the corner, Ron kneels and finds the *ourobouros* – the carving of Itzamna, depicted as a coiled serpent eating his tail. Using one of the jade amulets found on the necks of the dead Maya, which Ron 'borrowed' yesterday from the Belize Police evidence room, he inserts the amulet into the small cylindrical hole at the center of the *ourobouros* carving – while Kip grins salaciously at the sexual symbolism.

Then they hear a distinct click, followed by a loud and continuous grating, the sound of stone rolling against stone. With astonishing speed the huge sarcophagus swings towards the back wall – Ron scrambling to get out of the way – as the sarcophagus rides its stone slab along unseen stone rollers, before coming to a stop just a few feet short of the back wall of the tomb, settling to a stop with another distinct click, as the sarcophagus slab slots into an unseen groove.

In the place formerly occupied by the sarcophagus is a yawning hole in the earthen floor.

"Holy hell," Kip says. "How'd you figure this out?"

"You said there was 'no way' a secret room could be under this earth floor," Clive adds.

"I was wrong," Ron mutters. "On one of the breaks in the deposition, I glimpsed a passage in Kathleen Quinlan's diary, where she said the Reynolds painting, before it was damaged, showed a room just beyond the stone door, with '*writing on the wall*'. So I figured this sarcophagus had to be the 'stone door' in the earth that leads to the fountain of youth. Looks like I was right."

"But how'd you know to stick the amulet into the *ourobouros*?" Kip asks.

"I thought about the writing on the wall." Ron points at the ancient scratches on the wall behind the tomb. "Those numbers: 666-666-21-4-21-6. I realized they're a Biblical citation."

"But they're *Mayan* numbers," Clive protests.

"That's why it never occurred to me before," Ron says. "But even in the colonial period, there were Maya shamans who knew Christian scripture, and Catholic missionaries who learned to read and write Mayan. So either Father Sanchez left a Biblical message in Mayan, or Pel Echem cited the Bible in his native tongue – but those numbers are definitely a Biblical citation."

"What were those numbers again?" Clive asks.

"666-666-21-4-21-6."

"That's not the format of any Biblical citation I ever heard," Clive says.

"No," Ron concedes. "But '666' is commonly associated with the Apocalypse, so I assumed 666-666 was a short-hand for the Book of Revelation. From there, 21-4 and 21-6 took me to verses in the Book of Revelation I can't quote exactly, standing here now, but they go something like: *'And death shall be no more, for I am the Alpha and the Omega, the beginning and the end. To the thirsty I shall give from the fountain of the water of life'*. At that point, I got a hunch that what we have scratched on the wall back here is directions to the fountain of youth – telling us to start with the *ourobouros*, the Maya equivalent of the 'Alpha and Omega'."

"You brought me all the way back to Belize on a *hunch*?" Clive asks.

Kip and Ron exchange quick glances, which Clive fails to notice.

"The Reynolds painting gave me extra confidence my hunch was right." Ron gestures at the yawning hole. "And at this point, it appears I was."

"Maybe," Kip says. "But don't jinx it, till we go down and check it out."

Ron flips on a large portable floodlight and shines it down into the hole. The light illuminates two sets of stone rollers along the sides of the hole, and a set of uneven stone stairs, running along a rock wall, and disappearing down into the darkness beyond the floodlight's range.

To be sure they won't get trapped in the cave below, Kip and Ron place two stout wooden poles across the hole, wedging them between the sarcophagus and the opposite edge of the hole. Then Ron issues three spelunker helmets, with flashlights strapped onto the front of each, to Kip and Clive and himself; and instructs Kip and Clive to remove their shoes and walk in their socks, as Ron does, so that neither their shoes nor the oils from their feet will damage the surface of what is, after all, a virgin archeological site.

"I'll lead," Ron says. "You both stay close behind. Go slow, and look straight at your feet, so your headlight shows the next step. There's no handrail, so use the wall to keep your balance."

"Won't the oils on our hands disturb the site?" Kip asks, sarcastically.

"Yes, but you'll disturb the site a whole lot more if you fall off the stairs and bleed all over the place," Ron says. "Besides, I'm already breaking every rule of good archeological practice, by taking untrained novices along on the first exploration of a virgin site."

Down the dark stairs they go. Three steps down, the temperature plummets, and they fill their lungs with the cool damp cave air. Slowly Ron picks his way down three hundred uneven stone steps, until the steps end on a flat plateau by a narrow river filled with clear motionless water.

"Whoa!" Kip crinkles his nose. "Smells like rotten eggs down here."

"That's hydrogen sulphide," Clive says, bending and sniffing the river water. "Sulphur."

Ron finds a flat place on the plateau to set up his floodlight, and flips it on, revealing a cavern that looks just like the one in the India Reynolds painting. For a minute Ron slowly pans the light along the walls, revealing dramatic natural arrangements of stalactites and stalagmites, but no man-made artwork – no Maya cave drawings, no glyphic inscriptions, no stone sculptures. Ron pauses at ledges along the walls, with man-made holes, explaining that those were the places where the ancient Maya slaves must've mounted their pine torches. Then he aims the light out at the middle of the cavern, and braces it, so he can walk about freely.

Kip gestures at the stagnant river. "I thought the water down here would move."

"We've had a very dry spring," Ron says.

"Well if you think the river's a let-down," Clive says, "wait'll you see the fountain."

Ron and Kip join Clive, who's peering down into a small crevice in the plateau. Their headlights illuminate, about a foot down in the crevice, a small gurgling spring, pushing out less water than an average American suburban garden hose on a medium setting.

"This can't be it," Kip says. "The real fountain must be somewhere deeper in the cave."

"No, this is definitely it," Ron says.

"How can you be sure?" Kip asks.

"This same fountain," Ron says, "is in the Reynolds painting. Same stone stairs, same cave, same river. And the fountain wasn't gurgling much better in the painting than it is now."

While Ron and Kip debate whether this is really the right fountain, Clive begins collecting copious samples of its waters, in the three twenty-litre jugs he brought.

But as Clive holds the third jug under the fountain water, Ron trips and falls on top of Clive.

Clive drops the jug and rolls onto his back, wrestling Ron off of him. At the same instant, Kip thrusts a knife deep into Clive's jugular, and rips it across Clive's throat, from ear to ear.

Clive Phelps keels over dead, the blood from his throat spewing into the fountain of youth.

Ron turns away in horror. "How long till you get rid of me, too?"

"If I wanted to get rid of you," Kip says, "I'd've already done it. I told you, man, I can't market this treasure by myself. I need either you or Clive – and you're easier to deal with than him."

Ron looks less than fully comforted by this answer. But since his lips feel drier than they've felt in his whole life, he reaches for his canteen. It's empty.

"Shit," Ron says. "You got any water left?"

Kip holds his canteen above his mouth, but nothing comes out.

"No worries, partner," Kip says. With his knife he cuts the strap holding the two extra canteens to Clive's chest, and gives one to Ron, while taking the other for himself.

"To immortality!" Kip says, clinking canteens with Ron.

They both drink.

The next instant they both collapse, choking on the cyanide Clive mixed into the canteen water before they came. Ron Graham and Kip Hunter both die before Clive Phelps' blood dries.

* * *

Saturday 9 April 2011

Shortly after dawn Manuel Santoro ties up his launch at Lamanai, and escorts his somber visitors onto the dock there: Gemma Murray, Joyce Kerr and David Burns. Manny, carrying a large diving bag containing a large portable floodlight he uses on all his cave tours, is working hard to conceal from the whites how nervous he is, because he's risking his license bringing these unauthorized visitors to Lamanai – still a closed site, due to the cancer deaths four months ago.

But Manny's pretty sure no one can tell how nervous he is, because everyone's watching Gemma, who's a basket case. Gemma flew down to Belize Thursday with her boyfriend, Clive Phelps, and Clive's latest allies in the hunt for the fountain of youth, Ron Graham and Kip Hunter. The three men left the Jolly Roger Friday morning for Lamanai, with Clive promising Gemma he'd be back before dark, or call if they were delayed. Gemma hasn't heard a peep now for 24 hours.

Joyce and David also seem tense. They flew down to Belize Friday, on a celebratory jaunt after winning a lawsuit, with no purpose except to drink themselves silly, and find a realtor for some land Joyce inherited on Ambergris Caye. They were surprised to run into Gemma at the Jolly Roger – and dismayed to learn Clive and Ron and Kip are still hunting the fountain of youth.

Manny himself is worried not only about his license, but, more importantly, about his friend Ron, who's been keeping bad company with Kip Hunter lately, which is why Manny let Joyce talk him into ferrying these good people out to a closed site.

Manny leads the unauthorized visitors on a silent hike to the Mask Temple. Rather than break into the tomb, they climb the temple steps, and then descend to the tomb via the inner stairs.

Inside the tomb, Manny sets up his big portable floodlight, and flips it on. Immediately they all gasp, as they see that the stone sarcophagus has been moved from its usual resting place – with big timbers propping it against the wall – and in its place, there's a yawning hole in the earth.

After they all peer into the darkness, Manny picks up his big floodlight, and leads the way down three hundred stone steps, to a plateau in a cave, where he sets up his big light again.

When Manny aims his big light out at the plateau, everyone gasps again – this time at the sight of three dead bodies, sprawled near a small fountain beside an underground river. Gemma rushes to the body closest to the fountain, and starts to bend over it; but the grisly sight of maggots, already hard at work, causes her to stop, mid-bend, and view the body from a distance.

"Clive," Gemma croaks, her voice tinged with regret.

Manny sees that the other two bodies are Ron and his dangerous pirate friend Kip Hunter.

David bends close and inspects all three bodies carefully. From Ron's pocket he extracts a jade amulet; and from Kip's pocket he extracts something smaller. Then David rises to face Gemma, Joyce and Manny.

"I'm nobody's idea of a homicide detective or a coroner," David says. "But Clive's throat was clearly slashed open. Kip's the only one here with a knife on him, and there's blood on Kip's pants, like someone wiping off a bloody knife. There's also blood on Ron's sleeves and hands."

"What d'you think happened to Kip and Ron?" Joyce asks.

"Harder to say," David says, "with no marks on their bodies. Poison comes to mind."

"From the fountain of youth?" Gemma asks.

"Maybe – or maybe from those." David gestures at the canteens Ron and Kip are still clutching like death. "But gang, we gotta make some decisions, fast. Joyce and I invited you to join us here on the express condition, which you both agreed to, that this'd be a one-time-only trip to the fountain of youth, and you'd never tell anyone about coming here. Yet in fairness, when you agreed, you didn't know we'd find the door to the fountain already flung wide open, and you certainly didn't know we'd find a murder scene, with victims you were both close to. So all bets are off; you're free to do as you think right."

Joyce shoots David an alarmed glance, but David shrugs.

"But if we report these murders," Burns continues, "we'll all have to get into a huge international discussion of the fountain of youth, and the more we warn about its dangers, the more people will wanna come see it anyway. On the other hand, if we *don't* report these murders, in order to keep the fountain of youth secret, then these victims – your friends – will have to lay here, unburied, while we just close that big stone door on this cave, and walk away. In short, there's no good choice for us here."

For a minute they all stare at the three corpses, while the water from the fountain of youth gurgles quietly in the background.

At last Joyce breaks the silence. "What'd you take from Kip's pocket?"

David opens his hand and shows a small gold trinket. "Fiona's locket. So now we know who Clive hired for the river assault on her flat."

Joyce clenches her jaw in anger. "Well, I might be the closest thing Kip had to a friend in this life, so I'll speak for him. I didn't know he was a burglar – and I sure didn't know he was a murderer. But he brought this trouble on himself, and if Kip were here in our shoes, he wouldn't hesitate to walk away, and leave the dead unburied, in order to preserve the secret of the fountain of youth."

"I also didn't know Kip was a murderer," David says, "or a burglar, either. He seemed so genial at the depo."

"Kip was a cold and bloody bastard," Gemma interjects, with deep conviction.

David raises an eyebrow. "I guess we didn't really know him."

"Just like I didn't really know Clive," Gemma replies. "On those rare occasions when Clive let himself relax, he could be a very sweet man; but he was so obsessed with his quest to conquer death and give us all a new lease on life, he just – lost sight of his humanity."

They all stand in silence another minute.

"Then are you alright with leaving Clive here?" Joyce asks at last.

Gemma nods yes. "Better for Clive's reputation, if there's no story about his unhappy end. Better for Nigel, too. And better for Clive's rivals, so no one's tempted to follow his footsteps here."

David turns to Manny. "That just leaves you, Manny. How d'you feel about leaving Ron here, unburied, with no one but us ever to know what happened to him?"

"No problem," Manny replies. "Ron would understand. Leaving them all here as they lay – that's the Maya way."

Acknowledgements

The author gratefully acknowledges the wise editorial suggestions he received from Pamela Ahearn, Timothy L. Dickinson, J.D., Carol Diephuis, David Diephuis, Prof. David S. Gewanter, Gideon Hoffer, Dr. James Hughes, Kathleen D. Hunt, J.D., Susan Kessler, John W. Phillips, J.D., Craig Ross, J.D., Dr. Anne P. Rowe, Kyla K. Rowe, Rachel K. Rowe, Dr. Elizabeth Small, Janet L. Steinbach, and Prof. Theodore L. Trost. The author also acknowledges the following specific sources for the historical and scientific information contained in the novel:

Non-Fiction Sources

Rosila Arvigo and Michael Balick, *Rainforest Remedies: One Hundred Healing Herbs of Belize* (Lotus Press 1998)

Andrea G. Bodnar, Michel Ouellette, Maria Frolkis, Shawn E. Holt, Choy-Pik Chiu, Gregg B. Morin, Calvin B. Harley, Jerry W. Shaw, Serge Lichtsteiner, Woodring E. Wright, *Extension of Life-Span by Introduction of Telomerase into Normal Human Cells* (Science Magazine, 16 January 1998)

Jeremy Cherfas, *Hayflick Licked: Telomerase Lengthens Life of Normal Human Cells* (Science Watch, May/June 2000) – the source of the shoelace analogy

Michael D. Coe, *Breaking The Maya Code* (Thames & Hudson 1992)

William Dampier, *A New Voyage Round The World* (James Knaptan 1697; Hummingbird Press 1999) – Charles Darwin relied heavily on this amazing pirate's autobiography

Daniel DeFoe, *A General History of the Pyrates*, ed. Manuel Schonhorn (London 1720; Dover 1999) – still the most entertaining and comprehensive book ever written about the pirates

Arthur Demarest, *Ancient Maya: The Rise and Fall of a Rainforest Civilization* (Cambridge University Press 2004) – the leading non-fiction book on the Maya

Bernal Diaz, *History of the Conquest of New Spain*, trans. J.M. Cohen (Madrid 1568; Penguin 1963) – still the best account of the Spanish Conquest, by the plain-speaking old soldier

Peter Earle, *The Sack of Panama: Captain Morgan and the Battle for the Caribbean* (St. Martin's Press 1981)

David Eltis, *The Rise of African Slavery in the Americas* (Cambridge University Press 2000)

Keith Eunson, *The Wreck of the General Grant* (A.H. & A.W. Reed 1974)

Tom Kirkwood, *Sex and Death* (BBC Radio 4, Reith Lectures 2001, Lecture 3)

Charles C. Mann, *1491: New Revelations of the Americas Before Colombus* (Random House 2005) – the rare book that deserved every award it got

Victor Montejo, *Testimony: Death of a Guatemalan Village*, trans. Victor Perera (Curbstone Press 1987) – will help you understand why the Maya shun us

John Montgomery, *How To Read Maya Hieroglyphs* (Hippocrene Books 2002)

Diana & Michael Preston, *A Pirate of Exquisite Mind: The Life of Wm. Dampier* (Doubleday 2004)

Linda Schele & P. Mathews, *The Code of Kings: The Language of Seven Sacred Maya Temples and Tombs* (Simon & Schuster 1998)

Jerry W. Shay, *Telomeres and Telomerase* (Oncogene Reviews 2002)

J. Eric S. Thompson, *Maya Archeologist* (University of Oklahoma Press 1963)

P.A.B. Thomson, *Belize: A Concise History* (MacMillan 2004)

Fiction Sources

Miguel Angel Asturias, *Men of Maize*, trans. Gerald Martin (Editorial Losada 1949; Dell 1975) – still the greatest novel ever written about the Maya, by the 'James Joyce of Central America'

Carmen Boullosa, *They're Cows, We're Pigs*, trans. Leland H. Chambers (Ediciones Era 1991; Grove Press 1997) – terrific account of the daily lives of 18th century pirates

Eth Clifford, *The Curse of the Moonraker* (Houghton Mifflin 1977) – on the *General Grant wreck*

Gaspar Pedro Gonzalez, *A Mayan Life*, trans. Elaine Elliott (Yax Te Foundation 1995)

Ermilio Abreau Gomez, *Canek: History and Legend of a Maya Hero*, trans. Mario L. Davila and Carter Wilson (University of California Press 1979)

Norma Rosa Garcia Mainieri, *The Town of the Silent People and Other Stories*, trans. Susan Giersbach Rason, Ferando Penalosa, and Paula Gille Loubier (Caroline Grajeda 2001)

Fernando Penalosa, *Tales and Legends of the Q'anjob'al Maya* (Yax Te Foundation 2001)

Norman Spinrad, *Mexica* (Little Brown 2005) – historical novel about Cortes and the Conquest

Rob Swigart, *Xibalba Gate* (Rowman & Littlefield 2005) – a Maya scholar's novel about the ancient Maya

Dennis Tedlock, trans., *Popul Vuh: The Definitive Edition of the Dawn of Life and the Glories of Gods and Kings* (Simon & Schuster 1985) – the Maya creation story

9 780615 344102